DAVID F. FARRIS

ERAFEEN

BOOK 6

The Empires

David F. Farris

ERAFEEN: THE EMPIRES

www.erafeen.com

Written by: David F. Farris
Cover illustrated by: Alessandro Brunelli

This book is a work of fiction.
All material was derived from the author's imagination. Any resemblances to persons, alive or deceased, are simply coincidental.

Sphaira Publishing, 2020

ISBN 13 978-1-7323585-3-9

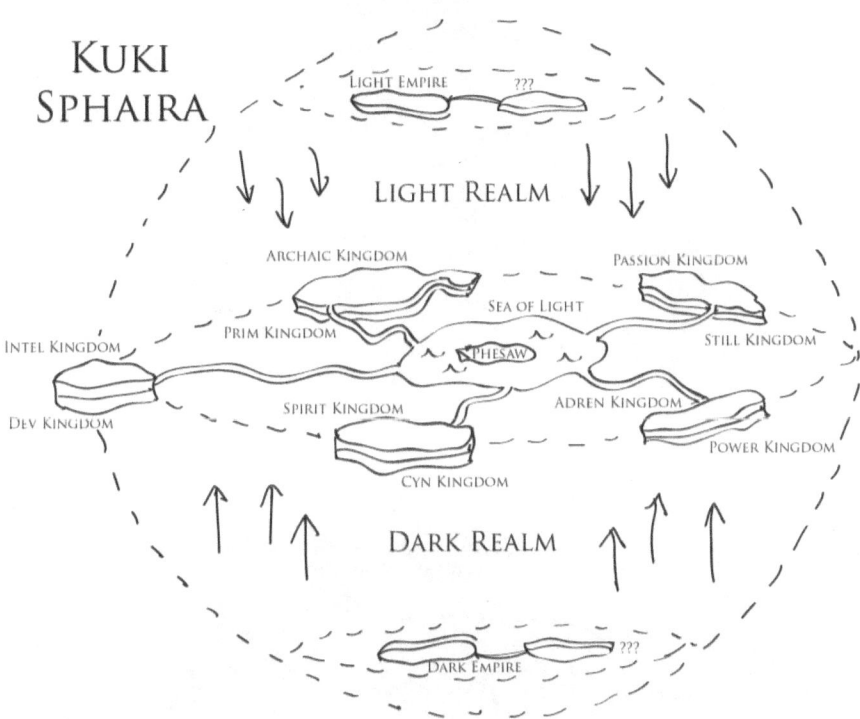

*This is a 3D diagram of Erafeen's world, Kuki Sphaira: a ball of air with floating islands and rivers. There are no landscapes or structures depicted within each kingdom because its purpose is a full-world view. Arrows represent flow of gravity. Dev, Cyn, Power, Still, and Prim Kingdoms (Dark Realm) hang on the underbellies of floating islands. Intel, Archaic, Spirit, Adren, and Passion Kingdoms (Light Realm) sit atop. More detailed maps of individual kingdoms ahead.

INTEL KINGDOM
(LIGHT KNOWLEDGE KINGDOM)

ARCHAIC KINGDOM
(LIGHT MORALITY KINGDOM)

CYN KINGDOM (THE VOID)
(DARK SPIRIT KINGDOM)

STILL KINGDOM
(DARK EMOTION KINGDOM)

ADREN KINGDOM
(LIGHT COURAGE KINGDOM)

DAVID F. FARRIS

Light Realm

Intel Kingdom (mind, electricity):
Bryson, Lilu, Jugtah, Princess Shelly, King Vitio, Yvole, Frederick, Gracie, Limone, Wendel, Benedict, Tonitrua, Sally, Geni

Passion Kingdom (heart, fire):
Olivia, Himitsu, Director Venustas, Fane, Horos, Barloe, Rayne

Spirit Kingdom (soul, wind):
Jilly, Tashami, Director Neaneuma, Queen Apsa, Thornstorm, Sephrina

Adren Kingdom (body, speed):
Toshik, Yama, Director Buredo, Saikatto, Kolver, Soraku

Archaic Kingdom (mind, ancients):
Agnos, Rhyparia, Itta, Prince Sigmund, Ophala, Musku, Gray Whale, Kaylee, Prakriti, Creep, Poicus, Senex, Pluzina, Joselina, Mengai, Kopios Soteria

Dark Realm

Dev Kingdom (mind, psychic):
Vistas, Flen, King Storshae, Illipsia, Tazama, Warden Gala, Mialo, Sylial

Still Kingdom (heart, ice):
Apoleia, Ropinia, Titus, Garlo, Moroza, Evelyn, Groto, Thyella, Hailey

Cyn Kingdom (soul, supernatural):
Ronossius, Chelekah, Nina, Halice, Lanor, Panelle, Ropper, Unry, Killui, Lu, Leslie

Power Kingdom (body, strength):
Vuilni, Jewel, Josie, Stonebody, Poten

Prim Kingdom (mind, ancients):
Arithmys, Pistimi, Nynis Yogo, Queen Inedibus, Atarax, Kakos, Therapif, Biaza, Moros, Dimiourgos, Brenson

Not all characters are listed

7

1

Light or Dark

The darkness was vast. Bryson didn't know whether he should call out for an answer or remain silent, possible threats lurking nearby. The situation stirred a suspicious feeling of déjà vu. He thought back to his nightmares of the classroom in which Director Senex had taught, the foreign language scribbled on the chalkboard, and the mangled faces of Saikatto and Musku—two of the original Jestivan—seated at desks. There had been a void to Bryson's left, where a wall should have stood, frigid to the bone and laced with the screams of his mother. In this void, only his breaths accompanied the quiet.

He thought nothing could have distracted him from the images he'd just witnessed: the electricity from Toono's finger, the T1 scar on his forehead, and his surprisingly heartbreaking suicide to become the tenth and final sacrifice ... Less heartbreaking when considering the demon's intentions with such a move. He had blindsided the world, granting a second life not to Dev King Rehn—also known as the Oracle—but to Mendac LeAnce, a twisted man who had raped Bryson's mother.

And the wings. You can't forget those wings. They had sprouted from Mendac's back the moment he stood in his casket, edges contorted in furling tendrils of black smoke.

But what clouded Bryson's mind was the uncertainty of the inexplicable void in which he stood and inability to move his feet. *Something* tugged at him in opposing directions. He couldn't tell if it was a physical or mental sensation until he noticed its directional peculiarity—up and down, not to and fro.

He looked up to where a celestial light hovered like a too-close star. Its shape was ever-morphing, edges in constant fluctuation. And despite its brightness, it did nothing to illuminate the void. He glanced below his feet to where a sphere of blackness—a shade so dark no human eye should have been able to detect it—lurked in the depths, making the void seem gray in comparison. These two entities were what pulled at Bryson, barring the lateral protest of his feet.

Doorways encircled him in the distance, seemingly sprinkled into the void almost at random. One of the doors was close enough for him to distinguish a feather hanging from its handle. Another door's handle was shrouded in gray dust, a cloud of ash revolving around the spherical shape. A metal plate was bolted to both doors, on which something had been inscribed, but it wasn't legible from this distance. Two other doors were bolted shut and stripped of their handles. While they intrigued him, they were irrelevant to his purpose for a reason of which he knew nothing. This chamber didn't feel of his world.

He looked up again, feeling the light's magnetism increase. The shifting ball of white grew larger while the pit of blackness minimized below. Whatever was happening here, it was clear the light was winning. It likely had been for a while, even before finding himself in this limbo. Had this war waged inside of him throughout his entire life? Had he slipped into depths of his subconscious that shouldn't have been obtainable? Or was this a physical location?

This feels right. A weight gradually lifted from his soul as he neared the light, reminding him of the sensation when first meeting Shelly's Branian or summoning his own.

Bryson raised his arms, fingertips extended toward the ball, partly to succumb to the euphoria it granted him and partly to get out of this nothingness. Luminescent tendrils peeled away and twisted around his fingers.

Then they punctured his wrists.

Heat rushed his energy canals, shooting down his outstretched arm and spilling into his chest, shocking his innards like a shot of the hardest liquor. It fuzzed and then lingered, teasing him with the slightest tickle.

This can't be it. There has to be more … I want more.

Just when it felt like it would dissipate completely—leaving him empty—the heat burst with an intensity that no alcohol could provide. It bloomed outward simultaneously, flooding his waist and legs while creeping up his neck and filling his skull. His ears and cheeks burned; his jaw slackened as he lost control of his facial muscles. Then the heat morphed into a subtle flame that ignited his eyes, triggering *something* within.

A cavity? A cell?

The moment became a constant, eyes resetting to their normal position. The heat wave that had stupefied him upon contact with the iridescent sphere had now found harmony. It was still there, but as a subtle undertone that pulsed in sync with his heart.

The void vanished, replaced by a room of Intelights and a crowd of people gathered around him at a forced distance. Shelly and many of the Jestivan stared at him—or at something *near* him. Rolling his head to the right, he followed their collective gaze. It seemed not only had he departed from the void, but so had the ball of light.

Only now it had reshaped itself … *into wings.*

11

2

The Skill Broker

Ophala Vevlu, Pilot of Spy and Sky, was changing. Her patience had worn thin years ago, after discovering her assignment in Rim to scout the Archaic Mountains had been a diversion. But now it was gone. She had no time for empathy or morality when it came to individuals who opposed her. To conquer evils such as this, she embraced that brutality herself. That explained the scene before her.

A man screamed for mercy, trying to squirm on the stone floor of a bare cell. His hands were tied behind his back and bound to a metal handle protruding from the floor. Same for his ankles, contorting him so his knees were bent back, ankles nearly pressed against his backside. Rope cut against his throat as it, too, was tied to a handle behind his head. It was just enough to irritate and burn the neck, but not enough to kill him and grant him the sweet mercy of death. The position strained his body like a nocked bow, back concaved, abdomen thrust outward. An inverted fetal position.

His face ... Well, Ophala couldn't see his face through the mass of black directly on top of it. A raven was perched on the man's head, talons tearing into hair and scalp while its beak tore at the man's right eye. Blood streaked the man's face, and the raven tugged at the pink rectus muscles that connected the eye to the brain. Lament was a rarely used bird of Ophala's. She had always been convinced it was more demon than animal. Whenever she entered its mind, she could feel the wildness more vividly than any other bird. She had always reserved Lament as an assassin bird of the night, but she could only remember twice when that had been necessary—with the vilest of targets.

This was different. This was torture, something she had never committed in her life. Lament feasted on the opportunity of mutilation, but that was exactly why Ophala had an iron grip on her ancient. She forced the raven to hold back, to focus only on the eye until this man spoke. If she lost even the slightest concentration, Lament would have progressed across the prisoner's body.

"*STOP! STOP!*" the man bellowed. He tried to say more, but agony arrested his words.

Ophala wove a litany of Archaic Chains and began fidgeting with Lament's will and motor functions. The raven stopped, but she had to peel its talons—and with it, skin—out of the man's head. The man heaved as the raven moved to the side. He gasped, sucking down fitful bursts of air. She had yet to see him like this. He'd kept his composure during previous tortures.

"You have something useful to say?" she asked from outside of the cell. He didn't respond immediately, but she granted him a moment to compose himself. Perhaps, she still had a little bit of patience inside of her. A doctor had rushed toward him from the side of the cell, tending to the wound just adequately enough to make sure he wouldn't die. He knew too much that Ophala didn't.

Mesitis Epidex, more commonly known as the Skill Broker among the circles of the shady elites, was the man responsible for resurrecting the Underground forty years ago, a criminal organization that hadn't seen its prime since the late 500's. He was the leader and had fallen into Ophala's lap almost by happenstance while her birds scouted the city of Balle in the dead hours of night. Of course, she hadn't leapt to any conclusions when encountering Mesitis through one of her bird's eyes, but after connecting some dots from ledgers in Lost Wisdom and speaking with elders who had once advised Archaic King Itta, she was able to deduct the importance of this man.

"I can speak on allies to King Itta's cause that the world isn't aware of," the man finally said.

"That does me no good," she said. It was true. Whatever allies Itta might have once possessed now held little to no consequence. Not only was the Light Realm united, but it had the Still Kingdom on its side. Given the current state of the Dev Kingdom, she saw no threat. Only the Cyn Kindom was a cause for concern. Speaking of … she still couldn't understand how Lost Wisdom had obtained a Cynnish woman for employment.

The memory of walking into that orphanage room, an elderly woman seated on a chair at its center with a gray sphere in her lap, put her on edge. The sensation that had overcome her was dread at first, but then followed by nothingness.

"Tell me about the woman with the stone."

"I know nothing about—*aargh*!" He roared and bucked at the doctor, who must have struck a sensitive spot of the socket.

Ophala waited for Mesitis to calm down, then asked, "Even after what you just went through, you still lie to me … Admirable."

"That woman was an acquisition of King Itta, not me. I know it's difficult to believe, but a Royal Head does have his own secrets and business conducted without my involvement. I appreciate the credit you give me, but I'm no royal."

She looked up and forced herself to not shake her head in annoyance. This could have been easier if she had the gall to ask for Kaylee's ancient. That eye of hers could read auras and reveal lies—unless the target had mastery over their emotional levels and mental fortitude. She believed that was probably the case with Mesitis. Still, she would have enjoyed having the option, but she couldn't stomach letting Kaylee see this. That girl admired Ophala, and this was too gruesome for her exposure. She could have asked to use the eye, herself, but that seemed tactless.

Eventually, Ophala came to a decision. She could wait for answers in regards to the woman and stone. There were plenty of other tortures through which she could put him. If he was willing to tell her anything at this point, might as well accept that small blessing. "Alright, what do you got for me?" she asked.

"A secret army," he said. "With special armory and weaponry. It's been in the works for decades now, and it was King Itta's original strategy to attack the Intel Kingdom before he jumped on the opportunity to ally with Dev King Storshae. But, it has continued to build itself over the past several years in the background. I've remained in touch with the leader. Their plans shifted focus when the Amendment Order was established and King Itta died. They've been preparing to march on the capital and overtake the kingdom, unhappy with the current state of reign. Sigmund has no clue—"

"*King* Sigmund," Ophala said tersely. The fact that Mesitis gave Itta the proper respect but not his son bothered her.

"King Sigmund has no clue how to lead a kingdom," he said. "There is reason to believe King Itta never passed down any of the information to his son that would have been vital for a Royal Head. The Loess Lord is not happy."

"The Loess Lord?"

"The man who rules over the Thousand-Layer Loess and the secret army of which I just spoke."

"My birds have flown over that Loess hundreds of times and have never seen armies. And if they're underground, I would have seen entrances."

"Your birds don't see everything, Pilot. You'd think the Generals' Battle would have taught you that."

Her grip on Cheiraskinia tightened. He had the audacity to taunt her while in his condition? But she said nothing. The Thousand-Layer Loess was a large stretch of mostly farmlands and woodlands from what she knew, but if Mesitis's warning had any merit, she needed to look into it.

"What's the Loess Lord's name?"

"Kopios Soteria."

She released a long, cathartic breath. She cursed and turned on her heels to take her leave, forcing the raven to follow. That name gave her reason to believe. She had seen it in Lost Wisdom's ledgers as one of the people who had placed a child in the orphanage.

Kaylee had been that child.

3

Ocular Rings

Shelly didn't know how much more she could take. Weeks had passed, yet her mother's wails continued to haunt the palace's royal quarters. Between that and the uncertainty of Bryson's status as his coma dragged on for a third week, she couldn't escape the air of dread suffocating the hollow corridors. Staff continued to roam the halls, but nothing could fill the gaping hole left by her dad's joviality. Every time she thought stepping outside might clear her mind, the aftermath of Toono's invasion—the capital in ruins—reminded her that her problems extended far beyond her family.

Her dad, Intel King Vitio, was dead, leaving Shelly as the woman who'd take his place as the kingdom's Royal Head. Recovering from the war now fell on her shoulders. From architecture to infrastructure, she'd oversee the rebuilding of the city. It was crippling to think that the grief of her mother and incapacitation of her fiancé had to take a back seat to matters that held no immediate weight in her mind—a selfish debilitation, and she knew this.

The nature of a sovereign required personal sacrifices, a directional prioritization of empathy.

Delilah belted out a scream, voice shaking from the straining of her vocal cords. Lilu squeezed Shelly's hand in response. The two sisters stood side by side at the foot of their parents' bed ... their *mother's* bed. She was in hysterics, slouched at the mattress's center.

Shelly glanced at Lilu, so impressed by her fortitude. While they were both Delilah's daughters, Shelly didn't share the same bond with their mother, yet Lilu had only broken into tears a few times over the weeks. Lilu returned Shelly's gaze, and that triggered the fourth occurrence of waterworks from the accomplished weavineer. Shelly embraced her younger sister. Lilu rested her head on Shelly's and wept. Four times was still impressive.

Shelly had yet to shed a single tear, a factor resulting from shock according to Olivia. She liked that explanation. Because if not shock, then only callousness could have brought forth such little sorrow ... right?

Then why do I feel so empty?

Why couldn't Shelly cry alongside Lilu, granting her that comfort of knowing she wasn't alone?

"I admire your strength," Lilu said, stirring Shelly's guilt. This was cowardice, not strength. "You're already prepared for the role this kingdom needs you to fill. The people will find great stability in you."

Shelly remained still as her sister leaned against her, despite the desire to flinch away. The role ... Royal Head. A queen. It required a level head and actions driven not by emotion, but by logic. So yes, she would continue to carry herself this way. There was no time for grief or—

The door burst open. Both sisters whirled, their mother paying the intrusion no mind. Vistas stood in the doorway, and for once—ever since the night his identical brother had murdered the king—he appeared unbroken ... maybe even hopeful. "Ladies, Bryson is awake."

Shelly's feet moved before she had time to think. And the tears ... they finally came.

*   *   *

Bryson wasn't sure how much time passed in silence as he studied the strange new appendages jutting from his shoulder blades. Others, too, ogled them with wide eyes or scrunched eyebrows, seemingly oblivious to the fact that his eyes had opened. Footsteps squeaked atop marble floors somewhere in the corridor outside the room, drawing his attention back to the people around him.

He blinked to rid the stars from his vision, reminding him of early weekend mornings when Debo would train him to the point of dehydration as a child. These stars, however, didn't disappear, nor did they swirl or sway as his gaze shifted directions. They remained in fixed positions, pulsating behind peoples' eyes in rhythm with Bryson's heart. Some burned brighter than others. Like Agnos, whose eyes might as well have been two full moons when compared to the dying stars surrounding him.

The footsteps reached Bryson's room, and the crowd of visitors split to make way for Shelly and Lilu. Upon seeing his fiancée's cheeks streaked with tears, he forgot about his wings, the void he'd just escaped, and the pulsing lights. He saw only Shelly, her pixie cut having grown into a green curtain of straight hair that flirted with her shoulders.

Her eyes lingered on his right wing before brushing it off as an afterthought and wrapping him in an embrace. He returned the gesture and observed Lilu, who, along with Vistas seated next to the door, was the only other person here now that everyone else had left. She had been crying, but he could tell those tears had been different than Shelly's.

"What's wrong?" he asked. "Is L.K. alright?"

Shelly let go of Bryson and sat on the edge of the bed. She looked back at Lilu—a gesture that tested his patience. *Spit it out already.* He tried to prop himself up with his elbows, but Shelly rested a hand on his chest. "Leon is fine."

He looked between them. Lilu managed to squeak out two words: "Dad's dead."

She broke down. Shelly stood and grabbed her sister's shoulder, guiding her to the bed. Lilu plopped into the sheets and collapsed atop Bryson's chest, alarming him enough to momentarily paralyze him. He raised his arms, but then stopped. He looked to Shelly, who offered an approving nod. He placed a hand on Lilu's back and rubbed gently, confused as to what made him a suitable pillar for her in this moment.

Tears slowly trickled down his cheeks, and Shelly watched. The world felt worse than it had when Toono was alive. Vitio's death. Mendac's rebirth. A new era of evil had descended upon Kuki Sphaira, and it made the force that had been the Rogue Demon seem trivial in comparison.

"How's Delilah?" Bryson asked.

Shelly shook her head. Lilu's sniffles became sobs, mouth open against Bryson's sternum.

"Who did it?" he asked after waiting for Lilu to relax.

"Flen," said Shelly.

Anger replaced anguish as Bryson stared daggers into Vistas, whom he had ignored up until this point. The Dev servant had remained in that chair, electing to remain quiet. "Vistas, we trusted you!" His back flared, a white-hot flame that scorched his spine.

Lilu jumped back. Shelly gasped, wide eyes finally acknowledging Bryson's wings. He didn't have to look at them to know they had brightened. He saw it in the reflection of their eyes. He didn't care.

Vistas's gaze had lost its signature placidity, filled with the heaviest of sorrows. "I didn't know …" He trailed off and paused. "But I should have. My dismissal caused this kingdom its leader. I'm sorry."

Bryson opened his mouth to retaliate, but thought better of it. Nobody wanted to hear a tirade. Nobody deserved such wrath—nobody in this room, at least. Especially not Vistas, a man who had shown nothing but kindness to this kingdom since it enslaved him. If anything, his loyalty served as an insult to his homeland and likely piled guilt onto his shoulders.

You're desperate to place blame, Bryson told himself.

The light softened, the pulsing in his spine settling into a dull *thump-thump*. Shelly looked away from his wings and shook her head. "What is that?"

"I think … it's *Tahara*."

Lilu straightened, wiping her cheeks with both hands as she stepped closer to Bryson. Without the tears, he could finally see the slivers of light that circled her pupils and irises, like four halos. Compared to Agnos's, they were dull. She leaned in to give the wings a closer inspection.

"Remember the lecture I gave you after finding Mendac's lab notes in Brilliance?" she asked.

"Yeah ... mostly."

"Well, I said he believed there was a cavity in the eyes that stored Tahara and its opposite. Do you sense anything different?"

He looked between the two sisters. "There are slivers of light in your eyes, circular and celestial."

She paused, her gaze rolling toward his. She leaned in, narrowing her eyes like the scholar she was. She wanted to make a big deal out of this. Anyone would. "Yes, I see them. It seems Mendac was—"

"Stop." He closed his eyes and softly exhaled. He didn't want to interrupt her, understanding what this revelation was for her: a distraction. Alas, he couldn't keep hearing that name.

She backed away, the studious glare melting away as she realized her mistake. "Sorry."

"No worries." He forced a smile, looking elsewhere for a distraction. His attention landed on Shelly. "I still want you to be my wife."

She cocked an eyebrow. "We were thinking about delaying the wedding."

"You're out of your damned mind. We're getting married." He paused. "By the end of the month ... if that's okay with you."

With a smile, she whispered, "I want my husband."

4

Half Human, Half Corpse

The atrium down the hall from Bryson's medical room was a massive waiting area, one side open to the corridor and the other a curved wall with tall windows, granting a breathtaking view of the hedge mazes and gardens of the western grounds. Olivia sat on a bench facing one of the windows, separated from the core group that mingled near the center: Tashami, Agnos, Himitsu, and Vuilni. A few benches down, Toshik stared out his own window in solitude.

"That was the craziest thing I've ever seen," she heard Tashami say.

The topic of Bryson's wings—or whatever they were—had consumed them. Olivia focused on what mattered most: Bryson's life. He had woken up; she could breathe easier now. She thought she was going to lose her twin brother. If she had, that blame would have belonged to her. While the war between True Light and SCAPD had hit its climax, Olivia had been off in a neutral kingdom, unable to provide support to her peers. Even the information she'd acquired about Kadlest and Mendac had come too late.

DAVID F. FARRIS

Olivia was desperate. Her father was alive again because she and the rest of True Light had been duped by Toono—a man with whom she had once allied for a brief period, and all while knowing the atrocities he'd committed. She could have killed him a long time ago—or at least tried to. A good person would have.

She looked up from the grounds below and beyond the perimeter walls, where Dunami's western half remained unmarred. Buildings stood erect and those civilians who hadn't chosen to uproot their lives in favor of new homes in Continon or Acu mingled in the streets. Such life didn't fool Olivia, for she knew about the wasteland that sat outside the windows on the other side of the palace to the east. What she saw here felt like ever-ice jewelry on the necks of traditional Stillian women—something pretty to distract eyes from spotting the void within.

One war may have ended, but a grander one that had been brewing in the Empires was now hitting its stride and leaking into the kingdoms. Spy Pilot Ophala has been holding group and individual meetings with the Jestivan and a few other important people over the past few weeks. After hearing everyone's stories, linking similar facts, and using deductive reasoning to fill in the holes, she determined that Kadlest had used Toono to resurrect Mendac. She convinced him when he was still a child, lying about the terrible things Mendac did to her, when the reality was that she loved the man and wanted him back in her life.

It was a twisted ruse. How could a mother manipulate her son like that? Of course, it was possible that Mendac had actually abused Kadlest just like he had done to Olivia's mother. The only difference lay in their responses. While Apoleia had despised him after he raped her, Kadlest may have been conditioned to the abuse. *Still, to involve her son?*

The man who became known as the Rogue Demon had never looked at himself as such a thing. He thought himself an avenger. Then, when he made the decision to offer his own life at the end, he died thinking himself a martyr as he attempted to pass the baton off to Bryson. He couldn't have predicted the smile on his mother's face at the sight of her abuser ... the love in her eyes. Connected hands. Black wings. A flight that saw them escape as a pair.

23

Mendac LeAnce was alive and about. Olivia looked at the sky, charcoal clouds looming overhead. Thunder reverberated through the floor, and she thought of Meow Meow—or Dimiourgos, as she had recently learned. The kitten hat—fabled lynx and one of ten Originators—was dead, his ninth life now powering Mendac's body. Meow Meow had once been her best friend ... No, part of her. They had shared minds for over a decade. She grew up with his guidance—a beacon she greatly appreciated. He'd been the counterweight to her mother's influence.

This most recent event felt like his second death. Her connection to him had been severed long ago, when Toono had taken him from her. But this was permanent. There were no maybes onto which she could hold.

"I bet you're happier than anyone right now."

Himitsu hopped the back of the bench and took a seat next to Olivia. His smile was genuine and full of life. Behind Jilly, he'd always been the best at expressing his happiness, a trait largely due to his parents. They were a family of comedians.

Olivia nodded. "I am ... pleased."

Chuckling, Himitsu shook his head and turned his attention toward the city outside. "Oh how I missed the calculated responses."

"Calculated ..." She mulled over the word in her mind. "Do you think that's what's holding me back?"

"From what?"

She turned in her seat, watching as Agnos, Vuilni, and Tashami exchanged laughter amidst upbeat conversation. She faced forward again. "I don't know ... from my potential."

He frowned and then twisted his lips. "I think so, which is odd when considering how I first thought of you years ago."

"What do you mean?"

He turned to face her, folding his leg on the bench and laying his arm across the back. "The Jestivan saw you as this brick wall. It's why nobody from your original team questioned your captaincy. They saw your emotional invulnerability as a strength, and it was up to a certain point." He smiled. "But everyone has their limits. You hit yours a long time ago and burst ... I'm sure you recall that moment."

24

She glanced down at her wrists and nodded. Wrists and necks reminded her of Mother's scars. Fingernails that ripped through flesh, drawing blood that seeped down her palms. There had been one night when she walked in on her mother naked, blood flowing from her neck and down her chest as she gambled with her own life. At her worst, she would hurt herself and then freeze the wound right before it could kill her. Mother had tried to make Olivia kill Bryson, leading to the moment of which Himitsu spoke.

"That had been a success ..." Himitsu trailed off and sighed. "Then, I don't know what happened. You reverted. Sure, you'd manage an occasional smile, but nothing beyond that. Learning how to repress emotions as a child is one thing. Forcing yourself to do it after relinquishing those constraints is a whole different story. I don't think your mind can process trauma properly."

"Meow Meow," she muttered. "He was taken from me immediately after I betrayed my mom."

Himitsu pursed his lips and inhaled, posture stiffening—as if preparing himself for his next words. "This may sound harsh, Olivia—and I understand he was a companion—but, more than anything else, he was nothing but a crutch for your broken heart. An entity in which you could empty your feelings."

"A scapegoat," she whispered. Warmth crept up her neck and into her skull, eyes glazing over. *No way. This feeling.*

He placed a hand on hers. She flinched backward and ripped her hand away, the motion nearly knocking a tear free. He tilted his head, his hand now on the bench. "Do you know where your fear of physical affection comes from?"

"Knowing what Mendac did to my mom."

"And the rare times you do allow someone to hug you ..."

"I don't hug them back," she said, finishing his sentence.

They studied each other in the silence that followed. She was surprised to find wetness in his eyes. He hurt for her.

"Once you realize that you don't need Meow Meow to cope with all of the pain, those insecurities will lessen. Your power will expand." He smiled, dropping his leg and facing the window again. "It's frightening, in a way. That you're as much of a force as you are while being held back. I know I'm giving weird advice, but tragedy *should* hurt you. You're doing yourself no favors by trying to filter out pain."

A tear slipped down Olivia's cheek as she scooted toward Himitsu. She placed her head on his shoulder. "That's a start," he said. He pressed his lips against her hair. "Bryson is a brother to me, which basically makes you my sister. I would never hurt you, nor would any of the other guys in the Jestivan."

They sat in silence after that. Olivia could feel the glances of others in her direction, shocked by the display: the emotionless girl who couldn't stand physical affection pressed against another person. Himitsu's assessment had been correct, and his words made her hate the fact that she'd seen so little of the Jestivan over the past few years.

She wiped her eyes before another tear could fall, but the sky seemed to cry on her behalf—just like Meow Meow used to do if the pain was bad enough. Rain hammered against the windows, distorting the palace grounds. *So much water.*

The sight of it brought her back to that day she'd betrayed her mother in favor of Bryson. The outpouring of emotions had caused her to create an intense columnar vortex of water—the first and only sign of weaving ability in her life. The events of that moment had replayed in her head every day since then. It was the true reason why she had reverted instantaneously. Meow Meow may have played a part, but it had never been the key.

She'd met a man in that twister of water—a very powerful one who had appeared out of darkness. Recognizing the situation immediately, her mother had made one last request of Olivia, and, consumed by the grief of betraying her mother, Olivia promised to never summon that man again.

Olivia's eyes closed, head limp on Himitsu's shoulder, the pattering of rain growing distant as her mind slipped into sleep and a dream …

… "He's your *son*! He's my *brother*! He's our *blood*!"

Olivia had never felt such a rush of emotion in her life. In a way, it felt like a betrayal to herself. But, it felt *right*. Her fists were soaked in Bryson's blood. Their mom held a frozen stake inches away from his heart.

It's too much, Olivia said to Meow Meow in her mind.

I know, he said. *I feel it, too. It's okay. No more holding back.*

Something hot and fluid ripped through her energy canals. A single tear ran down her cheek and clung to her chin. Her mother had turned her attention away from Bryson and Thusia, who were both pinned to the side of a building in Wealth's Crossroads. Olivia's outburst had surprised all of them.

The tear fell from her face and splashed against cobbles. Waves erupted, encircling her and her mother, separating them from everyone else. Heat rushed out of her and into the water that now curled inward hundreds of feet above. Apoleia looked up, slack-jawed, exposing dozens of self-inflicted cuts across her neck. Errant droplets splashed against her skin, burning it upon impact. Steam filled the aquatic vortex that had now begun to spin as it crashed down toward the two women at its center. And Olivia—a girl of Stillian genes who loved the ice—thrived in the sauna. Just as the wave was about to crush them both, she did something that reshaped the vortex into a spiraling dome.

You just wove, Meow Meow said. *YOU JUST WOVE.*

Steam swirled within the dome, figures from outside not visible through the wall of water. The crystallized ice on Apoleia's skin was melting away, revealing her natural color below. Tendrils of black fog began to appear around them, creeping within the steam before gaining speed. It swirled with the water, and the atmosphere shifted. Her body became heavier, but her insides felt hollow save something that clawed at her organs. The sensation wasn't pleasant, like butterflies if they had razors for wings.

Apoleia's eyes followed the black fog, her face impassive—an oddity on the typically animated woman. Her gaze then fixed itself on Olivia. "If today has triggered all of this, then it's obvious with whom you side."

"What is this?!" Olivia screamed, fearful of the desperation in her tone.

The black smoke peeled away from the dome and converged at the center into a blob of shadows. Its edges ebbed and flowed into a shape—a *humanistic* shape. It grew four limbs and a head, but remained shrouded in fog that encroached along the skin.

Olivia backed away, placing her hands behind her until her fingers punctured the wall of hot water, sending more steam upward. She didn't like the aura of this *thing*, appearing outside of her body while somehow rattling inside of her, gnawing at her innards. Her mother remained unfazed, hands clasped behind her back as she studied the entity. The shadows dispersed, revealing either a human or a corpse.

And I thought Rhyparia's mom was ugly, Meow Meow said. *What the hell is that?*

This man stood just north of six feet, his hair a kinky mass of graying curls. He was dark-skinned like Adren Director Buredo or King Supido, but that was hard to tell with the gaping holes in his body. Most of his face—the nose, mouth, and left eye—had no skin, exposing muscles, cartilage, and even the bones of some of his jaw. The left eyeball was spherical and black enough to absorb light. Because of this, it didn't seem to move at all, even though his right eye—the normal one—moved in different directions, surveying its surroundings.

The rest of his body was more terrifying. Absent of a shirt, he donned a hole in his chest that revealed a gray heart ribbed with blackened veins. Something crawled around it. It beat like any normal heart would, pumping the inky substance throughout the rest of the body. Sinuous muscle surrounded the hole, umber skin eventually growing another few centimeters outward. Another chunk of skin was gone from his obliques and abdomen, exposing more pinkish innards until they disappeared beneath his beltline.

"Unfortunate," Apoleia said, drawing the attention of the half-cadaver-half-human. It turned unnaturally slow, revealing a bloodied hole in the back of its skull—only the blood was, of course, black.

He turned back to Olivia. "My name is Preloz Henye, a Gefal of the Dark Empire, assigned to you as your Bewahr."

She balked, caught so off guard that she'd forgotten Stillian customs in regards to the royal firstborn's Bewahr. Her mother was quick to remind her. "Dismiss him."

Olivia couldn't regain her wits, but Meow Meow understood. *Remember, you don't have to*, he said.

"Are you in danger?" Preloz asked, deadpan. His eyes roved across the dome of water. "Peculiar."

"Dismiss him!" Apoleia screamed. "You can at least do that for me!"

Preloz seemed unbothered by Olivia's mother. He continued to acknowledge only her. "I know the Still family has a track record of rejecting male Bewahr," he said.

Olivia couldn't get over this man's image. When he spoke, the muscles around his mouth tore, shreds of it hanging loosely from his face. And she made it a point to not look at his left eye, the depth of its blackness too terrifying to face. What kind of Bewahr was he? She didn't recognize the name. If Gefal were once powerful humans before death, why had she never heard tales of this man's first life?

He obviously Cynnish, Meow Meow said.

She agreed, recalling the tales of her fellow Jestivan's adventure into the Cyn Kingdom. They'd mentioned people and animals with rotting skin, but nothing close to this. It looked as if a ghastly beast had ravaged his body.

Behind the Bewahr, her mother fell to her knees, losing composure as she spotted the contemplation on Olivia's face. Apoleia clawed at her wrists, breaking scabs with ease. Blood joined the sweat that trickled down her hands, the water's heat refusing to subside. Then came the crying, maniacal enough to cause her to convulse. Her body furled forward, back shaking as she tried to catch her breath.

Now, the Bewahr turned. "*You* are a Stillian? That despair in a Stillian woman?"

Apoleia looked up through sopping wet strands of hair. Her hands moved up her body, fingers ready to tear into her neck … But then they continued upward, past her mouth and nose. Her fingers hovered in front of bulging eyes. "Will this make it all disappear?" she asked, voice coarse and deep. "I see darkness everywhere now, ever since looking at Mendac. What good are my eyes?" She whispered, "I don't want to cry anymore."

There's no way, Meow Meow said.

That was it. The neck and wrists were one thing; Olivia had grown up around that and—as sad as it was—become accustom to it. But the eyes …

"*LEAVE!*"

Apoleia's fingers relaxed. Preloz regarded Olivia with a frown—or what she thought was a frown. It was difficult to decipher among the muscles and bones. Thankfully, he gave a single nod and dispersed into shadows.

After a few seconds to recollect herself, her mother stood. Olivia couldn't return her gaze.

"I suppose I should take solace in the fact that you at least had the gall to do that," Apoleia said. "Now, get us out of this damned furnace before I melt into a puddle."

"I'm sorry, Mother."

"A pointless sentiment. You're not my daughter."

5

One Moon

The sun had set, allowing Intelights to spark to life as they worked to bathe the atrium in a golden hue. Agnos appreciated these older models, as they closely mimicked the flames of candles. Newer Intelights were a harsh, sterile white that hurt the eyes. Looking directly at one was like staring at a miniature sun.

Rain continued to fall, a tranquil, constant noise to backdrop the conversation between Tashami and Vuilni. Spirits were high since Bryson awoke a few hours earlier, but nobody had been allowed to visit him since the royal sisters had rushed everyone out. Agnos didn't mind; he needed time to process what he'd seen. Bryson's eyes had been glowing. And wings constructed of celestial light? He knew what it was because it had been similar to the shield protecting the Thunder Queen's chronicle in the seafloor cave, but why wings?

Add that to the long list of the world's mysteries to which he wanted answers. Luckily, he believed he was close to discovering them. All he needed were a couple more scholars to join him, for tackling the Warpfinate's depths alone was ill advised according to the Thunder Queen.

Two young women entered the atrium from the end of the hallway opposite of Bryson's room. Evelyn and Kaylee hadn't known each other before arriving in Dunami a couple weeks ago, but they had developed a bond through their mutual friendship with the Jestivan. They viewed themselves as outsiders—no matter how many times Agnos or Himitsu tried convincing them otherwise. It made sense, he supposed. Kaylee may have played a big part in discovering Neeko's grave with Himitsu, and Evelyn had been crucial to Agnos's pirate crew toppling the SCAPD fleet, but those were recent events that happened on the war's peripheries. It would take some time before their presence in the core group was normal, but it would definitely happen. Vuilni was proof of that, for she had once been in a similar situation years ago.

Evelyn took a seat with Agnos, Tashami, and Vuilni, while Kaylee split away to join Himitsu near the windows. The two of them had apparently become a budding romance during their time in the Archaic Kingdom hunting down Neeko. Agnos turned to watch as Kaylee gave Himitsu a peck on the lips. Olivia, who had been leaning against Himitsu's shoulder, stirred and straightened.

Agnos looked away, annoyed that he had even cared to watch the affectionate exchange in the first place. He was beginning to question his own disregard of lust throughout his life. He'd never desired intimacy—a fact many would blame on his preoccupation with his personal dreams. That might have been the case, but now he wasn't so sure. He was beginning to pine for that touch, even if he had no idea what that "touch" was exactly. But he saw it. In the eyes of Bryson when he looked at Shelly. In Himitsu's sucker of a smile when Kaylee entered the room … In Queen Delilah's wails as she mourned her husband. Whether through bliss or anguish, that touch exposed itself with such alluring intensity.

"Why is everyone out here?" Evelyn asked.

"Bryson woke up," Vuilni said. "The princess …" She trailed off, knowing her mistake. "The queen is visiting him."

"That's good," Evelyn said. The news didn't bring the same excitement to her face like it had for everyone else. Nobody blamed her. She'd never met the rambunctious captain of the Jestivan.

Agnos crossed glances with Tashami for a moment, knowing what was going through his head. He wanted to mention the wings, but Agnos shook his head.

"What was the great Ophala up to today?" Tashami asked, turning toward Evelyn to change the subject.

"We walked the city's wreckage and visited construction crews, discussing areas that needed the most attention and how they could be tackled efficiently."

"That woman doesn't stop," Vuilni said.

Tashami laughed. "It's a miracle King Sigmund hasn't driven the Archaic Kingdom into the dirt without her there."

"She's been keeping in touch with him through broadcast meetings," Evelyn replied. "Although I must admit that I've never seen someone be so exasperated with another person."

As Tashami and Vuilni spilled into a conversation about Ophala's portentousness, Agnos noticed Evelyn frequently glance at Olivia, who had separated herself from Himitsu and Kaylee to sit in front of a different window. As a Stillian woman, Evelyn was awestruck by the presence of royalty. Olivia was her princess, next in line to take the Frozen Throne after Queen Apoleia. Agnos had a hard time putting himself in Evelyn's shoes. The possibility of meeting Archaic royalty meant nothing to him. Honestly, based on Ophala's comments, he probably wanted nothing to do with King Sigmund.

"Have you introduced yourself to her yet?" Agnos asked.

Evelyn shook her head.

He smiled. "This is not the Evelyn I met on the ship."

"Yes, well … my *princess* wasn't on that ship."

Agnos regarded Olivia, spotting her face's reflection in the giant wall of glass. He narrowed his eyes, catching sadness in that gaze. Had she been crying? *No, of course not.*

A hand hit his shoulder, and he flinched. "What was that for?" he snapped at Evelyn.

"Don't stare, or she'll see and come this way."

He rolled his eyes and turned back to—ah, yes. Olivia was on her way over. "Sorry," he said, fighting back a laugh as Evelyn's face twisted with horror.

Olivia stopped between the two armchairs occupied by Agnos and Evelyn. Spotting Evelyn's hesitance, he tried to introduce her, but Olivia beat him to the punch. "Hey, you're the Stillian I've been hearing about?"

Silence.

Tashami leaned in from across the centerpiece. "She's busy pissing herself. Give her a second."

"Yes, she is that woman," Agnos said, steering the discussion in the right direction. "Iced an entire chunk of river."

"I want to hear the story one day," Olivia said. "From the mouth of the woman who did it."

"Definitely," Evelyn muttered.

Tashami released a pent-up breath, scooting back from the edge of his seat. "She did it. Words."

Vuilni giggled. "I'm proud of you."

"Tomorrow we'll go for a walk or something," Olivia said.

"I'd love that, Princess."

Olivia opened her mouth, but then shut it. Agnos had expected her to ask Evelyn not to address her with such formalities, like Bryson.

"Oh, my apologies, Princess," Evelyn said, standing up and offering a bow. Agnos, Tashami, and Vuilni exchanged apprehensive looks, but Olivia wasn't fazed. She looked down at Evelyn … and, very slowly, a smile crept onto her face.

"You are kind," said Olivia as Evelyn returned to her seat. "Now, I believe it's about time I go visit my brother. The royal sisters can share."

As Olivia left, Evelyn sunk deeper into her chair. "I hate myself."

They burst into laughter, and spirits remained high for the next hour. The pattering of rain disappeared as the storm subsided, creating a rare sight for the Intel Kingdom. Despite the late hour, the city outside was illuminated in a luminescent light. Some could say it was because of the absence of Intelights in the city streets, but to those with trained eyes who had been in the Intel Kingdom for the past couple of weeks, there was something far grander at play.

"Guys, look at this."

Everyone turned to look at Himitsu, who stood in front of the glass wall with Kaylee by his side, both looking up. They all approached the massive window and regarded an open night sky, marking the first time such a spectacle had occurred in the Intel Kingdom in years, explaining the abundance of light.

But that wasn't what caused eyebrows to furrow and jaws to drop. They saw the stars, the underbellies of the two celestial islands, and a moon. And there lay the problem.

A *single* moon.

Agnos scanned the entire star-strewn canvas.

"Agnos," said Himitsu. "Tell me we aren't losing our minds."

He shook his head, jaw rigid. "You're not."

He didn't know what to say after that, his mind reeling from the inexplicable events of the past couple of weeks. News of Mendac's rebirth. Reports of black wings and the ability of flight. Bryson's awakening accompanied by wings of his own, except glowing with white hot light. Celestial rings that burned around Bryson's pupils and irises.

And now, their moon was gone.

*   *   *

Migraines were a new experience for Spy Pilot Ophala. It felt like the earthquakes and avalanches of the Archaic Mountains were happening just behind her eyes. For all the talk of sobriety's benefits, she was seeing very little to back it up.

What would help me see clearer is a tankard of vodka, she thought as she sorted through her bird mail. It was too bad that a recent revelation—dawning upon her during a drunken night after learning of a falling moon in the Power Kingdom—had convinced her alcohol was to blame for all of her judgmental errors throughout her life. She'd been so confident about Rhyparia's right to freedom that she'd gone out of her way to help her escape execution, believing she wasn't a danger to society with proper

35

guidance. And then Rhyparia went and murdered hundreds of thousands of people … and likely destroyed a kingdom. This was, of course, an assumption. She didn't know how the moon actually fell, but she knew who had gone there with very meaningful intentions. And if anyone's ancient and skill could manage the feat, it was Rhyparia's.

Ophala's fingers were busy massaging her temple as she squinted at Yvole's sorry excuse for cursive. He had taken control of Phesaw after Director Neaneuma's death. His penmanship was awful under normal circumstances, and this vain attempt at cursive for the sake of seeming more official didn't help the problem. He was asking about the proper time to start recruiting new staff for the school's reopening and … *ugh*. She tossed the letter to the side.

She leaned back and sighed, her chair squealing with the shift in weight. She eyed Vistas, who sat at the far end of her office in an armchair while casually sipping red wine—as if taunting her. He had brought news of Bryson's recovery from his coma just an hour ago. She would need to pay him a visit tomorrow. For now, she awaited an important call.

The rain cleared, bringing a hollow quiet to her temporary office—a space she would have liked to make permanent. Alas, she'd have to return to her proper kingdom soon.

Vistas set down his glass of wine on an end table and stood. "She's ready, Pilot."

"Very good."

His right eye burned burgundy while his left eye dilated, projecting a holographic display in the middle of the office. The picture depicted Joy's perspective. The Dev servant stood inside a chamber, looking out a pair of double doors that led to a balcony where Spirit Queen Apsa stood.

"Milady," said Joy, "I have Pilot Ophala and Vistas connected."

Apsa turned her head slightly, exposing half her face. Despite the minimal exposure, Ophala could read the look of hopelessness in that one eye. It had been ten days since the last update, but it seemed nothing had improved.

"How much longer?" Ophala asked.

"Take a look for yourself," Apsa said, turning back the other way.

36

Joy stepped onto the balcony and approached the banister, where the capital of the Spirit Kingdom, Sodai, lay below the palace. Only, no longer did it look like a city. The Gulf of Sodai had burst, the tides reaching heights that swallowed most streets and buildings. The only areas not submerged were the hilltops, but there was no telling how much longer before they, too, became nonexistent. Small vessels dotted the waters, rowed by rescue teams of navy sailors as they scoured the drowned neighborhoods for survivors. Battleships floated in a line in the distance, acting as barriers that prevented other vessels from accidentally steering toward the submerged city.

To the east should have stood the most powerful naval base in all of the Light Realm. It, too, had been claimed by the gulf, now rotting in the belly of the beast. Queen Apsa had only a few weeks before she'd need to evacuate like her citizens. The capital and royal headquarters required relocation, a transition that would prove difficult for even a small town, much less a sprawling metropolis. The pirate city, DaiSo, was experiencing the same disaster. The Spirit Kingdom tolerated the city because it had been a bubble, as piracy and criminal behavior remained contained in their grimy streets. Now, the bubble had burst, forcing miscreants to scatter across the land.

Ophala thought she had her hands full here in Dunami, trying to ease the transition from princess to queen for Shelly, like she had done with Archaic King Sigmund. But the problems here were fixable. Queen Apsa's enemy, nature's wrath, was undefeated. And the source of the catastrophe? A lone moon in the night sky, its little brother now gone. Rhyparia's stunt—again, a logical conclusion on Ophala's part—had hurt more than just the Power Kingdom. Had she foreseen the apocalyptic results that'd befall the rest of the world?

No. She hadn't seen past her own rage.

6

A Journey for Family

Despite her location, Shelly didn't recognize the moon's absence. Lost in the stars and her thoughts, her gaze was unfocused as she lay on the floor of her room—a room that she'd soon abandon. As the Royal Head, she needed to relocate to an area of the royal quarters that sat near the palace's heart in case of emergencies. The seclusion of this tower made reaching her in a timely manner too difficult. She needed to be accessible— a logical train of thought that didn't make the move any less heartbreaking.

She loved this place and all of its memories. It'd been built specifically for her at the age of six. A spherical room with curving glass walls and a ceiling, allowing her an endless view of the sky, for it sat above the kingdom's low-hanging clouds. At thirteen, her father decided she was old enough for a balcony that circled its perimeter. The first steps outside had been breathtaking, figuratively and literally, for breaths at such an altitude didn't come easily. Two years later, Lilu drew the blueprints for the platform at the center, which a weavineer from Brilliance then built to replace the spiral staircase.

Sometime after that, she brought Bryson here for the first time. It was an unforgettable night, during which they'd both summoned their Branian. They learned a little bit about the Light Empire and witnessed the friendly relationship between Thusia and Suadade. It was also when she'd learned Suadade might have been gay, a topic her Branian never let surface again.

Shelly located the crusted underbelly of the Light Empire. It had been several months since she'd last summoned her Branian, and not from a lack of trying. She missed him and feared that imprisonment was the cause of his absence. Bryson had told her what Thusia said about the state of the Empires. They were experiencing turmoil that had spilled into the kingdoms, evident in the events of the Blizzard of Blood. Linsani didn't just fly beyond the Cyn Kingdom's Edge without proper influence. These had all seemed like minor problems when compared to Toono and Storshae, but that didn't mean they hadn't existed. In fact, they'd been brewing in the background, and the resurrection of Mendac might have accelerated everything.

Angst riddled Shelly as she thought about that man. Bryson hadn't mentioned his father after waking from his coma. The one time Lilu let the name slip, he had instructed her to stop. Shelly didn't know how it would change Bryson, but she knew it would ... somehow. She only hoped that it wouldn't break him, which could have happened in any number of ways: rage driving him toward vengeance or sorrow sinking him into depression.

She had to take matters into her own hands. It was time to repay her fiancé for all of the sacrifices he'd made to protect this kingdom, his family, and his friends. Yes, she'd made sacrifices of her own—her freedom by remaining locked in this palace for the sake of their child—but this was solely for him. Shelly only hoped that woman showed up. She would be the most important guest at their wedding, but the trek across the Diamond Sea was difficult, so the chances were slim.

Please, for the sake of Bryson, be our guest.

*　　　*　　　*

Apoleia adored journeys across the Diamond Sea. It was an opportunity to escape the pressures of royalty while appreciating the frivolities. She sat in a covered seating chamber on the back of a royal tram ram—a massive, furry beast that dwarfed horses and barrelers. As far as communal animals, there was nothing like it.

Titus—her husband as of two months ago—sat at her side. Her sister, Ropinia, sat in the row of seats behind her. Gennaio, father to both women, sat in the rear with an entire bench to himself, cushioned with plush padding and pillows. It was a throne when compared to the more modest seats of everyone else—a throne he deserved in the eyes of both of his daughters. He'd spent most of his life as an afterthought in a culture dominated by women, followed by a lengthy stint of complete paralysis caused by Mendac LeAnce. Apoleia and Ropinia would spoil him for the rest of his life.

"This might be the most unwise thing we've ever done since your arrival to the throne," Ropinia said.

Apoleia flippantly waved her hand over her shoulder. "Kindoliya can last a month or two under your husband's leadership."

Titus nodded and turned in his seat, a footfall of the tram ram thundering in the background. "Have faith in General Valp, Milady."

"Stop calling me that," Ropinia said.

Gennaio wheezed out a laugh from the back. "Some Stillian women you two grew up to be."

Apoleia grinned, natural in the gentle curl of her lips. Hearing her father's voice—regardless of its fragility—brought her peace. His ability to form words had vastly improved since Nyemas Jugtah—a man now dubbed as *Miracle Weaver* in their kingdom—cured him of his paralysis. That Intelian man's actions had balanced her mental state. There was subtleness to her expressions now, and the scars on her wrists and neck—although permanent—were now over a year old. She didn't have to rely on self-harm to distract her mind from the emotional pain. That was liberating.

"Besides," she said, noticing the air of concern from her younger sister, "it's good for the city to see a man lead. This is a monumental moment for our culture; no male has ever held such authority. The vast majority of our female population has yet to accept the shift I'm trying to implement, so what's a better way of convincing them than by showing results?"

"A great mindset," Titus said.

Ropinia sucked her teeth. "Oh please, Titus. Weren't you the one telling Valp to keep his head on a swivel, fearing an assassination attempt by one of the women in the palace?"

"I know you're a Still-blooded woman, so tone alteration beyond the spectrum of bricks isn't your specialty, but I was being sarcastic."

Apoleia could practically hear Ropinia's chest puff in response. "Your head is a brick."

Titus laughed at himself, and Apoleia's smile widened.

"Just because you're in-laws doesn't mean you must bicker like actual siblings," Gennaio said.

The banter didn't stop. Hours passed, during which Apoleia sat mostly in silence, only providing input in efforts to fuel their fire. She had missed this in her life. It was not something she had ever experienced, not under the roof of her strict mother, nor the years spent trapped in her maniacal mind. This felt like a true family, and soon, she'd meet the rest.

By nightfall, they had reached a sparse settlement of frozen barracks sprawled at the base of the Still Mountains. Somewhere at the center of these rectangular buildings were the kingdom's teleplatforms. Fort Nalula was a young settlement. Apoleia had ordered its construction following the Blizzard of Blood. With the Still Kingdom's shift in alliance to True Light, she had feared potential retaliation from SCAPD forces such as the Cynnish, Powish, or Devish. While she felt the threat had greatly diminished, she enjoyed the added comfort of knowing a military base sat here. Granted, Fort Nalula was still in its infancy, but she counted ten barracks already. They lacked the refinement of Kindoliya's crystalline structures, but soldiers needed practicality, not aesthetics.

"The first settlement outside of Kindoliya in over a millennium," Titus said in awe. He had left his seat and was now standing at the front of the coach, hands on the guardrail as he leaned forward eagerly.

"I guess we're ignoring the tribes in the mountains," Ropinia said.

"Obviously. They're *tribes*."

While this place did draw awe for its uniqueness, Apoleia's anticipation stemmed from something else entirely: the beings inside one of the barracks. She hadn't informed her sister or husband of this, partly because it had been a recent development, but mostly because it needed to remain secret for the time being. When she had received news from Ophala Vevlu about the situation, it was explained as a sensitive topic. If she wanted to avoid unrest, then practice delicacy and patience when confronting it … whatever *it* was.

They dismounted the tram ram at nightfall via a long rope ladder that didn't lend well to heels or bare feet. That's what the special shoes were for, which Apoleia removed with haste after reaching the frozen surface of the Diamond Sea. She had equipped her crown of crystalline ice, a symbol of her sovereignty to those below her. The special concoction of gems and frost could only be found at the peak of the kingdom's tallest mountain, Mount Stillinia. The crown refracted moonlight in hundreds of directions, turning her into a beacon of prismatic light.

After getting her father settled in a room for the night, Apoleia split from Titus to seek out the "beings" that Ophala had written to her about. Titus opposed the notion of her roaming the base on her own, but quickly shut up upon seeing the look on her face—a look that was by no means fierce or exaggerated. She'd given him that thin-lipped, empty gaze, unnerving in its coldness.

Thus, Titus went to check on one of his lower officials who had minor authority in Fort Nalula, turning what should have been a vacation into an excuse to speak logistics and tactics. Apoleia made her way toward barrack number four, an abandoned building by the looks of its lightless windows and vacated perimeter. Guards seemed to make a point of avoiding it. A single woman sat next to the front door on a frozen bench, filing her nails with crystal teeth sharpened to a point like a shark's. She was a rare specimen and the true authority figure of this place—a tribal woman who'd fled her home in the mountains years ago.

Apoleia had to force length in her strides as she neared the woman, betraying the part of her that wanted to turn the other way. She'd never admit it to anyone else, but there was spontaneity to the Mountain Stills that made her anxious. Those teeth weren't natural, and the barbarian carried herself with the casual apathy of a bored drunk, despite possessing the reputation of jumping at someone's throat when given the tiniest of reasons. At least she stood and bowed as Apoleia stopped in front of her, however lackadaisical it might have been.

"Mrs. Trulin," Apoleia said, an air of royalty returning to her posture.

"Good evening, my Queen."

"What is it I'm getting myself into?" Apoleia asked, glancing at the door.

"I wouldn't know. My instructions were clear: Do not investigate."

Apoleia cocked an eyebrow at the frozen door, a maze of grooves etched into the surface. Such an intricate Stillian lock for a mere barrack. She thought that after the disappearance of a moon and the rising tides, nothing could spook someone this much. They'd seen it all, had they not?

Stepping past Mrs. Trulin, Apoleia placed three fingers at different spots on the maze. She wove with the grooves, following the proper paths until they converged at the door's center. It melted, and she walked through, the officer returning to her seat outside. The frozen door reformed behind her, swallowing the barracks in shadows save faint moonlight from the frost-coated windows.

"Skyrise," said a woman's voice from the darkness, initiating the code that Ophala had provided in the letter.

The Still Queen recited her part, though she had no idea what it meant. "An Omen of Shadows."

Flames erupted upon torches lining distant walls, revealing not a barrack but a massive rec hall. Long tables were pushed to the sides, leaving an empty floor at the center. Figures occupied the far end, some seated on the floor while others lay across benches. And she said "figures" because not all were people. There was a woman and a man, who she'd soon learn to be Rayne and Saikatto, two of the original Jestivan and former teammates of Mendac. This news should have triggered hate in her, but her mind had to come to grips with the other figures surrounding them first.

A fox with three swords at its hip, arms crossed as it sat on a bench and leaned back against the table; a sneering wolf seated on the floor with an abdomen that would have put a Powish to shame, a leg kicked up and hands behind him as support; a honey badger that stood between the two

Jestivan; a rabbit with its face buried in an open book on a table; and a weasel that hung from a torch by its tail.

The fox opened one eye, regarding Apoleia. "We're sorry for the intrusion on your lands, Queen Apoleia, but we must ask for passage into the Light Realm with you. Also, we request your beautiful kingdom be used as a haven for several hundred, maybe thousand, Powish refugees."

"That's it?" Apoleia asked dryly. "I think I need questions answered first."

The fox stood. "My name is Atarax, and you can ask me anything."

7

The Dark Empire

Rhyparia NuForce had heard the stories depicting stone as black as a starless night sky, the miners who would dig and excavate caves to find it—caves deep enough to make people lose themselves. Like most of Kuki Sphaira's tall tales, she had never believed them in her earlier years. After her botched execution, she had reason to become a believer of almost anything. Riding the back of the legendary beast, Gale Thrasher, and meeting the unknown race of dimiours could make a believer out of anybody. Then there were the wings of furling shadows presently folded against her back. Wings that had prompted the appearance of otherworldly beings with mentions of an empirical war and a god, claiming she would become a divine soldier and there was nothing she could do to negate that.

They were right. She'd tried countless times to take her own life since the abduction, but each attempt was stopped by an invisible force that took control of her body.

Despite all of these phenomena, it was her journey through Realmular Tunnel that had squashed any legitimacy to the tales of black stone, for it was said to have existed underground, halfway between the two realms. If that had been true, she would have seen evidence.

Now she believed she was seeing it, transfixed by the architecture of her cell. She'd spent two weeks trapped in here, yet the glossy black walls, laced with parabolic white lines that resembled wood grain, continued to beckon her attention. She'd made a habit of running her fingers across the floor or down a wall, feeling not a single bump in its surface. It was as if someone had sliced through the stone like butter and then polished it for centuries, as its blackened surface reflected the moonlight that trickled in from the small window at the top of the cell—not that there was much moonlight to begin with.

She regarded the small window, wondering what was outside. She had yet to see the "outside" since arriving in this cage, but something told her the Dark Empire's day-night cycle didn't follow natural law. *Nor did this stone*, she thought as her attention returned to the wall.

She scooted backward. As her back neared the wall, her wings grew more chaotic. Shadowy tendrils whipped out, attempting to latch onto the black stone. They yearned for a connection as if the wall was its partner. The only problem was that the wall never responded, lacking mutual desire. It all made no sense. Either natural law was a sham or the commoner's perception of it had been severely limited in scope. Agnos would have argued the latter; Rhyparia agreed.

Years ago, if someone would have told her that her umbrella could have been used to drop the moon from its fixture among the stars, she would have suggested a couple mental facilities for them to attend. But, with the two decades lent to her by Musku, she had discovered the sheer power of her ancient.

If finely woven enough, she could make her Archaic Chains stretch for thousands of leagues. The beginning of her training spent in Musku's time warp was spent contemplating methods of redeeming her atrocities. She brainstormed peaceful solutions at first—ways of freeing Powish slaves without using her ancient. She had viewed her ancient as nothing but a tool to get through the Realmular Tunnel. Then the years passed, and her patience declined.

She began contemplating ways to make up for all of the lost time. Those methods became aggressive in nature. She learned to exert Archaic Energy from her body into her ancient, then expel it externally where it'd proceed to collide into billions of Archaic Currents. She'd then spend every day narrowing these billions of energy-current clusters into invisible tubes as wide as her arm. Weaving so many clusters into such a fine space created massive thrust, which compiled exponentially as each cluster fed off another. Then, when her tube of Archaic Chains reached her desired target, she'd loosen her weaving in order to entrap it in a gravitational fluctuation. She'd crush trees in distant parts of the forest, and Musku never knew any better, for around Rhyparia it felt no different.

The farther she reached, the greater and deadlier her aspirations became. Once she had hit fifteen years of training, Rhyparia—accelerated into her lower thirties—would have been unrecognizable to those she once knew. And not just because of her physical maturation, but her process of thought. The naïve girl was gone, replaced by a hardened, scornful woman.

That night during her fifteenth year of training was unforgettable. She'd lain next to Musku in the grass as he told her a story about the two moons, how one belonged to Kuki Sphaira while the other belonged to the strange blue planet in the Dark Realm's sky. The smaller one was Kuki Sphaira's, its purpose unknown. Musku explained theories. A light source was the most obvious, but many scholars also believed it controlled weather patterns or even the tides. Rhyparia's mind, however, ventured elsewhere. Somewhere far darker.

Could she reach the moon? She had become an expert weaver, her Archaic tubes—terminology she'd given them herself—now as narrow as a quill's tip. She could reach the opposite end of the Archaic Kingdom if she'd wanted, though there were factors that would have made that difficult, such as mountains, plateaus, and other manmade structures that would force directional weaving. But the moon ... Well, that was above her, which meant a straight shot would work.

That had been the last four to five years of her training with Musku. Of course, he was unaware of this. She'd already mastered lateral gravity, the one skill necessary for traversing the Realmular Tunnel, but she feigned negligence in order to distract him from her personal lessons elsewhere.

The day eventually came when she touched the moon for the first time, but it was the larger one—the one that belonged to Earth, as Dev King Rehn had called it nearly three decades prior. Euphoria washed over her that no drug could have ever provided, teaching her that the moon—or at least Earth's moon—was more than just a rock in the sky. It was a different world entirely, not belonging to the same history as Kuki Sphaira.

The revelation spooked her. She wanted to use Earth's moon as a weapon to drop on the Power Kingdom, thinking it was better to leave her own world's moon untouched, but that first contact dispelled that notion. Earth's moon didn't belong to her, but some other peoples. Some other species. In a strange way, some other *sky*. She vowed to never touch their moon again, instead placing her focus on its little brother, where she then found familiarity.

Now Kuki Sphaira's moon was embedded in the crust of the Power Kingdom with a few generations of lives lost beneath it. And now she was here, sharing a prison block with the most unlikely person.

Rhyparia looked up, eyes trained on the cell across from her own. A man sat in the middle of it, seemingly unbothered by their foreign surroundings. In fact, he was engrossed by sheets of parchment strewn around him. Their jailers hadn't bothered stripping either of them of their personal belongings—except her umbrella.

The man in the cell across from her had taken imprisonment in stride. It seemed that as long as he had his papers and a writing instrument, he was happy. She supposed that made sense. Mendac LeAnce had always been revered as not just a mighty general, but a transcendent scholar. She hadn't expected such charisma and pageantry, which displayed itself in spades the first time they spoke. They shared few words, providing nothing about their personal lives or the decisions that had landed them in this predicament. Bryson had never spoken much of his father, uncomfortable with the shadow created by his name, so Rhyparia had to simply guess at what Mendac could have done to sprout those wings on his back and put him in her company. She was only certain that his actions couldn't have come anywhere close to her atrocities.

Plenty of questions sprouted in her mind. Why did he invade the Dev Kingdom and enslave so many of its people? Why was Debonicus—a mighty Pogu of the Light Empire—sent to execute him? That was the last information of interest she'd learned about him. She'd have to save those questions for another time. They'd likely be seeing a lot of each other from this point forward, as they'd both been told they were becoming soldiers fighting for—

"Emperor Mialo would like to speak with you."

Rhyparia scrambled forward, heart hammering from the unexpected voice. It had come from behind her, but there should have only been a wall there. She flipped onto her butt, pressing her back into the gate's bars as she gawked at the back wall … where a woman's face protruded from the black stone. Shadows shifted and crept along her skin. An arm extended from a separate part of the wall, hand open as if in waiting. Rhyparia didn't move toward her, but turned her head to see Mendac's reaction. He watched, but didn't seem perturbed.

As Rhyparia regarded her guest again, the woman narrowed hazel eyes, skin smooth and brown with golden undertones. "The rumors are true," she said. "You're stubborn and naïve." She sighed. "I guess we can take the long way to the emperor's energy room." She stepped out of the wall, long tan legs forming out of shadows as they broke free from the stone. She wore a pink dress that stopped halfway down her thighs, straps thin at her shoulders.

Rhyparia scuttled to the side as the woman strode directly for the gate, paying her no mind. She grasped the lock, her hand becoming shadows as it merged with the material. The gate squealed as it swung open.

"Are you Yasmine Cordelia?" Mendac asked as the woman stepped into the corridor that ran between the cells.

She turned to look at him, straight black hair shifting loosely against her back. "Ah, a fan of my work?"

He chuckled. "More like the bane of my existence."

"Yes, I heard about that. Couldn't find what you were looking for?"

"What do you think?"

"The effort was there at least," she said. "Poten will serve as your escort to the emperor. I believe he's finishing his twelfth meal of the day—

the smallest of his twenty-four, so it shouldn't take too long." She turned and raised her chin before walking out of sight. "Rhyparia NuForce, let's go. We don't keep Emperor Mialo waiting."

Rhyparia couldn't move, or she didn't want to. She'd just witnessed a woman appear out of a wall, and no ordinary woman at that. Yasmine Cordelia was a person on equal footing to the Light Realm's *Of Five*. That was all Rhyparia really knew about her though, considering she never took Dark Realm history courses at Phesaw.

Mendac had returned to sifting through parchment, but he had found a blank sheet on which he could jot down notes. "Twenty-four meals?" he muttered to himself. "How many calories ... Must be Powish, but I don't know the name."

An invisible force lifted Rhyparia onto her feet and pushed her out of the cell. It then guided her down the corridor, Yasmine several dozen paces ahead of her, her reflection stretching across the glossy black floor.

"Learn to walk on your own," she said. "Otherwise, you'll never know freedom again."

*   *   *

After five minutes of more ebony walls laced with ivory, it dawned on Rhyparia that she hadn't seen a single window. Even the light from torches created a paradoxical situation that made the blackness seem to stretch into forever. If it weren't for the white grains in the stone, she wouldn't have known the boundaries of the corridors through which she walked.

Yasmine said nothing throughout the trek absent of staircases, leading Rhyparia to believe they were either going in circles or that this building sprawled into eternity. Although enough questions raced through Rhyparia's mind to fill the span of time in silence, she stifled the inquisitive urge. She didn't know which topics were safe to mention and with whom she could discuss them. Yasmine could be her enemy, opposed to the idea of a commoner cursing the Dark Empire with her presence. She could despise this arrangement, secretly wanting any reason to snuff Rhyparia's candle of life on a mere whim. What better way to give her reason to do that than by prodding her about the cryptic remark she'd made to Mendac about his efforts to find something long hidden, or to ask her about her life before dying and being reborn as a Gefal? She might have wanted to forget that past, or possessed no desire to share it with someone of which she knew so little. Rhyparia could understand that. If Yasmine began interrogating her, she'd feel a certain type of way. The woman—however mighty she might have been—didn't need to know.

They crossed into a section of the structure where the walls had grown somewhat translucent, still a glossy black and reflective, but thin enough to show light on the other side. Rhyparia breathed cathartically, finding familiarity in what must have been chambers nestled between hollow corridors. This building was more than just a maze, but a functioning fortification of some sort. She caught glimpses of humanistic shadows moving around, silhouetted by torchlight beyond. They didn't move sluggishly or aimlessly like prisoners, but with purpose. Were they other Gefal or staff?

No, something is still wrong, she told herself as she studied the walls of her infinite corridor. Where are the doors?

A shove in her back goaded her forward and snapped her out of her trance. Emperor Mialo—or the Dark God—had enforced his will. Apparently she had stopped walking, her attention drawn to the walls. Yasmine was now far enough ahead to make her fear losing direction.

Rhyparia jogged to close the gap. She lost a shoe in the process and nearly jumped from the frigidity beneath her feet. The floor felt like ice, something she hadn't noticed in her cell. What caused that? She pushed this to the back of her mind with the dozens of other questions, electing to not aggravate Mialo any further.

Eventually they reached a fork in the corridor, two others splitting diagonally to the right and left, a square panel of black wall between them. Rhyparia slowed, waiting to see which route Yasmine would take, but the woman continued forward and ... walked straight *through* the slab of stone. The wall became swirling shadows around Yasmine's body, resembling her unnerving entrance into Rhyparia's cell.

Rhyparia froze, observing the black marble, eyes tracing the curving white lines. She didn't know what she was looking for. A puzzle? A pattern in the ivory threads that needed to be solved? Or perhaps the simple answer was to step through, but her logic—developed from decades of natural law in the kingdoms—automatically rendered such an option as asinine.

Expecting a nudge from Mialo, Rhyparia waited longer than she probably should have. A couple minutes passed before she took a few steps closer. The frigidity of the floor had weakened over time, which she'd attributed to the fact that she'd grown used to it—either that or her feet had gone numb. She pressed a hand against the wall, but felt solidity. Her face stared back at her in the glossy void, illuminated by the torch just above her, confusion furrowing her brows. Even compared to the forest-city capital of the Prim Kingdom, where massive willow trees served as buildings, this was foreign.

Her wings flared, extending outward as their edges flittered like black seaweed caught in the currents of a hurricane. She felt their thirst right as they flapped forward, extending like two arms to grab hold of the wall. Her stamina began to drain, as if her energy stores neared empty. It reminded her of the energy exhaustion she'd experienced after collapsing the restaurant as a Jestivan. Were these wings formed from her body's energy? If so, why couldn't she control them? They had a mind of their own—a mind that only wanted to bond with the stone.

A hole began to form, shadows and black smoke furling back, creeping along the stone. Her wings recoiled behind her back, tightening in efforts to shrink. They did have a mind of their own. At this moment, they were puppies frightened by whatever had caused the stone to morph.

A cavernous chamber sat beyond, sable walls rising and curving upward into a dome ceiling. A city block could have fit in the space, yet it held nothing. Moonlight streaked through dozens of holes in the ceiling, peppering the inky floor with luminescent spotlights. She saw no carpet, torches, or furniture—just a large panel of black stone that stood randomly at the center. A wall out of place.

Yasmine Cordelia stood out like the sun, her pastel dress of pink muting the black stone. She didn't move, but regarded Rhyparia as she entered the chamber, observing her reaction. A light drew Rhyparia's gaze elsewhere. It was more of a subtle glow than anything else, similar to what she'd seen in the barren corridors on her way here. Golden backlight seeped through the central wall's gemlike transparency, revealing the rough outline of a person on the other side. However, the light didn't seem to stretch and wane beyond the broken wall, somehow contained only directly behind it. It created a sense of disillusionment in Rhyparia's mind, tricking her perception.

The veiled person stepped closer, his or her shadow growing. Just as she questioned how much longer it'd take for the figure to collide with the wall, the shadow became part of the stone. The two converged, and a human's form pushed outward from the other side—the side that faced Rhyparia and Yasmine. She couldn't decipher finer details, but with the way the stone pressed against the figure's chest and folded around its crotch, mimicking someone who had tangled themselves in curtains, she knew he was a man.

He spoke in a foreign dialect, a mixture of hisses and clicks. Considering the vastness and emptiness of the rotunda, the lack of an echo unnerved her. The stone moved with his mouth, stretching as he clicked and snapping shut with each hiss. *This* was Mialo? This *thing* was the emperor ... the Dark God? He had size; she'd give him that. Seven feet, perhaps? But, blasphemies be damned, this appeared entirely too animalistic to be called something so holy.

The hissing ceased. No longer did her wings try to stretch for the structure's raven stone. Instead they clung to her back, flexed and tense. Yasmine turned to Rhyparia. "Emperor Mialo is unhappy with your reservations."

"You understood that?" Rhyparia asked.

"He expected a connection by now," she continued, ignoring Rhyparia's comment. "Mendac's shown great strides already."

"I sit in a cell all day. What do you expect of me?"

Mialo released a rapid series of clicks, making her question what kind of tongue movement such a noise would involve. Yasmine shook her head and clenched her jaw, as if pleading with Rhyparia to at least feign cooperation. "You reject yourself, which makes the onyx reject you."

Rhyparia's gaze shifted from Yasmine to Mialo, then focused on the marble of which he'd been shaped. Onyx? Her eyes narrowed as she crouched to study the floor. "This is *real* black onyx?"

"Of which there is almost none in the kingdoms," said Yasmine.

Rhyparia tilted her head slightly. "You're right. I had a feeling when I first saw this, but ..." She paused, trying to wrap her mind around the phenomenon. "But onyx is a gemstone of Dark Realm fables, lost enough in obscurity that even those who live in the realm don't know the origins."

"I suppose the depth of the onyx's blackness stems from the shadows that seem to infuse them." The deep, grating voice came from Mendac, who had just entered the chamber. Rhyparia twisted her body, supporting herself with a knee. "It's the only thing that'd make sense. Raw onyx tends to be brown or grayish, sometimes dark green. Yes, it looks black at a glance, but nothing like this."

Mendac had entered behind another man, who now stood to the side next to Yasmine. He had slightly darker skin and a patchy beard that he might as well have shaven off. At least the hair on his head looked neat, buzzed close to the scalp and faded down the sides. As for his outfit, she couldn't tell if it was comprised of clothing or bed sheets. Cloth cascaded down from his arms and legs, piling in layers atop the floor. It looked like he'd tied more cloth around his waist, knees, and shoulders as a means of keeping his clothes from falling off. It was all too grand, even for the giants she'd seen in the Power Kingdom, yet calling this man six feet would have been generous.

Yasmine held a steady expression while looking at Mendac, but there was a hint of displeasure somewhere in there.

Mialo released a long hiss that ended with two clicks. Yasmine translated: "You've progressed nicely, Mendac." More clicks. "The onyx senses your will."

"What is this onyx exactly?" he asked.

Yasmine answered without the need of Mialo's response. "It's a conductor of Mulawi, the Dark Energy of nature and what Gefal use to weave shadows."

Mendac's lips spread into a smile. "So that's what you call it. I've always known Light Energy as Tahara, but could never discover the name of its opposite. Is that what these wings are? My Mulawi?"

The Emperor's response stretched on for a couple minutes, as he broke into a monologue. Yasmine didn't miss a beat in her translations: "Your wings are an extension of your Mulawi, yes. The black veins that web out from your pupils are the roots of a special set of energy canals, pumping Mulawi out of its stores and into your body. The reason why controlling your wings is difficult is because of their natural inclination to interact with the Mulawi Currents in the onyx architecture around you. In your case specifically, Mendac, the onyx has begun to respond. I'm sure you've noticed it."

Yasmine's eyes veered toward Rhyparia. "You're a different story. The Mulanyx, which is what we call the combination of onyx and Mulawi, senses your absolute rejection of yourself and, therefore, *it*."

Rhyparia finally stood. "So, I must accept my actions in the kingdoms … what I did in the Power Kingdom … with the moon."

"No, not accept it. That you've already done. You know what you did. In fact, you understood the weight of it beforehand. But that didn't stop you. It was premeditated. You *wanted* to do it." She paused and lifted a hand. "And that has nothing to do with acceptance, but embracement."

Rhyparia stared through Yasmine for what felt like an eternity, processing the weight of her words. Premeditation. Implications of calculated terror. She'd told herself over the years that everything she was doing had been acts of passion, yet Yasmine had approached it from a different angle—one much more frightening.

"What did you do?" Mendac asked.

Rhyparia shook her head.

"She made you look like a saint," said the man dressed in bed sheets.

"Shut up, Poten," Yasmine drawled.

Mialo interrupted with a quick hiss, proceeding to speak more in his foreign tongue. "Rhyparia NuForce, you're far behind Mendac in terms of progress," Yasmine said, "but your ceiling might be higher. We need you to figure out what you are. In order to expedite the process, we will release you from your cell and allow you free exploration of the building. Speak with as many Gefal as possible and integrate yourself in our culture. Find yourself, but remember that I can take over whenever I see fit …" She tapered off, of course speaking from Mialo's perspective. Her next words sent a chill up Rhyparia's spine.

"You and Mendac aren't only to become soldiers of the Dark Empire, but a pair. Get used to each other. You will carry out operations in tandem.

Become friends and learn that against the force that is the Light Empire, you two will die for each other if need be. This means that Mendac, you—more than anyone else—will help guide her to the epiphany she needs. The epiphany that lurks in the depth of her ethos, waiting for her embrace."

8

Escorts of the Empress

Bryson saw the relief on his sister's face as she stared at him from his bedside. A subtle smile. Eyes wet with tears. Bags set beneath them, which he'd attributed to a lack of sleep. As foreign as the expression was for a woman like Olivia, he didn't acknowledge it verbally. He was just happy that she had returned from her mission in the Prim Kingdom without harm. Seeing her reminded him of Meow Meow, however, who was now dead, his life source flowing through Mendac's resurrected body. Had anyone told her about that?

Olivia dragged a chair closer to the head of the bead and then took a seat. Lilu and Shelly had departed minutes ago to allow the other pair of royal siblings a chance to catch up. The Intels and Stills ... two royal families that had once despised each other were now the closest of allies.

"How did that happen?" Olivia asked, referring to the folded wings of light beneath Bryson.

"I don't know. It's nice though ... their heat." She didn't respond to that, so he studied her eyes during the silence. The rings of light around her pupils and irises were slightly more vivid than Shelly's, but not Lilu's. And they were dull when compared to the celestial fire that emanated around Agnos's eyes.

"What was the Prim Kingdom like?" he asked.

"I was almost executed, as well as Vuilni and Fane." His eyes widened, but she cut him off before he could overreact. "Misunderstanding. We would have deserved it."

"What'd you guys do?"

"Well, I tried infiltrating their headquarters, and Fane committed arson."

Bryson pursed his lips in disbelief. "Okay, that was stupid, but it shouldn't earn death as a penalty."

"Different culture, Bry, which means different laws."

"Both in need of reevaluation, apparently," he said, turning his head and frowning at the ceiling in defiance.

She laughed, and he raised an eyebrow. Her ability to express herself didn't surprise him, for she'd been doing it for a few years now. It was the ease of it that struck him as odd. Her reactions were natural—casual even—which meant there was willingness behind each displayed emotion. Before, these interactions had felt manufactured, as if she'd been forcing herself to engage with depth despite reluctance.

"How much do you know?" he asked. "Of everything regarding what unfolded during the battle?"

"Most of it is calculated assumptions," she said. "Because of your comatose state, we've all had to connect dots and use deductive reasoning without your input. You were the one who fought Toono. Nonetheless, we have strong reasons to believe that Kadlest and Mendac had once been lovers. And considering a discovery Himitsu made about Toono's dream in life, we believe Kadlest was his mother ... and Mendac may have been his father."

Bryson exhaled through his nose, closing his eyes to brace himself. "It's the truth," he breathed. "Toono was our half-brother. And he basically told me to avenge our mothers on his behalf."

Olivia's nose curled up, as if disgusted by something. She snapped her head to the left, cracking her neck. "I worked by his side for an entire summer. I've beaten myself up for it every day since then, and now I hate myself even more."

Words didn't come easily after that; he didn't know how to react. Olivia *never* expressed self-hate or pity. He didn't like it. "We were all led astray. And that situation had been something specific to you, our mom, and the Still Kingdom." After not getting a response, he asked, "Why did he need to seek revenge on Mendac? The Light Empire disposed of him. He received his punishment by the blade of Debo."

"It's possible that hadn't been good enough for him. He may have wanted to give Mendac a personal exit from the world. Or, possibly, he wanted to torture him … anything to make the man suffer."

"Then why did I see Kadlest smile and take his hand?" Bryson asked, frustration mounting. The rage he had for that woman blinded him to the point of seeing black.

"That's when things become convoluted again, but based on the story I heard from Prim Queen Inedibus, I think Kadlest manipulated Toono with horror stories of the Mendac that our mother knew. It's possible Kadlest experienced something similar, but it seems her reaction to it was the complete opposite of Mother's. Regardless of how Mendac treated Kadlest, she loved him deeply. I think she used Toono to get her love back."

Bryson didn't realize how hard his jaw was clenched until a pain shot through his molars. Kadlest had always been the root of the problem. She drove Toono to become what he did, and who knew at how early of an age she'd began grooming him, taking advantage of the youthful, unconditional love a son has for his mother.

"Like you, I want to break something," Olivia whispered, her voice shaking. "Yes, I'm mad at myself, but I'm absolutely livid with Kadlest. I want to break her in half."

"I'm going to break her in—"

"But," she said, interrupting him, "Mendac is the true evil here. Let's not forget that. It would be hypocritical for us to treat Kadlest with such disdain while disregarding the damage Mom has done to this world, using Mendac's treatment of her as an excuse. I can attest for the innocent men she's killed in her lifetime. Kadlest is driven by that same treatment, only hers looks different. I think she became conditioned to the abuse and reliant on her abuser."

"I hate you sometimes," Bryson said. He had nothing left to express after that, upset she'd painted their mother as a villain. Olivia was right, per usual. Her habit of diving into multiple perspectives to properly inspect a situation or problem annoyed him, but that rational way of thinking was fairer than his tunnel vision. Kadlest had committed sins, but so had Apoleia.

And Mendac LeAnce was their common denominator.

*   *   *

Olivia stepped out of Bryson's medical room to find Lilu leaning against the corridor's opposite wall with arms crossed. Olivia slowed as she closed the door, vexed as to why it looked like Lilu had been waiting for her. "Can Bryson and I not speak without someone lurking outside?"

Lilu grinned, an orange lily in her hair accenting a yellow sundress. "I was waiting."

"He said he didn't want any other visitors unless it's Shelly," Olivia said, standing in front of the door like a shield.

"Waiting for you," Lilu said. "We need to talk."

Olivia couldn't remember the last time she'd conversed with Lilu one on one. There had been a point in their lives when it was a typical occurrence, as Lilu had been part of the Jestivan that fell under Olivia's captaincy. The two women had spent many nights discussing training regimens and giving updates on the progression of their peers, whether it had been academics, weaving, or fighting. However, once the Jestivan disbanded following Phesaw's indefinite closure, they'd seen little of each other. Lilu's tumultuous relationship with Bryson didn't help the matter, either, forcing Olivia to choose her brother over a woman whose mind she very much respected.

They proceeded down the corridor in the opposite direction of the lobby where some of the others had conjugated. "I bet he was happy to see you," Lilu said, an obvious attempt at small talk to cushion the transition into her point.

"We were both relieved," Olivia said. "What did you want to talk about?"

Lilu nodded, looking forward with a smirk. "The day of Phesaw's invasion, you had that moment …"

"There were many moments," said Olivia, forcing her voice to remain still despite her lack of patience with the subject.

"Yes, well, I heard of one specifically. And I believe most people saw it even from distant areas around the campus. You created water."

Olivia paused and turned to face Lilu. "And that was the only time."

"Do you know how it happened?"

"My emotional dam burst … in a sense," Olivia said. "I suppose that's the simple answer. If you're speaking on a scientific level, then no, I don't have a clue."

"Do you ever wish to tap into that again?"

Olivia paused, giving it thought. She'd grown frustrated with what felt like stagnancy in her progression over the past few years, which she'd recently attributed to her reluctance to summon her Bewahr. Lilu had just presented another roadblock. Since that day, Olivia hadn't been able to replicate that water ability.

"I would like to," she finally said.

"Listen, I have a friend named Frederick who came up with a theory about your unique ability. We found Mendac's lab notes about energies and how they're passed onto children. He believed those who had parents from two different realms were able to carry two energies within them. It's why we're beginning to believe that Bryson possesses the potential to weave ice like a Stillian. He has Mendac's Intel Energy and Apoleia's Still Energy." She paused, eyes tracing Olivia's face. "No questions yet?"

"I have plenty, but what good is asking them now if you're likely going to answer them in the rest of your explanation?"

Lilu laughed. "I'm so used to Bryson's impatience. He'll interrupt me constantly." She paused again, and Olivia continued to wait. Lilu smirked and continued her discourse: "Frederick believes that Mendac and Apoleia's combination gave both you and Bryson the potential to have two of four energies. Bryson got Intel and Still. You, on the other hand, got Passion and Still."

"But Passion Energy has nothing to do with Mendac or my mom," Olivia said.

"Not according to Mendac's notes. Passion and Still Energy are both produced in the same cavity located in the heart. Intel and Dev come from a cavity in the mind, which would mean it could have been possible for you or Bryson to have acquired Dev Energy, but I don't think that's the case."

"So you think I have fire and ice abilities," said Olivia. Lilu raised her eyebrows, as if waiting for more. Olivia got the hint. "Fire and ice make water."

Grinning, Lilu folded her arms in a triumphant gesture. "It makes a certain sort of sense."

Olivia glanced down as she contemplated the weight of this revelation. She had Passion and Still Energy flowing within her. That day she'd exploded in a fit of anguish over seeing Bryson fall victim to their mother's merciless assault, it had triggered her clout, expelling both energies out of her, but as a combined entity rather than separate. It would explain her comfort in extreme climates such as the Still Kingdom's Diamond Sea or the Passion Kingdom's hot and humid Lallopy Forest. Yet, while this provided an understanding of her water ability's source, it did nothing to explain its functionality—a problem to which she'd yet to find answers. Four years had passed since that aberrational occurrence.

She looked up at Lilu, who had possessed enough patience to wait for a response. "But how do I make it work?"

"I think that answer is obvious."

Olivia nodded and extended a hand. Lilu's lips remained flat, but there was a pitying smile in her eyes before she walked in the direction of the waiting lobby.

After twenty years spent completely suppressing her emotions, Olivia would have to overcome the fear of vulnerability her mother had instilled in her. She had tricked herself into thinking she'd fixed that part of her these past few years. Both Himitsu and Lilu had brought that falsehood to light tonight.

Hurt, love, fear, anxiety, lust, rage … embrace it all. The only problem? It required accepting the part of her that was Mendac, and the part of her that didn't want to become that younger version of her mother who'd fallen victim to him.

*   *   *

Agnos watched as Olivia returned from the corridor that stretched toward Bryson's medical room. Once again, she seemed perturbed by something, evident by the emptiness of her gaze as she found a seat separated from everyone else. Vuilni broke away to join her. After their mission in the Prim Kingdom, the two had become close. That left Agnos in the company of Tashami and Evelyn, which was what he wanted all night.

"Now that Bryson's awake, I can focus on the Warpfinate," he said, turning toward the other two.

"What about the wedding?" Tashami asked.

Agnos flopped back in his cushioned armchair, forcing out a breath. "I suppose I'd be a jerk if I wished they would call it off."

Tashami's eyes flattened. "Definitely."

"I don't know why you're in a rush," Evelyn said. "There are a couple giant roadblocks in your way. Those must be dealt with first, and that could take time."

Despite her correctness, Agnos continued to mope. Everything involved a chase. As much as he adored research and discovering new information, this particular hunt had become infinite. Where he thought lay answers to prior questions only lay guideposts. He'd found Gray Whale, the woman who possessed knowledge of the sea and Marigium, the ancient that allowed communication with and manipulation of sea life. Those two things—along with Toono's ancient, Orbaculum—got him to the cave on the seafloor. After retrieving the Thunder Queen's chronicle—and losing his arm in the process—he spent months translating the ancient text only to discover he needed to reach the Warpfinate's deepest chamber. And in order to achieve that never-before-done task, he'd have to recruit minds on par with his own. He only knew of a few people in his lifetime—three of whom were dead—with that level of intellect: Neeko, Director Senex, Toono, and Spy Pilot Ophala, who was too important to the Light Realm to join him. Even then, he needed someone of the Dark Realm.

That left Agnos with a barrier he couldn't get around, but he suspected someone knew of a way to help him. Every time he mentioned his qualms with the Warpfinate mission, Evelyn became unusually quiet, to the point of forcing her gaze anywhere but on him. There was something she wanted to tell him, and he could see it again right now as she forced out a cough.

"Do you have a solution?" he asked, eyes narrowing at her.

"To what?"

He paused, nearly chuckling at the exaggerated lightness in her tone. "To my lack of intellectual friends." He glanced at Tashami. "No offense."

Tashami shrugged. "Everybody is dumb in your company. I'd try Lilu. She built those travolter things."

Agnos frowned. "I respect her mind beyond belief, but her focus is here. Also, she doesn't possess a Dark Realm energy. Besides, it's not her type of intellectual path. She'd mock me if I told her my mission ... call me a mini-Accus or something."

"What's wrong with that?" Tashami asked. "Who doesn't want to be compared to the First of Five?"

"In the Dark Realm, we're taught about your realm's *Of Five* heroes," Evelyn said, sounding suddenly interested in their conversation. "Supposedly, they're all frauds, and Gatal Accus is one of the worst ... besides Mendac, of course. A priest and philosopher? A silly man chasing irrelevant knowledge and part of the reason why the Archaic Kingdom fell behind the Intel Kingdom over the centuries."

"Harsh ..." Tashami said.

Agnos rolled his eyes. "She's right in a way, although her warped perception grossly exaggerates it. Gatal has always been one of my favorite historic figures to study, but that doesn't make me blind to the fact that people perceived his intelligence as wasteful. Lilu will think the same of me if she knows I'm chasing answers to Earth's existence."

"Don't get me wrong," said Evelyn, crossing her arms as she shot a glance at Olivia on the far side of the rotunda. "Every kingdom, including mine, has their disgraces." She regarded Agnos and pointed her thumb over her shoulder at Olivia. "She's different, but many royal Still women before her did abhorrent things. Queen Francine, for example."

"Gatal was no Francine," Agnos said coldly.

"You both are losing me," Tashami groaned.

"Not much of a history buff, are you?" she asked.

"School was always a bore."

Agnos cocked an eyebrow, finally realizing the reason for Evelyn's awkwardness when discussing the Warpfinate. "You … you're smart enough to go with me."

"You think?" she asked with sarcasm, eyes widening.

Shaking his head, he laughed at himself. "Of course. You're a Stillian woman. You experience some of the toughest schooling in the world."

"Took you long enough to find the very thing that's been sitting in front of you for months," she said.

"Why didn't you say something?"

"Well, for the longest time it had been pointless with our attention pulled elsewhere. The war was more pressing. After that battle on Knowledge River, however, I'd been bothered by your automatic refusal of viewing me as a potential candidate."

"Because you're so strong!" he said, leaning forward and slapping his forehead. "Physically powerful and talented at combat-weaving." He shook his head and groaned. "I'm sorry. After seeing everything you did during the voyage, I had subconsciously grouped you with others I felt fit that stereotype—fighters, not scholars … Bryson, Toshik, Yama, Himitsu, Vuilni, and …" He trailed off, glancing at Tashami, who chuckled in return.

"Go ahead."

"And Tashami," Agnos said.

She nodded. "Apology accepted. But, we still can't enter the Warpfinate with only us two. The more we know as a collective, the deeper we can get, right? That means the more transcendent minds we have entering that building, the better our chances of not succumbing to the enemies it holds."

"Bringing us back to the original issue," Agnos said, growing frustrated with each passing second. "Who, that's capable of doing so, would go with us?"

"I told you when I first met you that a few of the Diatia weren't bad people. Vuilni over there is a good example of that, and I like to think that I am, too."

"Definitely," Tashami said.

She smiled at him in thanks before continuing. "While the Diatia was mostly fragmented, the group did have an unbreakable pair. They were the smartest people I'd ever known before meeting you, reigning from one of the most brilliant kingdoms in the world."

"Dev?" Agnos asked, thinking of Jina and Halluci.

She shook her head.

"Prim?"

"Yes, and they were good friends of mine before the group imploded a couple years back."

"Are you still on good terms?"

She rocked her hand back and forth and narrowed one eye. "We were cordial before I finally gave my leave after hearing about my kingdom's shift in alliances. But I think, with some convincing, they'd join you—*us*—on this little adventure."

Agnos fell silent, allowing the implications to settle into his mind. "How do we get in touch with them?"

"We visit Ipsas."

The buzz of conversation around them filled their silence. Himitsu was being particularly loud as he attempted to make Kaylee laugh. Agnos leaned back, placing his left elbow on the chair's arm and entwining his fingers with thought. Ipsas—basically the Dark Realm's version of Phesaw—would be quite the detour. He had wanted to find an easy solution, but he was beginning to realize he'd been naïve with such hopes.

"Can we ever just sit still for a year?" Tashami asked, no longer sporting an air of positivity.

Agnos regarded his best friend, not understanding his frustration. Had Tashami not just spent months stationed at the Intel Kingdom's teleplatforms while he voyaged across the Sea of Light for the third time in as many years? For a brief moment, Agnos felt he should have been the one to complain. Then he thought of Tashami's experience at the teleplatforms. The carnage of the invasion. The fight he'd described with Dev Warden of

66

Ipsas, Gala … Spirit Director Neaneuma's lifeless body, a woman who had once mentored Tashami and Jilly as Jestivan.

"I get the appeal of that," Agnos said, choosing his words wisely. "But time doesn't sit back and wait, nor do I." Tashami's posture slumped, and Agnos turned toward Evelyn. "Are we going to sail there? Teleplatforms to the Dark Realm are all shut off."

"I'd rather avoid using a whirlpool," she said. "I'm sure we can convince someone to allow us passage. The teleplatforms can easily be switched on. But, fair warning: I don't know how the school will react to my presence. The High Warden is not a friendly man to those who he deems disloyal."

"We'll deal with that some other time," Agnos said. He studied Tashami, who was picking at his cuticles. "Will you join us on our little adventure?"

Tashami's head snapped up, eyes squinted in disbelief. "Dumb question. I'm not going to miss out on what will likely be our last adventure together."

Conversation became light. An hour later, they visited Bryson before going their separate ways for the night. The weight of Tashami's words, however, lingered like a storm cloud above the heads of both young men. Together, they had searched for Tashami's father in the Void, joined a crew of pirates, gone to war at sea, and hunted the greatest historic treasure in Kuki Sphaira's history.

Alas, the Warpfinate's depths were no place for Tashami.

*　　　*　　　*

An hour of solitude had passed for Bryson since Lilu and Shelly's departure. They'd gone to help get there mother in bed safely, as she'd been stricken by grief over her husband's death. He, too, struggled to come to grips with the news. He'd never imagined King Vitio as a dead man, thinking his habits of fleeing from physical confrontation would always keep him alive. Bryson liked to think the king had gone down fighting, but he wouldn't know until he could confront Vistas about it … He wasn't sure he wanted to.

The image of a flying Mendac continued to haunt him. Nobody had seen it coming. Toono had played the world for a fool.

After a few visits from friends, Bryson managed to drift into slumber despite having been in a state of comatose for at least a week. He welcomed it after the last few overwhelming hours.

The backs of his eyelids blazed red, and heat washed over his entire body. Thinking fire, he opened his eyes only to squeeze them shut again. A blinding light, much stronger than any Intelight, filled the room, reminding him of the first time he summoned Thusia.

Then his eyelids darkened, the temperature somewhat restoring to normalcy. He opened one eye, hesitant of what he would see. That hesitance became bliss he hadn't felt in a long time, as the face of his Branian, Thusia, stared at him from the side of his bed. Even better was her condition. Last time he'd seen her, she'd been bruised and dirty, which she had blamed on a period of imprisonment in the Empire—punishment for all of the lines she'd crossed by revealing secrets of the Light Empire to him. Now her hair was long and healthy, her face kissed by the sun. His attention was drawn to the luster of her cerulean eyes. Sometimes this image of a woman in her early twenties made him forget how long she'd actually been alive. Had she never died saving Mendac, she would have been in her early forties.

"Hello, Bryson." Her voice expressed friendliness, but she didn't smile. She looked regretful. Something was eating at her.

Two other faces appeared behind hers, one familiar and the other foreign. "Suadade …" Shelly's Branian, who hadn't been seen since before Bryson's departure to Brilliance several months ago, was now here … but not for Shelly. And this other man—wide-faced with tiny eyes, like two dots hammered into a stone block—was a mystery. His trapezius swallowed his neck and shoulders, making him look like a stack of angular rocks.

"How are you feeling?" Thusia asked, her gaze raking over his wings.

He'd grown used to their warmth, so he kept forgetting their presence. It was difficult to ignore them now; they had unfurled in the presence of his guests. "I don't know."

She nodded. "I'm sure this is overwhelming."

She didn't know the half of it—or maybe she did. The wings, while unexplainable, didn't bother him. It was Toono, Mendac, Kadlest, and that girl who had once been Simon's friend a few years ago. Everything about that day upset him. "I've missed you, though."

She placed a hand on his elbow and finally smiled, but it disappeared quickly.

"That's enough of that," said the stranger. "It's time to go."

Bryson furrowed his brows at the man's audacity. He didn't care how strong he looked. "And who are you?"

Thusia closed her eyes and sighed, while Suadade's gaze shifted uneasily toward the man. The stranger merely grinned. "Quincy Gralth."

"Is that name supposed to mean something?"

"Depends how much you know about world history."

"Very little."

Quincy's beady eyes slid down Bryson's body, inspecting his casts and bandages. "Quite bold for being in no condition to put up a fight."

A ball of electricity expanded next to Quincy's head before collapsing in a thunderous clap.

Thusia's gaze grew stern. "Bryson, enough." Quincy appeared unfazed, that self-satisfied grin a fixture on his face.

"Why is he here?" Bryson asked. "Are they still mistreating you up there?"

Quincy chuckled and took a few steps back, possibly electing to stand and watch for a bit longer.

"They're not," Thusia said, "but we've been given instructions to bring you to the Light Empire. Those wings mean you can now. They're the only way a mortal can visit."

"You're cracked."

"Is that how you allow your charge to speak to you, Thusia?" asked Quincy, his arms now folded as he leaned back against the wall. "It's been well over a decade since Ataway mentored you, so that lack of discipline should be gone by now."

"Wait a minute," Bryson said, triggered by Debo's real name, recalling information Thusia had given him a couple years ago. "Are you the third Branian in their trio or are you—"

69

"I'm their Pogu," Quincy said. "I am their leader."

For once, Bryson shut his mouth not out of fear, but selflessness. If this man was a Pogu, it meant his authority greatly outweighed Thusia and Suadade. Bryson's insubordination could result in punishment for both of them.

"I'm sorry."

Suadade and Thusia's eyes widened in unison, but then he saw their relief. If only he could swallow his pride more often. He and Lilu really were two of a kind.

Quincy laughed. "Not the typical royal firstborn."

"Not at all," Thusia echoed, eyes lost on Bryson's wings until refocusing on his face. "You need to come to the Empire."

"Look at me," Bryson said, reevaluating his approach to this conversation.

Her eyes scanned the rest of his body. "We have someone who can take care of this much quicker and more efficiently than anyone down here."

Of course they did. He sighed, glancing at Quincy as he debated on asking a favor in front of him. He would have lifted a finger to motion for Thusia to inch closer, but his hand was heavily wrapped, fingers immobile. He'd broken a few during the fight with Toono. Instead, he croaked out two words: "The wedding."

Thusia's face softened. Quincy's eyes narrowed, pushing away from the wall and uncrossing his arms. His forearms were as big as Bryson's thighs … such a stout man.

"I forgot," she whispered.

Suadade stared at her, noticing her sudden hesitance. "Stop that, Thusia. Haven't we already been reprimanded enough for our insubordination? And all on his behalf no less."

Quincy returned to Bryson's bedside, eyes fierce. "If you were a proper charge," he said to Bryson, "you would show empathy toward your Branian in this situation. These orders have been given to her by Empress Tonitrua, yet it seems you try to instill her with guilt, a manipulative technique of scum."

"Two weeks," Bryson said, focus still on Thusia.

As Thusia chewed on her bottom lip, Quincy shook his head. "Do you forget I'm the one with sway here, not her or Leon."

Bryson continued to stare at Thusia, ignoring the Pogu who had taken Debo's place long ago. He sensed a strange aura among these three Bozani. Quincy may have had authority, but something kept him from enforcing it. Otherwise, Bryson would have been gone from this bed minutes ago. Quincy studied Thusia's face before pursing his lips and exhaling through his nose. Suadade looked up and closed his eyes, as if trying to quell his frustration.

"We can ask, right?" Thusia asked, turning toward Quincy. "For two weeks?"

"Why must you complicate my life?" he asked.

"You allow her to," Suadade said.

"Shut it," the Pogu barked, his gaze becoming a glare as he regarded Suadade. He looked at Thusia again. "I'm going to be the one who has to ask, which means I'll be the one who hears the backlash directly. We're in the midst of an empirical war, if you recall. And the Dark Empire is desperate."

She gave him a side-eyed glance. "I'm aware. And if she denies the request, pin the blame on me and return to get him."

Suadade was clearly biting his tongue, annoyed by the conversation.

Quincy stared at her, but then nodded and vanished into a cluster of white light. It seemed Bryson's evaluation had been correct. While Quincy was the Pogu, Thusia had established some sort of power over him. "That guy's lacking a backbone," Bryson said.

"Lacking an ability to ignore his feelings toward Thusia," Suadade said. "He's a puppy around her."

Bryson cocked an eyebrow, finding the relationship odd. He refrained from comment, however, seeing that Thusia had gone out on a limb for him. It did explain Suadade's disgust of the man when it was brought up a few years ago. Quincy played favorites, and Thusia had him wrapped around her finger.

"If the request is denied, you'll see us in the next few hours," Thusia said. She leaned over and kissed Bryson's forehead. "I love you."

Then, she and Suadade burst into orbs of white light. Bryson would not receive that visit, and because of that, he slept peacefully.

9

Mother's Arrival

Bryson was freed of his medical room a week later. The timing was less than ideal, seeing that he'd gone mad with impatience days ago. The thrill of seeing his friends as they trickled in to wish him good health after waking from his coma hadn't taken long to dissipate. He had also grown tired of their ogling of his glowing wings. Most had the common sense to remain quiet on the subject, but a few—mainly Agnos—peppered him with questions, reminding him that he didn't miss the genius's inquisitive nature. He couldn't vent his frustration, however, considering how far Agnos had gone out of his way years ago to help Bryson decipher the reoccurring dream. Despite Agnos's lack of social awareness, he was kind—maybe to a fault.

Bryson gazed down at his son, who was quickly approaching a year of age, for the first time since before the battle with Toono. With concerns of airborne pathogens, L.K. couldn't visit Bryson while in recovery. He felt guilt while studying the boy's features. The morning of the attack, he hadn't the chance to say goodbye to his son, for the palace's defenses and the safety of civilians had taken precedence. Ophala's words from months ago were all that quelled his shame over that decision: "Without the world, what would you give your son?"

He was forever indebted to and grateful for the Spy Pilot because of that advice. It'd live on in him forever. Without it, would he have rushed to the palace's perimeter with such haste? He might have prioritized Shelly and L.K. by making sure they escaped the city, only delaying their inevitable doom while allowing the city to perish. By confronting the enemy directly and immediately, he'd prioritized the populace, effectively lumping his fiancée and son in with the group. Ophala had forced him to look at the bigger picture, an ability she'd naturally obtained as a woman who regarded the world from the sky.

L.K.—or Leon Kawi, named after two lovers from centuries ago: Leon Suadade and Ataway Kawi—grabbed hold of Bryson's finger with tiny hands. This was the gift of love. *He* was the gift of love. The passion and devotion shared between Bryson and Shelly had created this beautiful bundle of untainted bliss.

"He's been different since Mother stopped visiting him."

Bryson didn't turn away from the crib, recognizing his fiancée's voice, solemn in its softness. "You can tell?" he asked, trying to read an expression in the baby's face. L.K. seemed fine as he tried to pull Bryson's finger into his mouth.

"Yes." Shelly approached, coming to a stop next to him. "His patience has thinned. He cries hysterically at the times of day when she'd usually take care of him."

"He's smart," Bryson muttered. "Likely senses the unease around the palace, especially if he sees it in you or Lilu. Or maybe he's noticed Vitio is gone."

Shelly sighed. "I know you're still in pain, but are you ready to—"

"More than ready," he said, thankful for the change of subject. "How are we going to restore this kingdom?"

Shelly reached down and gently pressed her hand against their son's temple. "Lilu has been so helpful. Her preexisting relationship with the leader of Brilliance has come in handy. The man has offered to help fund the rebuilding of Dunami. I've already had Father's team of advisors do the calculations, and it turns out his wealth alone will cover thirty percent of the damaged area. With another thirty percent coming from the Archaic and Passion Kingdoms and a small percentage from the Brench family, that leaves roughly thirty for us to cover ourselves."

"The Brench family?" he asked.

"Their estates are still operating. However, it's run mostly by an Archaic Kingdom beneficiary, its headquarters stationed in Balle." Shelly removed her hand from the crib and leaned against the rail, studying Bryson. "The Brench Crafts business didn't give us that money though. It came from Toshik."

Bryson's brows furrowed. "I didn't know he had his own wealth. Thought it all came from the family name."

"He received a large sum of money from his father's will, and a substantial percentage of the company's stakes. Toshik is filthy rich—even more than he'd been while his father was alive."

"I don't want to take that money from him."

She shook her head. "Neither did I, but he was persistent. He said it could do nothing to help him, for everything he wanted is now gone."

Bryson lowered his head, gaze falling back to L.K. Toshik had lost his parents, sister, and girlfriend. And, in the swordsman's eyes, each death was his fault.

"Which leads me to another concern," said Shelly, taking advantage of Bryson's hesitation. "And I'll admit that I hate myself for thinking it, but …" she trailed off, breathing deeply. "That man isn't stable. He roams the palace like a ghost, staring into emptiness like a statue. I don't know him that well—and I shouldn't even be thinking this when considering all the help he's giving us—but is he prone to outbursts?"

"Outbursts?" asked Bryson, confused. "What kind?"

"Those that would threaten the safety of innocent bystanders."

"No," he snapped. After that, however, words came slower. "Toshik has been steady ever since Jilly's death." Noticing her look of doubt, he added, "Yes, he's been steadily depressed and angry, but more melancholic than explosive. And clearly he's no threat to us if he's handing us his fortune." She twisted her lips, but decided against saying anything. "If you know something," he said, bothered by that reaction. "Spill it."

"He's not melancholic. He's bitter, projecting the faults of his shortcomings onto that woman who killed Jilly."

"Yama?"

"Yes, and I've seen the devastation of his rage ... the erratic nature of his emotions when confronting an opponent when sparring."

Bryson began thrumming his fingers against the crib's rail, losing patience as Shelly continued to speak about Toshik as if she knew the swordsman better than him. How could she? How many times had they ever interacted with each other personally? Before he could voice his questions, she answered them.

"Has Toshik mentioned his training regiments?" she asked. "From before he joined you on the mission in the Dev Kingdom."

Bryson recalled the weeks sitting in the palace after the Blizzard of Blood, as True Light began planning ways of discovering more information about Toono and Kadlest. On several occasions, Toshik had been seen with excessive bandaging, bruises, and even a sling a time or two. He'd told everyone it had come from combat training, but never revealed the identity of his mystery trainer. "Yes," he finally said.

"I witnessed those practice duels," Shelly said. She paused and forced out a single, unconvincing laugh. "Practice is a terrible word for it, honestly. I could have sworn they'd been fighting to the death every time. Toshik almost lost his life on many occasions. Most of the time, it was because he couldn't harness his emotions. He'd begin to view his trainer as Yama, resulting in a loss of temperament. His power and speed would increase exponentially, but his technique became sloppy. He would have killed any normal sparring partner." She closed her eyes. "Luckily, nothing about this partner was normal."

"When did you guys even do this?" Bryson asked. "I would have noticed your absences."

"You did."

He stuttered, dumbfounded, remembering the nights he'd questioned her absences. Had it been to watch Toshik train? And why would Toshik go to such great lengths to make sure nobody saw him, but then allow Shelly's presence? "Who was his trainer?" he asked.

"Toshik approached me with a request a while back actually … after the whole ordeal in the Archaic Mountains, right after the events of the uprising in Phelos. He sought an elite swordsman in hopes of receiving guidance." Bryson's head snapped toward Shelly, finally understanding. She nodded. She'd turned away from the crib, leaning back against it with arms folded. "Apparently, he knew who my Branian was. I'm assuming you—or someone you told—told him."

"Himitsu," Bryson murmured.

"Either way, I thought it a stupid request." She shrugged. "He was grasping at straws. But, taking into account Jilly's death and his feelings, I entertained it by bringing it to Suadade's attention. I was shocked when he accepted."

"He can't do that," Bryson said. "A Branian shouldn't even be seen by a non-royal, let alone be trained by one."

"And how often have we seen Thusia break that rule?" Shelly asked, regarding Bryson with a judgmental glare, effectively shutting him up. "I think she rubbed off on him. And he had a soft spot for Toshik after I introduced the two of them."

"Why?"

"That's obvious, but I guess a man wouldn't see it with such ease. Toshik reminded Suadade of a younger Debo. I think it rekindled false feelings."

"That's definitely not it," Bryson stated, matter-of-fact.

"Whatever. The point I've been trying to make is that I witnessed those fights between Toshik and Suadade. And while Suadade succeeded in making Toshik an elite swordsman, he also fueled his fire. He will burst. It's only a matter of time."

As Bryson dwelled in his thoughts, Shelly kissed his cheek and exited the nursery. He slumped forward, forearms crossed atop the crib's rails. Toshik was already leagues down a dark path, and there was nothing Bryson could do to stop it. When the two Adrenian Jestivan eventually clash, the clang of their swords will pierce the realm.

*   *   *

Bryson waited on the eastern grounds of the palace, seated on a low-rising brick wall that circled a manicured hedge. Lilu was just within eyesight, as she and Gracie split ways outside the demolished gate. The two women, best friends and former students of the Intel Weavineering Academy in Brilliance, had completed another morning of making their rounds throughout the eastern part of the capital. He was impressed by Lilu's hands-on involvement with the rebuilding process.

"Good morning, Bryson," she said as she approached. "How are your hands?"

"Healing … slowly."

"Well, that's better than the alternatives." She came to a stop and looked down at him, choosing not to take a seat on the bricks. She must have had somewhere else to be. "Enjoying the fresh air?" she asked. "Or, perhaps, the view?" She turned toward the wreckage of the city, a little too flippant with the morbid irony of her joke. He decided not to point it out. Her father's funeral was tonight, so it didn't surprise him to hear such comments. If humor was how she'd deal with it, then so be it.

"I've been thinking about politics," he said.

Lilu frowned. "You?"

"Yes. I know you've been focused on rebuilding the city in a literal sense, but I think your attention is also needed in the ethics of our policies."

"Barring obvious exceptions," she said, speaking of Mendac, "we've always had an ethical culture."

"There is nothing morally just about the socioenergenic system Vitio implemented based on your advice." Bryson knew he was coming off as stern and bitter, but he couldn't fake cordiality when it came to blatant discrimination.

"I get it," she said. She glanced back at the city before narrowing her eyes at him. "I suppose the policy was flawed anyway. After all, it didn't stop one of the greatest catastrophes in our history from happening. If you want to tackle its abolition while I continue to resuscitate the geographical and structural infrastructure of the city, then I don't see why not. Your moral compass has always been truer than most."

Her big words and pompous tone didn't distract him from her message: *If you believe you have what it takes, then prove it*. He didn't know what to say, flustered by the ease of which he'd argued his point. He'd expected a fight.

"While I'm woman enough to admit the error of my ways, I would still advise against outright abolishing the idea of socioenergenics. It does have its uses, but the methods of achieving them should be retooled drastically from what my father and I did. If you try to force this change without due process and a well thought out explanation, there are many people in this city who might rebel against you. And those people are powerful ones, with deep pockets and even deeper holes in their hearts."

Once again, silence from Bryson. He hadn't thought that hard about it, a result of his sensationalized mind. Lilu—a realist, but not quite as extreme as someone like Olivia—had shone light on factors he would have never considered. With the current socioenergenic system, the monarchy had made enemies out of the poor and unable. And while they were many in number, they didn't have the power to do anything about it. With his proposed abolishment of that policy, however, the enemies would become the citizens who could actually harm the monarch: those with money and certain talents. And if they didn't go after the royals in retaliation, they'd likely target the poor—something Bryson viewed to be just as bad, if not worse.

"On that note," Lilu said, "I have a meeting to attend. I'll see you tonight, Bry."

He raised his arms and slapped his hands into his face, annoyed by how complicated politics were. And this was just *one* issue. He'd only gotten his feet wet and already felt like drowning.

*　　*　　*

"I ... I ... I don't know!" Through the panting, Bryson could barely manage words as he sprinted through the palace's grand atrium toward the massive front doors.

Olivia was still yards away from the doors, moving at a more leisurely pace, when he blew past her. "What's going on?" she asked.

He was the first to stumble into the daylight, hands on his knees as he gasped for air. Debo would have scolded him for the improper form. Olivia followed, breathing normal and skin absent of sweat. Soon, Shelly and Lilu followed. He squinted not because of sunlight—the kingdom was blanketed beneath clouds as usual—but because of an approaching carriage in the distance.

"Who is it?" he asked, turning toward Shelly. She'd been the one who had broken into a smile after reading the note from Radon, one of Ophala's falcons, speaking of a surprise in the courtyard.

She shrugged, playing ignorant. She was in on this. She might have orchestrated it. His head flopped backward as he stared at the clouds and groaned. The carriage was more than a mile away, meandering down the abandoned street. It came from the south, which made sense considering the condition of the eastern gate and its crater-dotted and rift-slashed street—remnants of Bryson's clash with Toono.

By the time the carriage had reached the palace grounds and came to a stop, his impatience had become apathy, convinced that whoever was in the carriage wasn't worth all of this. Then he saw Titus, the man who had hidden himself in the city years ago before being found during the raids of the socioenergenic process. He had proposed the alliance between True Light and the Still Kingdom. If Titus was here, then surely … No, she wouldn't have left her kingdom.

Ropinia followed, and Bryson's mood soured shamefully. Her presence made more sense since she wasn't the Royal Head of the Still Kingdom. They could survive her absence. He should have been happier to see his aunt, but all he could think about was his mother's void … until his mother stepped out of the carriage.

Queen Apoleia Still wore a crystalline dress that hugged motherly curves. The material sparkled with diamond and ice, bright despite the overcast sky, as if challenging the sun's veil. Crystals coated her skin until reaching her upper chest and lower legs, where it dispersed into scattered scales and then to glittering dust near the ankles and neck. Frost dusted violet hair, pulled back in thick braids ribbed with snowflakes, completing her scintillating aura.

Bryson's attention, however, was drawn to her neck, mostly empty save the glitter and aged scars of a once-terrorized woman. The self-harm had stopped, and this brought tears to his eyes for which he hadn't been prepared. His hand went to his mouth to smother his sobs, and he hated himself for allowing such emotion to be ripped out of him. After all, Vitio's funeral was tonight, and he saw no pain in the faces of Shelly and Lilu. How could he shed tears over the sight of his mother, who was still very much alive?

Shelly's hand went to his back, as if to reaffirm her support of these emotions. It did nothing to calm him, however. His arms were shaking, his body convulsing as heat wafted through his shoulders and up his neck. He'd experienced so many tears that sprouted from painful roots throughout his life that his body had no idea how to react to those of felicity.

Apoleia reached back into the carriage. She pulled out a feeble man, who somehow managed to step down from the carriage despite atrophied limbs. Bryson recognized the man as his grandfather, Gennaio Still, the linchpin to shifting the Still Kingdom's allegiance from SCAPD to True Light nearly two years ago. Once a victim of complete paralysis, he now could move—albeit, with great strain and peer assistance—thanks to the Miracle Weaver, Nyemas Jugtah, an Intelian man with masterful weaving skills.

No longer did Bryson feel Shelly's hand on his back, nor did he see her in his peripherals; he was closing the gap between him and their guests. His family. Family that shared his blood. His feet had moved on their own, willing him forward while his mind and heart had stunned him into immobility. And as his mother waited with a smile, one arm wrapped around her father's waist as support, Bryson's legs churned faster until he ran into her other arm.

For a woman who possessed a chill, her touch warmed him. That cold might have been "home" all along, the thing his body had been searching for throughout his life, reminding him of his homesickness with each shiver that raced up his spine. Even as a child, he'd worn a hoodie, as if blaming the clouds of the Intelian sky for his chills. Even when his peers were sweating in what they claimed to have been sweltering heat, rarely had he shared their sentiments. The sun was no different than the moon to the sensory receptors in his skin, which he knew now to contribute to the dormant Still Energy inside of him. That controlled his body temperature more than the environment.

Apoleia grabbed the back of his head and kissed the yellow bangs on his temple. "It's good to see you," she said.

He didn't say anything, only remained in her one-armed embrace. Gennaio sported a crooked smile, his facial muscles not fully operable.

Someone tapped Bryson's shoulder. He turned to see Olivia, expression plain. He backed away from their mother, wiping his cheeks and allowing his sister a moment. Apoleia chuckled, more proof of the strides she'd taken in recovering from her past. There was balance in her ... harmony.

After greeting Bryson, Ropinia took over holding Gennaio, allowing Apoleia full range of motion as she regarded her daughter. She placed an open hand against both of Olivia's cheeks, lowering herself to match her height. Apoleia's eyes scanned her daughter's, and pride ignited within that gaze. "You're figuring yourself out," she whispered. "Becoming a proper woman, complex in mind and heart. Unafraid of an outsider's perception."

Bryson glanced at his sister with an arched brow. "All that from a look?"

"Eyes speak more than the tongue," Apoleia said, focus remaining on Olivia as her right hand moved upward, raking through violet bangs. "But hers have always been mute. A result of the lessons I had instilled upon her during her childhood." She beamed. "Now, they whisper. And that's a start."

Olivia's arms slowly crept around her mother's torso for an embrace, but the act might as well have been a clap of thunder in its impact. Heads tilted and brows furrowed. Even Titus's jaw dropped slightly. Olivia reciprocating a hug would have been shocking enough, but to initiate the gesture? To many, a hug was friendly, platonic even. For her, it was intimate.

Maybe ... just maybe, Apoleia's assessment was correct.

10

Harmony

A year and a half had passed since the Blizzard of Blood. On the day following the battle, Bryson lay in a private chamber somewhere deep in the family quarters of Kindoliya Palace. Ice accumulated along the edges of furniture. He fingered the bed frame, frost flaking beneath his nails. It'd become a habit of anxiety throughout the day, fearful of who would come to visit him first—mostly worried about it being his mother.

He enjoyed the peace since waking hours ago. Even if he had wanted to get out of bed, it wouldn't have been possible. His body wouldn't move beyond a couple inches. The effort to lift his hand and scratch his nose was excruciating, and injuries weren't the source. Tongku Feilong, the Linsani of Fear, might have assaulted his spirit, but nothing had physically hurt him. That explained his stationing in a luxurious residence chamber rather than an infirmary. He simply needed to recover his stamina.

The previous night's events replayed in his head. Thusia's original efforts to flood Bryson with spirit as he stood on the window's ledge of a wall that rose thousands of feet in the air, ready to jump and end his life, had failed. It looked like the Linsani would obliterate the Stillian army without any resistance. Then his mother arrived, taking his hand in hers and giving him the counterweight to quell the fear instilled by the Linsani's screeches. Together, with his mom and Branian, who had filled that motherly role for the time being, they defeated the skeletal beast cloaked in shadows.

He had collapsed after that, not blacking out, but growing weary. Thusia's worried face had blurred as she crouched in front of him, his eyes trying to close. He fought back the exhaustion, the heaviness, for the sake of the woman who stood behind his Branian. His mother didn't collapse in a fit of panic as his body tried to shut down. She watched from a controlled distance with a discerning look, as if trying to manage a grip of what emotions she should have been feeling while watching the miniature Mendac—at least, in appearance—suffer for the sake of her kingdom.

Bryson wanted to absorb all of her. That's what had kept him floating in a pool of consciousness.

He wanted his mother to love him.

She wouldn't visit him that day, nor the next. Olivia, Toshik, Vistas, Vuilni, Director Jugtah, even Titus and Still General Valp, stopped by to wish him well or thank him. Each visit, however, became more hollow than the last, as Bryson realized he only wanted Apoleia's company.

It was on the third day, when he could finally move his legs, that he left his room and sought her out. Had her act during the Blizzard of Blood been a ploy to motivate him? Had she known to pull at the strings of his heart with such a gesture in order for him to save her kingdom? Olivia had always said their mother was highly intelligent, and that might have been the sort of manipulative technique she'd use.

He lumbered down deserted corridors lined with portraits, torches, and the occasional sculpted head atop a marble stand. He passed closed doors, but entered none, feeling intrusive by simply walking the halls. At this rate, he would never find Apoleia or any other sign of human life. His fascination with the patches of frost accumulating in random areas remained firm. He craned his neck, looking up as he passed beneath a row of icicles hanging from a rafter.

He paused, gazing to his right as he stood at an intersection of corridors. His heart fell into his stomach as he inhaled, eyes widening. A painting hung from a wall at the end of the corridor: the Still Mountains, draped in ice as they towered over the Diamond Sea. Olivia had described that painting to him during the retelling of their mother's story.

Slowly, he walked down the corridor, rage flooding the place in his chest from which his heart had just collapsed. The closer he got to the painting, the clearer he could imagine the secret room just beyond it. Although more than two decades in the past, he could envision his mother at the age of eighteen seated on the twin-sized bed, smiling freely without fear of being ogled by subordinates for such an emotional display. A lyre in her lap, beautiful and carved of mahogany, strings plucked by a plectrum while she held still the rest with gentle fingers. It was such a shame, he thought, that she had to hide her sentiments from the rest of the world. *Be as rigid as the Diamond Sea*, a notion marred by the fact that humans were organic creatures, ebbing and flowing in ways more akin to water.

Bryson stood in front of the painting for close to an hour, debating on reaching out to pull it from its hinges. Part of him hoped he was wrong, that there was no secret doorway on the other side. Alas, he felt it. The abandonment of this corridor, seen in the dust collecting along the lips of the frame. The dents and holes in the walls, products of Mendac's fight with Gennaio as he tried to escape, the father risking life and limb to bring retribution to the man who raped his daughter. Gennaio would lose something far worse: expression and communication. He'd spend the next two decades as a spectator, mute and paralyzed, unable to stop his family's collapse … unable to tell his daughters he loved them.

"Would you like to see?"

The hairs on the back of Bryson's neck stood at attention, bumps rising in his skin. He remained facing the painting, unsure of what would happen within him if he turned to find his mother.

Still Queen Apoleia stopped next to her son and eyed the canvas. She stood taller than him, a trait he and Olivia had somehow missed. "I suppose nobody would 'like' to see," she said. "But I know you're curious, and I think I want you to see." Lifting a hand, she pulled at the frame's side.

Bryson sucked in air. Cuts raked her forearm, fresh and still seeping blood down to her hands, twisting around her fingers.

"Don't worry," she said. Her arm and the blood began to freeze, ice creeping from her fingertips to her elbow. "It was a brief relapse. I'll do better."

What lay beyond struck Bryson harder than any fist or weapon had in his life: drywall peppered with holes and scalded with electrical burns; a bed that tilted on a broken leg; a piano, untouched and stoic in the midst of tragedy; a splintered lyre, strings spooled across the floorboards. There were no words that came to mind as he and his mother absorbed the scene, memories undoubtedly clawing at her mind.

"This was the room of my childhood," she whispered, as if fearing her disturbance would wake the room's demons. "A haven from my mother and the overbearing restrictions on a woman's expressive freedom in Stillian culture. Once, I had found solitude and peace here … *harmony*." She hissed the last word, not out of spite but longing, as if pleading for its return. She shambled forward, unbefitting of a royal lady, and knelt next to the broken lyre, placing the fingers of her unfrozen arm on fragmented wood. "Then that day came, bestowing my sanctuary with a wave of horrors." Her hand clenched into a fist. "An epic symphony interrupted by a downpour of glass tableware from the heavens, shattering upon cobbles. He broke the harmony within me."

A gasp for air. Her back shaking as she heaved. Shoulders slouched and head bowed over her favorite instrument.

"Only now, am I beginning to repair it."

*   *   *

There was something to be said about Apoleia Still, the anomaly of Stillian women standards. At a young age, she expressed emotions more than her peers, and their parents found it odd enough to risk staring at a royal firstborn. Her laugh was more akin to a guffaw, hand clutching at her stomach as she'd topple onto her side, while every other child remained in a seated position with legs crossed and faces of stone. Her cry was a miserable thing—wretched and dramatic, enough to make her mother freeze her lips together. Once, the great Queen Salia iced the bubbling tears on Apoleia's eyelashes before they had a chance to slip down her cheeks. The seven-year-old spent that day with eyes as dry as any desert.

Apoleia didn't possess the stereotypical balance all Stillian women strived to obtain. While others struck a steady, monotonous note that she saw as bland, she fluctuated like any great song. She sought not balance, but harmony. Her peace stemmed from self-acceptance, including the erroneous highs and lows of life.

Her first cleanse changed all of that. The brutal week had ravaged her insides while staining her favorite clothes. She'd cried well over a dozen times, but not just because of the pains of transitioning into womanhood. The first cleanse marked the last time she could ever call her father "daddy." And each time she tried running to his safety when the cramps grew unbearable, her mother was there to slam the door shut.

Apoleia changed after that. As a teenager, she remained expressive through music behind closed doors, but everywhere else she became that steady, monotonous note that she hated so much. A glacial force that glided through halls. She lived two lives, one of which remained hidden. She saw no balance in that.

While a young soldier named Titus did his best to pry out those sides of her, her mother countered by prying him away from her in favor of Mendac, hoping the relationship could lead to a deal of commerce between the two kingdoms. Queen Salia found success with the deal, but at the expense of her daughter's innocence, virginity, and mental stability—not that the woman cared.

Apoleia Still became a radical in her adulthood. While her emotions became as wild as an active geyser, she taught her daughter not balance or harmony, but nothingness. *Don't let anybody—especially a man—read you.*

Nothing.

And that was what Olivia grew to become. A force in combat and a respectable mind in school, yes, but above all else, a void.

Don't settle with internalization, Apoleia had lectured her daughter. *There are more steps than that, my love. Take the fears, joys, anxieties, and depression that you've smothered deep within you and destroy them. That way you can forget. Memories are nothing but aftershocks. Symptoms of relapse.*

Olivia, my frozen daughter, if there's one thing to always remember, it's to forget.

*　　　*　　　*

Olivia let go of her mother, who smiled and raised a finger to Olivia's cheek, catching a falling tear. The scars across the Still Queen's neck were faint. Her eyes were steady and calm. Olivia had never seen her mother like this, even after the Blizzard of Blood. Seeing this change inspired her, sparking her own evolution with a hug as its inception.

"I spent so long telling you to let go of emotions," Apoleia whispered, "while I held on. I'm proud of you."

Olivia didn't know what to think. She hadn't envisioned a visit from her mother, let alone this version of her. Now, someone had to break the news to her that Mendac was alive again. It would break her. And how would Olivia approach the topic of wanting to summon her Bewahr for the first time since the day she chose Bryson's side?

Straightening, Apoleia looked past her children to where Shelly and Lilu stood.

"Welcome to Dunami Palace, Queen Apoleia," Shelly said.

"Thank you, Queen Shelly and Lady Lilu."

"We'll have your belongings taken to your quarters," Shelly said. "Lunch is prepared for us, but I understand that you have prior arrangements to which you must attend first."

"My family will join you for lunch, but I need to find this infamous Spy Pilot."

Olivia and Bryson exchanged glances. They were sure Apoleia and Ophala didn't know each other. What business would they have together?

Shelly smirked. "Just follow the scent of liquor."

11

A Coward's Funeral

"I'm offended," said Ophala, who rummaged through drawers with a quill pinned between her teeth. "I'm five days sober."

Apoleia watched the woman many believed to be the key to True Light's victory over SCAPD with keen interest. The two had never spoken, but Ophala's reputation had stretched far and wide in a short time. And seeing that Apoleia possessed intellect far beyond most, she wanted to measure her own to what many called the smartest person alive.

"And that's an ... accomplishment?" Apoleia asked.

"Of course it is."

Apoleia fell silent, eyes roving the office. Besides the generic bookcases, desk, and armchairs, there wasn't much else. This was a temporary space, evident by the absence of personal decorations such as family paintings and knickknacks. Still, she did smell some kind of alcohol.

"Ah, yes." Ophala backed away from an open drawer and beamed, a flask now in hand. She unscrewed its top and wafted the scent of its contents toward her nose as she lowered herself into her chair. "Can't get intoxicated from inhalation … or at least I don't think you can." She paused and extended a hand, offering the flask. "Can I indulge you?"

Apoleia waved her hand dismissively. "I appreciate it, but I've never been a drinker."

After setting the flask on the table, Ophala kicked one leg over the other and leaned back in her chair. "It's an honor to finally speak with you."

"Likewise. Written word is such a tired means of communication."

"We'll have to see if there are any Devish siblings who are willing to split. If you can take one back to your home, interrealmular broadcasts might be doable." Ophala sat up and reached for her quill, jotting down a note. "I'll get someone on that tomorrow."

"I'd rather not," Apoleia said. "I don't want any Devish, for I fear they'll communicate with their home kingdom and provide them with information I don't want them having. While Toono and Storshae are both dead, we still don't know the state of the Dev Kingdom. Their allegiances could remain with places like the Cyn Kingdom."

"That would be all they have," Ophala countered. "The Prim Kingdom remains neutral, and you're with us. As for the Power Kingdom, well …" She tapered off, glancing toward the window.

Apoleia followed her gaze, knowing her implication. It may have been daytime, but the absence of the smaller moon still lingered. "You know … you may not see it here in the Light Realm, but it's visible in certain areas of the Dark Realm."

Ophala tilted her head. "What do you mean?"

"In my kingdom, the Still Mountains block the view, but I've received word from peers that the top part of the moon can be seen on the horizon in the direction of the Power Kingdom." Apoleia shook her head, unable to process such an image. "Devastation. It's embedded in the kingdom's crust. Who knows how many people lay crushed beneath it?"

"Somewhere between tens and hundreds of thousands."

Apoleia pursed her lips, appreciative of Ophala's bluntness. Loss of life was nothing to be coy about, and—

"How many innocent lives have you killed?"

Apoleia's jaw slackened, eyes narrowing. Not just blunt, but bold. And … correct. "A handful of men."

Silence dragged between them, and Ophala nodded. "I'm not asking that to diminish the significance of what happened in the Power Kingdom. I only wanted to know the amount of blood on your hands. I, too, have killed someone. And no matter how much I feel he deserved it, it remains a weight of grief. He was someone's father."

Apoleia inhaled deeply, shoulders rising before exhaling and entwining her fingers on her lap. "I suppose a good person would share those sentiments. I do now, but at the time of the murders I committed, I felt no remorse. If you're testing my moral compass, disappointment is all you'll find."

"Mine is the one in question," Ophala said. "Are you familiar with the Gravity Trials?"

"Bryson told me about them."

"I freed Rhyparia against the will of my kingdom, sending her to a place of which the world knows nothing." She paused, then admitted, "I believe she might have been involved with the moon's plunge."

"That's a hefty assumption."

After staring into space for a few seconds, Ophala nodded and asked, "Did you bring the dimiours?"

"I did."

"And they're in the correct building?"

"Awaiting your arrival."

"Thank you, Queen Apoleia."

*   *   *

For the first time since waking from his coma days ago, Bryson saw Delilah Intel. Despite the bleak picture her daughters had painted of her, the royal lady stood composed at the lectern next to her husband's casket. Steady. No tears. There was significantly more gray than green in her hair than he last remembered.

"I overheard a staff member the day after my husband's death," she began, not bothering to use a prepared speech, speaking from the heart.

"I'll stress two words: *staff member*. A woman who has worked in this palace for five decades, beneath the reign of two kings. 'The man was a sweetheart, and for that he died a coward.'" She paused to acknowledge the casket, allowing the quote to sink in. "That's what she said."

Anger nipped at Bryson, but guilt drowned it. There had been a few times when he thought of Vitio as exactly that: a coward. The man had spent his reign closed off in this palace, reaping the benefits of successful kings before him. Even the "accomplishments" of his reign were happenstance, credited to the vile Mendac LeAnce. And those weren't accomplishments in Bryson's eyes. When conflict approached, Vitio's reaction had always been to run or hide—or that's what it seemed like from the outside looking in. The truth was that he took his job as a father more seriously than that of a king. His focus was on Shelly, Lilu, and Delilah, while Bryson's shield—a shield that was also treated as a weapon— protected everyone.

"Vitio Hinacio Intel was a kind, gentle man forced to follow the footsteps of his hardened predecessors—the likes of his father and grandmother. The people expected the same from him, and they believed he delivered it at first. It was the whole intent of making Mendac his general. If Vitio couldn't exert that level of tenacity, then employ someone who could do it for you. Mendac went on to invade the Dev Kingdom and enslave many of their people before visiting other Dark Realm kingdoms in order to initiate trade deals for raw materials our realm doesn't possess. While doing so, he committed atrocities in the colors of our kingdom."

Bryson turned from his seat in the front row of the chamber to look at his mother, who sat near the back. She didn't flinch or display any discomfort at the implications of Delilah's words. In fact, her placid gaze remained locked on the grieving widow.

"I'm the only one who witnessed Vitio's dolor every time Mendac returned with his reports. He hated what his general was doing, but felt he couldn't do anything about it because it's what the kingdom expected of him. Unfortunately, he didn't even know the worst of the man's crimes." Delilah's eyes settled on Apoleia, or at least in that direction. "When he did discover them, a rapid change occurred in this palace. He went to great lengths to achieve them, dabbling in a practice that had been outlawed in the first century of our timeline." Murmurs bubbled in the crowd of royals, aristocrats, and elites. "He paid a great price, but it triggered the actions that led to Mendac's death."

Skeptical looks were shot back and forth in the small audience. Most knew of Mendac's death as a result of a suicidal maneuver that had saved the life of a young Princess Shelly. Had they never questioned the identity of who that enemy might have been? The kingdom had always kept that information confidential. Of course, Bryson knew it had all been a sham, the truth in the form of a mighty Pogu sent to execute the Fifth of Five. His bafflement stemmed from something else: Delilah's claim that Vitio might have initiated that execution, and it reminded him of something Vitio had said to him three years ago when Bryson was frustrated with being locked in the palace.

Bryson had said that Mendac never served his time, as in a proper punishment for what he did to Apoleia and others in the Dark Realm. Vitio had retorted with a ferocious line: *Mendac's punishment was death!* Bryson had been thrown off by the outburst, and asked the king to explain himself, to which he replied with a dismissal. The whole exchange had been odd, leading him to believe that Vitio knew more about Mendac's death than he let on. Was this what he meant?

"My husband knew he couldn't fight well. If he ever tried, it would have been in vain and probably would have hindered this kingdom more than help it. But, Mendac was gone, and in that he found hope. He strove to revert the reputation his general had bestowed upon his reign. He did this not by *becoming* a peace-lover, but by *unveiling* that part of him. What everyone might have seen as cowardice, I knew as philanthropy. And while he was not without his faults, he was *always* a good man and an extraordinary father and husband. A part of me died with him, but the love remains the same."

Delilah approached the casket and fell to her knees, head bowed atop clasped hands. An image of taboo.

She was praying.

*   *   *

Bryson felt like crap, but that didn't stop him from remaining firm by Shelly's side during the reception. His thoughts were tugged in a dozen directions, but he consciously pushed his focus toward her. She was the one who had lost her father. To become preoccupied by Delilah's vague comments would have been selfish.

"I can't do it," Shelly breathed.

The engaged couple sat on a bench in the corner of the chamber, shrouded by two fake plants as tall as Himitsu to either side.

"Do what?" Bryson asked.

"Lead a kingdom. I'm not ready."

"You don't have a choice," he said, drawing a look of surprise from her. He could show his audacity to her sometimes. "But regardless of that, I believe in you."

"Lilu has shared news of occurrences outside the palace. There are people unhappy with the state of the capital and this kingdom, people who believe it's the fault of my father. They don't trust the Intel name anymore."

"It'll be your job to prove them wrong."

"But what if they organize?" she asked. "This would be the time to try to do something about it ... after such a disaster."

He bit his bottom lip, studying her face. This was more than fear of potential rebels. This angst pertained to her father, worries of trying to fill the shoes he left behind ... being reminded of his absence every time she placed the crown on her head. Even she—as strong as she was—couldn't deny her sorrow.

"Shelly, we can postpone the wedding."

She shook her head. "Never."

*   *   *

Toshik Brench stood with his former sparring instructor, Kuiku Fito, as they stared at King Vitio's casket. It was polished white marble, rimmed with gold along its edges, a spherical diamond placed along every foot. It got the young swordsman thinking about the cost of the gaudy thing—he didn't much care about the man inside since he hardly knew him—which drove him to memories of the family business, the wealth of the Brench name and the estates on which it was built. With the Adren Kingdom now unoccupied by Kadlest and her soldiers, it had returned to its True Light dominion. He had gone too long avoiding his home kingdom, and it was time he faced those demons. If he crossed paths with Yama along the way, even better.

"I hope you find what you're looking for at the estates," Kuiku said softly. Toshik had briefed the man on his plans earlier, and it seemed he just now figured out how to respond.

Toshik shrugged. "Brench Crafts reserved a percentage of its revenue to a stash for the Brench family. Emergency funds. Considering my disdain for the family business, my father never passed down its location to me. I want to find it."

"And what need do you have for money?" Kuiku asked, nodding politely to a tearful aristocratic passerby.

"I can give it to the Intel family to help rebuild this mess."

Kuiku regarded his former pupil with a raised brow. "And what of your own kingdom? It has no Royal Head, its firstborn still an infant. Word is that Kadlest and her hodgepodge army of darkens treated the capital poorly. The economy has quickly plunged into ruin without proper leadership."

"The money I give to the Intels is being distributed proportionally between the Intel, Spirit, and Adren Kingdoms, as they have suffered the most." Toshik paused, then asked," And did you hear? Pilot Ophala said Yama was likely responsible for King Supido's death. She caused that."

"And so we find the reason for your drive," Kuiku breathed. He plucked a finger sandwich from a server's platter. "Grief, bitterness … rage. It always circles back to her. She didn't take the lives of Jun or Alina."

"But she took Jilly's."

"And whose fault is that?" Kuiku asked casually, using his teeth to drag a tomato slice from between the bread.

Toshik's chest swelled, fury palpable. The man knew where to place blame, and he knew that Toshik held that weight on his shoulders for years. "It's mine," he snapped.

"No … love's, with a smidge of unfortunate luck." Kuiku finished his sandwich and raised a hand, placing it on Toshik's shoulder without turning away from the casket. "I know you seek reflection, and it's possible you'll find that in the estates. Alas, you'll never find peace if you don't believe in the possibility that there were women who loved you, despite your self-hatred caused by your father's words. There were three who loved you dearly enough to make the ultimate sacrifice. That is no fault, but a blessing."

Kuiku turned and left Toshik to his thoughts.

It wasn't long before the place next to the swordsman became occupied again. Approaching as a whisper, Toshik thought nothing of it until he heard the boy's voice. "You've always been a talented swordsman, but now I sense skill."

Toshik slowly turned his head with narrowed eyes, finding red hair tied atop a head, loose ends splayed every which way like fire spit from a torch. Simon, now sixteen years old, continued to surprise Toshik despite already knowing of his incredulous transformation into adulthood over the years. He still pictured that little boy with freckled cheeks and tattered clothing, fawning over his idol's glory. Of course, at that time Toshik had never understood the boy's endearment of Bryson.

"What do you know of swordsmanship?" Toshik asked.

Simon tilted his head side to side with a frown, as if searching for the right answer. "A little."

"You're Intelian."

The boy paused before saying, "I know of swordsmanship and gifts. You are not gifted—that is a birthright—but I know of people who can take that talent of yours and mold it into something resembling a gift."

Toshik turned toward the casket, jaw set. Since when did Simon speak like this, and where had that arrogance come from? Toshik knew of Simon's marksmanship as an archer, the nickname of Torchtop, but the art of the sword and the bow and arrow involved two completely different canvases. This confrontation was infuriating.

"If you ever plan on crossing swords with the lady known as Yama Fuuna, you'll need more training than—"

"Have you ever trained beneath a Bozani?" Toshik asked, his fury overtaking manners.

"No ..." Simon muttered, gaze thoughtful. "My tutelage has come from mortal beings far rarer than any celestial entity."

Toshik turned, eyes slanted fiercely.

"If you seek similar guidance, you can find my family in Yinyon," Simon said. And then he gave his leave.

*   *   *

Olivia had watched her mom glance at the casket from a distance multiple times throughout the reception. Only now was she finally acknowledging it fully. Olivia joined her, noticing a forced distance between her and it. "What are you thinking, Mother?"

"Nothing." After extended silence, she added, "Rather I feel nothing. I didn't know this man, but even if I did, I feel I wouldn't grieve his loss. He sent Mendac into the Dark Realm."

"Nobody would have blamed you for skipping this event," Olivia said.

"I know, but I didn't want to miss it. The Intel's have become my kingdom's greatest ally as of late. I want them to know they have my support in every aspect, including those that might bring me pain."

"I'm proud of you, Mother."

Apoleia smiled. "Besides, King Vitio sent me the Miracle Weaver, which is a kindness I could never repay." She turned and scanned the room. "I was hoping to see him here."

"Director Jugtah is in Brilliance."

Apoleia's gaze darkened, lips thinning. "That was the city responsible for raising Mendac, correct?"

"Until his teenage years," Olivia replied, forgetting the city's connection to her father and regretting her words.

"I suppose it's good to see it can spawn a variety of human beyond scum. I like that Jugtah fellow. Along with Bryson, they helped heal that place in my heart where men went to rot." She scoffed. "I may even like these people."

Olivia exhaled cathartically, knowing her mother spoke of Intelians. She never thought she'd see the day when a Stillian woman attended the funeral of an Intelian man, and not just for the satisfaction of seeing him dead.

While Apoleia's reasoning wasn't grief like the others around her, at least it wasn't pride. Also, she wasn't posturing to gain favor with her allies. This was her truth, her way of showing support for a kingdom that had fallen from glory's graces in a span of days. Olivia decided now was the time to tell her mom.

"Mendac's alive."

And just as sudden as the Intelians' plunge, Apoleia's face fell, too. A hand went for her forearm, fingernails pressing into skin. Then her grip slackened, fingertips sliding around her wrist and massaging her veins. "How?"

"Toono," Olivia muttered. "King Rehn was a red herring all along. Mendac, his father, was the goal."

"His father?" Apoleia whispered, grip tightening around her wrist. "And Kadlest ..."

Olivia finished the sentence. "His mother."

Apoleia bowed her head and closed her eyes, processing the revelation. Olivia noticed her breaths had become more controlled ... steady with focus.

"Bryson wanted to tell you immediately after he woke from his coma, and Pilot Ophala agreed to do so depending on my thoughts." Olivia guided her mother's fingers away from her wrist and held her hand. "This was my decision, Mother. Don't blame anyone else. I wanted to tell you this in person, so I told Pilot Ophala to wait. She warned me of the decision's dangers, that you'd be unprepared if Mendac came after you before I told you."

"He can go for it," Apoleia spat. Olivia looked up into her mother's blue eyes, a familiar iciness creeping back into the irises. "He'll realize I'm not that princess anymore."

Olivia squeezed tighter onto her mother's hand, recalling the woman's daily training sessions in Lallopy Forest. While Olivia had attended Phesaw during the day, her mother perfected her ice abilities. Rumors had spread throughout the northern area of the Passion Kingdom about an inexplicable chill that would blanket the forest. Sometimes, the temperature would dip well below freezing, causing frostbite for multiple bandits who ventured too close to her cave.

She had also physically tormented herself. While the scars on her neck and forearms were products of past demons, there were others she'd inflicted upon herself in order to increase her pain tolerance. The whole idea behind making a temporary home in the Passion Kingdom was to suffer in its notorious heat. At fourteen, Olivia spent two months of her summer break alone in their cave while her mother journeyed to the Volcanic Quadrant, where she set up camp at the rims of the volcanoes, lasting a week at each of them. On the final day of each week, she froze the bubbling magma within. The Volcanic Quadrant became inactive for the next three months, even after Apoleia's departure, becoming its longest stint of dormancy in Known History ... Or that's what Olivia's mother had told her. Temperatures capable of freezing magma? She didn't want to accuse her mother of lies, but that had always seemed too farfetched.

Silence stretched into eternity, flooded by the soft-spoken conversations of the reception's guests. Olivia didn't know what to say, and for a moment she regretted prioritizing the revelation of Mendac's rebirth over informing her mom of her plans to contact her Bewahr. No, she made the right choice. Her mom just needed ...

Apoleia's hand fell out of Olivia's as she turned and walked away. All the way to the exit, where Bryson watched with concern etched in his face.

Olivia stood alone at the casket, hearing the ghostly voice of Meow Meow in her mind: *Just give her time. She'll be okay.*

12

Kadlest and Mendac

"Have a seat," Ophala said as she settled into her office chair. Vistas, a prestigious Dev servant of the Intel family and last remaining brother of the Inson triplets, stood behind her with hands clasped behind his back. He had gravitated toward the Spy Pilot since Vitio's death, feeling most comfortable around whoever seemed to hold the most authority. While that should have been Shelly—now a Royal Head—it was clear she had yet to fully embrace that role.

Olivia settled into the chair across the desk, nodding toward Vistas. The Devish returned the gesture, but didn't smile. He had done very little of that since everything that happened the morning of Toono's invasion. Of course, having a man—a *king*—die in one's arms can do that to a person. The slender, ink-haired man hadn't attended the funeral yesterday, which had struck many of those who knew him as odd.

"You don't mind if I have the story recorded?" Ophala asked, gathering loose sheets of parchment from her desk and stacking them in a pile. "It's why I have Vistas here. Do you trust him?"

"Of course."

Vistas's eyes flared burgundy, signaling the recording process was underway. Ophala leaned back and placed folded hands on her lap, eyes focused. "The story of Kadlest and Mendac from a third-party perspective," she recited. "Told by Olivia Still, second-hand. Original source: Prim Queen Inedibus." She paused, glancing back at Vistas, who offered a nod of approval. Her gaze slid back to Olivia. "Go ahead."

*   *   *

Mendac leered at Kadlest, who sat beneath moonlight on a bench outside the onyx headquarters of the Dark Empire. She wore tan breeches rolled up at the knees to expose bulging calves. The sleeves of her beige tunic were missing, cut off at the shoulders, allowing powerful arms to breathe freely. She fidgeted with Baldum, her acidic ancient in the shape of an armlet, twisting it around her bicep. She was built like a Powish barreler—a mass of muscle with a presence like a steel building in Brilliance.

He kept his distance, trying to find in her what she had always seen in him: someone worthy of love. To any outsider who had witnessed the pair's time together in the Prim Kingdom, her feelings for him would have been confounding. She was the first woman he pursued after Thusia's death, but he held no emotional investment. This made certain individuals—Prim Queen Inedibus, for example—question his motives.

There was no affection in Mendac's eyes when he looked Kadlest's way, nor was there an effort to feign it. Yet the battle-hardened woman, once the general of the Prim army, had tricked herself into seeing it. If there was one trait of hers he absolutely adored, it was her foolishness, her delirium ... her desperation.

Okay, perhaps there was more than one redeeming quality of note.

It all stemmed from a father who had disowned her at an early age, realizing she didn't possess the religious acumen of her ancestors, rather drawing one's blood in murder and not sacrifice. This drove her toward the Primmish royals and away from the zealots, separating her from family.

Knowing this, Mendac took full advantage by preying on that familial void not by consumption—for a void is empty and thus impossible to consume—but by filling it. He provided her with hollow words and mindless gestures that she interpreted as love and support. Occasionally, those false kindnesses were followed with a swift fist or a jolt of electricity up her spine.

Tough love. Disciplinary love. Or that was how Kadlest viewed it. How else would he have kept her eating from the palm of his hand like a robin picking seed?

She was so different from Apoleia, the stubborn glacier of a princess he'd eventually meet a couple years later, whose attention he had to fight for. He thought he'd made great progress, but she continued to refuse his advances, forcing him to take matters into his own hands. He closed his eyes and shook his head, thinking of how much easier it could have been, how excessive force could have been avoided had she simply given in to his desires. She was to blame for her suffering, not him.

Kadlest, on the other hand, had thrown herself at him. Even when he hurt her, she stayed with him because she was loyal. She didn't fear the consequences of an untenable, so he didn't have to convince her that sex involving people from separate realms wasn't an unforgivable sin. Intimacy came easy to her, love fueling her drive; physicality came easy to him, goals fueling the motions. What she viewed as love-making, he saw as nothing more than a job needed to be done. It was the only way to create a child of both realms.

Kadlest gave him that child … his firstborn. A boy they would name Toono. And despite the boy's many failures on the operating table, his tiny body bucking and squirming beneath the blade of his father, Mendac was appreciative of his role. Toono was a prototype, his energies not capable of achieving what Mendac wanted of them—a fault of his mother. Mendac would conclude that Kadlest wasn't elite enough of a partner, her energy too weak.

When Toono was three years old, Mendac abandoned both of them with gaudier aspirations in sight. If a general couldn't give him what he wanted, then he'd have to hunt bigger game, and the only people above generals were the royal families they fought to protect.

Thus, Apoleia Still became the Fifth of Five's next subject, Toono serving as the prototype after which Bryson would be modeled.

T1 and *T2*. *Trial 1* and *Trial 2*.

*   *   *

Kadlest twisted her armlet, anxiety eating at her insides as she tried to orientate herself within this black world. She knew nobody and saw not many more. She had roamed these courtyards and fields for a week, or something close to it. Time was a difficult concept on which to grasp in the Dark Empire, the sun misbehaving when it conquered the sky, its rays lighting the land with grays rather than enriching nature's saturated greens. She saw no doors to the raven building, a structure built more like a sprawling hedge maze than a skyscraping castle, but she could have missed it in the darkness, seeing how the lines between shadow and structure blended together.

A fountain made of the same black stone stood at the courtyard's center, spurting water from its top in four separate streams. Its design was simple, a circular basin with a narrow, gently-curving pipe erected in the middle. She'd seen more extravagant sculptures in the kingdoms.

She surveyed the grassy courtyard, unadorned aside from the fountain. Benches dotted the perimeter, some disappearing in the building's shadow. She had arrived here hours ago by sheer luck, somehow passing through a mass of shadows that she thought had been a wall. A week of wandering, yet she didn't know what she was searching for. Mendac, perhaps. Some sort of familiarity. She had seen a total of three people throughout the week, each of whom either ignored or rejected her inquiries.

She hadn't consumed anything since arriving, yet she didn't feel deprived. She counted it as a blessing. She didn't have to try drinking from any strange sources. She didn't know who or what she could trust in a world of history's most elite Dark Realm citizens. Still, there must have been a catch that came with this self-sufficiency.

Something stirred in the shadows across the courtyard. She instinctively stood, prepared for any possible threat—not that she would achieve much when faced with the caliber of talent up here. Her body relaxed, however, as Mendac stepped into the moonlight.

He was so handsome, as he always had been. Even now with the grizzly scar of a sword wound across his face—starting in his scalp, where hair now refused to grow—it only added to his image. She loved a man who had seen his fair share of war. And knowing that this wound came from a mighty Pogu—Ataway Debonicus Kawi, Third of Five—she could only revel in the glory of his power. For a human to push a celestial being to his limit ... Well, there were no words.

However, Kadlest didn't love him anymore. Those feelings had slipped away a long time ago, the morning she woke to a wailing Toono. The toddler was strapped to the operating table with a small hole along the side of his head, freshly carved by Mendac's knife. Only, Mendac was nowhere to be found. A slip of parchment with his handwriting lay next to her son: *Thank you for your love and the gift it gave me, however mediocre it may be. You've served as a great lesson for me. You're responsible for my next move, so find solace in that as I take my leave. Don't bother trying to find me.*

It took that morning to realize she loathed Mendac. To see through the veil of his wry grin. To see the manipulation of her weaknesses when it came to love. He had never given a damn about her, evident in the splotches of purple on her skin from his fists and the constant muscle spasms from his shock therapies. What had made her think that was love and why had she been so desperate to seek it?

As Mendac reached Kadlest with an outstretched hand, wings of smoky black curled against his back, she accepted it. He pulled her up and looked her in the eyes, the devil's touch curling up one side of his lip. "I missed you," he said.

And in that moment, as she felt the emptiness of his presence, the magnitude of her duty filled that void. She had worked with Toono to bring this man back to life with the purpose of torturing him, showing him that the mother-son duo he had abandoned because of disappointment had become a pair that he could not best. Proper retribution for the ghastliness of his sins.

Alas, Toono died, sacrificing himself in order to allow his mother a chance at avenging herself. Without her son, this task became exponentially more difficult, her method forced to adapt to the circumstances. If she wanted Mendac to suffer, she need him think her a lovesick puppy. Like he had pulled at the strings of her heart, she would caress the lumps of his bloated ego.

Toono was a kind boy. A son she didn't deserve. And that's what she told herself as she whispered back to the thing with a demon's smile, "I missed you, too."

13

The Request

Rhyparia had found an area of the Black Labyrinth's grounds where the sun acted like normal. The grass was green and the bark of scattered trees a healthy brown. Even the sky flooded blue, not a cloud to be seen. It might have taken a lengthy walk away from the Dark Empire's maze of a headquarters, but it was worth it. She had missed this resemblance to home, tired of the gradient scale of grays at the empire's heart.

This was her first time away from the Labyrinth proper. She was shocked to find a city surrounding it, a collection of obsidian edifices carved through by tar-paved roads, eliciting a sense of imprisonment despite her location outside of the Labyrinth's walls. The blackness was suffocating even with the sunlight.

She sat at the cusp between the city's heart and its extremities. There was no barrier or moat to protect the Labyrinth, only a vast field dotted by an occasional oak. The city's buildings and roads began at random intervals across the field's perimeter. It seemed the Gefal didn't have a threat to worry about, or they had enough faith in their skills that if someone foolish enough were to approach headquarters, they could easily eliminate them.

Rhyparia narrowed her eyes. There were *people*, and enough to make her question the population of the Dark Empire. On one street alone—what she could see of it before a bend disappeared behind a cluster of townhomes—she spotted a dozen humanistic figures. If that trend continued throughout the rest of the sprawling metropolis, there had to be no less than ten thousand—a number far too egregious when compared to the stories of the mainland.

The Empires—both the Dark and Light—should have held just north of a couple dozen people each. Roughly twenty-four Gefal should have resided in the Dark Empire, and a similar amount of Bozani in the Light. If that was the case, then who were they?

She stepped out of her momentary stillness to approach the street. She wanted to question one of them. Maybe they'd talk to her, unlike the elites inside the Labyrinth who wanted nothing to do with her. Aside from Yasmine Cordelia's escort to speak with Emperor Mialo, she had spent two weeks in the Empire in silence.

A force stopped her in her tracks. She could lift her feet off the ground, but not forward. She also had control of her arms, neck, and just about every other body part save her wings. Those had anchored her, as if pinned to the air behind her. That was the presence of Mialo, who she had learned recently—after several suicide attempts—controlled her body through her wings. She cursed them. They served no purpose other than to hinder her. She couldn't move them, let alone fly. At first, she had tried flexing them like muscles. After deciding that had been a stupid train of thought—they were energy, not muscles—she tried manipulating them like she would her Archaic Energy. While it didn't work, she discovered it was the right thought process. She could feel them through her energy canals, but could achieve nothing beyond that.

Mialo didn't want her entering the city. He might have released her from her cage, but she was still a prisoner. And this might have been worse; she was bound by someone else's will. She needed to find a way out of this.

This scenario granted her one positive: a chance to work alongside a man like Mendac. She didn't know what he had done to land here in the

Dark Empire, but it couldn't have been anywhere close to her atrocities. And she had come to realize that not everyone in the Labyrinth were evil people—at least, not based on the legends. Yasmine, for instance, had been a trailblazer for Dev Assassins during a time when they had been faced with extermination. The world had decided they deserved the same fate as other races of assassins who had already been eliminated, such as the Adren Assassins. In order to save her people, she had to commit heinous crimes. But in hindsight, had it been her or her oppressors that were truly evil?

This gave Rhyparia reason to trust Mendac, though she was curious about the timing of his placement here. He had been locked up just like her, granted his first audience with Mialo at the same time, yet he died decades ago. And when he spoke with Mialo, he sounded just as enamored by the strangeness of the Labyrinth as she.

The pressure on her wings released. Despite the desire to continue toward the city, she turned back toward the Labyrinth. Mialo's restrictions were clear: remain at the heart. Defying him would prove useless. She wasn't inclined to learn what the reprimands of a god comprised. Death would have been welcome, but she knew he wouldn't give her that blessing. Torture was the only route.

As she trekked back toward the Labyrinth, she stuck her hands into her pockets and bowed her head. Still confiscated by the Gefal, she felt naked without her umbrella ancient, like an Adrenian without their sword. They didn't trust her with it—not yet. And as depressing as its absence was, she found solace in the measure's hidden meaning ...

Mialo had control of her Mulawi and physical body, but he couldn't stop her Archaic Energy. All she needed was an ancient, and perhaps she could regain her will.

*   *   *

Bryson, Himitsu, Toshik, and Simon found themselves resting in the ghost town of a chamber that was Dunami Palace's royal library. They had finished a two-hour training session a field over from the Intelian army, during which Bryson spent most of his time rehabilitating from injuries. While the kingdom sat in a state of transitioning, the army continued its normal functions. There was no vacation for soldiers, a maxim that intensified with the return of Mendac LeAnce. Nobody knew where he was, including Ophala's winged scouts. There was comfort in that, leading many to believe he was nowhere near Dunami. Every inch of the city had been scoured after the invasion. But that didn't mean the rest of the kingdom— or True Light for that matter—was safe. What was most concerning was the mystery behind Mendac. At least the world knew Toono's intentions— mostly—when he'd been alive. There was a chance Mendac only wanted to live a normal life now that he was back from the dead, but Bryson didn't believe that at all.

The palace's main library existed in a state of abandonment save the frequent visits from Lilu, Pilot Ophala, and a few advisors. It was a strange paradox in a kingdom supposedly known for its intellect, but that identity had fallen off in recent centuries as the royal family had grown comfortable in their position as the world power. Most money had gone to the army, which Bryson saw now as a waste. If it hadn't been for Lilu's travolters— invented in a city that actually valued technological advancement—the invasion would have ended much differently: Dunami occupied by SCAPD forces.

"What happens when you can't stand to sleep in the same bed?" Himitsu asked, flipping through the pages of a book as if he had any intentions of reading it.

"That will never happen," Bryson said, lying back on a bench of a study table. "She needs my embrace."

"You need her cuddles," Simon quipped, grinning as he thumbed the feather of one of his arrows. Himitsu laughed and bumped fists with the boy, tossing the book atop the table.

"Done pretending to know how to read?" Bryson asked.

Himitsu flippantly pointed his thumb at the discarded book. "Too many pictures and not enough words for a scholarly mind such as mine."

"Knocking boots with Kaylee doesn't make you smart by association," Toshik said. "It's not a transmittable disease."

Bryson and Simon guffawed, and Toshik grinned at his rival—an expression of which he'd shown very little since Jilly's death.

Himitsu puffed out his chest. "That joke's not funny since we haven't even 'knocked boots.'"

Bryson rolled off the bench in hysterics, Simon began dry heaving, and Toshik shook his head at the Passion Assassin. "You just made it funnier."

Himitsu's brows fell flat, clearly not amused. "How?"

"You've spent every day with that girl for how long now?" Simon asked.

"Virgins can't talk," Toshik said, redirecting his instigation toward the redheaded archer, flinging verbal jabs regardless of relation.

Bryson had begun to recover from his hysterical fit when Himitsu dug himself into an even deeper hole: "I'm a virgin, too."

This time, Bryson and Toshik went quiet, exchanging looks while Himitsu and Simon laughed at their own expense, appreciating the bafflement of their peers.

Toshik stammered, "You haven't …" He trailed off and squeezed his eyes shut in disbelief. "You've been with her for months."

"Not everyone just thoughtlessly swings their sword around."

Toshik frowned, as Himitsu's declaration got Bryson thinking. He rose from the floor and returned to his bench. "How many of us do you think are still virgins?"

"Define 'us,'" said Simon, his arrow now resting on the table, his attention fully on this conversation. It was juvenile and stupid, but this was the kind of topic that could make them forget the seriousness of the world … at least for a few minutes.

"The Jestivan."

Toshik leaned forward, feet on the bench opposite Bryson. "Strike off myself and Bryson. Yama lost hers years ago. She is older than all of us by at least a couple years." He paused. "And Jilly. I was her first."

Silence. Toshik didn't seem to realize the weight of mentioning her name until after the fact. He regarded his friends with pursed lips. "Let's not tread eggshells around me. I tolerate it from others, but not you guys." He glanced between Bryson and Himitsu. "And definitely not you two."

Bryson nodded, and the swordsman continued, "I don't know about Tashami or Rhyparia. My guess is Olivia and Agnos, but that's an admittedly shallow assumption based on their personalities."

"Olivia hasn't had sex," Bryson said, matter-of-fact and suddenly regretful of mentioning the topic. When he had thought of the private matters of the Jestivan, naturally, his sister hadn't entered the equation.

"Offended?" Toshik asked.

Bryson's nose curled up, bottom lip pushing upward into a frown. "I just don't like it." He heard crinkling parchment and turned toward the sound right as a crumpled ball collided with his face. He froze, a lazy gaze at Himitsu. "Why?"

"Knowing your story, Bryson … How you came to be. Your mother's story." Himitsu sighed. "You're the last person I would have expected such a comment from."

Bryson stewed in the painful truth of his friend's words. His mother had been robbed of her freedom of expression by the force of an evil man. He had taken her will into his own hands, deciding her purpose for her in that moment. By expressing disgust at the thought of Olivia in bed with another person, Bryson was mirroring that act. What his sister did with her body had nothing to do with him. He bowed his head and slumped. "You're right. I'm sorry."

Simon cocked an eyebrow, scanning the faces of his former idols. "Wow, you guys are way less idiotic than I remember."

Toshik smirked. Himitsu chuckled, patting Simon on the back. Bryson continued to stare at his knees. *Am I that ignorant? Mom would have scolded me if she'd heard what I'd said.*

"You forgot about Lilu," Himitsu said.

"Oh yeah," Toshik said. "She's in a similar boat as you and Kaylee, except she's known that Frederick dude for a couple years longer. You'd think the two of them would have done something by now, but Lilu's a bit on the straitlaced side of things." He sucked his teeth. "Hell, she's resigned the poor guy to an inn. He can't even stay in the palace."

"A bummer," Himitsu said. "I'd like to get to properly know the guy … see the creature who can handle her quick tongue."

Toshik grinned something evil. "Oh, you know how quick it is?"

Again, laughter erupted from the guys, each of them either clutching at their stomach, keeling over the table, or gasping for breath. It lasted for minutes, dwindling to near-sighs before their tearful eyes connected, which then caused a hysterical explosion of fists pounding atop the table. This euphoria—the kind that expelled all anxiety from the soul—only happened when three or more of the Jestivan congregated, especially the trio of Bryson, Himitsu, and Toshik. Simon proved himself a worthy addition.

Bryson's temple was pressed atop the table's polished wood, sides cramping and head flooded with heat, when a woman's voice carried through the study area. "Such perverse humor."

Heads snapped in the direction of the library's double doors, where a woman with violet hair pulled back into a crystalline bun leaned against the frame, arms crossed in front of her. Stunned silent, the young men sat motionless as if the Still Queen had iced them.

"Don't shrink on my account," she said, a gentle smile on her lips. "Making me rethink the whole cultural shift I'm attempting back home. Maybe the men belong where they are."

"How long have you been standing there?" Bryson asked.

"Long enough."

Feeling blush flood his cheeks, Bryson glanced at the table. He wasn't sure if he was embarrassed or ashamed … Definitely both.

"Well," said Himitsu, eyebrows raised with a shrug. "My mom would have congratulated our comical genius."

Apoleia nodded, entering the library and pausing at the end of one of the tables. "After having a few meetings with the Spy Pilot, I find myself not surprised."

Not paying attention to his mom, Bryson watched as his peers failed to keep their focus on her eyes. He picked up the book Himitsu had discarded earlier and threw it at the assassin's shoulder. "Stop, idiot."

Himitsu rubbed his shoulder and frowned, but didn't rebuke.

Apoleia smiled. "I'd like to speak with my disgraceful son."

They all bowed and sauntered out of the library. Simon glanced back just before disappearing around the corner, his lingering gaze directed downward. Bryson shook his head. He would have a proper conversation with that boy soon—one that would probably come off as hollow after everything they had just joked about. He exhaled and covered his face.

Apoleia took a seat at the head of the table, pressing the bottom of her glittering dress against the back of her thighs. She sat back, hands clasped in front of her as she leaned to one side, an elbow on the chair's arm and the other on her hip. He wasn't used to seeing her hair tied up, exposing the entirety of her slender neck. Though faint scars traced the width of her neck, he smiled. She had done well since the week following the Blizzard of Blood.

"Did Olivia tell you?" she asked.

He lifted the book he'd thrown at Himitsu, smoothing out a few of the pages that had folded beneath its weight. "Tell me what?"

"She told me about Mendac's revival."

He slowed as he closed the book and slid it to the middle of the table, eyes distant. He knew his sister had plans to tell their mother, but judging by her reluctance when Bryson had brought it up last, he didn't know it'd be this soon—not that this surprise upset him. He was relieved to know Olivia hadn't stalled. He glanced at her neck again, hardened eyes skipping to her forearms and trailing to her wrists, as if he may have missed something before.

"You fear relapse," she whispered. "No need."

He looked her in the eye with skepticism. "You're … alright with this?"

Her gaze drifted in thought. "I wouldn't say that, but I can cope in ways different than before. I have friends …" she smiled at him … "family …" she unclasped her hands, an open palm waving in front of her … "and allies. I have control over my emotions, so fury will not drown me."

"What are we going to do about *him*?" he asked, referring to Mendac.

"What we can, which isn't much at the moment. Pilot Ophala is handling that." She gave him a mother's smile. "I come with advice, my son. Do not fear your father, and do not fear him on my behalf."

He studied her, then nodded. "Yeah, alright."

"Now that that's out of the way, let's discuss your big day on Saturday."

"That's all anyone wants to talk about."

"You'll be the first Jestivan to marry. And besides that, it just *is* a big deal. You'll have a wife, and I, a daughter-in-law."

He hadn't even thought of the existence of in-laws. That meant Lilu, the girl he had crushed on during his first two years as a Jestivan, would soon be his sister-in-law. Strange.

"Queen Shelly rocks the Stillinia Ring well," Apoleia said. "Not quite as well as my grandmother, but she does it justice."

Bryson beamed, recalling the many times he'd seen Shelly admiring it on her finger when she thought he wasn't looking. Because of the ever-ice at its gem core, it shined brighter than any diamond—perfect for royalty, especially someone with Shelly's taste.

"I feel guilty," he said.

"Why?"

"That ring should have gone to Olivia for whenever she proposes."

A single laugh slipped from Apoleia's lips. "That's a difficult image to grasp. However, if that time comes, there are other rings for her to use. Also ..." she tapered off. He almost said something, but then her gaze refocused. "She'll have the crown when I die, and not even the ring compares to such regalia."

He smiled, picturing the bittersweet image of Olivia on the Frozen Throne. While he wanted her to have that position, it meant they'd spend their lives in not just separate kingdoms, but realms.

"My daughter: Queen and Royal Head of the Still Kingdom. My son: King of the Intel Kingdom, married to the Royal Head."

Bryson fidgeted with the cuffs of his jacket, thinking of where he'd been years ago. Consumed with self-loathing, incapable of filling his father's shoes. Ignorant to the fact that those shoes had trampled thousands of lives ... Marcus, Tristen, Vistas, Flen, Toono, and ... He regarded his mother, tears welling and tickling his eyelashes. "Will you walk with me down the aisle?"

The mother's smile returned, a twinkle in her frigid blue stare.

"I will."

14

Piece of Family, Peace of Mind

Saturday came, and Bryson remembered little of the morning. It was impossible to soak in the moments that led to the wedding as his pulse thumped in his eardrums, skin slicked in clammy sweat and breaths rattling in his lungs. He had never felt anxiety like this before. He'd soon marry the love of his life, confessing his commitments in front of everyone he cared about.

He stood in a grassy pathway between hedges, gray clouds hanging low above. Just around the corner, his and Shelly's audience—fellow Jestivan, friends, and future in-laws—awaited in wooden chairs. He took a deep breath, preparing himself for the void—the man who mattered most. As a little boy, he had never imagined life without Debo. His father-figure's absence stung deeper now than it had since the months following his death. He should have been the one to walk Bryson down the aisle.

A hand gripped his, a biting chill jarring him away from sorrowful memories. Looking to his right, he found his mom. Creamy skin and pink lips, parted to reveal a toothy smile. Blue eyes between curling lashes. A crystal crown perched in violet hair, woven into a single war braid down her back. Crystalline pins, shaped like miniature snowflakes, spiraled along the braid's length. Sparkling beads spilled from the braid's tail like soundless wind chimes. Her dress wasn't gaudy or big, but minimal. It was olive green in the empire style: an intricate lattice of straps in the back, a plunging V neckline, and a thin waistband that accentuated subtle hips. The skirt fell effortlessly around long legs, its hem cut to reveal only the toes and bottom straps of her heels.

He squeezed her hand. She wasn't Debo, but she was his mother.

"Ready?" she asked.

"Now I am."

She took the first step, and he quickly corrected himself by leading the pace. As they rounded the corner, he inhaled sharply as butterflies erupted in his stomach, millions of wings slapping against his insides. A field stretched before him, manicured hedges circling the perimeter. Rows of ivory benches ran its width beneath a central pergola, ivory framework casting the people below in a lattice of shadows. Orchids in all shades of violet dotted snaking vines that wrapped around the pergola's skeleton, dozens hanging from above like a floral chandelier. In the empty space between the pergola and the hedges, orchids lay scattered throughout the grass like the fallen leaves of Phesaw Park's cherry blossoms, the pink replaced by purple.

He and his mother walked the lone clear strip of grass that ran down the middle of the congregation, through a tunnel of four arbors toward the pergola. He eyed the orchids that twisted up snow-white beams. The flowers grew in scattered pairs along the vines, symbolizing the union of two souls, as Lilu had explained to him months ago in Brilliance.

As they stepped past the back row, all eyes on the mother-son duo, he felt brewing tears. His breathing grew difficult, nose already beginning to clog. He knew he wouldn't make it through today without crying, but he thought he'd at least make it to Shelly's walk. Every guest beamed, minds wiped clean of the recent disasters as they absorbed this momentary bliss. Women wore all kinds of dresses, and the men wore their finest suits. Himitsu's hair, which had grown to a respectable length since he'd last been forced to cut it, was tied back into a knot. And for the first time since Jilly's death, Toshik had applied product to his hair, a part splitting the right side of his scalp and brown locks slicked to the left.

Lilu's hair fell in leafy waves, layered to give it bounce. Her plus-one, Frederick, wore a modest blazer of gray, unbuttoned to reveal an absent tie. Simon's red hair didn't stand atop his head like the flame of a torch, but hung down his back with a glossy sheen. He'd bathed, which said a lot about how serious this was to him. There were many others of note in the audience, but Bryson had already reached the front before he could single them all out.

There was no stage, only a circular patch of green grass at the center of a carpet of orchids. Aside from the officient—a trusted elder of former King Vitio—two others stood in the circle. Following traditional Intelian wedding customs, both Bryson and Shelly were allowed one honorary witness to stand with them during the ceremony. For Shelly, that was her mother: Delilah Intel, dressed in a fine silken dress of lavender, L.K. in her arms. As for Bryson, he'd chosen Olivia Still, who wore not a dress, but a black suit with a purple tie.

Apoleia let go of his hand and leaned in, cold lips touching his cheeks. She placed a hand on his back and guided him forward before taking a seat on an empty section of bench at the front. Bryson had gone through a few notable transitions in his life. A few years ago, he had dropped the name of LeAnce, replacing it with his mother's. In minutes, that would change once again as he took on the name of his wife.

He approached Delilah first, wrapping her in a one-armed hug as L.K.'s face delighted at the sight of his father. Bryson smiled and leaned over his son, kissing his temple. L.K. squirmed, tiny fists raised at his chest as he giggled. Bryson let go of Delilah and stepped across the circle toward his sister. He stood in front of her, but didn't move toward her, aware of her discomfort with physical contact. Despite the rare gesture of intimacy she'd shown their mother upon her arrival to the palace, hesitance held his arms at his side … especially in front of this many people.

Olivia closed the gap and squeezed her brother, head buried in his chest. He stood there for a moment, dumbfounded, arms slack within her embrace. He then lifted his arms and wrapped them around her, placing his cheek atop her head. The tears finally fell out of him, without shame. He could accept this.

Olivia let go and stepped back. She gave him a nod, and he turned to face the congregation, eyes trained on the gap in the hedges across the field. He'd hated the spotlight in his youth, unable to handle the added pressure it brought. But that had come from focusing on all the eyes that were on him. In this moment, everyone else slipped into oblivion, his thoughts on one woman, regal and imperfect in all the ways that made her perfect to him.

He wondered who'd walk with her down the aisle, seeing that her mother and sister were out here. Would she walk alone, unable to allow someone to fill the role her father should have had? It'd make sense considering the freshness of his loss.

When she stepped from behind the distant hedge, Bryson's eyes widened. She did have someone by her side, elbows hooked as she held a bouquet of orchids in front of her. Vistas wore a black suit and tie, classically cut with a burgundy pocket square—the lone tribute to his home kingdom of Dev. His hair hung in a loose ponytail down his back. Having spent weeks wallowing in the grief over his shortcomings in how he handled his relationship with his brother, blaming himself for that leading to Flen's murder of King Vitio, Bryson was ecstatic to see him walking his soon-to-be-wife down the grassy aisle. The Dev servant had been largely responsible in raising the royal sisters.

Shelly's hair had been cut and stylized into a pixie cut, buzzed short on one side with layered locks that flicked effortlessly to the other side. Her bangs swept across her forehead, narrowing into a spiral down the side of her face. She had dyed her roots black, lightening to a shamrock green at the ends. Her dress was pure ivory, crashing to the ground in loose folds, embroidery in the shape of orchid vines climbing from the waistline up to her shoulder straps. White gloves stretched just above the elbow, and a golden crown blazed atop her head, the first obvious sign that Shelly was now this kingdom's Royal Head.

She stepped into the circle, and Vistas sat in the final empty space on the bench at the front. Bryson Still stood across from Shelly Intel, eyes only for each other while the elder drawled out the ceremonial script. He would have said this had been the longest he'd ever stared at someone, but that would have been a lie. There were a few nights spent watching the princess sleep, elbow propped on his pillow and head resting in his hand, the moons—so close when in the sky tower—splashing her in a bluish hue.

Shelly started her vows with a bittersweet tribute involving her father. She cried somber tears, silent as they trickled down her cheeks. But she continued her vows, transitioning to Bryson, triggering a smile that parted rosy lips. A couple tales earned her a few laughs from the audience.

Bryson reached behind the lapel of his tuxedo and retrieved a folded sheet of parchment when his turn came. Shelly giggled as he unfolded it, shaking her head. She knew his memory was poor and likely hadn't expected anything less. What she didn't know, however, was that he'd written this on his own. No help from Agnos or Lilu, his saviors when it had come to other writing assignments in his life. He looked up from his scrawl and said:

"Our relationship began with a lot of sass, mostly from your end. I'm pretty sure you hated me, and King Vitio's immediate friendliness toward me didn't help. I guess you were just jealous." He waited for the laughs to dwindle. "I learned a lot that first day: You have the mouth of a sailor, the sass of a pampered cat, and the first-impressions of a Cynnish ghoul. While it humored people like Himitsu, it terrified me. But, how we interacted evolved over time, and you broadened my perspective of what you were. You ran away with me to a different kingdom, displaying a sense of adventure. You trained me in my electrical weaving, proving your worth as an instructor. You circumvented your father by allowing me passage into the Archaic Mountains to find Olivia while knowing you were pregnant, displaying a mother's courage. And you forced me to leave home and family in order to help the kingdom—selflessness of which I find myself and this kingdom undeserving."

He folded the parchment and returned it to his inner pocket. These next words he didn't need to write down, for they had run through his mind every day for the past couple of years. "I love you," he breathed. "You and L.K. will always be what I live for."

Following vows, Bryson and Shelly exchanged rings with shaky fingers. The announcement of their marriage and a kiss sealed the deal. Applause erupted from the audience, as the two newlyweds—L.K. cradled in one arm—sauntered down the aisle and out of the courtyard.

They were, officially, a family.

*   *   *

It was difficult to believe that what came after the wedding—the reception—was called the same thing as what had followed Vitio's funeral, the two atmospheres polar opposites. Guests laughed and conversed around scattered tables in a separate field. Assigned seats be damned; people hopped between tables as if this was the commons area during school lunch.

Toshik was seated on one of the tables as he listened to a story from Agnos, who had gathered quite a crowd. Aunt Ropinia sat by her father, keeping him company as he indulged in cake. Lilu and Frederick danced to an energetic melody played by a stringed quartet, the two weavineers showing off footwork that would have made anyone jealous. Shelly tried the same with Vistas, but the Dev servant didn't possess the same rhythm, resembling a newborn deer as he wobbled across the dance floor. Other pairs were Queen Apoleia and Titus, Himitsu and Kaylee, Pilot Ophala and Horos, and Simon and one of his archer peers. Bryson vaguely remembered her from one of his visits to the archery store where Simon had worked. He had made her an impractical bow, and she had called herself an archer assassin.

As daylight faded to a starless gray, Bryson having spent most of the festivities making his rounds of the tables and thanking people for their attendance, Intelamps ignited and the guests grew louder, their wine glasses heavier.

"Your vows were impressive," said Agnos. Somehow, he and Bryson had found themselves alone at the open bar on the stone patio. Most guests had chosen to simply lift their drinks off of the platters of passing stewards. "Are you sure you didn't cheat?"

"My brain is capable."

Agnos grinned. "I believe it." His eyes drifted toward Bryson's wings. "You know I have to ask ..."

"If I had any answers, I'd give them to you." Bryson had yet to tell Shelly about the visit from Thusia, Suadade, and their superior, so he wasn't going to share that information with Agnos. "They're useless, honestly. They don't do anything, nor can I control them."

"And your eyes?"

Bryson cocked an eyebrow. "What about them?"

"The rings of light around your pupils and irises."

Bryson stopped stirring his virgin margarita, looking up at his friend. He had noticed the same trait in others, but this was the first time someone else pointed it out. He supposed it shouldn't have surprised him, seeing that Agnos's eyes glowed brighter than anyone else's. Maybe those with—

"I've been hanging with Lilu a lot lately," Agnos said. "We like to get together and catch each other up on our intellectual progressions."

"Nerds."

Agnos raised a glass of water. "Proud nerds."

"Definitely wasn't an insult," Bryson said.

"All those years ago, you went to me for help about your dream, yet Lilu's the one who cracked the code."

Bryson nodded, turning to lean back against a stone column and survey the festivities. "Just waiting for the day I can shoot ice out of my fingers."

Agnos laughed. "As if you aren't overpowered enough."

Taking a sip of his drink, Bryson shrugged. "Everyone's going their separate ways after this, so what will the great ..." he trailed off, chuckling softly ... "Sixth of Six be getting himself into?"

"Infiltrating the central school of the Dark Realm in efforts to recruit two of the Diatia."

Bryson coughed up some of his margarita, wiping his lips with the back of his hand. "Do you ever take a break?"

"I know of no such thing. I have answers to find."

Shaking his head, Bryson asked, "So ... what do you need two Diatia for?"

"To assist me in my journey through the Warpfinate."

"Screw that place." Bryson rubbed his eyes, memories of study sessions with Lilu at the Bricks exhausting him. "I'd rather visit the Linsaniun Mounds."

"If there's one thing I've never been scared of, it's books," Agnos said.

"Nothing scares you these days."

"Depends on if I'm alone or not." Agnos looked in the direction of Evelyn and Tashami, the latter waving him over. "Anyway, congratulations, Bryson."

Bryson sipped on his margarita, watching the reception from a distance. The patio gave him a higher vantage point, and he had resigned to absorbing the scene before him. Stewards swept past, replacing empty serving trays with full ones at the bar, ten glasses seemingly glued to the top as they wended between guests. He spotted two heads of green on the dance floor, Shelly and Lilu goofing off as they wiggled their romps, placed a finger on their noses, and stuck their tongue out at each other.

Perhaps he shouldn't have been a spectator at his own wedding reception, but there was something about taking a moment to appreciate it as a whole rather than only glimpsing segments, which was what he'd experienced as the nucleus.

A figure glowed across the field, towering in a gap between hedge walls. His face was wide and square-jawed, beady eyes inspecting the crowd, trapezius that swallowed his neck. It was a miracle the man could find a tunic with a collar wide enough to accommodate such a form. Bryson recognized him immediately as Quincy, the Pogu who had visited him with Thusia and Suadade a couple weeks back. Their assignment had been to bring Bryson to the Light Empire, but he was granted an extension for the sake of his wedding. Why was he here now? Could they not wait until after the reception and give him a few days to appreciate married life? *Why* did they even want him?

Bryson wondered if anyone noticed Quincy's conspicuous presence. He stood in the open, illuminated by the two Intelamps that hung at both sides of the hedge's gap. The Intelian guards who stood a couple yards away from the entrance didn't acknowledge him. The Pogu must have had a way of concealing his presence.

"Why not give your guests a show."

Bryson turned to find his mom. Pink lips and creamy skin, faded scars on her neck. A violet war braid embroidered with crystal snowflakes. He glanced back at the entryway to find it empty, the Pogu gone without a trace. His heartbeat slowed, breaths steadying. "What do you mean?" he asked.

"Well, that quartet over there seems ready to pass out." She extended a hand holding a glass of wine in the direction of a group of four men playing stringed instruments. "I'm sure you've noticed the piano, which has yet to be touched."

Truth be told, Bryson hadn't looked that way all night. While he'd heard the music, he never bothered to study the space from which it came. The musicians were tucked in the corner of the field, melodies amplified by strange boxes scattered across the base of the perimeter hedges. Lilu had apparently smuggled them out of Brilliance, storing them in hidden compartments of her travolters for when the time came to deploy.

Despite the quartet's secluded location, that wasn't the cause for Bryson's tunnel vision. Ever since that day Storshae, Toono, and Apoleia invaded Phesaw, and he had learned the origins of his musical talents and his favorite song, *Phases of S*, he couldn't stomach the thought of sitting at a piano again. In fact, he downright starved himself of music, with the only exception being Jilly's funeral. Every time he looked at a piano, he pictured his mother, fingers racing across the keys as ice crept around its body, rage flooding throw her veins as she hammered away the notes that represented the disdain she had for Bryson's father. He couldn't envision a piano without imagining Mendac pinning Apoleia to her bed.

His mom took a deep breath, nodding with pursed lips. "Shelly told me about your abandonment of music. She wanted to have a pianist at the reception, but was reluctant, fearing how you'd react."

"So, she didn't get a pianist," Bryson muttered. "But she has a piano to serve as decoration."

Apoleia frowned, tilting her head indifferently. "Why employ a pianist when she already has two?"

He regarded his mom, skepticism narrowing his eyes. "I've retired."

"That's a shame. I hate to hear you've dismissed such a critical talent of many Stillian women. Do you want to disrespect your roots?"

He turned fully, shoulder pressed against the stone column as he faced her. "I thought music was just something you were good at, which made you different. Women aren't supposed to express themselves passionately in Stillian culture. Music *is* passion, and it's as raw as it gets."

"Exactly." She placed an icy hand against his cheek. "And it's where Stillian women direct their emotions behind closed doors. I wasn't odd because of my love for music; I was odd because of my perspective of men, how I found them to be equals to women, and my animated personality as a child. But music … that was any woman's scapegoat. For some, like me, it was creating music. For others, it was dancing. Take your Aunt Ropinia for example. She could figure skate to any song. Hell, even without skates, she knows how to find a melody and put it under heel."

He eyed the dance floor. After spending most of the reception tending to Gennaio's needs, Aunt Ropinia had finally joined the dancers. She moved with purpose, knowing exactly which steps to take in accordance with the quartet's harmony.

Apoleia laughed. "She doesn't even know this song, yet you'd think she's heard it a thousand times with the way she's moving."

"That's a lot of confidence for a woman from a culture that forces such expression behind closed doors."

"Well, times change. I've worked hard at shifting my kingdom's views of such customs. And if it's going to happen, it starts with those who will lead by example. That means my sister and me."

He regarded the piano once more. "I don't think—"

"You don't have an excuse, Bryson," she said, grabbing him by the hand and dragging him down the patio's steps and toward the musicians' corner. "Smother the bad imagery with good! Let's make new memories today, and it starts with gaining power over the tools that you view as instruments of pain." She grabbed him by the shoulders and placed him on the piano's bench, waving off the quartet in the process. "Take a break, gentlemen."

Bryson's indecisiveness morphed into frustration now that someone was forcing his hand. Were his declarations of discomfort not enough? His mom took his wrists and raised them, but his fingers only hovered above the keys, a mental force field between them. She sat next to him on the bench, a floral perfume wafting past his nose, a chill that nipped at his side from her touch. She spread three sheets of parchment across the stand just above the keys. It was sheet music, pitches and rhythms racing across countless stanzas—the only other language Bryson knew outside of Sphairian. At the head of the first sheet was a title: *Piece of Family, Peace of Mind.*

"You took the pun route, eh?" Bryson asked, his nerves calming.

"I've worked on this ever since the Blizzard of Blood, inspired by your actions during your visit ... *You* are that piece of family. It's a song of bliss."

"I can tell," he whispered, lost in his mental translations of the notes. He pointed at a section on the second sheet. "I like that."

"Fitting," she said. "It represents the moment you, your Branian, and I joined hands to defeat the Linsani of Fear." After a stretch of silence, his eyes still scanning stanzas, she took his hand and placed it over the keys again. "As you can tell, I made this with two pianists in mind." She raised her hands and tapped two keys. "Will you join me?"

Bryson caved.

They played in perfect unison—mother and son. The song clocked in at roughly nine minutes, certain stanzas requiring loops. While he couldn't look away from the sheet music—this was his first time playing it and thus couldn't rely on memory—he could feel his mom's gentle eyes on him. She needn't see the keys; she knew them like the back of her hand. Music coursed through her blood.

As they struck the final notes, applause rung out from the direction of the gathering. Having lost himself in the sheet music, he'd forgotten where he was. The entire congregation faced him and his mom, whistles piercing through the applause. Shelly stood at the front, the only person not clapping. Her arms were crossed, a smug look on her face.

As if to say, "It's about time."

15

Dawn of Revolution

The waiting game exhausted Bryson. Thusia had said they'd return after his wedding, but they never gave a specific arrival date, leaving him in a constant state of anxiety, jumping at the slightest bump in the night. One thing was certain. He needed to tell Shelly.

The problem was finding a gap in her schedule. She had wasted no time in diving headfirst into her royal duties. Today, Lilu was taking her into the ravaged eastern sector of the city with an escort of over a dozen soldiers. Despite the precautions Lilu's arguments that they could defend themselves, Bryson made sure he accompanied them.

He trudged along, too wary of their surroundings to focus on the two sisters' discussions. Uliji, advisor to the crown, walked with them, providing input when needed. Bryson caught mentions of some rather gaudy numbers in terms of money when it came to repairs. Again, something he had a difficult time caring about, seeing that he'd soon be abducted by celestials.

"This is the spot," Lilu said, the group coming to a stop at a vast expanse of empty cobbles bordered by collapsed buildings.

One of several marketing hubs scattered throughout the city, Griva's Plaza was the second largest in terms of square footage and third most profitable—before it had become this wasteland, at least. Bryson lumbered forward, hands in his hoodie pockets, peeling away from the guards to join Lilu, Shelly, and Uliji in their inspection.

"Its prior use is unsustainable," Lilu said. "We can completely repurpose its functionality in the rebuild."

"You need all of this space?" Shelly asked, both hands on her hips.

"And then some."

Bryson had no idea what they were talking about, but he figured he'd wait for them to elaborate on their own.

Uliji, who had reserved his input in sparing dosages, cleared his throat. "Our allies who aid our efforts in the city's rebuild might not appreciate the allocation of their funds into such a project … however small the percentage might be."

"I know that," Lilu snapped. "Which is why none of the foreign donations are going into it."

"Then who is—"

"The LeAnce family," Lilu said, eyeing Uliji.

"That's dirty money!" Bryson shouted, forgetting his apathy.

Lilu rounded on him with deadly ire in her glare. "And what makes it dirty?"

He shrunk, reminded of Lilu's height, a trait that had skipped Shelly in favor of the younger sister. Stammering, he realized he didn't have an answer.

"The name?" Lilu asked rhetorically. She knew that was the answer, and now he knew it to be, too. Shelly's hands had moved from her hips to behind her back, clasped as she looked the other way, pretending to not see the altercation.

Wounded, Bryson's instinctive response was to return the accusation, show her the hypocrisy in her words. She had expressed disdain for Brilliance's League of Weavineers simply because of their last name. She'd lacked trust in Wendel LeAnce, the commissioner, because of it, yet she had the nerve to scorn Bryson about that same logic? He ground his teeth, debating on his next move.

Lilu made it for him, sighing as she shook her head and gazed longingly at the plaza. "I'm just as guilty, but these past few weeks have put things into perspective. Petty squabbles I might have with the LeAnce family— squabbles that are possibly undeserving, for I don't know what role they played in sculpting Mendac into the man he became—will only get in the way of this kingdom's priority … the people." She paused, eyes narrowed at the plaza. "Do you know why Brilliance is the safest place from outside threats? Why it bests even the capital in terms of security?"

Bryson's nose curled up. "I don't know … Maybe the massive, hundred-foot wall that swallows it."

"Partly, but the truth lies in its technological advancements, which is credit to the culture shaped by the LeAnce family. They value education more than anything else. They're the reason why Dunami Hospital is as notorious as it is, for they invented the devices within. The travolters that stopped the SCAPD fleet on Knowledge River wouldn't have existed had it not been for the tools and inspiration I received from IWA in Brilliance, which, once again, is credit to the LeAnce family. That is why I cannot decline their aid. I have shown Wendel LeAnce little respect since meeting him years ago, yet all he's done is put me in positions to excel."

"You put yourself in those positions," Bryson said. "Since when do you give credit to others for your successes?"

Lilu smiled, nodding. Shelly walked away with a slew of guards and Uliji in tow, seemingly interested in something in a nearby alleyway. Bryson eyed them, but remained with Lilu as he waited for a reasonable excuse for her shift in attitude toward the LeAnce family.

"Let me rephrase," she said. "While many have recognized my skills throughout my life, none had allowed me access to the tools to strengthen those skills or the authority to do with them what I want. Wendel did."

"And what about Mendac's lab hidden in the sewers?"

"Do we even know if Wendel knew about it?" Before he could rebuke, she added, "Think about it. That false door could have been constructed by Mendac long ago, to protect his research from the wandering eyes of his foster family."

"I don't believe it," he rebuked. "Then why have a statue of the man built in the busiest intersection with a hidden entrance into the sewers?"

She inhaled deeply and gazed off to the side, pursing her lips. "I understand your mistrust. I still waver, too. But in this moment, neither I nor my sister has the luxury of investigating the possible evils of those who raised Mendac just because of their last name. We need to focus on the places where our kingdom is suffering, which are here in the capital and the port city of Continon. If Wendel is willing to help us rebuild, then I will accept it for what it is. And I believe a Weavineering factory is the perfect start."

"Princess Lilu!" cried Uliji from the alley behind her.

Lilu hovered for a moment without response. She eyed Bryson and narrowed her eyes. "We aren't children anymore; we can't think that way … minds focused on revenge and petty grievances … actions based in passion rather than logic." She craned her neck, gazing upward at the overcast sky. "King Damian, King Supido, my father, Grand Director Poicus, Directors Senex, Buredo, and Neaneuma … all dead. As Pilot Ophala reminded me recently—" her head lowered, gaze returning to Bryson— "we are the next generation of leaders. The scope of our concerns must stretch beyond our own insignificant lives to encompass the populace."

"*LILU!*" This time, the bellow came from Shelly. "Get over here!"

With her signature eye roll, Lilu turned and jogged toward the alley in her heels. Bryson stood for a moment, mulling over her words of wisdom and the advice of Ophala contained within. The Spy Pilot had a knack for summing up his convictions as naivety, making him see the true depth of issues of which he could only perceive the surface value. She had done it again. This was more than—

"Bryson, get over here!"

His gaze focused on the alley. He could only see some guards from his vantage, four posted at the alley's mouth. He pushed through the crush, stepping out of the other side to find Shelly, Lilu, and Uliji. They stood in front of a wooden wall, where a mousey boy with blond hair sat limply against it—only his head lay on the ground next to his body. Blood splattered the wall and pooled across cobbles.

Lilu crossed her arms. "Another reason for the factory. To protect the kingdom from enemies within."

Bryson's horrified gaze skated up to an insignia carved into the wall above the corpse. Three triangles meant to symbolize mountains, a brain as their backdrop, halfway hidden as if it was the sun in its descent.

"They're growing bolder," Uliji breathed.

"What the hell is this?" Bryson asked.

"Remember when I mentioned rumblings of rising rebels?" Lilu asked.

He turned toward her, eyebrows furrowed. "Yes … rumblings."

"It's happening," she said, kneeling in her sundress, a solemn curve to her lips. "They're on the rise. This is a statement."

Minutes passed in silence, all eyes on the headless corpse. This wasn't supposed to be the conflict the kingdom faced. Bryson regarded the mountains once more, now realizing the brain wasn't setting, but rising.

The dawn of a revolution.

16

Lost Ancestry

Spy Pilot Ophala's sobriety gave her a new appreciation for the heat. The sun had always been her nemesis, but no longer did she feel lethargic and queasy as the sweltering rays squeezed the alcohol from her sweat glands. Instead, she was vivacious, a bounce in her saunter as she finished a ten-mile walk to the eastern edge of Dunami. Of course, the Intel Kingdom's customary storm clouds hiding the sun helped, but that didn't mean it was any less humid.

She traveled alone without need of concealment, for the ravaged streets of the capital's suburbs didn't contain life outside of herself—for the most part. With the focus of artisans and engineers closer to the heart of the city, it would take some months before they gave this area any attention.

As she traversed the final stretch of tar before her destination, her eyes combed the surrounding homes, all of which had been evacuated during the Rogue Demon's invasion. Many of these families had been wealthy and were now likely in Acu or Continon, trying to make a new living. She hoped they avoided the latter, as the port city was presently suffering from similar issues of flooding to the Spirit Kingdom's capital, Saido. The unfortunate risks of a city built below sea level.

She was relieved to not see her husband lurking on a roof or behind a tree, though she supposed that meant little when dealing with a man of stealth. She had wanted to come here without company, a reckless idea according to the love of her life. Horos had a habit of pointing out the obvious, and today that meant repeating the warning: "You're the Pilot of Spy and Sky, Love. People want you dead!"

She would have accepted protection had it not been for the confidentiality of this task. Only one other person knew where Ophala was, and she'd visit later, but only because that person deserved it.

She reached a beautiful home on her right. A sidewalk stretched from the road to the front door, cutting between a picket fence. She paused at the start of the sidewalk, raising an eyebrow at the lush grass, freshly cut and a healthy green. The neighboring properties housed tangled weeds and untrimmed grass, unruly blades curling over the sidewalk's edges. Her years as a spy made her cringe. A hideout should have blended in. And who had the time to maintain the yard?

She crept forward, placing a hand on the white picket gate that led to the yard. There was nobody outside to keep watch, and all curtains were drawn shut. Still, she found it hard to believe nobody was watching her at this very moment. Without her ancient—she had left it at the palace on purpose—she wouldn't be instantly recognizable to those waiting in the house, so she extended an arm and waited for her signal.

Wings fluttered behind her, and two black starlings perched on her arm. She had developed such a great relationship with creatures of the sky that she no longer needed her ancient for simple tasks. Many species— especially starlings—always remained near, waiting for communication through body language.

She smiled at the two ebony beauties, then turned toward the manicured lawn again. As she waited for a response, she studied the house. It was a single story, but the beauty spoke in its architectural design rather than its size. Built with brick, it possessed a chimney, shingled roof, and a multi-faced front, the right half receding further back into the structure, granting space for a bed of flowers beneath a grand rectangular window. Someone with substantial money had once owned this home. She would have expected nothing less from …

She sidestepped left as a figure stirred in her peripherals. She hadn't seen or heard anyone approach. A man stood in the yard, leaning casually against the fence, each elbow resting on a picket. He wore a long black trench coat, buttoned to the collar, broad shouldered with bronze buttons on the lapels. Patches of gray splotched a full black beard, hard eyes nestled in the crevices of a wrinkled face.

"Where'd you come from?" she asked.

Raven eyes slid her way before locking onto her—no, they skittered just around her face. "Do you want the smart-ass answer or …" He smirked, noticing the flatness of her eyebrows and lips. Nodding, he stared across the street. "Side yard. I'm the lookout. Saw your bird trick and came to invite you in."

She glanced at the side yard, expecting to find some sort of cover he'd used to reach the fence without her knowing, but it was only open grass. She frowned, the revelation insulting. As a spy—and not just any spy, but the Spy Pilot—she had plumed herself on her awareness, yet this man had gotten within twenty feet of her without her knowledge.

He pushed himself away from the fence and stood straight, adopting an exaggerated posture of an arched back as gloved hands entered his coat's deep pockets. Inhaling deeply, he closed his eyes and said, "Love the morning dew around here." He glanced at her out of the corner of his eye before turning to cut through the yard, toward the front door. "Welcome. The gate's open."

Ophala hated gate locks. They were simple and unnecessary—anyone could reach over and unlock it—but their crude design forced her to twist and yank several times before finding success. The rust from years of rainfall didn't help. Give her a locked vault, and she'd open it before this stupid … *Ha!* She swung the gate open and sauntered through, pride unscathed.

The man waited in front of the house, back to the front door as he stroked his beard with gloved hands. "Awfully clumsy for a woman who likely grew up picking locks."

"How do you know in which manner I was raised?"

He turned as she approached, opening the front door and stepping to the side, allowing her first passage. "I know the manner in which you were trained, unless the kingdom has completely overhauled the assassin and spy programs since I left."

That gave her pause, turning in the entry foyer to eye him. "You're an alumnus? And from which program did you graduate?"

"Both," he said, closing the door.

Her eyes narrowed, drifting from his face to the door. It didn't make a sound as it closed, not even a click. "That would make you …"

"A hybrid," he said while sweeping past her, heavy boots noiseless atop the floorboards.

She lingered for a moment, watching him walk deeper into the house where she could see the bar of a kitchen. Academes that trained in the arts of stealth and reconnaissance had stopped granting hybrid honors four decades ago, long before Ophala graduated from Swift Secrets—the Archaic Kingdom's most revered academe for future assassins and spies. During the first two years, students were trained in hybrid classes, learning the basic skills of both professions, but upon entering year three, they were forced to choose a side as they delved into more complex curriculum.

Still, even before the retirement of hybrid honors, they were seldom awarded to pupils. She believed the average had been two students every seven years graduated a hybrid—a miniscule number when considering dozens graduated as either a spy or assassin every year. This man was talented, and she didn't recall Apoleia warning her of such company.

Before heading for the kitchen area, she looked to her right to find a narrow hallway leading to a few rooms. To her left was a parlor wherein sat a grand piano. Her curiosities of the wraith-man vanished. When was the last time that young man had visited this place? Or had he completely erased his home from his memory?

She pushed through the hall just ahead, opening up to a kitchen to the right and a living room to the left, a breakfast nook split between them.

Pausing at the hallway's end, she absorbed those scattered throughout the three rooms.

The wraith-man stood at the kitchen's bar, eyeing a pan of eggs that sat over a fancy fire pit in the counter. A woman, dark-skinned with graying braids tied into a tail down her back, handled the pan, occasionally poking the yolk with a fork. A little girl—maybe five or six years of age—of the same complexion sat on the floor of the kitchen, keeping close to the woman and serving as a tripping hazard while reading a book—or trying to, judging by the upside down cover and narrowed concentration in her eyes.

Two men sat at the breakfast table, both at an angle that allowed Ophala to see the striking resemblance between them. One was more youthful in his features. Both were dark-skinned like the woman and girl, but their hair was left kinky. The oldest of the pair looked to have a twenty-year gap on the other based on the few coils of gray in his unkempt beard and the wrinkles in his forehead, but his body spoke of strength far beyond youth's grasp. A chiseled chest and abdomen peeked out from behind a baggy tank top as he curled over a plate of eggs and hash. His arms were ripped, skin taught against every curve of muscle. His younger clone—likely in his mid-twenties—looked like a stick in comparison despite possessing muscle mass that would have made most young men jealous.

In the living room were three figures that weren't human: a honey badger, rabbit, and a fox tall enough to best her son's height. In all the years leading up to this moment, she had told herself that if she'd ever gotten the chance to meet the dimiours—a species divided by the Archaic Mountains since the beginning of time—she wouldn't react. She couldn't carry through with that promise, as her eyes widened before her brain had a chance to stop them.

"Your eyes are going to get stuck like that," said the wraith-man. He was cutting around the yolk of his eggs after getting a plate from the woman cooking.

Ophala named them as her gaze shifted between the dimiours. "Atarax … Therapif … and Biaza."

"Pilot Ophala," Atarax said. The fox's voice was deeper than any she'd ever heard. "It's a pleasure to finally put a face to our good friend's name."

Biaza pushed herself off the sofa and walked toward Ophala, extending a paw. The pilot shook it, hiding her bemusement. Therapif nodded from his spot on a gray rug next to the fireplace.

"Aren't you missing someone?" asked the young man at the table. He glared at Ophala, no faith in those eyes. Knowing the hell he'd just escaped, she didn't blame him.

She smiled gently, words just as soft. "She'll be here soon. She had some things to attend to in the palace."

He glanced at the older man across the table, who nodded in return. "Patience, son."

Ophala turned toward the living room once more. "And aren't there more of you?"

Therapif looked up from his book. "Moros and Kakos are still sleeping. Prakriti is tending to a park somewhere nearby."

"Sit," Biaza said, returning to an armchair in the living room. Ophala chose a spot at the breakfast table, enraptured by the scent of the eggs.

"Would you like some?" the woman in the kitchen asked, likely noticing the Spy Pilot's fleeting glances toward the plates.

Ophala eyed the three dimiours, knowing their discomfort with the treatment of an animal's body as food. Apparently, that hadn't stopped the humans from enjoying their chicken offspring. The dimiours might not have even told them. Noticing Biaza staring at Ophala, almost expectantly, and Therapif's left ear unfurling to stand tall, as if waiting for the pilot's response, she declined the offer. Atarax, who sat with arms crossed and eyes closed, nodded with approval.

The little girl pattered over from the kitchen and climbed into the chair across from Ophala. She stared at the Spy Pilot, head tilting. "Where are your muscles?"

Ophala paused, glancing down at flabby arms, then to her waist, where love handles had begun developing beneath her shirt. She was suddenly aware of the ample cushion in her seat, yet knowing it wasn't credit to the chair. Still, she smiled as her gaze returned to the girl. "In my brain."

The girl's jaw dropped as she glanced at the older man. "Papa, there are muscles in your brain?"

The father leaned back, studying Ophala for a second. "Yes."

136

"Dad, stop spreading—"

The man cut off his son with a glare that could have burned holes through steel. "I'll spread your nose across your face."

As the younger man's gaze fell to his empty plate, Ophala returned her focus to the girl. Obviously, there were no muscles in the brain, but it was the best explanation for a child so young. "Why'd you ask?"

The girl shrugged. "You look strong, but you have no muscles. How can you be powerful without them?"

"How do you know I'm strong?"

"I can see it. In your eyes, the way you stand and talk." She muttered, "Like the taskmasters."

"She is nothing like them," the father said sternly. That didn't stop Ophala's heart from sinking.

"No," the girl said. "Not in the scary way. But she tells people what to do, like a boss. I know it."

Ophala leaned in, arms flat on the table, and whispered, "You can be a boss and a good person. I take care of those beneath me, and I train them to become the best spies they can be ... that way they can one day take my job."

The son scoffed. "You want us to believe that you want people to take your job?"

"I want them to be capable of it." She leaned back. "That doesn't mean I won't put up a fight." She quickly raised a finger at the girl, seeing the misunderstanding in the downward curl of her lips. "Not a physical fight ... a theoretical one. I'll use my experience and knowledge to prove I'm still the best person for the Spy Pilot position."

"Thee ... rechical?" the girl asked, trying to repeat the word by sounding it out.

Ophala laughed. "Don't worry about it, sweetie. Just know that I use my brain to fight people."

"How do I train my brain?"

"You were just doing it."

The girl's brows furrowed with confusion.

"That book," Ophala said. "The one you were reading."

"I was just looking at the pictures."

"Well, that's a start." Ophala looked at the father, who continued to watch with interest. She didn't want to assume the entire family was illiterate, but she knew it likely to be the case. Powish slaves weren't allowed books. She reached across the table and placed a hand on the girl's forearm. "Now that you're away from that place, there are plenty of people who can teach you how to read. The central school of the Light Realm, Phesaw, will be reopening soon."

"She's from the Dark Realm," the son spat.

"I can pull some strings."

The father's eyes narrowed. "For us?"

"Nobody is better than anyone else."

He nodded. "I respect that, but we don't know where our new home will be. It could end up in the Still Kingdom with most of the other refugees."

"I guess we'll see how it unfolds."

"Let's relax on the humanitarianism lessons," said the wraith-man, picking at his teeth, plate of eggs now empty on the bar. "Especially from a spawn of Swift Secrets."

"And which academe did you attend?" she asked, turning in her seat to face him.

"Same place," he grunted. "And I am spawn, as was my senior and every single other alumni. That place breeds killers." He shrugged. "Not that there's anything wrong with that to certain degrees. What bothers me is someone trying to feign philosophies as if it hides the trail of bodies."

She couldn't conjure up a counter. She had sent many people out to do the killing for her. Then there was Toth Brench—interim king of the Archaic Kingdom—who she had poisoned. Memories of Swift Secrets swum to the forefront of her mind, training beneath hardened masters of stealth, murder, and cunning. Such memories were unwelcome, scabbed wounds marring her psyche.

She turned away from Creep, regarding the trio of dimiours. "Rhyparia. What has come of her?"

Atarax finally opened his eyes, gaze sliding over to the breakfast area, pointed fox's ears twitching at the name. "Dead, we believe."

Her stomach dropped, gaze falling slightly, fearing she knew what had caused such an end: complete energy depletion, draining her energy canals and sending her body into a fatal state of shock. Dropping the moon would do that to a person, even though she was assuming she had done that. Nobody had verified the cause for the moon's plunge. She looked up and asked, "And was it—"

"—Perhaps," interrupted Atarax, gaze veering to the other humans around Ophala. "Not in front of them."

The father looked to his daughter. "Ahzedan, go wake Moros."

An evil grin appeared on the girl's face. "Like, wake him ... or *wake* him wake him?"

"Like it's the end of the world."

Ahzedan leapt from her chair and rushed down the hall before turning down another. The father nodded, acknowledging the fox. "That'll keep her occupied for a few minutes."

Ophala raised an eyebrow, but decided not to ask.

Atarax hesitated, regarding the family with scrupulous eyes. His reluctance to discuss the matter hadn't been focused on only the girl, but on the rest of the family, too. He turned forward, arms still crossed as he closed his eyes once more, resigned to their defiance.

"Rhyparia wanted to do more than just save the slaves," he said, his voice low enough to require Ophala to lean in. "She wanted to punish those who committed the atrocities, benefitted from them, or just simply spectated without a word."

A heavy silence blanketed them, the woman—who Ophala assumed was the mother—had stopped cooking, now listening from the other side of the bar. Ophala's stomach felt just as hollow as the room. Had it only been the Gravity Trials that had shaped her into such a vindictive soul? Or had she experienced something else beyond the Archaic Mountains? That shouldn't have been the case, not with Musku's guidance.

"Did you know about it beforehand?" she finally asked.

"Of course not," Therapif said, closing his book and laying it at his side. "Not until after the fact."

The wraith-man grunted. "We all saw signs ... or inklings of it."

"None more than you," Biaza said from the sofa. "You were the one she ended up entrusting most, after knowing you for only a couple of weeks."

"Prakriti warned us many times," Atarax said. "He saw it in her—the evils behind the stoic veil."

"Who is this Prakriti person?" Ophala asked. "And why didn't you listen to his warnings?"

Atarax opened his left eye to regard her briefly. "The same reason you didn't listen to the warnings of Rhyparia's past actions, or the words of your equals in the Amendment Order, who feared her capabilities … we believed in her … and, in you, Pilot Ophala." He bared his pointed fox teeth, clearly angry with himself. "Musku told us all about what led to Rhyparia's arrival in Epinio. The catastrophes, her mother, the trials … your desperate measures to assure her escape of the gallows." He shook his head. "It seems we are all fools."

Another logical, albeit brutal, rebuttal. Ophala searched elsewhere for the actual answer to her question. The wraith-man offered it: "Prakriti is an insufferable prude, but a correct one in hindsight."

"He's Musku's son," Biaza said.

Ophala's eyebrows rose, unaware such a being existed outside of Bryson and Olivia: a child of an original Jestivan. "When is he to return?" she asked.

The wraith-man shook his head, fingers combing through his beard. "Nightfall, likely. He likes to spend the entire day tending to any areas of nature."

Deep thought crinkled her brow, but she could wait for another day to meet the man. She didn't have the luxury of waiting for nightfall. She had other business in need of her attention. She heard a scream from somewhere in the house, followed by maniacal giggles.

"Seems she took full advantage of your rare command," said the mother.

The father smirked. "Damned weasel deserves it anyway. Too clever for his own good."

Putting aside the possibilities of what the girl had done to startle Moros out of his slumber with such alarm, Ophala turned to the dimiours again.

"Do you know what you want to do?" She paused, choosing her next words carefully. "About your situation in regards to the world?"

Atarax, Biaza, and Therapif exchanged glances before coming to silent agreement. They had likely discussed this in detail for weeks. "We'll reveal ourselves through the Devish broadcast witchery at a later date," the fox said, eyes closing once again. "For now, we return to our home of Epinio."

"When you do show yourself to the world, don't expect the public to stop eating eggs and dairy," said the mother, a single eyebrow arched. "Especially meat."

"That's fine … Just don't expect us to stop eating the livers of your children." The threat came from a hulking frame that entered from the hall. Ophala's eyes widened. A wet nose perched at the end of an elongated muzzle. Large, pointed ears stood at attention, and a thick coat of brown fur covered everything but his front, exposing the troughs and hills of his abdomen beneath matted fuzz. He stood on two hind legs, making the wolf taller than any human Ophala had ever seen. Kakos was more intimidating than she would have imagined. Musku had always said that Atarax was the leader of the bunch, and she supposed that reflected in the fox's tranquility, but this wolf was of an animalistic sort. His toothy sneer and piercing black eyes seeped with a desire for carnage.

As Kakos looked the humans over, gaze lingering on Ophala for only a second, Therapif said, "That's a lie."

"Not where Atarax and I come from. They would despise what we've become today."

"Quiet." The fox's command was short and stern.

Kakos chuckled. "Atarax carries great shame over our ancestry."

Ophala looked between the two mighty dimiours, Atarax's passive expression unreadable. She decided to steer the conversation elsewhere. "Queen Apoleia and I have been discussing the logistics of refugee placement. She seems eager to accept most of them, while the rest can be divided throughout the Light Realm." She paused. "Hopefully, we can find a way into the Power Kingdom."

A throaty laugh rumbled through the room. "That is impossible," the wolf said. "The entire northern section of that kingdom is crushed, including the teleplatforms and the bay."

141

"Good riddance," said the son, tone laced with venom.

Ophala eyed him once more, but said nothing as a knock came from the front door. All eyes turned toward it. "Way to do your job," Kakos said, facing the wraith-man at the bar.

"I can't hear crap over your barbaric growls, nor can I smell crap beyond …" the wraith-man trailed off, sniffing at the air. "My apologies. It seems that is *actual* crap in the air—" he eyed the wolf with a raised brow— "care to explain yourself, mut?"

Kakos growled, but the wraith-man pushed away from the bar and stepped past the wolf with little care. Ophala watched curiously, wondering why she had never heard of a hybrid of this caliber. She was the Spy Pilot, after all. She should have known about every spy and assassin within the Archaic Kingdom. The silence of his steps, again, wasn't lost on her.

The door opened. Kakos turned and leaned back against the wall, opening a sightline from the breakfast area to the foyer. A young woman entered past the wraith-man, black braids spilling out of her raised hood and down her chest. Her skin was as dark as the family around Ophala, the muscles in her arms threatening to split the sleeves of her jacket. She peered down the hall, oblivious to the humanistic wolf standing off to the side. The Diatia had eyes for only three people: the son and father at the table, and the woman now visible at the bar.

Tears flooded wide eyes, a well of hope filling a forlorn pit. The Diatia ran, footsteps like thunder compared to the wraith-man's whispers, and threw herself into the older man's arms. He barely had a chance to rise from his chair. He swung her around, a weight lifted off his shoulders despite his little girl—who was quite the opposite—in his arms.

"Dad!" she screamed, grip tightening around his neck.

Ophala watched with sullen eyes. How many years had they spent apart? How much had this man sacrificed by slaving away in the provod mines of the Malanese Peaks to ensure the safety of his family? A smile brightened the son's face. The woman at the bar stood next to the pair, an arm outstretched as she waited her turn. The father let his daughter fall to the floor and kissed her forehead.

"Oh, how I've missed you, Vuilni."

*   *   *

Spy Pilot Ophala couldn't shake the wave of emotions from earlier that day. The reunion between Vuilni and her family had been both tragic and serene, knowing the years of turmoil that had led to it. And while they deserved a happy ending, she still couldn't salvage any sort of appreciation for the events that had allowed it to happen. Rhyparia had murdered tens of thousands of people, and using the excuse of "a means to an end" justified nothing.

In a guest chamber of Dunami Palace, Agnos busied himself by dusting a bevy of glass figurines on a shelf out of his reach. An ottoman sat beneath his feet to aid his lack of height. Sure, there was an entire staff whose job pertained to cleaning and serving, yet the Archaic Jestivan—or pirate captain or Sixth of Six, whatever moniker he might have gone by now—had taken the duties upon himself, claiming the staff had enough on their plates already. She supposed he had a point, seeing that the guest wing of the palace was emptying quicker than a brothel at sunrise. Tomorrow, most would return to their own lives and goals, which had brought Ophala here.

"You take your leave tomorrow, too?" Agnos asked, the duster's handle in his mouth as he grasped a figurine with his fingertips and slid it over, proceeding to dust its former spot. His face was red from the reach's strain, the ottoman granting him little favor. He was remarkably skilled with only one arm.

"I do."

They had just finished a discussion about the moon, though she didn't share its location after he inquired about its departure from the sky. She'd feigned ignorance, and the pair conjured hypotheses of its fate. She sought an end to this meeting before it delved deeper into arguments of philosophy and life, which was bound to happen with two Archain minds of their acumen.

No rabbit holes. He deserves to know.

She squeezed a slip of parchment in her hand. "You know about the raid on Lost Wisdom?"

Agnos paused, hand slowing as he placed a figurine back on its spot. He didn't turn to acknowledge her, the mention of his former orphanage undoubtedly jarring, yet he let his arm fall to his side, duster hanging limp in his hand. "Himitsu told me about it."

She eyed him, choosing her words cautiously. "We learned a lot from it. The horrors of the place." Silence. "Why didn't you tell anyone?"

He lowered himself, placing bare feet on the carpet and sinking into the ottoman's cushion. He faced the wall, an elbow on a knee. "You make yourself forget those things."

Ophala relaxed in the armchair, loosening her grip on the parchment. "Do you ever think about all of the children you could have saved had you come forward?"

"With all due respect, Pilot Ophala, that's a stupid question."

"You're right."

Agnos sighed. "I think about it all the time. Worst part is I never received punishment anywhere close to the level of my peers. My position as Neeko's pupil granted me the benefit of avoiding any sort of abhorrent reprimands. Even before he took me under his wings, I had been too young for the worst of it. I avoided the 'field trip' to Accus Canyon and I never saw the inside of a weeping chamber."

He paused, and Ophala let the silence ask her questions.

"My experience with such evils stems from seeing its aftermath in the gazes of my fellow orphans. The haunted hollows of their eyes. The blank canvas of their faces. I don't know what was in the weeping chambers, but I feel the name was accurate."

"And Neeko didn't put a stop to it?" she asked.

"He had no power. I argued with him on several occasions, but he was right. Once I was older and away from the orphanage, I realized what he meant. King Itta's reign was merciless, and Lost Wisdom was one of his focal points. There was too much invested in the orphanage … for whatever reason. In fact, according to Neeko, Dolomarpos was the one who began its shady practices. Itta was simply carrying on his father's work."

"He could have come forward when the Amendment Order was formed," Ophala said.

"I wasn't in contact with Neeko then," he replied, back still facing her. "However, I assume there was too much uncertainty. Those were confusing times for the kingdom, after all. Foreigners holding office as a collegium? Then Toth Brench rising to power?" He trailed off, giving it thought. "But, that doesn't mean he didn't try."

Ophala remained mute, though she had a feeling she knew the truth at that point. Himitsu and Kaylee had told her one of the orphans noticed a shift in Neeko's demeanor during that period. The man had been mourning the losses of Mynute Senex and Praetor Poicus, two of his best friends from his younger years at Phesaw, which had likely killed any drive he might have possessed—confirmed by the man's death in the Central Grasslands.

As for the weeping chambers, it turned out she knew more about them than Agnos. It was an image she'd never forget: walking into that room, an old woman seated on a rickety chair at the center with a stone sphere in her lap, a curtain of dread collapsing atop her and rot creeping across the floorboards. After hearing Himitsu's recounts of his journey into Accus Canyon—the leechers siphoning energy from children—she hadn't been prepared for something even worse. Mesitis Epidex, Skill Broker of the Underground, still had yet to reveal information about that woman.

A shiver raced up her spine, recalling the horrified looks of the scholars who had entered the room with her, immediately recognizing what it was they had walked into. The elderly woman had been a powerful Dredge of the Cyn Kingdom, a class of Cynnish that didn't venture outside of the kingdom's capital. How Itta had wound up with one in his employ befuddled her. Accessing Batilearsh was the most difficult feat for any spy or assassin.

Dredges were weavers of Cyn Energy whose skill surpassed most others. They did more than decay the physical world around them; they decayed the spirit within people. With enough time, they could spiritually gut even the mightiest, most driven warriors. Some believed they could rob the Spirit Queen of her soul. Knowing Queen Apsa, Ophala doubted that.

While the Spy Pilot had spent the past few weeks dealing with the Intel Kingdom's issues by lending Queen Shelly a helping hand, she had kept a team back home in efforts to understand the mysteries of Lost Wisdom. The explanation of a Dredge's presence this far from Batilearsh and the origin of the leechers in Accus Canyon aside, they had succeeded with one massive discovery: ledgers of every child who'd ever fallen under the orphanage's care, including information such as date and age of arrival and induction, the tithe paid for the orphanage to accept said child, and—perhaps, most importantly—the identities of the parents who'd made the transaction.

There were many notable names among the hundreds of folders, yet Ophala had skimmed through them in order to find a specific one. Her team in the Archaic Kingdom was presently undergoing a closer inspection of those other names while she'd taken the file that mattered most to her … at least, at this time.

"You were sold to Lost Wisdom younger than most," she muttered.

"I was one of the youngest ever, I believe," he said. "Young enough to not remember it."

"Eight months," she breathed. "An infant."

He turned his head, his body following as he pivoted on the ottoman. Suspicion crumpled his brow. "How would you know that?"

"I know more than that. How much you were sold for … who your parents are."

The lines between his eyebrows disappeared, face softening. "You found the archives during the raid. I didn't even think about that."

She leaned forward with an eager smile. "Do you want to know who—"

Agnos stood faster than she could track him, eyes lagging behind. "Why would I ever want to know the filth that didn't just *give* me to an orphanage, but *sold* me to one? How eager were they to get rid of me? And if I remember correctly, the younger the child, the heftier the price!"

Ophala's lips thinned. She'd been stupid to expect the heartfelt and gleeful reaction of Vuilni. The two situations were nothing alike. Agnos's face flushed red with rage, an open hand trembling at his side. His body was rigid, knees locked and voice shaking. She hadn't thought him capable of such an outburst.

"Even if they didn't want me, they could have offered me to any orphanage free of charge! Instead, they fed a baby to a monster's stomach while simultaneously stuffing its pockets."

Her grip on the parchment slackened as she watched the young genius's shakes become convulsions, chest heaving and eyes watering. This wasn't a chance for a reunion. He hadn't been a child forced away from his family like Vuilni. He had been abandoned, had never known a father, mother, or siblings, leading him to trust individuals like Toono even when their intentions and actions turned sour. He sought not reunion, but nothing at all.

Ophala rose from the armchair and stood for a moment, observing him as his gaze fell to the carpet. "I'm sorry, Agnos. I'm ashamed of my shortsightedness ... It's not like me. I don't blame you for how you feel." She took her leave, but on her way to the door, she placed the slip of parchment—crinkled from the press of her fist—atop a circular entry table.

What he would do with it, she didn't know. But it was there, and that was all she could offer.

*   *   *

Pilot Ophala didn't waste time in reaching her next audience. She sat in another guest chamber, this one grander and with a bed big enough for two adults. She regarded it for a moment before shifting focus to the two others in the room: Himitsu and Kaylee. Both were seated on a large closed chest. She wondered if they had explored the depths of their relationship yet, in the physical sense. As much as her son enjoyed joking about the lusts of a woman when with his friends, she knew that changed the moment a woman was within earshot, especially one with whom he had fallen in love. While cute at first, his respect for personal space might have become intolerable for Kaylee. Ophala grinned.

Himitsu raised an eyebrow. "What is it?"

Shaking her head, she rested an elbow atop the chair's arm, grinning still. "Nothing ... I trust the two of you are doing well."

"We're great," Kaylee said, her amber eye—her ancient piece—making Ophala wonder. What did the girl see when she looked at her? Ophala was a master at blocking others from gaining access to her thoughts or emotions, specifically for the threat that Devish could pose, but did that transfer into her aura? And what was an aura, exactly? A sibling of the mind, heart, or soul … or all three?

"Good," she replied. "I'm still waiting on some grandbabies."

Himitsu rolled his eyes. Ophala chuckled, noticing Kaylee's sidelong glance as she gauged his reaction. If only he had noticed it, too.

"Look," Ophala said, readjusting herself in the armchair. "What are your plans going forward?"

"Mom, stop trying to get us to—"

She waved her hand. "I'm not on that topic anymore. I mean where are you going next? Do you have a journey planned? A goal to reach? I know it involves something with travel, seeing that none of the Jestivan have ever decided to call it quits and settle down in a humble home."

The two lovebirds exchanged looks. Himitsu shrugged. "Go where the wind blows. Or hunt someone. There are plenty of people in need of assassinating … Mendac, Kadlest, Flen, or that girl who everyone thought was Simon's girlfriend a few years back."

"Illipsia," Ophala said.

"Yeah, her." He looked to Kaylee. "Or we can finally focus on her dreams."

"I like the sound of that," Ophala replied.

Kaylee tilted her head. "With all due respect, Pilot, but why? There are matters of more importance than my career goals."

"Your studies with Neeko made you want to become an apothecary, correct?"

"Yes, Pilot."

"Then go become one."

Silence followed. Himitsu observed his woman, wondering what her answer would be. Ophala allowed the simplicity of her statement to wash through Kaylee, saying nothing else.

She twisted her lips into a frown. "I feel like everything Himitsu and I've been doing are auxiliary missions that aren't of dire consequence to the real goals the realm is trying to achieve, Pilot."

"You're not auxiliary pieces, first of all. The information you've acquired about Lost Wisdom, Neeko Lefolli, and Accus Canyon have been vitally important. I cannot stress that enough. However, Kaylee, you were

148

thrust into this conflict recently, and while I admire your willingness to abandon your dreams in order to help save the world …" She went silent, staring deeper at the young woman with ivory hair. "The world no longer needs saving. Not now, at least."

The words hung there as the love birds contemplating the truth of such a claim. Ophala was lying, and while they may have suspected it, they didn't know for a fact. Mendac was alive again, but nobody knew his purpose. And he'd need time to recover his strength and gather information about Kuki Sphaira's new political climate. A lot happened in the sixteen years since his death.

"Himitsu's told me about your original plans of visiting the Thousand Layer Loess," she finally said. "Understandable, considering their prowess in chemical and herbal medicines, or so I've heard. My birds don't hear or see much of anything in that area." After another pause, she added, "I want you to go there, and Himitsu should tag along. Maybe you can work on getting me those grandkids."

Himitsu's head fell back against the wall, shoulders slouching and back curling awkwardly.

"The melodrama," Ophala drawled.

Kaylee narrowed her eyes, displaying an uncertainty Ophala hadn't seen before—at least not directed toward her. "We'll discuss it, Pilot."

Ophala offered a nod, knowing it was best to not push her luck beyond that. She rose and approached Himitsu to kiss his forehead. "I'll let you return to your packing. I love you."

As she turned to leave, she smiled and winked at Kaylee. With all of the recent horrifying discoveries in the Archaic Kingdom, secrets lurking beneath the bloated belly of a former regime's corpse, she feared there were likely more. If Dolomarpos and Itta's corruption extended as far as the Archaic Mountains, what would have stopped it from reaching the Thousand-Layer Loess in the far east? And then there were other revelations within those Lost Wisdom files that had piqued Ophala's interest.

As she left the guest chamber, she made her way for the bird tower. She'd have a note delivered to Himitsu later, giving him his own mission in the Loess. She hated to do it to her, but Kaylee couldn't know the truth.

17

A Ghastly Beauty

It took a couple of days after her mother's approval before Olivia gained the courage to summon the man she had forced out of her life the moment he'd entered it. Preloz Henye. She'd not forgotten the name, despite only hearing it once among the chaos of that day. The fact that she knew nothing about the Bewahr unsettled her. Anyone powerful enough to be reborn as a Bozani or Gefal should have been notable in Sphairian history, yet the name Preloz had somehow evaded all history books. Her efforts had yielded no results, and it wasn't like she could ask anyone for help. Aside from her mother, nobody knew she possessed a Bewahr—and she planned on keeping it that way. Not even Bryson could know.

She wanted to do this before departing to the Still Kingdom with her mother and many others. A solid week on the ice-capped Diamond Sea wouldn't lend well to privacy, so her window of opportunity was closing. She didn't want to wait for their arrival to Kindoliya; that'd take too long.

Standing in a tiny chamber beneath the palace, a cellar in which sat one of Mendac's secret teleplatforms, the same one she, Bryson, and friends had used to travel to the Still Kingdom with goals of gaining a new ally a year ago. They should have destroyed it after that, as it then became the method of Illipsia's infiltration a month ago, leading to the murder of King Vitio and the retrieval and revival of Mendac's body. The platform had been specially made to not allow inbound teleportation, but Vistas believed Flen had rigged it via his weaving skills.

Unlike weaving, summoning her Bewahr was not difficult. Once she had broken that threshold of awakening in the aquatic vortex, it had become as simple as giving a command. And while she had no experience to warrant such confidence, she just *knew*. And thus, when she called to that blackness somewhere in her eyes, the man freed himself from his place in the Dark Empire and stepped out of a spiraling vortex of shadows ahead of her.

She absorbed every grotesque detail: chunks of skin missing from his face; sinuous, pinkish muscles stretched and tattered along the jaw and cheek; ivory bones of teeth jutting out from the pinkish flesh around his mouth. One eye was blacker than the bowels of the sea, incapable of casting a reflection. The other eye was a dazzling blue, almost enough to mistake him as human. Umber skin covered that side of his face, but it peeled at its edges, stopping just short of his right nostril—nothing more than a small hole in pink and white cartilage. His forehead stretched up his skull until kinky curls of gray began halfway across his scalp ...

But even all of that paled in comparison to his bare chest.

A tattered hole revealed the depths of his entrails, soft pink dusting his ribs, as if his skin had been torn straight from his body with enough force to leave only the residue of muscles. Behind the sternum lay a heart, gray and ribbed with black veins, pulsing as it pumped ink into the rest of his body. Something bug-like crawled around it. He was a corpse, not a man. A walking, breathing corpse with a stench capable of putting a funeral pyre to shame.

He regarded her blankly, one bottomless black eye unreadable, the other more human in its brilliant blue, expressionless. A lipless and skinless mouth bore teeth incapable of smiling or frowning. A chill raced down her spine. Despite her life of emotional suffocation, she feared this man … was disgusted by him.

"A surprise I had not foreseen," he said, voice proving just as deep as that black eye—oceanic, reverberating through her soul.

"I suspect reluctance to engage in conversation," she replied, nearly gagging from the stench punching the back of her throat.

"I suspect reluctance in your desire to breathe around me." His assumption rang true, though any signs of bitterness over it didn't reflect in those eyes.

Not a great first impression, she thought. *Wait. I already screwed that one up, which makes this a poor second impression. Great.*

She'd do her best to stifle any other crude gestures, no matter how involuntary. Wiping at the tears in her eyes—these caused not by emotion—she nodded. "I apologize, as does my mother."

"Yet I see her nowhere," Preloz said, his human eye scanning the tiny chamber.

"She doesn't know I'm doing this right now."

His gaze returned to her. "No matter. The rejection of males aside from viewing them as cannon fodder or sex objects has existed in your culture for centuries. I felt no ill will toward you the day of our awakening."

Olivia's stiff shoulders relaxed, having fully expected resistance. Perhaps, this was going to be easier than she'd thought.

"What is it you want from me?" he asked. "So badly, it seems, that you'd risk summoning me whilst in the Light Realm."

"How do you know where I am?"

"I feel it in the air. I do not know exactly where we are, but I know in which realm it falls."

"And what does it matter?"

"They will sense me."

She paused, then asked, "Who?"

He regarded her for a moment, contemplating something. "Once again, why have you summoned me? I see no threat to your life."

"To get to know each other … Offer a hand of cordiality of which to grasp."

Silence befell them. She tried reading his eyes, but it proved impossible. Not only did the deformities render expressive analysis useless, he simply possessed a demeanor of tranquility, reminding her of herself. This must have been what had felt like for her fellow Jestivan to speak with her in the past. What had made him this way? Knowing the horror stories of the kingdom dubbed the Void, it could have been anything.

"I wish not to discuss personal lives," he said. Footsteps thundered beyond the door at the top of the narrow stairwell, his human eye roving toward it. "I must take my leave. If ever you find yourself in grave danger, summon me." Indistinguishable shouting grew louder now. "Take this not as bitterness or anger toward the day of our awakening, but reluctance to compromise the sanctity of my role as your Bewahr. I do take this seriously, and a relationship beyond one of duty threatens the grip a person can have on their impulses."

The door jarred open, casting a strip of sunlight down the stairwell and into the cellar. It hit Olivia, but Preloz remained in the shadows.

"I swear something's dead down here!" a man's voice bellowed from the top of the stairs. "Rot and crap. I've killed enough people to know it."

She turned, spotting a tall silhouette at the door. Another figure—burlier and shorter—joined it, keeling over and puking the moment the putrid scent smacked him in the face. She looked back into the shadows to find no one. Preloz had returned to the Dark Empire.

"Olivia, is that you?" asked the man, boots thumping down the steps. "What'd you kill?"

She turned to look at Himitsu. The other man—she vaguely recalled his name as Sal—remained at the top of the steps, slumped on his knees and in the midst of his second round of vomit. "Nothing," she said.

The lanky assassin combed the cellar, one hand over his mouth and nose. Slowly, he acknowledged her with a raised eyebrow. "You know … there are bathrooms all over this place."

At any other time, that joke would have earned a smirk from her, but not now. Instead, she playfully punched Himitsu in the chest before walking past and up the stairs. She edged around the puddles of puke at the cellar door, casting Sal a pitiful gaze before continuing down the corridor.

Preloz Henye had a story to tell.

*　　*　　*

Rhyparia hated her wings. They defied her, cowering against her back within the Labyrinth's confines, but lashing out when outside. They obeyed someone else entirely despite being attached to her own body. She didn't need walls and bars to understand she was a caged animal, being trained to act as a weapon for the Dark Empire's war. It was a bloodcurdling bit of irony that she had avoided Itta's desires for her as a weapon of mass destruction to ultimately land in that same role, but for someone infinitely more dangerous.

Her wings were currently pressed against her back, resembling nothing of wings at all. They cowered in the presence of her new partner, as if to give ample space for the man to spread his own wings. Mendac LeAnce carried himself with a sense of knowing. Not only did he understand himself, but he owned it. The wispy black tendrils of his wings stretched toward the walls to his right, licking at the Mulanyx material, sometimes sticking to it and stretching as he continued to walk farther along.

Mendac had flirted with the topic of Rhyparia's reasons for being in the Dark Empire. He was curious, clearly, but held the common decency to not approach it so sloppily and forthright. She supposed she owed him insight. She did know a lot about him after all. He had been the Fifth of Five, a legend and hero, savior of the Intel Princess by sacrificing his own life. But that raised a vital question: How had he wound up here?

"If we are to be partners," he said, "I'd like to know more about you. All I know is your name." He turned and stepped through a wall, the Mulanyx becoming shadows that roiled around his body. After passing through, the wall opened, manipulated by Mendac's hand submerged in the blackness. Rhyparia stepped into a chamber beyond, a massive rectangular skylight casting gray hues across the raven interior. She still wasn't used to the sun's strange behavior over the Labyrinth.

"I'm a murderer," she said, absorbing the grand training hall. There was an ovular depression in the center of the floor, a few steps circling its perimeter. Practice dummies lined the raised floor around it. A long rack stretched across the opposite wall, stocked with swords, rapiers, daggers, flails, spears, battleaxes, and any other melee weaponry one could imagine.

Mendac walked around the depression and surveyed the assortment. He wrapped a whip around his fist and then pulled to test its tensile strength. "There is more beneath that, certainly," he said as she began poking about. "While the Light Realm views me as a hero, I'm sure there are many of my enemies—especially their family members—who'd view me as a murderer, too."

She looked away from a pair of onyx knuckles hanging from an open frame on the wall to survey him. A scar from an ungodly wound stretched from the front half of his scalp down his face. Someone had dealt him a mighty blow with a sword, and she couldn't imagine how someone would live through a wound like it, so she assumed that had been the fatal blow.

He narrowed his eyes, lifting a black rapier from the rack. Its edge was finer than glass, but it looked to be just as brittle. "You can pick these up," he said, flipping the rapier over to study the other side. "They're made of regular onyx. I'm guessing they don't bother infusing their practice weaponry with Mulawi."

She eyed the knuckles, then, carefully, reached out to grab them. She had learned over her weeks in the Empire that Mulanyx didn't like her, evident in her first contact with it on bare skin. Fortunately, her body didn't respond poorly to the weapon. Her fingertips didn't stain an unnatural black.

She equipped the knuckles, admiring their razor sharp peaks. These weren't meant for crushing bones in a brawl like most sets of brass knuckles, but puncturing skin and tearing muscle. But seeing that they were made of regular onyx, they'd break quickly. Returning them to their frame, she moved down the rack and stopped at a row of long swords. Mendac had already taken his whip and stepped into the depression. She felt his eyes watching her.

She perused her options, looking for something that'd feel similar to her umbrella in her hands. She missed its familiarity. She passed over the claymore, not trusting her strength and balance to wield the mighty two-handed sword; the sabre, intimidated by the backcurve in its spine; the katana, knowing she couldn't match the expertise of Adrenian elites who wielded such a blade; and broadsword. She ultimately settled with a simple backsword, a sidearm to most soldiers in any military.

"You have sword training?" Mendac asked as she entered the depression, gray sunlight forcing her to squint.

"None," she said, holding out the sword and getting a feel for its weight. She shuffled her feet, trying out different stances she'd seen from Yama and Toshik when she'd been a Jestivan.

He tilted his head. "What'd you kill people with?"

"The sky."

Eyebrows crept up his forehead. "And what'd it take to kill you?"

"I'm not dead," she said, stepping back in a ready stance, two hands on the hilt.

His eyebrows flattened, face grave, as he mirrored her stance, but with only one hand on the whip's handle. "Yet you're in the Dark Empire."

"Alive," she breathed.

She charged, his whip cracked, and so began the story of the most pestilent duo in the history of Empires.

*   *   *

Preloz returned to the raven halls of the Dark Empire's central keep, blackness swallowing him on all four sides. Ivory tendrils laced smooth Mulanyx walls. Faint lights beyond the wall exposed shadowy figures. Some walls revealed private quarters, others libraries or a kitchen. The Black Labyrinth was a sprawling maze akin to the hedge gardens of the Passion Kingdom. It was mostly a single story, but there were areas that stretched beyond that—three floors maximum. Perhaps, the most important parts of the Labyrinth, sat below it.

The Cynnish Bewahr walked with one purpose: reaching the girl he loved. She was beautiful, ghastly so. Hair as dull and gray as the broken flagstones of Batilearsh's most trodden sectors. Eyes that sat in shadowy bags from sleepless nights. Skin, ghoulishly pale. Lips, equally so. The shadows at the base of her neck, where the collarbones converged, displaying the decades of depression she'd endured through her atrophied body. And a shaky hand pressed to a hole in her stomach, intestines peeking between fingers as she tried to hold her guts inside.

He'd walked for what felt like miles and months to reach this woman. The truth was he'd walked for hundreds of leagues and several centuries. To the other Gefal of the Black Labyrinth, they saw no more a human than a corpse that should have been six feet under. A rotting cadaver that wandered the Mulanyx halls with no direction, movement unnatural, a ghostly afterimage drifting behind him. Most avoided him. He stank like a bucket of rat carcasses.

Despite this, most heard him before they smelled him, warning others to find a new route lest they desired contact with the undead. Strange, considering his utter lack of sound when moving. His feet whispered across the floor, breaths as empty as a beggar's cupped hands. He needn't much to fill his soul, like most who had survived a life in the Void's capital. But there was one person who provided the smidgen of substance that drove his life force, who made his breaths—as shallow as they may have been— worth it. He howled her name every so often, haunting the black halls with anguish, alerting his peers despite whispering feet and shallow breaths.

He had chased her for centuries, the girl who had his gray eyes, but not his umber skin. That had come from someone else, as did the smile that teased her lips, instigating in its efforts to defy Batilearsh's blanket of soullessness that smothered the hollow streets. A sturdy, vibrant oak at the apex of the Almawt Woods, a forest of decrepit trees cloaked in mists.

He'd continued to wander. He'd find her one day. After all, it had only been months—at least in his eyes.

Nothing could separate a man and his daughter for long.

Not even their king.

18

A Parting Gift

The war corridor had become a unique chamber in Dunami Palace. While the entire building elicited memories of King Vitio, the war corridor pried forth emotion along with them. He had spent most of his time over the past couple years here, holding broadcast meetings with fellow Royal Heads, buildings strategies for war, and fending off insubordinate quips from some of True Light's most elite warriors—mainly, the Jestivan. The only other person who'd spent more time in this room was the man currently standing near the three-dimensional module of Kuki Sphaira hanging in the middle of the room: Vistas, loyal servant to the Intel family … former captive of Mendac LeAnce.

Bryson didn't feel the same grief over the king's death as others. Thus, the newly married man could sit and listen to Ophala speak without distraction while others felt the kingly ghost prickling the back of their necks. Vitio's death had hurt, but compared to those of Debo and Jilly, it was something he could brush off. Most of his pain had resulted from seeing it in Shelly, Lilu, and Delilah, each of whom showed it in their own way.

The Spy Pilot was giving her final briefing to those with the most influence in the Intel Kingdom before departing the next day. This meant the usual faces occupied the room, but there was one with which Bryson wasn't familiar. Aside from Vistas, Shelly, Lilu, Horos, and Fane, a man in a trench coat sat at the front of the room. He was older, somewhere in his fifties, evident in his graying beard. While Bryson couldn't see him because of his positioning behind the man, he'd still noticed the shiftiness of his eyes earlier. He didn't like it. And there was something else that just seemed off about him. But, Ophala had begun the meeting with an indictment of her trust in him, which was enough to quell Bryson's doubts for now. Of course, she had followed such an announcement with his name, which only stirred more suspicion in Bryson. Nobody named "Creep" made a living with any sort of honest work.

The meeting was well underway, spanning a vast assortment of topics. They discussed the appointment of a new general, which had gone unoccupied since Lars's death the night of Toth Brench's assassination, settling on three names viable of such a position. A lot of time was spent on the flooding in Continon and the logistics involving the deployment of resources and rescuers to help, which had gathered a death toll in the hundreds. While it may not have been the same scale as what was happening in Saido, it was still of vital importance. Continon was the Intel Kingdom's main port city, lathering the northern shoreline of the Knowledge River's widest stretch.

Following an update on the rebuilding of Dunami's eastern half, Ophala's focus narrowed to Griva's Plaza, the location of a new Weavineering factory Lilu was spearheading with help from the LeAnce family.

"Two members from the League of Weavineers' board of directors will be arriving in the capital within the week. They want to personally see the construction of the new factory, which is understandable considering their investment in the project." Bryson tried opening his mouth to voice his opinion, but Ophala raised her hand and silenced him. He frowned, sinking lower in his chair, unhappy with the thought of two LeAnce family members in his vicinity again. "They're also visiting to discuss the state of our relationship with the Power Kingdom." She paused at that, glancing at the gathering before her.

Bryson raised an eyebrow. This time he wouldn't let her silence him. "What does that matter to them?"

"Provod," Lilu said from her chair a couple spots down his row. "When the Power Kingdom ceased their treaties of commerce with us, that meant we lost our access to the resource native to the Malanese Peaks. And provod is the most important raw material involved in the development of Permanence technology ... Travolters and Intelights don't exist without it." She looked to Ophala. "I'm guessing their cache is running low."

"They keep that information to themselves, but I would assume so."

"The Powish want nothing to do with us," Bryson said, "so let them be. With Toono gone and SCAPD's collapse, they're not going to cause us problems. I doubt they try being friendly with us again."

"They were never friendly with any of the Light Realm's kingdoms," Fane said. "They only admired our economies and politics, which is why they're the only kingdom in the Dark Realm that uses our currency."

"Access to provod is impossible at the moment," said the man with shifty eyes.

"Why?" Lilu asked.

Ophala's eyes narrowed at Creep. "Yes, do tell us why."

The man didn't respond, and Bryson looked between the new guy and the Spy Pilot, noticing something peculiar about their interaction. Creep said nothing, only shrugged.

"Speaking of Creep," Ophala said, continuing after allowing her gaze to linger on the man, "he will head the investigation into the new rebels, who recently showed they won't shy away from murdering aristocratic sons." She paused, shaking her head and glancing down at her notes on the lectern, as if trying to stomach those words. "Creep's position has been discussed at length with Queen Shelly, and she's accepted his aid. As difficult as his personality is to swallow, his credentials and references speak for themselves. He is one of the most accomplished hybrids ever, learning from a much younger Praetor Poicus."

"A hybrid?" Fane asked, eyebrows furrowed. "They did away with those long ago."

"I'm one of the last," Creep said.

As if sensing the confusion on Bryson's face, Ophala explained, "A hybrid is a person who mastered both the arts of reconnaissance and silent murder, making them both spy and assassin. There aren't really any left in the world. Creep is a rarity."

"With all of these credentials, references, and even a title to which only he can lay claim, how come I've never heard of him?"

Creep turned, eyes flittering around Bryson's face. "Because you're not supposed to have heard of me. If you had, that would mean I royally screwed up my job. In a painting of a grand tree at the center of a prairie, I'm a single blade of grass hugging the frame."

"We get it," Ophala said. Creep turned forward, leaving Bryson with his nose scrunched, lips pinched in skepticism. "Creep was the spy who alerted Grand Director Poicus of Toono's first sacrifice in the Prim Kingdom. He's spent decades there, but now he's back."

Bryson's face relaxed as awe pried open his eyes. Fane and Horos regarded the seasoned hybrid with smirks, perhaps of admiration?

"Why didn't you tell us that in the first place?" Fane asked, looking to Ophala.

"I shouldn't have had to. I'm the Spy Pilot, which means I steer the legion of stealth. You would have done as I told anyway."

"Yeah, but now I'm happier about doing it."

Ophala forced a laugh. "As if that matters to me." She grabbed the stack of parchment from the lectern and straightened it. "I'll be taking my leave tomorrow, but know that my presence will remain through the wings above. Besides that, Creep, Fane, and Horos are a capable trio in regards to sniffing out rebels." She smiled. "Dismissed."

*   *   *

Toshik bailed later in the day, packing his bags and leaving the palace in route for his family estates in the Adren Kingdom. He had stopped briefly to speak with the man named Creep, calling to attention a blade the hybrid had been inspecting while leaning against a wall. While others didn't possess the same haste as the swordsman, it was clear they were preparing for their own adventures. Bryson didn't like it.

Having everyone together in the palace had been a welcome change from the empty chambers and corridors the place usually was. He'd grown spoiled, frequently turning a corner and wondering which friendly face would surprise him next, an atmosphere reminiscent of schooldays at Phesaw. That would soon change as his friends trickled out, and there were no more pre-wedding preparations, something he never thought he'd miss.

Pilot Ophala's stay was nearing its end. News rolling in from Archaic King Sigmund had grown increasingly worrisome. The young king was struggling to handle a dispute between two of Phelos's top merchant guilds, leading to an economical regression, so she was cutting her stay short. "I have faith in Queen Shelly," she had said to a pouting Bryson. "She's way more competent than the boy my kingdom is dealing with."

Bryson sat on the floorboards of a Dunami Palace chamber he'd never been in before. His back and head were against the wall, elbows on raised knees, as he watched a crew of stewards usher out chairs, bed sections, candles, a wardrobe, and other bedroom furniture. He eyed each of them carefully, all too aware of the lengths some would go to for subterfuge. If any of these men or women were rebels, he'd filet them before they had a chance to hurt anyone. His eyes narrowed, a beefier man walking past Shelly with the post of a bed frame—a possible weapon. He watched him all the way to the door.

The room was emptying out quickly, the new Intel Queen standing at the center of it all, watching every move of the stewards, directing traffic, and reprimanding anyone who may have misheard a command. Shelly possessed a regal air that her father hadn't. For someone who frequently doubted her own ability, she seemed to have molded to the role like wet clay to a potter's hand. It seemed that the extra time she'd been spending with Pilot Ophala was worth it.

This had been Vitio and Delilah's room, but now it experienced a transition it hadn't seen in decades—a passing of the torch. With the former king dead and Delilah wanting nothing to do with politics or this room's nightmares, it awaited its new occupants: Shelly and Bryson. As the room was stripped to bones and skin, Bryson pondered on the morality of it all. Was Shelly being too crass with her father's belongings? Did she wish to rid herself of his memory? She had expressed her reluctance to hold onto things of his—at least, not too closely—but what did it mean that she was currently having the man's keepsakes hauled off to a dingy storage area of the palace? The coping mechanism seemed crude to Bryson, but who was he to talk? He had been guilty of something similar. When was the last time he had visited his old home, where Debo raised him?

But part of Bryson realized what actually bothered him about this move. While Delilah continued to mourn her husband, cherishing his memory via daily walks in the hedge mazes as she had with the burly man, his two daughters were showering him beneath shadows with the intent of drowning him from their minds and easing their grief. He felt Shelly could do that because of her husband, son, and mother. She'd lean on them through it all. But how much longer would Bryson be here to provide that support? What would happen when the Bozani come to abduct him?

As the final stewards trekked out of the room with a rolled carpet on their shoulders, Bryson closed the double doors and turned to his wife, her green eyes pooled with doubt. She wasn't sure if this was the right decision.

"What are you doing?" she asked. "More of them are soon to return with our furniture. I won't be sleeping on the floor."

A breeze swept in from open balcony doors, rustling the hem of her silken gown while kissing the ends of her spiraling pixie bangs. He released a cathartic breath, heart hammering against his ribs. "I need to tell you something."

"Is it some philanthropic nonsense about my father? If that was what I desired, Vistas would be my husband."

Blinking away the hypothetical image, he replied, "No."

"Okay, then what?"

"Uh …" He trailed off, every possible angle of attack he had prepared for this moment failing at the cusp of his lips. "These wings came with a tithe."

"Yeah, stealth. You're a walking star."

He frowned. He hadn't thought about that. While the celestial gifts didn't illuminate his surroundings, they were still bright. He shook his head, forcing his mind back on track. "I spoke with Thusia recently ... and Suadade."

Shelly's eyebrows creased down the center. "What? I haven't seen Suadade in months. He answers nothing!"

"I didn't call for them ... They just ... showed up."

"Why?"

"To take me."

A long, painful silence followed, his wife's arms now crossed in front of her. Her nostrils flared slightly as she ground her teeth. "Well, what does that mean?"

"Apparently, I am to be brought to the Light Empire at the goddess's request."

Shelly's eyes narrowed. She looked up at the ceiling. Tapping her foot, she glanced back down at Bryson only to stare off to the side, peering into a distance that didn't exist. Lips twisting, breaths growing deeper with either agitation or disbelief, she finally refocused on him and asked, "The goddess?"

He nodded slowly, tiptoeing around the subject as if Shelly were a caged lion. "And it wasn't just Thusia and Suadade, but their Pogu."

"Like Debo?"

Another nod.

She barked out a laugh, tilting her head back and bringing a finger and thumb to closed eyes. "Just grand. Just marvelous. It never ends with you."

"You ... believe me?"

She threw up her hands. "How would someone even conjure up such a lie? And I don't see you lying about this, anyway."

He relaxed, but after a few seconds of watching her turn the other way and shake her head, his eyebrows furrowed. "What do you mean by 'It never ends with you'?"

"The insanity!" she breathed. "All of the world's crap revolves around you."

His voice lowered to a mumble. "I have no control over this ..."

"I get that," she snapped, still facing the balcony.

A knock came from the door. "My Queen, we have the first of your furniture," said a man's voice from the corridor outside.

"Just wait a moment!" she yelled.

For some reason, Bryson hadn't envisioned it going this poorly. This was a reaction he'd expected from Lilu, but he supposed a revelation such as this would rattle the strongest of composures. It wasn't as if he hadn't seen it from her before—she'd shown this side of her temperament plenty of times with her father. This was just the first time she'd directed it to toward him.

She exhaled slowly before turning to him with wet eyes. "It's not your fault, but that's not going to make me any less annoyed."

"I'm going to keep fighting it," he whispered, stepping closer and taking her hand in his. "They wanted to take me last time, but I managed an extension for the wedding. If they want me, they'll have to drag me away."

Her gaze, which had been on his shoes, veered up to his eyes, darting between them. A tear slipped down her cheek as her expression morphed from frustration to rage. "When did this happen?"

"When I woke with my wings."

The tear caught in the crease of her pursed lips. "That was weeks ago."

He said nothing, and that would prove to be his biggest mistake ... maybe, of his life.

She dropped her hand from his and swept past. He didn't turn to watch her leave. Instead, he waited for the door's slam.

It never came.

*   *   *

Bryson stood glued to that spot for a few minutes, staring blankly at the balcony across the room. Shelly had departed with grace despite her rage. He had waited too long to tell her, and she felt betrayed by that. He imagined what she was thinking. What if he had been taken before he could warn her? How would she have reacted after noticing his absence and realizing he was nowhere to be found? With the rise of Mendac LeAnce and murderous rebels, her mind would have instantly gone to the darkest of places.

He studied the empty chambers, once belonging to a man who had never left his wife's side in order to always be a presence for his family. It had led to Bryson once calling him a coward—something he regretted deeply. It had been a callous and ignorant claim. Vitio's decisions to remain in his palace had been for the sake of family and love. Bryson, on the other hand, constantly abandoned them. And now, only a week into marriage, he would disappear again. While he wanted to believe he could continue to stall the Bozani and the goddess, how realistic was that?

"Bry."

Bryson looked away from an adjacent spare chamber and to the balcony, spotting a figure standing tall on the banister, fiery hair whipping in the breeze of the high altitude. A quiver of arrows was slung across his back, a bow pointed over the other shoulder. "Simon?"

The boy stepped off the railing with no effort, landing with impeccable balance. He walked into the room, sunlight dimmed by rain clouds at his back. As he entered, Bryson narrowed his eyes and created a temporary Intelight with his finger, waving it toward Simon. The light illuminated a freckled face, angled jaw, and long red hair ... and a sword sheathed at his hip. What was he doing with *that*? Better yet ...

"How did you get up here?" Bryson asked, looking past Simon toward the balcony.

"Depends. Can you keep a secret?"

Bryson thought of his conversation with Shelly. "Too well, perhaps."

"I'm going to tell you something," Simon said, a hand resting on his hilt, the other in a pants pocket. "Something about me, my roots. Then I'm going to leave the palace to return home for a time."

"You're not an Unable," Bryson said.

Simon's eyes widened. "Just now figuring that out?"

"It clicked during a lesson from Lilu a few months back. She told me Unables can't see the Empires, yet you've pointed them out to me on several occasions."

Simon laughed. "Leave it to Lilu to ruin the mystique of any of the world's wonders."

Peering at the sheath, Bryson asked, "So, what are you?"

"Adrenian."

Bryson searched his protégée's eyes, feeling an unsettling sense of déjà vu. This wasn't the first time someone had hidden their true identity from him. And, coincidentally, it had also been an Adrenian in disguise: Debo, or Ataway Debonicus Kawi, Third of Five.

"Before you bombard me with questions or possibly even scold me for lying—which I would not blame you for—there was always a reason for the secrecy. Believe me when I say it's always been a matter of life or death ... existence or extinction, in quite a literal sense."

"What are you?" Bryson asked. "Some sort of demon child? A bastard child of a promiscuous lord?"

Simon shrugged. "Worse, if history was the judge. I'm an Adren Assassin."

Bryson's jaw fell from its hinges, his face frozen still. "No ..."

"How else would I have gotten up here?" Simon asked.

"Rope."

Simon guffawed. "Have you seen the architecture outside this balcony? Do you know what room you're standing in? If all it took was rope to get into the private quarters of a Royal Head, reigns would last no more than a few months before a knife entered someone's back." Simon paused to study his idol's face. "I ran up here, Bryson. Up the damned wall."

"But ... you ... Adren Assassins were eliminated over a millennium ago."

"So the world has been made to believe. Don't get it twisted, however. They almost succeeded. Got our numbers down to the single digits, but ultimately, it's near impossible to exterminate a race. Someone will always escape or hide."

"Show me," Bryson said.

Simon's feet and legs blurred, body lifting higher as the speed increased. Craning his neck, Bryson watched the marksman approach the vaulted ceiling in awe. It had been a long time since he'd seen someone's movements as a blur, for he was faster than anyone he knew at this point in his life. But Simon was an anomaly. It took only a split second before he was back on the ground with a smile.

Anyone else would have missed it. They wouldn't have seen the boy move. Bryson had only tracked it because of his training with Debo years ago. He raised a hand to his temple, fingers combing through his bangs. "You just flew."

"Not exactly. I just ran on the air."

"*HOW?*"

Simon laughed, amused by the incredulous look on Bryson's face. "That's a matter of genetic mutation in my Adrenergy. Nothing you must worry about." His eyes drifted to the celestial wings. "Besides, it looks like you have the potential to actually fly."

"These don't do anything," Bryson said.

"That's a shame."

"Are there more of you?"

"A few," Simon replied. "You could count us on one hand. That's why I'm leaving. To return home and regroup."

"And where is home?"

That question gave Simon pause, as he contemplated the risk of answering. "You visited it once," he finally said.

"That doesn't narrow it down at all."

Simon sighed, lowering himself to the floor and sitting cross-legged. "I forgot you're an epic adventurer. Let's see … what if I told you that Shelly and Vistas had accompanied you on this journey?"

Bryson's eyes widened as he, too, sat on the floor. Memories of a farming village at the Adren Kingdom's Edge. An inn with no tenants. The loss of his virginity. Two oaks at the top of a cemetery's hill, a tombstone at the base of each, one belonging to a hero and the other a legend. "Yinyon," he whispered.

"And I believe you met my older brother," Simon said.

"Your brother?!" Bryson screamed. As fleeting as the interaction had been, he couldn't forget the innkeeper—a boy the same age as Bryson at the time—who had told him the real story of Ataway Kawi and Leon Suadade. The first two citizens of Yinyon to enter the Adrenian military, rising to the ranks of major and corporal before being discovered in intimate acts by a superior, sparking the climax of the Fifth of Five's epic tale.

"I can't remember his name," Bryson said, pounding at his head. "But I can remember the goat … William!"

Simon tilted farther back on his butt and burst into giggles. "Wait until Kolver finds out William stole the spotlight!"

"Kolver! That's it!" Bryson shook his head in disbelief. "It makes sense. There was this moment when I saw him at the back door like fifty feet away, then I looked down for a second and suddenly he was behind me."

"Kolver's not an assassin," Simon said. "He's just really fast, a side-effect of training beneath Adren Assassins. While the assassin trait is a blood trait, that doesn't mean everybody who shares the blood of an assassin will become one. Only one child does, and the trait ended up bypassing my brother and attaching to me a few years later when I was born." His eyes fell to the sheath at his waist. "In fact, I'm the only child Adren Assassin in existence. The next youngest is in his forties."

"That means you're pretty important," Bryson said.

"My full name is Simon Skimentis, and I belong to the historical family that led the Adren Assassins before their genocide. They call me the heir."

Bryson smirked. "They call him Simon Skimentis, Torchtop, Sharpshooter of the Millennium, and Heir to the Throne of Assassins."

"Spine," Simon said.

"What?"

"It's not a throne, but a spine."

"Whatever that means," Bryson said. "Heir to the Spine of Assassins."

The assassin grinned. "Did Kolver talk to you about Ataway?"

"Yes, he wasn't particularly fond of the biography I was reading. Called it a farce. Spoke of the real story."

"That 'real' story was also a farce," Simon said. "Do you think he'd really just tell some random person who arrived in his village the truth about Ataway Kawi and Leon Suadade?"

Bryson frowned. He had rested easier since that day, believing he'd learned the truth of Debo's former life.

"If it makes you feel any better," said Simon, "it was a somewhat truer farce than the one known by the masses. Ataway and Leon were lovers; that part is true. And they were judged because of it, making their lives in the Adrenian military harder than most. But that was never the straw that broke the camel's back." He paused before saying, "I didn't even realize it until the day of the restaurant collapse over Generals' Battle weekend, when I witnessed his abilities with my own two eyes, but Debo—*Ataway*—was an Adren Assassin, too."

"No way," Bryson said. "Himitsu was around him all the time, yet never said anything about sensing an assassin in his vicinity."

"Because Debo never used his abilities save that day of the restaurant collapse. In order for assassins to sense each other, they must be using their abilities."

Leaning back and placing his hands atop the floor, Bryson shook his head in wonder. "So that's why Ataway and Leon were chased all the way to Yinyon, where they had to then defend the village. Because the royals wanted to eradicate all traces of Adren Assassins that they must have missed from the proper massacre centuries before."

"When the Adren Queen finally took matters into her own hands," Simon said, "she arrived in Yinyon, besting Ataway and Leon with the aid of her Branian before slaughtering every woman, man, and child in the village ... or so she thought. Some lived, sent away under orders of Ataway and Leon before the queen had a chance to arrive. Eventually, some fifty years later, they returned to Yinyon to resettle."

"And your ancestors were part of the group that survived," said Bryson.

"Yes. The story is actually much longer and more intricate, but we don't have time for that. So, I brought you a gift." He reached into his leather bag and pulled out a leather-bound book, bare of lettering or engravings. "I snuck this out of my father's office during my last visit. I'd guess he's not pleased. It's the real story in all of its glory, of Ataway and Leon. Don't lose it."

Taking the book, Bryson flipped it in his hands, inspecting both covers. He scoffed, balancing it in one hand to admire its weight. This was a tome, not a book. He flipped through the pages, but saw no numbers. "How many pages is this?"

Simon rose to his feet and shrugged. "Just north of a thousand, give or take a few hundred."

Bryson cocked an eyebrow at the boy. "What does that even mean?"

"It means nobody is dumb enough to try counting them."

They stared at each other for a moment before Bryson glanced down at the book again, running a hand down its front cover. "Kolver told me if I wanted to hear the full story, I'd have to borrow the book from the mayor's office."

"The mayor's our dad." Simon pointed a finger at Bryson and winked. "It's nice, huh? Having connections."

Chuckling, Bryson also returned to his feet. Something ate at him though. "If Debo was an Adren Assassin, why didn't he save himself when Bewahr Fonos dropped him off the cliff?"

"Adren Assassins can't stop mid-fall and begin running across the air. There's a takeoff before flight, and that requires solid ground beneath our feet. Secondly, Debo didn't really have it in him in the first place. I recall you telling me he'd been away from the Light Empire for over a decade, and I'd imagine that weakened him substantially. Perhaps, using any of his assassin ability would have drained his energy quicker than he would have liked. A conservative approach."

Bryson huffed. That day still bothered him. He blamed himself for Debo's death. The Adrenian who disguised himself as the Intel Director had warned Bryson countless times not to chase after King Storshae and Olivia. He wasn't ready for such a task, which turned out to be a correct assessment. If Debo hadn't pursued them, Bryson, Jilly, Himitsu, Toshik, and Vistas would have died that day. And Olivia would have remained a captive of the Dev Kingdom.

Fear had struck Bryson on several occasions, but never quite like the horror of watching Debo plunge into the hardened crust of Necrosis Valley. Truth was, he had expected the man—a father figure and hero in the eyes of a youthful Bryson—to somehow save himself during the fall, as if he'd sprout wings and take to the sky. Even when he had hit the ground, a part of Bryson had believed he would survive.

Debo ... dead? He could never come to grips with it, evident in his inability to revisit their home.

"Seriously," Simon said. "Take care of that. Sleep with it if you must." Adjusting his bag on his shoulder, he exhaled. "Tell Queen Shelly I appreciate everything she did for me. Without her, I wouldn't have acquired a position in the archery unit. Without her, I wouldn't have gotten to visit Lingen's Rainforest." He grinned, reaching up to tie his long red hair into a messy bun atop his head. "And without her, they would not call me Torchtop."

Bryson laughed and reached out for a hug. "Don't be a stranger."

Simon, now a couple inches taller than his idol, ruffled Bryson's hair, stinging the Jestivan's pride a bit. "Never." Simon walked onto the balcony and leapt atop the banister with ease. He turned his head, revealing only half his face. "Read it to L.K. as often as you can. I want him to know the weight of the legacies behind his name."

*   *   *

Bryson stood outside the south side of the palace, a caravan waiting a couple hundred feet away—one carriage for the Stillian royal family and four others for their company of soldiers. He had already said his goodbyes to Aunt Ropinia, Gennaio, and Titus, which left the two most important people of the bunch.

Apoleia and Olivia Still stood side by side, near spitting images of each other, the daughter lacking the curves, slight crow's feet, and wisdom in her eyes. He had told Olivia the previous night about the Light Empire's plan to take him away. He told her about an empirical war at the cusp of its climax. And, in the most Olivia way possible, she'd taken it in stride and questioned nothing—the complete opposite of Shelly's reaction.

Apoleia, meanwhile, knew nothing of this. He either didn't want her worrying or he was scared to discover if she'd even care in the first place. Olivia had deemed the reasoning shallow after the events of the past several months, culminating with his mother's hand down the aisle, but she didn't press much beyond that. It was his decision, and she'd leave it at that. He did tell her, however, that she could inform their mother once they arrived in Kindoliya. That way, if the ice queen wanted to turn back, she couldn't.

"It was a pleasure," Apoleia said with a toothy grin. "Getting to finally meet everyone."

"Any favorites?" Bryson asked.

"The Spy Pilot I'm quite fond of." She glanced at the sky. "Though I may be uneasy around what feels like an ever-seeing presence."

"Don't worry," he replied. "With her in the Archaic Kingdom, she's too far to see directly from their eyes in the present."

She looked down at Bryson, eyes dulling. "I think I would have liked Delilah, but I never truly got a chance to speak with her. There is so much suffering in her, and understandably so. Wounds of the heart take a long time to heal."

Bryson pressed his lips together, looking deep into his mother's icy blue eyes. If there was anyone who knew about that, it was her. Her heart had ruptured long ago, now scarred earth, hardened magma. Only recently had it begun to thaw. The signs were clear, the most obvious showing itself the day of his wedding, when she had urged him to play the piano by her side. If she could conquer such demons, he could, too.

"Olivia and I got you something," he said, turning to a guard behind him. His sister stepped away from their mother to stand by his side for a moment. Apoleia tilted her head, eyebrows raised in interest.

"A present?" she asked.

He took an object wrapped in brown paper from the guard, gripping its base and side before handing it over to his mother. "Be careful with it. Don't grab the middle."

Apoleia's eyes narrowed the moment she took hold of the gift. She didn't open it immediately, rather testing the weight and feeling up its length. Bryson and Olivia studied their mother as she realized what it was without having to open it. Her teenage years were now in her hands. The tears welled, and he couldn't tell if it was pain, longing, or relief.

Carefully, slowly, she peeled back the brown paper, knowing exactly where to grip the gift in order to avoid harm to it. She shuddered, absorbing the gift: a wooden bar at the top that stretched between two slender arms, both of which curved up from a wide base. Seven strings stretching vertically between the base and the crossbar. A sharp intake of breath was accompanied by flowing tears, one hand raised in front of her mouth as she held the classical instrument in the other, admiring its beauty.

"You always said there had been engravings in an ancient tongue on the arms of your original lyre," Olivia said, "but Titus couldn't remember them, so we improvised. The carpenter pulled through."

Apoleia looked between her two children, smiling more genuinely than Bryson had ever seen from her. He had feared what the instrument might trigger. In a way, it had been the most damning image painted by Olivia when she had told him the story of their mother—the shattered lyre on the floor surrounded by broken strings as Mendac took away her will.

"It's beautiful," she breathed. She glanced at it again, running a finger down one of the four inscriptions. Both arms had two names engraved in the wood, one on the front and back: Olivia, Bryson, Ropinia, and Gennaio. They were her blood, four family members on which she could always rely. Daughter, son, sister, and father.

The Still Queen laughed, wiping tears from her cheeks. "A carpenter did this?"

"Yeah," Bryson said. "Apparently, Delilah knew a pretty good one and was more than willing to contact him for this purpose."

Apoleia's gaze drifted toward the palace looming behind her two children. "That poor woman. Thank her for me. I feel I owe her a great debt."

Bryson closed the gap between him and the queen and wrapped her in an embrace. "I'll miss you, mom."

"We'll only be a couple weeks away."

He nodded into her shoulder, squeezing harder, knowing the falsehood of that statement. Still, he said nothing; she couldn't know.

He didn't know when he'd see anyone again.

19

She Falls; He Rises

Bryson had seen little of Vistas since returning from Brilliance weeks ago, which explained his company during dinner tonight. He had reserved this meal for the two of them, wanting to spend some time with the Dev servant who had acted as a mentor to the two Intel daughters. He wanted Vistas to know Bryson appreciated him. He'd never forget everything this man, Tristen, and Marcus had sacrificed on behalf of the Light Realm.

Vistas had accompanied a very young and inexperienced group of Jestivan in Bryson, Himitsu, Jilly, and Toshik into the Dev Kingdom in order to rescue Olivia from King Storshae's grasp. Marcus had extracted truths from Archaic King Itta, revealing the man's efforts in using Rhyparia as a weapon of mass destruction, only to be murdered alongside Passion King Damian. And while that may have sparked the Gravity Trials, resulting in Rhyparia's abduction for litigation, that didn't cancel the fact that he had done it on the Light Realm's behalf.

And then there was Tristen, the often-times forgotten Inson triplet. He had acted as a spy for Intel King Vitio, betraying his home kingdom. He was the one who discovered Olivia's location after she'd been abducted during the Generals' Battle. He could have said nothing, favored his own life over that of some girl he didn't know. Instead, he made a reckless decision to contact Vitio while in Storshae's presence to show him Olivia's capture. That caused his death.

Bryson eyed Vistas, who was taking a sip from a glass of wine. He then dabbed his napkin against pursed lips and returned it to his lap. He was a sophisticated man. Intelligent, too, but not as intelligent as Flen, the third brother of the triplets who had held the most talent within him— unbeknownst to Bryson or anyone else of the True Light alliance, of course.

If anyone had known about the level of acumen possessed by Flen, Vitio would have still been alive. Flennigan Inson had been a scoundrel and a snake, though the moment of his flip to Storshae's and Toono's side was unclear. Vistas believed the partnership formed recently, while Bryson's cynical mind was sure it had been years in the making, though he never voiced it out loud.

What angered Bryson the most was the fact that Flen had a valid reason for his betrayal—if it could even be called that. Truth be told, he might have been more loyal than Vistas—the man who helped the very kingdom that had ripped him from his home, enslaved his friends, and set fire to his villages. At its core, the two men had different loyalties, which Bryson assumed was the most confusing dilemma warring in Vistas's head. Was Vistas not the original traitor?

Bryson was considering these thoughts while mindlessly pressing fingers against his glass of water, trying to ... Well, he wasn't sure. He'd been told by Lilu and Frederick that he harbored the ability of ice like his mother. And even before that, he'd experienced hints of that fact. Alas, it appeared either his Still Energy lie dormant or he didn't have any at all, which wouldn't have surprised him considering he was as close to freezing this glass of water as Agnos was to finding the Warpfinate's end.

A zap of electricity. Shattered glass and water spilling over Bryson's hands. He scowled at the spot in which his glass once stood, now a dampened patch of white cloth. Glass shards were scattered across the table, in his steak, and … he raised a finger to his cheek and pulled it away to find blood dripping down his palm. A piece had nicked his face. "Damn the world."

"Is it wise?" Vistas asked, setting down his fork. "Trying to force your clout while not knowing how to even detect the Still Energy in your canals?"

Bryson pressed his napkin—which had been less eloquently crumpled on the table—against his check. "Probably not, but how else am I to learn?"

"Your mother might be of assistance."

"She already left, and I didn't want to bother her with it. Besides, she has no experience in regard to manipulating two separate energies in your body." He paused, staring at the blood-stained napkin. It wasn't that bad; his steak had received the worst of it. He frowned, eyeing the ruined meat. "Nobody does, really."

Vistas nodded. "It is a peculiar situation."

A curious maid poked her head around a dining room door in search of the ruckus. As she spotted Bryson using the sleeve of his tunic to dry the cloth, she rushed in. Her eyes widened at the sight of the table. Her gaze drifted to the plate. "Let me get you another meal, Milord."

"Just get me a brush and dustpan, so I can get the glass," he said. "You can take my food. Don't worry about getting another plate. Vistas and I will leave you to tend to the tablecloth once I dispose of the glass."

She smiled. "Of course, Milord. Luckily, it's only water."

She took her leave, and Bryson moved the plate out of the way. "You treat them like equals," Vistas said.

"Because they are."

"While Shelly has left an impression on you, you have also inspired a change in her. I cannot wait to see the shift this kingdom takes under her reign. That is largely credited to you."

"You're the one who guided her throughout her childhood and into her teenage years," Bryson said.

"I tried my best. She did not make it easy."

The maid returned with the requested items. Bryson thanked her. "I'll only be a minute."

"I also brought some gauze for your cut, Milord," she said, pulling cotton, gauze, and adhesive from her apron pocket.

He raised an eyebrow. "Thank you so much." She bowed and went to leave, but he stopped her short. "You don't have to call me 'Milord' or bow to me."

She turned, lips slightly parted. "But … I owe you that," she muttered.

"You definitely don't. What's your name?"

"Saphron," she said, a smile curling her lips. "Saphron Jessim."

"I'll remember that." He stood and began brushing glass into the dustpan. "Thank you, once again, Saphron."

The maid left, and Vistas stood, glancing at his wristwatch.

"Is it seven already?" Bryson asked.

"Almost, so I must leave if I want to make my meeting." He folded the napkin that had been on his lap and placed it to the side of his empty plate. "Thank you for your company, Bryson. I will see you tomorrow."

Bryson nodded, though he wasn't entirely confident in it. "For sure."

The Dev servant left the room, and Bryson stared at the wooden dustpan lathered with water and glass. He didn't know why, but his stomach had just dropped, leaving an unsettling void in his gut. His eyes scanned the room, anticipating the appearance of something celestial.

Nothing came.

Breathing a sigh, he took a seat and began cleaning his cut.

*   *   *

Dunami Palace was a shell of its old self. With so many departures, the palace felt like an outbound teleplatform. Only Ophala and Himitsu's crew remained, but even they'd be gone by the next morning. Silence was all that flooded the vast corridors and massive chambers, making a pin drop audible from across the palace.

L.K.'s screams pierced the length of a corridor. Shelly removed her heels and placed them beneath her arm as her stroll became a jog, though there wasn't much cause for concern since she knew her mother was currently taking care of her baby. L.K. was likely throwing a tantrum—however rare they may have been—or begging for his mother's milk.

179

The jog became a sprint, hand gripping a bulk of her gown, as she realized a different sound to L.K.'s screams. She'd never heard something so visceral from him. That was a problem, a cause not for concern, but *panic*. The final stretch of corridor felt miles long, her breaths coming too fast for her lungs. With the auspicious silence lingering around her, L.K.'s hair-raising cries took on a different meaning in her mind.

Something was wrong.

Finally, she reached the door, wasting no movements as she burst into the nursery's vast chamber, a massive window bathing the space in the amber glow of dusk. L.K. was gripping the beams of the crib's banister, propped on his knees as he wailed, looking in the direction of the open window ...

Shelly only caught a glimpse before it was too late. She screamed.

*　　　*　　　*

Benedict Ronal was the head steward in Dunami Palace, putting him in charge of several branches of staff: stewards, maids, servants, and sometimes the cooks. But the responsibility he had always valued more than any of that was his counsel to the Intel family—specifically, the women. As great of a man Vistas was with his philosophical and intuitive advice, he had always been too trepid. Benedict was a force that would push back whenever Shelly, Lilu, or Delilah needed it. He'd never seen anyone else— not even Vitio—have that luxury or power over the trio of women.

Thus, it was strange to feel what he was feeling right now. Known as a stoic, unyielding presence around the palace, the head steward was now racing through corridors, crinkling perfectly pleated slacks and ruining undershirts with sweat stains. He had even loosened his collar to allow an influx of air. He wasn't built to run like this, lungs breaking down from overexertion. But he'd rather them collapse before he stopped for breath.

Pure adrenaline surged him forward, panic and dread fueling it. A servant paused her mopping and held out a hand, eyes wide, as she shouted, "Mr. Ronal! Be careful, the floor!"

He didn't care. He sped past, nearly slipping across the suds. The servant stared, uncertain of how to react to seeing her normally calm superior in such frenzy.

Benedict's shoes squealed as he turned a corner and rushed down the corridor to a set of twin doors on the left. Bryson was supposed to be having dinner with Vistas on the other side of those doors. Two guards flanked the entrance, helmets held between biceps and ribs. Their conversation ended as they heard the head steward. "What's wrong, Mr. Ronal?"

"I need ... to ... get Bryson!" Benedict exclaimed between breaths. "The queen needs him ... right now!" Brow lines creased at the center of both men. "It's an emergency!" Benedict didn't wait for permission; he blew past the men, hands outstretched toward the door.

*   *   *

Bryson approached the dining room's window and stared out to the western half of Dunami, untouched by Toono's invasion. Buildings stood tall, tar roads unblemished. Even the coliseum—the location of the annual Generals' Battle—remained sturdy on the western edge. Thankfully, Dunami Hospital also towered over the rest of the city. He pressed a finger against the adhesive strip he'd used to pin the gauze to the cut on his cheek. It was already peeling off after only five minutes. He may not have been a doctor, but he should have been able to apply bandages.

Part of him wished he was traveling with his mom and sister to Kindoliya. He had only visited the Still Kingdom once, but he had fallen in love with its capital. Kaleidoscope buildings of ice that reflected violet, azure, magenta, and green lights throughout the streets in hundreds of directions. Hills of snow pushed to the sides of frozen streets to make way for massive tram rams transporting dozens of citizens through the city. And while Toshik and Vuilni had hated the freezing temperatures, he hadn't minded it as much. He supposed he had his mother to thank for that.

Blissful memories were short-lived, as he spotted something in the window's reflection behind him. As he turned to the twin doors, his stomach sank.

*　　　*　　　*

Benedict fought through the steel-clad arms of the Intelian guards, trying to stomp forward, shoving their shoulders and cursing into the air. As much power and sway as he had—enough to argue with the royal family itself—he held no jurisdiction over the guard or military. They could stop him if they wanted. And at a time like this, with the active threat of rebels, they wouldn't trust him unless he showed them proof of Shelly's request for Bryson. That wasn't possible.

"Guards!"

The bellow forced both men to freeze, all too aware of whose enraged voice that had been. "Lady Lilu," said one man. "We were just—"

"Let Benedict go," she said sternly, annunciating each syllable. They did, and Benedict didn't wait for her permission. He plowed through the twin doors and came to a stop on the other side, heaving as he absorbed the scene at the window across the dining room.

*　　　*　　　*

Bryson swallowed, as a celestial light took a human's shape at the door. He heard fighting in the corridor—a struggle of some sort—but his path to the doors was now blocked by an escort of the empress. Except, this wasn't Thusia, Suadade, or even their built-like-a-brick-wall Pogu, Quincy.

A woman stared at him, eyes too big for her face, voluminous hair wider than her shoulders. A tattoo rested on her temple between parted bangs: a circle with four dashes intersecting it, one on each side—like crosshairs. He'd seen her before, but not in person. She'd been in the memory Debo had given to Vistas. Debo had called her Naipa, mentioning the oddity of someone in her position visiting the kingdoms. It had been clear that she outranked Debo—a notion Bryson could never wrap his head around. But now that she was in his vicinity, in the flesh, he could feel the power radiating from her. Had the Empire feared Thusia's connection to Bryson would continue to stall his abduction? If so, they clearly weren't take any more chances. There'd be no bartering with this woman.

182

"You're Naipa?" he asked.

She sauntered across the chamber, the rings of light around her pupils and irises a translucent, blinding white. Agnos, who possessed the brightest rings of light in his eyes from what Bryson had seen, came nowhere close to this woman's intensity.

He narrowed his eyes just as Naipa closed in on him, certain he'd just heard Lilu shriek the head steward's name from somewhere outside. The woman placed a hand on his shoulder and they drowned within an orb of luminescence.

Just before vanishing from the room, he saw the twin doors fly open to reveal Benedict Ronal. He was ... crying?

And then Bryson was gone.

*   *   *

Shelly sprinted across the nursery, unable to shake the image of a figure stepping off the grand window's ledge. A cold shot through her insides, effectively killing off any bit of hope or happiness within her. She ran past a changing table, sofa, armchair, toys scattered across the floor and, finally, a crib wherein sat a petrified child. She rambled incoherently to herself as words tumbled over trembling lips, a wad of blubbering nonsense. Snot drained from a red nose, tears spilling from tired eyes. Hands slapped against the ledge as she leaned over and looked down.

There, in the amber rays of the sun's dying light, lay her mother. Twisted and mangled, head open, the container of her soul shattered atop the shingled roof of a separate sector some eight floors below.

Another parent, gone.

20

The Light Empire

Bryson Intel sprouted from a deep basin of light, punching and screaming for his release, as he was dragged onto a shore of white stone by Naipa. His wings burst with celestial power, a surge of warmth flaring from his eyes down his neck and into his spine, ultimately spreading across the width of his back and flaring white hot at his shoulder blades. He seethed, clawing at the woman's dainty hands, yet gaining no purchase against her mighty grip. She pulled him up from the floor with one hand, the collar of his tunic suffocating within her grasp, and threw him across the room until his back collided with a wall harder than steel.

His wings wilted, the warmth rescinding to a kindle—his dignity right along with it as, against all common sense, he rose to his feet and bolted toward the woman who stood several inches shorter than him. She watched him with hardened eyes, unbothered as if he was no threat, yet annoyed with his persistence.

"You have no right!" he bellowed. "They needed me!" He reeked of desperation, knowing that something had gone terribly wrong and he had been ripped from his home right before learning of it. For Benedict Ronal to have displayed such horror, it had to have been of a personal matter—something regarding the royal family, a family to which he now belonged.

A ribbon of light unraveled from the white stone floor and twisted around his calf, tightening with a vice grip as it seared skin with icy heat. His leg was yanked from beneath him, and he lurched forward, face-planting into the hard floor. Screaming, he rolled onto his back, pulled his knee to his chest, and wrapped his hands around his shins, celestial ribbons unfurling back into the floor.

Through it all, Naipa said nothing, only observed. She shook her head as he writhed in pain, then looked up and muttered something under her breath.

"Are you done yet?" she asked, her gaze falling to the mortal again.

Tears welled in his eyes as he rolled onto his side, fists balled atop the floor. He could only picture the worst: Shelly dead, L.K. dead. Rebels swarming a palace void of the Jestivan. Why did the human brain have to work that way? Couldn't he immediately assume Benedict's sudden intrusion in the dining room had been a misunderstanding?

Footsteps approached. He pressed his forehead into the floor and turned his shoulder as if that would hide him from Naipa. A touch on his shoulder, this time with a delicacy more appropriate from such small hands.

"Come on," she breathed. "Stand up. Chin up. There's nothing you can do about this situation, so accept it and establish some dignity."

He turned with a glare, sparks of rage igniting within him. She had lowered herself to a knee, black breeches and a beige sweater vest beneath billowing robes that crashed to the floor. The robes, white with black trim along its hems, were split at the front. A strange symbol was patched into the left side of the chest.

"I think you have a lot of questions, and you're well on your way to finding the answers." He continued to stare in silence, so she sighed and stood. "I tried the soft way." She grabbed his wrist with lightning speed and dragged him across the floor, around the edge of the strange basin of light.

He tried wriggling free, tugging in its direction, as if jumping in would take him back home. "That will only get you killed."

At this point, that sounded more like an invitation than a warning. "I don't belong here!"

"Honestly, you belong in a grave. Ataway, however, saw differently."

Bryson fell still at the name of his dead father figure, realizing exactly who this woman was: Debo's superior.

Idiot. If anything, his antics were wasting his energy. "Let go of me."

She paused and turned, looking down at what must have been a pathetic image. Narrowed eyes relaxed as she released her grip. He pushed himself to a stand, his posture as straight as he could manage. There was no way he could sully the image of the person for whom Debo had abandoned the Empire. He had once roamed this place for hundreds of years, likely with that same formidable aura he'd always had in the kingdoms.

Naipa studied Bryson, all too aware of exactly what he was thinking. He was a child standing on tiptoes, trying to show his father just how tall he'd grown. She didn't point it out. She only turned and walked straight … toward … the wall.

He wiped tears from his cheeks, tilting his head at her before spinning to truly inspect the room. It was a vast rotunda, its floor and a curving wall made of some kind of stone, blindingly white except where patches of translucent off-whites shifted throughout. A pool of a softer light occupied the center of the rotunda, disappearing into the depths of the floor. He looked up to find a glass ceiling, expansive and not segmented by any panes. The larger moon—the smaller one having disappeared weeks ago— spilled a blue light into the rotunda, intensified by the white stone.

Turning toward Naipa, he gaped at the impossible. The woman stepped *through* the wall, white stone liquefying around her body, morphing with her movements. She stopped halfway through, looking back with an outstretched hand. "You'll need to take my hand. Otherwise, you'll be trapped in here."

After a moment's hesitation, he took her hand and was pulled through the stone. It liquefied around him, drenching him in heat. It didn't hurt— quite the opposite, in fact. It was euphoric.

They entered a corridor constructed of the same ivory material. This time it made up the ceiling, too. He followed Naipa, and while his eyes remained glued to the glossy stone, he couldn't fully admire it—not with Benedict's panicked eyes burned into his mind. He was curious about the illumination. He saw not a single window, torch, or Intelight, yet it was brighter than a sterile room in Dunami Hospital. Frowning, he shifted the path along which he walked closer to the wall. He studied the gray patches that swam along the ivory and realized they were easier on his eyes. The wall was infused with light. Naipa's footsteps caused the floor to ripple as if she was walking across the surface of a pond, but his did nothing of the sort. The stone remained firm beneath him.

After a stretch of silence down the infinite corridor, he broke it. "Why didn't Quincy come get me?"

"Because Quincy is a child with a backbone smaller than his heart. He was supposed to have gotten you thrice since his first arrival with Thusia and Suadade, yet that airhead of a woman persuades him to stall each time."

"Did you just call Thusia an airhead?"

"I called her what she is," Naipa said. "Don't get me wrong. It is charming in certain ways, but her buffoonery tends to overstep its boundaries—as it has in this instance. The empress can only show so much patience, especially with the recent events. She needs you here … for whatever reason."

"The empress?" Bryson asked. "As in the goddess?"

"She's only an empress, but mortals know her as a goddess, so you'll see the terms used interchangeably at times when Bozani speak to you."

"What do I matter to her?"

"A question I've been asking myself for sixteen years, ever since she allowed Debo's resignation to shelter you."

He stopped at that, eyebrows furrowed. She took his hand with a warning. "This will burn."

Their physical bodies became two clusters of lights, radiant orbs darting toward the ceiling and merging with the stone. It felt like his entire body was set aflame despite not seeing his physical self. He emerged as a shower of lights from the stone, which was now the floor, in a chamber above, screaming as he slapped at invisible flames on his arms, shoulders, and chest.

Naipa, who stood next to him with regality and poise, eyed him sidelong. "You're not truly ready for it … no matter how much she wants to believe it."

He calmed and stared down at his arms, absent of flame or scorched skin. He could have sworn he'd been swallowed by an inferno. Heat lingered in his eyes and back, however. They mimicked that movement several more times in order to switch rooms or floors. The succession didn't alleviate the pain. His body didn't grow used to it. Thankfully, after north of ten minutes of travel through ivory corridors and chambers, they arrived at their destination after permeating another ceiling.

Bryson stood in the sky, atop a tower erected hundreds of feet above dozens of others scattered miles apart. His heels flirted with the edge of the roof as he stared in awe at a massive sphere of light, larger than an aristocrat's manor, hovering above the tower. It was a lucid white that radiated no heat or light beyond its invisible container. A strange, radiant liquid spilled down its sides, a circular waterfall enclosing its base before crashing against the ivory roof. The substance ran across the stone, splitting in front of Bryson's boots and spilling over the roof's edge, where it then cascaded down the stone walls of the tower.

He turned and peered over the edge, stomach lurching at the bottomless drop, the ground some tens of thousands of feet below. Skyways and tunnels ran between the separate towers at varying elevations, creating a lattice-like network of walkways—a massive spider web suited only for catching comets. At random distances along these skyways were bulbous structures punctured by several other tunnels, small buildings suspended in air by the appendages reaching from auxiliary towers. It seemed the bigger the structure, the more pathways that led to and from it, jutting out in a multitude of directions, either toward sibling structures or one of the massive towers anchored to the ground below.

Bryson counted six towers, including the one on which he and Naipa stood. Each also held a sphere of celestial light above them, sizes differing, but that could have been a visual trick of the varying distances from his tower. The brilliant spheres looked like stars plucked from the night sky, millions of distant siblings serving as their backdrop.

"What ... is this?" he asked, turning back toward the sphere on their tower.

"One of six of Tahar's Cavities," Naipa said. "The other five rest above the other towers, providing power to the Starlight."

"Starlight?"

"That is the name of this sprawling ..." she rocked her head side to side, eyes narrowed as she searched for the right word ... "palace, I guess would be the closest word."

He turned and admired the structure once more. "Metropolis is more like it."

"I suppose that works, though this isn't the actual city of the Light Empire."

"A city?" he breathed. He tried looking over the roof's edge, but the sheer drop made him stumble backward. He'd expected his feet to slosh in the liquid light, but instead he felt solidity below him. He looked down again, lifting a foot and noticing the liquid's behavior as unnatural. It closed where his foot had been, covering the stone surface, but when he placed his foot down, the liquid diverged immediately. His physical presence didn't obstruct the liquid; the liquid simply chose to avoid him.

Naipa, who had reached out a hand to grab him before he fell on his butt, pulled him back to her side. "Be careful up here. When this close to a Cavity, circumstances can become dangerous—at least, for someone like you." She looked at his wings.

He looked over his shoulder, acknowledging them for the first time since yesterday. They had enlarged, rippling along illuminated edges. Glancing down around his hip, he noticed the bottoms of his wings were reaching for the flowing liquid below. He peered at the globe of light looming above the tower, just out of hands' reach, and recalled Lilu reciting parts of Mendac's lab notes.

"So, these Cavities are the source of Light Energy—Tahara—in the world?"

Naipa continued to stare into the waterfall of light that crashed from the sphere's base to the roof. His words seemed only a distraction she wished to avoid. Eventually, feeling his unrelenting stare, she looked his way. He noticed the hems of her robes and her feet had fused with the liquid light.

"Think of the world as a human body," she said. "A human has five cavities within them, each of which creates one of two energies. Intel or Dev Energy from the Knowledge Cavity in the brain's right half. Passion or Still from the Emotion Cavity in the heart. Adren or Power from the Courage Cavity in the muscles. Spirit or Cyn from the Soul Cavity in the soul. Archaic or Prim from the Morality Cavity in the brain's left half."

She turned toward the edge and gestured toward the five fallen stars on the shorter towers scattered below. "These are the world's cavities." She proceeded to point at each one in succession, naming them in the process. "The heart. The muscle. The soul. The right and left halves."

Bryson couldn't help but notice she'd left out one of the spheres and, quite possibly, the largest one, floating directly behind them on the very tower they occupied. He also questioned the accuracy of her explanation. According to Lilu, Mendac believed the human body had a sixth cavity. This sphere behind them was the sixth sphere. He turned, hands on his hips and head tilted.

"You only named five cavities," he said.

She turned and whispered, "There is a sixth."

"The eyes," he said.

"I wager you found Mendac's notes." He nodded, and she said, "The Judgment Cavity. It holds the parent energies. What more ancient people called the mother and father of the lesser ten energies. Tahara, the Energy of Light. Mulawi, the Energy of Dark. In a human, it leaks both into the body, but the ratio leans heavily to whichever realm you were born ... Still, the ratio can flip according to one's life, but that's astronomically rare. Here, in the Light Empire, directly in front of us, it leaks only Tahara." She paused before adding, "The world's source of Mulawi is in the Judgment Cavity of the Dark Empire."

"Is that why it's bigger than the rest," he said. "Or are my eyes deceiving me?"

"They're not, but it's still nowhere near its proper size or radiance. While the other five burn in all their glory, this cavity is only a piece of its grander self."

"Where's the rest of it?" he asked.

"Lost in the bowels of the world, apparently."

"And nobody can find it?"

She shook her head. "I believe the empress and emperor tried before the Known History timeline, when they were known as Originators. They never reached it."

With each statement Naipa made, a dozen more questions sprouted in his mind. And he wanted to keep asking, thoughts of Benedict, Shelly, and L.K. drifting beneath the awe of his surroundings, but Naipa held up a hand as a request for silence, eyes focused on the waterfall again. "She's here."

He regarded the cascading liquid of light, glowing brightly but illuminating nothing around it. A woman's body, or at least the front of it, formed in the falling liquid, shadows collecting beneath her neck and bust, hollowed divots for eyes, and hair that dripped with radiance. She was a moving statue of alabaster—white and translucent, yet not as sturdy as quartz.

She spoke in a tongue that clicked and hissed, sending Bryson's hairs on end. Naipa translated: "Do you know what I speak?"

He shook his head.

Naipa scoffed before the empress even had a chance to respond. "Of course," she muttered.

The empress spoke again, but this time in Sphairian. "I expected more of Ataway."

"I don't know why you're surprised, Empress," Naipa said. "His track record with squads he's led should have been telling enough. They're miscreants, all of them."

The liquid woman chuckled softly. "That's why I liked him. Thusia, Leon, Quincy, and Aestys are some of this empire's brightest stars, are they not?"

"Our perspective on what is bright and what is dull doesn't share common ground, Empress."

191

Bryson's gaze shifted between them, perplexed by the casual nature of the conversation. Was this liquid woman not a god who ruled with an iron fist?

Nodding, the empress said, "Yes, well, I find them to be most promising—even if a bit rambunctious, especially as of late. And Ataway is the one responsible for molding them into the Bozani they've become."

"Was I supposed to know that language?" Bryson asked.

"Mind your tongue," Naipa said. "Address her as Empress."

"This is fine," said the liquid woman, hollowed gaze turning to Bryson. "I don't think Empress is the proper title for him to call me, anyway." A smile—nothing but a crease in the liquid—formed on her face. "Bryson LeAnce."

"Intel," he snapped. "Don't ever call me by that name."

A pause as she processed his correction. "Intel?" She looked at Naipa. "Didn't he just marry? That was Quincy's reasoning behind the postponement of his abduction, correct?"

"Yes, Empress."

The empress's eyes narrowed at him. "And now your last name is Intel? Did you go and marry—"

"An Intelian royal?" he asked. "Yes."

The laugh echoed across the vast night sky and reverberated against the stars, white light stretching between the lips of her open mouth. "What a twisted turn of fate," she said after a few seconds. She shook her head. "Ludicrous really. And Leon and Thusia thought it wise to not inform anyone of this development."

Naipa's brows furrowed. "I doubt they knew it was noteworthy, Empress. Even I find myself confounded by your intrigue."

Bryson, annoyed by the vagueness of the empress's comments, was confused by more than just that. Thus, he repeated his earlier question. "Was I supposed to know that language?"

The empress sighed. "I thought Ataway would teach you. He was one of the few Bozani who could speak it with me. Along with him and Naipa here, only two others share the knowledge."

"I only know Sphairian."

"Not a problem. Maybe I will teach you Technous one day."

"Wait." He paused, flabbergasted by the connection that name served to a reoccurring dream he had during his second year as a Jestivan. A classroom with shadows swallowing one wall, ice creeping across floorboards; the original Jestivan seated around him; Director Senex standing at the front of the classroom with strange symbols written on the chalkboard behind him.

When Bryson had gone to Agnos for help translating the foreign language, Agnos said Director Senex called it Technous—a complex, ancient language lost to time, containing more than a hundred letters. The Archaic Director, however, couldn't do much beyond recognizing it. Deciphering it was impossible, and he wasn't sure why Bryson would have been seeing it in a dream. Nobody—aside from Agnos with the aid of his glasses—had the knowledge to read it.

"What is it?" the empress asked after a long pause.

"Technous is a language with over a hundred characters, each of which is determined by the character that precedes or follows it in a word," he explained, trying to remember Agnos's description. "A brain-breaking puzzle."

"So Ataway wasn't completely useless," she said.

"He didn't teach me that. In one of my past dreams, words were written in Technous on a chalkboard."

"How did a dead language enter your dreams?" Naipa asked.

"How am I supposed to know? It could have been Mendac since the word had to do with him and my mother."

"Doubtful," the empress said, more to herself than them. Her gaze veered left, toward nothing, as if in thought. "Do you know why you're here, Bryson?"

He had to stop himself from groaning with impatience. "No clue."

"To take someone's place."

His eyes narrowed. "I have no place up here. My place is with my wife and son."

Again, the empress smiled. "My name is Tonitrua, once known as the Queen of Thunder. I ruled the Light Knowledge Kingdom before Known History began. That was a much different time, when only ten people known as the Originators harnessed abilities. We acquired those abilities via

Essences that lived in our kingdoms. My Essence had resided in the Valley of Thunder, or what you call Thunder Alley in present day. He went by Intelius, and he was the metaphysical form of Intel Currents. Billions of them clustered in that one area of the world. When he wasn't a brilliant shower of lightning, he took the form of a man when I came to harvest him for that power."

"He was lightning?" Bryson asked, dumbfounded.

"*Is*," she said. "Only difference is, now he's up here, but on the neighboring island."

"Okay, and what does that matter?"

Her face became still, incandescent liquid spilling down her body. She spoke her next words tersely:

"He is your mark."

21

Lay Low

When Lilu turned the corner into the nursery and found her older sister slouched on the floor below the window with her face between her knees and hands clasped over her head, back heaving as she moaned in anguish, she broke down, too. She didn't race toward Shelly; she inched across the nursery, wobbling on shaky legs, hand to her mouth as she tried muffling her own sobs.

L.K.'s screams continued to pierce the empty corridors and chambers around them while the queen's howls served a haunting backdrop, reminding Lilu of her journey into the Void. Suffering lay thick in the air here, and she couldn't avoid it.

She paused at the open window, hand atremble on its ledge. Staring out at the starless night sky, she contemplated looking down, knowing what the image awaiting her could do to a person ... to a daughter who had already lost her father. Tears stained the mahogany wood of the ledge. She decided not to look down outside, but inside, where her sister now slumped against her leg. Shelly's fingers dug into her scalp as her howls became screams, violent and shrill, as if her throat had been scarred by several minutes of lamentation.

Lilu lowered herself to the floor. The two sisters leaned against each other. She wrapped an arm around Shelly's hunched back, feeling her shudders reverberate against her ribs. While Shelly gasped for air between dreadful plaints, Lilu tried to wrangle in her own emotions, knowing the volatility of her sanity in that moment. And as comforting as a sister might be, the queen had called for Benedict to retrieve her *husband*, not *Lilu*.

But Bryson was gone.

*   *   *

Three women made fools.

Illipsia, Homina, and Tazama stood in the antechamber to King Storshae's living quarters. The Dev Kingdom now lay in the hands of a toddler. Telos Dev, next in line to sit on the throne, currently sat on the floor among a gathering of wooden toys. He bashed soldier figurines together, pretending they were in the midst of war. Of course, true carnage wouldn't have been achieved without a few soldiers crushed beneath the wheels of a military convoy. Illipsia debated on stopping the child. These games seemed awfully dark for someone so young. He had to have learned it from someone, and she was willing to bet Storshae had been the culprit.

Three women made fools.

Illipsia remained numb, as she had been since fleeing the Intel Kingdom. She had disliked Storshae. She may have listened to her once-king as a child, but that had been because of fear and not knowing anything else in life. Toono had showed her true compassion, and she supposed she had Storshae to thank for assigning her to the man who became known as the Rogue Demon. But in the end, that man—that demon—revealed himself a liar. He hadn't taken Bryson's life as the final sacrifice to rebirth Mendac, but his own, robbing Illipsia of a life with the closest thing she'd ever known as a father or older brother. And to make matters worse, Kadlest had taken Mendac's hand with a smile as she was pulled into the sky.

196

Kadlest had betrayed Toono; Toono had betrayed Illipsia.

Three women made fools.

Homina pitied her daughter, understanding the tithe of unconditional trust. She had shown that same vulnerability to a woman once before. Halys Dev, wife to Dev King Rehn, had fallen in love with a lowly servant of the royal family some twenty years ago. That servant was Homina. King Rehn had never suspected a thing, but when Homina began speaking in her sleep, Halys didn't like what she had heard. Comments about true heirs. Talk of Originators. It had spooked the queen enough for her to give that information to Rehn. The Oracle, as intelligent and prophetic of a man he had been, had taken swift action, locking Homina away in the Confines of Consciousness, viewing her as the Dev family's greatest threat. Halys then died a few years later from a mysterious disease, or so the Dev King claimed.

Illipsia had rejected all of Homina's efforts to provide comfort. A gentle hand pushed away with a more violent one. Soft words met with empty silence. A game of mental probing in which the daughter's walls remained rigid. There was no getting through to her. And while it hurt Homina, she knew Illipsia suffered more than she, for betrayal cut deep.

Three women made fools.

Tazama experienced not apathy or sorrow, but rage. Unlike Illipsia, who had known of the Rogue Demon's true mark for resurrection, and Homina, who hadn't known Toono long enough to care about the betrayal, Tazama had known nothing. She had poured every ounce of herself into the Dev Kingdom's efforts to bring back their proper king by fooling Toth Brench and Prince Storshae and picking the exact moment to flee both of their sides, predicting their demises. Fabulous ruses conducted all for the sake of Toono's goal of bringing the Oracle back to life. Little had she known, her subterfuge was insignificant when compared to the demon's hell of black curtains.

Thus, she glared at Telos—toddler king of the Dev Kingdom—with gaudy aspirations of revenge. She'd mold him, sculpt him, *carve* him into the hardened man he'd need to be to achieve the goals she'd hammer into his head throughout his childhood. She would maintain a manner of cool temperament, but only as a façade. Within her festered a bubbling, callous wound that would receive penance one day.

Toono had rebirthed Mendac LeAnce, the man who had set fire to villages and the Cosmos Meadows. The man who had raped princesses. The man who had abducted Devish citizens from their homes and made them slaves. The man who had killed the king. And the man who had stolen the master blueprints of teleplatform construction from the Consortium in Prayoga, leading to the forced resignation of its president—her father.

Tazama Bandia smoldered, eyes alight with ire as she repeated those accusations in her head. One day, either years or decades from now, the world would fear the names of Tazama and Telos.

*   *   *

Yama Fuuna sought out direction. She could think of no story more pathetic than her own. She had once dripped with conviction, aspirations she had deemed heavy only recently realized as illusions. They had been hollow, a cluster of balloons that took up too much space in a room, but in reality occupied none at all, each filled with nothing but more empty space. All of her life, she had been a skin suit swollen with dreams lacking substance. And all it had taken was a slight puncture to send her spiraling through the world, dreams deflating in the blink of an eye.

Ironic that her lack of direction in recent years had sent her down many paths. She'd been in a mad scramble for purpose, searching for it in her time spent as Toono's adversary, bitter over Jilly's decision to place her heart with Toshik, or her return home with hopes of being trained by relatives she didn't even know she had. Perhaps, she simply needed a return to form. She knew Toshik's feelings toward her—the utter hatred. And while those sentiments were reciprocated on her end, she hadn't focused enough on it, preoccupied with mourning Jilly's death.

That led her to Katashi, capital of the Adren Kingdom. The Light Realm had regained control of the kingdom, which had experienced a temporary period of instability under the reign of Kadlest. The mysterious partner of Toono had had no interest in the wellbeing of the kingdom, using it as nothing more than a staging ground for SCAPD troops as they prepared to ambush the Intel Kingdom. Yama had no idea as to how True Light was handling its vacant throne, with Supido's infant son not ready for the role. She supposed it wasn't her concern.

With the Adren Assassins of Yinyon—and a mother who wanted nothing to do with her—now in her past along with everyone else save Jilly and Toshik, she stood in front of the steps leading to the Adren Assistance Academy. If she wanted to improve, she needed to look elsewhere. What better place than under the tutelage of the woman who had been the tyrant driving a younger Yama toward galvanized years.

Hopefully, she wouldn't turn her away, too.

22

One's True Nature

Following the conclusion of Bryson's meeting with Empress Tonitrua, Naipa escorted the confused Jestivan to his new home for the foreseeable future. It was another journey of permeating through walls and floors, his skin now suffering from a constant fire. She told him there were faster ways, but she couldn't risk it with his Tahara in its infancy stages.

Naipa was odd. She didn't seem to know the layout of this unorthodox palace named Starlight. Hadn't she spent centuries in it? Sure, the place was gigantic and convoluted in its layout, but a being of her stature shouldn't have had to stop every few minutes to read a sign.

Bryson sighed as the woman paused at a dead end, a strange architectural choice he didn't bother questioning. Transportation through the Starlight was clearly unconventional and divine, apathetic to natural law. But Naipa only frowned, eyes drifting left, right, up, down. "Where is it?"

"What?"

"The sign. My directions."

"Are you kidding me?"

"I carve lettering into wooden planks and plant them around this monstrous place so I don't lose myself." She tapped her foot. "There should definitely be one right here. I placed it just the other day, knowing I had to come in this direction soon."

"May I ask where we're going?"

"Squad Three's capsule," she muttered, still focused on absorbing her surroundings. He didn't know why that would help, for every corridor they'd walked through up to this point had looked the same: white.

"Maybe if there were windows," he suggested, "you could look outside and orientate yourself."

"That's cheating. I want to remember this place from the inside."

He balked, unsure of how to take that. Naipa's face had pinched at the center with concentration, the center of her lips pushed up toward her nose. He recalled making that face many times as a teenager, confronted with any sort of written exam. He grinned, amused by the thought that a celestial being of her status couldn't memorize centuries' worth of repeated directions. He nearly laughed as she stepped forward and knocked on the square wall of the dead end, placing her ear against it as if testing the sound. She paid him no mind.

"Ugh, it's no use," she breathed, stepping back, defeat felling her expression. "You win this round, humanity."

Bryson didn't have a chance to fully question that statement before the white surrounding him became a milky haze. He let slip a scream as the walls, floor, and ceiling seemed to dissolve, exposing them to the moonlight. Glancing down, he saw the ground hundreds of yards below. He panicked and grabbed hold of Naipa's shoulder. She raised an eyebrow. "And you were the one questioning my sanity?"

Hesitantly, he stepped in place. Each time his foot hit solid ground despite his eyes showing nothing there. He released his death grip of her shirt and, once his wits were gathered, he studied the sprawling web of ivory tunnels laced between towers. The tunnel they were currently inside was only one floor, but there were others elsewhere that may have been multiple stories, thick enough to contain auxiliary chambers. Dotting the gargantuan web of white stone were egg-shaped buildings suspended in the air by several intersecting tunnels. There were dozens of them, all of varying sizes. One sat right next to Bryson and Naipa, its curving walls rising above and sinking below them. It was dotted with windows save a vertical stretch of wall that was inscribed with foreign lettering. Bryson recognized it instantly as Technous, recalling the strange symbols from his dreams.

"Wow, I can't be this bad," Naipa said, sounding genuinely upset with herself.

"Is this thing a capsule?" he asked.

She turned and looked the other way. "Yes, but not the one you're supposed to be at."

After allowing his gaze to linger on the capsule, he turned. "So, even celestial beings can be as dumb as I am, apparently."

She shot him a glare of contempt. "I'm not dumb, just human."

He kept his mouth shut after that, recalling the authority she'd possessed over Debo in his father-figure's old memory.

"This is Squad One's capsule, which explains my missing sign. Rhysel is a nefarious bastard who enjoys ruining my progression. He spends a lot of his time here since it's his old squad." She huffed, displaying a demeanor akin to Jilly, but more reserved. Her eyes flitted between capsules, some too far to read the letterings in their sides. "There it is," she finally said, pointing downward. Not only was the capsule at a much lower elevation, but it seemed smaller than Squad One's.

The rest of their journey was easier, as Naipa decided to ditch the signs in favor of dissolving the stone around them as they walked, using the exterior of Squad Three's capsule as a beacon. She was unhappy, more of a pout on her face than a scowl. Bryson didn't recall this sort of attitude in Debo's memory. She almost seemed like a different person.

A wooden sign leaned against the base of the dead end's wall that divided the tunnel from Squad Three's capsule. Like the massive inscriptions along the structure, this too was carved in Technous. The milky haze solidified into ivory stone as they lost sight of the outside world. She knelt down and ran a finger along the grooves of the symbols in the wood, gaze suddenly distant.

"You okay?" he asked.

"Familiarity is a trait often disregarded by humans, but is vastly important to our subconscious. We take it for granted—perhaps, our greatest source of comfort." She paused, pulling her finger away from the sign. "It's not until we're plodding around in the dark in a foreign environment when we miss that familiarity, the thing that turns hesitant steps into thoughtless strides. Now imagine if the entire world, including your own home and the people who call you family, were always foreign to you."

She rose from her knee and knocked on the wall, then turned and walked away. He watched her leave. After only a few paces, luminescent wings sprouted from her back and blazed outward, quadrupling the wingspan of Bryson's. She leapt and fazed through the ceiling, disappearing somewhere beyond, incandescent liquid dripping to the floor from a hole in her wake.

He had been naïve to call Naipa Levlin dumb. There was a story there.

*   *   *

A hand grasped the back of Bryson's tunic and pulled him backward through the wall. He grimaced as a surge of heat compressed around him once again. He whirled once free on the other side, exasperation getting the better of him, as he shouted, "Can people stop that?!"

A massive hug. A squeal of delight. Thusia wrapped her arms around him and lifted him off his feet to spin him as if in a dance, only to think better of it and drop him back to his feet. She arched her back and groaned. "You gettin' fat?"

"More like ripped."

As she guffawed, he smiled at her, already finding a situation in which to apply Naipa's final words before departing. For most of his short time spent here in the Starlight, he had been annoyed. Fascination only dampened the frustration in spurts. However, now that he was with Thusia, the woman who had saved his life on a couple of occasions now, the frustration died. His familiarity with her could make this easier.

Sorry, Naipa.

He also found comfort in the architecture of what looked to be an expansive antechamber, not a speck of that unnatural white to be seen. A hearth sat ablaze against the far wall, an overlook hanging above it as it curved along the back wall, set with a polished wooden banister. Five closed doors were spaced evenly along the wall of the overlook, a tall, rectangular window placed between each, the door in the middle complete with Technous engravings and a brass knocker. Two doors flanked each side of the grander one. A staircase curved up both the right and left side of the antechamber to the overlook. From Bryson's vantage point, it didn't look as if the overlook stretched into any corridors beyond the side walls.

A familiar head of greasy red hair could be seen just above the back of an armchair next to the hearth, a sheathed scimitar leaning against its side. "Hey, Suadade," Bryson said.

The Adrenian twisted in his seat and waved. "Bryson."

The middle door of the overlook opened, and out walked Quincy Gralth, the man who had taken the place of Pogu from Debo and became the leader of Squad Three. If Bryson had referred to himself as "ripped" earlier, then this man was shredded. Quincy was the last image any mortal being would conjure up when discussing Bozani. There was no elegance to his posture, no regality in his attire. He looked nothing more than a ruffian—a street urchin turned hardened criminal.

Dressed in a white tank-top, straps thin along sharply angled muscles in his neck, he folded a pair of bulging arms atop the banister as he slouched and eyed their guest. "They finally got you, ay?"

Bryson nodded, his wave of appreciation for Thusia and Suadade in allowing him to experience his wedding extending to this man. "They did. And thank you, by the way, for doing what you did."

Thusia was wrapped to his arm, torso bouncing as if she was holding back her excitement. Quincy returned the nod. "If she cares that much, then I care that much."

Bryson looked over at his Branian, her head now leaning against his shoulder. The anger he felt over his abduction from the dining room in Dunami Palace had melted away, Benedict Ronal's feverous gaze becoming less crisp in his memory. It was possible that he had overreacted to the head steward's intrusion, misjudged the severity of it. That was easy to trick himself into thinking now, when accompanied by Thusia and Suadade. But what would happen when he tried sleeping in a few hours?

"So this is where I live now?" he asked, patting Thusia's shoulder and walking deeper into the antechamber after she'd released him. He surveyed the furniture of brown leather gathered around the hearth, the blood red carpet that swathed the entire floor. Gold accented the designs in polished wooden end tables and a coffee table in front of a sofa. Dozens of paintings hung from cream drywall. Three bookcases—reaching higher than the overlook itself—stood between two doors to the side of the main floor. And all of it was illuminated in the orange light of a candle chandelier that hung from the vaulted dome ceiling.

"Think of it as your new Lilac Suites," Thusia said, opening both arms wide in presentation.

"It is beautiful," he said. "I don't see a pulley system to lower the chandelier. I'm guessing you guys just fly up there?"

Quincy's chuckle thrummed through the capsule. "You think just any of us have wings? We're not all Strasan."

"True," Suadade said dryly from the armchair. "In fact, only three of the Pogu have them … and our dear Quincy isn't one of them."

"Easy there, brat."

"Debonicus had them." Suadade looked up at the Pogu with that jab, but Quincy only shook his head.

"One day you'll get over him," Quincy said. "Besides, those frilly wings aren't going to lift this body."

"That's right!" exclaimed Thusia.

Slowly, Bryson turned to look back at her, disgust contorting his face. "That's right?" he repeated. She shrugged.

"And that's why his head is too big," Suadade drawled.

"Well, that and the pile of rocks," said a new voice.

Bryson turned toward the overlook again. A woman had exited the first door to Quincy's left. Brown hair tried to fall to her shoulders, but it had to fight through fizz and matted clumps. She wore green silk pajamas, the top a loose-fitting button-up and her pants barely long enough to reach her ankles. She yawned as she approached the left staircase, grimacing. "Someone shove manure in my mouth while I was sleeping?"

"Aestys, we have company," Thusia said.

She paused halfway down the stairs, squinting in Bryson's direction until her eyes became slits, wrinkles fraying out from the edges. "Where are those damned things?" she said after staring at him for a few seconds, patting her chest pocket and a trouser pocket before finally finding a pair of glasses with thick black rims resting atop her head. She put them on and studied Bryson. "He's scrawnier than I thought he'd be ... considering all those achievements you listed off, Thusia."

Bryson's eyebrows flattened, but he ignored it and introduced himself anyway. "Good to meet you, Aestys. Name's Bryson."

"I'd shake your hand," she said, continuing down the stairs, "but it'd be better if I brushed my teeth first."

"You have a nap?" he asked.

"Pssh, no," she said, grabbing a pastry from a platter on the centerpiece. "Got my full eight hours."

He scanned the room for a clock, and found one behind him at the top of the wall through which he had entered. "It's eleven at night."

"Yeah, so what?" she asked through a mouthful of mashed pastry. "Don't know what nocturnal means?"

"It just seems ..." he trailed off, a hand placed on his shoulder as if in warning.

Thusia smiled at Aestys. "He's new. We're still getting him acquainted."

The woman stopped chewing, mouth frozen in a pinched position, cheeks swollen with breakfast desserts. She eyed him for a moment before shrugging and heading toward a door to the left. "Gotta squeeze one out. Maybe I'll practice my multitasking and clean my teeth while staining the bowl." She paused and stared at the door, then swallowed the last bit of pastry and sighed before opening it and disappearing beyond.

"Thanks for sharing," Quincy mumbled.

"She hates doors," Thusia said. "Doesn't like how our capsule is set up to mimic mainland architecture. She'd rather just faze through everything."

"What is wrong with everyone here?" Bryson asked incredulously. "Between her sleeping schedule and disdain for doors, you flirting with that meathead, and that Naipa woman getting lost in a home she's lived in for hundreds of years, I don't know who to take seriously."

"Firstly," Thusia said, "Aestys is a bit crass and blunt, but her work ethic is unmatched. And her nocturnal habits are perfect for the job she has up here. As for Naipa, I wouldn't be so quick to judge. While all the Bozani had interesting human lives before dying, hers is one of the more unique and devastating ones."

"I never even heard of her until seeing Debo's memory," Bryson groaned. "How am I supposed to know?"

"You're not gonna know a lot of us," said Quincy from his perch on the overlook. He continued to lean against the banister. "Especially considering your poor acumen. A lot of our stories from our mortal lives were contained to smaller areas than what you're used to. The Light Realm didn't have Devish servants to transport information through broadcasts between cities and kingdoms until two decades ago. Our names and stories fill obscure books that can probably only be found in remote locations. You wouldn't find them unless you were some sort of intellectual savant. But that doesn't mean we weren't powerful."

"But there are people from the past whose names became legends despite not having Devish abilities to spread the word," Bryson said, now leaning back against an entry table and facing the hearth and overlook. Thusia, using the feathery grace of her Spirit Assassin abilities, leapt, flipped, and grabbed hold of the chandelier with her legs. Her arms and straight blonde hair dangled beneath her. Fortunately, she was wearing pants with a tucked-in shirt rather than her typical sundresses.

"Yes, and they're anomalies," Quincy said, laughing. "But there are a few of those up here, too."

"Really? What about the *Of Five* legends?"

The big man winked, and Bryson's gaze dropped to the carpet. He didn't know how he felt about the heroes of those fairy tales. What he'd learned about Mendac had sullied everyone else in his mind. What dark secrets had escaped the pages of the other stories?

"They're not all Mendac," Suadade said, still facing the hearth in his armchair. He must have read Bryson's thoughts in the extended silence. "And if you ever find yourself doubting that, think of Debo. He'd been known as Ataway Debonicus Kawi, *Third of Five*, and you know what kind of man he was."

Bryson knew he had a point, but his father's darkness overpowered everything else. He couldn't see past it. He decided to change subjects. "When do I get more clarity for the purpose of me being here? The liquid-light woman made it sound way simpler than it probably is. I have to eliminate some kind of electrical essence?"

"Again, two things here," Thusia said from her upside-down perch above, face red as blood rushed to her head. "Don't call her liquid-light woman. She's the empress. Or goddess, if you must call her that, though she's not technically a deity. Also, she said you have to eliminate Intelius?"

Quincy grunted. "He obviously heard her wrong. A mortal child cannot kill a metaphysical entity—especially one considered a demigod."

"I'm twenty-one."

"A child to my nine-hundred and six years."

At that, Bryson shut his mouth.

Thusia curled upward, either displaying considerable leg strength or the luxuries of a weightless body, and grabbed hold of a rung of the chandelier with her hand. Unhooking her legs, she dropped them and fell to the floor without a sound. She looked worried. "Empress Tonitrua said your assignment was to eliminate Intelius?"

Exasperated with the repetition, he forced out a breath. "Yes. She called him my mark, like I'm an assassin or something."

"Strange," Suadade said. "I know Intelius and the empress despise each other, and Intelius has been a major reason why we can't advance in the war, but if the Bozani can't do it how can you?"

"So, you guys know about as much as I do. Fantastic."

Suadade rose from his chair, placing a book down on the coffee table. He wore a maroon cloak pinned at the middle of his neck, cut down the middle in a style that widened in its descent, revealing a simple tunic and trousers. "Empress Tonitrua is highly selective in how she rations information. Strasan and certain Pogu are the only ones who speak with her directly, so consider it another anomaly that you've done so."

"She's grown desperate," said Quincy.

"Forgive me," Bryson said. "But I see no signs of desperation or war here."

"Imagine yourself a lowly civilian who stumbled their way into Dunami Palace sometime in the past two to three years," Thusia said. "Had you seen the royal family and the peaceful nature of palace operations, would you have known there was a massive war happening?"

Bryson paused, reflecting on his time in the palace when he wasn't on missions, trying to view it from an outsider's perspective. Unless one had been present in the war corridor or map rooms, they wouldn't have heard the brutal discussions of war.

"There is war, and you will learn it soon," said Quincy. "You'll get more answers in a week. The Pogu were told today that you'll have a meeting with us in the coming days. We are to prep you for the more important meeting, one involving the three Strasan. That will happen at a date determined later down the line."

Bryson nodded, deciding to let his many other questions lay in wait. For now, he wanted to get a head start on sleep. Something told him shutting down would prove a struggle. He kept thinking of Shelly and L.K. "Do I get a room?" he asked, grabbing a pastry from the centerpiece.

"First door, next to Aestys," Quincy said. "It's a prime spot suited for quiet nights since she's never here in these hours."

As if on cue, the woman exited the bathroom. Her hair was wet and combed, eyes rimmed with black charcoal, and her silk pajamas were replaced with a maroon cloak, its hems edged with silvery etchings. A silver fist coated in flame was embroidered into its back. "Well, I'm off. A city to patrol and all that."

"Say hi to Nora for me," Suadade said.

"Will do." Aestys grabbed a slew of drinking flasks from a skinny table against the wall, where glass figurines served as decoration. She hooked the flasks to her person somewhere beneath her cloak, then looked up, eyes locking on Bryson. "Don't ever drink from these if you value your life."

And then she was gone, pausing only briefly at the front wall of the antechamber to smile, before fazing through it and into the corridor beyond.

*　　　*　　　*

It had been over a month, yet Rhyparia's wings remained disobedient to her will. They surged outward when free of the Black Labyrinth, but if she came within a few feet of a Mulanyx surface, they wilted against her back. Mendac's wings behaved oppositely, their smoky tendrils snaking toward the Mulanyx, slipping inside the stone with ease. Sometimes, the stone responded itself by stretching and meeting his wings halfway. If Emperor Mialo's advice was correct, that meant Mendac knew who he was and not just accepted it, but embraced it. A teenage Rhyparia would have found this unfair. Of course he could embrace himself; surely, nothing he'd done was anywhere close to her atrocities. She was supposed to embrace her … what, exactly? Her conviction? Tenacity? Perhaps, her aggression? Dropping the moon had been necessity—proper penance. It was a measure she hadn't taken lightly. A statement was made.

She looked across the table at Yasmine Cordelia—Dev Assassin and Gefal—kinky hair fuzzed into an afro. She had abandoned straightening her hair a week and a half ago, claiming she rarely had the patience for such a task. Yasmine was one of the Dark Empire's five Fuhren, a class of Gefal similar to the Light Realm's Pogu. They ranked above Bewahr, of which there were fifteen. She was one of the few who spoke with Rhyparia beyond a few words, but that didn't necessarily mean the woman liked her. She could have been assigned this task by the emperor in order to make Rhyparia "discover herself." It was all a special kind of torture, but she didn't complain. A part of her enjoyed Yasmine's company during dinner.

"Did you embrace what you are?" Rhyparia asked, setting down her seltzer.

"Yes, I knew myself very well even during my mortal life," Yasmine said without looking away from a sheet of parchment resting next to her plate.

"You're okay with being a bad person?"

The Fuhren looked up at that. "And why I am a bad person?"

"Don't you have to do terrible things to end up here?" Rhyparia said, leaning back from her now-empty plate.

"So, that's your logic …" Yasmine said, intrigued.

"I got my wings the moment after I crushed Ulna Malen. Mendac must be here because of his invasion of the Dev Kingdom, enslaving so many

Devish. And some versions of his tale spoke of battles with mercenary armies and arson."

"Just because you're in the Dark Empire doesn't mean you're evil, at least not in all instances. Mulawi is a very complex energy. It's not like where a person falls on the spectrum between Tahara and Mulawi is only determined by acts you've committed in your life. There are many other factors, some at odds with others. For instance, internal demons such as guilt, anguish, ire, lust." She paused and then added, "Denial."

"I feel none of that," Rhyparia said.

"You're at peace."

Rhyparia nodded.

"Those people of Ulna Malen deserved it?" asked Yasmine.

"They did."

Yasmine studied Rhyparia, allowing a few seconds to pass before asking, "So the question becomes: why *those* wings?"

"I answered that already. Because of what I did."

"You see ... I think you were heading down this path for a long time. Dropping the moon wasn't some kind of magic lever that sprouted your wings. Would you call what you did immoral?"

"It was just."

"Not the same thing," Yasmine said. "Was it immoral?"

"Yes, but justified."

"Which makes you feel at peace with it regardless of its unethical and abhorrent nature."

Rhyparia closed her eyes and inhaled, waiting for a point to her ramblings. She didn't voice her frustrations, however. She was the one who had brought this topic up, though she wasn't sure how its focus had been flipped onto her.

Yasmine tilted her head and narrowed her hazel eyes. "You don't see it, do you?"

Rhyparia shrugged. "People with power sometimes have to go to the blackest of depths to protect those without power. My fellow Jestivan have killed plenty of people. You understand this."

Yasmine laughed. "Are you trying to find parallels to what you did? You'll be searching for a long time."

"I freed the—"

"I'm going to say this," Yasmine said, interrupting Rhyparia. "You said you're at peace, and that's fine. But you're in denial, which is one of those internal demons I mentioned. I don't even know if it's denial. Honestly, after speaking with you tonight, the past several weeks make sense. I think it's ignorance." She stood, wiping her mouth with a napkin and dropping it on her plate, her rant broken in its fervor. "You annihilated an entire population and felt no remorse. Serenity, in fact. And you were at peace with it even before you did it. You knew what you wanted to do. You succeeded. Now, you're satisfied."

The gears began spinning in a part of Rhyparia's mind she had shut off a long time ago, when she'd been alone with Musku for nearly twenty years, wasting her life away.

Shaking her head, Yasmine said, "I have an assignment for you: self-reflection. Break down everything I just said. Figure out what it means. Also, ask yourself a couple questions. Was freeing the slaves or slaughtering the free more important to you? And do you seriously believe you got every slave or servant out of that city?"

Rhyparia watched the Fuhren take her leave through a Mulanyx wall, black smoke furling around her form. She stared at the spot, suddenly angry … and not at herself, but at Yasmine …

For speaking to her with such disrespect.

23

The Bribe

Agnos had said his goodbyes and given his thanks to Still Queen Apoleia and crew for their hospitality. He and Evelyn had appreciated the few nights of rest in the barracks of the Still Kingdom's frozen teleplatforms. He sat on a platform's edge, watching Evelyn in the midst of an extended farewell with Vuilni Gesluimant. The two former Diatia had tried recruiting each other to their own missions over the course of days, but neither budged. While he knew Vuilni was firm in her decision to travel to Kindoliya with her family, where Queen Apoleia promised extended lodging for refugees until they could get on their feet, he wasn't exactly sure where Evelyn stood in regards to his goal of getting to the end of the Warpfinate. He didn't expect loyalty from her; he had no right to. Truth be told, the two Diatia knew each other better than he knew Evelyn.

Thus, he was pleasantly surprised when the blue-haired Diatia woke him this morning with urgency, a leaf of vellum held over his face. Once he regained his bearings from being jarred awake and he'd buried his mouth and nose under covers to protect from the cold, he had read the letter. It had been a few paragraphs scrawled by Queen Apoleia, allowing his and Evelyn's passage into Ipsas, accompanied by her signature and a wax insignia.

"They can't turn us away now!" Evelyn had whispered, careful to not wake Vuilni and her family in the neighboring cots.

"Awesome," he said through the covers.

She stood and admired it from a distance, arm outstretched. "My queen is generous."

Agnos sat up with his one arm, using his teeth to pull the covers up with him. A coat alone wasn't enough to contain his body heat. "You spoke with her without puking?"

She nodded, then noticed the blanket slipping down his chest. She pulled it up and tucked it behind his shoulders, pinning it to the bedframe. She had grown comfortable around him, a far cry from the distance from which she'd used to watch him while on the Mythmaker, observing him like an exam proctor. She'd wanted to know what had separated the Jestivan from the Diatia, a fractured group that had experienced only disarray. While she said she learned that difference at the whirlpool and on Knowledge River, where he had swallowed his fear and taken charge of his crew as they sailed into certain demise, he didn't truly notice a shift in her mannerisms until spending the past few weeks in Dunami. The Jestivan when gathered in the same place were an infectious lot. They possessed the camaraderie a person like Evelyn craved. He recalled the bounce in her step when she had joined Lilu in the fight against Powish giants on the frozen river. Nobody could manufacture that joy.

His mouth curved into a grin as Evelyn and Vuilni embraced. He found a certain sense of pride in the transformation the two women had taken since meeting the Jestivan. This group was more than a specialized force of elite soldiers, evident in the inclusion of individuals like Jilly and Agnos. They were humanity at its finest, role models after which children could shape themselves. They were hope, courage, and integrity. Each Jestivan possessed flaws, but most of them had persevered despite them, proving no amount of baggage would hold them back.

Evelyn pawed at tears as she separated from Vuilni and headed in Agnos's direction. She wore a light jacket, nothing like the multiple coats squeezing the life out of him, making movement near impossible. He envied her cold blood and the Still Energy that made her prosper in temperatures such as this. A couple bags were slung over each of her shoulders, the signed writ of passage tucked away in one of them.

"Let's get this show on the road, marshmallow," she said, helping him to his feet. The nickname was recent, poking fun at his bloated appearance when stuffed with so many layers of pants and shirts. He liked it and was quite fond that it stemmed from his image rather than his personality. Marshmallow was something that would have used to be an insult to his character … soft.

As she and Tashami boarded the platform, he eyed a tram ram just beyond the outer barracks. He took a moment to admire the beast, for it had been his first time seeing one outside of sketches in texts. It was being prepped for departure, the capital waiting hundreds of miles across the Diamond Sea. He spotted a hand waving from the coach on the tram ram's massive back. A smile from a girl who had once been incapable of such a feat. A head of violet hair and absent of the feline deity.

He returned the wave to his former Jestivan captain for whom he held nothing but respect. He adored Olivia Still. Along with her brother, they had always been the two pillars of the Jestivan. And if this world ever needed saving, he'd bet his last arm on those two being there.

*   *   *

The teleplatform spun to a stop. Because of his handicap, Agnos had to adopt a peculiar position in order to remain on the device. He was pinned between Evelyn and a support beam, burrowed in her embrace. In order to maintain the balance of two people, she had frozen her forearms and hands to the beam, a shell of ice extended between them. It led to an awkward entrance to Ipsas's island and embarrassing first impression on the guards stationed around it.

215

"Let me handle this," she whispered as guards marched to the platform's perimeter with haste. Her hands thawed, and she released him from her embrace.

Tashami inched toward his friend's side. Agnos knew what he was doing and didn't mind the protective stance. As much as he hated his cowardice, seeing the ivory-haired Spiritian step up to his defense had always been comforting, reminiscent of another old friend in Lost Wisdom. As far as the relationship he had shared with Toono, the two men were very similar in his heart.

A man whose uniform was edged with knots along his shoulder, marking him as an officer of the school's defense force, stepped forward, breaking ranks from the circle of guards. "You've come outside of the Head Warden's allotted arrival hours," he said, scanning the faces of the two men specifically. "State your business and names."

Evelyn's hands nested on her hips, head tilting. "Really. You ask that of me?"

His gaze, which had been lingering on Agnos and Tashami, drifted toward her, face falling flat with realization. "Evelyn Tesai, you dare show your face here again?"

"Not the surprise you were looking for this morning, Jewel?"

He spat, biceps growing noticeably larger, nearly ripping his sleeves. "As impudent as ever."

"As 'jeweless' as ever, still?" she asked.

The officer leapt onto the platform, sending quakes across the Permanence floor as he landed right in front of Evelyn. Tashami stepped closer to Agnos. Jewel's face was inches away from hers, as he grumbled, "You are no longer a student here. I can dispose of you if I please."

"Before you do that," she said, stepping back and dropping one of her four bags. She untied one and, after some digging, pulled out a leaf of vellum. She lifted from her knee and thrust the sheet in his face, nearly punching him in the nose. "A signed and sealed writ of passage from the Still Queen herself."

He snatched it and straightened to his normal height, eyes racing across the document. "You think the word of a traitor holds any weight here?"

"If I recall, this school has never been aligned with any of the kingdoms, so what do matters of their wars and politics mean here? You, of all people, should understand that, seeing that you live on bended knee for the wardens as if they were lords and ladies."

"No matter the queen. *You* are a traitor to this school."

"Yet I'm still alive, and those who were deemed favorites by the High Warden are now six feet under." She smirked, closing the already-tiny gap between them, and whispered, "Bruut, Gina, Halluci, Groto. They join your other jewel."

Agnos's eyes spread wide, breath caught in his throat as he dug a finger in his ear, as if clearing it would help him hear her better. He blinked several times in efforts to restore an image he'd developed of her since meeting her. Was this Evelyn in her natural environment, when not faced with strangers on foreign ground?

Tashami leaned back and whispered out the corner of his mouth: "She wasn't lying when she said she hated this place."

Jewel lowered the vellum and narrowed his eyes at her. "Would you like your friends to join them?" He snapped his fingers, and two guards flanking the platform boarded it. Their forearms swelled as they reached for war hammers on their back, marching in Tashami and Agnos's direction. They only made it a few strides before a hole opened in each of their shoulders, red liquid spraying from their backs. The men roared in agony, grasping at their wounds.

Tashami's arms were crossed, index fingers pointed at both men. "It's not going to kill you," he said. "I missed any vitals."

Evelyn's lazy gaze turned from the seething guards to the officer. "That was dumb." She stepped around him and off the platform, ignoring the other guards as she found a bench in front of a lone inn. Blue hair glittered with frost beneath the first-day sun as she took a seat. "Do what you need to do. Let the High Warden know we're coming if you must. We'll wait."

Tashami circled Agnos, eyeing each and every guard, as if daring them to try something reckless again. But Jewel had learned his lesson, or so it seemed. "Relax, soldiers."

Agnos cocked an eyebrow. Soldiers? Were they not guards? Perhaps, Evelyn hadn't been lying when she'd said this school operated as its own nation.

Jewel's scowl turned from the two Jestivan to Evelyn on the bench some thirty feet away. "Let me fetch a Devish who can connect me with High Warden Sylial. We'll see how welcome you are here after he finds out who has showed up on his doorstep."

Agnos and Tashami eventually joined Evelyn on the bench, the perimeter of guards breaking formation to help the two wounded men to their feet before rushing them to a simple wooden building across from the inn. Agnos assumed it was a barrack.

With the commotion of their entry receded, he could finally absorb his surroundings. The teleplatforms sat near the shoreline of the Dark Sea, small waves shrinking to subtle humps until a rippling, bubbling tide drifted up the sandy beach. A pungent scent of fish laced with notes of crisp salt lay in the air, providing him with familiarity on which to grasp. DaiSo, city of pirates, had carried that same scent when on the beach, although the deeper into the city one went, the heavier odors of animal manure, pirate grime, and sometimes blood drowned out the gulf's fragrances.

A lousy pier extended over shallow waters, a ship anchored at its end. It was nothing close to the mighty galleons Agnos had grown accustom to in his brief life of piracy. Instead, it was a caravel, three masts that stood in a tight row with ivory sails not as vast. It was beautiful, though. Well maintained and graceful in its humbleness. Beyond the beach was a grassy field wherein sat the teleplatforms, inn, and barrack. It was a pocket of grass, surrounded by a curving wall of trees on three sides, the sea at its front. Agnos knew of this forest. He'd read about it during his studies under Neeko's tutelage. It was called the Infested Forest, and he didn't much fancy the idea of experiencing the details listed out in that textbook firsthand. Luckily, the text had also mentioned carriage rides and escorts who guided students and guests to the main campus—that way injuries and fatalities could be avoided.

He spotted potential transport among a cluster of sheds angled errantly behind the inn. Two carriages and four horses, each with a sleek brown coat and golden manes. They were healthy beasts, muscles taught in their legs.

He breathed easier, confident the Infested Forest couldn't rival the Almawt Woods, a dead expanse of forest that swathed much of the Cyn Kingdom's central landmass. He had traveled atop a rotting, undead horse with its pink flesh and skeleton partially exposed.

"That Jewel guy too scared to oppose you?" Tashami asked, not removing his eyes from a group of guards who watched them from the front of the barrack.

Distinguishing them by kingdom was impossible save the Powish, whose unnaturally muscular frames stuck out like a sore thumb. A few looked feeble—decrepit like the trees in the Almawt Woods, hollow cheeks and sunken eyes—which made Agnos think they were Cynnish. As for the Devish, Primmish, and Stillians, they were indiscernible, if present at all. They all wore the same uniforms, sleek gray accented with jungle greens along the hems, buttons, and shoulder straps. He needn't see the campus to know this was nothing like Phesaw.

"Fear is definitely not his issue," she said, digging through another bag for something. "Don't let that man's lack of temperament fool you. His explosiveness isn't limited to his voice. He can hang with the best of them, including the Diatia. It's duty that keeps him from unleashing on us at the moment. Because if there is one man he truly fears, it's High Warden Sylial. And I don't blame him." She pulled out a gem. "But I know his biggest vice."

Agnos eyed the gem with a smirk. "Greed for wealth?"

She nodded, gaze distant as she flipped the small gem between two fingers. "This is pure ever-ice, residing about as close to Mount Stillinia's summit as a human can get."

"Is that why he's called Jewel?" Agnos asked.

She snorted. "No."

"Where'd you get it?" Tashami asked, frowning. "Is that where the chill's coming from?"

"Queen Apoleia gave it to me for this purpose. And yes, this tiny thing is capable of dropping the temperature by twenty degrees anywhere within five feet. Only Stillians can touch it with their bare hands. Centuries ago, the royal family used it to identify foreigners in the city. It was a flawless strategy, really. The person usually dropped it the moment it touched skin."

Tashami leaned in and narrowed his eyes at the stone. "Centuries ago? Why'd they stop?"

She grinned, bringing it closer to his face. His entire body recoiled as his hand went to his face, accidentally shoving Agnos off the bench and into the sod. Agnos lay still for a moment, inhaling deep as he contemplated life and how he'd ended up in this position. Evelyn guffawed, and Tashami leapt to his friend's aid, grabbing him by his arm and lifting him to his feet. "Sorry, buddy."

"It's okay," Agnos said, trailing off as he noticed a bright red rash on Tashami's cheek. He'd read about the increase in severity of ever-ice's effects according to its purity—or its source's proximity to the summit— but seeing it in person was an entirely different experience. He balked. "It did that?"

"And I didn't even touch him with it," she said. "While it drops the temperature twenty degrees within a five-foot radius, the same can't be said if you're within inches."

"It burned him!" Agnos yelled. Before he could turn on her, Tashami grabbed his face, using his thumb to wipe at something on his forehead. "What are you doing?" asked Agnos.

"Dirt stain."

Evelyn nearly toppled off the bench in hysterics. The brief anger slipped from Agnos's mind, as he, too, could only find humor in their situation. Stepping back to admire his work, like a painter trying to see his canvas in its entirety, Tashami pursed his lips and nodded, seemingly oblivious to the ice burn on his face. They returned to the bench, three friends cramped shoulder to shoulder as they waited for an update from the officer.

"So yeah," Evelyn said, "the practice was ceased due to a nasty string of amputations resulting from frostbitten hands. There's a whole story behind that fiasco. One of the more popular Stillian plays."

"Sounds dark," Tashami muttered. He had just applied water to his burn from a waterskin and was now lathering on some kind of oil, both of which had been lent to him by Evelyn.

"Depends on the version being told. There's a genius parody that will have you peeing yourself laughing."

"There he is," Agnos said, drawing their attention to the inn. Jewel sauntered toward them with a sneer that didn't bode well for the trio. "His chest is wider than Tashami's and mine put together."

"Once again, let me talk," she said, her tone suddenly austere as she rose to her feet. The two Jestivan remained seated.

"What's the verdict, Jewel?"

"You are to be escorted to the campus and served to High Warden Sylial as prisoners of the school."

Evelyn remained quiet for a long pause, possibly perusing her options. Younger Agnos would have thought it obvious. He would have seen only two options: run or forfeit. Even with two elite fighters at his side, he would have pled for mercy or given himself over in hopes that the less he struggled, the less severe his punishment. But now, Agnos—notorious pirate captain, conqueror of the Region of Raging Tides, Sixth of Six, and protégé of the most elusive man in history: Neeko Lefolli—couldn't fathom the idea of settling for anything less than his greatest desires. He went to stand, but an open hand of warning from Evelyn stilled him. After months on the Mythmaker, chasing down whirlpools and SCAPD fleets, it was her turn to lead him.

"Let's find common ground here, Jewel," she whispered, not wanting the man's underlings to hear. Guards scattered around the field only had eyes and ears for the Diatia and their officer. "I don't wish to create a scene."

He stared at her, then glanced her comrades' way. "I'm not stupid," he breathed, gaze returning to her. "I know who they are. Everyone with authority in this school has studied the likes of these two. That armless scholar serves no threat. You should have brought more of the reputable Jestivan."

It was Tashami's turn to stir, always eager to defend his best friend, but Agnos clamped a hand over his wrist.

"It's still Tashami and me versus ... what ..." she visually combed the guards ... "you?"

"You forget about your dear friend, Ronossius." She hesitated, and he jumped on that weakness. "Take a look over there." He raised a massive hand that had probably crushed a few adult heads in its life, and extended a finger.

Agnos looked in that direction and noticed a young man seated on the edge of the barrack's roof. He sat with legs crossed, elbows resting on knees and hands limp in front of his shins. He wore a guard's uniform, but it was bare compared to the medal and pin-adorned tops of his peers. No ribbons, gold, or other laurels. And Agnos found that plainness far more distinguishing. The man watched them from his perch, expression unreadable. Eyes set in dark bags contrasted with ghostly white skin. His hair was as gray and brittle as an old man's, falling in strings around his ears and down his back. He was a man teetering between boyhood and elder years.

"This is his job now?" Evelyn asked. "Oh, how the Diatia have fallen."

"He vowed to protect the realm when he became a Diatia," Jewel scorned. "As did nine others. Don't fault him for upholding that honor. Not all can be as spineless as you."

She looked at him, head tilting. "That vow was broken by the wardens, squabbling over nothing and sucking us into it in the process."

"Mind your tongue."

"Mind your pedestal upon which you think you stand." She took a step closer. "How easily a *chill* can cause glass houses to crack and shatter."

Noticing he hadn't released his death grip of Tashami's wrist, Agnos relaxed. He was waiting for the climax.

Jewel smiled and then laughed, loud and deep, his gigantic mouth spread wide to reveal more teeth than normal for a human. His barrel of a chest swelled with each gasp for breath. "Do I look made of glass?" he asked after recovering his wits.

Bricks are more like it, Agnos thought. *Or marble.*

Evelyn reached into her pocket and pulled out the ever-ice gem. Holding it in two hands, she cupped them to shield from curious eyes. "Let us enter the forest unaccompanied, and I'll let you have this."

His grin melted, jaw slackening as he regarded the gem with rising eyebrows. "Purity percentage?" he asked.

"Eighty-seven."

Shock crossed Agnos's face. Queen Apoleia had been willing to give Evelyn something *that* valuable? Ever-ice with such purity could have bought her mountains of the Intel Kingdom's iron. And Jewel seemed to have realized that in a breath's span, eyes glinting up to hers. "What kind of game are you playing at?"

"One of honor … to make up for that I was lacking when I departed this school and abandoned the fragments of what was the Diatia."

"Clever tongue smothered with lies," he said. However, despite firm words, he couldn't hide the growing lust with each glance down at the gem. This man made of stone looked to be on the verge of breaking.

Evelyn shrugged, returning the ever-ice bead to her pocket and looking toward the man on the barrack roof who Jewel had called Ronossius. "Fine, I guess we can battle it out. Good ol' fashioned winner takes all. Perfect show for the gang of thugs you run here." She cracked her neck, the sudden movement causing beads of frost to fall from her blue hair. "Besides, Ronossius and I never had a real chance at a fight back in the day."

"We're going to put on a show here," Jewel muttered, "but not one of violence or truth." He thrust forward, snatching her by her neck and lifting her on her toes. Both Jestivan leapt to their feet, but couldn't move beyond that, the bottoms of their shoes and clogs frozen to the grass. She still didn't want them to interfere. A raucous arose among the guards, some jeering Evelyn while others cheered on their superior. Ronossius had raised to his feet on the roof, displaying a spindly stature, the uniform baggy on his frame.

Jewel's arms enlarged, muscles tearing the seams of his sleeves. He pulled her in close, their noses an inch apart, and muttered, "I'm going to get angry and shout at you, rant about that annoying defiance you Stillian women have when threatened by a man. Then, I'll threaten you with not just my wrath or Ronossius's abilities, but with the High Warden's arrival to handle you himself. That final bit will shut you up, and you will rescind your combative efforts. I will have you and your two friends here escorted to three separate holding cells in the barrack, where you'll have to wait for the High Warden's arrival. Those rooms are made of holy wood, so forcing yourself out will be useless. There will be a loose floorboard in your room, specifically. I'm sure you're smart enough to find it. You will place the ever-ice in the compartment and wait until I retrieve it via the ceiling of the room below. Once I have my hands on it, I'll make sure neither I nor Ronossius are anywhere near here to put up a fight when you break yourself out. When Warden Sylial arrives later today, it'll all look like a mishap."

Throughout the entire explanation, Evelyn had gagged and hacked, her toes barely on the ground. Agnos saw the ruse here, and it wasn't just in Jewel's words. If this man had truly been choking her with all of his strength, she wouldn't have been able to make any noise. He wondered if anyone else recognized this through their blinding bliss of witnessing a traitor receive the punishment she deserved.

Agnos regarded Ronossius, who had now crossed his arms, eyes narrowed. Agnos knew the names and titles of the Diatia who were dead, so that left three possibilities. That young man with the hair of an elder was either one of the Prim Diatia or the only remaining Cyn Diatia. Agnos was willing to bet the latter—a product of the Void.

Jewel's voice became murderous as he roared, "THE HIGH WARDEN WILL SERVE YOU WITH THE MOST GRUESOME OF—"

A hand connected with his face like a clap of thunder, his head nearly spinning off his neck. Grip slackening, he dropped Evelyn to her feet as she grabbed her own wrist and wrung out her hand with a grimace. "Frost of Francine, man must have a mouthful of marbles!"

He roared and twisted back into a stand, eyes bulging as a massive hand clutched at his frost-burned cheek. "*YOU FROZEN HAG!*"

Agnos no longer knew if this was an act or the real thing. But then she waltzed past Jewel and waved him off. "Where do you want me?" she asked, digging her hands into her trouser pockets as if all of this was nothing more than a bother. "I'll happily wait for your phony king."

The ice gluing Agnos and Tashami to the ground melted to nothing. Jewel's glare shot toward them, and Agnos expected to die in that moment. Thankfully, the officer stretched his mouth open and wiggled his jaw, ice from Evelyn's blow cracking with the movements. Then Agnos saw it—not in the man's lips, but the eyes. Jewel was delighted with the possibility of landing such wealth.

He turned toward the platforms and bellowed, "Show them to their cells!"

Ronossius's sunken eyes didn't follow Evelyn as the guards swarmed her, but remained fixated on Tashami Patter, son of the Unbreakable, the man who had founded an orphanage in the depths of the Void with hopes of healing broken children ... only to fail them all.

Four had survived that night of slaughter and suicide. Just four.

Ronossius bit his lip and drew blood. Sucking down the tang of metal and salt, he imagined it belonging to someone else. And he watched that someone with dead eyes from the rooftop.

24

Decay

Agnos was tossed into a cell on the highest floor of the barrack. He skidded across floorboards before finishing with a single roll into the back wall. His head made first impact. He didn't grunt or gasp, for the blow had knocked him unconscious for a span of maybe three seconds. When he awakened from that black, he struggled to push himself out of a crumpled heap and into a respectable seated position. He keeled over, hands grasping his head to keep his brain from leaking out of his ears. While Jewel knew the ruse for what it was, these other guards believed this was the real deal, that they were going to witness proper retribution for the Still Diatia who had betrayed the High Warden of Ipsas, and the Spirit Jestivan who had wounded two of their peers as an introduction. Thus, despite Agnos's scrawny frame and lack of combat ability, his companionship with them made him equally as guilty.

The scholar gritted his teeth once the pounding subsided, finally lifting his head to glare at the woman who remained standing at the gate. She was obviously Powish with a physique nearly as intimidating as Jewel's. His glower dissipated into something more pathetic at the sight of her. She had pulled a blindfold off him right before tossing him in here. She grinned at the shift in his demeanor. And for added emphasis, she pounded both fists against the wooden bars of the gate and growled, teeth bared and nose wrinkled. Then she left, leaving Agnos in a figurative puddle of his own piss.

Agnos's reliance on others terrified him. He thought he had a better grip of his fear and insecurities in regards to physical confrontation, but apparently that had been because of friends and allies around him, people he knew would have stepped up when he backed down. Alone in this cell, he was reminded of his frailty. His mind and will meant nothing when faced with a fist.

He inspected his cell, running a finger across the umber wood of a floorboard, feeling slight bumps in the grain. This was holy wood alright, and of the highest quality. Vuilni or Olivia would have had trouble pounding their way through it. It was why the Powish guard had been comfortable banging her fists against the gate's wooden beams.

Two more cell doors closed somewhere along the corridor. One sounded like it might have been his neighbor to the left, while the other had shut with a more violent bang that echoed from a distance to the right. That didn't sound like holy wood. Footsteps of guards trailed off to the left and right, as there must have been exits on both ends of the corridor. Agnos approached the front of his cell and pressed his face against the gate, eyeing the closer end. The Powish woman responsible for his concussion sat across from a leaner woman at a small, foldable table. One was shuffling a deck of cards while the other smoked something rolled in a leafy material. A scent of cinnamon and vanilla wafted over him, gray smoke filling their end of the corridor.

"Hey, do you two mind if we talk?"

The question came from the cell to Agnos's left, voice belonging to Evelyn. The two guards, who sat maybe a couple cells down from Evelyn's at the landing of a stairwell, looked her way and shrugged.

"We can't stop you," said the woman opposite Agnos's jailer. "High Warden Sylial wants you alive and in good condition."

"Agnos, you okay?" Evelyn asked.

"Aside from the future brain damage? Just great."

"No worries. Grumpy over there has been taking out her anger on everyone since Jewel's debacle."

"She's testing me," said the Powish guard, eyes focused on her hand of five cards. "I will kill her."

"Pay it no mind, Josie," her counterpart said.

"Debacle?" Agnos asked.

"Do you know why the students call the Might Commander 'Jewel'?" Evelyn asked.

Turning so that his back was pressed against the gate, he frowned, believing he'd had the nickname figured out already. The man's lust for the ever-ice gem seemed telling. "He loves sparkly things?"

"He has one testicle."

Agnos's eyes widened just a little, recalling Evelyn's tease when they had arrived earlier. "Ah … that makes sense."

Tashami's laughter rang out from down the corridor, and a growl from Josie followed. "I'm going to kill them."

"Easy," said the other guard.

Agnos, too, found himself disappointed in his two friends. The humor was distasteful. "I don't think that's our business to poke fun at," he said.

The laughter stopped, and if he knew Tashami, the Spiritian was suddenly questioning his heart. Agnos had a habit of making people do that.

"It's a well-earned moniker," Evelyn said. "You met Bruut Schaap, right—the Power Diatia?"

"Unfortunately," Agnos muttered.

"Well, the Might Commander thought himself mighty enough to torture the boy during one of his many detentions. Bruut was a frequent troublemaker, you see, and the High Warden—wanting nothing to do with the grandson of the Power General—decided to make his commander responsible for dealing out punishment. Jewel, known as Rasha at the time, thought he could gain even more respect from Warden Sylial if he could get the boy to never stir up trouble again. He thought terror would do the trick, which it did for a short while. Whippings, beatings, and being thrown into the Infested Forest without clothes or weapons can do that to a kid."

Silence shrouded the cells save the footsteps trailing down the stairwell. Josie had left her post. Finally, Tashami asked, "So, how'd it happen? The nickname."

"Ipsas received a personal visit from Bruut's grandfather along with a horde of Powish soldiers. Rasha was taken into the Infested Forest, where he was strung up from his ankles from a branch. They lashed his face into eternity, then the general tore out half of Jewel's manhood with only his hand." She paused. "No incisions. Just a single grasp and tug. A surgeon had been on standby following the ordeal, and he had sewn and stitched everything back together save a single jewel. It's said the Power General kept that as a trophy. And that is how Rasha became Jewel."

Agnos's face had contorted from a slackened jaw to a grimace, his entire body cringing with each sentence of the story. A slow whistle from Tashami cut through the lengthy silence. Agnos had thought the scars littering Jewel's face had come from war or a battle of some sort. Torture had never crossed his mind, partly because he couldn't envision the boulder of a man in a position of submission.

"So laugh away, Tashami," she said. "He deserved it. Because while Bruut may have been a pain in the ass and on his way to evil, he was still just a boy, misguided by the very men and women who served as his mentors. Beatings and lashings are one thing; the Infested Forest—especially whilst void of clothing, sustenance, and weaponry—might as well be the Voidlands."

Once Agnos's blood stopped curdling and his nerves settled, he shook his head and exhaled, head drooping between his knees. He had never questioned the morality or sincerity of the directors in charge, but this tiny glimpse of Ipsas's outskirts—not even its main campus—had shone the Light Realm's central school in a new light. Phesaw was a paradise. Even the one man with a questionable past in terms of ethical decision-making, Grand Director Poicus, had dedicated the latter half of his life to becoming a better person for the sake of the youth.

Ipsas is as bad as Lost Wisdom, he thought.

"Are your cells Permanence, too?" Tashami asked.

"No," Evelyn replied. "They have different cells for different types of prisoners. Usually, holy wood would be effective for a Spiritian, but your weaving skills are far too dangerous to gamble. Those wind bullets could likely pierce holy wood."

"Your ice can't?" Tashami asked.

"If it could, I would have dealt with the SCAPD fleet's leviathans with ease. Electricity is about all that'll work ... and special skills like yours."

Just for experimentation, Agnos swung his fist at the floor in a hammer-strike motion. Rather than splintering wood, however, he might have splintered bone. He opened his mouth and released a soundless scream, toppling over on his side and squeezing at his wrist, clenching and unclenching his fist.

"Agnos, are you dense?" Evelyn asked.

"Bored," he wheezed, writhing on the floor.

Footsteps sounded from the stairwell. Agnos rose to his knees and placed his right cheek against the wooden beams. Josie had returned with newfound composure. "He's at the far end in the Permanence cell," she said.

Another figure emerged from the shadows of the stairwell, and Agnos's stomach dropped like a stone in water. Gray hair, wispy and thin, dangling to his shoulders. A boyish face despite eyes set in heavy bags from sleepless nights. A naked, gray uniform, excess fabric folding around the tops of untied boots. The Diatia named Ronossius glided past Agnos's cell without sparing him a glance, sucking the life out of the atmosphere around him and replacing it with heat. For a second, the scholarly orphan who had spent his entire life pursuing dreams grander than divinity itself felt utterly hot and vengeful. A pit of rage consumed his soul.

Ronossius was at the other end of the corridor by the time Agnos was able to shake himself free of the sensation. Slowly ... clumsily ... Agnos crawled toward the gate, trying to spot the walking carrier of anguish, but he and Tashami's cell were too far away to see around the side wall of the cell.

"Tashami ..." Agnos muttered. He repeated himself, but louder. *"Tashami."*

Evelyn had moved to the front of her cell for the first time, eyebrows furrowed in confusion. She was trying to get a look at Ronossius, too. Then the heat that had followed Ronossius dissipated as the entire floor grew unnaturally cold—the kind that iced one's innards. That feeling of foreboding that made a person dread events to come. Faint and weak, he heard weeping from his best friend's direction.

"*TASHAMI!*" Agnos screamed, banging fists and his entire upper body against the bars.

Josie chuckled. Rage joined Agnos's fear, bubbling like magma to fill that pit in his soul. If they hurt Tashami, he would …

He would do nothing. The realization hit him like a Powish fist. He was incapable—not just physically, but mentally. He couldn't stomach hurting someone even if they hurt him. He banged the gate again. "*TASHAMI!*"

And if he hadn't been in an emotional fit, he might have noticed who Evelyn truly looked at in that moment. She wasn't trying to see Ronossius and Tashami; she was watching Agnos break down at the thought of losing the most important person in his life. He was blacking out—she'd seen it enough to know it—with such madness that he didn't notice Ronossius had retreated from Tashami's cell and was now descending the stairwell. Agnos continued to scream his friend's name, and all she could think in that moment was …

Does either of them know the depth of love they have for each other?

*　　　*　　　*

Agnos was panting. His hands squeezed the gate's beams as he continued to whisper Tashami's name. He hadn't known how much Tashami meant to him until the several months spent apart, sailing the Sea of Light absent of his proper quartermaster. All he wanted was a response.

"He's fine," Evelyn said. "We're fine."

Agnos glanced at her, but only saw Josie's sneer just beyond. She was enjoying the show. Had she fetched Ronossius out of bitterness? To spite Evelyn for telling Jewel's story? She had missed her target, but the delight in her eyes meant that didn't matter. Agnos's suffering proved satisfactory.

"I'm okay."

The voice—albeit, weak and ragged—inflated Agnos's aura. His back straightened, rising to his feet as tears of relief flowed down his cheeks. "Tashami!"

"I'm okay," his friend repeated. "I wasn't ready for that. Now I know and next time I'll be prepared."

"What happened?"

"Misdirected vengeance."

"Huh?" said Agnos, unsure of what that meant.

"Seems that Josie wench wasn't happy about Evelyn's story," Tashami explained. "Couple that with what I did to the two guards at the teleplatforms, and they saw sending that guy to deal with me was fitting retribution."

Agnos's eyes narrowed, skeptical but satisfied for now. Not only was Tashami still alive, but he was talking. He didn't know what condition his friend was in, but if it was anything worse than what Agnos had felt when Ronossius had glided past the first time, it was best to not push Tashami. He wasn't familiar with Cynergy. It could rot inanimate objects and disintegrate the soul, as well as other more advanced techniques out of the realm of understanding for foreigners.

Something clicked to his left. A gate swung open in his peripherals. He turned and saw Evelyn strolling out of her cell, the two guards stunned in shock for a moment before dropping their cards and leaping to their feet. Drawing their weapons—a granite maul for Josie and an impractical sickle made of stone for the other guard—they opened their mouths to scream warning only to be silenced by a sheet of ice over each of their mouths, a frozen pillar connecting them to Evelyn's hands. Next were their feet, as ice crept from the soles of Evelyn's shoes across the floor, pinning them still.

Rage peeled Josie's eyes wide; fear did the same to her colleague. Evelyn regarded them as Josie tried lifting her maul and swinging it, but without a steady base, she couldn't gather enough momentum to follow through. The Stillian glanced at the unnamed guard. "Drop it. I have no intentions of hurting you."

The woman complied, letting the sickle fall from her grasp. Josie, meanwhile, continued to fight, ice cracking around her boots and ankles as she tried to wriggle free. Evelyn stepped closer, and the unnamed guard watched her intently as she feared for her colleague's life. Evelyn grasped Josie's wrist, a frozen shell encasing the woman's skin. It crept down the hand that wielded the maul, and before the weapon hit the floor with a bang, a hand of ice sprouted from the floor to catch it.

Ice continued to climb Josie's arms, and now the terror etched its way into the wrinkles in her forehead. Her jaw pulsed as it tried to free itself from the frozen mask that muffled her screams. Ice encased her shoulder, and for a second Agnos could only marvel at its strength to hold a Powish down. Evelyn's EC chains must have been rigid. But as Josie's neck and chest began to crystallize, he realized the lengths Evelyn was about to take.

"Stop it!" he hissed, having to hold back a shout and risk alerting others below.

The ice slowed and halted just as it was about to converge with the frozen gag and swallow her entire head. Frost crept outward and thinned from the ice's edge as Evelyn's slow torture subsided. She turned to regard him, eyes as dead as any of the legends said about Stillian women. "Does she not deserve it?"

"Not by our hand," he said. "I don't advocate murder."

She tilted her head. "The Jestivan have murdered."

"You're right, though usually in order to defend themselves or others." Noticing the counter brewing, he added, "This isn't self-defense. You've apprehended her, and she can't harm us."

"Should I remind you what she caused you're good friend back there?"

"Doesn't mean—"

"—a piece of his sanity."

Agnos paused at that. She had made it sound like something permanent. "Well, get me out of here," he said tersely, "so I can check on him. And don't kill her."

She turned back to Josie. "You're lucky," she said, releasing her grip on the guard's wrist. She then raised a wall of ice between the corridor of cells and the two women, eliminating sight of what Evelyn was about to do. She didn't want anyone knowing she had a key, otherwise guards might have questioned Jewel. They would have definitely told the High Warden. She approached Agnos's cell and stuck the key in a steel mechanism installed within the holy wood, twisting it and jarring the gate loose. He ran straight to Tashami's cell, who had said little during the time Evelyn was trying to ice people.

He saw little different in Tashami. There was no blood or injury. His hair was a stark white as always. His face was clean save a slight pimple in front of his ear. As Evelyn opened the gate, he tried to get a good look at his friend's eyes, feeling as though those would reveal the most. The most damning aspect of a Cynnish attack was nothing physical—not usually, at least. They involved the soul of things.

He'd been sitting against the back wall of the cell—a canvas of gray Permanence rather than the umber tones of the holy wood. He stood effortlessly, smiling as he waved a dismissive hand toward Agnos. "I'm fine, man. Truly."

Seeing nothing to prove otherwise, Agnos decided to believe him. The two Jestivan hugged—Agnos capable of offering only one arm—while Evelyn watched from the cell door. "Let's go," she said. "The High Warden will be arriving soon."

After Evelyn returned the key to its compartment in the floor of her cell, they ran to the corridor's opposite end and down the stairwell, leaving the wall of ice in its place. She claimed she'd woven her Still Chains compactly enough for the wall to last hours. The guards would likely break it before it melted on its own.

They met no resistance on their way through the barrack, down two more flights of stairs and across the commons area of the main floor. They didn't cross paths with guards until they were outside in the moonlight of second-night. It seemed Jewel had held up his end of the bargain. Tashami shot down enemies before they had a chance to engage. Evelyn erected glacial walls to their right as they ran, daggers impaling the other side, while she used a makeshift shield of ice constructed on her forearm to knock away telekinetically thrown projectiles from other directions.

"Screw this!" Evelyn screamed, raising a hand to her side and bringing it over her head in a sweeping arc. Ice spilled from her hands and formed a tunnel around them.

Agnos fought to speak words between ragged breaths. He hated running. "Is this ... a good ... idea?"

"It's the only way we're getting into the forest!" she screamed. "At least if you want to do it without killing people!"

"But we're ... in a bottleneck now. They'll wait ... for us ... at the exit."

"That's what Tashami's for!"

Agnos glanced at Tashami, who was purposely slowing himself down to stay by Agnos's side. The Spiritian grinned. "I got it!"

The tunnel continued to stretch as they ran. Evelyn extended her arms in separate directions to produce waves of ice that froze to form the tunnel's curving walls. Behind them, the other side was closed off, so nobody could attack their blind side.

A man with glowing burgundy eyes stepped into the mouth of the tunnel ahead, a belt of throwing knives at his waistband. He was recording the events, paired to another Devish who was broadcasting it elsewhere. The tips of the knives rose from his waist, vibrating as they defied physics and gravity. Suddenly, Agnos saw several flaws with Evelyn's plan. Not only were they running through a bottleneck, but she was leading and therefore in the way of Tashami's sightline.

"*SHOOT!*" she screamed.

Tashami lashed his arm out to the right and whipped it across his chest, a single finger extended. Agnos couldn't see the bullet itself, for it was woven with air, but he had a feeling it could have been a rock and it wouldn't have made a difference. A gash was ripped into the tunnel's right wall by the wind bullet's trajectory, shaved ice exploding around them. Displaced air blasted Agnos off his feet, and Tashami's timely grasp of his collar was the only thing that kept him from flying backward several dozen paces.

They continued their dash through the haze of frost, and the lack of flying projectiles told Agnos the Devish guard at the entrance had been hit. The clearing haze verified his assumption, as a body was seen crumpled on the ground ahead. The attacker was now stirring in the grass of the ever-forming tunnel. Tashami had obviously aimed for his legs while staying wary of vital arteries. Hopefully, he'd live.

Clang! Clang! Clang! Clang! Clang!

Agnos flinched at each sound, ducking and covering his head with one arm. When he looked up again, he saw throwing knives impaled in the ice walls around them. Evelyn looked back at them, anger crossing her face. "If you had killed him, we wouldn't have had to worry about that!"

"Just keep running!" Tashami exclaimed. "I took care of it, didn't I?"

Agnos hadn't even seen it, but the Devish man must have telekinetically flung his arsenal of knives while feigning debilitation. And Tashami had likely deflected all of them with wind bullets. It was astonishing how skilled a person could be in battle. Agnos didn't care how much he had been around the Jestivan, he would never get used to it. The soundness of their technique. The power of their blows. The speed with which they moved. The reactionary times and instincts. The sixth sense for danger. They did it all without thinking, while he had to count seconds between breaths during a sprint to keep himself from passing out.

The Infested Forest finally welcomed them, but they didn't stop at its cusp. They continued running into its depths, shadows swallowing them as the treetops blocked the light of the moon and stars. Leaves crunched beneath their feet, partially embedded rocks daring their footwork. They heard shouting behind them, but it grew distant as they fled. It didn't sound like they were giving chase.

Evelyn came to a stop, throwing her back against a trunk and slipping down into the grass, breaths heavy. Tashami slowed, holding Agnos's arm and helping him to the ground. Agnos splayed out across the grass, but Tashami pulled him up to his knees. "Nope," he breathed. "Lying down is the worst thing you could do right now. You need oxygen."

Agnos knew this, of course. But there was something about the shock of shredded muscles—muscles he didn't know he had—and burning lungs that trumped his rational mind. He gasped and heaved, gulping down air in ragged chunks, attempting to refuel his blood. Meanwhile, Tashami knelt next to him, holding him upright with a hand pressed against his chest and back.

Catching her breath, Evelyn raised an eyebrow at the scholar. "Is he going to be okay?"

"I don't know. I've never seen him run like that."

It took several minutes before Agnos had the strength to respond. "You didn't see me chase down a kid who tried taking a book from the Warpfinate."

Tashami's stare became a smile, and then laughter. Evelyn quickly hushed him, but only half-heartedly. Agnos plopped down into the grass and focused on steadying his breaths, looking up into the canopies. He didn't know why they had stopped moving, but he didn't hear pursuers. And as odd as that was, he didn't question it. Evelyn was the one who knew this forest and this school, so if she felt safe enough to settle here, then he did, too.

"How big is this place?" Tashami asked, rising to a stand and looking at the trees around them.

"About as big as Phesaw's Rolling Oaks," she said, now up and inspecting the bases of trees.

"What about provisions? We seem to be off any kind of trail."

"Stop worrying," she said. "It's all right here, boys." They looked her way, where she was using the bottom of her foot to push away a log. Beneath it were two sacks, fewer in number and much lighter than Agnos remembered arriving here with. She stepped back as the two Jestivan rummaged through the contents.

"The essentials are there," she said. "Like your glasses and the diary."

Agnos grabbed the primordial tome and flipped through its pages, checking for any blemishes. Once satisfied, he fell back, pressing it tight against his chest, and muttered, "It's a *chronicle*."

25

Sunshine, the Butcher

Toshik stood at the gate to the Brench Estates, peering in through golden poles. Despite the family's vacancy, the grounds had remained in pristine condition. Gentle hills rolled for hundreds of acres, dotted with an occasional tree with yellowing leaves. The building itself was a sprawling expanse of multi-leveled wings, constructed of woven bamboo and shingled roofs. It loomed atop the tallest of the property's hills. He was happy to see the Archaic Kingdom hadn't allowed his childhood home to fall to ruin after the transitioning of its ownership from the Brench family. While business headquarters were now in the city of Balle, the foundation of Brench Crafts remained here at its original home in the Adren Kingdom. What would the family crest on hilts across the world mean if the blades didn't come from the spines of actual spunka?

Lazily, he turned his head and pressed his cheek against a bar. "Okay, let me in."

The guard nodded and then motioned approval to his counterpart. Both women were new to the staff, likely employed by whoever was now in charge of that sort of thing. Nevertheless, this place still brought forth memories: waiting for his mother as she returned from a hunting trip abroad; playing with his little sister in the pond; his father's smile as he placed a gentle hand on his son's head, something he never experienced again after Jun's and Alina's deaths. The treetops of Spunka Forest just beyond the estates ripped the nightmares from the bowels of his existence.

His mother and little sister gutted on the forest floor.

He stepped through the gate, sheathed spunka sword at his waist. Cool winds nipped at his skin through his elastic suit. He had made the decision to adopt the style of many modern day Adrenian swordsmen, appreciating the improved aerodynamics. He felt quick and light, unbothered by loose folds of clothing.

He strolled up the pathway flanked by gardens and frog ponds of the first rolling hill. Groundskeepers, landscapers, and gardeners waved at him with delighted smiles. There were many he recognized, making him feel a little less like a stranger in his own home. Maybe the changes were minimal.

His first stops were the forge and workshop, where he was happy to smell, feel, and hear the familiar sounds of bladesmithing: the clang of hammers on anvils, the squeal of furnace doors opening and the bang of them slamming shut. The high-pitched scraping sound of a nearly finished blade on the whetstone. Dozens of men and women chattering between each other from their stations. The air was filled with the must of sweat, burning coals singeing the hairs in Toshik's nostrils. Sweltering heat wafted across the chamber from over a dozen furnaces, the breeze flowing in from a wall that had been retracted on the far side, doing its best to ventilate the inferno.

He pictured his father among the smiths. Toth Brench's favorite aspect of the family company aside from the number crunching was the craft itself. Wealthy patrons would oftentimes request a blade crafted specifically by his hands, but not many had such money to throw around. Still, Toshik's father would sometimes partake in the process of any commission as a helping hand. His favorite weapon to make had been the katana, which explained Toshik's blade. Even though Toth detested his son's interest of hunting over crafting, analytics, and accounting, he still personally made the boy the finest katana he'd ever made for his seventh birthday.

Toshik gripped its handle, seeing his father's ghost manning an anvil.

His next stop in the estates was probably the most depressing, not because of bad memories—though there were many rooted here from his teenage years—but because of its current state.

The business wing was deserted. Cubicles empty, desk drawers left open, entrails of scrap parchment spilled out onto the floor in some cases. Chairs were scattered around the aisles between cubicles, impeding any flow of foot traffic. Why did it look like the employees had either bolted in haste or ransacked the place?

He turned toward an office at the front of the maze of cubicles. The blinds along its glass wall were open to reveal his father's throne behind a beautiful mahogany desk, sunlight spilling in from another glass wall at its back. Even from his position on the opposite side of the cubicles, he could see the lush Spunka Forest outside.

His steps were reticent as he approached his father's sanctum. He'd received many stern lectures on the other side of that desk, his father displeased by any minor error Toshik might have committed. He recalled a quill in the man's hand as it raced across countless parchment, signing his name and stacking them neatly off to the side, where they'd then sit until the end of the day when he'd hand them off to an assistant for mailing. Five-year-old Toshik had boldly proclaimed the task a "snooze fest", drawing a genuine chuckle from his father.

But there was no chuckle emanating from that office today … No, something far worse. He heard giggling, lighthearted and maniacal. And as he stepped into the doorway, he saw none of the verbal reprimands or boring lessons, but his most cherished memory from this office.

A young Spiritian woman whirled in his father's chair, legs kicked out ahead of her, a hand grabbing the desk with each pass to propel her torque. Straight blonde hair trailed behind while her other hand was raised above her head, pinning a ridiculously large sunhat to her head. She vomited laughter and radiated bliss, her presence as warm as the Passionian sun. She had been his muse … she still was.

Toshik watched the apparition through bubbling tears. Jilly stopped herself and jumped onto her feet, only to fall sideways from a spinning room before collapsing in a hysterical heap. Her violet kimono, red and yellow flowers printed in patterns, splayed around her hips and revealed the upper reaches of her thighs. Caught in the comedy of it all, she was oblivious to her state.

The process of standing up was arduous, dizzy from the spins. Knees and hands first, then feet. She locked eyes with him, love splitting her lips into a toothy grin. She sat on the desk's edge and untied her waistband, overplaying the seductive role as she always used to do. Rarely could she take anything seriously. He needed to look away. He had come here to find closure, and this wasn't it.

Jilly's waistband came undone. The front of her kimono opened to reveal ... a slash wound across her bare chest, blood cascading down her abdomen and legs. She gurgled. More crimson spilled over her bottom lip and down her chin as she struggled to say the final words Yama had robbed from her.

And then she vanished, her ghost dying in silence just like his mother and sister.

*　　*　　*

Lilu had heard it all over the next several days. Reports from scouts across western Dunami spoke of suspicious gatherings inside the roughest taverns of the ghettos, usually no more than three to four people contained to a table in a corner farthest from the reaches of any candlelight. Somehow, despite all her efforts to keep the news of her mother's death within the palace's walls, that information had leaked and then spilled across the city's streets, infecting them with gossip. The public had also caught wind of their queen's loss of sanity, spending hours of her days in the sky tower she had recently emptied to move into their parents' former quarters. Witnessing one's mother step out of a window and to her death would do that to a person. Couple it with their father's murder and Bryson's abduction to the Light Empire, and Lilu could only wonder what kept her sister breathing. That fear was the reason why she had either

241

Frederick or Fane posted in the sky tower at all times. They alternated shifts, watching to make sure the queen remained safe from herself.

This meant Lilu lost most of the help Fane should have been providing with investigating the growing rebels, but she'd risk it, knowing the likes of Horos and Creep were up to the task. Ophala had already recruited what she felt were the most valuable spies in the Intelian stealth. The two men were now a week into their mission. And while she didn't trust Creep as she did Horos—the father of fellow Jestivan, Himitsu—she was appreciative of his skillset. Pilot Ophala had spoken highly of the older man, the hybrid who had spent the past couple decades in a culture that protected its secrets with more vigor than its royals. He moved as silent as a wraith and had worked under Praetor Poicus before the man became Phesaw's Grand Director. He was a well-accomplished concoction of spy and assassin.

Lilu stood on the balcony that circled her sister's old room, elbows resting on the railing as she watched the clouds roll beneath her. She turned her head and spotted Shelly lying on a sofa, the only piece of furniture Lilu had ordered be returned to the tower for her sister's sake. While Benedict and Vistas had pushed for a bed, Lilu refused. She didn't want Shelly to have a reason to spend her nights here, too. Alas, that had done nothing to stop the queen from doing exactly that.

She sighed and looked up at the underbellies of two floating islands, one smaller than the other by half. From this height, she could almost see individual nooks and crevices in the crusted undersides, but that wasn't what she sought. Bryson was somewhere up there at this very moment, and for once in her life she was utterly stumped. She had no idea how to retrieve him, let alone get up there in the first place. Her first solution had been Branian Suadade, but Shelly had refused summoning him, claiming betrayal and uselessness.

She forced out a breath through flapping lips, a combination of emotions making sleep impossible to achieve. Frustration. Exhaustion. Hopelessness. Anguish. What seemed to make Shelly spend most of her time in slumber, as if her brain was shutting down in order to force the passing of time and therefore the healing of wounds, only made Lilu constantly wander the palace's corridors or the city's eastern streets.

Someone needed to keep their eyes open for threats. Nobody knew where Mendac, Kadlest, Tazama, Flen, or that raven-haired girl and woman were. For all she knew, one or many of them could have been the forces driving the rebels. That was what required her focus—not Bryson. The security of her kingdom, once again, was at stake. And with the queen wallowing in the chasms of nightmares that were her reality, the princess would become this family's pillar and its battering ram.

*   *   *

Creep had spent the better part of a week scoping out the many establishments of western Dunami. He spent his mornings in bakeries, pastry shops, market squares, and inns, while reserving the taverns—of which there were near a hundred—for the evenings. He'd split the sectors between he and Horos, and the city blocks of each sector were split between the teams of spies Ophala had assembled from Intelian Stealth. The responsibilities of the two men had expanded in area vastly since Fane's reassignment to acting as Queen Shelly's personal bodyguard. Creep had found this an unnecessary annoyance. While he felt for the girl, she was doing significant damage to the kingdom by sulking in misery.

Creep oversaw northwest Dunami. Scouts reported to him thrice a week, but that didn't mean he had deprived himself of the action. He had spent too many years in Asalka doing nothing. Yes, the job of integrating himself into their society had been difficult, taxing, and time consuming—taking the better part of seven years—but once he'd rooted himself in the company of the zealots, he'd grown comfortable. In the decade plus following that, discovering the secret of the Prim Prince's assassination had been the closest he'd gotten to actual spy work … Well, until Rhyparia NuForce came along.

He entered a tavern he had frequented a lot lately. He made sure to limit his marks, only visiting a handful of establishments within the same stretch of blocks over the week. He'd adopted a scruffy look, beard more unkempt than usual. His signature trench coat was kept at a room assigned to him by the royals under an alias. Save his boots and gloves, the ancients already appearing old and worn, the only thing recognizable about the man to anyone who knew him were his eyes. He could never stop them from skittering this way and that, an old habit developed in his younger years as a hybrid. He needed to see every corner, shadow, door, and window at all times. Awareness was the most important skill of any spy or assassin.

The tavern known as The Electric Eel was nothing of the sort. The barroom was dull and dirty. Pathetic illumination provided by a handful of candles stood erect on a table here and there. Vacant tables sat in gloom, unlit candles as a centerpiece. There wasn't a single Intelight in the building, reminding Creep of taverns in Phelos.

He took his spot at the bar, slumping atop the counter as he groaned and raised a finger to the barmaid. "Three shots, whiskey."

She eyed him from behind the bar, standing several stools down from his own. She was in the midst of wiping down a length of counter that had just been sullied by a slew of youthful, drunken patrons. "I hope you show a bit more courtesy than my last guests."

He lifted his head with a bastard's grin. "Honestly, Sally, when have you ever seen me lose my stomach over a bit of alcohol?"

"Your stomach?" She barked a laugh, turning to the back shelf and grabbing his favorite bottle. None of her product was labeled, but he knew the whiskey in that particular bottle had the best kick to it. "It's your wits I'm worried about."

He chuckled, turning slightly in his stool to get a better look at a cluster of booths near the front entrance. He may have enjoyed Sally's company during his nightly visits to The Electric Eel, but she wasn't why he continued to return. The booths were empty for now, but he suspected they'd soon find occupancy. While the average spy targeted the poorest of establishments where the shadiest of citizens might gather, searching their blackest corners where schemes might fester in the darkness, Creep had learned such plotting—the *true* subterfuge—often happened in places of average standing.

The Electric Eel might have been void of Intelights and other riches, but it was no shanty. Sally ran a tight ship here, keeping her shelves well stocked and the furniture clean. She might have been swindling her vendors and the customers with deceptive tactics such as unlabeled bottles, but it wasn't a plight against the moderate success she'd obtained. And her deception always remained on the conservative side, making her profits average, effectively keeping her out of the spotlight of tax collectors and other royal officials on the prowl for dishonest business owners. She knew exactly what she was doing.

That mediocrity, however, attracted many customers of the lower-middle and middle class. Lost in the barroom, which would soon increase tenfold in customers within the next twenty minutes, would be the cleverest criminals in the city. Usually, these were con artists with many skills; more rarely, they were recruiters. And Creep believed he had stumbled upon that rarity here in the Electric Eel, hiding in plain sight right next to the front door. He didn't have much evidence, simply chalking it up to a hunch, but that was enough for someone with his instincts.

Despite being distracted, he saw the three shot glasses before they thumped against the counter. Many would have cursed eyes like his, but these instances made him appreciative of them. Had that been a knife rather than those glasses, an average person would have already been bleeding out onto the counter.

"Thank you," he said, reaching for the first glass. He reached into his pocket and pulled out a tiny glass vial. After unstopping it, he tilted it over the glass until a single drop fell into the whiskey. He studied it, searching for a shift in color along the spectrum of black, lest he wished a death of poison. Once satisfied with the stubborn shade of amber in the liquid, he tossed it back.

"Why must you offend me every time?" Sally asked. She had retreated to the back counter of the bar, where a slew of glassware was stacked next to a wide sink, her butt pressed against the edge as she watched him with arms crossed. After not getting a response, she said, "I've never seen someone check their drinks for poison—not here. I'd hate to see the amount of enemies you've accumulated over the years."

"My clients aren't always the most forgiving."

She tilted her head. "Why must they be?"

"You don't know my line of work."

"You're a butcher."

He raised an eyebrow after tossing back the second glass. "And what kind of butcher would have as much free time as I do?"

She turned and ran her hands under a faucet, shrugging. "You've been kind enough to not question my practices, so why would I do that to you?"

He downed the third glass, grimacing from the heat. "Kind of you."

"But—" she turned and dried her hands with a rag— "since you've invited my inquiries, I now wonder if you're actually a butcher."

"Of the unconventional mold," he said, holding up three fingers.

She poured him three more shots, the bottle still on the counter next to him. She knew his drinking habits well—or, at least, she knew what he wanted her to know. He could have poured himself the shots, but he'd learned on his first night here to not touch the barmaid's bottles. An unfortunate drunk had gone home with a broken hand that night.

Creep's profession was a lie, of course. Lilu had pulled a lot of strings, setting him up with a falsified license in butchery and lending him a vacant shop for the course of the mission. He spent little of his time there, but an apprentice—also a spy—by the alias of York held down the fort most of the day. This was all by design. York's real job was to spread word that Creep—known as Sunshine in this grand ruse—was not the typical butcher, specializing not in animals, but humans. Those kinds of rumors, however, took time to set up. York couldn't exactly tell each of his customers, "Hey, the owner here butchers people for coin. Let me know if you need anyone … taken out."

Sally nodded, glancing toward the door as three women entered. After waving at them, she regarded Creep again. "I guess I'm not surprised. A butcher named Sunshine? Ha."

He smirked. "With that hair, you're the one truly deserving of such a name."

She laughed, striding down the length of the bar to greet the three newcomers. It had been more of a pity laugh than anything else. He was obviously too old for her taste. He was in his fifties and she was probably in her early forties. She was a red-head. He'd always gravitated toward women with hair color that strayed from the normal browns, blacks, or blondes. During his mission in the Power Kingdom with Rhyparia, it had been Rose. In Yinyon under orders from Poicus, he had fallen in love with a woman with hair of violet. That had been a mistake, and a sudden itch rose along his forearm where a spunka knife was strapped—a knife crafted by an

Adren Assassin and the finest bladesmith in the Light Realm, Soraku Fuuna.

He squeezed his eyes shut, ridding his mind of those memories. He'd nearly betrayed that woman by revealing the existence of her race to Poicus. Instead, he chose to flee the village and return to his home kingdom, reporting to Mynute Senex, a man known for having much more empathy. He never saw her again.

He tossed back all three shots in rapid succession to drown the woman's image, each glass smacking the table with a thud. His face twisted in response to the swathe of heat, and he licked at tingling lips. Sally had already taken the orders of her new customers and was now mixing clear liquors with orange juice she had retrieved from an ever-ice box somewhere below the bar. He glanced at the three women to find them staring at him. They turned back toward each other, however, after making eye contact.

He continued to study them, not as bothered by etiquette standards. Each wore a blouse and skirt of muted gray, conservatively cut to only reveal the neck and below the knees. Their hair, each a shade of 'normal' and thus no interest to Creep, was tied back in buns or ponytails—not a single strand out of place. They were white-collar workers trying to enjoy their happy hour. He decided to not invest much focus on them, but he'd remain somewhat wary.

Throughout the next twenty minutes, customers poured into the building. Four members of the staff showed up for their night shifts. Sally sent one of them home after he strolled in seven minutes late, telling him to not bother showing up tomorrow either. The front door was propped open to give its hinges a rest through the busy evening hours, and the curtains in the front window were parted, allowing Intelamps from an inn across the street to illuminate the barroom with white light.

It was the best time of night, and oftentimes the most difficult part of Creep's job. He couldn't lose himself in the splendor, atmosphere thrumming with the collective anticipation of the weekend ahead. He had to pick his way through the laughter and banging of fists against tables to catch conversations of meaning. Still, it was hard to believe that this was a city with a wasteland as its right half and a couple dead royals to mourn.

He was on his tenth shot with no signs of slowing down. Most customers had given him a wide berth, fearful of the contents that might have hurled onto them. This stumped him. He had yet to vomit this week, and tonight he was pacing himself. Couldn't they tell?

Sally slammed three more shots on the counter, laughing at him in the process. "You'll lose your stomach one of these days, old man!"

He plopped an elbow down and pointed a wobbly finger at her, torso swaying on his stool. "What if I lost my coin purse?"

Her laughter died, and for a split second, he saw the mixture of rage and fear in her eyes. Then he guffawed, a bit of whiskey trailing down his chin and into his beard, as her eyebrows flattened and lips pursed. She threw the rag that had been slung over her shoulder into his face and walked away.

Chuckling, he spun on his stool to face the barroom, throwing his elbows back atop the counter. He allowed his mouth to remain slightly open in a bemused smile, facial muscles loose to express a severe lack of control of his expression. The whiskey coating his lips was a heavy perfume beneath his nose, and the stool was like a cloud beneath him. His body was reacting well to the copious liquor; back slouched and upper arms splayed across the counter. His mind, however, was without ailment. Obscured by the drunken, sloppy façade were keen eyes and an alert mind, for the substance he had dropped into all of his shot glasses was more than just a precaution to signal for poison.

Known as limpincy, this unique sap was produced in only one area of the world—the willow trees of the Prim Kingdom's capital, Asalka. It was a marvel, and one of Creep's favorite discoveries of human kind. Nobody outside of the forest-city knew of its existence. Aside from detecting poisons, limpincy negated the effects of alcohol on one's mind while empowering the effects on the body. Of course, this could also be an annoyance, as a person would frequently find themselves incapable of achieving simple tasks while knowing—in their unfazed minds—that they would have been able to do it under normal circumstances. Fortunately, limpincy's effects were perfect for Creep's line of work. He could remain attentive, but to those surrounding him, he was nothing more than a clumsy, blubbering distraction who'd likely wake in the street the next morning absent of memories of the night before.

While darting in multiple directions, his eyes spent the most time locked on the huddle of figures in the two booths next to the front door, gaze holding there for only a second longer than anywhere else. But for Creep, that short span was long enough to be considered as "locked." Each time he stared that way, he absorbed more of the gathering's details. He reached back, twisting his body to snag a shot glass only to knock it over, amber liquid camouflaging well atop the polished wood. He could have sworn his mind told his hand to open sooner before trying to grasp the cup. The fool man who had chosen to sit next to him—a first-timer by the looks of such a mistake—cursed and stabbed a disgusted glare at Creep, before picking up a pair of spectacles from the bar and marching off to the far end of the counter. Creep thought he had caught a muttering of something like "Bums can't get their lives together."

The hybrid chuckled softly to himself, turned and wiped the spill with the long sleeve of his sweatshirt. It was a stupid decision—his sleeve was about as effective as a piece of cardboard would have been—but a calculated one, playing into that role of bum. He snuck a glance at the two booths of suspects and noticed nobody had looked his way. This was good. He had developed a reputation, meaning the drunken antics that had drawn him attention the first few nights had lost their charm on the regulars. This sort of thing was expected from him, so nobody paid him much mind. In the coming days, that meant he could begin executing plans of nearing those gathered at the booths in efforts to scavenge information with keen hearing.

"You lose your wits yet, old man?"

He spun back toward the bar and smiled ... only to spin too far, slide off the stool, and crash into another fool man who'd sat next to him. To the stranger's credit, he didn't budge. He had shoulders and arms the size of a miner's and a jaw and chin that protruded out farther from his face than his nose. Creep, now a pathetic ball on the floor, looked up at this fool man and suddenly felt the fool, himself. He laughed awkwardly, as if fully expecting what came next: the toe of the man's boot to his face and warmth gushing from his nose.

Creep pushed himself up to his hands and knees, all eyes finally on him. He had done nothing quite as idiotic as this since his first night. His attacker simply returned to his tankard of "man's ale"—because that was likely his drink of choice if Creep were to go by surface-level analyses—and paid his victim no mind. Eventually, the hybrid returned to his stool, head pounding and nose leaking blood into his mouth, and held up three fingers.

Sally slapped three shot glasses on the counter and filled each with a generous portion. These he didn't bother dousing with limpincy before downing them. He sighed with satisfaction into the dead silence of the barroom, smacking tingling lips. Then he turned to the man and extended a gloved hand. The man eyed it for long moment, then lowered his tankard and shook Creep's hand.

The hybrid nodded. "I deserved it. Name's Sunshine."

"Connely," the man grunted.

And with that brief exchange, the people of this bar knew both his name and the kind of guy he was. He didn't need to survey the room to know the people seated at the front booths were staring him down. Of course, this wouldn't gain enough interest for them to invite him over. But over the next few weeks, the name Sunshine would gain traction throughout underground operations with the help of York's word at the butcher's shop. And every time one of the suckers in those booths heard it, they'd think of this night.

They'd know where to find him.

26

The Infested Forest

Evelyn and Tashami took turns carrying the group's bags during the first few hours through the Infested Forest. Agnos offered to sling one over his good shoulder, but they rejected him every time. They were babying him, and while they thought they were being nice, he hated it. With second-day's arrival, the rays of the evening sun split through the broken canopies, casting strips of grass and leaves in golden light.

The journey had been easy up to this point. Aside from the occasional noise in the distance, there were no obstacles or causes for alarm. Evelyn walked several paces ahead of the two Jestivan, taking advantage of the lessened load while the bags were currently in Tashami's possession. She had taken the role of a hunter: combing the forest floor for tracks, inspecting the bark and branches of trees, sniffing at the air, and covering their own tracks when necessary. Thankfully, the healthy grass meant that last part required little work. The blades would flatten beneath their feet, but return to their upright position quickly. As long as they avoided patches of dirt, footprints weren't a danger. That didn't stop here from taking other precautions such as taking multiple paths to confuse pursuers. The three of them had split up on several occasions already for that very reason.

"What kinds of dangers lurk in this forest?" Tashami asked, breaking the white noise of chirping crickets and whistling birds.

"Do you know what a barreler is?" Evelyn asked.

Agnos froze. "No way."

"Yep, there are three of them. High Warden Kwami, whose tenure lasted from 1232 to 1256 K.H., purchased some from the Power Kingdom, claiming the horrors in the Infested Forest weren't intimidating enough. He was quoted as saying 'We have entities of oddities and creatures of finesse, but where are the beasts of strength? Those will strike fear in anyone who dares try to infiltrate our campus ... and in any student who dares defy our codes.'" She turned, raising both eyebrows. "Ipsas's High Wardens aren't known for their sanity."

"That was nearly three hundred years ago," Agnos said, his eyes erratic as they shifted between trees in the distance. "Barrelers only have a lifespan of forty."

"Yes, well, they procreated. Warden Kwami bought six back then, and like I said earlier, there are only three now."

Tashami's eyes narrowed. "Barrelers are those reptilian gorilla things, right?"

"Good job," Agnos said. "I'm impressed."

"I'd die to see a gorilla," Evelyn said.

"Guess we have to take a trip to the Oros Jungle one day," said Tashami.

Agnos sighed. "Let's focus on one adventure at a time."

"You're the boss," she replied, stepping onto a fallen tree that had been caught by the lower branches of a neighboring one. She climbed the incline until she found a spot to stop and survey their surroundings from above.

"You know where we are?" Agnos asked. Tashami plopped down on a cluster of rocks to one side of the grove, taking a bite out of some jerky.

"Yes. I've spent my fair share of days in this place. The Infested Forest was a favorite of the wardens in order to train the Diatia. They'd throw us in here to hunt."

"Ever kill a barreler?" Tashami asked.

"Who said anything about hunting animals?"

Tashami and Agnos exchanged uneasy glances. Then they heard Evelyn chuckle to herself. "Funny," said Agnos.

"Well, it's not as ominous as I made it sound. We hunted animals mostly, but sometimes each other. Other times we had to reach a location first, following trails or clues. It was almost always fun … almost."

She wove a slide of ice from her perch to the ground, then sat down and pushed off. She hit the ground and bounced in the air, pumping a fist as if she had stuck an acrobatic landing. "Not fair," said Tashami, who ran to the angled tree, dropping the bags by the trunk.

Agnos took the bags now that they were free, slinging them over the shoulder of his only arm. They were heavy enough to drag his one side down, but he forced himself to straighten, concealing his grunt with a fake cough. Tashami slid down the frozen ramp on his belly, head first. Evelyn wove an extra several feet of ice at the bottom as a landing strip, sending the Spirit Jestivan gliding across the forest floor. His expression morphed from joy to horror, however, as he noticed a snarl of thick roots just ahead. Evelyn grinned and added a ramp in front of the trap. He hit the ramp and flew through the air, arms flailing hopelessly before crashing into a distant bush.

She placed hands on hips, shaking her head. "Tashami, are you trying to attract attention?"

Plodding over, Agnos stood next to her and regarded the hole in the bush. "You're a different person here."

"Same person. More comfortable."

Tashami yelled, leaping out of the bush and swatting at his arms, prickly leaves tangled in his hair. A gooey substance was stretching between his hands and sleeves as he slapped. "What is it? What is it? What is it?"

"You found a slugger nest," Evelyn said, approaching the bush as Tashami ran the opposite way. His shoes were leaving goo tracks.

She spread several branches apart and peered into the bush. "Come look, Agnos."

Agnos cocked an eyebrow at Tashami. He'd never seen the Spiritian this squeamish. "Sluggers are harmless," he said as he joined Evelyn.

A ring of stones lay on the ground at the center of the bush, holding eight massive eggs. They were black and shaped more like spheres than a normal egg. Two on the right edge lay shattered, innards splayed across the rest, victims to Tashami's fall.

Evelyn placed a finger against the ground just outside the nest and scooped up clear sludge. She eyed it, then wiped her finger against her trousers. "Their father's been gone for somewhere between two to four hours. He'll be back soon."

"Really soon," Agnos muttered. "He's going to be devastated."

"Luckily, sluggers are the most docile creatures around."

"I feel terrible."

She turned to regard Tashami. "That man is a nut. I wish he could have come with us on that last voyage."

Agnos pulled his head from the bush and turned, readjusting the bags as he stood straight. Tashami was rubbing the entire right side of his body against a tree. "You done yet?" Agnos asked.

Tashami groaned and pushed away from the tree. "Are there any streams nearby?"

"Not quite," Evelyn replied. "But we can get to one tomorrow. I think we should call it a day."

Tashami tilted his head. "How big is this forest?"

She stuffed her hands in her pockets. "Depends where you are. The forest circles the entire campus, but at certain spots of the circle it's only a few miles wide. We could have been at the campus by now, but I can't risk waltzing straight in. We're flanking the campus to the south and will end up entering from the west."

"But won't that give the High Warden time to return from the teleplatforms to the campus and station guards at the perimeter."

"Perhaps, but that's not something I'm worried about. Just trust me … I attended Ipsas for ten years. I know things."

*   *   *

The trio had situated themselves among the boulders at the grove's edge by the time second-dusk arrived, the tangle of trees choking out the sun's dying light. Evelyn volunteered to keep watch for the first few hours while the two Jestivan slept. She sat on a lower branch of a tree with her back to the trunk, one leg kicked over the edge and arms crossed in front of her. Her thoughts were on Ipsas, the school that had treated her well during her ten years. She didn't realize how privileged she was until a few months after becoming a Diatia. Most students hadn't shared the same positive experiences as her—and she had either been blind or apathetic toward it.

Ipsas was worse than a monarchy, for its leader—High Warden Sylial—sought advice from nobody. He had no family to keep him in check. He ran a tyranny, and he dished out consequences whenever someone stupid enough tried challenging that idea. There was no greater example of this than his rampage when the Diatia and Energy Wardens began to form factions. He loved the idea of owning an elite squad of fighters who could defend the school from any threat, but that love became fear when he realized that members of that squad could turn on him. The world outside of Ipsas became irrelevant as conflict became internalized. Subterfuge, betrayal, and violence. In some ways, Evelyn had helped spark the fire, believing she could make a difference in the school's culture. Arithmys and Pistimi, the two Prim Diatia, had been two of her biggest supporters. She couldn't wait to see them again.

Movement in the shadows of the boulders below caught her eye. She looked down and saw Tashami rise from his slumber. Agnos, who had been pressed against his friend for an hour, rolled over. It seemed sleep came easily to the scholar when Tashami was around. She didn't know what to make of their relationship. The chemistry between them was ignitable.

She figured Tashami was going to urinate, but the Spirit Jestivan instead made his way to her tree, climbed its trunk, and sat on a branch next to hers. "Hey," he said. "Can't sleep."

"Really? The cold ground isn't comfortable enough?"

"Not at all."

She rested the back of her head against the tree. "I thought Agnos might be warm enough."

He gave her a sideways glance, then shrugged. "He's a small guy. Doesn't produce much body heat."

"The sparks that fly between you two would make me think otherwise."

He didn't respond.

They watched the nighttime forest for a few minutes, their eyes having adjusted to the darkness. The patches of moonlight helped give a sense of location. "What did Ronossius do to you?"

"Nothing."

"Don't feed me lies. It's insulting. I know that man very well, and it doesn't take a psychiatrist to know those screams you were belting out in the barrack weren't those of pleasure."

"He tried rotting off my foot," he said.

Evelyn's neck slackened, her head rolling against the tree from annoyance. "That's it?"

"Yep."

She released a cathartic breath, not sure what to believe. Tashami knew a good bit about Cynnish abilities. Agnos had told her about their mission in the Void years ago. If the rotting story was a lie, it was a good one. Ronossius could have very well tried that as a method of punishment. But she knew what else the Cyn Diatia was capable of, and part of her feared those possibilities. An attack on the soul could prove more damning than one on the body.

"Just let me know if you feel strange," she said.

"Will do …" He trailed off and sat up higher, squinting at the far edge of the grove. "What is that?!"

She lurched forward, fearing the arrival of a nocturnal creature, but then relaxed. A fat tube of blubber slid into the grove, a translucent trail of slime in its wake. It had white skin with yellow dots, a coat of slime dripping down its sides before reaching the underbelly and transferring to the ground, acting as a lubricant to propel the legless creature forward. It was twelve feet long with a girth that was half that. Its middle curled upward and then straightened again to move forward a few inches. "That's a slugger."

He balked. "And is that slime the—"

She interrupted him with a small laugh. "Yes."

"I hate your school."

The slugger paused at the bush with the hole, two flimsy antennae wiggling frantically. "It's scared," she said.

Tashami's jaw dropped as he watched what came next. The creature slipped through the bush's leaves and branches as if it was made of liquid, its entire body disappearing within. A segment of its skin was visible through the foliage's hole.

"How'd it just do that?"

"Sluggers can mutate between a solid and liquid state."

He turned to look at her. "Do I have a liquefied animal on me?"

"I don't know how to answer that."

"What do you mean?"

"I mean ..." She squinted one eye and inhaled. "I don't think the real answer's any better, so I'm thinking we should just go with that."

His eyebrows flattened. "What can be any worse than liquefied animal?"

"Well, when a female slugger lays eggs, the male gains responsibility of caring for the eggs. And part of that care is fertilization." Tashami's nostrils flared, eyes widening. "And sluggers don't fertilize like other animals. Instead of a singular process, it must be done multiple times ... dozens of times ... once a day in fact. A male slugger must return to the nest every day and dissolve atop the eggs to fertilize them. In the resulting solution is a mixture of chemicals, and one of those chemicals is sem—"

"You stop right there," Tashami said coldly.

Evelyn fell back against the tree, one hand to her heaving chest and the other over her open mouth to stifle her laughter. She kicked the heel of her dangling leg against the tree repeatedly, trying to redirect the expulsion of her amusement.

"I hate you," he said. "They need to be exterminated."

It took a minute to regain her composure. She pushed herself into a more comfortable position and sighed. "I disagree. They're adorable, harmless, and most importantly, useful. If extracted properly, two chemicals from their slime can cure burns."

"Agnos is going to be upset he missed seeing one," Tashami said.

"There's plenty of other stuff out here at which to marvel."

He leaned back against the tree, elbows up and hands behind his head. "Go get some sleep, Evelyn. I'll keep watch."

"Are you sure?"

"Yeah."

She eyed him, but then repositioned herself on the branch. "Wake me whenever you get tired. It's not fair that you didn't get any sleep."

"I got an hour. Unfortunately, my dreams aren't cooperating tonight."

"Alright," she said, dropping from the branch and catching it, using her dangling feet to feel for the next branch. "Again, make sure you come to me if you feel different."

"Sweet dreams, Evelyn."

*　　　*　　　*

They stopped at a brook the next day. It was a couple arm-lengths wide, peppered with rocks, and barely deep enough to submerge someone's foot. Tashami had no complaints, however, for it was enough to wash his shirt and body. Agnos stood a hundred paces away, spreading water along his chest, fingers running along the bumps of exposed ribs through the skin. He hated his body enough to always remain clothed. Even when swimming, he kept a shirt on. That was why he stood around a bend in the brook, a thicket of trees obscuring him from Tashami. It was an unnecessary precaution, knowing his friend wouldn't have looked his way anyway. Tashami knew of Agnos's bodily insecurities and thus would grant him that privacy.

"So why do you let me near you when you're shirtless, but won't let Tashami?"

He turned to Evelyn, who had already washed up earlier and was now seated in the grass. Their bags lay next to her. "I've never minded women seeing me," he said.

"Interesting. And why is that?"

"Because their bodies don't intimidate me."

Her gaze dulled. "Only a man's body can? There are strong women."

258

"I know that," he said. "Vuilni and Olivia have biceps like cantaloupes and abdomens like washboards, but for whatever reason, I don't compare myself to them."

She nodded. "You ever think it might be something other than intimidation?"

"Like what?"

"Well," she looked toward the group of trees, "I've seen you sneak glances that way about ten times now. It seems you don't give Tashami the same privacy you expect from him."

Heat flood Agnos's cheeks. "I have not."

"It's possible you actually think that," she said. "Your brain is in automatic denial of such a notion. But you have glanced that way several times."

He stepped out of the brook and stood in front of her. "What are you implying?"

"Maybe you don't want men seeing you because your body is sacred in regards to them. It's embarrassing for you to expose skin around them, like a group of girls in a changing room at school when a perverted, disgusting boy decides to sneak in."

Agnos narrowed his eyes, an understanding dawning on him. He'd never really attacked it from that angle. So caught up in his dreams and studies, concepts such as lust, passion, and intimacy never entered his mind. He looked through the trees, this time uncaring of Evelyn watching him do so. Tashami was running both hands down the length of his thighs, back turned toward them. Agnos shivered.

"There's nothing wrong with it," she said softly. "Attraction is fluid."

He turned toward her again. "How long have you been analyzing us two?"

"I wouldn't call it analyzing. It's not like I've been looking for it. Both of you just make it obvious, so the signs have been gathered through general observation of your habits."

"'Both of you?'"

She smiled, eyebrows climbing her forehead. "Yes."

He didn't know why, but his heart fluttered at those words. He had wanted to discover … His eyes shot up, scanning the trees behind Evelyn.

He'd heard a snap and seen something within the lower branches. He was thankful for the first-day sunlight. Otherwise, the panic would have ravaged him a lot faster.

She twisted on the ground to look behind her. "What?"

A long branch bent downward beneath the weight of an animal, its figure obscured by dense leaves. The branch snapped upward and rustled as the animal leapt to a higher one. Agnos caught a glimpse of a long tail, four legs, and a lean body before it disappeared again.

Evelyn rose to her feet and pressed a hand against Agnos's chest, backing him across the brook to the other side. "A pericul," she said.

Now his heart began to race, breaths quickening. "Pre or post-host?"

"Post, judging by the scent."

He took a moment to properly inhale, then nearly gagged.

Death.

They had backed far enough away to now fully see Tashami around the bend. He was kicking a leg into his trousers, yanking them up by the beltline. Knowing the pericul had already spotted them, Agnos didn't bother with subtleties. "Tashami!"

The Spirit Jestivan turned, chest and abs wet and exposed. He read the scene immediately, noticing the hesitant steps of Evelyn as she held an arm in front of Agnos, and ran over to them. "What is it this time?"

Agnos pointed forward, where a creature dropped from the branches and landed nimbly in the grass. Its skin was fleshy pink save the patches of dull brown fur that peeled away in places. It had a narrow head and long neck, facial muscles stretching and contracting with the snapping of wide jaws. Its eyes were black voids, and it was missing half of its left ear. The head closely resembled a hairless lynx's, but the long, lean body and legs were those of a greyhound. If it chose to run, it'd catch all three of them without much effort. The stench of rot overcame them, as two more dropped out of trees at either side. These had more fur and less flesh.

"We should have gone straight to the campus," Tashami said, now standing on Agnos's either side, serving as another shield.

"There are only three," Evelyn muttered. "Doable."

"I'm not complaining about a challenge," Tashami replied. "It's the fact that I have to deal with abominations like this in the first place. I can shoot each of them down from here."

Agnos shook his head. "It's not that simple with these periculs. If they were pre-host, sure. But post-host periculs require finesse and precision to kill."

"I don't know what that means."

"You have to kill the host."

Tashami straightened and shot a barrage of wind bullets at the trio of periculs, peppering their skulls with holes, black blood spraying out of the back. The beasts flinched, blackness seeping from dozens of holes in their faces. They paused, bore fangs a foot long, and charged.

"Good job," Evelyn said. "Just marvelous."

Conversation stopped, and Agnos was pushed backward by the force of Evelyn and Tashami's arms. He lost his footing and threw back his one arm to cushion the blow. Thankfully, it was nothing but a blanket of grass around him. He scampered backward as his two friends began fighting the periculs. Evelyn—familiar with the strengths, weaknesses, and habits of the animals—moved with precision and purpose, while Tashami relied on pure skill. She screamed out instructions as they battled, but implementing the strategies was difficult in the heat of it all.

"Don't let them bite you!"

Tashami thrust out his hand, creating a gale that toppled one of the less-deformed pericul, its body tumbling across the ground before hitting the base of a tree. He snatched back his arm just as the monstrous one— the one who had shown itself first—snapped its jaw shut where the arm had been. She likely didn't have to scream such an obvious warning. Clearly, nobody thought it wise to allow fangs that big to puncture skin and muscle. But Tashami didn't know the true dangers of a pericul's bite.

They were animals native to the Cyn Kingdom, lurking about the northern reaches of the Almawt Woods. They were similar to typical wild species of cats or dogs in the fact that every pack had an alpha. There was one pericul that had dominion over the rest, usually because of strength.

When periculs approached death, they attracted umbra fairies, shadowy orbs the size of someone's fingertip. While they were called fairies, they were nothing of the sort, for such creatures didn't exist. Umbra fairies were floating bugs that collected Cynergy throughout their lifespan. The more they collected, the more swollen the shadows around their body became. And their method of collecting energy was what made them a parasite.

The two smaller periculs charged Evelyn from either side. She skewered both with separate spires of ice. The periculs hung in the air with the spires straight through their abdomens. Black blood dripped down the ice, flesh peeling unnaturally around the wound. Despite what should have been a fatal blow, the animals continued kicking their legs, heads bucking with fervor. They had another hole in their chest, exposing a gray heart, which hadn't been a result of any attacks. Those had likely been there for some time now.

Tashami was still struggling to tame the monstrous pericul. He effortlessly dodged its attacks and connected with plenty of wind bullets, but he wasn't targeting the right spot. No matter how many wounds littered the beast's body, it wouldn't die unless he killed what was keeping it alive.

"Pin it!" Evelyn yelled.

The pericul lunged and pounced, but Tashami sidestepped, grabbed its tail as it passed and flexed. It yelped like a wounded dog, barks becoming whimpers as its head smacked the ground. He pulled it up by its tail and slammed a foot atop its throat, placing the pericul in an upside down position like a fisherman holding up his trophy catch. The animal writhed beneath his foot, but couldn't beat his strength.

"What is wrong with its heart?" he asked, eyeing the exposed chest.

Evelyn walked over while Agnos remained far away. She knelt next to the pinned animal and pointed at the hole in the chest. "That thing there … the thing roiling in shadows."

"Looks like a blackened leech," he groaned.

"It's an umbra fairy," she said. "It's a parasite that feeds on negative states of being … such as rage, sorrow, or hopelessness. Once it feeds, it digests and excretes it with twenty-times the potency. It keys in on the heart—hence the circling of it—and infects the blood with the excrement, effectively intensifying the aforementioned emotions."

"It feeds off a wild animal's feelings?" he asked, face twisted in disbelief.

"All living creatures have them," she whispered.

"Put it out of its misery already," Agnos said.

"How?"

"Spirit Weaving," Evelyn said, rising to her feet. "Weave a mighty gale directly at the heart. It will negate the umbra fairy's Cynergy, forcing it to flee its home, effectively killing the host."

One hand around the pericul's tail and a foot to its neck, Tashami raised his other hand and released a blast of wind at the chest. The animal went limp, back slouching. He dropped it, then did the same to the other two periculs skewered in the air. A black bug crawled out of their chests, and Evelyn stomped on each one before they skittered away.

"It's best you kill them in their depletion phase," she said, noticing Tashami's look of disgust. "Since you just emptied their Cynergy, they're at their weakest and cannot fly."

Tashami collapsed, crossing his legs on the ground and shaking his head. "I think I prefer the Void or the Sea of Light."

"I just don't think you saw the worst of the Void," she said, letting her frozen spires melt, the two periculs landing in the grass. "It is the worst kingdom, by far."

"Do these umbra fairies leech onto any animal?"

"In rare cases," Agnos said. He kept a forced distance away from them. The thought of black leeches festering around the carcasses made him want to puke. "But periculs are their ideal hosts. Because of how poorly the alpha treats the weaker periculs in the pack, those weaklings become bitter and angry, which makes them desperate. And the most attractive emotional state to an umbra fairy is desperation. It makes the potential host vulnerable. So when a pericul that has spent its life being humiliated and beaten by an alpha nears death, it knows it has one option if it ever wants to return the favor: find and ingest an umbra fairy."

"They *voluntarily* allow these parasites shelter in their bodies?" Tashami asked.

Agnos nodded, but Evelyn continued the lecture. "Because the umbra fairy grants its host eternal life ... if you call constant decay and misery a life, that is. Over time, the host's skin rots, their muscles degrade, and their happy memories vanish. They become a vessel of depression." She shrugged. "The silver lining? They get the momentary satisfaction and glory of killing the alpha that made them so desperate in the first place. But is that worth the eternal emptiness that follows?"

Tashami sat speechless for a few moments, gaze shifting between the three carcasses. "So what we did wasn't really that cruel ..."

"No," she breathed. "We put them out of their misery. And they attacked us first, so it was self-defense."

Looking up, Tashami's final question was a whisper: "Have humans ever tried ingesting an umbra fairy?"

She held his gaze, studying him. "A few, yes. I remember learning in my Cynnish History class about a man named Preloz Henye, who was alive in the 900's. He was the captain of the Mound Guard, which is a force of soldiers who patrol the eastern reaches of the Linsaniun Mounds, granting or blocking access to and from the capital. He got caught smuggling citizens out of the capital, people who wanted to relocate to the southeastern cities and towns of the kingdom. They couldn't handle a life that close to the royal family and the Linsani. It crippled them. Batilearsh is known as a pit of despair capable of sucking the soul out of any foreigner.

"Anyway, Preloz's punishment was to watch the king feed his daughter ten umbra fairies, knowing that meant a life of rapid decay without an end. The king then sent her into the Linsaniun Mounds to spend an eternity of wandering and suffering in the atmosphere created by the Linsani's screams. He couldn't fight back or rescue her after that. A common man cannot defeat a Royal Head."

"That's awful," Tashami muttered. Agnos shared his sentiments, surprised he'd never heard such a story.

"On his deathbed ten years later, Preloz decided he couldn't leave the world without finding his daughter and ending her miserable life. So he ingested an umbra fairy, dooming himself to eternal damnation, and sought out the Linsaniun Mounds. He killed many officers on his way there, including the Cyn General. But he never actually made it. The king intercepted him. They fought. The king won. Preloz was executed by the winds of a hired mercenary from the Spirit Kingdom."

Tashami was hunched forward in attention. "What happened to his daughter?"

"Don't know. The legend says she's still out there, enduring the roars of the Linsani and wandering those mounds like a wraith."

He shook his head. "I was hoping for a happy ending."

"Stories meant to instill lessons don't have happy endings," she said, dragging two pericul bodies over to the cluster of trees that had stood between Tashami and Agnos's bathing spots. "Get the other one for me."

The Spiritian complied and followed her across the brook. Agnos watched, gaze distant. Would he ever go to such lengths to rescue someone he loved? His gaze focused on Tashami, hearing the screams from that night in the barrack again. He grunted in frustration, the idea triggering tears. He stood and gathered their bags, wiping his eyes against his shoulder.

No negativity. Move forward.

27

Steam

The property of Pluzina Senex, widow to former Archaic Director Mynute Senex, had seen better days. Himitsu wasn't sure why he'd expected that same vibrant cottage to appear before him as he and Kaylee stepped out of the prairie grass of the Central Grasslands, but he had. Seeing it in this condition—pea plants in brown rot atop dirt, vines of weeds overtaking the building's exterior, dead plants drooped over ceramic pots hanging from the porch's roof—was devastating.

He, Kaylee, and Sal had left Pluzina's cottage the day they discovered Neeko's grave and the ancients buried with him. And while not without a proper goodbye, it had still been sudden and rushed. The elderly woman had moved a lot less frequently over the course of their stay, and Kaylee had worried about how much time she had left in this world. Alas, they had to prioritize the fate of True Light over her, and Kaylee believed she could still live with help. Sal had offered to stay behind, but Himitsu had thought of a better idea. They would soon discover if that idea worked as they ran down the stone-lain path to the porch. That idea swooped down to the porch's roof and perched itself on the wooden gutter.

"Skyrise!" shouted Himitsu, nearly slipping on the path's rain-slicked stone. "How is she?"

The falcon screamed and flew through a window on the second floor. Himitsu and Kaylee burst through the front door and bolted up the staircase, turning sharply at the landing and following the banister to the master bedroom.

Pluzina sat in a rocking chair, an open book on her lap and narrow spectacles low on her nose. She looked up and smiled. Skyrise was perched on the chair's arm, head twitching, beak nipping at old feathers beneath his wings as he sped up the molting process. A bowl sat atop a small circular table at the chair's side, fruits of different varieties piled within.

"Atta boy, Sky!" Himitsu exclaimed.

Pluzina gave a raspy laugh. "He has been a reliable friend."

"You're up and about. That's good," Kaylee said, entering the room and heading straight for the woman.

"Oh, don't go prodding me just yet," Pluzina fussed, waving the eager apothecary away and causing Skyrise to dart for the windowsill. The falcon's massive wingspan knocked a decorative plate from its stand on a desk, sending it shattering across the wooden floor.

Himitsu winced, then apologized. "I hope that wasn't important."

As Kaylee reluctantly retreated, taking a seat on the bed's edge, Pluzina shrugged. "That's not the first thing he's broken in here. Falcons aren't meant for the indoors, honestly. I don't fault him for it."

"Where's your broom?" Himitsu asked.

"Don't worry about it. Sit with your beautiful woman here."

He looked at Kaylee, and she returned his stupefied glance with a smirk, brushing a stray strand of ivory hair behind her ear. He'd never told her about his infatuation with that habit, but she must have known.

Pluzina waited for them to get settled before grabbing a cluster of grapes from her bowl and popping one in her mouth. She chewed, observing them through wise eyes. "Did you find his grave?" she finally asked.

Himitsu hesitated, unsure of how to answer that, but Kaylee's response was immediate. "Yes."

"I appreciate the honesty. Did you sully it?"

"We ... We did dig it up and retrieve the ancient pieces."

"So you're grave robbers."

Himitsu's mouth remained closed with guilt. Kaylee didn't hold back. "I guess by definition, yes. But every Archain knows a person cannot be buried with ancients. If the person had a written will, it must be checked for successors of the ancient. If there is no will or there are no successors, then the ancient piece is handed over to the monarch."

Taking her time chewing on another grape, Pluzina shook her head. "Don't pretend your motives were lawful."

Kaylee's gaze fell. "You're right. We needed them. They were, potentially, massive clues behind Toono's story. We believed it could help True Light win the war."

"Alright," the widow said. "For how long should I expect your company?"

"Through the night, if you'll allow it," said Kaylee. "Then we're headed east to the Thousand-Layer Loess."

"That's a journey ..."

"I'm still unsure about it myself," Kaylee muttered.

"Well, you're welcome to any food in the kitchen. I don't know everything Skyrise has scavenged from the fields, but I'm sure there's plenty of rodent meat."

Himitsu's nose curled upward with disgust.

*   *   *

Himitsu lay in the guest room bed, the same one he and Sal had slept in during their last stay here. Staring at the ceiling, moonlight casting the space in a deep bluish hue, he contemplated his next move in life. There was something comforting about his and Kaylee's destination. To visit the Thousand-Layer Loess was more than a simple dream of the aspiring apothecary; it had implications for him, too. His mother had tasked him with an important mission, but he had learned more and more recently of his desire to settle down. He may have only been twenty-two, but his experiences were that of an old man.

Whether it was the past year and a half spent with Kaylee or experiencing the wedding of Bryson and Shelly, he knew he wanted her. He knew he wanted a normal life with her. He wanted children, several of them, for he could never make a son or daughter of his go through life without a sibling on which to lean. Bryson and Olivia, Shelly and Lilu—he admired their relationships. He, like so many of the Jestivan, had no siblings. He supposed his situation was better than Tashami's or Rhyparia's, whose siblings had mostly died in tragic ways. He never had anyone to lose in the first place.

He slipped into a shallow sleep, dreams teasing his desires: a home in the Loess, secluded far away from the disasters of Kuki Sphaira; Kaylee returning home at dusk, a smile on her face as she hung a massive satchel of medical equipment on a hook next to the front door; five children sprinting to greet her, asking whose lives she saved that day; Himitsu watching from a parchment-strewn dining room table. They were balance sheets depicting yields, profit margins, and inventory for his tavern that was finding a lot of success in its infancy. While he had given up on drinking alcohol, he'd apparently not lost his desire to be around it.

Ice stabbed his left side, jarring him awake. Still on his back, he turned his head to see Kaylee, pale skin and hair glowing from the moonlight. How could a human body be so cold?

"Mind being my hearth for the night?" she asked.

He shook his head, pulling out his arm from the covers and extending it beneath her. She pressed against him as he enveloped her. He lay there like that for a few minutes until she looked up at him from his chest. Some timid part of him kept him from making eye contact, as if he was oblivious to her gaze, but she knew the battle in his heart at that moment ... the one between fear and passion. That discolored eye saw all.

"Don't worry," she whispered. "I've stopped weaving around you. Out of respect for your privacy, I don't read your aura, but I can see it through other means."

He looked at her, the bridge of her nose a gentle curve. Thin lips moist. Eyes unmoving. She pushed herself closer, lips parting, and they kissed. An inferno blazed through him as their tongues entwined, breaths flowing. His heart thumped as she pressed her hands against his chest. His hands explored her waist, fingers tangling within the straps of her nightwear.

Then came everything he'd physically desired since laying eyes on her for the first time, everything he'd feared, knowing the weight behind the act. He was ready.

Goddess, it was about time.

*   *   *

Olivia rode with refugees for the latter half of the journey to Kindoliya across the Diamond Sea. Transporting hundreds of people across the massive sheet of ice was dangerous with the hail storms, so they had been split into smaller groups. She rode on the second tram ram of this group, about two dozen refugees cramped inside the covered seating chamber atop the beast's back. She sat at the front alongside Vuilni, whose family was somewhere in the back rows of seats.

With Lady Ropinia and Titus remaining in Fort Nalula to oversee the deployment of the other groups of refugees, Olivia's tram ram followed the one carrying Queen Apoleia, Gennaio, and several people who had apparently been very important to saving the slaves in the Power Kingdom. They had been leaders in an organization called the Slave Liberation Operation, or SLO for short. Olivia had spoken briefly with a young girl named Yesenia Itria, orphaned after her parents died in the freeing of the slaves. While most of the SLO leaders were adults, Yesenia was the one exception. Perhaps twelve years of age, she was also the only one willing to tell Olivia what happened that night.

The moon that had gone missing from the sky, that everyone in the Light Realm saw to be Kuki Sphaira's greatest mystery of the past month, was now embedded deep in the crust of the Power Kingdom. It had been dropped directly onto Ulna Malen, the kingdom's capital, crushing hundreds of thousands of unfortunate souls within. And its impact had likely been powerful enough to have caused deadly earthquakes or other natural phenomenon to ravage the farther reaches of the kingdom that weren't buried beneath the moon.

Without a shadow of a doubt, Olivia knew who had done it. Yesenia hadn't needed to tell her. Olivia and Vuilni had run into Rhyparia in Asalka. The girl once known as the youngest Jestivan had almost been unrecognizable to the pair, having grown a few inches in height and swelled several more around the bust and hips. Her hair hadn't possessed the same sheen as before, and slight frown lines had become a fixture around her mouth and between her eyebrows. She had hardened, her outlook on the world bleak and bitter. That conversation had said a lot about Rhyparia, mostly that she was no longer the girl Olivia and Vuilni had known. It stirred uneasiness in them, but to pester her beyond their already-accusative inquiries would have damaged everything about that reunion. That had been before the disappearance of the moon. Rhyparia must have been on her way to the Power Kingdom in that moment. Had she known what she was going to do beforehand?

Olivia and Vuilni steered clear of the topic since learning of it, focusing on the promise of the future for these slaves-turned-refugees rather than the catastrophic events of the past that got them here. Rhyparia had achieved her goal in rescuing the slaves, but had all the death been worth it? And how many slaves or servants hadn't made it out? How many were buried beneath the moon with their owners?

The frozen wall of Kindoliya eclipsed the barren, ice-capped horizon. They were almost home. The ice here wasn't like the rest of the Diamond Sea. Instead of one vast sheet of white and blue, craters dotted the surface, boulders of ice strewn throughout. Olivia spotted a body here or there, carelessly missed by crews responsible for cleaning up the battlefield. The corpses hadn't decomposed—credit to the Still Kingdom's sub-freezing temperatures—but were instead covered in frost, skin a ghostly shade of blue.

A year later, yet the remnants of the Blizzard of Blood remained—a ghostly afterimage serving as a permanent reminder of the side the Stillians had chosen that day, shifting from SCAPD to True Light. Most of the corpses save those in allied uniforms had been disposed of into the sea via holes in the ice formed by Bryson's electrical storm that day. Those holes had since been filled by newer ice-caps, evident as shallow depressions along the surface. It was unlikely this section of the Diamond Sea ever returned to—

Cries from behind. Olivia and Vuilni stood and whirled, catching sight of restlessness in one of the middle rows. Several people had huddled around something, screams of distress ringing out from a few of them. The rest of the refugees, too far away from the focal point to have the same reaction, stood and craned their necks to see, murmurs creeping across the crowd.

"He's dying!" a man screamed from the center of the crush.

Olivia ran. She reached the end of her seats and fought her way past the crowd along the side of the seating chamber. She reached the commotion and forced her way through the crush, shoving people awkwardly into their chairs as her strength proved its worth.

The boy was blue, lips pale and freckled with frost. The Powish hadn't dealt with the cold well since arriving to the Still Kingdom, and while some had grown ill, none had died. Olivia's mother had made sure everyone was provided with thick wool coats and plenty of layers beneath. Only the nose and eyes were exposed of each refugee, turtleneck collars pulled up over their mouths. That apparently hadn't mattered for this boy. And that made sense. He was tiny, maybe seven years of age. If anything, he needed a heat source aside from his own body.

She placed a hand against his cheek and felt no warmth. She dropped to a knee, leaned in, and tilted her head so that her ear was below his nose.

Nothing.

Placed two fingers against his neck.

Nothing.

The man next to the boy was the only one still seated, his torso twisted as he squeezed the boy's gloved hand. "My boy's not dead!"

Olivia looked at him with sullen eyes, then back to the boy. Administering CPR would prove useless because this wasn't a matter of forcing his lungs into functionality. His body had simply stopped, shock-induced from the frigidity. The final defense mechanism to deal with the cold. Instead of fighting and losing, it had chosen to shut down.

She placed a hand against the boy's cheek as the father cried, trying to manipulate the energies within her and force them out to produce hot water. Mimic something close to the anomaly of that day of Phesaw's invasion, if only on a miniature scale. Alas, her hand remained dry and the boy remained dead.

She dropped her hand, letting it fall into his tiny lap bundled in pillowed layers. And as the father grabbed the boy's head and tugged it into his chest, spilling tears into the fur along the hood's hem, Olivia watched and allowed the shame to fill her. Her younger self would have funneled that grief into Meow Meow. A more recent her would have looked away to spare herself the trouble of grieving.

She couldn't do that anymore.

Himitsu had lent her new perspective with his lesson of empathy and sentimentality. He had helped her see the unhealthiness of the walls she had erected within her heart and mind. So she watched the father hold onto his lifeless son, and heat flushed through her body. She fell onto her butt between the cramped rows of seats, back smacking Vuilni's shins, and felt the tears stream down her face. She clamped her hands in fists and felt warm wetness on her skin. She opened them and studied her palms through the tears. Water seeped out of her skin, steam rising from the droplets.

She would try to save the boy that day, but either it was too late or the water too little. And despite the progress—the first signs of her ability in years—it felt more like failure.

28

The Five Pogu

Bryson awoke on his fourth day in the Light Empire to an eyeful of sunlight. He kept the window of his room open as the sun's rays proved a fitting alarm. The altitude of Squad Three's capsule allowed a continuous breeze to drift inside, casting his bangs sideways along his temple. He lay still momentarily, eyes locked on the ceiling.

It had been another rough night, dreams riddled with his wife and son, only to wake at odd hours to find her not next to him. The feeling was alien. When he'd traveled to the Still Kingdom to gain their allegiance or to Brilliance to get into Mendac's laboratory, he'd known them as temporary stays. That had been a pillar for him when away from family. Here, he didn't have that luxury of knowing. He hadn't come here of his own accord, and nobody made it sound like he'd return home anytime soon. In fact, they continued to call Capsule Three his home.

Efforts to find out information from his actual home from Suadade had been useless. The Adrenian, who, like Thusia, had neglected his charge's summons for months due to imprisonment, claimed that she was now neglecting his efforts of reaching her. He quickly quelled Bryson's first concern: her death. Bryson couldn't shake that split-second glimpse of Benedict, worrying the nefarious crimes of brewing rebels had spilled into the palace. Suadade, however, made a point that if Shelly were dead, he would feel it. If her life was in danger, he would feel it. It was how Thusia came to aid Bryson during the Blizzard of Blood.

Suadade's words of comfort only extended so far. Because while he proclaimed Shelly didn't stare death in the eyes, he was apprehensive about something stirring along the string that connected them—that sixth sense Branian apparently had in regards to the royal firstborn they were tasked to protect. She was alive and in safe company, but struggling mentally and emotionally. He and Bryson chalked that up to her husband's disappearance. And Bryson was pleased to know Suadade was equally aggrieved about the crass nature of his abduction.

As for the queen's refusal to allow Suadade's summoning, Bryson believed he knew Shelly well enough to know it stemmed from bitterness. He had told her about Suadade's arrival at his bedside with Thusia and Quincy. She felt betrayed and hated the Branian for it. Hopefully, her rational side would trump the emotional ... and soon. Bryson was dying for an update, and she must have been, too.

Bryson got out of bed and studied the bulletin board above the desk. It was a canvas of brown, absent of any pinned parchment or notes. This room typically belonged to potential Bozani—those who died in the real world and were strong enough to be reborn here, yet weren't at the stage of maturity to be called Bozani. They were students sequestered to a squad as the celestial equivalent to an intern. According to Quincy, most died within the first few months of their existence in the Empire, unable to handle the Tahara that seeped within the Starlight's walls of quartz. According to Thusia, that said a lot about Bryson, a mere mortal. He'd only been here a few days though.

Today was huge. After spending the first few days acting as a tourist with Thusia as his exuberant tour guide, he was finally going to receive some real answers about this place, the war, and his purpose in it all. Sure, he met a few interesting Branian while passing through the ivory

275

corridors—even stumbled upon a nonhuman servant, its humanistic figure and features sculpted of the same quartz that made up the Starlight—but nobody of real note from what he could tell.

He walked with Quincy today, the mountainous man patient with Bryson's more human-like gate. Not everyone could cover four paces with one stride. Not everyone could faze through walls without holding someone's hand. The Pogu understood that, displaying another trait of the many Bryson found likeable in the man. First impressions notwithstanding—the hardened, dutiful pet of the empress sent to escort him to the Empire—he could see why a woman like Thusia gravitated toward him. He was a teddy bear.

"Nervous?" the teddy bear asked.

"Antsy. I just want direction. It's clear the Empress views me as a soldier, which isn't unordinary for me. I've been fighting for the past five years. But being a soldier is easier when there is reason … motive … stakes … of the personal sort."

Quincy grunted. "Many want to believe this war is a matter of grudges—a personal matter to Empress Tonitrua. But I don't believe she'd allow a war of this magnitude—on an empirical scale that will determine Kuki Sphaira's fate—to happen because of petty grievances." He reached upward and slipped a massive hand into the ceiling, his other grabbing Bryson's wrist. They warped through the quartz to a corridor above, the wave of heat consuming him. They began walking again, and Quincy continued.

"Personal motives don't always equate to passable validation. And Empress Tonitrua knows that—or at least I believe she knows that. There is a bigger picture here, one wherein people like you and I sit, but because of our periphery position are oblivious to all of it." He gazed sidelong at Bryson. "The stakes are order … the balance of this world, preventing a slip into chaos. There's a reason why killing a royal firstborn is an Untenable. It causes the scales to tip in favor of one side, and in a rather literal sense." He shook his head. "It started with the Prim Prince's assassination. That tiny event in the kingdoms triggered something massive here. That's when the Dark Empire struck at us."

"I don't understand. How can they strike when they're not even in the same realm? Are there teleplatforms here? And if so, can't they be turned off as a precaution?"

Quincy chuckled. "You are a simpleton, which isn't your fault I suppose. We have our own methods of travel between the empires. Something less predictable, unfortunately. There's no way of stopping them if they chose to enter and no way to pinpoint locations of entry. The only safe space is the Starlight, which has to do with Tahar's Cavities and these quartz walls."

He paused in front of one such wall as they stepped into an empty chamber, a domed ceiling with a circular skylight at its center. Sunlight refracted off the quartz architecture, adding translucent rays of gold that crisscrossed throughout the rotunda. It was a wide rectangular wall of quartz, breaking the gently curving pattern of the rest. Its texture was different, too, jagged edges webbing across the surface. It looked like a true gemstone, uncut and ripped straight out of the crust, splintered from some kind of physical blow.

"What happened here?" Bryson asked.

Quincy placed his palm against the wall, but it didn't faze through like it would have anywhere else. In fact, the quartz looked to be rejecting his touch, as his skin sizzled and popped against it. The scent of scorched skin hit Bryson. The Pogu's right eye twitched, but he didn't grimace or show any signs of pain beyond that. Slowly, liquid light crept through the cracks of the quartz, and as it progressed to the panel's outer edges, the wall became a waterfall of gold.

"Take my hand," the Pogu said, reaching toward him with the free one.

Bryson took it, fearing what came next but refusing to back down. Quincy stepped through the blinding liquid with Bryson in tow.

Fire, or that's what it might as well have been. Luckily, it lasted for only a split second before they were on the other side.

The chamber beyond was humbler in size than the previous. A sturdy wooden table occupied the center. Six chairs were set at the table, five of which were gathered at one end—one at the head and two flanking each side. The sixth was placed at the opposite end, where Bryson assumed he'd be sitting. The room was constructed of the Starlight's familiar quartz, but shattered and uneven like the wall through which he and Quincy had passed. Clearly, it served as a protective measure, keeping unwanted guests from entering or eyes from seeing.

"Go ahead and take a seat," Quincy said, gesturing toward the chair at the end of the table.

Bryson obliged while Quincy settled down in the first seat to the right of the head chair. He wasn't sure if that had been the Pogu's choice or someone else's. Quincy had adopted a more sophisticated look today, opting out of his tank-tops or raggedy tunics in favor of a stunning maroon cloak. A pin shaped in the Technous symbol of "3" connected the collar of his cloak at his right collarbone. Beneath he wore a fine silk shirt of silver tucked into sturdy black pants.

Bryson sported a spare maroon cloak from Suadade, which he had come to learn was Squad Three's color, the stylized Technous "3" their insignia. He had been borrowing Suadade's clothes daily since he was never offered the chance to pack personal belongings before being abducted.

"You ready?" Quincy asked. After Bryson nodded, the Pogu stomped a black boot atop the cragged floor. White lights shot across crevices in the quartz floor and up all four walls of the room.

Four figures entered the chamber from Quincy's end, stepping out of the wall as if it were the surface of a glowing pond, quartz rippling outward from their bodies. Bryson recognized none of them, though each possessed distinguishing traits. There was an air about them that emanated power and aristocracy, including a somewhat disfigured man who had entered in a wheelchair. They took spots at the table without fuss, making Bryson believe there was an order to it.

A woman sat in the head chair, directly across the length of the table from Bryson. She had removed a bouquet of a dozen roses from her back, held in what looked to be a quiver meant for arrows. He only got a glimpse before she placed it somewhere on the floor, leaning it against a leg of the table, but that had been enough to appreciate its slender, lengthy craftsmanship of ivory leather. The woman was tall and bald. Sunspots dotted her scalp. She had black eyes, olive skin, and earlobes that stretched an inch longer than most. She wore a cerulean kimono secured at her midsection by a white cloth waistband. It was tied in the back in what must

278

have been a huge bow, its loops wide enough to be seen from the front, jutting out from both sides of her like wings of ribbons. The Technous symbol for "1" was etched down the upper length of both lapels, explaining her position at the head of the table.

She wasted no time in commencing the meeting, which felt more like an interview or disciplinary panel from Bryson's perspective. He was far enough removed from them to make him feel isolated. Only Quincy and the Squad One leader visually acknowledged him. The other three perused parchment that had already been stacked in front of their seats.

"My name is Withornis Storm," the head woman said, her voice terse and dry. "You may address me as Thornstorm. We're here today to lay down the ground rules of the Starlight and Light Empire. Rules you must prove to understand and to which you comply before the Strasan take you on for their own meetings. Think of this as a prerequisite."

The name didn't ring any bells for Bryson. His education at Phesaw suddenly felt lackluster. Surely, he hadn't been so poor a student he couldn't remember the name of someone strong enough to not only have been reborn as a Bozani, but risen to the rank of Squad One Pogu. Was Withornis Storm ... *Thornstorm* ... one of those obscure heroes from a secluded home like Quincy had mentioned? At least the name made sense, considering the quiver of roses she had removed from her back. Besides, he didn't know Naipa, too ... And she was a Strasan.

"We'll start simple," she said with a brief glance down at her parchment. "There are twenty-four total Bozani in existence. There can never be any more or fewer. If one dies, they are replaced within days. Death, however, is rare. Retirement is far rarer."

Bryson, who had been preoccupied by the absence of any sort of introductions from the other Pogu, raised an eyebrow at the word "retirement." Thornstorm's explanation followed immediately.

"If a Bozani chooses to retire, he or she is, essentially, forfeiting their second life."

"So retirement is basically death?" Bryson asked.

"Voluntary."

He said nothing. Who was he to question the decisions of beings who were centuries old?

"There are four tiers to the Bozani hierarchy," she continued. "The lowest are the Branian, of which there are fifteen separated into five squads of three. The next tier is us, the Pogu. There are five of us, each one assigned as the leader of a squad. As you've come to learn, Pogu Quincy Gralth is the leader of Squad Three, making him responsible for the Branian trio of Thusia, Leon, and Aestys."

"Why'd they throw this boy in with the messiest of squads?" asked the man in the wheelchair. He sat on the left side of the table, in the position farthest from Thornstorm. He had long blonde hair that fell in strings to his shoulders. His arms, chest, and abdomen were strong, but his legs had atrophied from disuse. Each time he turned to look at Bryson, he revealed a damaged left side of his face. His ear was missing and he seemed to have popped vessels in his eye, blood filling the iris with red. When shuffling through parchment, Bryson noticed the man was also missing two fingers on his left hand.

"That's grand coming from a Pogu who leads the most useless squad," Quincy retaliated. "When's the last time a Squad Five Branian was assigned to a royal firstborn? I have two currently."

"Three centuries," said a toffee-skinned woman seated next to Quincy, positioned farthest from Thornstorm on the table's right side.

"Enough," Thornstorm said. She glared at the man in the wheelchair. "Don't interrupt me again, Zenoss."

"You're not our superior. You may be the Pogu of Squad One, but you're still a Pogu like us."

"We'll test that theory when I speak with Naipa, Magnifica, or Rhysel."

He shook his head, disgust in his face. "Yes, run to the Strasan. As if spending your life in pursuit means you're going to catch up. Again, you're just a Pogu."

The room fell silent, and Bryson made sure to study every reaction. He could learn a lot about a person by simply getting a gauge of their reactionary impulses. Aside from Zenoss and Thornstorm, the other three remained mute, lips pursed as they watched their two peers stare each other down. Zenoss's glare of contempt had shifted into a smug grin, perhaps satisfied with the woman's silence. Bryson couldn't help but feel like he was looking at the Jestivan. It appeared it didn't matter if a group of comrades were mortals or divinities, there would always be friction built from complex relationship dynamics. He liked it. This short exchange had made them appear more human—on his level.

Thornstorm didn't retaliate. Her expression remained passive as she nodded and gazed down at her parchment. "Well, Zenoss, I think we can all agree that the last place we want to be at the moment is here, laying down ground rules to a boy. So, I ask for you to limit your interruptions in hopes that it will expedite the process." She looked up with a casual smile. And though her next question was directed toward everyone, she only had eyes for Zenoss. "How does that sound, everyone?"

After a swift round of confirmations, Thornstorm redirected her attention to Bryson. "Our apologies. Where was I?"

"You mentioned the fifteen Branian and five Pogu," he said.

"Thank you. Above the Pogu are the three Strasan. Of the four tiers, they are the second most powerful. If the Branian are guardians and the Pogu executioners, consider the Strasan as specialists. They have specific skillsets that fit specific needs. And they are not to be crossed if you value your life."

He thought of Naipa, who had come across as a forgetful woman. He knew not to question her status, but couldn't rid himself of the image of her wandering around the Starlight halls in confusion.

"Only one person occupies the highest tier, and that is Empress Tonitrua. She is absolute. She is law. Any questions so far?"

He shook his head, and she flipped to the next sheet. "Aside from the twenty-four Bozani, there are creatures that live in the Starlight. I'm sure you've ran into a few of them. They are constructed of quartz and fueled by Tahara. We call them *luzens*, and they serve as the Starlight's staff.

"As for matters of more importance, know that as you grow into your wings and develop use of your Tahara, the more the Starlight's quartz will respond to your touch. Thankfully, this growth will come naturally to you. Most people don't know themselves well enough to rein in their wings. Remember that this building isn't an inanimate object; it's a living thing … at least while Tahar's Cavities are spilling energy into it. When you begin weaving your Tahara with its walls, it's like having a conversation. Tahara is everything to the Light Empire." She paused, as if for effect, and hardened her stare. "*Everything.*"

Bryson nodded during the pause that followed, thinking she was looking for some kind of understanding. There was a weight to that final word and the way every pair of eyes looked at him when she said it. All five Pogu wanted to read his reaction.

"A lesson on lore that predates the Empress herself," Thornstorm said, sliding over a leaf of parchment to eye the next. She studied the new sheet for a moment, eyes narrowing.

"Yes," said the man who sat to her left. He was the only one who hadn't spoken yet, hair a deep black save for graying roots. Judging by his massive beige toga, he was feeble and perhaps the shortest of them all, though Zenoss's position in the wheelchair made that difficult to distinguish. Despite weak forearms extending from the toga's elbow-long sleeves, Bryson reserved hasty critique. The man's blood red sash had the Technous character for "2" embroidered in gold, marking him the Pogu of Squad Two. "I find it odd how much Empress Tonitrua is willing to reveal to this boy."

The other three followed suit, finding the parchment of which they spoke. The two Pogu who sat closest to Bryson—the handicapped man named Zenoss and the toffee-skinned woman—looked up at him as if searching for something. Quincy could only lean back and shake his head, smiling as if he wanted to chuckle.

Thornstorm continued, deeming it unnecessary to point out her obvious agreement with the man in the toga. "Bryson, while you didn't know her name or if she truly existed, you and other mortals called the Light Empire's leader a goddess. Truly, she isn't anything of the sort, which is why we refer to her as an empress. In her first life, she was an Originator, Queen of Thunder. Kuki Sphaira has five true gods, but we'll place our focus only on two in this meeting because they are what matter most to the empires: Tahar and Mulawith, neither of which holds gender."

"They're something other than gods," said the man in the toga.

Thornstorm held up a hand. "We don't want to hear it." She continued, "Tahar is the God of Light, Mulawith the God of Darkness. Their existences flirt between the border of metaphysical and tangible. On one hand, they can't will themselves into action or manipulate the world, making their presences seem conceptual. On the other hand, they exist in plain sight and can be interacted with in a physical sense, giving them a concrete foundation."

Bryson plopped an elbow on the table and held up a finger. "I'm going to stop you there. I have no idea what you just said."

"Fair enough," Thornstorm said, letting slip the first smile he'd seen from her. "Let me help you visualize it since this is vital information. Think of Tahar as a god with human traits. You have a body, right?"

He glanced down at himself, then looked up and shrugged. "Looks like it."

"The Starlight is Tahar's body. This quartz is its skeleton, nerves, and arteries."

"We live in a god?"

Quincy burst into laughter deep enough to thrum through the table. The Squad Four Pogu grinned, as did Zenoss and Thornstorm. The man in the toga, Pogu of Squad Two, did not.

"The actual answer veers back toward my original explanation that you weren't fond of, so we'll just go with yes … the Bozani live inside of a god."

"Does that mean the luzens are parts of a god?" he asked, finding himself fascinated by details they probably didn't care to give attention.

"Again, sure," she said. "But can we get back on track?"

"Go ahead. Sorry."

"The Starlight has six Gate Towers, which are skyscraping towers that hold radiant orbs of light above them. You met with Empress Tonitrua, so I'm sure you saw them … like six stars plucked from the night sky. Those are Tahar's Cavities, feeding its quartz body—the Starlight—with liquid energy. This mimics the human body, which has six unique cavities in the heart, soul, muscles, right and left half of the brain, and eyes, each one capable of spilling one of two energies into your body. That means each Gate Tower holds an important element of Tahar's being. When you spoke with the empress, you were standing beneath Tahar's eye—the most important cavity of the six."

"Explains its size," he muttered. His eyebrows crumpled, and he pinched his temple. This was giving him a headache. "But, why don't the other cavities spill out Passion, Spirit, Intel, Adren, or Archaic Energy if those are the energies that correspond to them in a human's body? From what I saw, all six spilled Tahara."

"Because those energies you just named, in their base forms, are the same. They were created from the parent energy, Tahara, which is the energy of the god, Tahar."

"You skipped the bit about Essences," Quincy said.

"The notes specifically say to not mention them," said the Squad Two Pogu. "Leave that for the Strasan meeting. We're already on a tangent as is."

Thornstorm glanced at a wristwatch and frowned. "Alright, let's wrap this up. The Starlight is the body. Tahar's Cavities are both the body's life force and shield."

"So what does that mean if one or all of them were to stop functioning?" Bryson asked. "Is that even possible?"

Thornstorm's lips pursed. "And why do you think we're at war? Because we don't want to find out. With each death of a powerful mortal in the kingdoms—especially a royal firstborn or Royal Head—Tahar or Mulawith weaken depending on the energy of the person snuffed. When the Prim Prince was assassinated years ago, the Dark Empire felt that loss. Mulawith's Morality Cavity vanished, the balance between the two realms thrown askew. Just recently, every royal of the Power Kingdom was annihilated, marking the disappearance of the Courage Cavity… and Emperor Mialo has grown desperate because of it."

Bryson sank in his chair, the epiphany a mighty blow.

Thornstorm nodded, appreciating his realization of the situation's hefty significance. "So Mialo and the rest of the Gefal wish to attack Tahar directly, either to restore the balance or entirely destroy it in their favor. And they do that by targeting the Cavities, for the only thing that can damage Tahar's Cavities is Mulawi, the energy of darkness … of shadows."

"The Energy Gates hold them pretty far out of reach," Bryson said.

"That's our saving grace," she replied. "The Gefal can enter the Light Empire through darkness or shadows outside of infused quartz. Tahar's

Cavities prevent them from being able to step right into the Starlight or onto its grounds, forcing them to enter through darkness in the outskirts of the city. Alas, even that's still a threat."

"There's no way they could get to the cavities with a start point that far away," he said.

She tilted her head and exhaled shortly. "I advise not trying to predict the capabilities of Gefal and Bozani. You will always end up underestimating them."

He didn't argue, seeing the flawed arrogance in his statement. They began gathering their parchment into stacks. "Is that it?" he asked.

"Pogu Quincy and Branian Aestys will take you on a menial assignment in the city whenever they feel you're ready. Based on the results of that night, you will either be granted a meeting with the Strasan or you will go again." She finished tapping the edges of the parchment into a neat stack and looked up. "Any questions?"

Bryson regarded the Pogu of Squad Two, dressed in a beige toga and crimson sash, his hair black with silver roots. He looked at the Pogu of Squad Four, the woman with smooth, light-brown skin, wearing a shamrock green trench coat adorned with golden tassels that hung from its pockets and shoulder patches. "What are your names?" he asked, gaze shifting between them.

"Gatal Accus," the man said.

"Sephrina Jordan," the woman followed.

And for the first time since arriving in the Light Empire, Bryson recognized a historical name. He was sitting within a few paces of fairy tale legends: the *First* and *Second of Five*.

He watched them leave, slack-jawed. Quincy stayed behind, an eyebrow raised at the mortal. "Can you move?" After not getting a response, the man chuckled. "I guess they were more of what you expected up here." He walked over to Bryson and placed a hand on his shoulder. "Don't forget they were once human, too. They aren't gods."

Bryson knew this, but it didn't quell his admiration. As much as he had feared comparing them to Mendac, when he looked at them, he saw Debo's equals—no one else. And Debo, in all due respect, might as well have been a god. How else did a boy view his father?

285

29

Royal Rage

The Adren Assistance Academy had been Yama's home at one point. From the ages of four to eleven, she trained and was housed here until she was sent to the Archaic Kingdom to meet her first charge: Toono. Calm slipped over her as she stepped into the academy, familiarity and nostalgia taking its roots in her memories.

The architecture followed the same trend of traditional Adrenian buildings. The main lobby was a sectioned off area of a grander chamber, separated from the sparring area by a low-rising wall, where parents typically sat to watch their children. She remembered how distracting that had been for the young ones, as they'd constantly look toward the lobby for smiles of affirmation and words of encouragement. Given her parentless upbringing, it was something she never had to worry about. Her audience had consisted of herself and Master Ichi.

A class of roughly thirty children, likely senior students judging by their prepubescent frames, went through foot-stance drills, wooden swords with rounded edges swooshing through the air. They wore the modernized elastic tight suits, while the instructor stood at the front in a traditional kimono, covered from the waist down by a loose hakama, seven pleats ironed perfectly into the front and back. While Master Ichi allowed the students to adapt to the evolution of swordsmanship, her staff was required to maintain Adrenian customs. Yama had always adored the elegant outfits of her instructors, and they made moving in them look easy.

Yama lingered at the lobby's rear, sidestepping down the building's front wall until she found a spot in the corner next to a tall potted bamboo plant. The parents were seated on the floor at the low-rising wall, pillows beneath them as cushion, a chorus of shouts from the students with each strike. She didn't recognize this instructor, a tall man with dark skin and fierceness to his glare. Yes, Master Ichi really knew how to pick them. The woman's fondness for Adrenian traditions extended beyond clothing and architecture, seeking staff members who fit the mold of their kingdom's mightiest swordsmen and women in history: tall and lean, with a personality of either a   bear—stoic and unyielding—or a lion—ferocious and unrelenting. Nothing timid entered Master Ichi's doors, and if it did, it was shown its way out.

Yama smirked for the first time in years, salt and must faint in the air, open window shutters struggling to combat it. Aside from the moments marred by Toshik's arrogance, she could only revel in the atmosphere here.

A door to the right side of the lobby opened, and Yama had to force herself to not visibly react at the sight of Master Ichi. She was tall and olive-skinned, raven hair sleek and long, the ends cut in a perfect line. It shifted loosely with even the slightest movement of her head. The only times she let it hang naturally was when she wasn't training or instructing. Otherwise, she tied it into a tight bun against the back of her head. A white kimono was visible on her upper torso, a red hakama tied at her waist as skirt legs fell in wide pleats to her ankles. She wore tabi—a type of Adrenian sock that had a divide between the big toe and the rest, allowing placement for the thong of straw sandals, the material thin and bendable beneath her feet.

She stepped behind the front desk, tucking her hair behind her ears as she looked down at something behind the raised counter, and began a conversation with the secretary. Yama stared at the woman, hesitant about her next move. She hadn't expected the opportunity to come this fast. Master Ichi was only a dozen paces away and not preoccupied with students or parents, though many of the people in the building had turned to get a glimpse of her.

A mom entered the building with a boy around the age of six. She had a handful of his collar wrapped in her fist as she practically dragged him to the desk. His arms were crossed in defiance, shoulders twisting as he tried to rip himself free, mouth curled downward in a boyish scowl. "He deserved it!" he screamed.

Master Ichi looked up, expression passionless. Her eyes slowly dragged from the mother to the boy.

"Please, take my son," the mom breathed, clearly exhausted from trying to restrain the little monster.

Master Ichi rounded the desk, an empty scabbard at her waist. She stood over him, her six-foot frame swallowing the child. The top of his head reached only her thighs. Most adults would have knelt to meet the boy's level, but not Ichi. She remained on her feet, and Yama—knowing the woman like she did—saw the back grow rigid to embellish her height even further. The boy's bucking, however, didn't cease from intimidation. If anything, the mother's fight to restrain the boy weakened instead, and he struggled harder.

"Why did he deserve it?" Master Ichi asked, chin tilted up as she stared down her nose at him. Yama doubted she had any idea who "he" actually was.

"He was yelling at our teacher!"

"A classmate at school?"

"He called our teacher a hippo! He said everyone hates him!"

The lesson currently happening in the training area didn't stop—a credit to the discipline of the academy—but most of the parents in the lobby stared. Master Ichi fell silent for a moment while the boy continued to exhaust himself in his struggle.

"And what did you do about it?" Ichi asked.

"He almost killed the—"

Ichi's gaze shot to the mother, and that alone was efficient enough of a command to shut her up. The master looked down at the boy again, repeating her question. "What did you do about it?"

"I beat him up." He grunted, trying to tug his arms from his mother's grip. "You don't disrespect your elders! Especially anyone who's trying to help you be a smarter person!"

Ichi smiled gently. That got the boy to calm down. "Do you love your teachers?"

"Yes," he squeaked.

"Here, we have the greatest teachers. Perhaps, we can teach you to gain control of that rage of yours. While your classmate deserved reprimand, you overstepped."

The boy turned to the lessons, eyes wet with tears. "But you teach fighting."

"We teach responsibility and self-discipline, two core values of our kingdom. We also teach honor." She stepped back, eyeing the boy from a distance. "How old are you?"

"Six."

"You're big for your age."

He nodded with pride. "Which is why I fight on behalf of those who can't. My teacher wouldn't fight a kid, so I did it for him."

"And how did you approach this classmate to fight him?"

"I jumped on his back at the potty."

Snickering from the parents, and Yama grinned. The mother, however, flushed red with embarrassment.

"And where is the honor in that?" Master Ichi asked, the brief smile from earlier fading into nothing. He shrugged. She regarded the mother, eyes unreadable. "I will take on your cub and do my best to make him a proper lion."

"Thank you!" she breathed, extending an open hand … a mistake.

Ichi stared at it and said, "That is not the way of tradition."

The mother looked at her own hand, open-mouthed, before letting it fall to her side. She bowed curtly. Master Ichi nodded and stepped to the desk. The secretary handed her a few leafs of parchment, a quill, and inkwell, which she gave to the mother. "Scribe all of his information. The fee is significant, but I'm sure you were aware of that before deciding to come here in the first place. I will be looking forward to his first lesson." With that, she returned to her office, sparing a fleeting glance at Yama.

Yama's jaw tightened as she strode across the lobby. Master Ichi hated tepidness, so her best bet was to address her now. Knock on that door and demand an audience. But as she reached the door, the secretary stopped her. "Are you Yama?"

Yama turned, not sure how this woman knew her name. She was young—lower twenties—and hadn't been an employee here when Yama was a student. "I am."

"I was just informed by Master Ichi to request your leave from the premises."

Yama's fists clenched. Not again. This was the same welcome she'd received from the citizens of Yinyon—from her mother. She was not going to leave another opportunity unexplored. She was tired of wandering. She would knock down this wall if—

"She said to stop by in a week's time. You've arrived during testing week, and she can have no distractions."

Yama relaxed her hands, lifted her chin, and inhaled deeply. That made sense. Testing weeks were intense. She stared at the door, which stood a few inches in front of her. Then she turned and exited the building.

*   *   *

A week had passed since Olivia and her family's return to Kindoliya. A congregation had been waiting for them on the final road leading to the palace's frozen wall, split to two sides as the royal family and refugees were escorted down the middle atop tram rams. It was essentially a parade orchestrated by Still General Valp, husband to Aunt Ropinia. The man had been overjoyed for the Still family's return, claiming the responsibilities of being the man in charge too daunting. Apparently, running an army was child's play compared to running a kingdom. Either that or the two entities simply weren't comparable, requiring much different skillsets.

Olivia had appreciated the festive welcome, the refugees reveling in the high spirits of the Stillians. Considering their lives as slaves in the sewage of

Stratum Zero, the witnessing of their land's apocalypse beneath the moon, and the debilitating trek across the Diamond Sea, they deserved this. Alas, she couldn't shake the image of that father who had pleaded for her to save his son as he froze to death. No amount of spirit could heal that void.

A couple days had passed since their return to the capital, and they were spending them in leisure. Vuilni wobbled on the ice, unfamiliar with skates despite having been here once before, when they had traveled here with other Jestivan, Director Jugtah, and Vistas to heal her grandfather's paralysis. Olivia had a hand on each side of her friend's waist to steady her. The Still Princess didn't wear gloves or a scarf like most people on the ice. She could handle the cold even better than the average Stillian—a benefit of her royal blood.

Most people at the rink today were refugees granted this treat by Still Queen Apoleia. Many hadn't come, electing to remain in their temporary homes, finding the warmth of their hearths a greater advantage of which to seize hold. Those who were here, however, were enjoying themselves— even if it meant wearing enough layers to make them look like ripened fruits.

"Your legs are as stiff as tree bark," Olivia said, looking down at Vuilni's scooting feet. "Bend the knees and relax the muscles."

"Why do the Stillians lock their knees?" Vuilni asked, teeth chattering.

"Because they know what they're doing, and even then it's only at certain points in their strides."

"How am I doing?"

Olivia looked to the ice at her right. A six-year-old girl, black braids falling out of her hood, was sliding past them on all fours. Every time she tried standing, she had slipped and fallen on her rear, so she had resorted to crawling. Vuilni could have done the same, but the cuteness was less redeeming from a grown woman. Ahzedan—who didn't know Vuilni despite being her little sister—could glide across the ice on gloved hands and padded knees without being humiliated. If people did laugh at the girl, it was because they found it adorable.

"You're doing great," Olivia said. The girl smiled and continued onward.

"I'm going to stomp my foot into this ice and tread my way across," Vuilni said.

"Look, this is a skill that takes time. The more you do it, the better you'll get. My mom used to drill me a lot harder than this."

"I'm surprised she wanted you to do something this expressive, knowing how she used to be with you."

Olivia's gaze unfocused, staring over Vuilni's shoulder in case she needed to steer the Diatia to the right or left. "I was a child," Olivia said, turning the pair of them left to follow the rink's bend. "My mother understood she couldn't just shut off a child's emotions. Children are impulsive and emotional. They don't know enough of life or the world to understand composure. I was only four, so she tried to find a scapegoat for me, originally thinking it might be music."

Ahzedan crawled her way to the middle of the rink, where the crush of skaters was nonexistent save for a few couples who chose the secluded center to spin in circles or dance.

"I was awful at every instrument she tried putting in my hands. The piano, violin, clarinet ... all failures. She even tried drums, and she despises drums. Calls them primitive and unrefined. After realizing I had no musical talent, we tried artistry. But I couldn't even draw a straight line, much less a circle. Then she gave me a pair of skates, thinking if I hadn't gotten any of her talents in music or artistry, then maybe I picked up my aunt's talent that she had gotten from my great grandmother. And I did. I could skate."

Olivia paused, thinking back to those days at the edge of the Diamond Sea in her early years. They had lived at the base of the mountains. "I'd skate every day, improving with each fall. Whenever mom would sense my loneliness of a life secluded from civilization, or my anger at her for giving me such a life, she'd tell me to skate out my melancholy and frustrations. I learned to funnel everything through ice skating, not knowing I was being sculpted into a girl of apathy. I just thought it was fun and, sometimes, healing. For my mom, it was the only way to teach me how to not feel anything outside of skating ... not until I got a few years older at least. Then she told me her story, and with it the real strategies of invulnerability."

"When did Meow Meow enter the picture?" Vuilni asked, losing focus on her fear of ice skating, enamored by Olivia's story instead. Her strides were lengthening.

"When my mom realized I was never going to get over my loneliness, she gave him to me as a gift of companionship. And that's what he became, while also becoming the emotional half of my mind. I stopped skating more and more, and I learned to consciously reject empathy. If anything happened that was too devastating even for my conscious efforts, then Meow Meow absorbed the blow on my behalf."

Vuilni shook her head. "That's messed up."

"I don't blame her," Olivia said. They avoided a man who had slipped onto the ice, this time without her steering. "She was trying to protect me by teaching me values she felt she had betrayed in her teenage years, which she felt directly resulted in the incident with Mendac."

"Vulnerability doesn't equate to weakness," Vuilni said. "It's not about the emotion itself, but how you react to it. Like, what are you going to do about it?"

"That's what I plan to find out," Olivia said, releasing Vuilni's waist.

"And I'm glad you're on this journey. You deserve to feel human. You deserve to …" She trailed off, likely just noticing the absence of her crutch.

Olivia grinned, watching the gears tick in Vuilni's mind as she processed what that meant. She was alone, at risk of crashing into the ice with nobody to stop her. "Don't freak out. You're doing it."

Vuilni's timid shuffling of her feet had become gentle steps. Her arms were a little stiff and spread like wings, but that was ignorable considering the progress in her legs.

They skated side by side after that, though Olivia now felt confident enough in her friend to skate ahead sometimes, pining for the nip of brisk winds against her cheeks and through her hair. Eyes followed her path around the rink. She'd grown used to it over the years, starting with gazes from students at Phesaw when she became a student. This was no different. They found it odd that a royal would mingle so casually with civilians, but Olivia refused to bunker herself in the palace. She didn't grow up a royal, but a civilian. Some might go as far as saying she'd been a recluse.

She leapt and twirled, landing backward on one skate, leg kicked behind her. Sounds of admiration came from the surrounding crowd, giggling from the children. One girl tried following the princess's lead, but was caught out of the air by an older gentleman at her side. "You're not ready for that," he said.

"Never pegged you for a show-off," said Vuilni. Olivia had finally slowed next to Vuilni after passing her on three laps.

"I do it for myself."

"I know. Just like giving you a hard time."

Up ahead, a teenage girl—Stillian judging by the thin jacket and lack of a hat, scarf, or gloves—dashed through the crowd, displaying impressive speed on her skates. She cut her way to the inside line of the rink's ovular track, seeking out open space. She hit the turn at full speed, and Vuilni gasped. The girl leaned with the sharp bend of the track, extending an arm and letting her fingertips skim across the ice. It was a highly skillful maneuver, one that Olivia wouldn't have tried with this many people around. The risk of endangering others—especially in a setting where ninety-percent of the people were novices or worse—was too great. But to the girl's credit, she was pulling it off.

She was three-quarters of the way through the elongated bend, knees bent and butt low to the ground, glittering skirt above thick trousers rippling behind her, when a boy fell out of the crowd ahead of her. He toppled, and she was moving too quickly. She turned her skates and tried to stop, shaving gouts of ice from the rink floor. An eruption of white powder swallowed a portion of the crowd.

Olivia lost her in it all, but as the air cleared, she saw the boy lying on his side, wailing. The teenage girl was seated ten feet down the ice, one leg bent as she squeezed her knee. There was a rip in her trousers and skin, blood trailing into the thick material. She appeared furious rather that in pain. A woman peeled away from the crowd somewhere farther back, skating toward the boy. This was another Stillian, and probably the teenager's mother based on physical resemblances.

The woman lifted the refugee boy up from the ice and slapped him without hesitation, expression hardened but controlled—yes, she was a proper Stillian woman, which was the exact thing Olivia's mother was trying to rid their culture of. Shouts of anger came from the refugees as they swarmed the woman, the flow of the rink now at a standstill. "You move out of a woman's way next time," she said tersely. "That is my daughter, and I will not let her be treated like a man." She shoved the boy, and the crush swallowed her.

Olivia skated toward the chaos. The temperature dropped several degrees as she neared, alerting her of the woman's attempt to weave frigidity into the air. She wasn't a great weaver, but she was no amateur. If the refugees felt the dip, it didn't matter how many of them were packed together like this. Working her way through the weakest part of the throng she could find, Olivia sought out the fallen boy, fearing he'd be trampled by skates. The refugees wisely moved around him. He was curled into a ball, face tucked into his chest and gloved hands squeezed tight over his head. Men and women collapsed around them, losing balance on the ice. This was madness and stupidity all in one.

She grabbed the boy and dragged him out of the mob, anger overcoming her. She was mad at the Stillian woman for her flawed cultural beliefs and the refugees for their irrational response, putting this child's life in danger. All it would have taken was one clumsy person to kick out a leg in distress to catch their fall, and a skate could have gone across the boy's neck.

Once free and sure he was absent of injury, she swung a fist into the ice. Tremors coursed across the rink. The ice split in several directions, racing toward the wooden fence circling the rink. The mayhem stilled, and she rose to her feet. She marched through the crowd of stunned and irate faces, stopping in front of the mother. The woman didn't flinch. "Princess, they're foreigners, yes, but that doesn't excuse them from proper punishment. We must not lose our pride for their sake. I was simply laying down the groundwork." She glanced left, where the girl was somewhere beyond the wall of people. "And besides, Princess, it was my daughter."

"Your daughter was the one at fault," Olivia snapped.

"The boy got in her way, Princess."

"She shouldn't have been skating like that in the first place. And you lost your pride the moment you slapped a child in the face—a child, need I remind you, that isn't yours."

"That is my right as a wo—"

FWAP! Olivia's palm collided with her cheek. The woman's neck popped as her head torqued atop it, her entire body jerking sideways with the motion. She lost her footing and fell to hands and knees, mouth open as she stared at the ice in shock.

"That is my right as your future queen," Olivia said. "So let this be a lesson to you. We do not allow bias between men and women anymore in this kingdom. You are no greater than that boy. And hopefully this image will stick with you forever." The boy walked over, a red handprint on his cheek, eyelashes matted in tears. "A male standing above you, by your princess's side."

To the mother's credit, she didn't lash out. Her features remained unmarred by wrinkles of fury, though Olivia could only imagine what was running through her mind. At least she was proving to be a Stillian woman on all ends of the spectrum. When faced with a woman of higher ranking, comply in a rational manner. "Yes, Princess," the mother said, attempting to stand.

Olivia grabbed the crook of her elbow and helped guide her up. "I want you to take your daughter to the nearest medical building to get that knee patched up."

"Yes, Princess."

Olivia turned to the rambunctious teenager, whose rage had become flabbergast after witnessing her mother be reprimanded by a royal. "I hope you were paying attention. You were raised one way, but that needs to change."

The girl nodded, and then was taken by her mother toward the rink's edge. Olivia's gaze scanned the surrounding refugees, some of whom were still rising from their falls. "Unless someone's life is in danger, don't react like that again. I understand the anger, but this is still a learning process for my people. From now on, report any grievances to your SLO leaders. They will transfer that information to the queen, my aunt, or me. And we will see it dealt with."

Eyes began to drift downward, toward her feet. She looked down. Her feet had sunken a few inches into the rink, ice melting beneath her then evaporating into steam almost instantaneously.

The boy's eyes widened as he knelt next to her boots. "What kind of power is that?"

*   *   *

Olivia entered the Icebound Confluence, a central chamber in Kindoliya Palace that served as a junction between several of its wings. At the center of the chamber stood the Statue of Gefal, twenty-four humanistic statues carved of ice separated on tiers of a layered mount— fifteen to the bottom, five on the next, then three, and one at the very top. All of them were women despite the obvious evidence—Olivia's current Bewahr—that there were men in the Gefal.

It was nine P.M. and therefore outside of busy hours. The chamber was mostly empty, the sunlight of second-day streaking in from the circular opening several stories above. This chamber had no roof, making it more of a frozen courtyard. With the wall that circled them, however, it didn't feel that way.

Apoleia sat on a throne she had erected from the floor out of ice, the lyre gifted to her by her children on her lap. Titus stood by her side, hand placed on the throne's back. He wore a soldier's cloak—powder blue with a crystalline snowflake on the back. They spoke while watching a woman hammer a stake into a massive block of ice. During the Confluence's active hours, when messengers, advisors, officers, and other staff trafficked through it between wings, that block stood ominously over the crowds, a length of rope encircling it as symbolic warning to not approach.

Olivia stopped at the throne's left side, eyes fixed on the sculptor. This had become a nightly routine for the queen and king since the project began three days prior. She hadn't asked what it was supposed to be, but she knew it to be integral to the Still Kingdom's cultural shift. Why else would her mother spend all of this time treating its creation as a spectating event? And why would it stand this close to the Statue of Gefal while also nearly matching half its height? That meant it served to lessen the landmark's appeal, rob the historic monument of its glory.

"How was your day, Olivia?" Apoleia asked.

"Eventful."

"The good or bad kind?" Titus asked.

"Both. It was one of those situations where in order for there to be good, the bad had to happen in the first place." She paused, watching as the sculptor hammered a stake into the top of the ice block from her perch atop a ladder. "There were lessons learned today, and I'm sure that will be the case for years to come as we try to weed out old ideologies."

"It requires patience," Apoleia said. "Baby steps."

"I slapped a woman."

The statement ripped their eyes away from the sculptor and onto her. "Excuse me?" said Apoleia with the unusual expression of genuine shock on her face.

"She hit a young boy for nothing and then tried to argue her case— rather boldly might I add—in front of the refugees who had seen it. She refused to respect my attempt at talking her down, which made me angry and ashamed of our kingdom, so I hit her in the face."

Titus smirked and then chuckled. Before a few seconds passed, he broke into laughter. Apoleia grinned. "They made you ... *angry?*"

Olivia shook her head, reliving the events in her mind. "I couldn't believe it, Mother. That woman had the nerve to attack a child in front of dozens of foreigners, thinking she was actually in the right. That's a sense of entitlement that is so deeply embedded it might as well be a genetic trait."

"A lot of women here believe that's the case. Still Queen Francine was a huge supporter of the idea that women, genetically, were superior."

Titus shook his head. "Who needs genetics as proof when the scars on my back tell all?"

Olivia looked at the man. He was her stepfather now, though she didn't think of him as that. Apoleia reached up and grabbed Titus's hand from the throne's back, placing it on the arm and entwining her fingers with his. "And I'm making sure no other man has to experience that again. I'm so sorry, Love."

"It's nothing compared to what you've gone through."

Olivia's gaze fell to the lyre. Not many people had experienced a life like her mother's. She returned her attention to the ice block. "What's it going to be?"

"A surprise," Apoleia whispered.

"Do you not fear destroying the sanctity of this room?"

Her mother scoffed. "You sound like the pompous elders. There is no sanctity in here—only lies."

Olivia agreed, so she didn't argue any further.

"Any progress with your Bewahr?" Apoleia asked.

"No." Olivia hadn't summoned Preloz since that day in the cellar of Dunami Palace, when the man had told her to respect the boundaries of their relationship. He wasn't a friend or even an acquaintance—just a guardian. He would treat her like a commission project, only willing to show up when his skills were needed. But that didn't mean she'd give up.

"I showed abilities again," she said.

Her mother clapped her hands together. "That's good! When?"

"Today, when I hit the woman."

"The rage brought it out of you, just like the grief over the boy on the way to Kindoliya." Apoleia was running a finger down the left arm of her lyre. "I know I hindered you for a long time, but I'm glad to see you're overcoming it. I'm so proud of you."

Olivia said nothing. She didn't want it to require heartbreaking or rage-inducing moments to trigger her powers. She wanted to control it, to will the energy out of her of her own volition. Because if her abilities proved useful only in reactionary scenarios, then how many times would she be too late? She needed to be proactive ... to initiate. How would she get to that point?

"Hm ... if anger's what you need," said Apoleia, "perhaps I'll wake you every morning at five o'clock with some out-of-tune violin notes. All while stomping across your bed."

The queen and king spilled into hysterics, and Olivia gave them a lazy, sidelong glance.

30

The Thousand-Layer Loess

There weren't words to properly describe the marvel that was the Thousand-Layer Loess. Himitsu stood at the precipice of its highest plateau, looking down into a valley wider than Necrosis Valley or Accus Canyon. The descent beneath him was a series of plateaus arranged like stairs meant for mountainous gods. They converged at the bottom with the valley's opposite wall, where another series of plateaus ascended toward the sky a hundred miles in the distance. Buttes, towers of earth, jutted from the Loess in random locations throughout the valley, circled by grassy plateaus that wrapped around the formation. Some reached higher than the bluff on which he and Kaylee stood, others barely ascending beyond three layers of plateaus.

The only spectacle that could rival the Loess for Himitsu was Kaylee's face. It took a lot to make someone's jaw hit the floor. And the way her eyes had locked straight ahead, twitching only slightly instead of scanning the behemoth, he knew she was currently absorbing all of it at once—from the dead center to her peripherals. She'd even placed a hand against her chest, taking long breaths to steady her pulse. He couldn't blame her. He had traveled to many places as a Jestivan, but nothing came close to this.

They walked along the bluff's edge, appreciating the view from different angles while they searched for a way down. The plateau directly below them seemed to house hundreds of farmlands and pastures for as far as the eye could see across its length, dotted with barn houses, ranches, and ponds. The next plateau was covered in dense woodlands, but trails of smoke could be seen rising from the canopies, suggesting there might have been cottages within, where fires crackled in cozy hearths.

"What's that?" He pointed to the depths of the valley, toward the bottom plateaus and far south. Up the opposite side of the loess was an enormous, circular patch of rock. It was a lone smooth surface that ran up the valley wall, cutting into the tiered plateaus, like a bald spot in the back of an elderly man's head.

Kaylee squinted, placing a hand over her eyes. A squat butte nearly blocked the sightline, a mountainous shadow swallowing that part of the loess. "Looks like it might have once been a mine, but I don't see any equipment or machinery nearby that would imply it's active … and I don't see an entrance. It's either dried up from years of excavation, it's simply being ignored, or it caved in."

"Was the Thousand-Layer Loess known for mining?"

"They haven't been known for it since the first century, and nobody outside of the Loess even knows that much. The mineral inside was outlawed when religion was abolished, so that's why I think they're probably ignoring it … the law says so. The brunt of the war on religion was felt here, for the Loess was a holy land, and that mine was the heart. But what is known about this place is lost to time mostly. That's why it sounds so obscure. I was simply lucky enough to have a mentor like Neeko who had books people shouldn't have."

Himitsu paused to study the lower plateaus, realizing they were nothing but lush grass as opposed to the farm and forest-filled top five or six. "It's beautiful," he said, "but seems boring. I didn't know these apothecaries you were looking for were also farmers."

She laughed. "That's a good reaction. It means their façade is working."

"They're faking this?"

"Well, no ... not completely. These upper tiers are actual farms and forests, and the residents are real farmers and foresters, but they're also a red herring to distract strangers from seeing the real Thousand-Layer Loess. The people who live here want you to believe they're only a nomadic culture, but they're actually one of the most advanced civilizations in Kuki Sphaira."

"Like Brilliance?" he asked.

"Eh ... not a fair comparison. Cities like Brilliance and Prayoga are far beyond anything else because of their relationships with the monarchy of their respective kingdoms. The Loess has secluded itself from the rest of its kingdom, so they don't receive support or funds on that level."

They found stairs that had been carved out of the rock in the cliff and descended them. "Why don't they ask for help?"

"They don't want to, nor does the Archaic Kingdom. There's a rough past between the two sides. Like I said, this was a holy land and the Archaic family back then was trying to destroy anything holy. Did you know Gatal Accus was rumored to have grown up here?"

"No. I don't think the *First of Five* mentions it." He racked his brain, trying to recall the many times he'd been told the story as a child.

"That's because it's a fairy tale and not an origin story. Fairy tales tend to skip what most people would find boring in favor of the immaculate ... such as summoning a Bozani to redirect a meteor. But the story did say he traveled west through the kingdom."

They reached the next plateau and trekked across a couple miles of open plains, admiring cattle that lay in the grass and horses drinking from a spring. Despite seeing several homes across the stretch of prairie, he saw no fences. How did they keep track of whose animals belonged to whom and where properties met?

As Kaylee proceeded toward the front porch of a ranch, Himitsu froze. "We're just gonna walk up to someone's house and knock?"

She continued onward without a response, marching up the front steps and rapping her fist against the door. Himitsu remained motionless only momentarily before sprinting to her side. He didn't know who would answer the door, but he'd be there just to fend off any potential threats.

Kaylee might have had daggers hidden up her sleeves, but he was her favorite dagger … He laughed at himself, then shut his mouth at Kaylee's glance of exasperation. "Whatever you're thinking, stop it."

A young woman answered the door. Her hair was tied back in a bun and she wore strange clothes that covered all skin save her face and hands. Her expression darkened. "I don't know you. And I know everyone here."

"We're strangers to the Loess," Kaylee said with a friendly smile.

"You're lost? How bad are you at directions to end up all the way out here?"

"No, we want to be here. I have business with the apothecaries."

The woman went quiet, eyes tracking up to find Himitsu. He wasn't looking at her, instead peering over her head and surveying the home's interior for danger. "You looking for something?" she asked.

"Funny business," he said.

At that, her expression lightened. "You'll find no mirrors from there."

Laughter from Kaylee. Himitsu looked down at the woman, lips quirked up in a smirk. "That was good. It just so happens, however, that I *am* funny, so your quips are compliments."

The woman stepped to the side, extending a hand behind her. "Come on in. Supper's almost done and Jacoby should be returning from the stable anytime now." Himitsu and Kaylee walked past. "Name's Elana, by the way."

"It's a pleasure," said Kaylee, stepping into the living room, a staircase plastered against the wall directly ahead. "I'm Kaylee and this is Himitsu."

Elana closed the door and turned, gesturing toward three pairs of dirty shoes against the wall. As they kicked off their shoes and placed them in the row, Elana asked, "And both of you have dreams of becoming an apothecary of the Loess?"

"Just me," Kaylee replied as Himitsu handed over their bags. Elana hung them on a coat rack nailed into the wall.

"Lofty goals." The woman crossed through the living room and entered a kitchen, where Himitsu tried his best to lounge on a stiff wooden chair at the table. Kaylee stood to the side of the counters while Elana displayed a technician's speed and precision in her knife work, the sound of rapid knocking as she cut through a bundle of carrots.

"What are you making?" Kaylee asked.

"Roasted chicken stew, complete with a medley of carrots, potatoes, and onion."

"Smells delicious," Himitsu said.

"Thank you."

"Does your family run a farm of leisure or servitude?" Kaylee said.

Cringing, Elana shook her head. "Ugh, I forgot that's the outsider words for it. I guess you'd call us a farm of leisure, even though there's nothing leisurely about it." She guided a pile of diced carrots with her knife across the counter and into a bowl. She then dumped the bowl into a pot that hung over a stone fire pit in the floor. "It's hard work running a farm. Doesn't matter if you're providing for just your family or the general public."

"So you did your time already," Kaylee said.

Elana nodded, using two hands to stir the contents of the pot with a wooden ladle as long as Himitsu's arm. "Ten years of servitude, as you put it."

"What's that mean?" Himitsu asked through a mouthful of bread.

Kaylee, just now noticing her man's thievery, shot him a death stare. "Did you ask if you could snatch from their loaf of bread?"

Elana chuckled. "It's alright. If anything, he's doing me a favor. Now the children won't fill up on bread and neglect their protein and vegetables."

Himitsu's hand slowly crept toward the loaf again, his narrowed eyes on Elana asking the question for him. "One more chunk is fine," she said.

Arching her neck and gritting her teeth at the ceiling, Kaylee gathered a soothing breath.

"Every half-century, every family of the nomad plateaus must serve ten years as a public farm. Meaning we have to provide raw materials and food for the population of the inlanders."

Himitsu tossed another chunk of bread into his mouth. "What are inlanders?"

Elana turned to Kaylee. "He knows nothing."

"The inlands are what would be considered the Loess's city," Kaylee said. "And they are what hide beneath this veil of farmlands and forests. People who live in the inlands are called inlanders."

"I didn't see any cities when we got here."

"Because they're inside the Loess, you imbecile," Kaylee explained. "Underground. A system of tunnels and caverns."

"That's awesome," he said, swallowing. "But it sucks you have to feed them."

"We are paid well," Elana said. "Well enough to last forty years in 'leisure' before needing to enter servitude again." She pulled the ladle out of the stew and lifted it to her lips, blowing on it before tilting its contents into her mouth. She smacked her lips, nodded, and then returned it to the pot. She exited the kitchen and stopped at the foot of the staircase next to the front door. "Children!"

Footsteps thundered above. Himitsu smiled at the ceiling, feeling an unexpected sense of comfort. Kaylee took a seat next to him and nudged his shoulder. "What's that look about?"

"I don't know …"

Two girls and a boy sprinted into the kitchen behind their mother, tiny legs freezing at the sight of their guests. "Have a seat," Elana instructed, goading them forward. "This is Himitsu and Kaylee."

The children sat on the opposite side of the table, eyes locked on the strangers. "What are your names?" Himitsu asked.

"Gretchen," said the girl with a bowl cut.

"Glade," said the girl with long, frizzy hair in need of a wash.

"Grant," said the boy.

As Elana set the table, she said, "Kaylee is going to be an apothecary."

The two girl's faces lit up. "Can you take us?" Glade asked.

"You're not ready yet," the mother said, dumping stew into her bowl.

Grant, the boy, had lost interest in their guests. He was frowning at the platter of bread at the center of the table. "No fair. Someone already ate half of it."

"Which means you'll have to eat more stew than normal tonight," Elana stated. Grant crossed his arms and scowled at his bowl.

Himitsu heard the front door open, though it couldn't be seen from the table. This time it was Grant's turn to perk up with excitement. He was just about leap out of his chair when his mother eyed him down from the stew pot. A man entered the kitchen. He had a full brown beard and matching hair circling his head, the top of his scalp bald. "Daddy!" Grant screamed.

The father kissed Elana and turned to the table, his smile dissipating as he spotted their guests. "We have ... company?"

"Foreigners," she said.

The man stared, but then offered a nod and approached the side of the table where his children sat, giving each of them a kiss on the temple. He sat at the head of the table, tucking a napkin into the collar of his shirt and grinning at the stew lain out before them. "You're in for a treat," he said to Himitsu and Kaylee.

Dinner was filled with a lot of small talk and laughs provided by the children, who had taken advantage of the lax nature of their parents in the company of guests. The two girls wanted to be apothecaries when they got older, while the boy wanted to continue his father's legacy on the farm. Noticing the rivalry between the two girls when they spoke of their futures, Kaylee whispered into Himitsu's ear that only one of them would get that opportunity, for the other would marry into another farm family. He felt bad for them, knowing how primitive such a custom sounded.

He grew a bond with the children in the short span of thirty minutes. While Kaylee spoke of mature topics with the two parents, he entertained the younger ones with funny faces and instigative rebukes to their jabs at his height. "At least I can get to the cookie jar" and "I can beat you up" got the best reactions. The dinner became reaffirmation of those creeping desires to settle down and start a family—a big one, nothing like the household he grew up in ... void of siblings, and his parents away on missions.

Dinner finished with an invitation to spend the night. Apparently, reaching the inlands from the upper plateau would take a few hours even by horseback. Jacoby offered to loan a couple of his steads to them, and he'd guide them to the innards' closest entrance after tending to the farm's morning duties.

"I'm assuming you have a letter of recommendation from a Loess-trained apothecary?" Jacoby asked as he and his wife cleared the table, the children already preparing for bed upstairs.

"No," Kaylee said. "But I have one from the king."

Jacoby didn't flinch, but Himitsu saw Elana hesitate as she scrubbed a plate in a water bucket. "The king?" the father asked. "And which unfortunate or corrupt soul holds that position now? Last I checked it was King Sigmund, but with the rapid turnover as of late, I suppose it could be a blacksmith for all I know."

"It's still King Sigmund. And it should stay that way until he passes it on to a future firstborn. Stability has been reestablished in the capital."

"Good to hear," he said, wiping down the table with a damp rag. "Well, the man might not be an apothecary, but he is the king. As long as your documents bare his seal, then you should be fine."

Himitsu watched Elana, who hadn't looked up from her bucket since the mentioning of the Archaic King. Did this have to do with the friction between the Thousand-Layer Loess and the monarchy? When Kaylee had told him about the relationship, he had chalked it up to superstitions set in a distant past. But perhaps it was more concrete than he'd believed. Maybe the citizens of the Loess really did despise the royal family. Or maybe it was fear. This must have been part of the reason why his mother sent him out here—aside from the more straightforward tasks.

He sighed, feeling the weight of the convoluted mess he'd spend the next few months sorting through.

*   *   *

After a morning of playing tag with Gretchen, Glade, and Grant, Himitsu and Kaylee departed from the ranch with Jacoby as their guide. They rode horses down switchbacks to the plateau below, where a dense forest lay in wait. Himitsu flirted with death a few times, unfamiliar with the wildlife within. His horse had decided to break away from Jacoby and Kaylee upon reaching a fork in their path, seeing that it reconnected a few hundred feet ahead. It turned out Jacoby had chosen the other one for good reason, and by the time he'd shouted warning to Himitsu across the median of trees and brush, the Jestivan had decided to reach up from his mount and snag a tangle of low-hanging vines. Only the vines squirmed at his touch, dropped into his lap and around his shoulders, and hissed.

He almost fell off the saddle in alarm, realizing the dozens of looped green ropes he had mistaken for vines were actually massive boas. The only thing that saved him was the horse's instinctive bucking, jarring both the snakes and Himitsu loose. He was tossed forward and, upon hitting the ground, was nearly trampled by the galloping horse. He rolled out of its way and wove a ring of black flame around himself, not to hide from the snakes—wherever they had landed—but to torch the life out of them if they tried approaching.

Jacoby's horse came galloping from the opposite direction, Kaylee waiting at the merger of the two paths ahead, Himitsu's horse at her side. "You have a death wish, young man?"

Himitsu let the fire disappear, but ran to Jacoby and leapt onto the horse, fighting to mount the beast. Luckily, Ebony was the finest horse in the man's stable and was used to carrying the weight of multiple people—usually carrying Jacoby and two of his children at once. The man laughed as they joined Kaylee and the other two horses ahead. If he had any reaction to discovering Himitsu was not just a Passionian, but one of assassin blood, he didn't show it. That had been a careless mistake to reveal his powers.

It was on the fourth plateau some five hours later when Jacoby dropped them off at the gaping mouth of a tunnel the size of a villa, set into the base of the cliffside. This location must have been strategic, for it faced the west and couldn't be seen from the eastern cliff, from where foreigners would approach. The farmer and his three horses departed, commencing the long journey back to his home three plateaus above.

Stone barracks lined the tunnel's walls just inside the entrances, their structures seeming to mold flawlessly with the rocky earth. The guards' armor made little sense. Aside from the rusted chainmail protecting their chests, stomachs, and backs, the rest of the ensemble was tanned leather. They didn't wear helmets and their joints were unprotected. They were a shabby bunch, causing Himitsu to relax despite the sheer volume of guards roaming the tunnel.

Tall torches lined a makeshift road running down the middle of the tunnel, leaving plenty of empty space between the road and the buildings on the far sides. Sunlight spilling in from the tunnel's entrance illuminated the base, but at night Himitsu assumed they'd light the hundreds of torches. Otherwise, this place would suffer from blinding darkness. When he'd pictured the inlands described by Kaylee, the thought of illumination hadn't even occurred to him. With their lives underground, there must have been hundreds of thousands of torches throughout the Loess's inner network of tunnels and caverns.

They didn't make it more than a few yards into the tunnel before a woman stopped them, her chainmail missing a few links. Despite the disorganization apparent in the meandering nature of the guards—certain groups roaming the tunnel while others sat at wooden tables and conducted games of gambling—that didn't mean all of them were oblivious. He wondered if they ever faced real threats in their lifetimes. It'd explain the lack of quality equipment and state of their base. Who lived in stone buildings anymore?

"Are you recruits?" the guard asked.

"What? No," he said, pulling his arm away from her grasp.

"Then why are you here?"

"We're trying to enter the inlands."

"Through a military base?" she asked incredulously. "Are you dense? There are civilian entrances on plateaus seven, eight, nine, and twelve."

Kaylee stepped forward, speaking before he could respond. "We're foreigners, and I'm here to pursue a career in medicine. Our guide couldn't bring us all the way to the civilian entrances, lest he desired to return home after dark."

"I can't let you in through here," the woman said. "It's a security risk to the Loess's defense. Unless you're a member of the Soteria family, you better turn around. Force can be used if necessary."

Kaylee turned and opened one of the bags on Himitsu's shoulder. The guard drew a poniard from a sheath at her waist and bellowed, "Enemies!" Dozens of guards around them snapped into a similar position, each drawing different kinds of blades. Some held strange items that had no business being flaunted as weapons. Himitsu had to choke back a laugh at what looked to be a hula-hoop in one man's hand.

Kaylee withdrew a vellum slip and held it in the air, wiggling it as if to show that it was clearly not a threat. The woman didn't lower her guard, but others slackened. Kaylee untied the wool string that kept the slip's contents secure and pulled out a sturdy leaf of vellum. She held it in front of the guard, whose eyes scanned the missive. They held still at the bottom, where the Archaic King's signature and wax seal sat. She looked at Kaylee, then back at the seal. "Are you a spy?"

"Honestly, I'd be a pretty bad one if I answered that truthfully."

The woman narrowed her eyes, sheathing her poniard. Normal activity resumed around them. "The king desires a personal apothecary trained in the healing arts of the Loess," said Kaylee during the guard's silence. "He's developed a fondness for the more unorthodox methods of eastern medicine. Turn me away, and I assure you there will be consequences. I doubt you want the royal army impeding on your territory." She turned to observe the shoddy military base. "Something tells me you don't have the talent or provisions to hold up."

"Follow me," the guard said with annoyance.

Himitsu was impressed by Kaylee, though he shouldn't have been shocked. He recalled the day they'd returned to Lost Wisdom, when she had waltzed up to the front desk and demanded the location of one of Neeko's students. She had gone so far as to placing a knife against the neck of a security guard and threatening to burn the orphanage down.

They waited outside one of the smaller barracks on a wooden bench, its stone walls better maintained when compared to the others. Grass grew in front of it—another oddity when surrounded by the brown crust of the tunnel's floor. A rock outcropping surrounded it to act as a marker for the end of the property.

"Steel?" Himitsu asked, eyeing a trio of guards who walked past the front yard.

"Probably iron," Kaylee said. "While the Loess is very wealthy, that wealth is reserved for the top two percent."

"You'd think their security would be important enough to warrant more funding for better equipment."

"They have no threats. They're comfortable."

He scoffed. "And that's when someone should be on the highest alert."

"So cynical."

He gritted his teeth. "My mom had once been comfortable stationed in Rim and scouting the Archaic Mountains. Meanwhile, King Itta and King Storshae were scheming to form an alliance with Toono as a puppeteer in the background. And we all know everything that happened because of it."

She blew out a breath and nodded. "True. I guess I'm just thinking our luck can't be that bad. There hasn't been any serious turmoil here since the first and second centuries."

"You know of any specific apothecaries you're looking to train under?" he asked, deciding to change the subject.

"A few. Of course, the person I most desire would never teach me."

"You have a penned letter from the king. I'm sure that could grant you any favor."

"Not with the Loess Lord."

"Well, that's quite a title," said Himitsu. Of course, he knew about the Loess Lord—probably more than her—but he couldn't let her know that.

"He rules over the Thousand-Layer Loess, making him everything just short of a king or queen. He'll have no interest in taking on some random orphan. I don't think he shares his knowledge anyway."

"It's good you have a few options then," he said.

The front door opened. Himitsu expected to see the female guard from earlier, but a man looked outside instead. He wore a cinnamon brown uniform with white trim and a white robe billowing down his back. He was clean-shaven, gray hair buzzed short against his scalp. Spotting the waiting pair on the bench in the yard, he approached.

"Commander Shulith," he stated, stopping in front of them. Before Himitsu or Kaylee could give him their names, he extended a hand and asked, "May I see the missive?"

Kaylee handed it over, and he read through it. He flicked the seal to test the wax. Himitsu couldn't get a read of the man, his expression rigid. He returned it to her and placed his hands in his pants pockets, observing them for a few seconds.

"You will be housed in the family apartments a little deeper into the tunnel. I am going to send a squad of my guards to the lord's estate with word of your unannounced arrival and peculiar demands from the king. Forgive the Loess for our suspicions, but we haven't received communication from a royal in quite some time now. When my squad returns with instructions on what to do with you two, we'll see where to go from there." He paused, then added, "Either that or you can leave the Loess."

Anger darkened Himitsu's face. "And if we don't comply? We can go find another entrance into the inlands."

"That would have been fine with us had the king's letter not been brought to our attention, but we are skeptical now. We don't know what you might be."

"You'll find out if you try anything while we're here."

The commander smiled. "So does that mean you're staying?" His back had developed a slight arch to it, hands still tucked in his pockets. A casual display to prove he didn't fear their mysterious guests.

Himitsu glanced at Kaylee. "I can wait," she muttered. "We're in no rush."

"How long will it take?" he asked, turning to the commander.

"There and back?" He shrugged and frowned, as if to give it thought. He could have spit out the answer automatically—as the commander of the guard, he had to know distances between important landmarks. This was just another act of flippancy. "Nine days. The Thousand-Layer Loess isn't just deep and wide, but long. The Heresy Butte is far north from here."

Kaylee stood, and Himitsu followed. She offered her hand, which the commander shook. "I'll send back out Mazie, the guard who brought you to me. She'll take you to the apartments. And who knows? When all is said and done, you might find yourself an audience with Lord Kopios Soteria."

As the commander walked back to the stone house, Kaylee was left with a delighted glint in her eyes. Himitsu couldn't say the same. He had turned to watch Shulith disappear into the building, his eyes wide. Mazie returned and instructed them to follow. Kaylee grabbed his arm and pulled him down the road with gusto in her strides. He dragged his feet. When his mother had informed him about the details of this trip, she had told him about Agnos's mother. He was to find her.

But there was someone else here who was even more important, and that man was the Loess Lord.

31

In Business

In order to properly thank individuals belonging to a family as accomplished as the LeAnce's, Lilu had to execute a gala with a level of showmanship that would put any other to shame. That meant setting aside the internal torture of her mother's suicide, blocking out her father's corpse in his casket, and pinning her faith of her sister's safety in the hands of Fane. The fate of this city, this kingdom, needed all of Lilu's attention tonight.

The gala's location made that tricky, for she had decided—with support from advisors and encouragement from Benedict—on ground zero of the future Weavineering Factory, Griza's Plaza. Stalls and pop-up shops had been erected around the plaza, Intelamps illuminating the night with a steady white light. Honored guests laughed and conversed throughout the plaza. Lines gathered in front of food and pastry vendors. Children, who had been dragged along by aristocratic parents, had migrated toward the middle of the plaza, where a slew of horses were tied to a post. Among the scents of expensive perfumes and colognes were spices and cooked meats. A chill from an approaching winter hung crisp in the air. The atmosphere was almost enough to block out the rubble surrounding the plaza from collapsed taverns and stores from the battle between Bryson and Toono.

While her guests might have had tunnel vision for the festivities she'd strategically thrown in their face with bright lights and hollow fun, Lilu was very much aware of the backdrop. A few wagons were parked at the plaza's western edge, separated from the gala, their horses presently giving rides to children.

She stood alone in the shadows of the abandoned vehicles. She needed a moment's reprieve, which apparently involved standing in front of the broken alley where the body of the aristocrat's child had been found decapitated. Eyes adjusted to the darkness, she could see the revolutionary's symbol painted on the wall in blood. Itta, Storshae, and Toono were all dead—the last of whom was supposed to be the end of it all. She would have never expected her own people to rise up.

She turned, hearing footsteps behind her. Frederick, kinky hair tamed into a sphere of fluff, stared at her. He wore a fitted tux, white irises stark against dark skin. "Figured I should check on you. Gracie and I were getting worried."

"I messed up, Frederick."

He closed the gap and stood next to her, staring into the alley. "Stop trying to shoulder the blame. Something this complex is rooted in many different soils. There was just a war, and a lot of death resulted from it. With the battle on Knowledge River and the invasion here, there were a lot of families that day that lost brave family members."

"I did nothing to help the situation. I compounded it."

He looked at her, expression solemn. "You did everything to help. Without your travolters, a lot more people would have died. That SCAPD fleet would have pushed deeper into the kingdom, invading our biggest port city in Continon and ambushing Dunami from the western flank."

"I'm talking about the socioenergenic system," she muttered. "The identification cards that only complicated and widened the gap between social classes."

"You feared for your family's safety," he replied.

"And in doing so, jeopardized those who I'm supposed to protect as an integral part of the monarchy."

Frederick sighed. "Then abolish it."

"I'm trying, but it's a delicate, time-consuming process."

He tilted his head. "That seems to be the biggest hurdle in kingdoms like ours, where the royals try so hard to follow due process. Where politics are more stalling than doing, finding excuses not to change rather than just seeing the evidence for change."

"I should be impulsive?" she asked. "We saw how that worked out for Archaic King Itta."

"I'm not that knowledgeable of what happened back then, but I believe what King Itta did was personal, involving a grudge from centuries past." He shook his head. "You should never allow negative emotions to make you impulsive, which is not what I'm suggesting here."

They stood in silence, and he wrapped his arm around her waist, pulling her to his side. "This kingdom is crippled by a philosophical question at the moment. No emotion. Just what is good and what is bad." He pressed his nose and mouth against the begonia in her hair and whispered, "With Shelly crippled by sorrow at the moment, you must take a page from traditional Archains and make a decision based on the moral implications."

She breathed out a single laugh at the irony of it all. She had always been an Intelian mind through and through, never understanding the fascination a mind like Agnos had with the enigmatic nature of human existence and philosophy. Apparently, her next biggest decision would require her to adapt that very same way of thinking.

She could hear Agnos now: "I told you so."

The lovebirds returned to the heart of the gala, where Lilu dodged questions about her sister's and brother-in-law's absences as of late. Nobody had heard from the king and queen in weeks, amplifying the restlessness of the general public and, more importantly, solidifying the foundation on which the rebels based their rally cries. Shelly needed to make an appearance soon. While Lilu was more active than she'd ever been in the political and public realms, she was still only a princess.

Wendel LeAnce broke away from his sister, Periphan, during a dance to join Lilu. They moved slowly, faces pointed beyond each other's shoulders.

She had learned to avoid eye contact with him throughout the song, as she could only see Bryson in those blue eyes and blond locks. And the last distraction she needed was a dream of her being his partner during the first dance of their wedding. That opportunity was lost years ago, and it was a sad fact that she'd try to ignore for the rest of her life—regardless of who ended up sharing a place in her heart down the line.

"Who knew such a workaholic had this sort of glamor in her?" Wendel asked.

"You knew me as a student and a weavineer, but you never met Lilu Intel, the princess."

Low laughter sounded next to her left ear. "I appreciate it. I've never had a welcome quite like it."

"And I appreciate you," she replied. "Without your family's funding, my aspirations here wouldn't be possible. You are the star of this night. You are the reason why all of these people have come here to celebrate."

"I've heard rumblings of dissonance in the populace. Should I fear for my safety here in the capital?"

She tilted her head back to look up at him, an eyebrow raised. "And from whom did you hear that?"

He met her gaze. "A man like me does have connections, you see. We have customers who buy our Weavineering technology from all over the realm."

"You are safe," she said, eyes returning to the other couples beyond his shoulder. "I can make arrangements for body guards, however, if you'd like that."

"I would, but for my sister."

Lilu spotted Periphan in the crowd. The heavier-set woman with golden hair tied back in a single braid danced with Benedict Ronal. Lilu had made a habit of keeping the head steward around, finding she trusted him more than anyone. His task tonight had been to keep Periphan company, that way she didn't feel out of place.

"I can arrange that," Lilu said.

"Very good. Considering the state of the kingdom, I would have expected royal guards attached to your own hip, especially in a crowd like this."

"All entrances to the plaza are heavily manned," she replied. "No weapons of any sort are getting in here."

He laughed. "That I should believe. I still feel a bit violated from the thorough inspection upon entry. Still, that doesn't account for ability users."

"I can defend myself against that."

"And I've noticed Frederick remains behind you when he dances, no matter which way our turns take us."

"He thinks himself my guardian even though he's not a fighter."

"Are you thankful for everything Brilliance gave you?"

"And what's that?" she asked, face growing hot.

"A platform, purpose ... Love."

She released his hand and stepped back. "I've had those things. My bloodline gave me a platform, I gave myself purpose, and my family gave me love ... the Jestivan gave me love." She inhaled deeply and cracked her neck. "Don't get me wrong. Brilliance was good for me, but the only thing it gave me was an avenue to streamline my progress. Because with or without that city, I would have found success."

His expression faltered, and he began to look hurt ... or ashamed—genuinely so. "I'm sorry, Lilu. I wasn't trying to diminish anything. You were the person you are even before arriving in Brilliance. It's why I sought you out that day in IWA's labs."

"No, no. My apologies," she muttered, angry at herself. Frederick had just gotten done talking to her about impulsive reactions to emotional triggers—the same issue that had led to her and Bryson constantly butting heads. "You were right. Brilliance gave me Frederick, Gracie, and Limone. Brilliance sent me Director Jugtah, who showed me what a true education can look like."

That didn't seem to make Wendel feel any better. And she was seeing him in a more individual light now, rather than the general glow she had cast upon the LeAnce family based on the evils of Mendac.

The song stopped, and dozens of tiny bells rang from somewhere in the crowd. "It is time for the ceremony," Benedict said, who had broken away from Periphan.

"Ceremony?" Wendel asked.

She grinned, ecstatic with the timing. "Yes! You must leave a tangible mark on Dunami's future. Come on!"

He looked confused, but he and his sister followed the royal through the plaza.

Behind the roped-off section where the horses munched on hey strewn below them, Lilu stood with Frederick, Gracie, Periphan, and Wendel. The aristocrats and wealthy class amassed before them, separated by a vacated strip of the plaza where the royal guard stood. A lone man stood behind Lilu and company, sweating over a bucket as he stirred with a sturdy wooden rod.

Lilu concluded a rousing speech in support of those who stood next to her, thanking Frederick and Gracie—with an honorary mention of Limone, who had remained in Brilliance—for their roles in producing the travolters and stopping the SCAPD naval fleet. She then shifted focus to the LeAnce family, their acknowledgements being accepted by Wendel and Periphan. Their response from the crowd had been mixed, the stain of Mendac's reputation undoubtedly on some of their minds. She felt a tinge of pity at the pain on Wendel's face. The commissioner hadn't been part of any of Mendac's atrocities. Perhaps, now that he was away from the vacuum that was Brilliance, he could finally see the true meaning of his name in the world.

Lilu glanced back at the mason slaving over the bucket. He nodded, standing straight and wiping his temple with a rag from his work belt. Addressing the crowd again, she said, "Let's break ground on our capital's new future." She approached the bucket and instructed Gracie, Frederick, and Periphan to follow. The mason handed each of them a masons trowel from his work belt. Lilu dipped hers into the bucket and scooped out a slab of mortar. The others followed suit.

She knelt on the ground where a line had been drawn with chalk and slapped the mortar on the cobbles, lathering it thickly and smoothly across the marker's length. "Each of you take a spot," she whispered. "Apply up to where the line stops."

After they were finished, she called over Wendel. The mason pushed a wheelbarrow of rectangular stones over to the fresh line of mortar. Wendel stared at it, and Lilu said, "You will lay the first ten stones … with the mason's help of course." She winked. "Can't have any imperfections in the foundation."

The smile finally returned to the commissioner's face, growing slightly as he went to work with the mason's guidance. Laughter sprang from the crowd each time the man had to slap Wendel's hand away from a costly error. And Lilu watched, mind empty of her internal horrors if only for a blissful moment.

*   *   *

Two weeks. No, three.

Shelly was losing track of time, finding the concept useless ever since watching her mother step out of that window. It was said that time healed all wounds, but the queen's heart didn't hurt any less, leading her to curse the clichés of poets.

She sat on her sofa, the lone piece of furniture her younger sister had allowed be returned to the sky tower. She stared at the glass wall, but didn't really see it. Just her mother.

Falling.

Fane stood outside the wall, back turned to the banister as he watched her. They were terrified of what she would do. Count their blessings they weren't in her mind, lest those fears found more purchase.

She had nothing of promise. No purpose. No happiness. Her parents were dead. Bryson wasn't here. She'd felt Suadade's efforts to contact her, but her bitterness toward him was the one feeling of substance she could embrace, which she did by rejecting him.

Her infant son probably needed her, but she couldn't look at the doppelganger of her husband, nor could she stomach the shame of knowing she was the only person that baby had left.

Two weeks? No, three.

She had neglected her son for three weeks.

She hoped he could forget her face in that time.

*   *   *

Creep found himself staring at the sign hanging above his fake butcher's shop. He'd never been one for snarling, but that was the exact form his lips took. *This* was the name Lilu had conjured up for the headquarters of his grand ruse? SUNSHINE'S CHOPPED MEAT? Either that girl had a sense of humor or a knack for coincidental innuendos.

"I said the entire leg, not just the thigh!"

His gaze lowered from the sign to peer into his shop, where a counter meant for transactions sat close to the entrance. A larger chamber sat behind the counter, where stripped animal carcasses hung from the ceiling. An irate customer stood at the counter, the back of his wide neck flushed a vibrant pink. York, Creep's false butcher's apprentice, wiped a wad of the customer's spittle from his eyelid, leaving a streak of red from whichever animal he'd just hacked at.

"You definitely said thigh," York stated, betraying no emotion at the outburst.

The customer whirled, searching the faces of three others waiting in the line behind him, then two men seated on the lone bench along the front wall. "You all heard me!"

Creep watched the burly man unravel, curious as to which direction this would go. He supposed a proper owner of a butcher shop would take control of the situation, but that would betray the character of Sunshine that he and York had worked so hard to build. There was nothing proper about a butcher named Sunshine.

"Stop giving the kid a hard time," a man on the bench said. Creep took special interest in him, for he was one of the regulars who frequented the front booths at the Electric Eel. It had taken a long time and a lot of effort to prod the man into visiting Sunshine's Chopped Meat without actually interacting with him. "I'm pretty sure you said leg, but I'm sure the lad can cut you a new one. Honest mistakes happen."

Creep almost laughed. The man was fairly decent for someone who was likely involved in shady activities. That shouldn't have shocked him though. Most bad people had good qualities.

"I picked the perfect cow," the cheated customer growled. "There's an art to selecting the meat you plan on cooking."

"Ask for your money back."

The angry customer turned to York, waving off the man at the bench. "I want you fired!" By this point, one of the potential customers in line left the building, muttering something about the number of other options elsewhere in the neighborhood.

"Over a slice of meat?" York asked, a butcher's cleaver casually placed on his shoulder, compensating for the apprentice's spindly frame. "Besides, you said thigh."

A fist slammed the counter. "Where's the owner?!"

York pointed toward the entrance. "A problem?" Creep asked.

The customer marched outside, bringing the spectacle to the street. "What's your take on incompetence?"

"I hate it," Creep said, tucking gloved hands into his trench coat pockets.

"Then fire that boy!"

The hybrid's skittering eyes slowed for just a moment, scanning the street around them. Good, an audience had assembled. He looked at the customer again. He was a young man with a broad chest and shoulders, a layer of fat atop a strong abdomen, and some height. "Let's take this to my office, and we'll see what we can do to compensate you for the trouble."

"Fire the imbecile!"

Creep lowered his chin and hardened his stare. "My office, please."

The man replied with a barrage of lucid profanity, but ultimately followed as Creep swept into the shop, past the counter, and into the chamber beyond. The ill-tempered man squeezed himself upon entry into the back room.

"Forgive me," Creep said. "Those are the ever-ice panels set into our walls. I can't have the meat spoil." Once in his office, he turned behind his desk and tugged at the lapels of his trench coat. "That's when this thing comes in handy."

Just before the man slammed the office door shut, Creep saw the other customers now standing at the counter, straining to get a look into the back of the building.

"This place is a damned disgrace!" the man yelled as he stood next to the door.

Creep smiled, appreciating the commitment. "You're good," the hybrid said. "This way everyone in the lobby can still hear you."

"I'll chop that kid's head off!"

Glancing down at his desk to find a name on a leaf of parchment, Creep asked, "What was your name again? I need to remember. You have so much skill at this."

The man stomped toward the desk, grabbed an inkwell, and flung it across the room. It crashed into the door, shattering glass and coating the wood in black ink. "Do you like that?!" he bellowed.

Creep narrowed his eyes. "Okay, that's a little too much." He rounded the desk and closed his hand around the man's neck, gifting him one, two, three punches to the face, possibly doing more damage to himself than the customer. He wrung out his hand and choked down a groan, then recomposed himself before kicking open his office door and dragging the customer through the cold chamber.

All eyes followed the pair as Sunshine stepped outside his shop and flung the burly man into the tar-paved street. As pedestrians gave the limp man a wide berth, York stepped outside and handed his boss a towel. Creep wiped the blood from his knuckles and finally remembered the name Ophala had called this stupid, yet fiery, young man.

Thank you, Sal.

32

The Imperfect Storm

Simon's breaths had slowed and deepened ever since breaking free of Spunka Forest earlier in the day. It might have been a trick of his mind, but there was a difference in the crisp scent of the air when this close to the Edge. He was in the center of Yinyon, entering the mayor's building, where he was greeted enthusiastically with warm smiles from the staff. He made his way to the third floor, which might as well have made the building a skyscraper among the village's flat ranches.

There was no door at the top of the stairs, instead opening up to a long room that occupied the entire floor. Like any proper office, bookcases lined the side walls. The decoy book Simon had planted on one of the higher shelves after taking the true story of the Third of Five seemed untouched. He was in the clear, for now. The front half of the room closest to the staircase served as a sitting chamber, complete with two armchairs, a loveseat, and a coffee table. A desk dominated the far end, a door leading outside just behind it. The mayor—Simon's father—sat at the desk, hair a faded orange with gray dusting the sides of his temple. Soraku Fuuna, her hair a striking violet, sat across from him with her back to Simon. Recognizing the new arrival, his dad clapped his hands together, stood, and rounded the desk.

"My boy!"

Simon approached and gave him a hug. "Hey, Dad."

"Got back earlier than expected," Soraku said.

"I rushed here."

His dad stepped back and held Simon at arm's length, absorbing the boy's face. "Glad to see you're okay."

"They could have used your help," Simon said.

"That wasn't our fight."

Simon's mouth twisted, biting the inside of his bottom lip. He didn't like that excuse. They had gotten onto Yama for her actions in recent years—which she deserved—but then claimed they couldn't aid True Light in the war? The excuse was that if they were going to reveal their true identities to the world, it needed to be done when there was little turmoil. War added too many unpredictable variables. Simon had accepted that reasoning in his haste before leaving Yinyon a couple months ago, fearing the war's impending climax. The Adren Assassins had only allowed him to go because he had already established a connection with the power players involved.

The stipulation attached? He couldn't use his abilities for any reason. If he wanted to partake in the deciding battle, he had to use archery. The whole reason behind him learning it in the first place was to have a skill outside of his talents as an assassin. It was a cover-up.

Simon had broken that rule. Upon arriving to the Intel Kingdom and seeing the duels occurring at the teleplatforms—Tashami and Dev Warden Gala, Spirit Director Neaneuma and Tazama, Passion Director Venustas and Still Warden Moroza—he made a decision to do the only thing that would turn the tides. He had chosen his friends and their alliance over his family back home. He had run in the sky and rained arrows from above. How would he break that news to his father?

The mayor returned to his office chair, and Simon took a seat next to Soraku. "The war ended?" his dad asked.

"The Rogue Demon's dead, but the resurrection was successful."

Soraku set her jaw. "So the war continues, but now with that king as the enemy. So much for our return to the populace."

She was referring to Dev King Rehn, but with Yinyon's seclusion from the rest of the world, their knowledge of current events was sparse. The only reason why it wasn't completely nonexistent was because of Simon's occasional updates over the years.

"No, Mendac LeAnce was the benefactor of the rebirth. Turns out that had always been the plan."

Soraku turned, eyebrows slanted with bewilderment. "The Fifth of Five?"

He nodded. His father leaned forward, laying both hands flat on the desk, gaze unfocused.

"We can't go public," she said, looking at the mayor. "One war transitioned into another."

"I used my abilities."

All eyes turned to Simon, glacial in both speed and emotion. "Repeat that," she said, voice low and steady.

"I took to the sky."

Soraku sprung from her chair, toppling it backward, hands shooting to her hips as she instantly began pacing to blow off steam. If his father, Solace Skimentis, was the bear of traditional Adrenian customs, Soraku Fuuna was the lion. Simon had feared her reaction to the news more than anyone. This ... Well, this wasn't that bad.

Solace's hands went to his face, pushing his spectacles up his forehead as he rubbed his eyes. "Who saw you?" he asked.

"I actually don't know if anyone did. I think my speed percentage was too high."

"Obviously," Soraku snapped, still pacing, now twiddling a dagger between her fingers. "If you were sky-skimming then clearly your speed percentage was beyond the range anybody could track."

"That's right," Solace breathed, sighing in relief. "I didn't even think of that." He leaned back. "The shock kind of threw me for a loop."

"It was still reckless," she said. "As the only young Adren Assassin and the mayor's son, you should know better."

Simon stared at his father, who was watching Soraku pace. "He's a kid."

She stopped and turned toward them. "That doesn't excuse him. I told you he's too rambunctious."

As if attracted to disappointing people, Simon said, "I told someone what I am."

A laugh, crazed and loud, climbed from Soraku's throat. He knew she found no humor in his confession. That response was a weird coping mechanism, as if laughing would distract her from wanting to throw her dagger at him. "And we were worried about him accidentally *showing* his skills to people, Solace," she said sarcastically. "No, he only *told* someone *directly*. A conscious decision followed by a deliberate act."

The sounds of cows and chickens filled the silence that followed. Solace didn't reveal much in his face, but his body showed signs of ticking gears. He placed his hands on his flat stomach, thin fabric of his button-up crinkled at the waist band of his pants. He tapped his fingers, eyes locked on Soraku. "I recall a rather young woman who decided it wise she share our secrets with a man she'd claimed was the love of her life … only to wake up one day and find that man had left the village."

Simon glanced at her sidelong. Her expression was frozen in ire. His father had dealt her a blow with which she couldn't argue—a personal blow of a moment that had stuck with her for a long time.

"Centuries of secrecy, and you wound up being the person who had a lapse of judgment," Solace said. "That makes you the only person in this village without ground to stand on when trying to shame my son."

Soraku pivoted sharply and strode for the staircase. Simon didn't know what he expected from the lion when faced with such a challenge, but it hadn't been that.

"She's not wrong," Solace said once the footfalls faded below.

"She told someone?"

His father smiled, glancing down at the desk in memory. "Love makes us all fools at least once in our lives."

The wise words stabbed at Simon, finding truth in them. Though he was only on the cusp of seventeen years old, he had fallen victim to something that came close to such a concept. Illipsia had fooled not only him, but all of True Light. He thought he loved her; he still did. That could be the only explanation behind why he'd helped her return to the Dev Kingdom with the woman she had called her mother—even after everything she'd done in allowing the Rogue Demon to resurrect Mendac.

"Why don't you seem angry?" Simon asked.

"I'm guessing you told Bryson."

"Yes."

Solace nodded. "For some reason, I find comfort in that. You've told me a lot about that boy over the years. He became your older brother whenever you weren't here with Kolver, which was a lot of the time. And judging by the lengths to which he's gone and the goodness of his heroics, I'd say I could trust him with our secret." He closed his eyes and shook his head. "To think I'd ever say that about someone I haven't met. Says a lot about the kind of person he is."

"I've never known anyone more dedicated to good," Simon said.

"You've been lucky, Simon." His father had that twinkle in his eye whenever he was about to say something profound. "When we sent you into the world, you could have ended up down a similar path as Yama ... or worse. But you found great people and followed them."

It was an understatement, but his father didn't know everyone who helped mold him into the young man he became. He had never told anyone about Intel Director Debo, the man this village knew as Ataway Debonicus Kawi. He would keep that secret until he felt comfortable sharing it.

"Where's Yama now?" Simon asked.

"Who knows? The woman is lost. It's a shame, and I feel for Soraku. I really believed that little girl we thrust into the world would come back as one of the best assassins we've ever seen. Alas, she doesn't have the trait and she's lost her conviction."

"Do you think she's a danger?"

A ponderous gaze set into Solace's face. "I think if she's a danger to anyone, it's herself."

Simon stood, pulling a wrapped bundle of cloth from his pocket. He unraveled it and placed it on the desk, revealing a chunk of dark chocolate. "I'm off to see Kolver, but I wanted to give you this."

"Is that ..."

"Chocolate from the Volcanic Quadrant of the Passion Kingdom?" Simon asked, finishing his dad's question. "Yes. And you can thank Director Venustas."

"Yes, yes," he said giddily, reaching for the chocolate. "Give her my thanks ... which one is she again?"

"You need to pay more attention to my updates."

He chuckled, taking a bite out of the chocolate. "Go. Tell your brother his aunt said they'll bury him in that inn if he spends anymore time there."

Simon smirked. "As long as he's buried near his goats."

*   *   *

On the way to the inn that served as the village's figurehead, Simon passed the Fuuna ranch. Soraku was nowhere to be found in the fields, but her uncle was picking barley with the help of paid farmhands. A wave from the old man told Simon he hadn't been in contact with Soraku since the meeting in his father's office. He always marveled at the strength and endurance of Soraku's uncle, who was well into his seventies.

The gate to the Fuuna ranch was what caught Simon's attention. It was constructed with four horizontal and three vertical wooden rods, but the symbol carved into the center pole of the gate sparked a feeling of déjà vu. He had seen that somewhere—a recent memory just out of grasp. An "S" with a spine of spikes running along its two humps. He studied and burned it into his mind. Perhaps, he could make the connection later.

The Yinyon Inn had only been known as such for eight years. The building had been abandoned due to its lack of necessity—nobody traveled to Yinyon—but Kolver, at the age of fifteen, had convinced the village to allow him to put it back in business. They were all for it, believing it might stop the boy from playing with their livestock or trampling across their pastures. And it did.

Kolver didn't receive any financial or work help. He had cleaned up the abandoned building and then maintained it by himself. He built an animal pen behind the inn and took on any injured livestock from other farm owners. He tried healing them with limited veterinary knowledge, but usually without results. That didn't bother him, for nothing beat the satisfaction of knowing the animals had a home. Yinyon Inn served lodging to animals more than it did people.

Simon snuck into the lobby, a narrow corridor with an even narrower staircase pressed against the right wall, a host's lectern placed next to the bottom of the stairs. The place seemed empty, so he crept through the lobby and found a modest-sized barroom toward the back of the main floor. Kolver sat hunched on a stool at the bar, back to the entrance, the feather of a quill shaking next to his head. Making every use of the stealth skills he'd developed since learning of his assassin blood, Simon tiptoed his way to his big brother, saw the edge of a sketchpad from around his back, and roared in his ear.

The quill scraped across the parchment, an errant line in its wake, as Kolver's entire upper body twitched. He whirled with fiery eyes, but they softened upon landing on Simon. Kolver laughed and shoved his brother. Simon reclosed the gap and embraced the innkeeper, patting him on the back. "How's it going, Kol?"

Kolver's hand moved up to Simon's hair, squeezing at different parts of his scalp. "I have to make sure it's not a ghost. The guys and I had a bet on if you'd make it back alive."

They separated, and Simon lowered himself on the neighboring stool. "I wasn't gone that long."

"Yeah, and you were only here for a couple weeks before you left again. You think you're some kind of fairy tale legend?"

Simon shrugged, a smug smirk tugging at his lips. "They *do* call me Torchtop."

"Heir to the Sky-Skimmers," Kolver added, chuckling. "I suppose two cool monikers qualify for legend status."

Simon sighed, gaze falling to the sketchpad. Kolver had always been an exceptional artist, though he had a rather annoying habit—when it came to the village elders—of only sketching Adren Assassins in action. That meant a lot of drawings of humans running on air or up the sides of buildings. It was damning evidence if anyone unfriendly ever came around these parts. His current piece now had a slash of ink across it and a tear from the quill's point.

"Sorry about that."

"Eh …" Kolver tore the parchment from its holder, crumpled it, and tossed it in the vicinity of a waste bin. "Not one of my better works."

"You remember me telling you about Bryson a few times, right?" Simon asked.

Kolver scoffed. "A *few?*"

"Okay, a lot. The point is … why didn't you tell me he came here?"

With a snap of his fingers, Kolver said, "Ah, yeah. That was like three years ago now." He paused, taking a long swig from a tankard. He lowered it and wiped his mouth, noticing the look on his little brother's face. "What? I forgot."

"You forgot about a visit from outsiders?" Simon asked, baffled. "How often does that happen here again? Oh yeah, never. And one of them was the *Intel Princess* herself."

"That lady was a princess? I thought royal women all had long hair and no fun?

Simon plopped his face in one hand, his elbow braced on the countertop. "At least you stay true to your backwoods lifestyle."

"Whatever. We're educated here."

Shaking his head, Simon said, "You told Bryson *The Third of Five* was a lie and that you would tell him the truth, but then you proceeded to tell him a different lie."

"Ehhh … I look at it as a smaller lie. His version was a complete farce. My version was slightly altered. Ataway and Leon did face heavy criticism for their relationship in Katashi, and it made fellow soldiers uneasy around them."

"But it wasn't the determining factor," Simon countered. "Ataway was caught Sky—"

"Duhhh," Kolver drawled with an air of boredom, interrupting his little brother. "I know how it goes, but I wasn't going to tell some random foreigner that."

Simon stared at Kolver, and the innkeeper sighed. "Look, it's not like I didn't drop a hint in the story I told him. I did him that favor. It's not my fault he's not the sharpest set of horns in the flock."

"Birds have horns?"

"A flock of rams, you idiot."

Per usual, their brotherly love had shifted from displays of affection to hurling insults and wise-cracks. "What was the hint?"

"I told him Ataway and Leon headed west to the capital from Yinyon."

Simon slipped into a dumbstruck silence before inhaling deeply. He had no retort. His brother was right. The only place west of Yinyon was the Edge. The capital, Katashi, was to the northeast. Basic geography. He laughed at Bryson's cluelessness, then said, "He might have been too caught up in the story to catch it."

"You're a nice person," Kolver said. "Anyway, I did tell him we had the full story and he could read it, but he said he didn't have time."

"As if dad would have let him."

Kolver closed his sketchpad and returned the quill to the inkwell. "True, but I was practicing hospitality. He was my first human tenant." He frowned. "And now that I think of it, that lady was pretty stingy with her tips for being a princess."

Simon heard fluttering wings behind him. He spun on his stool to find a falcon in the open window. He was across the room in a heartbeat.

Kolver's eyes widened. "A falcon in Yinyon?"

Recognizing the falcon from its cracked beak, Simon unraveled the miniature scroll that had been tied to its leg. This was Radon, the falcon gifted to Intel King Vitio from Ophala as a carrier bird. Now she belonged to Shelly, and for a carrier with this kind of speed to have traveled all the way out here, something bad must have happened. He had told the Intel Queen to alert him the moment a problem arose.

His heart sank as he scanned the coded missive. Lady Delilah dead. Revolutionists rising. Queen Shelly in a crippling state of depression … Bryson gone.

Kolver must have seen the color drain from Simon's face. "I'm guessing this time you're not even going to last a couple weeks."

Simon's hands were shaking. "They need me."

*   *   *

There are people who swim atop the waves of loss; there are people who drown in the undertow.

It had been the quote of a patient woman in Toshik's life. A woman who, despite disciplining him swiftly and without mercy, had never given the entitled brat the true damnation he deserved. She had seen the kindle of anguish beneath the pot of boiling arrogance. And although she hated the boy, she had done everything in her power to help him rise above the pain of losing his mother and little sister, lest he continue down a treacherous road of chauvinism. He had been stubborn and dismissive toward her lessons at first, but, as stated earlier, she had showed patience he did not deserve.

He didn't know what Yama was up to these days or how she was coping with Jilly's death, but he decided to assume she was a person who swam, not drowned. She'd always been a woman of conviction. He remembered that look of misery in her face, the flash of regret in her eyes when her sword had slashed across their love's chest—the incongruity of it all when aligned with the woman's determined attitude. But he had a difficult time believing a woman like her could love someone enough to allow the loss to break them.

So he trained. He sprinted across a dock and leapt into the deepest pond on his estate. He hit the surface, cold shocking his muscles and lungs, trying to convince him back to the surface even as he released air to make himself sink. The pressure popped his eardrums, vision hazy in the murky water. The soles of his feet hit a soft, muddy floor. He drew a waterlogged wooden sword and began sparring drills taught to him by that patient woman, the pond's depths resisting his speed and strength.

He went through the motions until his lungs nearly gave out, until he was on the cusp of sucking in gouts of water. Then it was back to the surface only to dive right back down. As the days progressed, his endurance, strength, and speed increased. Before long, he could last five minutes submerged.

It wasn't good enough.

He'd keep going until his swings created waves at the surface a hundred feet above. Until he could split the pond in two.

Patience he could have only learned from one woman: Master Ichi.

*   *   *

Rhyparia's and Mendac's training locations had slowly shifted from within the Labyrinth's walls to the courtyards and now to the vast outer grounds, where the city could be seen in the distance and color filled the grass and sky. She took any opportunity she could to escape the monochromatic grays of the Labyrinth's heart, an effect for which she still hadn't found an explanation. The sun seemed to shine just as bright in the sky in the inner courtyards as it did the outer grounds, yet colors didn't penetrate the Labyrinth's walls.

A woman sat against the base of a nearby tree, watching the two empirical soldiers fight. Rhyparia wasn't familiar with her, though she'd gotten her name one day when overhearing a conversation between her and Mendac. He had called her Kadlest, and she seemed to be an enigma up here in the Empire. She didn't mingle with the Gefal nor did she have wings. It didn't seem like she belonged, making Rhyparia curious of her role here.

Mendac thrust out an open palm, electricity streaking toward Rhyparia. She raised a rubber shield—designed specifically to counter electrical attacks—and negated the blow. He was on her instantly, a wooden long sword jabbing beneath the shield and headed for her leg. She dropped the shield on the sword's spine, then brought it back up to connect with his chin. She heard the pop of his bottom teeth smacking against the top set, and she shoved him back with the shield.

She closed the gap as he stumbled, a wooden dagger aimed at his neck, but he planted his foot and regained traction as his torso dipped to the side. Her dagger skimmed above his face. He grabbed a weapon from his belt, a pair of metal rods connected by a chain, and thrust the chain into her wrist. He gripped the metal rods and crossed them, wrapping the chain around her wrist. He lowered his shoulder and twisted his body, flipping her with his momentum over his back. She let slip a scream as he also released a voltaic attack into the rods, which then transferred into her wrist as he loosened the chain's grip. She darted through the air before smacking the ground and lifting upward again, like a pebble skipping across a pond. Kadlest, who sat in her path, caught her with an outstretched arm.

"You should do better," whispered Kadlest.

Rhyparia knocked the woman's hand away and stood, brushing off her shoulder and chest.

Mendac let the tip of his wooden sword hit the grass, using it as a cane. "I don't know why you let me use my electricity. This would be a fairer fight if you had your ancient."

"Or maybe it's my utter lack of a cheerleader," she said vehemently, casting a glare back at Kadlest. "What is it that you even do?" She felt the poison dripping from her tone, but she'd had enough of the woman's sarcastic jabs and judgmental eyes.

"I aid Mendac."

"In emptying his piss bucket?"

Kadlest said nothing, eyes landing on Mendac as if hoping for his defense. He didn't give one. Rhyparia shook her hand as shocks continued pulsing through her nerves, returning her attention to him. She was curious of his relationship with Kadlest. The woman seemed tied to him like a dog on a leash, yet he seemed the kind of man who wouldn't bother taking the dog out to enjoy a walk in the first place. There was a disconnect, and Kadlest's loyalty to him was pathetic in Rhyparia's eyes. As far as she could tell, he had never abused the woman, but there was something about him that commanded Kadlest's will.

Was it in those piercing, yet studious blue eyes? He possessed the look and air of a well-educated soldier: the scar stretching into his scalp, his hair giving it a wide berth; the hardened jawline beneath a grizzled, buzz-cut beard of silver; wings of black folded tight against his back, under his control, for he was a man who knew himself. If Rhyparia hadn't been conscious of the mystery behind him, perhaps she would have allowed that strength to draw her in, too.

"And what are you?" he asked.

The question brought his blurry face into focus. "What?"

"You're perplexed by Kadlest's identity, her role. Do you not find it ironic that someone who has yet to find her own identity questions someone else's?"

Rhyparia could only blink away the shock of his directness. Okay, perhaps he did have some kind of loyalty to Kadlest. She could feel the woman's face growing smug behind her back.

Rhyparia took a moment to process his implication, knowing her initial reaction to hurl an insult back was impulsive and irrational. It had been a clever and accurate accusation. Yasmine had made her aware of this every single day. The legendary Dev Assassin had been the only Gefal to give her the time of day since arriving in the Dark Empire. This was a result of Rhyparia's self-obliviousness. The other Gefal refused to acknowledge her until she could acknowledge herself—an arbitrary rite of passage into their ranks. Mendac had gained that respect already. He was on good terms with several of the Gefal, while she floundered. Not even the team to which they'd been assigned—comprised of one Fuhren and three Bewahr—had spared a glance her way.

"Do you want to know who I am?" Mendac asked. She eyed him warily, not sure of the question's legitimacy. Recognizing this, he lowered himself into the grass and extended a hand, gesturing for her to do the same. She complied.

"I'm a scholar and innovator. A warrior and leader." His chin dipped, gazing at his lap, lost in thought. "But those are identities, and identities aren't traits. While scholars are skilled and impressive, that doesn't mean they're inherently good or bad. Same for the other identities I mentioned. Rather than stemming from identities, behavioral traits—what makes you, you—are mannerisms.

"While I was any one of those four identities—sometimes all four depending on the situation—in order to become them, I was aggressive in my mannerisms and apathetic toward those affected by them. And if we are to dig deeper into what makes someone what they are, beyond mannerisms, we find motives ... desires. For me, that was knowledge and power." His piercing blue eyes hardened. "What does that make me?"

"I don't know," she said.

He narrowed his eyes in disbelief, but repositioned himself on the ground for comfort and said, "If mannerisms and motives were all it took to make someone a bad person, than there would be no good in the world—and I find that hard to believe. I've known 'Good.' I watched her die."

Rhyparia stole herself, believing she knew of whom he spoke. The tale of Thusia's Sacrifice. The girl he once loved. How would he react if he knew she was alive as a Branian? That he could see her again? Or did he already know?

"Musku Rao," he said, "one of my fellow Jestivan, had a habit of teaching me things in which I had no interest."

Again, Rhyparia had to stifle a visual reaction. Musku was the man who had trained her for two decades over the span of a time-warped ten months. He had put his faith in her to guide the Dimiours through Realmular Tunnel with the ultimate goal of freeing the Powish slaves. He had preached compassion and temperance, knowing how to analyze a situation and determine a proper, ethical response … all ideas she had gone on to ignore.

"He taught me topics on the opposite side of the intellectual spectrum from me," Mendac continued. "The whole Archain versus Intelian debate. One day, he explained to me Yulis's Venn Diagram. Are you familiar with it?"

"No," she lied. Of course she knew it. Musku had drilled the diagram into their lessons on a weekly basis, the old man fearful of the monster she could one day become. He had never fully trusted her, and she had proved his doubts right.

"Three circles overlapping at the center to create four additional sections shared between them," Mendac explained. "One of many Archain methods to measure one's self. Archains believe the true nature of a person boils down to three questions: What is the motive behind your thoughts, the manner in which you feel toward them, and the action taken to achieve them? The three circles of Yulis's Venn Diagram contain 'Motive,' 'Manner,' and 'Action.' Motives can be revenge, greed, or pride—and one other thing, but that's it. Mannerisms aren't as constricting: belligerent, manipulative, calculated, violent, apathetic, regretful… the list goes on and on." He paused, studying her with those piercing eyes. "But 'Action' … Well, that's a simple 'yes' or 'no.'"

He exhaled sharply. It almost sounded like a single mocking laugh. "My motive was the greed of knowledge and dominion. The manner in which I thought of achieving those motives was violent and apathetic to those around me. And most importantly, I put it into action. Do you know what those three traits make me when overlapped on the diagram?"

She lied again, shaking her head.

"A bad person ... a very bad person."

"So what would the diagram have determined had you not acted?"

"A flawed person, like any other human."

Rhyparia nodded solemnly. Mendac had held no punches, laying it all on the table for her. "Do you regret it?" she asked.

"I killed their king, and they knew I was going after their kingdom's greatest secrets," he said, glare softening with internal pain, "so they tried all measures to stop me. I regret everything I did that went beyond the motive of avenging Thusia, even if it was self-defense. And that regret is the reason why I'm lucky enough to *only* be considered 'bad.'"

His wings flared unnaturally at that. Rhyparia found herself frowning, recalling the foul taste in her mouth after hearing Musku use that same word. "Bad" sounded juvenile to her, a perception that strengthened while rotting away in that time-warp.

"What about you?" he asked. "Applying the diagram to yourself, where do you fall?"

She turned to find Kadlest still seated against the tree. She held one of her boots in front of her face, inspecting its sole and pretending not to listen. Rhyparia wasn't a dunce. While she was willing to share her story with the man who had just revealed so much about himself, that offer didn't extend to Kadlest. She stood and retrieved her rubber shield, then said, "We'll talk in the bunker."

*   *   *

They didn't get a chance to speak again until early evening, just before the sun showed itself to begin second-day. Mendac arrived to the bunker covered in sweat, having completed another rigorous training session with Poten Copor, one of the Gefal's five Fuhren and the man who had escorted Mendac to Emperor Mialo the day they had met him for the first time. Mendac had the luxury of combat training with a Fuhren because of the strides made in knowing himself. Rhyparia would have to continue sparring Mendac until she could learn to do the same.

She needed to learn fast. Ever since receiving news that she would have to fight one of the Fuhren in the coming months as a test of her abilities, her angst had grown. She had preached not caring about this place or its war, but when matters of physical prowess were spotlighted, she couldn't stop herself from wanting to excel.

There were five bunkers in the Black Labyrinth, each of which housed a team consisting of three Bewahr and one Fuhren. Despite Rhyparia's connection with Yasmine and Mendac's connection with Poten, they had been stationed with a team led by neither. The Fuhren who led this team had not spoken with Rhyparia and therefore had never given her his name, but Mendac—the human encyclopedia that he was—had called him the Plague. It was the exact kind of ominous moniker she would have expected from someone who looked like him and lived in the Dark Empire.

Mendac walked past her in the commons area, shirtless, exposing the troughs and hills of his abdomen and the pronounced V-line that disappeared behind low-hanging trousers. She looked away, unfamiliar with the nakedness of a man's body. It was during times like this one when she had to remind herself of her age. She was no girl.

He didn't glance at her in his passing, leaving her questioning the motives of this man now that he wasn't chasing the knowledge and dominion of the mainland below. There were moments when he only had eyes for her and there were times she didn't seem to exist in his presence. She wondered if there was a calculated reason for that.

Mendac reached the middle of the bunker, where a recess cut along the length of the Mulanyx floor in a narrow strip, ramps at the edges meeting at a dip at its center. It was just wide enough for two people to walk through shoulder-to-shoulder. And the recess was low enough for someone to disappear beneath the floor. She heard the door to their room open and shut. They shared a room, for each bunker was only equipped with five, one for each Gefal and an extra for any trainees. The recess was lined with three doors on one side and two on the other, each leading to a room below the commons area's floor.

She waited while he cleaned himself up and changed into fresh clothes. The bunker was empty save him, herself, and the lifeless furniture and other objects within. She surveyed the Mulanyx walls of the bunker, the smoothness seen elsewhere broken here. Apparently, that fragmentation was actually a lock constructed by highly complex weaving of Mulawi. It was what kept other Gefal from entering or looking inside.

The only way she could enter or leave was via the help of one of the Gefal who resided in this bunker. Mendac, somehow, could do it unaided, able to come and go as he pleased. Her nostrils flared with annoyance at her shortcomings. She had been upset with her inability to kill herself after dropping the moon, the Gefal's intrusion as they swept her away to some world of no consequence to her. But she was slowly beginning to realize she hated her status here.

A fleck of dust, not enough to be a nuisance to anyone because of her insignificance, but still there, wandering aimlessly. Mendac had purpose here, and he was making her look like that incompetent, hapless child she once had been: when her mother had toyed with her to test her potential and when King Itta had dreamed of her as his weapon of mass destruction. If she was breathing, she needed to control her own will. She needed to assert herself among these legends, lest she desired a slave's life again. Too weak to grab the reins, too poor to grab attention.

Mendac returned to the commons area half an hour later. Candlelight shimmered off the ebony walls, making the bunker's reach seem an infinite void. He chose a sofa across from her armchair, sitting at the far end, one leg crossed over the other and his arm resting along the armrest. He eyed her without a hint of amusement or friendliness, understanding the nature of the story about to be told. She appreciated that genuine display. He would take this seriously.

Rhyparia told the man everything starting at a certain point of her life—or mostly everything. The story took one detour at the beginning, as Musku's name prompted questions from the old friend. After concluding with Ulna Malen's destruction, he asked for the whole story, starting from her childhood. She thought she had skipped that part because of the pain it brought her, but when he asked, she realized it was because it hadn't crossed her mind. Then, when she did recount her early years, the words came forth easily.

Mendac's eyes narrowed throughout the tragedy: a mother's exploitation of her young daughter's innocence, the collapse of a poor, rundown sector, and the loss of a newborn baby sister and the guilt placed on her shoulders. He was evaluating every aspect of her story—and not just the plot. This man knew how to listen and what to listen for. He heard tone alterations and spotted postural shifts. She saw him glance at her shoulder as it dipped, her head reaching toward the opposite shoulder and her neck releasing a pop in its stretch. She had done this when speaking of the Gravity Trials, when her verdict and the punishment of execution had been announced, pantomiming the anger she felt toward the moment.

When all was said and done, he said, "You experienced the grief of ten people in their nineties, yet you walked Kuki Sphaira's lands for a tiny fraction of that time."

"And I found solace," she said.

"In mass murder?"

She didn't answer. They had discussed this countless times. She was at peace; they had deserved it.

"Justice is a delicate concept," he said, proving he remembered her reasoning in their prior conversations. "When applied in certain ways, it can venture into areas of petty vengeance, which our friend, Musku, views as an evil doppelganger of justice. Sure, vengeance may appear honorable and deserving, but it's really just selfish. And, in the way you applied it, merciless and ..." He trailed off.

"And what?"

He inhaled and looked elsewhere for a moment, then posed a question. "You crushed a lower class sector when you were a mere child, killing an entire population, family and friends included. Your mother made you do that. You killed dozens in the restaurant collapse. Your mother made you do that. You killed a general, who had simply been following orders to apprehend you. Again, your mother. Unbeknownst to you, you were being molded into a weapon of mass destruction. That had been Archaic King Itta's doing. When I hear a story like that, I see more a puppet than a person—albeit, a puppet with claws, fangs, and bulk, but still just a puppet. No will. No dominion over one's own body."

"I am nobody's puppet." She was losing her wonder with this man. He was enraging her. She regretted telling him anything. Judging by the man's inward lean, elbows on his knees and intense gaze, it was what he had wanted. *Of course.*

"And I agree," he said. "And there came a point in your life when you learned that, likely during those decades spent with Musku. And you wanted to rid yourself of that image of a forlorn, hapless girl who couldn't understand why she did bad things. So you worked to erase it. You took the closest opportunity, which was getting through Realmular Tunnel and rescuing the Powish slaves, and you chose that as your defining moment … as your way of proving to yourself that you had control over your own body and mind, while masking the abhorrence of it all with a mission close to the hearts of your comrades. A mission that lined up with your selfish desires by mere happenstance."

Silence befell them, and she found herself looking past Mendac, toward the shattered Mulanyx wall behind him. Her reflection stared back at her, clear in the glossy back material, fragmented into a dozen surfaces. For the first time in a long time, she could see that little girl—that naïve version of herself. It was a part of her she had lost not just with age, but with cynicism caused by the events of her early years.

"Tell me again," Mendac said. "What did you feel when you watched Ulna Malen perish beneath the moon?"

This time, there was a pause before her answer. "Peace."

"No, what did you feel?"

Her gaze had dropped from the wall to the glass table between them, and she saw the answer he was trying to siphon from her. To an infant, glass was probably one of the most perplexing items in the world. They couldn't see it, so of course they thought it wasn't there, spurring amazement in them when they tried to reach for something beyond it only to discover "it" was in the way. To their eyes, it wasn't something, but … She looked up, giving the answer in a steady voice: "Nothing."

Mendac leaned back, returning his forearm to the arm of the sofa and kicking a leg back over the other. "Nothing," he echoed softly.

The epiphany was a massive weight dropped on her. Ironic that "nothing" could feel so heavy. In those final moments between the moon's landing and the Gefal's arrival, gazing at the ruin, she didn't think of Olethros, the Generals' Battle weekend, the Gravity Trials, or her family.

Even Vuilni and her family, who had suffered as Powish slaves, hadn't crossed her mind—and that was supposed to have been the main motivation behind the act. If those thoughts hadn't occurred to her, then had it really been justice?

"And do you know what that means?" Mendac asked. "The 'nothingness?'"

"Aside from me being a bad person?" she asked.

He raised an eyebrow. "Oh, no," he said. "In Yulis's Venn Diagram, you have what is referred to as the 'imperfect storm.' And this phenomenon occurs, firstly, when someone acts. Then that action must fall under a specific combination of motive and manner. I told you earlier that motive could be one of four things. I named three: revenge, greed, and pride. The fourth is spoken about the least, but doesn't make it any less important. That is 'demonstration.' What you did in the Power Kingdom was a demonstration. You made a statement: 'My will is my own. This is me and no one else.'"

Rhyparia gave no counter. She was beginning to understand it all. And perhaps she had already known all of this deep down, the reality suffocated by denial—an instinctive coping mechanism for someone who's experienced great trauma.

"So you acted in demonstration," he said. "But that's just two-thirds of what creates the imperfect storm. So we move to the next question: In what manner was it conducted? There are two answers in this case: violently and unapologetically." He narrowed his eyes. "You don't have regrets, right?"

"No."

"Then you've found yourself in rare company. Not many share your classification. The imperfect storm of an action motivated by demonstration and conducted in a violent, unapologetic manner causes a rare overlap in the diagram's circles."

Rhyparia nodded, that nothingness becoming heavier. He tilted his head. "Ah, that's right. You lied earlier about not knowing the diagram. There's no way you spent two decades with Musku and weren't taught it." He paused, then asked, "So, what are you, Rhyparia NuForce?"

"Evil," she replied. Her wings became frozen daggers in her back, flaring outward and revealing an impressive wingspan that may have

DAVID F. FARRIS

dwarfed Mendac's. She turned her head, acknowledging her left wing, its edges warping to touch the Mulanyx walls and floor. Per usual, she felt the Mulawi coursing through her, but now she felt control over it. She wove the energy escaping her back and pulled her wings forward. The Mulanyx responded, raven stone fuzzing into shadows that coiled upward to entwine with her wings.

The sensation that followed was sheer brilliance. A chilly rush spilled into her from the Mulanyx, teasing at untapped power. Her heart throttled into her throat, stomach growing feathery light, hair flying backward as if caught in a gale. She felt as if she was flying—no, racing at breakneck speed. She reveled in it, mouth slack as she gulped down ragged breaths of pleasure, eyes rolling back slightly.

She was conscious; she was present. But she was also cognitive of something else. This sensation had once belonged to whatever was in these walls: a primordial entity faced with death—and she had no idea what it was.

By the time she regained dominion over her wings and ripped them free from the Mulanyx, another presence had joined hers and Mendac's in the commons area. His greasy black hair fell in mangled strings. His pale skin was oily enough to reflect candlelight, his smell so putrid she made a conscious effort to breathe through her mouth. His ancient, a grated mask of wood, covered his mouth and nose, a strap along the back of his head holding it in place. He was the Fuhren of this bunker, and she knew him only as Plague.

"There aren't many of us," he rasped, his voice strained and weak.

She raised her eyebrows in question.

"He was in his room below," Mendac said. "Apparently, he was there the whole time, listening through the Mulanyx floor."

"Us?" she asked, standing to meet the Fuhren's gaze.

The mask hid his mouth, but she saw the smile in his red eyes. That was unnatural. "Evil," he said.

"Now you want to talk to me? I don't even know you."

"The name is Brenson Ulial. In 1127 K.H., I poisoned the air of two Primmish towns and a city, granting every man, woman, and child the slowest, most agonizing deaths. I believe, to this day, a person cannot step

345

foot in one of those towns without first stepping on bones." He extended a hand. "Not many like us."

She stared at his mask. So that was the ancient's ability: poison, toxins? She met his eyes and said, "I'm not shaking your hand." She headed for the bunker's side wall. She stared at it, tracking the ivory lines curling through the black. The sensation had disappeared from her body, but a lasting impression had been imprinted into her mind. This building was alive, once existing on a scale too large for the human mind to comprehend.

"I want to know everything about this place."

33

The Immortal Daughter

The Infested Forest had grown tiresome. Well over a week had passed, yet Agnos, Tashami, and Evelyn had yet to step foot on Ipsas's campus proper, despite sitting just a mile out of its reach. Agnos appreciated Evelyn's carefulness—they had combed the forest's edge and found guards manning the watchtowers with keen eyes—but he was beginning to question if she had a plan to infiltrate. She had sworn she did, but he was losing faith in it, mostly because it involved a lot of sitting on their thumbs and waiting for the actions of others.

They were stationed in a general location of the forest on the western side of the campus within a mile of the boundary. They moved each day, but only by a few thousand feet, always keeping a certain cottage in sight. According to Evelyn, it was the only manmade structure in the forest and belonged to a woman known as the Woodkeeper, Nynis Yogo. She was a Primmish woman, meaning she possessed a fondness for nature that stemmed from their religious culture. She lived in the forest, working to conserve it and the life contained within.

Evelyn proclaimed the Woodkeeper would help because of her great relationship with the woman. The first day spotting the cottage, she had found a hidden compartment within a uniquely shaped gnarl of roots. She used a knife to cut a lock of her hair and then placed it inside before departing. A perplexed Agnos and Tashami badgered her about it, but their answer didn't come until a middle-aged woman—her bald scalp slicked with oil or wax—approached the roots and dug inside. She wore a toga like Agnos remembered from Toono's earlier years. She pulled out the hair, inspecting it for a few seconds before looking around her. Then she returned to her cottage.

"Now we wait," Evelyn said, leaning back against a tree, arms crossed in front of her.

"For what?" Tashami asked.

"Before I left Ipsas to return to Kindoliya and pledge my allegiance to Still Queen Apoleia, I made sure I didn't burn all of my bridges. While most of the school hated me because siding with my queen meant siding with True Light, there were a few individuals who I knew wouldn't fault me for it, so I paid them visits and asked favors. The Woodkeeper was one of those people, and that was her. I'm sure she heard rumblings these past couple weeks about my return, so she's likely been checking those roots every day since. After all, we agreed on it being our communication. She knows who I am because not many have frosted blue hair. Now that she knows I'm somewhere around, she'll stow away food and messages in the roots while we wait."

"Why can't we just go to her or she come to us?" Tashami asked.

Agnos shook his head. "That would be reckless. What if there are guards around or inside the cottage? We need verification that it's safe first, I'm guessing."

"Yes," said Evelyn. "And I also want to know if the High Warden has come out this way to pay Nynis a visit. I'd suspect him to, seeing as she is the eyes of this forest. And while I don't know if he was aware of my good relationship with her, it's best to assume he did. He might interrogate her."

"Alright, so we wait a little bit longer," Agnos said, sighing and leaning against the trunk of a toppled tree.

The days following initial contact were filled with written communication and the little bit of food Nynis could offer. They learned there weren't guards nor had she received a visit from High Warden Sylial. Alas, she was hesitant in allowing them close to her home, predicting an impending visit from the man.

They had one more encounter with a pericul, but thankfully it was pre-host, meaning there was no umbra fairy they had to target in order to kill it. Other than that, their stay in the forest was relatively peaceful, which could be attributed to their proximity to Ipsas's campus. The animals knew to steer clear of the student life. According to Evelyn, they only came this way if in need of aid from Nynis. The Woodkeeper was a skilled veterinarian.

Tonight, however, was different. As the light of second-day splashed through the treetops, the trio eyed the cottage from a safe distance, hiding behind a fallen log, heads covered in a makeshift net of sticks and leaves.

The man who approached the cottage from its eastward side didn't bother with guards or soldiers—odd for someone who thought himself a king. However, this was a school, so were there any real threats to him? No matter how many times Evelyn spoke of conflict in Ipsas, Agnos had a hard time believing students would attempt rebellion or assassination. Besides, what kind of lunatic would make this guy an enemy?

High Warden Sylial was no giant or Powish brute, but he was tall and imposing. He could probably look Toshik and Himitsu in the eye, but he was built stronger, tight muscles running the length of his arms. He wore sleeveless, unbuttoned, and billowing robes, its hood draped down his back. He wore a simple tunic as his undershirt, the hems of its sleeves squeezing his biceps, and trousers that hugged most of his legs until crinkling at the calves and disappearing within high-top combat boots. His charcoal hair—black and striped with grays—was long and thin, billowing behind him in rhythm with his robes. When he reached the front door, knocked, and came to a stop, his hair fell down to his hamstrings. His face, spotted with light between leaves above, was a sun-kissed tan, jaw clenched and eyes fierce.

He looked more like a general than a king. It was obvious that he was trained in physical combat, yet Agnos couldn't shake the knowledge that he was also from the Dev Kingdom. He'd met so many Devish soldiers whose skills in weaving were all they had in their arsenal. Many were subpar in hand-to-hand combat and—Agnos's eyes widened. Did he have a sword sheathed at each hip?

The door opened, and the warden entered.

"*That's* your High Warden?" Tashami asked.

"Yep."

"Where is the elderly wisdom and professional uniform? His robes don't have sleeves; his hair reaches his legs!" he hissed.

"There is nothing 'conventional' here in Ipsas. You wear what you want, and aside from the rules regarding behavior toward Warden Sylial, codes aren't set in stone. Discipline comes in a more circumstantial basis. An act that one student might get overlooked for can send another student into a box with a swarm of bees."

Agnos squinted at a window, but it was difficult to see inside with the sunlight hitting that side of the cottage. "And she's not going to betray you?" Agnos asked.

"You can never be certain here," she replied, drawing looks of alarm from her two comrades. She added, "But if I were to trust anyone, it'd be a Primmish. Considering their neutral position in worldwide wars and politics over the centuries, they don't hold the same anger toward me for what most people in the Dark Realm consider my 'treacherous' ways. She doesn't care who I side with. Plus, I've established something solid with the woman."

Agnos looked at the cottage again. He had no reason to not trust Evelyn. She had been too good to him since joining his pirate crew.

Hours of second-day progressed without activity. A hand nudged Agnos's shoulder, waking him from a slumber. He blinked out dreariness and discovered he had slipped behind the tree and passed out. His neck was stiff, but when he tried to move, a weight atop his right shoulder made him stop. Then he noticed a steady breath brushing against his slightly-exposed collarbone. Tashami had fallen asleep, too, and he was using Agnos's shoulder as a pillow. Evelyn moved the Spiritian's head for him. "Real cute, but pay attention."

The two men turned, pressing the tops of their heads upward against the net. It had covered them in their sleep while Evelyn scouted the cottage. The sun was setting with midnight's approach, making sight difficult, but shadowy figures could be distinguished outside the front door. Agnos couldn't believe it was so late. How much had they needed to discuss?

"That's Sylial and Nynis," said Evelyn. "Looks like the warden is headed back."

As if on cue, the tall man set out east, toward the campus. Nynis stepped into her cottage and closed the door. "Now what?" Tashami asked through a yawn.

"We go to sleep," she said. "Nynis isn't going to leave her home until tomorrow. I'll check the roots around noon, in the darkness of second-night."

Agnos nodded, excited to escape this stagnancy. Tashami, however, frowned, slipping back behind the tree and placing his head against Agnos's hip. That couldn't have been comfortable—not with his bony frame. "Then what was the point of waking us?"

Ten seconds. That was all it took before snoring disrupted Evelyn and Agnos's amused silence.

*   *   *

Twelve hours later, Agnos watched Tashami from across a patch of grass. The Spiritian was still sleeping, but it hadn't been a smooth process. Since waking a few hours ago, Agnos had seen Tashami's eyes snap open multiple times, as if startled. His breathing would grow erratic for a few seconds before returning to normal, his eyes slowly closing again. This time his eyes opened more naturally. He pushed himself out of a slouched position against the log, smacking his lips, face twisting in disgust. They didn't have dental hygiene products out here.

"Good afternoon," Agnos said.

Tashami paused, blinking a couple times before glancing up at the blackened treetops, stars barely visible between branches and foliage. "How long did I sleep?"

"Half a day. It's a little past noon."

"Good grief. Don't let me do that again."

"Well, you kept waking up."

Tashami threw up his arms and arched his back. As he released the stretch, he rolled his neck, muscles straining with the motion. Agnos looked away, questioning why he was suddenly noticing these details. Evelyn had gotten into his head. He decided to force more conversation. "Did you have any nightmares?"

Tashami shrugged. "I don't think so. It was probably just discomfort."

That didn't explain the irregular breathing, but Agnos didn't gripe about it. He let the topic blow over. "How do you feel about the High Warden?" he asked.

"I only got a glimpse, but I'd say he's formidable. You can't be the head of a school like Ipsas and not be. Think of what Grand Director Poicus did as a man in his nineties. Could you imagine him in his prime? This Warden Sylial guy looks like he's in his prime."

Agnos plopped his head back against their bags. That wasn't what he wanted to hear. Tashami sat forward, eyes raking their surroundings. He rose to a knee and twisted, peering over the fallen tree. "Where's Evelyn?"

"On her way back, hopefully."

"And with good news," Tashami muttered.

"Good news!" came a voice from several paces to the side. Agnos twitched in surprise, nearly choking from sucking air down the wrong pipe. Tashami cocked his head as he tried to distinguish a figure in the shadows of a cluster of trees. Evelyn stepped into a patch of moonlight, blue hair luminescent.

"I didn't even hear you," Tashami said, seeming genuinely impressed. "I spent a couple years refining my hearing for assassins while training with Himitsu, so how did you just do that?"

"I know how to walk through this forest," she said nonchalantly. "As we're all aware, I've done it many times." She looked at Agnos with an evil grin. "You okay there, pal?"

Agnos nodded slowly.

"Good. Anyway, Nynis left me a message. She said to visit the cottage in three days' time. Warden Sylial's visit last night wasn't just about us. Apparently, a group of four students got in serious trouble yesterday. Their punishment will take place three days from now, with Nynis as the overseer."

"She punishes people?" Agnos asked.

"Only if they're truly deserving, which means something in a school like this. The High Warden picked that night because it's supposed to be one of the worst thunderstorms in recent memory. He wants the students tossed into the Infested Forest during it." She paused, frowning. "A miserable time, really."

"Alright," Agnos said, "and what do we do?" A thunderstorm in a forest didn't faze him as much as it should have. This was due to his experiences sailing open waters. He'd fought through many storms, but nothing quite like that night on the Whale Lord when he'd caught the mutinous rats aboard the ship. If it hadn't been for Tashami's weaving abilities in filling the sails, the massive galleon would have capsized.

"Nynis made a brilliant suggestion to Warden Sylial," Evelyn said. "She said to turn the punishment into a deadly game." Agnos's mouth curled downward with distaste. "She suggested releasing the students into the forest blindfolded, then tasking them to escape the forest before the sun rises to begin first-day. Sometime in that timeframe, we can enter the campus under cloaks amidst a thunderstorm at night. With that chaos and darkness, the conditions will be ideal. And if any guards just so happen to spot cloaked figures running out of the forest, they'll assume them to be the punished students."

"Not bad," said Tashami.

Agnos scratched his chin. "And what if a guard stops us to verify our identities?"

"They shouldn't. When I placed that ever-ice gem beneath the floorboard of my cell, I also placed a note inside, telling Jewel to make sure his worst soldiers were stationed at the western edge of the campus for the foreseeable future. None of them are going to bother stepping into the deluge and searching us. They suck and they're lazy. His best men and women are on the eastern side of the campus."

Agnos slapped his hands atop bent knees. "A gamble, but all we have at this point."

"And what do we know of this school?" Tashami asked. "I don't know the staff or any important students. I don't know what we're supposed to be doing once we're on campus, nor do I know its layout."

Evelyn sat next to Agnos on the ground, pulling an apple slice from somewhere in her shirt. She tossed it in her mouth and began crunching. "Well, that's what the next few days are for. Plus, I don't think you guys will be roaming the campus at all."

*   *   *

Manufacturing emotion was impossible—at least for Olivia Still.

The events of the boy's death on the tram ram and the mother's abuse of a refugee on the ice rink proved to Olivia that she could tap into her water ability if faced with severe sorrow or rage. Those were the only two times she was able to produce trace amounts of hot water from her hands. Outside of those instances, however, she accomplished nothing. So she had set out on achieving those feelings again.

In the past five days alone, she witnessed twenty-two people die. She had visited elderly homes and hospitals, offering her presence to people on their deathbeds. She often stood at their bedside, the patient's family surrounding them as their final breaths leaked out. Word had spread quickly of the Still Princess's daily routine. Most of the population thought it telling of her empathy, claiming she had a big heart and was simply embodying the new image of a proper Stillian woman. A few—specifically women against the cultural shift and royal family because of it—despised her for what they viewed as posturing.

Honestly, it was neither of those things. Olivia empathized with the loved ones of those dying, but not nearly enough. These people were strangers. She had shed not a single tear at any death. What did these families think when they saw their princess hold the hand of their loved one's corpse with an expressionless face? One daughter had tried hugging Olivia and wailing into her shoulder, but she could only stand there with her arms at her sides. She may have made strides in displaying affection or empathy to her friends, but not to people she didn't know.

Her mother had expressed disdain for Olivia's methods, not because she was staining their political and ideological foundations, but because she was essentially toying with very real concepts such as death and family. And while Apoleia understood her daughter's struggles to reach notches on the emotional spectrum, she wouldn't accept the callousness of Olivia's ignorant acts.

"Do not undermine the raw, tragic beauty of a family grieving over loss," Apoleia had said one night while watching the sculptor hammer at the ice block in the Icebound Confluence. "Do not patronize their humanity by using them as an experiment for personal gain."

Thus, Olivia found herself free of death for the first time in a week. Her mother had been right, of course. Her actions had been egregiously selfish, and she felt she had regressed because of it. She had been trying to fabricate emotion—a cardinal sin when dealing with energies such as Passion and Still, which thrived off authenticity.

She sat in her room, replaying her conversations with Himitsu and Lilu in Dunami. Her two friends—especially the former—had given helpful insight. Himitsu had pulled feelings out of her with relative ease, a testament to his heart. Out of the Jestivan, he might have cared more about his peers than anyone else, including the caring souls of Bryson and Jilly. She hadn't expected it, but that was what made that moment with Himitsu authentic, her tears real. The moment had crept up on her naturally.

Her quarters were huge, occupying nearly an entire floor of the royal sector. She had four chambers: an antechamber with walls covered in paintings, a round, elegant foyer table topped with an ever-ice centerpiece, and a few credenzas to the sides of the room; a washroom, complete with plumbing suited for a bath, sink, and toilet; a sitting room lined with bookcases and filled with plush furniture; and the bedroom, where a four-poster bed dominated attention over the wardrobes and nightstands, a desk at the opposite end.

She currently sat on the white carpet of the sitting room in front of a cackling hearth. It had been an abandoned feature of the quarters for a long time, likely because no Stillian really craved the heat. But she was biracial and appreciated some semblance of warmth, possessing her father's blood and—somehow, despite her father's Intel Energy—Passion Energy within her. That continued to befuddle her: the mixing of genetics from separate realms creating any kind of combination involving the cavities of the two parents. That meant Olivia could have ended up with any pair of Intel, Dev, Still, or Passion Energy, given they were opposite energies. It didn't matter that her parents were Intelian and Stillian, for Dev came from the Knowledge Cavity just like Intel, and Passion came from the Emotion Cavity just like Still.

She stared into the fire, then glanced at the ice accumulating in the upper corners of the room. She was working so hard to awaken her water ability for a second time, but could she also separate the two energies flowing through her, granting her the ability to weave both fire and ice? Such an arsenal of abilities—fire, ice, and water—would have been dangerous. There'd be no proper defense against her.

There was reason for hope. Since arriving to Kindoliya, she had reserved hours of her night to scouring the libraries of the scholar's wing. One of the most unique aspects of the capital's palace was that it held a school of sorts. The finest women dedicated their studies in that wing, boarding in rooms inside of the palace. The libraries held some of the finest reading material.

She had thirty books sprawled around her on the carpet, but it had only taken reading through twelve of them to find what she'd been looking for: the story behind her Bewahr, Preloz Henye. The book was called *Tragedies of the Dark*, and it was an anthology of morbid, depressing stories from the Dark Realm. As she read through them, she felt they were the opposites of the Light Realm's *Of Five* series, depicting anti-heroes or victims as the main character. Preloz Henye was a victim who had never found a resolution.

She didn't know how to approach her Bewahr about it. The logical decision was to not approach him at all, but she wanted to establish a connection with the man. However, she had to make sure she didn't come off as pitying, lest she wound the man's pride. Bryson used to react poorly whenever someone tried pitying his position in Mendac's shadow. It only reminded him of what he didn't have, and he didn't need the rest of the world rubbing it in his face.

Against her better judgment, she summoned her Bewahr.

Preloz appeared in a swirl of black smoke, skin peeling away from his face, patches of sinuous muscle exposed around his mouth. He wore a shirt today, so the damage to his torso couldn't be seen. That didn't mean she wasn't aware of that gaping hole in his chest where a gray heart with black veins pumped ink into the rest of his body. After reading his story, *The Immortal Daughter*, his ghastly physical state made sense. It wasn't simply a product of the Cyn Kingdom's atmosphere, but a parasitic insect known as an umbra fairy.

His head moved slowly as he searched the room. "Again, I see no danger."

She didn't know if the man had other speeds, but if he didn't, she couldn't imagine how difficult life would be when faced with the elite talents of the Light and Dark Empire. He didn't move as much as he did shift. Every response seemed delayed; every motion arduous. "No danger," she said.

His eyes slid downward, raking over the books. "Are you sure?" he asked. "Did one of these books attack? I will even avenge something as minor as a paper cut."

Her head fell limp against her shoulder, nearly looking at him sideways. Had that been humor? If so, he could have given Olivia's deadpan a run for its money. "I'm good," she said.

"Then I'll take my leave."

She blurted out a question: "Is it true you never found her?"

His eyes narrowed. Bait successful. "Her?"

"Your daughter."

The silence that followed lasted so long she began to count the seconds in her head. She supposed it shouldn't have surprised her, considering her previous observations. She reached the count of fifteen before asking, "Was she sent to the Linsaniun Mounds?"

Seven seconds. Then, he eyed the books again. "How do you know this?" he asked, tone solemn. "Is my baby in these books? You found her in the pages?" Laggardly, he dropped to his knees, hands dragging across the texts in search of the proper one. She saw his phalanges in two fingers.

Olivia was overwhelmed with pity. The man was in pain; he was broken—mentally, physically, and emotionally.

"Which book is it?" he asked, hands shaking as he opened the cover of a leather book. This was the man charged with protecting a royal firstborn? "Oh, I'm so happy. My search is over. I knew I'd find her."

She had to rip her gaze away from his face. She hadn't said she'd found his daughter, but his state of mind interpreted it that way. He wasn't all there—at least not when it came to his little girl.

"She's not in a book," Olivia whispered. "Or not her physical self. I was talking about your story, which is in this book." She held up a tome of obscure legends.

He stared at it, one eye a mass of black, the other leaking black into the iris and tears down his cheek. "Where is Pytatia?"

She glanced at the book, then back to Preloz. "Do you not know?"

He shook his head.

"You don't remember what the Cyn King did to you and your daughter?"

"No, but I know she's not with me."

She pulled the book toward her, eyeing it as a thought came to her mind. This poor man was existing without knowledge of his daughter's whereabouts or condition. Shouldn't he have assumed her dead if that was the case? His human life had taken place five hundred years ago. Had the umbra fairy degraded his memories, too? And what happened to that stoic, dutiful attitude from her last time summoning him?

"Do you remember anything of your human life?" she asked.

"Small things to an extent," he said. "But after a certain point, I don't remember anything. I know my daughter was in trouble ... and suffering. I was willing to do anything to save her, which might have been my demise."

Olivia nodded. "In the story, you were exactly that: a good person and loving father."

"What kind of father abandons his daughter?" he asked, lowering himself to take a seat on the carpet across from her.

"You didn't. Trust someone who knows what abandonment looks like. Mendac did that to me and much more. You are nothing of the sort."

Preloz paused, eyes finally shifting from the book to her. "Mendac?"

"He was my father."

Another pause. "And he hurt you?"

"He hurt my mother more than anyone," she muttered. "But yes, he hurt me in an indirect way."

Preloz scooted closer. "Tell me about him."

She almost backed away—younger her would have—but she remained still. That wasn't the reaction she would have expected. Hearing the name of her father had triggered something in him. She tried to determine his angle. Did hearing about a man who hurt his daughter upset him enough to make him genuinely curious? Or was Preloz looking for comfort in knowing there was another man out there who was a more terrible man than he?

"Why?" she asked.

"I want to know of a man like me."

"You are nothing like him." Olivia's retort almost sounded venomous, a shred of rage bleeding through her tone.

He must have noticed the nerve he had struck because his lipless mouth closed, exposed teeth pressed together. Reading his expression was difficult through the distorted and maimed face, but she was already learning to find hints. The left side and bottom portion of his face was completely stripped of skin, but the right eye wasn't a canvas of black like the other. While black leaked into gray iris, she could still decipher subtle emotion in the pigment.

She looked down at the book again, then extended it toward him. "Here."

He took it from her. "Are you sure?"

"Of course. Why would I try to withhold your own life from you?"

"Because, like Mendac, I'm a terrible fa—" He stopped short, either spotting the clenching of her jaw or remembering her reaction earlier.

"I don't want to tell you about him," she said. "Not now, at least. Just … just read the story called 'The Immortal Daughter.'"

He studied her, that spherical black eye unnerving, book held aloft in his hand. He nodded and vanished in a spiral of shadows.

Olivia gazed at the fire in the hearth that had been behind her Bewahr, his putrid scent still hanging in the air. Then she fell back and lay on the carpet, a tear streaming down her cheek. Conversations of fathers and daughters had apparently struck a sore spot in her heart.

She'd never known a father.

34

Celeste

Mendac couldn't properly bask in the sense of accomplishment he had gained after getting Rhyparia to realize what she was because of the cold. He lay on a sofa in the bunker's common area, three blankets smothering him. Rhyparia had gone to their room, and Brenson had left the bunker to meet with the four other Fuhren. The man had been eager to share the news of Rhyparia's progress. Only moments after the common area had emptied, Hailey Vonalitis had entered and taken a seat in the same armchair Rhyparia had been occupying just a few minutes prior.

Hailey was the second youngest of all the Gefal. She had died in 1352 K.H., which was only a century and a half ago. She was responsible for the bunker's current chill. Besides her year of death and name, Mendac didn't know much about her. They'd seen little of each other, which he figured was his own fault since he couldn't last more than a few minutes around her. He had once spent weeks in Kindoliya, the Still Kingdom's capital, yet even that might as well have been a tropical climate when compared to the temperatures this woman created. He was determined to fight it this time.

"That blue hair; it's rare," he said, conscious of his chattering teeth.

She was eating blueberries. *More like playing with them*, he thought. She'd grab one from a bowl on the small table next to the armchair, then place it between a top-row and bottom-row tooth. She'd slowly bite into it, her pointed teeth puncturing instead of squashing it. Each tooth was filed to a point, making her canines indistinguishable from the rest. That combined with the blue hair told Mendac a lot. One didn't find a woman like Hailey in Kindoliya—nowhere near it, in fact.

She acknowledged his presence as if she had only now noticed it, as if she hadn't been the one who had intruded on him. Her eyes were a stunning blue, skin ghostly pale. A crown of frozen horns encircled her skull, growing out of her scalp.

"A savant of observation, I see," she said dryly, which was enough to prove that while her physical traits might have differed wildly from Stillian women in the capital, her gender role as a woman was very much the same. She was smug and caustic, and likely had no interest in Mendac.

Having dealt with Stillian women, he didn't let it faze him. "Pointed teeth, pale skin and blue eyes, icy patches along your extremities … a Mountain Still."

She smirked, puncturing another berry. "You're Intelian, correct?" she asked.

"Yes."

"I don't know much about other kingdoms and their cultures, but from what I've studied as a Bewahr, you're exhibiting Intelian traits to a tee. It's quite funny."

"My knowledge?"

"Your ego," she said. "Your desire to flaunt all of the useless information you've accumulated over your life. I was really excited to observe more about you. After all, you and that woman are the first beings of the Light Realm to enter the Labyrinth. But you are every bit the cliché I've been told about Intelians." She tossed a berry in her mouth, catching it between her teeth and demolishing it. "What a bore."

He didn't flinch. With age, he had become less reactionary. He saw Hailey's tactics as instigative, trying to draw the "barbaric man"—as Stillian women would say—out of him. And for every backhanded insult she threw his way, he could have made that same claim about her. But he didn't. Instead, he'd shatter the mold in which her perception had already begun shaping him. Steer clear of the normal—all of that nonsense. The truth was that he was nothing like most Intelians; he was an exaggerated version of their culture. Most Intelians had lost their identities as scholars and innovators. He was the exception.

Thus, he grinned, dry lips splitting in the cold. "That's nice to hear," he said, "for I truly feel out of place here. I'm in a foreign—no, *alien* land. If there was one topic that wasn't covered in any of the books I read while in the kingdoms, it was the Empires. I know nothing now, and I feel like I'm starting from ground zero. But if you think I believe myself some all-knowing entity, then I must be painting a perfect façade."

She tilted her head and cocked an eyebrow. "Oh, so you're a clever one with your words."

"Not so clever up here."

He heard the sound of something cracking behind him. Someone was unlocking the Mulanyx shell of the bunker, which meant it was one of three people. With Fuhren Brenson's recent departure, he was ruled out, so that left two possibilities: one of the team's other two Bewahr. The sound stopped, and Hailey tilted her head at whoever entered. Mendac's sofa faced the opposite direction of the main entrance, so he couldn't see what had shocked her. But the sudden putrid smell that accompanied the cold said enough. Combine Hailey's cold, Preloz's scent, and Brenson's toxins, and Mendac was forced to question why this team was cursed with the foulest auras.

Preloz Henye walked past the sitting area, sparing both of them an uncomfortable glance, lingering slightly longer on Mendac. That was a first. He never made eye contact with anyone. And there was something else off about him. He wasn't drifting or wailing. Usually, one would hear his cries before they smelled the death. But now Mendac saw some life in him.

Mendac and Hailey watched the moving corpse take unnatural strides to the narrow recess at the center of the common area, where he then disappeared into his room. The scene had been perplexing enough to have almost made Mendac miss a book Preloz had been carrying at his side. That excited the scholar in him. He hadn't seen a single book since arriving to the Dark Empire.

Hailey frowned and dropped a blueberry back into the bowl, pulling the collar of her tunic over her nose. "Appetite ruined."

He didn't mind it, his nose accustom to the pungency. Between the villages he had burned and soldiers he had fought, there had never been a shortage of death in his life. The only thing that made Preloz peculiar was his existence in the threshold between life and death. The undead corpse intrigued Mendac. The Void was the one kingdom Mendac hadn't explored during his life save the short time he spent building teleplatforms to connect the realms. The idea of venturing deeper hadn't appealed to him, despite finding so much of Cynnish abilities, culture, and geography fascinating.

Maybe, he could learn a thing or two from Preloz.

*   *   *

Mendac and Rhyparia shared a small room, as Brenson's chambers occupied nearly eighty percent of the space on their half below the common area. They each had a twin-sized bed, which poorly accommodated Mendac's stature. He entered the room with a folder stuffed with parchment. Brenson had just given it to him after returning from his meeting with the other Fuhren.

Rhyparia was lying in her bed on the right side of the room, staring up at the ceiling, accompanied by the dim light of a single candle at her bedside. He wasn't fond of the Black Labyrinth's dreary atmosphere. During his time spent researching and experimenting in the sewers of Brilliance, Intelights combated the shadows well. He wove his Intel Energy into several Intelights that flew to the room's ceiling and scattered. Rhyparia's head rolled sideways, eyes squinting as they met his. Maybe he should have given her a warning. The difference in intensity between a candle's flame and an Intelight—especially several of them—was jarring and disorienting.

Her eyes dropped to the folder in his hand. Her wings were folded around her, forming a shadowy cocoon of sorts. "Any news?" she asked.

Mendac dropped the folder on his desk with a heavy thud. "Study material," he said. "We need to know it."

She sat up, wings unfurling from her chest and partially extending. The left wing converged with the Mulanyx wall, disappearing within it. He made a point to read her expression when it happened, but she didn't show any signs of discomfort. "How am I to study when I don't know what I'm studying for?" she asked. "I need a reason."

He opened the folder and sifted through the first few leaves of parchment. Thankfully, it was all written in Sphairian rather than the Technous he'd seen prevalent around the Labyrinth. "Wow ..." he breathed. "There are big names in here."

"Of what?"

"Legends of the Light Realm. They've essentially given us a database containing details of most of the Bozani. Gatal Accus and Sephrina Jordan to name a couple, but I think there are some missing."

One name gave him pause: Geni LeAnce. He'd heard it when he was a child, living a wealthy life alongside his siblings. The family had adopted him at a young age, so he wasn't their blood, but he grew to see them as such. They were big on ancestry, which meant they heralded the woman who was credited with bringing the LeAnce name fortune and success. She was responsible for birthing the city of Brilliance and starting it all. There was a statue dedicated to her in the family mansion.

"How do you know they're not all in there?" Rhyparia asked.

He blinked, forgetting where he was for a second. Then, he counted the sheets until the content shifted from the Bozani to landmarks in the Light Empire's city. "There are only twenty Bozani listed. There should be twenty-four ... twenty-three if we don't count the Empress." He looked through them again, this time counting the numbers of each rank. "Two Branian and a Strasan."

"What's a Strasan?"

"It's the equivalent to the Dark Empire's Versac, so the highest rank aside from Emporer Mialo. There should be three of them, but I only see two here."

After a pause, Rhyparia asked, "Do you actually care about any of this? What we're fighting for?"

He looked at her. "I do, but I have the benefit of actually knowing what's at stake in this war." He smiled. "And now that you've gained a sense of self, you'll learn, too. Brenson said he was going to take you to see a Cavity—you'll figure out what that is when you get there—but I managed to convince him to send you with Yasmine."

Her face brightened. "Thank you!"

Mendac lowered himself into his chair, chuckling. "I aim to please." And that was true. Every word he spoke, every action he took, was aimed to please ... *himself*.

*   *   *

For the first time since being brought to the Light Empire, Bryson was on solid ground at the base of one of the Starlight's six Gate Towers. This one was the Gate of Heart, which meant Tahar's Emotion Cavity sat at the top of it—an incandescent sphere of white liquid that spilled into the quartz material of the Starlight. Pogu Quincy and Branian Aestys, both wearing burgundy cloaks, led the way across the plains that sprawled beneath the complex structure. The Pogu was a massive shadow of black beneath the moonlight.

Angst filled Bryson, but not because of the start of his first mission. No, he had been informed that he could return home for a visit if he progressed through his assignments. He didn't know how many hurdles he had to clear in order to proclaim sufficiency, but apparently it was only a few. After asking if that included fighting his mark named Intelius, he had been told no. That task was too big in his current state. He didn't have the means of achieving it.

Knowing he had a chance of seeing his wife and daughter motivated him more than anything else. In truth, he didn't care about this empirical war. He saw the weight of it, but he didn't see a threat. How would anyone reach the Cavities of Tahar while they were so far out of the way? He assumed some Gefal had wings, but certainly it wasn't enough to fly thousands of feet into the air without being smacked back down by the twenty-four Bozani who called the Starlight home.

They reached the city of Celeste, its white marble buildings hypnotizing in their lucidity beneath the light of the moons and stars. The Starlight didn't extend above the city, so the night sky was easily visible. Intelamps lined the buildings, splashing white light across the stone-paved streets. This part of the city was mostly silent and still, save the occasional humanistic figure of quartz that either walked a perimeter or stood guard at posts in front of buildings. Thornstorm had called these creatures "luzens." Bryson eyed them curiously, noting the differences between these versions and those seen in the Starlight. These held quartz spears or swords. They didn't wear anything, but the weapons marked them as soldiers or guards.

What Bryson found interesting—and this had been a theme in the Starlight, too—was Quincy's and Aestys's reverence for the creatures, offering them nods of respect and smiles rather than the other way around. The luzens didn't really acknowledge them at all, even when confronted, making him question the state of loyalties in the Empire.

"So, what's this area?" Bryson asked. He regretted the question immediately.

Quincy's head snapped around. "You told me you studied."

Bryson winced, deserving the retort. Every time he saw the stack of parchment that was his study material, he found something else with which to distract himself. Usually, that meant an escapade with Thusia through the Starlight or training to manipulate the Tahara-infused quartz walls. He was getting better at that, and his wings were slowly responding more to his will. He had impressed Squad Three. Soon, he'd manage warping through quartz. Quincy had called him a natural.

Bryson and the Pogu had developed a solid connection. Suadade found it unbearable, making offhanded remarks about a "bromance." And that was true. Sometimes, Bryson saw the burly man as his new Himitsu. However, Quincy did have boundaries, which usually pertained to anything in the realm of discipline and responsibility. He wouldn't hide his displeasure if the young Jestivan stepped out of line, such as not taking his study material seriously.

"I may have fibbed," Bryson admitted.

Aestys, who hadn't bothered turning to acknowledge them, said, "He's been out prancing around with your woman."

"She's not my woman," Quincy snapped.

"It's that kind of attitude that's going to make you lose her to him."

Bryson's head recoiled into his shoulders. "I have no interest in Thusia! She's like a second mom."

"People have their kinks," Aestys said. She turned and walked backward, spreading her arms to the side and shrugging. "In my first life, my brother and I had plenty—"

"Enough!" Quincy shouted, more out of embarrassment than anger judging by the pinkish tint in his cheeks. Bryson showed his disdain with a pronounced frown. Bluntness was one thing, but when accompanied by such crassness, it became jarring. He still didn't know what to think of the third Branian in Squad Three's trio.

Aestys smirked and turned forward again, wet brown hair falling in strands down her back. She had just woken an hour ago and recently bathed. It was her wake-up routine—a morning routine had it not been midnight.

Quincy's glare of contempt lingered on her for a moment before he shook his head and redirected his attention toward Bryson. "The whole point of this mission is to test your studies."

"I was never good at school. I was a below-average student at Phesaw."

"You're Intelian."

"And Stillian," Bryson added.

Quincy nodded, and Aestys turned her head slightly at that, eyeing him sidelong. "True," the Pogu said. "But, if anything, you strengthened my point. Aside from emotional independence, Stillian culture is prided on intelligence."

"Yeah, the women," said Bryson. "The men are lucky enough to get any semblance of an education."

"An answer for everything," Quincy said. "Except for anything of relevance." He forced out a breath and gestured toward the surrounding marble buildings, all of which stood three stories high, constructed in the same rectangular shape. "The districts of Celeste that directly surround the Starlight are sentry districts. Unlike the luzens in the palace, which were created to be docile and subservient, these were created to be aggressive and hostile toward threats. Because of them, it'd be difficult for an enemy to cross from the outer districts to the Starlight."

"Who created them?"

"Tahar, we believe. Empress Tonitrua doesn't reveal much of the Empire's secrets to anyone below a Strasan."

Aestys barked out a laugh. "Even the Strasan don't know anything."

"Yes, let Magnifica hear you say that."

Bryson's legs stopped. Quincy turned and waited while Aestys continued walking. "Did you ... say Magnifica?" Bryson asked.

Aestys finally came to a stop, whirling on a single foot. "Damned hag has too much pride."

Quincy raised an eyebrow at his inferior. "You are pushing your luck, Aestys. As your Pogu, what am I supposed to do when I hear you insult a Strasan?"

"Nothing, *Quincy*. You'll let it slide, disregarding it as lightheartedness."

Bryson stared at both of them, stupefied. "Magnifica? Like the Magnifica from the First of Five's tale?"

Aestys rolled her eyes and began walking again, this time with longer strides. Quincy tilted his head toward her, instructing Bryson to follow. "Yes," the Pogu said, slowing his pace to match Bryson's. "Except those tales were grossly exaggerated."

Bryson shrugged. He'd never actually thought someone was able to redirect a meteorite. "Duh. Nobody is capable of that, not even a Bozani."

Laughing, Quincy shook his head and placed a giant hand on Bryson's shoulder. "Your naivety is showing; you've yet to meet a Strasan." Noting the mortal's confusion, he elaborated, "I didn't mean her heroics were exaggerated. Yes, she deflected a meteorite. I was speaking more on her character. I'm not saying she's a bad person, but I'm also not saying she's a good person."

"That's disheartening," Bryson muttered.

"It's not that bad. It's just that ..." he paused, furrowing his brows with thought ... "Aestys wasn't incorrect. Magnifica is a prideful woman who had come from a wealthy family in her human life. That shows even now, well over a millennium later."

"As long as she's not evil."

"Evil doesn't exist." The comment had come from Aestys, who continued forward despite meeting an intersection in the street that only gave them a right or left option. She stepped into an alley between marble buildings. Two luzen sentries who had been guarding the entrance let them pass.

"You must not know my father," Bryson said.

"I don't, but nobody is evil," she said. "There are bad people, and good people who do bad things. Evil means all-encompassing. Every single thing about you is bad and completely lacking in humanity. And I have never, in my entire life, heard of such a thing ... unless you count fiction."

"I guess we have two different definitions of evil," Bryson said.

"Sure, but yours is stupid."

That was it. He didn't like her. No, he *hated* her. If the rising heat in his face didn't scream his loathing of this woman, then the blackness festering around the edges of his vision sure did. His heart hammered against his ribs, awareness of anything aside from her lost. Who was she to call him stupid? She didn't know Mendac. Did Bryson have to rip off his cloak and show her the scars on his chest? Did he have to put her in his mother's shoes? His fists were balled at his sides.

Quincy forced out a laugh, his chest swelling unnaturally. "I'm glad we're having a great time! We almost there, Aestys?"

She glanced back, passing beneath one of the alley's dim Intelamps. "Seems like you need to study." She turned forward again. "Yes, this alley cuts the time by twenty minutes."

Bryson seethed, but his vision broadened as the black in his peripherals faded to the marble of the surrounding buildings. The heat dissipated from his face, heartbeat dulling. He allowed his hands to relax, suddenly conscious of Quincy's eyes on him. He had nearly blacked out—and that was not like him. At all.

They traveled for another ten minutes, now in a district with buildings constructed of duller stone—granite, possibly. The roads remained stone-lain, but not as evenly as the sentry's district. Bryson stubbed his toe against a couple errant chunks in the ground. Because of the time of night and it being a civilian district—according to Quincy—the streets were vacated, most Intelights unlit except for the few holding dim charges. Shops and trade buildings were closed; homes showed no light from the windows.

"There are civilian luzens, too?" Bryson asked, questioning the practicality of such an existence. "I understand the servants in the Starlight and sentries near it, but what use are civilians?"

"No," Quincy sighed, the journey wearing on him. As a Pogu who didn't have wings, he couldn't simply fly to destinations. "Only servants and sentries."

"Then who lives here?"

His question was answered almost immediately, as they stepped into a city square full of life. He thought he had heard the rumblings of a crowd, but nothing could have prepared him for the crush of people crammed in the street ahead of him ... *People*. At first, confusion creased his brows. Then, wonderment pulled them up his temple.

Aestys snapped. "Let's go. I'm already late for my shift."

Quincy, who had paused to admire Bryson's reaction, followed her, pressing a hand against Bryson's back. "I thought the Bozani are the only people in the empires," he said in awe.

"Celeste's population hovers around one hundred and twenty thousand," Quincy yelled, practically bending over to match Bryson's height and be heard over the din. "Again, something you should have known." Despite harping on the same frustrations from earlier about Bryson's lack of discipline, the Pogu didn't express it in the same manner. He was smiling, soaking in the atmosphere.

The crowd parted for the trio, Aestys leading the way. While many eyes shot in their direction, none lingered. They simply knew to move, handling the presence of Bozani like it was just another day.

One of the few surviving ideological remnants from Kuki Sphaira's religious era was that humans lived beyond death—no matter the magnitude of their accomplishments in life. Everyone received a second chance, given to them in the form of an afterlife in the Empires. That belief, however, was highly taboo in the modern world. Nobody spoke of it. A reward such as an afterlife was granted to only the elites, reserved for twenty-four individuals to each realm. He thought of Jilly.

"Are these people who have died in the kingdoms?" he asked. "I want to find my—"

"No," Quincy replied softly, face darkening. "Celestians are no different from you or someone else who is alive in the kingdoms. They are mortals, and when they die here, they die for good. The difference between them and you is that they're conditioned to our presence. Seeing a Bozani for a Celestian is like seeing a royal for a human of the kingdoms."

Bryson's posture slumped, his momentary optimism deflating. He would have loved to see Jilly again. When the Jestivan first formed, she had been the first one to accept him for who he was. She treated everyone that way.

"I'm sorry if I led you to think otherwise," Quincy said. "I should have started off with that."

"No big deal," Bryson said, forcing a smile. "After all, you shouldn't have had to be the one to break the news anyway. If I had studied, I would have figured all of this out myself."

Quincy nodded, standing tall again. "I need you to pay attention from this point forward. This mission isn't really a mission. It's more of a test."

"What?"

"I called it a mission so you wouldn't fight me on it. I knew if I told you it was a test, you would have hated it. If you pass, you'll have that meeting Thornstorm was talking about, the one with the Strasan. Not only that, but you'll get to visit home and see your wife and son."

"If I had been told about that sooner, I would have started studying weeks ago," Bryson said, hands now tucked in his pockets.

The street widened into a plaza, the crush dispersing to fill it. Aestys, who had pushed farther ahead of them, was barely visible through the throng. She was headed toward the plaza's left side. Bryson became distracted by a large expanse of the plaza that was empty. The masses walked around it as if something was there, but he saw nothing. He slowed, staring at the square patch large enough to fit a small house. He eyed passersby, wondering if any of them found the phenomenon strange.

Quincy grabbed him by the shoulder and goaded him forward. "Let's go."

"Do you not see that?" Bryson asked.

"Yes. What about it?"

"Is that normal?"

"I don't know; you tell me."

The peculiarity of the Pogu's response should have registered for Bryson, but he dismissed it and focused on Aestys, who had entered a bar. The sign above read: GARNETTS.

The interior was beautiful, the walls a lacquered white oak with vertical planks offset across the perimeter. Intelights breathed life into the bar, brightening the wood and spotlighting canvases of strange landmarks Bryson had never seen before. Circular tables were scattered with enough space for ample walking room, booths lining the wall opposite of the bar counter. The patrons were well-behaved, keeping conversation at a level volume, and the staff wore friendly smiles and twinkling eyes, accompanied by black vests over white button-ups and violet cravats around their necks. If it hadn't been for the absence of food, he would have mistaken it for a luxury diner.

The trio crossed the bar without obstruction, stepping onto a raised section at the far end. A single booth rested here, its bench curving with the back wall. The bench was padded with violet cushions, and a slew of silvery pillows were strewn across it. A low table sat at the center, like a campfire at the center of sitting logs.

Aestys fell into a cluster of pillows and sighed, closing her charcoal-rimmed eyes. Quincy accidentally shifted the table with his shin as he took a seat. Bryson sat carefully, as if he was lowering himself onto a bed of thorns. Since the Pogu's warning of this being a test rather than a mission, he was on even higher alert than before.

Without introducing himself or taking anyone's order, the server approached with a glass of brown liquor and placed it in front of Aestys, proving she was a regular patron. He looked at the two men and asked, "What will it be for you two gentlemen?"

Quincy frowned at Aestys's drink. She tossed it back with only a slight grimace, then slid it across the table toward the waiter with a belch. He took it, smiled, and then retrieved a narrow glass bottle from within his vest. He refilled her glass and returned it to the Branian.

"Water, for both us," Quincy said, shaking his head and forcing himself to look away from the woman.

The server nodded and walked away. Aestys smirked before taking a sip of her second glass.

"Is this the example you're trying to set for the boy?" Quincy asked. "Drinking on the job?"

"How else am I supposed to last through the night slog?"

"It's not a big deal," Bryson said. "I don't drink anyway."

She tipped her head as a salute. "More power to you, young man."

He cocked an eyebrow, confused by the respect. He expected humiliation from someone like her.

"Just because I drink like a drunk doesn't mean I condone it," she said. "Nasty habit."

Quincy's eyes scanned the bar before them. They had a perfect view from the dais, looking down at the rest of the patrons.

Aestys groaned. "This is the worst post ever. No action."

The waiter returned with water and refilled Aestys's empty glass with more liquor. Once he left, Quincy asked, "Where's Nora tonight?"

"The Crust. I swear if I miss something of note, I'm gonna revolt."

"So you're in charge of the plaza tonight?" Bryson asked.

"Yes, where nothing ever happens. It's too close to Celeste's heart. Gefal don't come this far in."

"And that comfort is exactly what's going to screw us," Quincy said sternly. "Wasn't it you who reported they're growing bolder, reaching as far as Featherwood?"

She shrugged. "Still nowhere close to here."

"What's the Crust?" Bryson asked.

"Celeste's eastern outskirts and the farthest point of civilization from the Starlight," she replied. "It's the most trafficked area for Gefal. That's where they slip out of the shadows."

Quincy rubbed his eyes, clearly frustrated with Bryson's questions. He should have known these things already. "And this plaza," Bryson said hesitantly. "I'm guessing it's always this packed at ... one in the morning?"

"It's the one positive of being here," Aestys said. "All the fine young men."

Bryson followed the Branian's eyes to discover she was tracking different men—all around Bryson's age, perhaps lower twenties—as they sat and drank. Actually, now that he was paying attention, he noticed everyone was within that same age group.

"You're currently in Founding Plaza," Quincy said. "Which is the social hub of Celeste University's campus, the only university in the city."

Bryson's eyes raised two levels. "They learn about their energy?"

"Celestians don't have energy," said Quincy.

"Like Unables?" Bryson asked.

"I guess. But the concept of an Unable doesn't exist here because there isn't anyone who is … *Able*. They're just Celestians."

"Then what do they learn?"

Aestys laughed. "Nobody can call me the dumb one anymore."

Sighing, Quincy said, "Bryson, you act as if there's no such thing as mathematics, science, history, philosophy, language, literature, geography … Hell, the list goes on and on. You ever think the problem in the kingdoms is the obsessive focus on weaving? Phesaw has become a trash heap of a school."

Bryson snorted. Weaving was the most important subject of any curriculum. He couldn't fathom attending a place like Celeste University, where nobody could weave. He eyed an Intelight above their booth. "Then where did that come from?"

"Empress Tonitrua powers all Intelights in the city," Quincy said.

A new presence interrupted them before Bryson could respond. A woman in her mid-to-late thirties stood at the top of the steps that led to the raised floor, wearing the Garnetts uniform for a server. She had hazel eyes and brown skin with undertones of gold. Her hair was a sleek black that fell to her shoulders. She was beautiful.

"Anyone ready for more drinks?" she asked.

Bryson stared like an idiot while Quincy asked, "What happened to the young man who was serving us?"

"Emergency, so the boss let him go for the night."

Bryson hadn't even thought of asking that question. Had that been part of the test? His eyes narrowed, roving down her body for any suspicious signs: a lump in the sleeve, bulk near the ankles, a weapon of any sort. He saw nothing.

"I hope that boy told you about my preferences," Aestys said.

She flashed two rows of white teeth in a grand smile, pulling a small bottle from her inner vest pocket. "Preferences? Your taste is singular." She shook the bottle. "Scotch, Branian Aestys?"

Aestys slid the empty glass across the table for a refill. Quincy waved the waitress off, but Bryson asked for more water. He had finished the first. The waitress's gaze lingered on him before walking away. She glanced back halfway across the barroom.

Bryson flopped back in the bench, relaxing his face and lowering his eyelids to look suave. "I don't know how she'll take it when I break the news."

"Of what?" Quincy asked.

"That I'm happily taken."

The Pogu bellowed out a laugh, broad chest heaving. "Okay, mortal."

Despite Bryson's confidence, he found himself peeking toward the door behind the bar, waiting for the waitress's return. Perhaps, he should have questioned her reasoning for going back there; there was a water faucet directly installed into the back counter. She returned a short while later with a glass of water and handed it to him. As she gave her leave, he watched her turn back twice more.

"Well, are you gonna do anything about it or sit there like an idiot?" Aestys asked, continuing to sip on her scotch.

He gulped down his water and then slammed the glass on the table.

"Woah, slow down there, sport," she said with a mocking eye roll.

"I have no interest in her," he said, wiping the back of his hand against his lips. "Not with the woman I have waiting back home." His gaze became distant as he stared at the empty glass, a smile tugging at his lips. He missed her so much, and he would see her soon. He just needed to take this seriously. He'd likely fail tonight's test—whatever it was—but he would study the moment he returned to their capsule. Thusia's been dying to …

His thoughts escaped him, fingers growing tingly before fading to numbness. He smacked his lips, eyebrows furrowed. Since when did water have a bitter aftertaste? He smacked his lips again and this time couldn't feel his tongue at all. He saw Quincy's face, his bald head shining beneath an Intelight. It was distorting, blurring around the edges. His eyelids grew heavy.

Idiot, he thought to himself as his head fell forward and thudded against the table.

35

Mad Dash

Yama's return to the Adren Assistance Academy a week after her first attempt to meet with Master Ichi was met with success. The owner of the academy—and its head instructor—was currently guiding a class of teenagers through advanced kata. Unsurprisingly, she moved like a butterfly, but struck like a nose-diving hawk. This wasn't a kata of slow, methodical movements, but light steps, graceful pivots, and an organic flow. Master Ichi's long raven hair was in a tight bun. Sweat trailed down the back of her neck. As she came to a stop, the class continued the kata. She wended between students, correcting footwork, stances, and hand positioning when needed. At six feet tall, she was a towering presence among the class.

Despite Yama's presence in the lobby, watching from the front wall, Ichi didn't once look her way. The master's eyes were always on her students, looking for something to make better. It was that kind of attention to detail that Yama had admired about the woman. Nothing distracted her from her duty of molding young minds and sculpting great fighters.

At eleven, Yama had left the AAA in order to become the protector of an orphan as part of one of the academy's charitable programs—and one Master Ichi was most proud of. She had persuaded Yama into entering the program, believing the girl ready for it. Yama gave up training at the academy and the chance of accumulating a lot of money down the road, when she'd be given the chance to showcase her skills against her classmates in front of wealthy clients in search of skilled guards.

Adrenian guards were invaluable—especially those of the Adren Assistance Academy. As a swordsman or woman of the Adren Kingdom, nothing trumped duty ... not family, not love, not money. If a responsibility was given to you, you fulfilled it to the death.

Yama was taken to Lost Wisdom in the Archaic Kingdom as part of the academy's charity program, where she then chose an orphan—Toono—to become her charge. She didn't receive pay, but that didn't bother her. She was simply happy to have purpose outside of that note she'd been given when abandoned at the AAA as a young child. When Toono left with that mysterious woman—who Yama now knew as Kadlest—Yama had lost her charge, and thus her assignment. When she tried to return to the academy, she was barred from reentry by Master Ichi, who had been disappointed in the girl's failure. That had driven her to Phesaw, where she saw the opportunity of training under Adren Director Buredo as her only viable option.

Part of her remained bitter about her master's cold shoulder. What could she have done to stop Toono from abandoning her, just like countless others had done to her in her life? Abandonment wasn't something anyone could just brush off—not even a woman with Yama's conviction.

Halfway through class, one of Ichi's inferiors took over instruction. The olive-skinned swordswoman stepped through a gap in the low-rise wall that separated the training area from the lobby. Many of the parents seated on the cushions thanked the master for her time. She nodded her gratitude for their kind words before heading to her office. Before entering, she looked back and said, "Yama, let's go."

Ichi's office was more akin to an exhibit in a museum. Blades of all types lined both side walls, some perched sideways on wooden holders, others standing tall in glass cases that hung from the walls. Ancient helms and armor sat in glass cabinets on the far wall behind Ichi's desk. A scaled breastplate and helm hung on a wooden pole in one corner, as if it were a person. Two banners hung from the ceiling, flanking Ichi's desk and nearly touching the floor. To the left, a violet banner with silver etching in the shape of a bear's head. On the right, an orange banner with amber etching in the shape of a lion's head. Not a single thing had changed since Yama's last visit here over a decade ago.

Yama took a seat on the other side of the desk, watching as Ichi untied her bun, sleek black hair crashing effortlessly down her back. As always, the master regarded Yama with little emotion. Ichi grinned infrequently. Even rarer were frowns, scowls, or laughter. She was a bear, which explained much of what Yama had become in her life.

"Yama, what brings you here?"

"An apparent dead end."

Ichi untied her empty scabbard from her hip and placed it somewhere behind the desk before sitting down. She crossed one leg over the other, brown eyes bearing into Yama. "So this is the forgery of a new path?"

"You used to tell us to make something out of nothing," Yama said. "A dead end is nothing but a road undiscovered."

Nodding, Ichi said, "And if all options seem impossible or unobtainable, then I will always be here to lend a helping hand in forging that new path." It was a quote taken from the master's first lesson with any student of promise. When Yama had lost Toono to Kadlest and tried returning to AAA to reap the benefits of said quote, Ichi had said there were other options aside from herself. Now here Yama was, trying again.

"You've exhausted all options?" Ichi asked.

"I feel like I have, yes."

Ichi inhaled sharply, straightening her back. "I know most of what you've done in the past few years. I try to refrain from matters of the kingdom's politics or the world's wars, but I've found myself without much of a choice recently, with the murder of King Supido and foreign occupancy of the capital's throne. It seemed the conflict was placed directly on our doorstep—no, smack dab in the middle of our living room. I know you had a role in a lot of it. I heard you betrayed comrades and killed one. I heard you stood by Toono's side while he committed atrocities. Why should I help you?"

Yama would choose her words wisely while minding her manners. She waited until Ichi completely finished talking, allowing the woman to string together trains of thought without interruption. That was another cardinal sin in this academy. One did not interrupt or talk down to a superior, especially the master.

"Jilly's murder should have never happened," Yama said. "It resulted from a lapse of judgment and break in emotional control. I allowed love, rage, and bitterness to blind me. But I was also fighting on behalf of Toono during that time, for I had already switched from the Jestivan's efforts nearly a year prior."

"I am pleased that you returned to your charge," Ichi said. "You were tasked to protect him long ago, until your dying breath. However, I want to know what drove you to return to him. A matter of convenience? Had you already known where he was, yet never tried finding him?"

A pause, then Yama replied, "He came to me. He was sorry for leaving me when we were kids, and he wanted me back by his side. I had an idea of where he was before that, but I thought he had made it clear to me that he didn't want me around. But once he gave me the chance, I took it." She paused, letting her explanation die there. She thought it better not to mention a lot of that decision had come from Jilly choosing Toshik over her, stemming from bitterness. Lying to Ichi wasn't wise, but it wasn't like the woman was an all-knowing god.

"So, you left your friends to return to your duty."

Yama nodded. "Yes. Duty over everything else. That is the Adrenian way, and the only thing that stopped me from fulfilling it was Toono's reluctance to allow it. I wasn't going to insert my will upon him. He was his own individual capable of his own decisions."

Ichi resituated herself, folding her hands in her lap and looking off to the side in thought. "But you left him again … or that's what I'm assuming. Why else is he dead while you're alive? Did you fail as his guardian? If he's dead, you should be dead, too. The fact that you're still breathing means you didn't do everything possible."

"It was the evils he was committing," Yama said, deepening her lies. "His ambitions were destructive to civilization. And, as Adrenians, we're always told there's nothing more important than the protection of those who cannot protect themselves—of the populace."

"There is honor in that," the master said. "Yet you didn't try stopping him. It seems you didn't pick a side. You were comfortable riding the middle."

"I couldn't," Yama breathed. "Call it cowardice; call it naivety. When I made the decision to walk away from him a second time, it had come after months of questioning myself. I had been struggling with Jilly's death, and I learned I had been trying to distract myself from it … and failing miserably. Because above the disappointment in myself and anguish over her was the anger toward Toshik."

"You went looking for a new purpose," Ichi said.

"By looking for an old one, yes," Yama said. She proceeded to tell the story of returning to Yinyon, searching for the family that had taken her to the AAA and left her there, believing the academy could help her reach her potential as a swordswoman. They had hinted at such a thing in the note they'd left with her. Yama didn't mention the fact that she came from a village of Adren Assassins.

"Ah, that Soraku," Ichi said, almost reverently. She even smiled. "Yes, I wouldn't expect anything less from her. She's more stubborn than I am. Makes me seem like a fencing sword, which says quite a lot."

Yama tilted her head. "You know her?"

"Depends … did Soraku tell you everything?"

"What do you mean?"

"Did she …" Ichi tapped her fingers against her thigh, looking for the right words … "reveal all of Yinyon's peculiarities?"

Yama didn't respond immediately. While her return to the village had been depressing enough to make her go as far as contemplate suicide, she'd never even entertained the thought of revealing her mother's secret—no matter how poorly the woman had treated her. She supposed that was because she knew she deserved it. She had made awful mistakes in her life.

"It's okay if you know," Ichi said.

Yama gave a nod.

"Good. Then yes, I know your mother. Why do you think you were brought here as a child? Mere happenstance?"

"How do you know her?"

"I'm her sister." Yama's eyes spread wide. "Which, naturally, makes me your aunt."

The revelation stunned Yama, waves of emotions—too convoluted to decipher—crashing down on her. Since leaving Toono's efforts in a war in which she had no interest, she had discovered a lot of herself and her roots. She had grown up with no family, yet while this was a constant topic of conversation in regards to the likes of Agnos, Bryson, and Tashami, nobody had ever questioned her solitude. She had never received that same treatment. The Jestivan could only see her as a woman too strong to need bonds. They figured she had everything figured out in her life—unyielding and fearless. In reality, they should have questioned her independence more than anyone else's.

To whom did she go home? Who did she know that loved her? What was she capable of when finally given love only to have it snatched out of her hands? Toshik and Jilly figured that out.

"I am like my sister," Ichi said, her voice having grown gentler. Another oddity coming from the mouth of a stoic Adrenian bear. "However, I'm the only assassin—aside from young Simon, I suppose— who lives away from the village. A very long time ago, during the transition into the Known History timeline, this building wasn't the Adren Assistance Academy, but the Adren *Assassin* Academy. Young assassins trained here to kill in the art of stealth.

"I'm not as firm as Soraku. And while I'm a bear—" she gestured toward the banner to her left— "your mom's a lion in a bear's coat. I'm disappointed that she turned you away, though not surprised. And I know I did a long time ago, but that was because I was sure you'd return to Yinyon, where your mother could decide what to do with you. You ended up going to Phesaw instead—a decision with which I held no gripes, considering the talent I knew was there. After all, you must pave your own path." She released a long breath, then uncrossed her legs and leaned forward. "What is it that you want to do?"

Finally managing to move her lips, Yama asked her own question instead of answering her aunt's. "You're an assassin?"

"Yes, but an unpolished one, which is why I find myself here. I can't do quite as much as Soraku, Solace, or Silk. I know what it feels like to be cast out, Yama. Soraku and I were in your shoes once, but I didn't develop quite like she did. You and Simon are quite similar, except for the sibling part. I've heard he's developed to become as great as—if not better than—Soraku and Solace, while you have fallen short like I did."

"My mom never told me," said Yama. "Am I an assassin, too?"

"You have to be tested, which I can do here. Assassin traits are solely genetic—nobody can be born with them without having gotten it from their parents—but that doesn't mean a child will always become an assassin just because their parents were. In fact, it's more common the child isn't one. But it takes years to determine if someone is an assassin or not, usually until their adulthood."

Yama's hand moved from the chair's arm to the hilt of her sword leaning against the chair. She ran a finger along its length. "Jilly was Toshik's charge. He was supposed to protect her, but she wound up protecting him."

"Protecting him from you," Ichi said.

"Yes." Yama's gaze dulled. That thought maddened her. "And I will receive my punishment one day, but not until I give him his. She died because of him ... because he made her love him. He broke codes of conduct between a charge and guardian."

Ichi stared at Yama. If she held any reservations, she didn't express them. She probably saw the flawed logic in her niece's thinking, but thought it wise to not state the obvious. It was as if the master of the AAA had become a different person since revealing the truth. There might have been compassion in her.

"I came back to you to learn," Yama said. "I want to regain the ambition I once had years ago. I fear my growth was stunted from leaving the academy too early."

The sternness returned to Ichi's eyes, but she nodded and leaned back. "I didn't think your mother could actually shun you. I can't do that, not as your last resort. I'll test you in a week to discover your capabilities, then I'll work you harder than you've ever been worked in your life." She paused. "Part of me believes Toshik has it coming to him. He was never kind to the girls. I hope he's evolved past that, but that doesn't mean I can't send him one last test of reprimand. He always thought I would cast damnation's judgment upon him eventually. Perhaps, this will be it."

And just like that, Yama had reason to live again.

*　　*　　*

After a week of scouting it, Agnos, Tashami, and Evelyn entered the cottage of Woodkeeper Nynis. It was a humble structure made of lumber from the forest, logs stacked on top of each other to make the walls. They dripped rain water onto the entryway's floor, an expansive open-floor plan spreading before them. The living room, dining room, and kitchen were all visible from the doorway, huddled around an unused section of floor space at the center.

A bald woman, scalp slicked with wax, approached from the living room in a toga. She had been standing at the window, staring into the storm outside. Thunder boomed, overpowering the hammering rain for a few seconds.

"I'm sorry, Ms. Yogo," Evelyn said, still dripping onto the woman's floor.

Nynis grabbed a bundle of blankets from the couch as she passed by the living room, handing one to Agnos and Tashami while placing the final one around Evelyn's shoulders. "No worries. I'm just relieved to know you're okay. Didn't know what was going to happen to you abroad."

"It was a breath of fresh air," Evelyn said. "By the way, this is Agnos and Tashami, two of the Jestivan."

Nynis, who was walking toward the kitchen, paused and turned. "Jestivan?" Her lips quivered, and then she laughed. "Only you, Evelyn. Only you." She walked toward them again, extending a hand. "Name's Nynis Yogo."

"Pleasure," said Agnos, shaking her hand. Tashami followed suit.

As the Woodkeeper returned to the kitchen, she said, "Have a seat at the dining table. I prefer you refrain from sitting on anything cushioned."

They gathered around the table, and Nynis placed a canteen of water at the center. She offered them each a cup. Pouring herself a cup, Evelyn asked, "Warden Sylial not tell you about my companions during his visit?"

Nynis was looking out of the window again. "He mentioned them, but didn't say anything about who they were." She eyed the two Jestivan. "And now that I know, can't say I don't blame him. After finally restoring a semblance of calm on the campus, he wants to keep a tight lid on this. Jestivan at Ipsas would create havoc."

"Nothing to fear from me," Agnos said. "Unless you're scared of one-armed scholars."

Nynis didn't respond, gaze remaining on the window. "So how did you end up with the Diatia's rivals, Evelyn?"

"A combination of luck and will," she said, grabbing a caramel cube from a bowl. "Knowing my old dream of sailing, Still Queen Apoleia sent me to the Spirit Kingdom to aid Queen Apsa's navy. One day, while attending a meeting between the Spirit Queen and her advisors, they spoke of infiltration strategies. Surprisingly, they began exploring pirate options rather than naval. They mentioned using a very accomplished pirate crew, captained by Agnos, the Sixth of Six. And when I heard the name and who he was, I threw my name into the hat to help."

"Sixth of Six?" said Nynis. "I thought there were only five."

"Now there's six."

Agnos purposefully avoided anyone's eye contact, uncomfortable with the attention and title. How could a one-armed weakling who read books all day be grouped with legends like Gatal, Sephrina, and Ataway?

"I see he doesn't believe it, himself," Nynis said, looking in Agnos's direction. She shook her head with a smile. "A Jestivan who became a captain of a pirate ship? What in the world goes on in the Light Realm?"

Tashami laughed. "With all due respect, I wouldn't call it any more normal down here."

A knock on the door. Agnos jumped. Tashami's eyes narrowed. "I thought the student punishments already started. Aren't they deeper in the forest at the moment?"

"They did," Nynis said, walking past the table. "We have another guest."

Tashami snapped his head toward Evelyn. "Did she tell you about this?"

Evelyn's gaze was on the door, a smidge of uncertainty in her face. "No …"

"Great," Agnos said. "She betrayed you."

"She wouldn't."

Tashami stood just as Nynis opened the door. Agnos's heart thumped against his chest. Evelyn remained still.

A young woman entered, dripping wet just like them. A gale carried a sideways wave of rain through the door behind her, and Nynis slammed the door shut. The Woodkeeper frowned at the fresh puddles dotting her floor. Evelyn pounded a fist on the table and leaped from her chair to dash toward the newcomer. "Eve!" the girl screamed, catching Evelyn in her embrace.

"Arithmys!"

Tashami slowly lowered himself back into his chair, jaw relaxing. Agnos watched with intrigue.

Arithmys was a spectacled woman with blonde hair and green eyes. She was short—Agnos's height probably—but developed far more than the average woman. She was round at the bottom, resembling an egg, and had excess fat in her upper arms and love handles. When Evelyn walked her friend over to the table and introduced her as one of the Prim Diatia, Agnos had to force himself to not physically react. It was nothing against her. If anything, he found himself excited. He'd always felt out of place when surrounded by the physical specimens that were the Jestivan. He was a twig, skin rising and falling with the contours of his ribs rather than those of Bryson or Toshik's abdomens. When in candlelight, the center of his neck was obscured in shadows and his cheeks were hollow. Himitsu could wrap his fingers around Agnos's ankle. He'd been insecure about it.

Arithmys had likely lived that same experience. Knowing the Diatia Agnos had seen or heard about in his life—Bruut, Vuilni, Evelyn, Gina, and Halluci—she must have felt like a fish out of water, only her body was the opposite of his. He stood and shook her hand enthusiastically. "Nice to meet you."

After they settled down, the two Diatia caught up. Agnos and Tashami held a conversation with Nynis, who was curious to hear some about their lives as Jestivan. She shared with them information about the forest and her religion's love of nature, how she wasn't a radical zealot, which allowed her to have a home constructed of fallen timber. A building such as this would have been blasphemous in the Prim Kingdom. She would have been labeled a heretic. When Agnos questioned her free expression of Primmish secrets, she brushed the details off as minor. Basically, she wasn't saying much.

Half an hour later, the time for relaxation came to an end. Agnos, Tashami, Evelyn, and Arithmys stood at the back door, heavy cloaks wrapped around their shoulders, hoods thrown over their heads, hems low enough to obscure the face. Arithmys had been part of the punished students, which Evelyn had teased her for at the table. Apparently, the Primmish woman had a reputation of being a saint. She had purposefully gotten into trouble in order to be sent out here and help Evelyn. When asked about what she did to receive such a brutal judgment, she blushed and went quiet.

"The other three won't make it back before us?" Tashami asked, putting on a pair of gloves.

"Oh, no," Nynis said, helping Arithmys tie her cloak. "I put them way out there. They'll be gone until dawn." Lightning lit the room, followed by a clap of thunder that dissipated into a low rumble.

"If they don't die first," Tashami muttered.

Evelyn glanced out a small, square window. "So we're hoping the guards at the campus's perimeter don't see us escape the forest in this mess. And even if they do, they'll assume we're the four students returning from their punishment and won't bother checking."

"Sounds like a well-thought-out plan!" Arithmys said sarcastically. She threw a fist into the air. "Hoo-rah!"

Agnos cocked an eyebrow at her while Nynis opened the door. Arithmys had a lot of flamboyant energy, which made him question his comparison to himself earlier. Evelyn stopped in the doorway, staring into the blackness. A lone lantern in the backyard illuminated a sphere of slashing rain around it. She sighed and lifted her fist halfheartedly. "Hoorah …"

And then they charged the forest.

*   *   *

Agnos tripped over his own feet several times during the sprint. He was running at a speed beyond his capabilities, pulled by Tashami through the thunderstorm, a wet hand in his. He was sure adrenaline should have kicked in by now, making him oblivious to his jelly legs and pincushion lungs—that was how others described it, at least—yet all he felt was physical pain. His mind should have focused on the potential of escaping the forest while the strikes of lightning and claps of thunder pumped endorphins through him, but it was his collapsing lungs that begged for his attention.

He slipped on a wet root, fell, and slashed his shin. His scream was drowned out by the storm. Tashami pulled him up, readjusting his hood to cover his face. Then they ran again, the gash in Agnos's shin screaming in pain as water and dirt coursed over it.

A wind hit them in their back—sudden, steady, and unnatural, aiding their sprint with a push. It also helped counter the crosswind from the storm. This was Tashami's wind, once again doing everything possible to stop Agnos from holding them back. Just like in the Chasm or at sea. Rinse and repeat.

Evelyn and Arithmys were elsewhere in the forest, planning to escape at different locations. They didn't run as a pair, for they were both capable enough alone—even Arithmys, who Agnos was beginning to realize didn't share much in common with him. He supposed he'd been shallow in his quick assessment of her based on her outward image. He'd gotten onto Bryson when they first became Jestivan for doing the same thing to Rhyparia. Agnos would apologize for his impertinence to the Prim Diatia later.

With his one arm occupied by Tashami's hand, Agnos could do little else to make traversal of the forest's terrain easier. The absence of light—thunder clouds looming beneath the stars and moon—made decisive motions impossible, yet Tashami seemed to defy the factors working against them. Agnos, had he been alone, would have hesitantly picked his way through the trees. The storm's gales would have knocked him sideways. One such blast of wind tore a tree from its base and tossed it toward the pair of Jestivan. Tashami stopped it momentarily with his own woven wind, making the behemoth jitter between the converging forces, before deflecting it adjacently. What kind of thunderstorm was this? And how were the winds this strong in such a dense forest?

It clicked as Agnos saw a gap in the trees just ahead. They were at the forest's edge, so the winds were at their strongest.

Panic swept over him as they broke free of the trees to sprint across an open field, boots sloshing through flooded grass. Winds howled against his ears, sheets of rain swirling around and tugging at his cloak. He looked up as Tashami continued pulling him forward, trying to see through the showers. He squinted as cold rain hammered against his face, bangs stuck to his forehead, his hood no match for the squalls. Watchtowers were distinguishable via distorted hovering torchlight nearby, but he saw no torches on the ground. Evelyn and Nynis had been correct. Nobody wanted to be outside during this. And he found it absurd that throwing students in a forest in the midst of it was considered punishment.

Agnos kicked up soggy chunks of soil with each stride, losing his footing a couple times from the poor traction. His breathing became ragged, a strained noise ripping from his throat. He couldn't get oxygen into his lungs fast enough; his brain was shutting down. His toes were wet and tingly in his boots, and a volcanic heat tore at his calves. And just as he was about to collapse and force Tashami to carry him, they arrived under the cover of a narrow edge of roof that extended beyond the building upon which it sat.

A wall of water splattered against stone, falling from the roof and separating them from the storm. They were against the building, Tashami standing and catching his breath. Agnos had fallen to hand and knees, windpipe on the verge of closing. Half his body was still in the storm, the wall of water crashing against his spine. He didn't care.

Tashami gently grabbed him and lifted him to his feet. "You have to stand. Put your hands on your head and breathe properly."

Agnos did so, but breathing was impossible when sobbing as hard as he was.

"Calm down," Tashami said, voice soft. "You're safe. I'm here." He placed a hand on each cheek and looked him in the eye. "Breathe with me." Agnos did. Slowly, the crying stopped. Tashami smiled. "Just a bit of anxiety. You're good to go."

Agnos nodded, eyes irritated and puffy. His body cold and wet. His pride wounded, and his knees buckling. "Thank you again, Tashami."

36

The Loess Lord

Peg courses were a staple of any Adrenian's training regimen. Toshik had watched his mother, Jun, train on the elaborate course of the Brench Estates for years as a child. The course had three sections in total: the middle over a strip of land that separated two ponds, and two areas that stood in either pond, their stilts embedded in the pond's floor.

Toshik bounded between stilts, currently maneuvering the highest of them over the deepest part of the deeper of ponds. What made the ponds' sections of the peg course difficult was the instability of the stilts. The pond's floor was muddy, the bottoms of the stilts not lodged deep enough to be firm. Thus, when he planted the ball of his foot on one and shot in a different direction, it would provide little purchase and give way beneath the force. It forced an Adrenian to land lighter on their feet and take off quicker. It was a test of balance, agility, burst, and speed—the most important traits for any elite swordsman.

This peg course was different than most, its inspiration stemming from his mother's life as a hunter of exotic beasts. Most of her missions took her to jungles or forests, where branches and vines served as alternative means of movement—a necessary measure when hunting animals known for living in treetops. To mimic the woodlands, many of the stilts were connected by horizontal rods between them, some of which were draped in rope to impersonate vines.

Toshik would lunge from the top of a stilt and dive down to a bar, grab hold of it, and swing himself back up to another stilt. He was doing his best to honor his mother's grace and ferocity, but he was clumsy when it came to anything outside of footwork.

He caught a rod and swung, releasing his grip and flipping midair. Instead of finding purchase on another stilt, he dove into the pond and swam to its bottom, letting air escape his lungs. His feet hit the muddy floor and he began sprinting across the depths, wending between the trunks of stilts. This was unorthodox, and he couldn't recall seeing anyone train like this, but it was the closest he could get to mimicking Rhyparia's gravitational manipulation.

He felt his right calf nearly tear as he tried to lengthen his stride. His eyes widened, but his Adrenergy quickly surged through the muscle to repair it—one of the critical advantages an Adrenian had over a normal person who could run fast.

He swam up to the surface and imagined three hands reaching for him from above, each belonging to a girl or woman he had loved.

Jun, Alina, and Jilly, all of whom died to protect his weaknesses.

No more. He'd never be weak again.

*   *   *

Creep sat at the counter in the Electric Eel, Intelights basking the barroom in a warm yellow glow. The sun had slipped past the horizon. Shadowed silhouettes of people walked past the front of the building, illuminated briefly by Intelamps lining the street. York accompanied him, standing against the stool next to him rather than sitting on it. He was laughing at something Sally, the red-headed bar owner, had said. Creep didn't pay them much attention, finding himself a bit jealous of their chemistry. He had developed a similar relationship with the woman, but she had noticed his hesitance. He liked to think there was only one reason for his trepidation: he was on a job, acting as a spy. He couldn't allow distractions like her get in the way.

The truth, however, loomed over him like a storm cloud—or clung to him like a monstrous demon, but in the shape of a dagger strapped to his forearm. He could never love another woman like he had Soraku, nor did he deserve that kind of love after abandoning her.

He glanced at the spindly York, propped against the stool like a cool guy, a mustache of foam from his beer swelling on his lip. Creep wouldn't have pegged Sally to be the kind of woman smitten by such an act—not with the amount of flirtation she must have gotten while working at a bar—but there was something innocent and playful about York's movements, laughter, and tone. He was genuine, absent of hidden agendas of the more predatory kind. Creep supposed he should have scolded the man for allowing her to interfere with their work, but in a way he was doing his job. His banter with Sally was convincing, cementing their roles in society as normal people.

As if right on cue, affirming this belief, another man sat to Creep's left. The hybrid turned his head lazily, recognizing him immediately. He was seen mostly in one of the two front booths. Very rarely, aside from walking to the back to use the restroom, did he ever leave his booth. He was also the gentleman of note in Creep's butcher shop when Creep, York, and Sal had feigned a boisterous and physical altercation. He had become a frequent customer since then, yet Creep didn't know if it was of a practical nature in regards to wanting meat for his family or a curious nature, wanting to learn more about the workings of the butchery and the man named Sunshine. After all, word had begun swirling around the neighborhood of a "specialist" butcher.

According to Creep's customer log, this man's name was Croinys—though that could have been an alias, knowing the kind of business he conducted. Anyone involved in the two front booths of the Electric Eel weren't individuals to be crossed. Horos and Creep had met twice over the past few weeks, and their separate information, when linked, revealed a lot about the bubbling conflicts in western Dunami. The royals may have held the palace, but beneath their pedestals rose anarchy. News of the socioenergenic system's abolishment had leaked, and it wasn't sitting well with many of the powerful families. With the destruction of half of Dunami and deaths of hundreds of soldiers during the recent war, King Vitio's reign had been a failure in the eyes of civilians. His death had been in vain.

Croinys was in that percentage of the population who believed the Intelian family was degrading with each successor, and they didn't want to see how much farther it'd fall with the induction of Shelly as their queen.

Croinys and Creep sat next to each other, but didn't speak. Croinys asked for ale, which Sally provided. He sipped on it, possibly waiting for Creep to speak. But the hybrid knew—thanks to many years in Swift Secrets, the most reputable academe for assassins and spies—the best way to siphon conversation was to not converse at all.

Sure enough, Croinys cleared his throat. "Not much business today, Sunshine?"

Creep took the alias in stride, allowing the costume to slip over him. "Too much. My shop needed a little cleaning."

"Butchery is a messy job," Croinys said, nodding.

"You have no idea."

Croinys snorted, finding humor in the hidden context. He removed a gray kangol hat and placed it on the counter in front of him. *Good sign. Getting comfortable.* He wore a thick, woolen blazer coat, a fine vest beneath with a black tie. He was the kind of man who likely had a pipe at home, resting on the end table next to his armchair. Creep imagined Croinys's lazy eyes and thinned lips as he sucked in the taste of tobacco, a neglected wife in the kitchen cooking up a meal that would go unappreciated.

York continued to banter with Sally when the chance presented itself—she was serving many others at the counter—but it was clear he had noticed Croinys's arrival. The butcher's apprentice was listening to every word of their conversation, proving Pilot Ophala had given Creep an astounding partner. The young man wasn't bad for an Intelian spy, which had always been considered the less refined of the nationalities.

"I haven't seen many of your customers cross you since the day you tossed that blubbering idiot into the street," Croinys said, downing half his mug.

"It was about time I set an example," Creep replied. "I've been too nice since opening the shop, and I mingle little with the average customer."

Croinys set down his mug and scratched at his chin. "True. I only see York in the front of house. Sometimes I wonder if you ever leave that office of yours."

Creep smirked. He allowed his shifty eyes to skate around them, making it look like he was uneasy of possible spies. Noticing the shift, Croinys leaned in as if to say, *It's okay; You can trust me.* It was the exact reaction Creep wanted.

Creep edged closer in his stool. "I don't bother with average," the hybrid muttered. "My office is my true shop ... for my privileged clientele."

Croinys raised an eyebrow. "So it's true ... the word around town."

"Stop by one day and find out. I've heard a thing or two about you, too, and the company you keep. I'll admit to desiring a piece of the pie—if the rumblings of a rebellion are true."

Silence. Creep's delivery of his knowledge was heavy-handed, purposefully so. In some instances, delicacy wasn't effective. But Croinys was high enough in his group of criminals to recognize a man of sway—like Creep, or Sunshine in his eyes—but low enough to fear the knowledge Creep had just shared. Everything about the hybrid's aura had just diminished any confidence Croinys might have had, any dominion he thought he possessed. The delay in his response was the most damning evidence. Both he and Creep knew the man was familiar with the rebels, and it was too late to backtrack.

Creep placed a firm hand on Croinys's shoulder, his gloves tucked into his trench coat pockets. "I'm looking forward to meeting with you."

York toppled into Creep, laughing like a maniac. The apprentice had heard the finality of his master's statement, and had caused a distraction to let it end there. Creep turned and shoved his partner back onto his stool, releasing a barrage of verbal jabs. Then he turned back to where Croinys had been sitting to find him gone, having slipped away the moment he had the chance. Creep didn't need to look back toward the booths to know the criminal had scampered that way. He was likely telling his buddies about the conversation right now, and Creep would receive a visit from someone higher up eventually.

Smirking, Creep propped an elbow on the counter and held his glass of scotch in a dangling hand. He was old and lonely, but he could always count on his wit.

*   *   *

Himitsu and Kaylee were escorted not by guards, like those they'd grown accustom to in the cavern they'd stayed in for the first week, but soldiers clad in armor far superior to any guard's. Most wore only chest plates of gemlike material, the rest of their bodies protected by steel. Ribbed leather covered their joints for flexibility. But there were a few soldiers—high ranking officers by their appearances—at the front of the transit atop horses. They wore full suit armor, visors of their helms lifted to expose their faces. Their armor wasn't steel nor was it smooth or polished; it was grainy like the surface of a weathered rock, gray with bits of violet and green that glinted in the sunlight. It was beautiful, but also intimidating. It looked impractically heavy and suffocating.

They had granted Himitsu and Kaylee horses, though most of the soldiers walked. It seemed a writ from the Royal Head, while making everyone suspicious, granted them a level of respect—just not enough to allow them passage through the Loess unattended.

They were traveling one of the Loess's lowest terraces, hugging tight to its western wall. Crude columns ran along the road's left side, connecting the crusted floor to the alcove-like roof. Healthy grass stretched across the terrace's expanse, kept alive by the sun and occasional rain. That carpet of green was what made the Thousand Layer Loess different than gorges like Accus Canyon and Necrosis Valley, which were decrepit lands of browns and grays. This road had been carved into the cliffside of the plateau above it, acting like a courtyard walkway with one side exposed and a roof over their heads. The purpose of this was to hide anyone traveling the Loess's outdoor roads from the western precipice of the Loess, where foreigners might have stopped to gaze down into the breathtaking formation. While most of the city, save the farmlands and woodlands of the upper plateaus, was inland, tucked away in a vast network of caverns and tunnels, there were some major trade routes that couldn't be underground—usually because of impenetrable rock in certain areas. Access to the Heresy Butte required such a route.

Himitsu's eyes were locked on the officers leading the company of one hundred soldiers. He couldn't see ancient pieces on any of them, but they did wield short swords at their hips. When first meeting the two men and one woman several days ago—this was day number eight of the journey—Kaylee had reassured Himitsu of their honor. With the use of her ancient, she had seen something in their auras that made her trust them. Alas, he couldn't allow himself to grow comfortable. They were in a strange land with its own lord and army, a big red flag in most situations. Kingdoms had one Royal Head, and depending on the size, a city had either a governor or mayor. Lords didn't exist, or at least they shouldn't have.

Riding atop a stallion next to Himitsu, Kaylee pointed somewhere ahead, mouth agape and eyes alight. A massive pillar of land erected toward the sky, a circular wall of cragged cliffsides disappearing beyond the road's roof. It was as tall as a small mountain, but more cylindrical than conical. Himitsu prodded his horse to the left, where it trotted just outside of the road's columns. Soldiers looked his way, ready to grab him if necessary. He looked up to find the butte's top. It was higher than the Loess was deep, rising out of the canyon. They'd seen several buttes during their journey, but none like this.

The alcove deepened into the cliffside, forming a massive chamber that served as an intersection. To the right was a tunnel that led into the Loess's inlands; ahead was the rest of the road they'd already been walking; and to the left was a narrower dirt road that cut through the grass of the plateau and led to an entryway in the massive butte. A clever roof stretched across the path, protecting from the elements and unwanted eyes high above. The company turned down this road, as those who stood guard split to allow passage.

The road took them into a tunnel that cut through the butte's wall. On the other side was a glorious sight. The butte's interior was hollow, the walls stretching upward to a circular skylight at the top. It was like being inside a volcano. The sector lain before them climbed a gentle hill that stretched for miles until meeting the opposite wall. Slate gray fortresses—perhaps gemstone like those seen in the armor of the officers—shone with translucent violets and greens, the sunlight striking a vast circular area of land. The sector was dense with giant buildings, making it look like a labyrinth. But as it progressed up the hill, space between fortresses expanded.

Himitsu, Kaylee, and the company stood at the base of the hill after exiting the tunnel. A thoroughfare stretched before them, lined with four-story buildings, smaller roads branching off every few dozen paces. Even with all the grays, the Hersey Butte was beautiful. There was little grass and few trees—a byproduct of such contained sunlight from the hole above—but there was enough to make breathing not difficult.

The company didn't slow as they entered. Throngs of citizens split to make way for the group. Himitsu didn't see the dense crowds of other cities, which made sense considering the Heresy Butte's status. The people who lived here were the wealthiest in the Thousand-Layer Loess, meaning it was only a small percentage of the Loess's total population. He liked this better than the inlands they had traveled through for most of the journey here, where buildings had been made of compacted dirt sculpted into tunnel and cavern walls, and people had to move with the flow of the masses. He couldn't understand how anyone could breathe in the inlands.

A soldier groaned to Himitsu's right. He looked down from his horse to see a man sweating profusely, his helm tucked under his arm. Himitsu pitied him. Undoubtedly, this trek up the hill was rough for anyone traveling by foot and clad in armor. He saw a few soldiers glance his way with jealous scowls. He slipped his hand toward his hip, placing it against the hilt of his spunka blade gifted to him by Toshik, something he hadn't been forced to use in a long time—years, it felt like. He had continued to practice, but had yet to experience much outside of simulation. Something told him he'd get his chance here. These people didn't trust him.

They traveled for hours until reaching the hill's highest point at the butte's opposite wall. Himitsu turned on his mount, observing the steep decline to the bottom where the entrance they had used sat. It was like looking down at a collection of squares, the flattop roofs of stone fortresses sprawling below.

He turned forward again. The company had come to a stop, waiting as an iron gate slowly rose, disappearing within the arch of a perimeter wall. Like the rest of the sector, the building protected inside resembled architecture of ancient fortresses. The only difference was the size, as this was much larger and had more turrets. Everything was gray and angular, blockish even, as if someone had taken stones and just dropped them into place. Himitsu wouldn't have labeled it a palace or mansion, but a proper castle like those depicted in ancient history books.

Soldiers manned the wall, standing at the top, heads visible between tooth-like stone rails. He could envision archers hiding behind the stone teeth, then peak into a gap and shoot when necessary. Windows in the wall implied there were interior walkways, where soldiers would run messages or carry supplies. There might have been barracks inside, too. Based on the clinking of gears, chains, and metal as the gate raised, a group of men were probably working an outdated lever to move the heavy mass of iron. It reminded him of the High Sever in Phesaw, the day they had entered the Rolling Oaks to hunt down Dev Assassins—just on a much smaller scale.

They entered the castle's grounds, which was mostly a floor of stone. There was some grass, but it was treated like the flower patches of mansions, reserved to square areas bordered by rocks. A single tree grew out of a few of them. Monuments lined the front of the castle. They were old, evident in the erosion in certain areas, and large, requiring Himitsu to crane his neck to appreciate their height. They depicted objects, not humans. One was a quill, its vane crumbling at the tips. There was a hooded cloak, its hems billowing in a nonexistent breeze, a stone set into the lapel at its collar. One monument drew his attention because it was wider than the rest and not as tall—a pair of glasses. A four-pointed star with a broken arm. There was likely a time long ago when people would have reveled at such artistry. Now, it looked dull and broken. He counted at least ten more, but the line of monuments turned with the end of the castle's front wall, disappearing around the corner.

More soldiers walked the rooftops of the castle, which were only a few stories high, treating it the same as the property's defensive wall. The front entrance was a pair of sturdy wooden doors. Here, anyone on horseback dismounted, where grooms then took the beasts to whichever stable sat nearby. Himitsu adjusted his pants, sore and uncomfortable from the extended trek on the saddle. The company of soldiers dispersed at the entrance, heading in different directions, while the three officers who had led them now personally escorted Himitsu and Kaylee into the castle.

Himitsu didn't expect the gaudiness. While the castle's exterior was weathered and dull, it was clear the interior had been renovated many times over. The foyer was massive, high enough to take up three levels itself. A vaulted ceiling loomed high above, ribbed stone running from the edges and converging at a point at the center. The bricks of stone in the wall glittered slightly, mimicking the armor of the officers. Pillars protruded from the walls, gold inlaid in swollen strips of stone. Candelabrums stood in rows along the foyer's perimeter, waiting to be lit as dusk settled on the land. A massive carpet covered the center of the foyer.

Kaylee held Himitsu's hand as they walked, two of the officers in front and one trailing. The lovebirds snuck glances at each other, but didn't say much. He wondered what she was thinking, what she was interpreting in his body language. She had promised him that she wouldn't use her ancient eye to read him, and he was thankful for it. While it was useful for reading strangers, it was a breach of privacy when dealing with loved ones. A person should feel safe in their own mind and emotions. He would have liked to say he had nothing to hide—any real man wouldn't have in regards to the woman they loved—but he did … and they were terrible things. His mother had sent him here for a reason.

Would Kaylee have been able to sense betrayal in his body language?

The thought made him look away from her, the smile slipping from his face. The price of being an assassin. The price of being the son of the Spy Pilot. Certain things were bigger than love. He was learning he didn't enjoy that notion; he was unsure of his ideologies. He had grown up wanting to be as important and cool as his mom and dad, but was that worth stabbing someone in the back?

They reached a lengthy corridor, big enough to be mistaken as a cavern. Windows lined its length on both sides, and Himitsu stared out at a central stone courtyard as they passed. He could see other wings of the castle surrounding the courtyard.

Phesaw's main entrance had twin doors tall enough to make someone feel like an insect when standing in front of them. The doors at the end of this corridor were nearly as big. An officer stepped ahead while the others remained at a forced distance with Himitsu and Kaylee. The man muttered something to a guard posted at the doors. The guard then nodded, glancing at the two guests before pushing open the left half of the door. The officer pushed open the other half.

A throne room lay beyond, just as vast as the corridor. Two rows of pillars lined the edges of the chamber, a strip of the mysterious gemstone seen elsewhere running down the middle of the floor, connecting the doorway to a set of wide steps leading to a dais. For the first time in over a week, Himitsu and Kaylee walked alone down the path as the officers remained at the door.

A middle-aged man sat on a crude throne of gray, its surface glinting with violets and greens. He had a brown mustache specked with gray, chin beardless. His eyes were small and beady, eyebrows short as if burned off at the edges. For someone his age, however, his hairline was immaculate, hair only slightly thinner than the rest at the edges. In a few more years, he'd begin balding. He didn't wear a crown, but the throne symbolized enough. A retinue of armored soldiers flanked him, branching out and descending down the steps to the chamber's main floor. Himitsu eyed each one, trying to spot any weaponry on their persons. Archains were tricky, however, as some of them may have had ancient pieces with abilities unknown to him.

The man on the throne flashed a merchant's smile, a glint of knowing in his eyes as he regarded the young woman at Himitsu's side. The man knew it without being told. What gave it away? The mismatched eyes or an uncanny resemblance that only he'd know? Most importantly, would the man tell Kaylee?

"You are Loess Lord Kopios Soteria?" Himitsu asked.

The man regarded Himitsu, as if just now noticing him. "That I am."

The Passion Assassin set his jaw and nodded. He had met his mark. Kopios Soteria was a bad man and the final remnant of Archaic King Dolomarpos and Itta's reign. He had conspired with the two kings to create a force that could one day take on the Intel Kingdom, but the catch was he would remain in the shadows—a stealth force of trained Archains gifted with ancients. When King Itta was killed and the Amendment Order took over the kingdom, Kopios's focus shifted to the capital. He wanted to march west, overtake royalty, and continue his former kings' dreams of toppling the Intelians. Ophala had only recently learned of this when researching Lost Wisdom's underground business. That was why Himitsu was here—not because of Kaylee's dreams of medicine.

Himitsu was to assassinate this man who called himself a lord, but he was faced with a major dilemma …

Kaylee was his daughter.

37

The Child and Her Monster

"A writ from the one and only Archaic King," said Kopios with sincere surprise. "You two must be very important."

Himitsu hesitated, recalling all the training his mother had given him when it came to first impressions. Small talk was everything but small. There were games of deception, context clues, and hidden agendas. Kopios would dissect every response, which meant Himitsu had to be careful.

"Kaylee healed several people close to the king," Himitsu said. "He sent her here to learn from the very best apothecaries, believing she had the acumen to impress one into mentoring her."

"Can she not speak for herself?"

"Of course I can, Lord Kopios," she said. Himitsu gave her a sidelong glance, shocked by the reverence in her voice. Usually, such a question would have caught a stern retort from the orphan. He shouldn't have been surprised, seeing that this man was the leader of apothecaries. She aspired to be as skilled as him.

"Then do so," the lord said.

"I seek an education in medicine, both herbal and surgical, from the best experts in the field. I read a lot about the Thousand-Layer Loess when I was younger, but didn't have the ability to make it this far east because of sheer distance and the Archaic Desert between. The king gave me this opportunity after working very hard to reach the level I have, displaying my skills by saving lives in the recent war."

Himitsu studied Kopios's face. That had been a lie. She had saved no lives during the war, nor had she participated in it at all.

Kopios stroked his mustache with index finger and thumb. "I haven't heard from an Archaic royal since King Itta was in power. And while I expected a lapse in communication with his death and the unstable ground on which the kingdom's politics stood as a result—the Amendment Order and that idiot businessman's rule—I thought that, *surely*, Sigmund would reach out to me once regaining power."

"Wars of the global scale tend to push domestic matters into the sludge pile," Himitsu said.

"And it's over now, yet he sends me—" he narrowed his eyes at Kaylee, searching for the word— "an aspiring apothecary to teach."

"Her presence should imply a lot," Himitsu said, drawing Kaylee's gaze. This mission was lost on her; Ophala had given it to him in secret. The comment was purposefully cryptic. If Kopios knew what Himitsu believed him to know, then the Loess Lord should have been able to interpret it. *You gave your daughter to Lost Wisdom, an orphanage when taken at surface value, but a breeding ground for youth of physical and mental talent in reality. Archaic King Sigmund knows the business his father and grandfather had with you, and his efforts to restore it are in the act of returning your daughter to you.*

Something along these trains of thought were processing in Kopios's mind right now, as he leaned forward in his throne, an elbow resting on its arm while continuing to stroke his mustache. He nodded and leaned back. "The girl will …" He paused. "What are your names?"

"Hymis."

"Kaylee."

"Kaylee, since the request came from the Royal Head, we will grant you the finest of apothecaries to train under. She has served the Heresy Butte for decades, and during that lengthy tenure, she has yet to acquire a death in her presence. Anyone in her care has healed."

Kaylee brightened, wide eyes wiping clean the suspicious crinkle of her brow line after Himitsu's vague remark. He wondered what she saw in Kopios's aura. Was the man dulling his inner emotions as well as he was his facial and postural reactions? Himitsu only hoped she was staying true to her word about not using her ancient on him.

"We'll provide you with luxurious quarters here in the castle. And if you require separate living arrangements, we'll also give—"

"We're a pair," Kaylee said, the bluntness like a hammer to Himitsu's gut. Here he was, deceiving and plotting behind her back while she remained blindly rigid in her loyalties and love.

Kopios smiled. "Then you both can stay there."

"Thank you so much," she said.

"You are esteemed guests." His lips flattened, expression grim. "However, I must take precautionary measures. During your stays here, you will always have multiple guards around you. Even in your private chambers, I will have the doors to your chambers manned."

"Understood," Himitsu said. It was an added wrinkle to an already difficult mission, but he couldn't become upset over it. Only someone guilty would react poorly, and Kopios would sniff that out immediately.

"Now," Kopios slapped the arm of his throne twice, "I want Kaylee shown to her chambers."

The three officers who had escorted them for the past week stood at the door to the corridor. One said, "Madam, follow us."

Kaylee and Himitsu shared questioning looks. Hers asked, *why is he only dismissing me?* His asked, *will you be fine by yourself?*

"Go. I'll be right behind you," Himitsu said with a smile.

And trusting him fully, she placed a hand on his shoulder, stood on her toes, and kissed him briefly on the lips. He shuddered, nearly collapsing beneath the weight of betrayal. Why had his mother tasked him with this? He knew she was not the same Spy Pilot who had patrolled the Archaic Mountains several years ago, but even this seemed too cruel for the hardened woman she had become. He was her son.

He watched Kaylee leave, two officers leading her and one behind. Four guards closed the massive doors as she walked the length of the corridor, turning back to give the love of her life—a smitten Passion Assassin—a genuine smile.

"Can we end the foreplay now?"

Himitsu dropped his head and turned, raising it again to look at the Loess Lord.

"You've been teasing me," the man said. "I'm assuming she knows nothing."

Bending over and reaching into one of his leather boots, Himitsu pulled out a folded sheet of parchment. The guards around Kopios drew swords crafted with the same gemstone-like material of their armor and the strip of floor beneath Himitsu's feet, fearing he was unearthing a weapon. He held up the parchment between two fingers, but they didn't relax. They were trained well, even if fearing some folded paper was stupid. He regarded it for a moment. *Could someone kill with this?*

"And that is?" asked Kopios.

"The *real* missive," Himitsu said. "Meant to be delivered directly to you from me—no middlemen."

"Von."

The guard to Kopios's left sheathed his sword and trotted down the steps of the dais. Himitsu handed the parchment over to him. As the guard returned to the dais, Kopios said, "I hope you don't mind one middleman. Forgive me for not wanting to get within striking distance of you. I don't know you."

"A decision any wise king would make," Himitsu said.

Von handed the parchment to Kopios, who unfolded and read through it. Himitsu knew the letter very well. King Sigmund had written it, but under the watchful eye of Pilot Ophala. Not a word in that letter was out of place, each one holding purpose. Himitsu had read it many times over. His mother had also briefed him on the ruse relentlessly before departing from Phelos. She was a queen of deceit, and most with sense in the Light Realm knew her as the real composer and orchestrator of many of True Light's key victories throughout the war.

Kaylee's father was her next victim.

Dear Loess Lord Kopios Soteria,

Allow me to preface this by introducing myself and stating my sincerest apologies. My name is Sigmund Archaic, son of Itta and grandson of Dolomarpos, and I am sorry for not possessing the faculties to get this to you sooner. With the turmoil following my father's death, I was either not in position to make anything happen of my own accord or didn't possess the information needed to properly continue my predecessors' legacies. That has changed recently.

I have regained my position on the throne of the Archaic Kingdom. Not only that, but the global war between True Light and SCAPD has come to an end with True Light as victors. Good news, of course, but I have better. Certain kingdoms find themselves crippled, desperate, and vulnerable—and one of those kingdoms has been our biggest rival for a millennium and a half.

I grew up learning about the Mind War, a war with no blood drawn for 1,500 years. The Intelians cemented themselves as a world power, while the Archains rotted as the realm's lowliest people, their ideologies lost to the rapidly-progressing technological achievements of the Intelian mind. I grew up hating the Intelians, our kingdom's beneficial relationship with them a product of necessity rather than desire.

When obtaining the throne, I began interrogating the elders who had worked with my father—some of whom had the pleasure of working with my grandfather. They shared secrets with me that my father hadn't deemed worthy of my knowledge when he was alive. He felt I was too young and, honestly, thought himself invincible. He never foresaw himself dying before having the chance to pass on the information I needed.

The elders urged me to vet many areas of the kingdom, and I did, but no place was as valuable as Lost Wisdom. Within the orphanage was a treasure trove of intelligence in regards to Itta and Dolomarpos's clandestine providence to propel our kingdom into a powerhouse that could rival the Intel Kingdom. To think they had disguised a mere orphanage into the hub of a back-channel society of galvanized men and women, all of whom desired international respect.

Lost Wisdom, apparently, held many purposes. It sculpted children who had the physical potential to become weapons, molded minds of the youth who had potential to outsmart the world's greatest spies and politicians, and had the boldness to experiment with peculiar phenomenon in order to technologically advance our culture in ways my distant ancestors couldn't. But through all of this, I found the system of raising children for future arranged marriages the most interesting.

Many have tried to bring together powerful families. In fact, we saw recent attempts with Toth Brench and Wert Lamay, who had a son and daughter who were to serve as the catalyst to a dynamic family tree. I never blamed them for that. Who knows how that might have turned out had it worked?

My grandfather initiated communication with your father seven decades ago. Dolomarpos wanted something from the Loess, and he was willing to help you obtain it. That deal brought the Soteria name glory and riches—and put to rest a stubborn enemy of yours. When Dolomarpos died, my father, whose goals involved influencing more than simple domestic affairs, stepped up and strengthened the relationship. Itta offered you, Kopios, a chance to join the royal bloodline via a daughter who could one day marry his son ... me. Of course, you are aware that there are two sides to every deal. Yours has yet to be delivered.

The Archaic family has been out of commission for a few years now, but we've returned to dominion. I send you Kaylee Soteria not as a threat, but as a token of good faith. It's my way of showing you her health and happiness. She is there because of her wish to become a Loess-trained apothecary. She doesn't know who you are to her. She doesn't know of arranged marriages or her potential life with me, which is why she's with the gentleman named Hymis.

However, once you complete your side of the bargain—its specifics redacted for obvious reasons—she'll return to Phelos and be my wife. And I would love for your attendance of the ceremonies.

It is time the east and west of the Archaic Kingdom unite to obtain the glory we deserve, the glory my forefathers worked so hard to one day obtain. And the Soteria name can join the Archaic in history.

It's still kind of surreal to know my father was grooming a girl hundreds of leagues away from me to become my wife, orchestrating a chance meeting between us two as if we were complete strangers. But, I am willing to accept it given the circumstances ... the promise.

I look forward to a long, accomplished relationship between the capital and the Loess.

Sincerely,
Archaic King Sigmund

Kopios lowered the scroll, letting it ravel in his hands. "And you're okay with this?"

Himitsu tilted his head. "With what?"

"Knowing my daughter doesn't belong to you."

"Firstly, she *belongs* to no one. If you were to spend more than a few minutes with her, you'd learn that very quickly. But I do know what you're trying to imply, and yes, I don't question my king's wishes. I accept everything."

Kopios smiled, then laughed. "This is great news!" The laughter lasted for several seconds before dying slowly. His eyes locked on Himitsu. "Finally!"

*   *   *

The Icebound Confluence stood silent and empty save two: Olivia Still and Preloz Henye. It was late, one in the morning, the night sky's star-speckled black canvas hanging high above in the circular skylight of the cylindrical chamber. Although the Confluence was normally empty at this time—messengers, aristocrats, and palace staff mostly asleep—Queen Apoleia had taken extra precautions on behalf of her daughter to make sure she wasn't disturbed. Every door leading to the chamber was locked and manned by guards on the other side, granting Olivia the privacy she needed when accompanied by her Bewahr. She wouldn't fall into the same trap as Bryson, who had developed a reputation for summoning his Branian on a whim … around anyone.

Preloz circled the Statue of Gefal, maimed hands clasped behind his back. The freezing temperatures weren't enough to combat the stench of death radiating from him, but Olivia had grown used to it—or as about as used to it as one could get. Not focusing on it helped a little.

"See any familiar faces?" Olivia asked.

He stopped circling to take a step back and observe it from a distance. His neck craned, mismatched eyes scanning the figures at the top. "A few," he said. He shook his head. "Leave it to Stillians to make their commoners think all Gefal are women, even if the royals know better."

"We're changing," she said.

"I know."

Olivia surveyed the figures and decided to ask a stupid question to carry the conversation forward. "Can you tell me which ones are correct?"

"No."

The answer was short and without hesitation, but calm. He understood her curiosity. What mainlander wouldn't be fascinated with the Empires?

"And what is this?" Preloz asked, approaching the unfinished sculpture Olivia's mother had commissioned and been watching as sport. It no longer looked like a tall, rectangular block of ice, but an amorphous blob as the sculptor worked the edges down to the figure's finished look.

"No idea," Olivia said. "My mother commanded for it to be built, and she's been watching the sculptor work on it every night."

Preloz stared at it for some time before looking at her. His movements were less sluggish and more natural now. She wondered why. He stared at her for what felt like an entire minute, one dead, black eye unnerving her. She smiled because that was what she had seen others do in her life when uncomfortable.

"Have you always been expressive?" he asked. "In your face?"

Her smile vanished. "No."

"I can tell. That was bad."

Her cheeks burned hot. Then she looked away, mortified that embarrassment had been her reaction. Bashfulness wasn't in her nature—at least not any time before this. She just wasn't used to hearing someone call her out like that. She wasn't naïve enough to believe the Jestivan hadn't found her efforts of expression awkward, but they had never confronted her about it. Perhaps, they had feared a fist to their gut. She supposed what made it worse was Preloz's deadpan delivery. The man had a sense of humor, however dry it may have been.

"I admire the effort," the Bewahr added. "But be genuine with your emotions. You are not one to fake laughter or tears, which I like. I can trust someone like you."

"I've always possessed genuine emotion; I'm just trying to learn how to free them."

He nodded. "Is it your Stillian upbringing that has caused you to lock them away from others?"

"I'd say it's deeper than that."

He strolled over to a staircase that curved with the cylindrical wall, taking a seat on the second step. She followed and leaned against the wall in front of him. "You're moving differently than I remember," she said.

"I feel more alive than I have in a long time," he replied.

"Why is that?"

"The book you lent me. It seems reading the story of me and my daughter invigorated me." He paused, his good eye—black spilling only partly into its iris—narrowing. "No, calmed me. While it's unsettling to know of her situation, wandering the Linsaniun Mounds as a corpse, at least I know where she is now. That beats being blind."

"What are you going to do with the information?" she asked.

He shrugged. "There isn't much I can do at the moment. A Bewahr's link to the kingdoms is through the royal firstborn. I must stay in your proximity. But that doesn't mean I won't have a chance down the road. Maybe one day I'll be assigned to a Cynnish royal. At least now I know where to go."

Olivia went silent, crossing her arms, shoulder pressed against the wall. She wanted to help him, but it wasn't practical. Aside from the Linsaniun Mounds' seclusion from the rest of the world, there was the matter of the atmosphere. If Cynnish could barely tolerate the cries of the Linsani, then how would a foreigner survive it? She wished she hadn't been barred from joining her team on their mission in Cyn Kingdom years ago. Such familiarity would have made her more comfortable with the notion of finding Preloz's daughter.

"I want you to find yourself," Preloz said, surprising Olivia. "If I can't save my daughter, I want to help you."

"I won't be able to fill that hole for you," she said.

"That's not what I want." He paused. "You said your father was a man named Mendac LeAnce. I know him."

"That's not possible. You existed in different lifetimes."

"True, but I do. He's currently in the Dark Empire."

Olivia's arms fell to her sides. She pushed herself away from the wall and cocked her head. "Also impossible. He's Intelian"

He shook his head. "I don't have the time or authority to explain to you the reasons why it is possible. I just need you to believe me. I haven't spoken with him, but I've observed the kind of person he is. That whole spiel about me trusting you because of your inability to feign emotion … Well, Mendac, I've learned, is the complete opposite. He is a master of molding himself to become what the person's he's talking to needs him to be. He's manipulative and very good at it, a shape shifter of natures."

"I went my whole life without showing people what I feel," Olivia said. "They'd call me stoneface. Is that not faking?"

"You were protecting yourself, and it was something you learned from your mother."

"I never told you that."

"It's a guess," Preloz whispered. "I can connect dots. A bad—almost evil—father who hurt your mother? That narrows down the possibilities of what he could have done. And the fact that you grew up stonewalling your heart? That came from your mother." He sighed. "Seeing what I have from him in the Empire, I can only imagine how he twisted your mother's perception." He looked up at her from his seat on the bottom steps. "You said you've been trying to free your emotions. What have you tried?"

She hesitated, trying to process the barrage of revelations and psychological evaluations. "Well …" She twisted her lips, uncertain of sharing that with him. He was right though; she needed to open up. "There were a couple moments when something happened around me and I instinctively reacted with a spark of anger or sorrow. But when I try to purposefully place myself in those situations, I can't feel it."

"Because you're not someone who can manufacture it," he said. "You're not your father. It must be natural."

"So says my mother."

"As a kid," said Preloz, "you have nightmares of monsters hiding under the bed or in the wardrobe, so you make your parents check before you go to sleep. Sometimes, you run to sleep in your parents' bedroom to avoid them. But those monsters don't disappear when you become an adult. They lose form, but gain mass, becoming less literal and more symbolic. We all have these monsters that haunt us."

Olivia didn't respond in the silence that followed, waiting for him to reach his point.

"Your mother passed her monsters down to you." He used a gnarled finger to pick at the crease between his molars. Because of the stripped skin and lips on the left side of his face, both rows of teeth were completely visible. He stared at her through the silence, then asked, "I'll take your silence as a yes."

She leaned back against the wall and stared at the Statue of Gefal. "I've dealt with those monsters."

"You've avoided them," he said. "Just like the child who ran to his mother's bed."

She looked at him. He had a father's intuition—not that she'd ever experienced such a thing. But it sounded like something she would have heard when Debo spoke to Bryson.

He reached up and grabbed the banister, pulling himself to his feet with that newfound limberness, wafting death's stench up her nose. He jerked his head to the left, popping his neck. Then he stared at her, shadows swirling at his feet and climbing his legs. "It's time to stop being that child."

And then he disappeared.

*   *   *

Olivia stood in front of her version of a child's wardrobe: a painting of the Still Mountains framed in gold. She stared at it from a distance, contemplating Preloz's words of wisdom. It wasn't as if she hadn't entered the room behind that painting before. She had done so once, when she had visited the Still Kingdom with her mother and Toono with the purpose of murdering Still Queen Salia—Olivia's grandmother.

The anguish she felt while inside the room had left a lasting impression on her, for she had never felt anything close to that in her life up to that point. Sharing her mind and emotions, Meow Meow was overwhelmed by it and had to remind her to calm down. But even he had issues trying to take all the pain away from her. She hadn't returned to the room since then.

Until now, she hadn't realized that. That was how deeply she'd repressed the memory.

414

Deciding she was fed up with her hesitancy as of late, she marched down the corridor. She had never been one for unnecessarily lengthening the inevitable. Then again, bashfulness had never been an issue either, but the heat in her cheeks earlier said otherwise. She was changing ... or perhaps not changing, but releasing. She wanted to free herself, but needed to understand the emotional spectrum was broad and layered, creating hundreds of byproducts beyond anger, sorrow, and bliss.

She reached for the painting's frame, then paused as she gripped the cold surface. Why couldn't she just yank it open? Why did she cower?

Olivia grunted, outwardly frustrated with herself, willing herself to rip the painting from the wall. It swung fully with ease, clapping against the wall hard enough to rebound and rattle. She stared beyond, already feeling the rush of emotion in her chest.

On the other side she stood in a small chamber, accompanied by a piano, broken bed, and burn marks across the walls. Why hadn't her mother permanently locked this room, destroyed it, or replaced the contents within? Did she need this reminder? Were the ghoulish memories not enough?

Olivia stood at the room's center. Her eyes raked her surroundings, and unlike last time, the dam broke. She saw the fight between Mendac and her mother, its violence and abhorrence, before spiraling into a clobbering as one side overpowered the other. She could see the Intelian on top of the princess and everything that followed—the snapping of two of the bed's legs, her head smacking the wall ...

A lyre broken on the floor, like her guarded heart, its strings spooled errantly, like her hair beneath the weight of her head, forced down by Mendac's forearm.

Olivia was now standing next to the bed, unaware she had even approached it. She fell to her knees, back furling as she bent over the mattress, the right side of her face pressed into it. Her outburst during the Phesaw invasion had been explosive, the fight between her brother and mother unbearable to endure. This was nothing like that.

She wept, the tears streaming from her left eye running across the bridge of her nose and joining those on the right side of her face before staining the mattress. This was steady, over a decade's worth of blockage finding any gap through which to seep. Her mother's monsters were her own, passed onto her like some kind of poisoned inheritance.

The monster had made this room its wardrobe, the piano's keys its many teeth, the bed its gnarled, broken body … scorched walls the evidence of its wrathful efforts to escape its cage.

Now, a young woman occupied the cage with it—a child in the wardrobe. Still crying, she climbed to her feet, hands pressing into the soft mattress. She would stand defiant to her and her mother's nightmare, but not defy the feelings it brought. Ears hot, snot leaking from her nostrils and down her lips, she cried and thrust out both hands.

A stream of water shot from each, obliterating both the piano and the bed with unbelievable force. The bed's frame shattered completely as the mattress was flung against the wall. As her attack rescinded, a hole revealed itself in the center of the mattress, steam rising from scalding hot water. The piano's metal melted where it had been struck, contorting around the target area.

Olivia heaved, breaths releasing in uncontrollable spurts as she tried to scavenge oxygen. Then she fell to her knees, water pooling beneath her, steam rising from where it contacted the skin of her legs.

Hurried footsteps grew louder, approaching from down the corridor. "*OLIVIA!*" It was her mother's scream of panic. Her beautiful, fearless mother.

She felt the heat surging through her, felt her energies draining from her hands. She had done it, but it brought no relief or happiness …

Only exhaustion.

Her mother entered the room, sobbing. And Olivia slumped into the puddle with closed eyes.

38

The Cavities of Mulawith

Bryson opened his eyes to Thusia's face, cerulean orbs fixated on him. She was leaning forward on a chair next to his bed next to his bed, a hand placed on his face and thumb caressing his cheek. Her lips split to reveal a pearly smile. "Welcome back."

He blinked several times, groggy and bleary-eyed. Smacking his lips, mouth cotton dry, he reached for his head and felt the heat of his temple. Thusia pressed her hand over his. "A lingering fever from the poison," she said. "Needless to say, you failed your test."

"They poisoned me?" he asked. He frowned immediately, morning breath amplified by what had probably been a few days' sleep.

She picked up a glass of water from the floor next to her and tipped it into his mouth. "Yes, but only a non-lethal dosage."

The sip turned into several gulps, and he took over holding the cup. She waited for him to finish. He did and said, "This place is mad."

"A bit." She took the empty glass from him. "But usually for good reason."

"Did you believe that when they had you and Suadade locked up?"

She paused, but then grinned. "Yes. Knowing the consequences, we had made our beds, and then we lay in them."

"I'll get it right next time," he said, propping himself onto his elbows. He squeezed his eyes shut as someone hammered drums inside his head. "If I want to see Shelly and L.K., I have to." He opened one eye and glanced at his desk, a stack of parchment waiting for his attention. "We have to study."

She nodded. "No more games."

He plopped back into his pillow and groaned. "What'd I do wrong? What'd I miss?"

"I can't tell you that. You have to figure it out yourself."

He sighed, replaying the events of that night. The most obvious red flag had been the waitress who relieved their original waiter of his shift. Her mannerisms were strange—the lingering gazes and crafty smiles, her retreat behind the bar to get him water, something that she could have gotten from the sink right behind the counter. Alas, that was likely too obvious. A red herring. The test had likely begun the moment they exited the Starlight. He'd have to retrace every step he took to get to Founding Plaza, then compare those events to the intelligence contained in that stack of parchment on his desk.

He took from Lilu's repertoire and rolled his eyes. It was a homework assignment.

*　　　*　　　*

Yama didn't know what to expect when Master Ichi opened the door behind her desk. The sides and back of the Adren Assistance Academy had always been blocked from view by healthy oaks that hugged the building's perimeter. Neighboring buildings squeezed against the other side of the oaks and a tall wooden fence stood between them, so there were no sightlines from the street. She guessed she expected a balcony; instead, she saw a series of wooden stilts stretching into the distance, multiple paths splitting in different directions across the city.

"The backyard is off limits to most of my students," Ichi said. "You know this."

Yama stepped to the door, where the floor abruptly stopped, a stilt seven paces away. She gazed down at a grassy backyard, a windowless back wall preventing anyone from seeing it. She looked up, following the separate paths. Stilts stood on roofs of varying heights, some large enough to hold several. She couldn't believe it—a peg course that ran across the city's skyline. "Why haven't I ever noticed this?" she asked.

"It was only built a couple years ago after King Supido's death. He had dreamed of making the world's largest peg course, and his wife made sure it was built in his honor. There used to be a smaller course contained to my property, but obviously this is better."

"So you want me to run it."

Master Ichi stepped back from the doorway, her glossy black hair falling flat against her back as she retreated from the breeze. "Yes. It's the first part of your test. Each path of stilts is marked with a different color line at the top. The first color I want you to follow is green."

Yama unclasped her scabbard from her waistline and placed it against the wall. She undid her belt and dropped it on the floor.

"Really, Yama?" said Master Ichi, unimpressed by the lack of respect.

Yama had begun acting differently around the woman after noticing a difference in her attitude. Since the revelation of their blood relationship, Master Ichi had shown a softer side. Unlike her mother, Yama's aunt seemed to put much weight in family ties. She leapt to the first stilt, then turned on the ball of one foot to face her aunt, waiting for the instruction to begin.

Ichi gave her a dead look, but it didn't hold the same effect it once had. Sighing, Ichi grabbed a stopwatch from her desk and held it in the air. "Go."

Yama whirled and bound toward the first stilt she saw with a green stripe. In the midst of her lunge, she scanned other poles around her for more green. She saw two to her right and bound toward them with her foot only brushing the top of the prior silt. The stripes were thin, unreadable from a distance of more than two dozen paces. With many of the stilts spread beyond that distance—many more of which branched into different directions—this became more than an agility and balance exercise. Her awareness and reflexes were being tested. How keen were her eyes, how precisely could her mind register deviations, and how quickly could she react?

She rebounded between stilts, suddenly leaping over alleys and streets. Nobody looked up because nobody could see her. In order to run a course like this, her speed percentage had to be at a level beyond the tracking ability of a normal person's eyes. Maybe some saw a blur of color, but even that would only cause them to question their own eyesight—a trick of the light.

Within thirty seconds, she was in the downtown districts of Katashi, miles away from the Adren Assistance Academy. Buildings stood taller— five to six stories—making the course riskier. If she fell to the street from this height and at this speed, she'd die, painting the cobbles in gore. She circled the grounds of the royal estate, a sprawling structure that sat atop a hill of grass and gardens. When constructing the peg course, they had obviously kept the safety of the royals in mind. The stilts didn't come within half a mile of the property. Growing comfortable with the course, she almost failed. The wind whistling past her ears, cool humidity dampening her pores … it was hypnotizing.

She reached a stilt that sat on a single-floored home, and the next closest was on a three-story building across a wide side yard. Knowing she couldn't stop—because then she'd lose momentum and thus the ability to thrust with the speed to cover the gap—she hit the lower stilt and propelled herself angularly upward. Her calf threatened to rip from the unexpected force, and her trajectory didn't take her high enough.

She arched over the higher roof's edge, but descended just as her head reached the top of the stilt. She reached out with both hands and caught the top of the stilt. She pushed upward with enough power to lift her body over it, essentially leap-frogging the pole and flying toward the next. She lost control and her body flailed. She plunged to a green-striped stilt on a lower roof while looking for others around it. She caught and swung around it, throwing herself toward the next, where she finally regained control by landing on the ball of her foot.

Her heart raced, but her breathing was steady. Proper breathing was one of the first techniques an Adrenian learned in their life. If an Adrenian couldn't provide ample enough oxygen to their lungs and blood, they'd die mid sprint—*literally*. It was an actual cause of death for people in their culture. While rare, there was a student every few years who would drop dead on a peg course or even during laps or sprints. They called it "Death by overdrive."

Yama finished the course with relative ease, careful to not repeat her earlier mistake. Peg courses seemed child's play ever since training with Illipsia and Toono. Dashing between coin-sized pebbles floating in the air—most of which moved or gave way beneath Yama's weight—by a child's telekinetic abilities made stilts seem like solid ground ... almost.

She lunged through the doorway and rolled across the floor, rising to her feet just before colliding with the desk's chair. Master Ichi was seated in said chair. She clicked the stopwatch, looked at it, then placed it on the desk before returning to wiping down her katana.

"Well?" Yama asked.

"Very good," she said. "But green is the easiest path."

"Am I an assassin?"

Ichi's eyes lifted toward Yama, but not her head. "I have no idea. Before I conduct the tests to determine if you're an assassin, I must first determine if you meet the speed percentage and equilibrium status thresholds to take those tests. Think of these peg course runs as preliminary exams to determine eligibility."

Yama closed her eyes, head tilting back, as she inhaled deeply. This was nothing to get upset about. If it was part of the process, so be it. At least Master Ichi was doing something to help. "What do you want me to do next?" she asked, gaze returning to the woman.

"To leave for the night and recover," Ichi said, pulling the cloth away from the blade to check her reflection in the spunka steel. "Tomorrow, you do the black path."

* * *

Rhyparia walked with Yasmine Cordelia and Mendac LeAnce through the Black Labyrinth, ivory laces of the Mulanyx walls rising, falling, and twisting along their lengths. She felt a chill in her bones, which had become a constant sensation since her conversation with Mendac, when she realized who she truly was a little over a week ago. Her wings of shadows extended from her back, their amorphous edges reaching for the Labyrinth's black surfaces, pulling away as Rhyparia walked past only to reattach a few paces down the corridor. It was as if she was breathing in sync with a greater beast—as if the Mulanyx walls, floors, and ceilings were the bones of something alive.

She appreciated the force's presence, however ambiguous it might have been. She was learning how to embrace it as time went by, practicing delicacy when drawing from its power. Engulf too much, and a person— including a Versac, though their threshold was significantly higher—would find him or herself paralyzed, and dead. There was also a dependence that came with the tethering of one's Mulawi to the Mulawi of the Labyrinth. The more Rhyparia took, the more she'd rely on it in the future. The only mystery that unsettled her was the source of the Labyrinth's power.

Yasmine stopped in an atrium, seven corridors branching off from it in different directions. The floor's center was shattered and cragged, a ring of smooth Mulanyx wrapped around it. The legendary Dev Assassin stood at the center and asked for Mendac and Rhyparia's hand. Rhyparia stepped from the smooth onyx to the broken, then took the Fuhren's left hand, Mendac taking the other. This was a lock, and only someone with the Mulawi weaving talent of a Fuhren could break it. Neither Rhyparia nor Mendac were skilled enough yet.

Rhyparia gazed down at the infused onyx, a blackness deep enough in which to get lost. Why was there a lock in the floor? Was there something down there? Besides the small recess in her team's bunker, she had yet to see any evidence of a basement in the Labyrinth.

Shadows crept from the soles of Yasmine's leather shoes into the cracks of the shattered onyx, following paths in a pattern unrecognizable to Rhyparia until reaching the place where broken met smooth. The circle vanished into shadows, and they dropped through, plunging into the water of an ice-capped lake that punched the air from her lungs. They didn't fall freely, but gently sunk into a chamber below. Yasmine had sprouted her wings and guided them to the chamber's floor. Her wings disappeared, rescinding into her back as they touched ground.

Rhyparia gaped at a massive dome of shadows that rose from the floor at the chamber's center. Clumps of its surface pulsed like a blanket of shadows over a pile of beating hearts, black smoke billowing outward from each visible thump before thinning in the air. Shadows sunk down the dome's surface, interrupted only by the pulsing, pooling atop and spreading thickly across the Mulanyx floor. In some areas, it was sucked into the floor, but most of it reached the chamber's walls and climbed to the ceiling. Rhyparia looked down at her feet; the carpet of shadows split just in front of her but converged again behind. Her wings wanted to reach for the shadows, but she harnessed that desire, noticing the unbearable bite of frigidity accompanying the strange substance.

"This is a Cavity of Mulawith," Yasmine stated.

Dumfounded, Rhyparia stared at the pulsing blob that stood at twice any of their heights. Mendac, the scholar that he was, stepped closer, eyes wide with rare, genuine awe. It took a lot to siphon such an expression out of a man who had seen so many things that broke natural laws.

"A cavity like those found in our bodies?" he asked.

"Yes."

He leaned in. A shadow bubble swelled on the dome's surface and burst into a plume of smoke. He backed away, possessing the common sense to know one didn't play with the unknown without proper research first. He stood straight and inspected the chamber. "The cavity of a god, and it's releasing its Mulawi into the onyx of the Black Labyrinth."

"The Labyrinth is Mulanyx's body ... or its skeleton," Yasmine explained. "However you want to look at it."

Mendac turned back toward the pulsating dome. Rhyparia wondered what he was thinking. Had a man with his acumen and experience seen anything close to this? Of course not. Nobody had. Not even the Bewahr, which Yasmine had explained during their trek here. The Bewahr knew of its existence, but had never seen it. And none of them had the weaving skill to unlock the floor above to gain excess.

Mendac knelt and placed a hand against the floor, roiling shadows circumventing the new obstacle. "So this is one of six?"

"One of four," Yasmine corrected.

He turned from his knelt position to regard her. "Spirit Cavity of the soul, Emotion Cavity of the heart, Courage Cavity of the muscles, Knowledge Cavity of the brain's right half, Morality Cavity of the brain's left half, and the cavity—its name unknown to me—of the eyes. Which of the six isn't accounted for?"

Yasmine stared at him for a silent moment, crossing her arms, the hems of loose sleeves hanging past her waist. She seemed either shocked or impressed by Mendac's knowledge of the cavities. "Your reputation as a theorist isn't all talk." She paused, looking up at the dome. "The Morality and Courage Cavities."

Rhyparia was utterly lost. None of this made sense, and she was growing frustrated. She felt like an extra in a play, Mendac and Yasmine the leads. "Anyone willing to clarify?" she asked.

Mendac, whose hand had lifted to rub his blond beard, clearly trying to connect dots Rhyparia couldn't see, looked at her as if he was just now noticing her presence. Then he looked at Yasmine. "Do you want me to explain it to her?"

She shrugged, then backed against a wall as if to say, "Go ahead." The mass of shadows climbing the wall didn't try to avoid her. She almost seemed to sink into them.

Mendac proceeded to lecture Rhyparia about the anatomical makeup of the energy system, from cavities to energy gates, and his Theory of Polarity and Connectivity. Being Archain, Rhyparia's only active cavity was her Morality Cavity, located in the brain's left half and responsible for creating and filling her body with Archaic Energy. Mendac's active cavity, as an Intelian, was the Knowledge Cavity in the brain's right half, responsible for creating and filling his body with Intel Energy. Yasmine's body used the same cavity as Mendac, but produced Dev Energy instead of Intel. Simple enough.

After the fifteen-minute lecture, Mendac observed the dome of shadows again. He was standing now, hands tucked into cloak pockets. "So there are six chambers below the Labyrinth, each meant to hold one of

Mulawith's cavities. But whichever usually holds the Morality and Courage Cavities are empty."

Yasmine hadn't moved from her post against the wall. "Yes."

"Why would that be?" he muttered to himself.

"I suppose you were a corpse when it happened," the Fuhren said, "but the Prim Prince was murdered ... or sacrificed."

He remained facing the dome, expression darkening. He was brooding, and he looked to know something they didn't. After a pause, he said, "This is why killing a royal firstborn is an Untenable."

Yasmine didn't respond, letting the silence answer him.

"If they die without passing on the genetic trait of their royal bloodline, so does Mulawith's corresponding Cavity."

Rhyparia's posture weakened, knowing what it was she had done ... why Emperor Mialo would treat her with such crassness.

"Over fifteen centuries ago, during the void between timelines," Yasmine said, "Kuki Sphaira experienced a cataclysmic transition, both geographically and metaphysically. Have you ever heard of the Essences?"

"No, I haven't," admitted Mendac, while Rhyparia continued to gaze emptily at the dome.

Yasmine began a spiel about the time before Known History, of Originators—the rulers of the kingdoms during that time—and Essences—the physical manifestations of the ten energies. The two entities fed off each other, each kingdom possessing one Originator and one Essence. It was what made Originators immortal while containing the Essences to remote locations. Over time, the Originators stopped harvesting their Essences, causing the immortal rulers of that era to die, which left the Essences without anyone to harvest them, causing them to swell and burst across the world as currents. Within those billions of currents were thousands of fragments of the Essence's being. While currents remained in nature forever, those fragments of Essence were absorbed by people, triggering their cavities into motion and releasing energy in their body. During the void between timelines, people learned how to bond their energy with the currents of nature, which was where the term, "weaving", was born.

At this point, Mendac interrupted the lecture. "Are you saying anyone who has energy in them is, technically, a descendent of an Essence?"

Yasmine tilted her head, pursing her lips. She had pushed away from the wall and was now standing at attention, likely excited to finally teach the man something. "Essences aren't human, and therefore don't have descendants per se. Using commoner's terminology, they're demigods—Mulawith and Tahar being actual gods. 'Byproducts' is better than 'descendants.' Essentially, anyone who has energy possesses a fragment of an Essence inside of them."

"A fragment of a demigod," Mendac said.

"Sure." She extended a hand toward him. "In other words, you possess a fragment of Intelius." She looked at Rhyparia. "You, a fragment of Archaius. And I, a fragment of Devissa. However, nobody could dissect any of us and find them; they're genetic."

"So how does this correlate to Mulawith's missing cavities?" Rhyparia asked.

"When an Essence burst into the atmosphere, sending chunks of itself into people, some were bigger than others," Yasmine said. "None were equal portions, but there was always one fragment far greater than the rest, which sought out a person most capable of harnessing it."

"Royals," Mendac breathed.

Yasmine nodded. "At the time, they weren't known as such, but they became known as royals. For instance, the Dev royal firstborn carries a genetic makeup closer to the Essence than anyone else in the world. So when a Dark Empire royal dies, specifically a firstborn before passing on the trait, that part of Mulawith dies. And the same applies to a Light Empire royal, except Tahar would become the victim."

"I'm confused," Rhyparia said. "How is Mulawith's cavity affected? If anything, it sounds like the Essence would feel it."

"Because the five Essences of the Dark Empire are children of Mulawith. This blob we're standing in front of now is the Knowledge Cavity. And while all you see is shadows, Devissa—the Essence of the Dev Kingdom—was born from this many millennia ago. Thus, if the Dev royal firstborn, who possesses the truest fragment of Devissa, were to die before having a child of his or her own, this would die, too."

Rhyparia stared at the dome, finally understanding. She tilted her head and narrowed her eyes. "What happens if all five of a realm's royal firstborns die?"

Yasmine's face grew somber as she regarded the cavity. "Mulawith will come as close to death as possible. This Labyrinth's skeleton will become normal onyx without the infusion of Mulawi, which means it'd crumble over time. Onyx isn't known for its durability."

"Why wouldn't it die completely?" Rhyparia asked.

"Because of the sixth Cavity Mendac mentioned earlier. It's called the Judgment Cavity. A portion of it is located in an undisclosed location somewhere beneath the Labyrinth. In the human body, it's found in your eyes and is responsible for producing Tahara and Mulawi. When you meet the three Versac, you'll notice their irises are streaked with black that then floods into the whites."

"A portion of it?" Mendac asked.

"Mulawith's and Tahar's true selves are hidden somewhere in the world of mortals. The theory is that they did it for protection, so no one could truly kill them. When five of their Cavities die, they enter hibernation as they work to rebuild themselves, a process that takes several centuries. It doesn't take all five, however, for the effects to be felt." Yasmine shook her head. "As I said, the Dark Empire has lost only two, yet the Gefal feel the loss. We're not as strong as we were."

"What is the Light Empire's state?" Mendac asked.

"Each royal firstborn is still alive, so all of Tahar's Cavities are intact."

"And that's the 'balance' spoken of in the Untenable regarding the killing of a royal firstborn," he said. "It's to protect these Cavities and, thus, the balance between the two Empires."

"Precisely. It's why we're at war. Everything in that petty squabble that's been happening in the kingdoms has directly impacted events up here, causing a grander spectacle of proportions beyond any normal scope of comprehension. We're dealing with gods here—Mulawith and Tahar ... if gods are what you call them. Most believe them to be the creators of life. We don't know what would happen, exactly, if Tahar or Mulawith were to enter hibernation, but it's safe to assume it'd be cataclysmic for one side or the other. When the Prim Prince was killed before creating an heir, and

427

Mulawith's Morality Cavity died as a result, it forced Emperor Mialo's hands to strike against the Light Empire, fearing the imbalance would beckon Empress Tonitrua into attacking. It turned general disdain into aggression seeded in terror."

"And when did the Courage Cavity vanish?" asked Mendac.

Yasmine looked at Rhyparia, who hadn't spoken in a while. "Why don't you ask the one responsible?"

Slowly, he followed the Fuhren's gaze, wide eyes landing on Rhyparia. "You?"

She snorted. "Didn't I tell you the story of what I did in the Power Kingdom?"

"Yes, but I guess ..." He shook his head and blinked. "It didn't click for me, but I guess it should have. While you didn't mention killing any royals, you did say you destroyed the capital. Naturally, the royal family was in the palace. It also explains the Emperor's treatment of you. He doesn't like you, finds you to be largely responsible for the Dark Empire's current status." Mendac was rambling, but he paused to collect his thoughts, then squinted at her. "An entire royal family?"

Rhyparia huffed, bringing a hand up to brush through her thick brown hair. However indirectly it may have been, she had slain a lofty percentage of a god. And now she was living inside that same god's body, breathing in its energy and life, flaunting its power as wings. She was throwing it in Emperor Mialo's face, like a victorious gambler dangling his bag of coin across the table from the loser.

Mialo had every right to hate her, but he was also a rational man—the Originator of the Dev Kingdom, the Dark Knowledge Kingdom. Because of this, he knew to use her for the weapon of mass destruction that she was. If he lost two of Mulawith's Cavities, the best he could do to make up for it was recruit two powerful individuals to add to his numbers.

She scratched her scalp at the top of her neck, a clump of hair in her grip, then dropped her hand. Regarding the shadowy dome—this one the Knowledge Cavity that birthed Devissa, the Essence of Dev Energy—she made herself see it for what it was: a source of life for the Dark Empire and now her own power. She could feel Emperor Mialo's presence in her subconscious, actively feeling for any doubts within her. He could search all he wanted; he'd fine none. Not anymore.

Getting to know Yasmine Cordelia, she had learned that not all Gefal were bad people. And she was certain not all Bozani were good. Dark didn't mean Evil, nor did Light mean Pure. Wasn't that the whole basis to the Sphairian Summit in the 700's, the whole reason for the shift in the kingdoms' nomenclature? She could fight on behalf of Mulawith, the Emperor, and those Gefal worth saving.

For all the evil she had done, could she still manage one good deed?

39

The Soteria-Accus Feud

Himitsu lay in a four-poster bed with a mattress vast enough to hold four grown men, staring at its tarp roof. The curtains were tied to the posts, sunlight spilling through a series of tall, narrow windows, cutting across the sleeping chamber of his and Kaylee's quarters. Loess Lord Kopios hadn't exaggerated the luxuries of their guest space, the overabundance of gold décor bordering on frivolous. He eyed the dark brown wood of the bed's frame, wondering what kind of tree could have created such sheen.

Look at me. Bored out of my wits. Mother never told me assassinations were a drag. Perhaps, this was his fault. A week of sitting on his butt, and he still had no desire to plan a way of killing the Loess Lord. He was stalling, and for good reason. *I've been tasked to kill the love of my life's father.*

His mother had told him Kopios was a bad man, but had given no evidence. She wanted him to trust her blindly—essentially the same thing she had done with King Itta during her assignment in the Archaic

Mountains. She was his mother, though. She wouldn't lie to him. She knew what kind of assignment on which she'd sent him.

He sat up before his eyes could close on him again, bored sleep trying to take him under. He needed to keep busy, discover information about the Heresy Butte and the Loess as a whole. With a mission such as this, proper scouting preceded any defining actions. While the Spy Pilot knew of treason in the Loess, she hadn't known anything about its civilization, from the populace to the politics. When he had asked her about what her birds had seen—for they saw everything—she said nothing. That had struck him as unbelievable back then, so now he found it downright impossible after seeing the skylight at the top of the butte. He was to believe not a single bird had flown over this butte, looked down, and seen civilization within? And what about the caves?

A knock came from the door to his quarters. The door was in the antechamber, two rooms over from his. He collected air and bellowed, "COME IN!"

The door opened and closed, and a woman eventually peeked around the arched entryway into his sleeping chamber. She stepped fully into view upon seeing Himitsu was in a presentable state. He stood and tucked his hands in his pockets, tilting his head. "Hello?"

"Sir Hymis?" she said.

He cocked a brow. "Sir? Is this the first century? I'm no knight."

She opened her mouth, then closed it. She didn't know what to call him.

"Just Hymis," he said.

She nodded and unraveled a scroll in front of her to read. "Hymis, Loess Lord Kopios Soteria has invited you to visit the Piety Mines. The three-day journey begins in two days' time at first light. He figures you would like to see your investment firsthand." She looked up from the scroll. "What is your decision?"

Himitsu didn't know what the Piety Mines or this investment was, but he couldn't let her know that. "Sounds good," he said.

She closed the scroll and bowed, then disappeared behind the wall. He smirked, rubbing the back of his head. This place didn't operate like the rest of the world. He gazed out one of the windows from the bed and thought of Kaylee. She was presently studying beneath a talented apothecary, viewing this journey as a scholarly retreat, not an assassination mission.

He wished he had that ignorance.

*   *   *

It was Kaylee's final day with her instructor of a five-day stretch. On top of the sixteen-hour days, she had spent the nights in the hospital, sleeping with one eye open, as her cupboard of a room was frequently invaded by a stressed nurse who required extra hands in a surgical room. It was all part of her instructor's rigorous training, believing before she learned the arts of medicine and healing, she must first understand the demands of the profession. That, apparently, involved strenuous hours and a selfless desire to forego any sleep in favor of patients whose lives were in danger. This five-day stretch was a preliminary method of discovering if Kaylee was truly ready to learn, for if she didn't have the ability to put others first, then she couldn't be a healer.

Thankfully, she was in the waning hours of her final day, heavy eyelids making it impossible to focus on her instructor's gloved fingers as they dug into a man's lower abdomen, the other hand holding a pair of skinny scissors. He had been put under, courtesy of Wrinkle Root scavenged from the uppermost plateau of the Loess's eastern edge.

"Kaylee," her instructor snapped. "Light."

Kaylee's hazy vision refocused, and she stared at a glass globe in her hand, two circular discs of Permanence on either side. Rays of blue electricity bounded between the discs, contained within the sphere, errant sparks disappearing as they hit the glass. It was an Intelight with only a few more minutes left of power, the stored energy in the Permanence vessels nearing depletion. Noticing her hand had drifted to the side in her stupor, she relocated it next to the incision on which her instructor was working. The woman shook her head, annoyed.

"Sorry, Doctor Mengai."

Doctor Mengai was an elderly woman who stood at four-and-a-half feet and needed a stepstool to see patients on the surgical bed. A gray head cap covered white hair. Wrinkled skin hung loosely from her forearms and elbows, age spots smattering her skin as if a painter had flicked his brush at her. Excess skin drooped from her chin into her neck, and that theme carried up her face, from her cheeks to the bags of her eyes. A mouse could have grabbed her earlobes and gone for a ride. In any respectable hospital under the authority of any sane board of directors, she would have been forced to retire decades ago. Kaylee ventured a guess at her age falling in the nineties.

But this was no normal old woman. She still had a surgeon's hand and caretaker's temperament, both rock steady. And she had the eyes of a hawk, spotting details in a diseased heart while standing in a doorway before any doctor directly operating on the patient could even glance at it. It was strange enough to make Kaylee internally question it every time. She wasn't yet comfortable enough to confront the doctor about it. Inquiring about someone's old age was typically frowned upon.

The more intriguing matter was Mengai's last name. Accus held historical significance. It didn't matter where you were in the Light Realm— even an unmapped village—people had heard the tale of Gatal Accus, First of Five. Mengai was a distant descendent of the hero from over fourteen hundred years ago. Kaylee knew the man had hailed from the Loess, but she didn't know the name would have remained prevalent. One, because of the length time between eras, and two, because of the social stigma attached to the name. Gatal had fought tooth and nail against the orders that moved to abolish religion at the beginning of Known History. While the rest of the world—aside from the Prim Kingdom—had successfully eradicated organized religion, the Archaic Kingdom's royal family was still trying to destroy it into the latter half of the first century.

Gatal had been that stubborn thorn in the royal family's side. He had a cult-like following, and they journeyed from the kingdom's eastern reaches to the west, slowly making their way toward the capital, Phelos, and adding more followers as he passed through cities and towns as checkpoints. He carried on his person a golden scepter ribbed with jewels, its handle a broad curve like the top of a question mark. He treated it like a walking stick, but the kingdom learned, as gossip spread across the lands, that it was the rarest category of ancients—a relic—and the source of conviction he'd instill in doubters. As the legends went, that scepter could summon manifestations of gods. Other versions of the story said he carried a book rather than the scepter. Civilians claimed to have witnessed it with their own eyes, while others refused to give Gatal a chance, finding the lies distasteful.

Gatal's story came to a climactic end in the city of Balle, where he supposedly summoned a god called Magnifica, who then redirected an incoming meteorite away from the city and into the vacant grasslands to the west, creating what was now known as Accus Canyon. Out of the *Of Five* tales, Gatal's was usually deemed the tallest of them all. Aside from the incredulous power level and weaving talent one must have to summon a god, there was the indisputable evidence of a missing meteorite in the canyon. Also, wouldn't a meteorite cause cataclysmic destruction across the entire kingdom?

Doctor Mengai extracted a clump of a crystalline substance from the man and placed it on a napkin on a foldable stand to her right. Kaylee stepped back, pulling the Intelight away from the incision.

"Ever had a kidney stone?" Mengai asked.

"No, Doctor."

"I've had seven in my life," she said. "I think I'd rather charge an opposing army and take a sword wound to the gut."

"Have you ever had a sword wound?" Kaylee asked, finding the comparison absurd.

"No, but I cut my finger once while dicing carrots." Mengai walked away from the patient and waved for a fellow doctor to finish the procedure, which involved reclosing and cleaning the incision. "Same thing, right?" she asked as they stepped out of the room.

As they removed their gloves, hair caps, and surgical gowns, Kaylee didn't respond. The question felt like a trap. Mengai had a habit of trying to catch her in them.

"It's a simple question, really," the doctor said.

Kaylee dipped her hands into a bucket of hot water. There were dozens of buckets lined against the wall on a table, each one designed for one-time use. She shrugged and said, "No?" It came out as more of a question than an answer.

Mengai said nothing else after that. They bathed separately in the hospital's staff washroom. Half-an-hour later, the two of them reconvened in the cavern garden, where herbs and flowers of all types grew in sectioned rows under dozens of Intelamps hanging from the ceiling. Kaylee followed Mengai down a path between two rows of floral assortments. Despite the woman's age and hunched frame, she didn't hobble. Her strides were steady and smooth—just like her hands during surgery.

She came to a stop halfway down the row and stepped onto a low bench that ran along the sides of each table, which had been built specifically for Mengai's short stature. Kaylee stood at her side, electing not to use the makeshift stool. Mengai gestured toward the general vicinity of several potted flowers, all of which looked identical. "Can you pick me a Rubber Topaz?" she asked.

Kaylee surveyed the flowers. All of them had broad petals that gently cupped inward to form a layered, cerulean bowl. Thick and leafy stems made it look like the bowl-like flower sat atop a stack of green leaves. She knew the Rubber Topaz was a flower native to the Passion Kingdom, as was most of Kuki Sphaira's beautiful plant life. It was sought after not just because of its beauty, but because of medical purposes. Its petals, when boiled, secreted a substance called laxer that relaxed the transitional epithelium, or the inner lining of one's ureter, bladder, and urethra. Doctors often used laxer to treat kidney stones, unless they were too big, in which case the amount of laxer needed would be too dangerous, for excess laxer permanently damaged the urinal system's tract. That was why Mengai had been forced to operate on the earlier patient.

"Well?" Mengai asked, several seconds having passed.

Kaylee leaned over, inspecting each identical flower carefully. She knew this was a trap. While she had read a lot about the medicinal field, she had very little real life experience with the supplements. Mengai had been assigning her this cavern garden as study material for the past week, but Kaylee had yet to reach this table. Clearly, the doctor expected her to have covered the entire garden already.

She inhaled and grabbed a pot of four Rubber Topazes, handing it to Mengai. The doctor looked at her and not the flowers, gaze unrevealing. "Do you want to embarrass someone?"

Kaylee's shoulders sunk, knowing she had fallen into the trap.

"Give a man that flower and he'll be pissing himself for the rest of his life, his bladder incapable of holding anything inside. Urine will essentially fall out of him involuntarily."

"My apologies, Doctor," Kaylee said. "I haven't gotten to this section yet." She went to put the pot back on the table. Mengai caught her wrist.

"Why would you put it back? Does it sound like it has any use in a hospital?"

Kaylee frowned, pulling it back toward her. "Why was it there in the first place then?"

"This batch went bad this morning," Mengai said. "The herbalists would have trashed them by now, but I instructed them to not touch these, seeing it as an opportunity to test you." She took the flower pot from Kaylee. "Look at the petals," she said. "Specifically, where they converge at the stigma. The petals of a Rubber Topaz are cerulean, but do you see the lines of darker blue—almost a navy blue—branching outward toward the petals' tips?" Kaylee nodded. "And how many do you count on each petal?"

Kaylee moved her head closer, as the navy blue lines were fine and abundant, requiring a keen eye. Knowing Mengai, she could have likely counted them from a few meters' distance. "Twelve," Kaylee finally said.

"Which is one too many," said Mengai. "Think of those lines as the rings of a tree; they tell the flower's age. That twelfth line on each of the petals appeared this morning, which means they're seventy-two days old. Anything under twelve stripes, and a Rubber Topaz is okay to boil and use for treatment. If it's twelve or above, sure, kidney stones will never be an issue of pain again, but you're damning someone to a lifetime of involuntary urination. And therefore, like a cooking-prep knife wound and a fatal blow to the gut from a sword are nothing alike, neither are all Rubber Topazes."

Kaylee scoffed. What a convoluted, bizarre segue into a lecture.

Mengai placed the Rubber Topazes down on the table and checked her wristwatch. She frowned. "And so our first week together comes to an end. A real shame. I like your brain."

"But I just failed a test."

"I expected you to."

Kaylee's eyebrows flattened. "Well, that's just mean, Doctor."

Mengai smirked. "Fun, I'd say. Figured we'd end the week on a lighter note—urinal humor and all that chaff. I want you to enjoy your day off."

"Doctor Mengai," said a man from the cavern's entrance. "A Soteria is here for a checkup."

Mengai sighed. "Duty calls."

"You do routine checkups?" Kaylee asked. "Wouldn't your skills be more suited elsewhere?"

"When the name 'Soteria' is involved, I have no choice. That family rules the Loess and pays my salary."

"When do you get a break?" Kaylee asked. "A day off."

"I don't."

"What?"

"I am an Accus," said Mengai. "Which basically makes me the Soteria family's lackey. I don't leave this hospital unless it's to tend to the Loess Lord in his castle. My amenities are far more lavish than even the wealthiest members of society, but I don't have any freedom. I should consider myself lucky, for the rest of the Accus family owns that same lack of freedom, but don't have the wealth to show for it."

"Do they live around here?" Kaylee asked.

"No. They're inlanders, residing in less-than-ideal conditions close to the Piety Mines. I haven't seen a family member in twenty-two years." Mengai gave a hollow grin. "It's the price we pay for having tried to continue Gatal's legacy of worship." She turned and headed for the doors. "We deserve this, no?"

Kaylee watched her leave, suddenly questioning everything. She had come to the Thousand-Layer Loess without a thought of corruption or evil. The Loess had existed for hundreds of years without help from the rest of the world or its kingdom—or so she'd assumed. She had believed, because of the absence of news from the Loess, that it existed in peace. Mengai Accus had just flipped that notion on its head.

There was a feud between two families here, one submissive to the other. She wanted an explanation because there was no way she could continue to learn under Doctor Mengai if she was basically a prisoner—however luxurious and wealthy her cage might have been. It made Kaylee feel like she was taking advantage of a woman who probably wanted nothing more than to exist without shackles.

40

A Martyr's Rally

"This seems lazy," said Creep, standing next to a wardrobe in a tiny tavern room. He shook his head. "I think the husband of the Spy Pilot should be capable of better."

Horos sat on the room's lone, twin-sized bed. He paused putting on a pair of boots to look up at Creep with an expression of amusement. "The husband of the Spy Pilot? Is that my title?"

"Does it bother you?" Creep asked. "She is grander than you, far more important and notable to the world."

"I get that," he said. "But you know my name, so please use it."

Creep nodded. "Of course."

"I'm used to operating with a partner," Horos said. "Fane was always the brains to my brawn. But, since he's stuck on suicide watch for the queen, I'm forced to shake the cobwebs off the pile of slush in the ol' noggin." He knocked at his temple.

"It's a plan," Creep said, rocking his head back and forth with uncertainty. "But I think it's rushed and unrealistic."

"My guy's already too far into the ruse to back out. The rebels have paid him, and he's committed to seeing it out to the end." Horos stomped his heel into his boot. "That comes in two hours."

Creep looked at the window, curtains open. They were on the fourth floor, so nobody could see inside their room. Dusk splashed amber across the carpet.

"Honestly, your methods are taking too long," Horos said. "You call me lazy and desperate for shortcuts; I call you meticulous to a fault, desperate for a perfect solution."

The hybrid chuckled, lifted his chin, and nodded. "Fair deduction. I suppose it doesn't matter. As long as someone gets an in with the rebels ..." he trailed off ... "Without compromising ourselves."

Horos stood, pulling his raven hair into a ponytail. The man had let it grow down to his shoulders over the past few months. "This isn't my first rodeo," he said. "Just keep a low profile in the crowd."

"And my eyes peeled," said Creep.

*   *   *

The crush was insufferable, the press of bodies so compact that Creep couldn't tell if three of seven people were touching him at the present moment. He occupied what he thought would have been a safe place in the crowd, but he couldn't have predicted this many people showing up for the rally. Thus, he fought his way to the rear of the crowd, prying women by their arms out of his path, shoving his shoulder against the biceps of men. Nobody retaliated; they were all too enamored by a young man standing atop a stone wall at the front of the crowd, addressing them with a rousing speech. Damned puppets. Had Horos been right?

Creep found salvation among dispersed groups at the perimeter. He turned to face the young man, but couldn't see him through the crowd. Scanning the street, he spotted the one bench on which nobody stood. He climbed atop it and located the man across the sea of heads, Intelamps intensifying the moonlight's bluish hue. Creep estimated over a hundred people had shown up, and many watched from the windows of bordering tenements. He tried to read their faces, most of which were disdain.

"… and why are we in the dark?!" shouted the young man, Creep just now focusing on his speech. "We've heard nothing from the royal family! Was half our city not just obliterated?! Does the new queen think those who uprooted their lives from the east can just restart somewhere else, as if it were as easy as flipping a switch?!" He paused, a smattering of angry shouts from the crowd. "I have friends in unique places! They tell me what's happening in the east! They're building a factory for machines of war! Tell me … HAVE WE NOT HAD OUR FILL OF WAR ALREADY?!"

A raucous eruption of cheers. Creep narrowed his eyes. This was risky. Wasn't this man supposed to be one of Horos's? Why did their ruse involve fueling the crowd? He scanned the tops of heads in the crowd, searching for anyone who either wasn't paying attention to the speech or didn't share the same excitement as the rest of the crowd. They would be the most suspicious. If their focus wasn't on the man giving the speech, then that meant they were searching for someone or something else. And if they were the one statue among the frenzy, that meant they saw beneath the surface of the man's words, for this man wasn't an actual member of the rebels, but was preaching as if he was, leading the masses astray.

"Is that where all their money's going?" the man screamed. "There are floods in Continon and overcrowding here in Dunami! The streets and alleys are filled with the homeless! Food is scarce! Prices are rising as inflation swells! The Still Kingdom, a kingdom of the Dark Realm, is the most stable kingdom in our alliance! Why are we getting bailed out by Stillians?"

As the crowd began to roar, Creep wondered how effective this was going to be. He had told Horos weeks ago about the people who gathered at the front of the Electric Eel. Horos then decided to send one of his men—his alias was Gore—into Creep's territory and infiltrate that group. According to Horos, Gore succeeded. The group brought the young man in, but didn't reveal any details about their intentions. Before they'd accept him, they needed him to hold a rally, denouncing the royal family and state of the kingdom, to prove he was serious about whatever their mission was. This rally was an initiation, which didn't surprise Creep. Several of his spies who were responsible for other territories had informed him about pop-up rallies like this. The difference, however, was that Gore wasn't an actual rebel.

If this ruse found success, the rebels would welcome Gore in with open arms. Creep's spies would have their first agent inside enemy lines to gather intelligence. They'd be well on their way to discovering the head of the snake: who was organizing and conducting the rebellion and who provided funding? Once they found the head, dismantling the body would be as simple as chopping it off. He would owe Horos a drink every night of the week once all was said and done.

"And where is our Royal Head?!" Gore asked. "Where's the king?! We haven't seen Queen Shelly or King Bryson in months! Why has Princess Lilu been the only one showing her face? Do the two people who lead us not care?"

The cheers became rumblings of anger as Gore began speaking sense. Scanning the crowd again, Creep saw someone pushing through the crush. The long hair made him think it was a woman, but she lifted a hood over her head as she reached the halfway point between the perimeter and Gore's location.

Creep leapt from his bench and sprinted into the crush, shoving people to the side, his sturdy trench coat a hindrance in cramped spaces. Curses were flung his way as he disregarded any delicacy in maneuvering the crowd, but their voices were drowned out by the swelling frenzy over Gore's inspiring words. Creep couldn't hear the young man anymore, not in his fervor and over the pumping of his heart.

He found the hooded woman and tackled her. They were ten meters away from the front. He sat on her back, her face pressed into tar, wispy strands of brown hair splayed out of the hood and around her head. As he tried to turn her over to see her face, the crowd around them stirred into a mob. His tackle had toppled two people, who had rammed into others, causing a domino effect. Now a boot connected with his ribs, peeling him off the woman's back. He rolled into someone else's ankles. He looked up to find the sole of their shoe plunging toward his face. He rolled the other way.

Fists were being exchanged between those still standing, while the unfortunate souls who had fallen to the ground were being trampled. He saw the hooded woman—not her face, but brown hair dangling from within the hem—through a throng of legs. She was pushing herself up to all fours, catching someone's foot who had tried kicking her. She yanked it, ripping her assailant off his feet. The man hit the ground with a crunch and scream.

Creep pushed off toward her, but two burly hands grabbed fistfuls of his trench coat's lapels, lifting him upward. His feet dangled over the ground. He looked the man in the eyes, then noticed the thick neck and square jaw. There was no way he was overpowering this guy. The man reached back with one fist, the other hand clasped around Creep's lapel. Creep kicked the man in the groin before he could get his punch off. He dropped Creep, knees buckling as he yelled for the empires.

The hybrid scanned the crowd. Some women fled; others held their own. Some people grappled sloppily while others searched for potential cheap shots on unsuspecting victims. It was a brawling pit, screams of the fearful piercing the grunts of the fighters.

Creep lost sight of the hooded woman. She had likely escaped by now. He turned and pushed toward the front of the dispersing crowd in efforts to find Gore. As he reached the stone rail on which the young man had stood, he found no one. Gore was gone, and the masses had scattered, a stampede heading for any building they could find. Creep stood there, confused, for a second, but then he saw the sole of a boot resting atop the rail. He walked toward it, ignoring the instinct of flight sounding alarm bells in his head. If people were running in a panic, it was for good reason.

He stopped at the rail and leaned over to look into the flower patch just behind it. A leg extended from the boot, accompanied by the rest of Gore's body lying in the flowers. An arrow was lodged into his temple, blood spilling down his face and soaking the soil.

The train of thoughts that followed took less than a second. Gore had been assassinated, and Creep didn't have the slightest clue by whom. It could have been a random person who thought they were doing good by eliminating someone who was rebelling against the crown, but that seemed unlikely—unless there was a faction that directly opposed the rebels. The hooded woman he had tackled and then lost in the riot was a culprit, but he would have felt a bow on her person when he'd been on top of her. She could have concealed a crossbow, but the size of the arrow in Gore's head implied it had been shot from a longbow, likely from somewhere on a rooftop or in a window. The other possibility was the rebels who had given Gore the task of holding this rally, knowing him for what he was—a spy—and taking him out after he did some of their dirty work.

That possibility was the most likely, which would mean they were somewhere in the vicinity at this very moment, observing the aftermath. Considering this, Creep needed to play the role this situation had just presented to him. Horos's plan may have failed, but Creep could make it work through improvising, and hopefully, make sure Gore's death wasn't in vain in the process.

Creep hurled himself over the low stone wall, gathered Gore in his arms and raised him so the world could see. He dragged the corpse over the wall and placed it against the stone, where it slouched lifelessly atop the tar road. He stood atop the rail and thought of the morning he had abandoned Soraku, knowing her secret wasn't safe if he stayed in Yinyon any longer. His eyes watered. A tear slipped down his cheek and into his beard. *Success.* Authenticity sold any decent act.

"Do you see what they've done?!" Creep roared, extending a hand toward the corpse. "The royals now treat common citizens who simply voice their disapproval like they're criminals! What has happened to the freedom of speech?"

"Get down from there!" a man screamed. A small group from the crowd had remained in scattered clumps.

"Do you want to end up like that guy?!" a woman asked.

"The crown doesn't scare me!" Creep bellowed. "They just assassinated an innocent man for speaking his mind! If I find myself meeting the same fate, know that I did so willingly! If this is what it takes to get the people to realize the truth, then so be it!" He paused to catch his breath, placing a hand against his heaving chest. He wished this was part of the act, but his heart was actually … in physical pain. It felt like someone had grabbed and twisted it into a knot. His eyes bulged momentarily. Heart attack?

"They're killing him with witchcraft!" someone from the crowd screamed.

Creep straightened his back, one eye closed. Witchcraft didn't exist; this was his own body failing. The pain slowly rescinded, and he released the last bit of stamina he had left to bellow, "*DOWN WITH THE CROWN!*"

He stood there, the hand that had been clutching at his chest now raised toward the night sky in a fist. Honestly, he didn't know what he expected in that moment. If the rebels knew Gore was a spy, then it was possible they knew of Creep and Horos's real identity. He breathed deeply, eyes skittering across the throngs of people then skating up the fronts of buildings. Was he going to die? The arrow would hit him before he saw it. He was gambling here, believing the rebels wouldn't want to kill the man known to the community as Sunshine, the Butcher. It would stir the entire populace into riots; they'd lose control of whatever refined system they currently had in place. It was better for the rebels to remain hidden, for that was their main advantage. If they wanted an uprising, now wasn't the time.

Thirty seconds passed, Creep unmoving. Deciding the threat had passed, spectators began to roar. They pumped fists in the air, chanting in a rhythm that boomed down the street. "DOWN WITH THE CROWN! DOWN WITH THE CROWN! DOWN WITH THE CROWN!"

Creep kept his face rigid, silent while the people shouted for him. He didn't know which rebels were watching him, but all that mattered was that he caught someone's attention.

He was a hybrid, a breed of stealth specialists that no longer existed. He was a master of deception—the man who would have likely become Spy Pilot had he not fled to the Prim Kingdom.

Tonight, he was a butcher named Sunshine, a shining beacon of rebellion.

41

The Nature of Brothers

The Cyn Kingdom—the Void—was never kind to its native inhabitants, let alone foreigners. Its reputation involved degradation of the soul and decomposition of the flesh. The Linsani's screams reached every corner of the kingdom, expelling the spirit out of people. The leading cause of death in the Void was suicide, but the lengths one needed to go to achieve death were unfathomable. Leaping from a rooftop or cutting one's neck wouldn't stop someone from suffering.

Considering these horrors, why would a Spiritian man uproot his family from their home to live in the Void? He was known as the Unbreakable because of the atrocities he had overcome in his lifetime, able to continue living with positivity and spreading it to those around him, but that didn't mean his wife and infant son possessed the same spiritual strength. And not only that, but he impregnated his wife again while in the Void, exposing a newborn to the hollow kingdom.

Tashami had been that newborn. Now he was three years old, a toddler, experiencing memories that shouldn't have stuck with him over the years. Nobody remembered events prior to five or six years old—only the rare few. But these were dreams, not memories—they only happened when he went to sleep—so did that mean sleep was powerful enough to draw visions from his subconscious? He had never experienced them before. He used to dream of his father—the Unbreakable—but they were nightmares depicting the day he had found the walking corpse of a man while traveling with the Jestivan. But even those dreams had faded over the years, replaced by blissful ones with Agnos by his side.

He was walking down the second floor hallway of his father's foster home, which rested just outside the city of Spachny—a city that was more likely a town. He was following one of the older orphans, a girl around the age of twelve. Her name was Nina. As a toddler, he didn't understand the concept of age; he understood little of anything—a blessing when considering he lived in the Void—but he did know that Nina might as well have been an old lady. Her hair grayed at the roots, her face shallow. He didn't know those features were a product of their environment. It made no sense, for his older brother, Joni, was a vibrant child, irises alight and hair full and healthy. For whatever reason, his family was different than the orphans.

Nina turned into a room—there were many in their home—and didn't bother lighting a lantern to fight the darkness. Gray mist suffocated the first-night sky and hugged the house's small windows, making this the perfect time of day for several rounds of hide-and-seek. It was Tashami's favorite part of the day, though not many appreciated the small child's enthusiasm, seeing him as nothing more than a nuisance. They expected him to hide on his own, but he wasn't smart enough—brain not yet developed to their level—to find any good spots, nor was he patient enough—his attention easily diverted from boredom—to remain still for long. These qualities made him a terrible partner with whom to hide. Nina was one of two orphans who allowed him to join her.

As she fidgeted with items and furniture in the room, Tashami's eyes widened, hearing the seeker's voice as he counted from the front door downstairs. Joni was the seeker this round, and he was one of the best, knowing each of the orphans' tendencies and where they would likely hide first. It was just another reason why Tashami admired his older brother. Counting down from sixty, Joni was now at ten. Tashami didn't know his numbers backwards yet, but he knew when he heard the word "ten", that meant they were running out of time. In past games, that marked the moment when the peculiar hiders grew desperate and began scrambling for a spot.

"Tashami," Nina breathed, volume lower than a whisper. In the Void, that was enough to catch his attention. He turned. She was crouched next to a massive armchair against the wall, its blue color a muted gray in the darkness. She lifted it by its left two legs only slightly, then twisted it an inch before setting it down again. It made a dull, muffled sound, but wasn't the piercing screech that would have resulted from pushing it across the floorboards. "Get in," she said, gesturing toward a hole in the cloth in the back of the armchair.

He tiptoed over, and she helped him climb in. The space was only big enough for a toddler. Even still, his left shoulder was pressed against a plank of wood that supported the armchair's back, his neck bent at a forty-five degree angle. Nina lifted half of the chair and placed it against the wall. She was strong for her age. Joni's countdown hit two, and she ran to her own spot with footfalls a little louder than she would have liked.

Tashami remained in that position, crumpled like damaged parchment. He was good at getting into tight spaces. He used his hand to stifle a giggle, thinking of the time he'd escaped his mother's pursuit through a hole in the backyard. He didn't know who or what had made the hole, but the fear of his mother drowned out any fears of the unknown. She wasn't mean or violent, but she was firm and loud.

Joni's footsteps thundered throughout the house as he found the easiest hiders first. Tashami heard Lanor—a six-year-old orphan who was less interested in the game and more desperate to become the first person to make Joni jump—scream, likely leaping out of his hiding spot the moment Joni neared. Tashami shook his head and muttered to himself, "Nothing scares Joni, dummies."

Joni found nine hiders in less than five minutes, blowing through the house with ease—an impressive feat, considering the building was three stories if the basement was included. He even entered the room in which Tashami hid and found Nina before leaving it to search other rooms. Tashami was so happy; he had never won a game of hide-and-seek before, but he could see victory on the horizon—not that he could really see anything at all.

He was inside an armchair, the hole pinned against the wall. Only three children knew of the hole. Panelle, a nine-year-old boy with brown hair and freckles, had been showing Tashami—who was always the most easily entertained—his skills with a sword the day before. The boy had made the mistake of slashing through the back of the armchair, which had been sitting in the middle of the room as it always had. Panelle nearly cried the moment he noticed his mistake, and Tashami sprinted out of the room to find his dad and tattle, but instead he collided with Nina as she entered the doorway. She assessed the situation and helped Panelle cover his error by moving the chair against the wall. The Unbreakable rarely used the parlor, so she guessed it'd be a long time before he noticed. She told the two boys to keep it their secret.

In hide-and-seek, you didn't win by being the last found; you won by not being found at all. When the second-to-last hider was discovered, everyone who had lost began counting down from sixty, giving the seeker one minute to find the last person. The chanting usually rattled the seeker, but Joni unflappable. He was Tashami's mighty older brother.

The countdown reached fifteen, and he couldn't believe it. He was going to win. Joni wasn't even searching the correct room!

Something landed on his shoulder—heavy, hairy, and many-legged—crawling toward his neck and placing two legs against his cheek. Tashami stiffened. In his position, there was no way to wriggle it off. Tears bubbled, breaths growing louder, his swelling chest constricted by the armchair's wooden frame. He was trapped in a dark, tight space with a massive spider on his shoulder—he knew it. But the countdown had reached ten, and he knew that meant he was about to win. He could do this; he was as strong as his brother, and he'd prove it by besting him in this match.

To quell his squeals, he bit his lip but instead bit the end of a hairy leg just as the critter tried to climb his face. He screamed. The spider nearly scrambled into his open mouth, but he quickly closed his mouth and spit it out, where it then fell onto his legs somewhere below. He wailed and threw his palms at the wall in terror, trying to push the armchair away from the wall while his foot was twisted awkwardly in part of the wooden frame beneath him. He was too small, incapable of moving the massive piece of furniture. He banged his fists against the wall, shouting his brother's name: "JONI! JONI! JONI!"

Footsteps thundered into the room; the counting had stopped—not that it mattered, for he had lost the moment he'd opened his mouth, surely. The armchair was dragged away from the wall, and his brother's arms reached in to pull him out of the hole. Joni fell to the floor, back against the wall as he held Tashami half in his lap, legs stretched before him toward the chair. Joni ran fingers through his little brother's ivory hair. He didn't whisper words of comfort, question his fear, or scold him for choosing such a stupid place to hide; he said the only words that he knew Tashami wanted to hear:

"Good job, Tashami. You were strong. You were brave. Because of that, you won."

The toddler sobbed, but he didn't know why. When infused with several emotions at once—terror from what felt like a brush with death, relief from escaping it, shame from requiring a brother's rescue, and then gratefulness from hearing his recognition—the confusion often consumed someone so young, someone who couldn't process all of it.

Joni was a great boy. To Tashami, he might as well have been a man. That was the nature of brothers.

42

Pain

Agnos was seated at a desk when Tashami woke. They were in a dark room, heavy brown curtains drawn shut to stifle the first-day sun. Ipsas's campus was buzzing with anticipation for the day, students leaving their rooms and walking the campus in order to make it to their first class. Agnos hadn't realized how much he missed school life until now. He had underappreciated its importance during his time there. He may have marveled at the Warpfinate each time he walked inside, reminding himself that Neeko had once wandered the same depths, but it wasn't until he retrieved Tonitrua's chronicle from the seafloor when he learned the answers for which he'd searched his entire life were in the Warpfinate's greatest depths the entire time.

He had seen next to nothing of Ipsas since fleeing the Infested Forest days ago—cooped up in this room during all of it—but based on the words of Evelyn and Arithmys, there was nothing close to the Warpfinate here. While part of him had always assumed that to be true, it still hurt to now know for a fact. Why was that? He was being greedy. He'd had access to a limitless well of books and knowledge at Phesaw, yet wanted more.

He looked back at Tashami, who had been shifting throughout the night, twisting in his blanket. The Spirit Jestivan had yet to have a single night of decent sleep. Agnos frequently woke to his friend's murmurs or sobs. Sometimes, he mumbled incoherently. Agnos had never seen him like this, and it had been happening since the day they'd been jailed at the teleplatforms, when the Cyn Diatia had done something to Tashami out of Agnos's eyesight. He didn't believe it was coincidence. That man had done something sinister.

Today, Tashami sat up slowly. Even from several paces' distance, Agnos could see the wetness in his eyes. "More nightmares?"

Tashami wiped his eyes with the back of his hands. "Yeah, but it's nothing serious."

Agnos turned back to the book on his desk: Tonitrua's chronicle. "Sure," he said. He wasn't going to argue with Tashami about it, for his efforts had been fruitless in the past. But he was scared. Since Ronossius was Cynnish, Agnos didn't know with what he was dealing. Cynergy was capable of destroying the soul and sucking the life out of the atmosphere, but such powers were vague. Nobody seemed to understand the specifics, no matter which books Agnos tried digging up on the subject. He had three off to the side of his desk—all of them useless—which Arithmys had scavenged for him from their library.

"Tashami," said Agnos.

Tashami had risen from bed and was now choosing between a total of four shirts that the two of them had been interchanging since departing the Intel Kingdom a month ago. Agnos particularly enjoyed when Tashami chose to wear one of his shirts, the smaller size exposing the bottom of his abdomen and squeezing his biceps. Agnos didn't know what to make of such a preference in his friend's image—that he was attracted to him? Had he always been? Ever since Evelyn's little talk with him in the forest, his senses when around Tashami had heightened.

"What's up?"

Agnos hesitated, then asked, "You wouldn't lie to me, right?"

Brief silence, during which Agnos remained focused on the Technous writing in the chronicle, though he was paying no attention to it.

"Never," Tashami said.

Agnos closed his eyes, disappointed in his friend's delayed response. Tashami was lying to protect him. Ever since meeting his father in the Void, Tashami had changed, opening up fully and becoming Agnos's defender and motivator. They were his methods of repaying Agnos's efforts to find his dad. Before then, he had been a boy scared to exert too much power, fearful it'd take him down a path of overconfidence, leading to demise equal to that of his father.

Tashami was a true Spiritian, invigorating spirit and instilling confidence in others, but only when it regarded Agnos. He wasn't Jilly. He didn't care much when it came to others. He had always liked the rest of the Jestivan, but he was quiet with them, tempered. Grand Director Poicus had used a great word during their first meeting as Jestivan: "prudent."

Now that soft-spoken nature was returning, but it extended to Agnos, which was worrisome. Tashami was beginning to close himself off again, which made Agnos believe Tashami was protecting more than just his friend here ... but himself.

Why?

What could have Tashami—the man who had fought off thugs in the Chasm, saved the Whale Lord amidst a storm, rescued Agnos from the waves of the sea, and defeated a warden at the teleplatforms—so rattled?

Agnos turned his head. Tashami was seated at the end of the twin-sized bed, smiling at him.

A mask, and he knew it.

*   *   *

Apoleia didn't leave her daughter's side in the days following the spectacle: Olivia slouched atop the floor of the room in which Apoleia was raped, scalding hot water pooled beneath her, a piano and bed in shambles. Olivia had taken it upon her own shoulders to exercise her mother's demons—a responsibility that didn't belong to her, nor should have ever been given to her. Apoleia blamed herself; she had raised the girl in fear, disguising it as apathy and flaunting it as strength. Apoleia's guidance had not been kind.

Olivia's face was tranquil during sleep, a trait that had remained since childhood. The stone-faced girl only allowed peace to reveal itself when she wasn't conscious. Apoleia smiled at her, remembering all of the times she had entered Olivia's cavern in their cave in Lallopy Forest just to watch her sleep. It was a reprieve from her insanity. She wondered what—

—a shadow spiraled up from the floor and uncloaked a corpse of a man, face absent of skin on one side, exposing teeth, gums, and an eye of pure black. She remembered him from the invasion of Phesaw, when Olivia had broken her emotional shackles after seeing her mother nearly murder her brother. He was Olivia's Bewahr, whose immediate dismissal had been forced by Apoleia.

The Bewahr locked eyes with the Still Queen, expression unreadable, then turned toward Olivia in the bed. Gore lined a hole in the back of his head, revealing gray matter. He lifted a gnarled hand. Apoleia's brows furrowed. Was he going to touch her? He pulled his hand away and dropped it at his side, possibly thinking better of it. She leaned back, allowing ... *this* ... to play out. Olivia had told her about the efforts to reconnect with the Bewahr, but Apoleia had yet to see it firsthand.

"How is she?" he asked.

"Exhausted ... emotionally and mentally."

His fingers twitched. "Physically?"

"Perfectly fine."

His hand relaxed. "Good."

She focused on breathing through her mouth, the man's putrid scent unfriendly. "I'm sorry," she said.

"It's your culture," he said, not needing to hear an explanation. They were on the same page. "If I hadn't been turned away, I would have thought something was wrong."

"Selfish of me," Apoleia said. "If anything, Olivia could have used a man in her life."

He turned his head, exposing the unharmed half of his face and decent eye. "I'm nothing more than her Bewahr. There are boundaries. Besides, she won't have me forever—a decade at most, likely."

"If you're only her Bewahr, you overstepped those boundaries the moment you gave her advice that didn't pertain to the protection of her life, but the preservation of her heart. You became a counselor, a therapist."

He turned toward Olivia again. "She helped me; I helped her."

"What do you see her as?" Apoleia asked.

"My charge."

Her gaze fell to Olivia. At twenty-one, she may have been an adult, but Apoleia would always see her daughter as her child. She didn't reply to the Bewahr, letting the man stew in the silence.

"Why'd you come down here?" she finally asked.

"I felt her discomfort."

"Are Bewahr capable of feeling the severity of pain or discomfort in their charges?"

"Yes."

"Had hers felt anywhere close to life-threatening?" she asked.

He paused, then said, "No."

"Then again, why are you here? Sounds undisciplined for a being whose sole purpose is to serve as a meat shield for a firstborn. Are you not stepping outside certain boundaries?" She paused, raising her eyebrows. "Using your own logic there, by the way."

A long pause. "Clever," he said. He sighed, then added, "I was worried and felt partially responsible."

"Oh, no," Apoleia said. "Don't take credit for my shortcomings as a mother. How do you think I feel? Downright guilty."

He said nothing, nor did she. She thought of her own mother, Salia Still, whose murder she had assisted. She'd led Toono to her, blaming the hag for how she wound up. Mothers had a lot of power over their daughters. Salia had forced Apoleia to dismiss her Bewahr the moment he appeared. To this day, Apoleia didn't know her Bewahr's name or legacy. She had tried finding information about him based on her brief glimpse of him, but hadn't gathered any results. She wished she could have gotten to know the man.

"I apologize in advance," the Bewahr said, "but has she told you about Mendac?"

Apoleia's gaze snapped to him, the name jarring her out of her trance. "Yes. Albeit, very little."

He turned toward her fully, revealing his mangled body in its full glory. She was scared to know what lay beneath his clothing. "She didn't tell me what he did to you, specifically, but I have my assumptions," he said.

Apoleia swallowed, a knot forming in her throat. Had Olivia really grown so comfortable with the man this quickly? She guessed it made sense, considering how she'd found her daughter in the secret room. "What did you tell her that made her do what she did?" she asked.

"To stop avoiding the demons you gave her and face them. Of course, it was a vague suggestion, for I don't know specifics, but I had hoped it would carry weight." He turned his head to regard Olivia. "Apparently, it did." He looked at Apoleia. "I see Mendac every day now; I know him for the metamorph he is, shaping himself in adaptation to the people around him and the situation in which he finds himself. He is good at it, and I hate people like him … slimy, but in that insufferable, charismatic way."

"Why are you telling me things I already know?"

He titled his head. There was a slowness in the way he moved that irked her. She didn't know if it was due to his withered body and joints or something more supernatural in regards to his Cynergy. The Cynnish had a reputation of making a person's skin crawl for good reason.

"You had good intentions with the methods in which you raised Olivia. If I knew of a world with men like Mendac in it, I would have also taken extreme paths to guide my own daughter to make sure she avoided them. Were the lessons you instilled in her enough to keep her away from those kinds of men?"

There was a time years ago when she would have answered that question with an emphatic "no" after discovering Olivia had been friends with Bryson LeAnce, the girl's twin brother and a near-doppelganger of Mendac. The fact that he looked like that man caused Apoleia to immediately pin him with the same character traits—and mostly the flaws. Now, the answer was simple: Olivia had steered clear of those men who would hurt her—even if she was capable of destroying them if needed. And Bryson might have been the best friend she could have made when away from her mother.

"Yes," she finally whispered.

"I can't think of a parent who hasn't passed on monsters to their children, intentionally or not. You're a great parent. I wish I could say the same about myself."

Having been the one to give Olivia the book of tales that held Preloz's story, Apoleia said, "You're being hard on yourself."

"I abandoned her," he said softly. "I may not be as vile a father as Mendac, but I wasn't a good one. I'd like to tell you that I can do something about Mendac since he's within my grasp on a daily basis, but I can't. I want to, but he is practically invulnerable with the protection he's under."

"I wouldn't expect that from you anyway. It isn't your fight. The fact that you told us he's up there is more than enough. Because of that, I've been able to send word to allies who have been worried about his presence in their kingdoms."

Preloz smiled. "Good." He turned to face Olivia again, and this time he placed a hand on the edge of her bed, clearly itching to touch her forearm. "I expect I'll be retired soon. By divulging Mendac's location, I've betrayed the Dark Empire. They'll find out eventually. A few days ago, I told Olivia I was happier because I'd discovered where my daughter was, and knowing that gave me hope. That was a lie, but only because I didn't need her knowing the truth—or else she'd try something rash. Pytatia is lost to the Linsaniun Mounds. I've come to grips with that. The levity that has befallen me since reading the story Olivia gave to me has actually come from a sense of peace, knowing I'd die soon, ending my two lives of misery."

Apoleia inhaled slowly, nearly shaking her head. For a parent to welcome death while knowing their child was alive and suffering? That was ... unfathomable. And he was choosing that option because the only alternative was Olivia risking her life.

"Maybe I'm not as bad a father as Mendac," he muttered. "I'm worse."

He was gone in a swirl of black shadows. Apoleia blinked, stunned. She looked at her daughter and saw that Olivia wasn't sleeping, but staring at the ceiling with a ferociousness that could only mean one thing.

*　　*　　*

Olivia wanted to help Preloz. Her determination to understand and gain control of her water ability had been the priority since her discussions with Himitsu and Lilu, but now that she had achieved that—with Preloz's help—she felt liberated to pursue other goals. She owed him. He had called his aid repayment for her giving him the book which held the story of his daughter, but she didn't see that as an equal transaction. What he did for her held far more substance.

She sat with Vuilni on a bench in a palace ice garden. The Powish was bundled in several layers, a collar pulled up over her mouth and nose, a hat covering the top of her head and ears. The cold didn't quell her excitement, however. Olivia had asked her to convene here, using hints about a breakthrough of some kind as bait. Olivia hadn't told Vuilni what she'd been trying to achieve these past several weeks.

Vuilni's legs bounced either from the cold or anticipation. Olivia held cupped hands in front of herself. She relaxed her body and mind, opening all five of her senses to the world. Warmth spilled through her body, and she directed it into her hands and out through her skin, hot water pooling in her palms.

Vuilni gasped, eyes widening. She peeled her collar away from her mouth and asked, "When did you start doing that?!"

"A few days ago," Olivia said, smiling. "The specifics don't matter, but I had an epiphany."

"That's amazing!" She paused in wonder, then said, "Water … It makes no sense. That's not an ability of any kingdom, nor is there an ancient piece that grants it."

"Makes perfect sense after speaking with Lilu," Olivia said. She went on to summarize Lilu's explanation, Vuini's cocked eyebrow rising further with each sentence.

"So Lilu's a genius, as we all expected," she said.

Olivia nodded. "Just one of a few people I have to thank. How's your family doing?"

"Dad's found a job as a server at a restaurant. There's not much else he can do. He spent his childhood as a slave and adulthood as a miner, so he doesn't have the skills to be any kind of tradesman. The only opportunities for mining jobs are the ever-ice mines way out in the Still Mountains, but apparently only Stillians can survive those temperatures. Mom's a line cook at the same restaurant. I think they're enjoying the chance to work in the same building. My sister spends most of the day in daycare."

"And what about you?" Olivia asked.

"Your mom didn't tell you?"

Olivia shook her head.

"Well, it just happened yesterday," Vuilni said, "and considering you've been out of commission, I suppose it wasn't in the forefront of her mind." She grinned. "I'm to be an honor guard for the crown and your aunt's personal guard."

"So you're going to be here forever?"

Vuilni laughed. "I guess for a while. Despite the cold, we like it here. Some of the women are judgmental, but I believe they'll adapt once they discover how helpful the refugees can be. Most importantly, we stand by you and your mother." She paused, looking at Olivia. "Look at that smile! I love it!"

"So do I," Olivia replied.

"As do I."

Both women turned. The Still Queen strolled into the garden, a crystalline figure of curves against a backdrop of glittering blue trees and hedges. She smiled sweetly at Vuilni. "May I speak with my daughter?"

Vuilni leapt off the bench and snapped to attention, bowing. "Of course, My Queen."

"I think General Valp is looking for you—something about trading your life for my sister's, if necessary."

Apoleia lowered herself onto the bench as Vuilni sprinted away. "Eager, that one is," she said.

"And capable," Olivia said.

Apoleia looked in the sprinting woman's direction until she turned a corner around a distant hedge. "Expected of a Diatia." She looked at Olivia. "Now that you've gained control of your powers, what are you going to do with all of your spare time?"

"Help the refugees assimilate to our society and culture," Olivia said, tilting her hands and letting the water spill into the snow. "Be a visible figurehead for the transition from old traditions into new. Lead by example, which I can do by spending a few days in a man's blue-collar job, working by their sides. Desegregate schools, allowing genders to mix in their education."

Apoleia hummed. "I see. Basically, everything I've been trying to do, but placing yourself directly in it. Instead of being the crank, you're a cog." She nodded, a grin quirking up her lips. "Humbling. As the Royal Head, I can't do that. Technically, as a royal firstborn, you shouldn't either."

"It's not like I haven't been risking my life every day for the past five years," Olivia said. "The life of a Jestivan wasn't exactly a safe one."

"Hence why I'm not fighting you on it."

"And who's the real royal firstborn, Mother? Bryson or me? We both were assigned divine protectors, he a Branian and me a Bewahr."

"Bryson was born first, beat you by twelve minutes." She narrowed her eyes at nothing in particular. "But I guess with twins, the royal firstborn trait is given to both. I did carry both of you at the same time." She shrugged. "That's my best guess. I've tried researching any instances like mine, but from what I can tell, a Royal Head has never created twins."

The two Still women fell silent, consumed by their own thoughts. Olivia was wrestling with the knowledge that she was actually the younger sibling—she had never asked her mother about it—when Apoleia said, "I'm sorry I could never give you a father."

The apology had dropped on Olivia like a lead weight. And even though she knew it to be unnecessary—no, downright *absurd*—she found herself crying. It was stupid. Tears? She didn't need a dad; she had never needed one. Her mother was everything to her; she'd raised her. And who was Olivia to expect a man in her life after knowing what a man had done to her mom?

Still, she *cried*. And she felt like crap for crying, which made her cry more. This was selfish. She should have told her mom, "No, you were all I needed." Alas, the words wouldn't leave her mouth.

Her mother wrapped an arm around her shoulder and pulled her tight. She placed her lips against her hair, tears of her own falling atop her head. "I know what you're planning to do," she said. "And I'm not going to stop you."

Olivia nodded, unable to verbally thank her.

"I love you," whispered Apoleia.

43

Collision Course

Kadlest could see the infatuation oozing out of Mendac every time he looked at Rhyparia. His attitude toward the Archain may have had everyone else fooled, but not Kadlest, who had known the man for what he was. He was currently working his relationship with Rhyparia with a surgeon's steady hand, cutting slowly and precisely with a fine scalpel. The poor woman had no clue that she was on her way to being used just like Kadlest and Apoleia. Kadlest supposed she could have told her the truth, but it would have been her word against his—a battle she'd likely lose considering the good terms Rhyparia and Mendac were on. The only person Kadlest got to spend time with in the Empire was Mendac. Nobody else paid her any mind. She wandered the grounds of the Labyrinth like a ghost, incapable of penetrating its black walls.

With such a lack of communication and human interaction, she was losing grasp of her identity. She didn't know if it was a natural development or something about the Labyrinth's atmosphere. When she was alone, there were times she didn't know where she was or why she was here. Mendac's existence slipped from her mind at times, sometimes requiring his physical presence to remind her. And as silly as it sounded, she had to look down at her body to confirm she wasn't disappearing.

Rhyparia and Mendac were training in a grassy field surrounded by the Labyrinth on all four sides. Kadlest watched from a bench at the edge, particularly invested in the presence of four others. A man with a grated mask, oily skin, and unkempt hair stood by Rhyparia and Mendac, critiquing certain aspects of their fighting techniques. Another pair fought on the opposite side of the field: a woman with a crown of frozen horns growing beneath her hair and a man who had cloned himself multiple times over. The final presence was a deformed man more akin to a corpse than a living person, half his face gone and a hole in the back of his head. He stood to the side. From what Kadlest could decipher in his one good eye, he was focused on Mendac, but she never saw him fight.

She sniffed, curious, then tilted her head. The stench of death must have been coming from him. If she hadn't been used to the smell from the hordes of corpses she'd been around in her life, she would have likely retched.

Rhyparia went flying backward, screaming as she hit the ground and rolled. Mendac stood several paces away, a fist extended. He wasn't holding back, and Rhyparia was hopeless against it. She pushed herself to a stand, unfazed. It didn't matter how many times he bested her, she went back for more, feeding off the frustration of inferiority. But she respected him for not treating her like a child. He didn't pull his punches or weaken his clout because he knew that would only make her hate him, and Kadlest knew he was in the process of drawing Rhyparia in.

Kadlest watched for hours until Mendac approached her at the bench and told her to leave. He didn't ask, for that wasn't their dynamic. She had been his punching dummy for years, and he didn't expect that to have changed. She didn't want him to, so she rose from the bench and found her way off the field through a cluster of shadows.

*   *   *

"Emperor Mialo is tired of sitting on his thumbs," said Brenson Ulial, voice deep and scratchy, somewhat muffled by his grated mask.

They were in the training field. Rhyparia, Mendac, and Brenson's three Bewahr—Hailey, Preloz, and Antigrafi—stood at attention in a semicircle.

"Over the past five years, we've been sending some of our ranks into the Light Empire on covert missions. Simple scouting jobs to acquire information on the Bozani's efforts to secure the city of Celeste. As far as aggression, we've done little since the initial attack following the Prim Prince's murder."

"I don't know why we play coy," said Antigrafi, the Bewahr capable of cloning himself via an ancient piece somewhere on his body. "The Bozani are growing lax. It seems I can penetrate Celeste deeper with each visit, their luzens retreating toward the center."

"Orias thinks it's a trap," Brenson said. "The Bozani want us to penetrate as far as we can. They're luring us into something."

"Is that why they keep letting us destroy their luzens in the outer reaches?" Antigrafi asked.

"I don't know if they're letting you or if it's just because they're too far away from the Starlight to put up much of a fight. You know the luzens grow weaker the farther from the Starlight they travel."

"And that's why they used to send a Branian or two to defend them." Antigrafi sighed, nearly pouting. "I miss my little bouts with Aestys. I'm telling you, I was this close to killing her last time."

"Stop treating this like a game," Brenson said. "This is war."

"Some war," Hailey said, exposing teeth shaved to fine points.

Rhyparia, Mendac, and Preloz remained silent during the conversation. Preloz seemed apathetic, gaze occasionally wandering toward Mendac. But Rhyparia simply had no idea what was going on. She'd spoken with Antigrafi once, but it was nothing more than a brief greeting. He was away from the bunker most of the time, his skills needed elsewhere. Apparently, he was one of the Bewahr who frequently visited the Light Empire as a scout, which made sense considering his cloning abilities.

"However, Emperor Mialo disagrees with Orias," Brenson said. "Like I said, he's tired of this game of patience. While Orias fears the Bozani are baiting us into a trap, Mialo believes we've gained the manpower to overcome most obstacles." He looked between Rhyparia and Mendac, as if to say they were the manpower.

Antigrafi followed his gaze, then shook his head. "The two recruits who only got here a couple months ago? The two recruits who aren't technically Gefal? They haven't even died in the real world yet."

"Which should say a lot about their talent, seeing that they have wings, something no Bewahr—including you, Antigrafi—can claim. Hell, the only Fuhren with wings are Yasmine, Poten, and I."

Rhyparia hadn't known that. She had assumed all Gefal, including the Bewahr, had the ability of flight. Now it made sense why she'd only seen Yasmine sprout wings, and Brenson must use them only sparingly and out of sight of those beneath him, for she hadn't seen him sprout any.

Antigrafi's gaze lingered on the two recruits. He nodded. "Makes sense. It's just odd, something I'm gonna have to get used to."

"Forgive me," Mendac said, "but when you say 'Orias,' do you mean Orias Grandeur?"

"We get it," Hailey droned. "You know everything. You're a scholar with no bounds."

"Yes," Brenson replied, ignoring her sarcasm. "Orias Grandeur is a Versac—one of three."

Rhyparia didn't recognize the name, but if Mendac was interested enough to ask for clarification, she knew the man known as Orias must have had historical relevance. Mendac didn't say anything further, however, instead keeping his face expressionless.

"I have orders from Orias, passed on from Mialo," Brenson continued. "It's been two years since anyone above a Bewahr has traveled to the Light Empire, but with the murder of the Power Prince, circumstances are now dire. I am to execute a mission, pushing deeper into Celeste's heart than we have since declaring war five years ago. Antigrafi, you will be joining me ... as well as Rhyparia and Mendac."

"Is that wise?"

The question came from Preloz, which caused everyone to react in surprise. Recently, he had stopped wailing while wandering the Labyrinth's corridors. Odd, yes. But to hear him speak was alien.

"Preloz!" said Antigrafi, slapping a hand against the Cynnish's back. "What's gotten into you?"

Preloz's good eye locked onto the Primmish, then glided to Brenson. "Is that wise?" he asked again. "They don't know how to retract their wings yet. The Bozani will be alerted by the heavy concentration of Mulawi in the atmosphere. They'll serve as beacons, guiding enemies toward their location."

"Already taken into consideration," Brenson said, not as fazed by the corpse's participation. "And it's not a problem. There is a plan in place, drawn up by Orias himself. There aren't many minds in the world better than his, the Emperor's being the only one I can think of that supersedes it. I've read it over, and it's promising."

Antigrafi's face was one of determination. "Sounds like a return to real warfare."

"It is," Brenson said. "And you'll likely have a chance to run into more than just Aestys."

"Will I get my ancient?" Rhyparia asked.

"No," he replied. "You're not ready for it."

In other words, Mialo isn't ready for it. Rhyparia had obtained near-mastery of her umbrella ancient; she didn't doubt her readiness. Alas, the Emperor wasn't sure he could put a clamp on her ability once she got a hold of it, so the real question was if he could handle it.

"The main objective of our mission?" said Brenson. "Attack Celeste University."

He let the implications hang in the air. They would target students.

"I don't know who looks more excited to die at the moment," said Hailey. "Mendac or Antigrafi?"

Both men wore galvanized expressions, lips flat, eyes furrowed, and jaws set—the kind of look a soldier had when marching toward the certain doom of an incoming army. Rhyparia wondered if that expression would falter for Mendac if they ran into the one Branian that had been missing from their study materials. He had noticed the missing number and had plenty of theories as to why, but none were correct. Rhyparia knew the truth and understood the purpose of Mialo not including that person in the list.

The Emperor didn't know how Mendac would react to knowing Thusia fought on the other side, so he'd delay its revelation until the day both of them collided.

*   *   *

Bryson thought it obvious why he failed the test in Founding Plaza. If anything, the signs of danger had been staring him in the face. The switch of waiters halfway through a meal, the first waiter not bothering to collect an eventual tip he would have deserved. The new waitress's inexplicable infatuation with Bryson, which he had arrogantly chalked up to his good looks—or supposed good looks, according to Thusia. And the waitress bypassing the sink installed in the bar's counter to get water from somewhere in the kitchens or store room, hidden from view of the customers. That last part was the most damning evidence, and he had questioned it in the moment, yet still drank from the glass. He was an idiot.

When he had brought these moments of suspicion to Quincy, the Pogu's response had been sarcastic. He chided Bryson for only noticing the obvious signs—signs that were apparently useless because they happened after the threat. Bryson refuted that, saying he drank the poison after the signs. But then Quincy made the point that the poison wasn't the threat, but the attack. The threat was the waitress, which Bryson should have noticed not just the moment she had walked up to their table for the first time, but before that. He had responded with a caustic remark under his breath—something about not being a damned prophet—to which Quincy served his fist as discipline.

Bryson sat on the carpeted floor of the capsule's common area, parchment strewn around him as he rubbed his left pectoral. That punch had left a lasting bruise. While reading through the names and bios of the Gefal, Bryson frequently lost focus on his objective in studying, instead becoming lost in the stories of these historic figures. From heroic accolades to the vilest of sins, it seemed every moment of a Gefal's life had been epic. A woman who took down a Still Queen who massacred hundreds of thousands of men; a man who could use clairvoyance, hallucinogenics, and teleportation; a man who could kill nature just by walking through it; and a

467

man who could grow to the size of a mansion. Those were just a few of the marvels listed in their ranks.

But he needed to stop focusing on the grandeur aspects of their lives. "Usually, the most important intelligence comes from the most mundane resources," Aestys had told him a few days after their journey into Celeste. She had been sitting on the toilet while he asked questions from outside the washroom door. Those were the only moments she'd offer real conversation, for she had nothing better to do to pass the time. "Intelligence leaks in subtle ways."

Thus, Bryson now scanned physical traits of the Gefal, Thusia watching from the other side of the sea of parchment. After Quincy had briefed her on the details of that night, it didn't take her long to figure it out. Of course, she couldn't tell Bryson the answers, so she waited.

He picked up a stack of parchment belonging to one of the Gefal's Fuhren. She squealed, and he looked up at her with a raised eyebrow. She bit down on her lip, failing miserably at hiding a grin. It had been a delighted squeal, which either meant he was on the right track or someone presented her with a plate of rice and chopsticks. Seeing no plate in her vicinity, it must have been the former.

The top page in the stack read:

YASMINE CORDELIA

Dev Assassin

796 – 841 K.H.

The parchment in this stack were flimsy and crinkled at the edges, for he had flipped through her bio several times, finding her story fascinating. Cloaking ships and buildings with invisibility, a trait Dev assassins should have only been able to give themselves. After the blueprints to learning how to achieve Grandeur's Three—clairvoyance, hallucinogenics, and teleportation—had nearly been stolen by a group of notorious mercenaries in the 800's, she'd taken it upon herself to cloak Orias's secrets in a cloaked fortress somewhere near the city of Prayoga. That was just one of many feats in her life.

Today, however, he didn't flip past the cover page. He focused on her physical attributes. He had to read through each trait repeatedly, his eyes glazing over from boredom. Thusia snapped at him, and he jerked upright, unaware of his body's sideways lean. Her gaze was intense, as if to say, "Pay attention!" If Quincy or Suadade were here, they wouldn't have approved of her gestures. He was supposed to receive no hints—not that Quincy had the gall to actually stop her. The Pogu was smitten with the Spirit Branian.

Bryson rubbed his eyes and studied the cover sheet again. This was for Shelly and L.K. If he wanted to see them, he needed to figure out why he failed the first test and then pass the next one.

He read through the attributes thrice more before spotting the connection: hazel eyes; caramel skin, accented beneath with a golden hue; sleek raven hair that usually didn't fall past her shoulders. Yasmine's appearance aligned perfectly with the waitress's, which meant she had been an actor disguised to look like the Fuhren. He pounded his fist atop his knee, victorious. He'd been too enamored by the fantastical when he should have been paying attention to the normal.

A crumpled ball of parchment smacked him in the forehead and fell into his lap, jarring him from his moment of achievement. He looked up, giving Thusia a lazy gaze. "What was that for?"

"Stop celebrating. You're one step closer, but there was still something from earlier in the night that should have been an immediate cause for concern. If you go to Quincy now, he'll tell you there is one other thing you're missing."

He looked down at his lap. He snatched the ball and unwrapped it. Someone had sloppily drawn a map of Founding Plaza. He felt wetness on his thumb and pulled it away from the parchment, finding a streak of black ink across his skin. He looked at the map again, lines indicating building and property boundaries smudged and splotched erratically. This was Thusia's handiwork. "Couldn't let it dry first?" he asked.

She shrugged. "You figured it out faster than I expected."

"You think so little of me?"

"You're dumb, Bryson."

He paid the insult no mind and scanned the map. It didn't take an architect to know the proportions were egregiously inaccurate. In what world was a bakery four times the size of a library? And why was there a library on a busy plaza in the first place? How did crowd noises affect the sanctified silence within? His gaze paused at the center of the plaza, where a large person was drawn. If this was supposed to depict realistic proportions, that man was the size of Power Warden Feissam. He almost questioned his purpose on the map before realizing a rectangular prism beneath his feet, as if he was standing on a block of stone. A statue? But Bryson had walked directly across the middle of the plaza that night and seen nothing of the sort.

His eyes widened. Literally, *nothing*.

There had been a square area of the plaza wherein nobody walked. The crowd walked around this empty space as if something important was there, though all Bryson had seen were cobbles. He looked up. "You got this wrong. There's no statue there."

"What does the map say," she asked.

"So it's invisible?" he asked. "And the Celestians just know to circumvent it."

She pursed her lips, implying she couldn't answer that. He studied the map again, knowing he was on the right track. He lifted the map and looked at the stack of parchment beneath it. Yasmine Cordelia's name stared up at him—an assassin capable of cloaking inanimate objects, from knickknacks to small buildings and boats. He grinned.

"That was the first sign of her presence," he said. "A statue doesn't just get up and move. Had I been properly prepared, I would have known a statue should have been in that spot, and seeing that it wasn't would have alerted me of Yasmine's presence." He shook his head and scoffed. Now that he knew the truth, he couldn't help but realize how easy and unsubtle they had made his first test, so much so it was impractical. None of the Gefal would have been that clumsy in their infiltration. The Bozani weren't trying to deceive him. They had probably hoped he would pass with flying colors. "I'm an idiot," he muttered.

"Also my fault," she said. "I served only as a distraction for you since arriving here."

Leon Suadade entered the capsule, having finished his afternoon shift in the sentry district. "He figured it out!" Thusia screamed.

The swordsman gazed at them, apathetically. "So go tell Quincy. The sooner you do, the sooner your next test."

Bryson leapt off the floor, parchment blowing across the carpet from the speed at which he moved. "I don't know where he is, so someone take me."

Suadade crossed his arms and tapped his fingers against his bicep. "After you clean that up."

Bryson groaned and threw back his head, returning to hands and knees to collect the strewn parchment. Thusia joined him, and he mocked Suadade under his breath.

"What was that?"

"Nothing," said Bryson. Thusia giggled.

He smiled, knowing he only needed to pass this next test. Then it was a visit home and a meeting with the three Strasan.

44

Piety Mines

Lilu held L.K. in her arms as she stood in the rotunda below Shelly's sky room. The platform lifted, raising her into her older sister's room, where everything glowed in sunlight from all angles. When used to the overcast sky of the Intel Kingdom, it was nice being above the clouds for once.

Shelly sat on the sofa, draped in blankets and in desperate need of a wash. Her pixie cut was flat and greasy, green bangs sticking to her temple in strings. Her oily skin had a sheen to it, her pores visible like grains of sandpaper. She was skinny, her neck and collarbones collecting shadows, only eating when her stomach was in dire pain.

L.K. wriggled in Lilu's arms, his pudgy face turning to find Shelly. He paused, recognizing his mother while some instinctive part of him realized there was something wrong with her. He cried.

"Get him away," Shelly said.

"It's been months, Shelly."

"He's better with you raising him."

Lilu paused. Following their mother's suicide, she had pitied Shelly for a long time, but the self-loathing had entered territories of exhaustion. She was the queen—the Royal Head. And with the Passion and Adren Kingdom's Royal Heads still toddlers or children, they couldn't have another kingdom absent of a functional leader. Besides, L.K. needed his mother, not his aunt.

She placed him on the sofa, seeing Shelly's reluctance to hold him in the way she turned her back. L.K. crawled toward his mother, crying, a hand outreached with each advance—as if begging for his mother's response. Shelly kept her eyes locked in the opposite direction, a cold shoulder turned. It was borderline monstrous. What kind of mother could act like this?

"Riots are happening," Lilu said. "Fueled by the fact that nobody has seen or heard from their king or queen in months. They're growing violent."

"You be their queen," Shelly said.

"In what world would that work?" asked Lilu, watching as L.K. grabbed the blanket at his mother's thigh. Shelly shifted her legs away from him.

"I don't know, nor do I care."

Lilu breathed deeply, but found no catharsis. Her head and ears grew hot. This wasn't like Shelly at all. She had always been a loaded boulder in a trebuchet, ropes on the verge of snapping as it prepared to strike any fortification standing in its way. Now she was a raindrop plunging toward the sea. What difference could she possibly make?

Lilu glanced at the balcony that circled the room's glass wall. Frederick watched from the banister, back turned to the sky, expression solemn. Nobody could comprehend the inner workings of Shelly's mind recently— not even Lilu, who had experienced the same losses. Vitio and Delilah had been her parents, too. But she still had Frederick she supposed, while Shelly had lost Bryson.

"Let me die," Shelly mumbled, barely audible over L.K.'s wails.

Lilu sat on the sofa, lifting the child and placing him on her lap. She bounced him on her knee as she tried gently hushing him. L.K.'s cries softened into sniffles. She looked at Shelly and whispered, "Never."

*   *   *

What haunted Shelly the most was the silence. When her mother had stepped off the balcony, she didn't scream—a fact that served as a reminder of her preparation for and acceptance of it. Nobody had pushed her, nor had she fallen accidentally. It was intentional. She had *willingly* ended her life, marking the love of her daughters and grandson as worthless. It had been a selfish act, and Shelly didn't blame her for it. She wanted the same.

She wasn't fit for motherhood. L.K. would benefit greatly without her. She couldn't even look the boy in the face without seeing Bryson or her father and then wanting to flood the world with her tears. She was drowning in misery, all her pillars collapsing around her.

She hated herself.

*   *   *

The entrance to the Piety Mines was miles deep in the eastern wall of the Loess. Himitsu had tired of the journey quickly, still exhausted from the trek to the Loess and then to the Heresy Butte. The thought of settling down in a home had never sounded so appealing. He was thankful these soldiers were nothing like the guards who had escorted him and Kaylee to the Heresy Butte. They had been instructed by Kopios Soteria to practically cater to Himitsu. When he was ready to call it quits for the day, they found the nearest form of lodging in the tunnels and caverns. They usually wound up as guests in a civilian's home, as taverns and inns were spread thinly throughout the inlands—especially this deep.

Himitsu stared into the gaping maw of the Piety Mines, rock and sediment glittering dully in the cave beyond, climbing its walls and crystallizing into frayed stalactites. It held the same gradient of violets, greens, and blues as some of the buildings in the Heresy Butte and the armor of the Loess's officers. This must have been its source material. He wanted to question its practicality, the colors displaying gemlike traits, which would make him think they'd be brittle and weak—unless they were more akin to diamonds. But they also looked like rock, grainy and non-translucent, so he didn't know what to think. Surely, if officers wore it as armor, then it must have been as strong as steel ... Stronger, perhaps?

The guards took him into the mines, leaving a cavern behind, where a single building had stood against a wall. They didn't enter beyond a few paces inside. Himitsu gawked at the spectacle, now noticing just how high the ceiling was. It would have made the vaulted ceilings of Phesaw's auditorium or any throne room quiver, thousands of stalactites hanging from a natural roof some twenty stories up. There were no torches or Intelights, but dozens of skylights—no more than a hand span wide—in what must have been the surface of the terrace above, streaks of sunlight peppering the mines' floor. If it hadn't been for the leechers in Accus Canyon, he would have claimed to have seen nothing like it.

How had his mother not ever seen this? While she had never traveled this far east—thus, not acquiring the proximity needed to see from the eyes of birds directly in this region of the kingdom—that didn't mean she didn't possess scouting birds that patrolled the Loess. When they returned to Phelos with updates for his mother, she should have noticed the holes in the ground when she used her ancient to delve into their minds. It was the same mystery as the massive skylight at the top of the Heresy Butte.

"Any questions?" one soldier asked.

Himitsu didn't respond immediately. Ask something with an obvious answer—something he should have already known if he'd truly seen Itta or Dolomarpos's plans for the Loess—and they'd question the legitimacy of his story and reason for being here. Ask nothing, and he was dooming himself to complete ignorance in a mission in which he was struggling to find reason to kill his target. He was searching for validity. Kopios was Kaylee's father, and a lord with vast amounts of wealth and power.

"Where are the miners?" he asked.

"Resting," the soldier said. "Pious mineral is less sturdy in moonlight. Trying to mine it during day hours is a waste of effort. Their shifts will begin at dusk."

"Are King Itta's reports true about its other traits?" Himitsu asked. It was best he kept his questions vague and hope they were willing to fill in the blanks.

"Nothing stronger in the world," the man replied. "It breaks steel. Holy wood is its only equal, but like holy wood with electricity, pious minerals also have a weakness in flame. But it melts slowly unless you held it next to the sun itself."

"A haul worthy of our king," said Himitsu.

"Forgive me," said the soldier, hesitance in his words. "But is King Sigmund as great as his father?"

Himitsu looked at the man, noting the leathery skin and wrinkles. He was older, somewhere in his fifties, hair gray save the infrequent streaks of black. "How long have you been a soldier of the Loess?"

"Four decades, starting at sixteen."

At that age, Himitsu found it strange why the man had asked him about Itta. Despite a few scars on his face, Himitsu looked no older than his mid-twenties. Then he remembered the position the people here were made to believe he held. He was a personal courier of the royal family. Many thought him an elite guard; why else would the king trust Kaylee with him alone? None knew he was an assassin, however, or that he was actually Passionian and a Jestivan. They had gotten one fact right: He would die on Kaylee's behalf.

"What did they tell you of King Itta?" he asked, seizing the opportunity of gathering information on their reverence for the former corrupt king. Maybe it'd strengthen his reasoning to assassinate the Loess Lord. His mother would be displeased had she known about this hesitance.

"Tell me?" asked the soldier. He shook his head. "I saw it myself. I was a head officer in charge of escorting a Soteria retinue to Phelos nineteen years ago, shortly after Lady Kaylee's birth. I stood guard in the throne room—a privilege—while Zyle Reklon, a high-ranking advisor to the Soteria family, personally announced the existence of a Soteria daughter to King Itta. I was there when we met Prince Sigmund as a six-year-old child. King Itta was a stern and driven man with dreams of grandeur seen in his plans of victory and conquest. He was everything one expected of

Dolomarpos's son, who I had only heard stories about. They were the kind of family suited for mixture with Soteria blood."

Himitsu looked away from the man, deciding to not press him further. Anything outside of what the man had said, he should have already known. And he did, if he were to believe what his mother had said about the intelligence they had gathered from Lost Wisdom and its president, Mesitis Epidex, known as the Skill Broker in underground circles. The Thousand-Layer Loess would send most of their soldiers westward along with whichever man was responsible for smelting and shaping pious minerals into armor, weapons, and other objects. In exchange, the Loess would receive a union with the Archaic family via an arranged marriage between Kaylee and Prince—now King—Sigmund. Eventually, they'd join the war that King Itta had begun alongside the Archains and Devish following the massacre at the Generals' Battle. It was supposed to serve as Itta's final trump card, for no one had seen Loess-trained soldiers or this material known as pious minerals.

But therein didn't lay the real issue, at least not in current events. What had bothered Ophala most was the apparent lack of communication between President Mesitis and Loess Lord Kopios following Itta's downfall. The tone of their missives had heightened to that of frustration, both seeing different futures for their alliance—an alliance that had only existed because of their king. In the end, Mesitis had decided to hold Kaylee hostage, using her safety as a threat to stop Kopios from marching westward in efforts to conquer the capital and usurping authority from the interim king, Toth Brench. With Himitsu's arrival here in the Loess, along with the safe return of Kaylee and promise of Mesitis's torture and eventual execution, Kopios saw that as a gesture of good faith. The Archaic family wanted to return to their original aspirations of uniting the western and eastern powers of their kingdom.

Himitsu peered into the distant caverns of the Piety Mines, seeing no end. "King Sigmund is all that and more," he said. A lie, but they didn't need to know that. The young Archaic King was a figurehead at best, Himitsu's mother operating as the Royal Head no matter how much she tried rejecting it.

"I'd expect no less from the grandson of Dolomarpos," the soldier said.

"What's your name?"

"Hal Lessus."

They didn't venture deeper into the mines. They turned back to the cavern and entered the lone building built into the side wall. The guards didn't enter with him. The first floor was completely open. From the tables and workbenches, Himitsu deducted it was a workshop. Against the back wall were three carts with piles of pious minerals in each. They sat on a track, their wheels lodged onto wooden rails. The track disappeared into the walls on both sides, swallowed by small tunnels that likely led to and from different areas of the Piety Mines.

A woman walked down a flight of stairs along one side of the vast room. She was short and narrow with poor posture. That and the gray hair made Himitsu guess north of sixty in years. She was wiping her hands and forearms with a rag—blackened from some kind of grime—as she reached the floor, turning to study her guest. After a few seconds, she said, "Welcome," and headed for the carts, walking past him without another glance.

She grabbed a pious mineral from the top of the pile, seemingly uninterested in weight or shape, and brought it to the closest table. "Well, do you want to see what the king has in store for him?"

He paused. He'd been given no instruction, yet she expected him to assume and then act with purpose? It was clear she possessed no desire for this, though he couldn't tell if it was his company or her life. He disregarded the disrespect and approached the table. An attitude wouldn't serve him well. He had a feeling he knew what this woman did. Staring at the table, however, he saw no tools of a blacksmith ... and where was the furnace? He didn't know much about the trade, but in his conversations with Toshik about the family business, smelting was the most important step in the process.

The woman cupped her hand over the mineral. Rays of black light shone from her palm and fingers and connected with the mineral. She began lifting fingers, sometimes slowly and other times flicking them effortlessly. She made use of every joint in each finger, occasionally curling one completely into her palm. She'd tilt her palm to and fro, her hand jerking up to one side if another quick movement was needed. And as she did this, the mineral took shape, rays of black light shifting in width, density, and length depending on the motion of her hand. She was manipulating the mineral without heat, a chisel, or hammer.

She finished a couple minutes later, lifting her hand and revealing a dagger in the wake of its weakening shadow. The weapon was a hand's length, black and grainy from hilt to the blade's tip, reflecting violet, green, and blue.

Himitsu closed his eyes and shook his head. He opened them again, head receding back slightly, as if seeing from a distance would dispel what should have been an illusion. It was still there.

"That is a small taste of what the king can expect from my ability," she said. "Will it suffice?"

Peeling his eyes away from the dagger to regard her, he asked, "And you can do this easily and frequently?"

"It's not a strain on my Archaic Energy," she said. "I used little to create this dagger. I could create thousands more without tiring. No, the difficulty lies in the complex weaving, which involves recognizing patterns and applying algorithms."

He scanned her body, trying to spot an ancient. She wore no jewelry or odd accessories, nor did she wield any items. She sported a simple tunic, trousers, and leather shoes, none of which he ruled out. Though rare, articles of clothing could be ancients he supposed. King Sigmund's scarf was the only example of which he could think. Her ancient could have been hidden beneath the clothing. He doubted it was one that implanted into the skin, for the ability of shaping pious minerals didn't involve morphing her body like Grand Director Poicus's shapeshifting ancient or Archaic Director Senex's resizing ancient.

She noticed his intrusive gaze. "You won't find what you're looking for."

He looked away, toward the dagger, and feigned ignorance.

"I've dealt with too many of King Itta's men back in the day who thought they could find and confiscate the ancient that allows me to do this," she said. "Not kind men, neither." Her eyes glazed over, but then they refocused seconds later. "The king wanted the power to manipulate pious minerals for himself, unaware such a desire is impossible. It seemed he didn't believe his father. King Dolomarpos had understood my ability, though that didn't make him any less brutal. Both were dangerous and vile; one was just significantly more intelligent."

"I don't want your ancient," Himitsu said.

She stared at him placidly. "So Itta passed his ignorance onto his son. What was his name again?"

"Sigmund."

"Well, King Sigmund should know that he needs me in order to make any use of the pious minerals from these mines. No one else can do it."

"He knows."

"And it's best he not forget about the auxiliary parameters of our deal," she said defiantly. She had the tone of a mother when faced with a thief in front of her children. She would show them her strength and lend them strength of their own while bargaining with the thief in a way that would see their lives spared in favor of her own and whatever fortune he sought. "My family goes unharmed, or else I'll gladly take my own life, making the bond between the Archaic and Soteria family pointless. The Accus's experienced enough brutality because of Dolomarpos and Itta. I will not let that continue beneath King Sigmund."

"Can you tell me the full story?" Himitsu asked.

She looked at him, eyes narrowing with mistrust.

"I'm nothing more than an elite guard and courier for the king's future wife," he explained. "In other words, a glorified meat shield. I'd like to know what is in store for my kingdom with such a union between families." These were mostly lies, requiring a simple fact check with Kopios—with whom Himitsu had provided a missive from the king that would contradict the ignorance he just declared. However, he doubted this woman spoke with the Loess Lord personally, nor would she have anything to gain from doing so. In fact, it sounded like she hated both the Archaic and Soteria name, seeing them as responsible for the Accus family's downfall.

She didn't respond, so he said, "Kaylee—Loess Lord Kopios's daughter—is training under a woman named Doctor Mengai." He glanced at a window in the front wall. The soldiers stood gathered in the distance, laughing and conversing. Once he realized they were all accounted for, and therefore not standing at the front door to try to hear his conversation, he lowered his voice and said, "Are you basically slaves of the Loess?"

The woman exhaled. "Mengai's loose lips will sink us all."

"Kaylee won't say anything. She doesn't even know what's happening here. She thinks she's here purely for apothecary tutorship."

"You're an odd enemy."

"I don't think I am your enemy," he breathed. She paused, and he was cursing himself in his mind. This was too reckless, but he was desperate in his hunt for that reason to kill Kaylee's father. Besides, this woman was unhappy, simply going through the motions. The only thing keeping her alive was the wellness of her family. Why wouldn't she bite at any bait he gave her if it meant possible salvation?

She grabbed the dagger and extended it toward him, hilt first. "Take this," she said. "Nobody will mind if I gave you this one dagger. I would still keep it concealed if I were you, though. If they find it and question you about it, you can tell them I gave it to you as a prototype—a taste of what else I have to offer the crown."

He stared at her, trying to determine her angle with the gift. He had been trying to lure her into divulging information to him, and now it seemed she had flipped the script, dangling an expensive dagger as bait— but for what purpose? He took it anyway, hoping she interpreted that as a gesture of good faith. And he saw no downside to it.

"May I have your name?" he asked.

"Joselina Accus."

She returned to the back of the room and grabbed a wheelbarrow before pushing it over to the mine carts. She began picking up pious minerals one at a time and placing them into the wheelbarrow. "I don't hear you leaving," she said. "I need to get these emptied before the evening shift begins."

He hurriedly tucked the dagger down the top of his left boot, but then realized his mistake as it cut sock and flesh effortlessly. He winced, feeling blood dampen his sock. It had cut him that easily? He repositioned it, this time more carefully. Straightening up, he eyed her once more. She'd only transferred an armful of minerals. A shovel would have been more useful, but he wasn't sure it would do her much good considering her stature.

"Do you not care to ask my name?"

A short silence as she continued her work. "I don't think I care," she finally said. "You will feed me a lie."

The accusation stung—because it was true. He couldn't let anyone know his real name. They didn't know if Lord Kopios knew of Spy Pilot Ophala or Himitsu. It was better to keep that under wraps so he turned and exited the building.

He approached the soldiers, who reformed into more dignified ranks at the sight of him, their relaxed congregation evaporating. He did his best to not walk with a limp, but the nagging presence of the dagger at his ankle was bothersome. And the bottom of his boot was wet and warm, causing him to question just how deep that cut had been. *Deep enough to hurt.*

The soldier who had spoken with him before in the Piety Mines, Hal Lessus, stepped forward, face grim. "Forgive me, Sir, but I must conduct a search."

Himitsu raised an eyebrow, careful to not react too strongly—or else they wouldn't need to search to know him guilty. "I haven't been searched since arriving in the Heresy Butte over a week ago."

"Nothing against you, Sir," Hal said, clearly uncomfortable. "But anybody who steps inside of Joselina's home is searched upon exit." He paused, then emphasized, "*Anybody.*"

The damned woman had planted the dagger on him. Had the whole woe-is-me act been a ploy? If so, she could have bested his mother on a theatre's stage. No, what he had seen in there had been authentic. She'd been as pale as a ghost. When was the last time she'd seen sunlight? And if she was the only person capable of shaping pious minerals, Lord Kopios would have kept her under strict watch. Her safety was the hinges that held up his plans. She was likely a prisoner in that building, just like Kaylee had said about Doctor Mengai.

He reached down to his boot, using one hand to peel back the leather and the other to, very carefully, pull out the dagger. Blood traced the grooves of its grainy surface. The little bit of pink drained from Hal's face.

"Did she give that to you?"

Himitsu tilted his head. That had been the man's first thought? There was clearly blood on the blade. Hal should have questioned *him* first—the stranger not from his land—not Joselina, a native inlander. The blood should have made him fear for her safety. He should have assumed Himitsu had wounded her and stolen the dagger ... Something an assassin would have done, which would have made more sense than her freely giving him a weapon made of a precious stone, knowing the ramifications of doing so. It was all beginning to click. These people despised the Accus name so much that they trusted strangers over them.

"Whose blood is that?"

Oh, now he asks. "Mine," Himitsu said, bending over to show his now-red sock. "Turns out I'm an idiot who didn't fully realize just what I was playing with here."

"Farley, Jet," Hal snapped. "Deal with Joselina. Pull no punches."

As the two soldiers strode toward the building with more pep in their step than any soldier should walk with, Himitsu said, "I took it." *Well, I'm stupid.* He wanted to call it clever improvising, but that would have implied thinking had been involved. This was purely impulsive. He wasn't going to let them beat that woman.

Farley and Jet froze in their tracks, and Hal's chin tilted upward, eyebrows crumpling in disbelief. He was tall, but not quite as tall as Himitsu. "Excuse me, Sir?"

"I took it when she wasn't looking."

Hal's chest swelled, nostrils flaring. Himitsu awaited the stern words of reprimand. Hal forced out a breath, then asked, "Why?"

So, no more 'Sir?' Himitsu had lost the man's respect. Great. "When I returned to Phelos, I was to give it to King Sigmund to show him proof of its miraculous existence."

"So you ask the Loess Lord," Hal said, face regaining color, but more red than pink. "You don't try sneaking it past us like a thief."

"I'm terribly sorry. I will return—*oof!*"

A fist to Himitsu's face. He teetered, but didn't fall. He was a Jestivan who had refined his hand-to-hand combat skills by sparring, daily, one of the scariest melee fighters he'd ever known in his life: Olivia. The punch had been strong, but nothing compared to the violet-haired, brick-faced royal. He straightened and wiped blood from his lips. His cheek burned hot as his fingers brushed skin. A definite bruise in his future.

Another fist, opposite cheek. An uppercut to the gut, up through his diaphragm. He dropped the dagger and spat out blood, air knocked out of him. He didn't fall, though. He'd endure this, for he saw Joselina watching from the window in his peripherals.

She had planted the dagger on purpose, knowing the ramifications. She had put her body on the line, knowing what the soldiers would have done to her had Himitsu ratted her out like she had suggested. But that risk had been worth it if it meant discovering she had an ally in the Loess who was also in with the Soteria family, which he was … and he hoped he'd still be after chalking this unfortunate turn of events up to a misunderstanding.

"No fight back?!" Hal roared, dropping an elbow on the head of Himitsu's hunched frame. His knees buckled, but he remained on his feet.

"I'll take what I deserve," Himitsu said. "Do you think King Sigmund hasn't done worse?" Another lie. Sigmund couldn't even swat a fly without remorse.

A knee smashed his face. His nose crunched. He yelled bitter agony, but did not crumple. Joselina had tested him, and he liked to believe he passed.

45

Six Feet Under

"Last chance to turn back," said Olivia, faced with the teleplatform they were about to onboard.

Vuilni stood by her side. Both women carried massive bags on their backs stuffed full of materials that would get them to the nearest town. It was more than usually necessary if traveling to a normal kingdom, but they weren't. The Void brought deprivation faster than natural law should have allowed. They looked like hikers weighed down by knapsacks, with heavy blankets folded and strapped to the top. "Give it a break," Vuilni said flippantly.

Olivia hadn't questioned Vuilni about her decision since departing Kindoliya, but she could grant her that mercy here. Many would have called this a suicide mission. Sure, a few of the Jestivan had survived their mission in the Void years back, but they'd been accompanied by two Energy Directors. Even then, they still hadn't penetrated its greatest depths. They had done their best to circumvent the Voidlands and gone nowhere near the Linsaniun Mounds.

Just days after acquiring the duty of protecting Lady Ropinia, Vuilni had asked to join Olivia after learning of her friend's desire to travel to the Cyn Kingdom. Both Olivia's mother and aunt didn't decline or argue, seeing greater benefit in the royal firstborn having a partner in foreign territory than Ropinia, who was safe within their capital's walls. Queen Apoleia may have swallowed her motherly instincts in allowing Olivia to commit to such a foolish journey, but she couldn't deny the importance of her kingdom needing its royal firstborn alive. The trait of a Bewahr guardian needed to be passed down. Her mother was gambling by allowing this. Only General Valp and Major Titus had aggressively voiced their objections, but to no avail. Just a few years ago, such behavior would have warranted immediate execution for a man.

Progress.

Olivia and Vuilni stepped onto the teleplatform, grabbed hold of a support beam, and flexed the muscles in their arm as the device kicked into gear, rotating with enough speed to cause Olivia's brain to feel as if it was sliding to one side of her skull. She closed her eyes in preparation for the dizziness once finished, knowing the ballerina or figure skater's trick of keeping her gaze locked onto a single point was impossible at this speed.

The platform slowed. She had arrived in a vacuum, air thin and wind nonexistent. It was just past seven o'clock in the morning, first-day's sun illuminating the golden, hip-high grass surrounding them. The light did little to quell the haunting quality of the Void. All sounds of life disappeared and heightened at the same time, the eerie quietness of the atmosphere lending to subtle sounds that carried from miles away: branches from the forest in the distance, creaking not because of wind, but age; the rustling of grass, and a rodent squeaking in its depths as it hunted smaller game; a man's grated cough, traveling from miles away; and the cries of the Linsani from across the kingdom, a constant backdrop that never died.

"Wow. Woah!" Vuilni clamped her hand over her mouth, eyebrows climbing two stories. She had either forgotten or disbelieved the stories about how sounds traveled in the Void. What would have been a whisper anywhere else in Kuki Sphaira became a raised voice here. Vuilni slowly dropped her hand, probably just now realizing all of those distinct sounds surrounding them that Olivia had noticed seconds ago. Despite existing in the Dark Realm her entire life, Vuilni was just as new to this as Olivia, apparently. Not even people of the Dark Realm wanted to visit the Cyn Kingdom.

There were three Voidlands in the Cyn Kingdom. The first was unavoidable, as they swallowed the teleplatforms. Olivia stepped off the platform and directly into grass, knowing that disturbance alone could have been heard a few hundred paces away.

"I have goosebumps," said Vuilni, running a finger along her forearm as they walked. "And despite it not being anywhere near as cold as the Still Kingdom, there is a chill that's unnervingly different." She paused, drifting into thought. "Reminds me of one of the other Diatia."

"What was he like?" Olivia asked, struggling to whisper. The notorious monotone she'd spoken with in her life had made whispering just as difficult as shouting. Maybe living here for a time would change that.

"Ronossius was …" she drifted off. "I guess … bad? He definitely wasn't a good person. He was damaged, and very much empty. Aside from Chelekah, he conversed little with others and shared even less. He never seemed to understand the repercussions of his actions—or maybe he did, yet didn't care enough to show it. Chelekah's death sparked the discord among the Diatia and wardens, and Ronossius was very much the soulless engine that powered it. But I guess being raised as a child in a place like this does that to you."

"And we're only a mile in," Olivia said.

A scream ripped through the atmosphere, and Vuilni looked up and ahead, as if toward the horizon. She needn't remark on its source: a skeletal wyvern cloaked in roiling shadows. They both were all too familiar with the beasts known as Linsani, of which there were seven. Well, now six, for Bryson had killed Tongku Feilong, the Linsani of Fear, during the Blizzard of Blood. Olivia and Vuilni had been on the battlefield during it, fighting SCAPD forces. Both had been lucky enough to avoid the Linsani's wrath, but they had seen hundreds of their comrades and enemies fall victim. Many had committed suicide after being drenched in the shadows; others had gone mad; a few hurt themselves in order to distract themselves from the fear.

And now Olivia and Vuilni were headed for the homelands of the Linsani, where they didn't feast on humans—for none were stupid enough to venture too close—but consumed the atmosphere, the very spirit of the kingdom. According to texts, those creatures were responsible for the Void's lack of life and air resistance, but also responsible for keeping humans alive in a miserable state—most wouldn't call it a life. Preloz's daughter, Pytatia, surely wouldn't. Olivia wondered if the poor girl was even aware of her misery anymore. It was sad to think of that as a blessing.

"When are you going to tell your Bewahr about this?" Vuilni asked.

"When we're deeper."

Vuilni nodded. "So if he tries convincing you to turn back, which you wouldn't anyway, you'd have the excuse of being too far in."

Olivia hadn't given Vuilni her Bewahr's identity, but she had told her friend this mission was to help him. When asked for a reason, Olivia conjured a half-truth on the spot. She had thought it a lie, but since verbalizing it, she'd seen the benefit of it. It had grown on her ever since. Perhaps, finding Preloz his daughter would encourage him to help Olivia. He had already shown he didn't care about betraying his own empire, so what would stop him from destroying it from within? She wouldn't bring this up forthright, but she could feel him out as they got to know each other more.

Could the Light Empire win if they had a saboteur within their enemy's ranks? Did she even want the Light Empire to win? All that talk of maintaining balance in the Untenables seemed a wash if one side destroyed the other.

She was getting ahead of herself. For now, she need to get this man his daughter back. It was a mission she could put her heart and soul into, for there was nothing sadder to her than a daughter without a proper father.

Then, just maybe, Preloz could help put her own father back where he belonged.

Six feet under.

46

A Bold Attack

Bryson was pleased to be in Founding Plaza again. As overwhelming as the midnight crush of bodies was, the youthful faces siphoned memories of Phesaw, cramped in the halls of the Knowledge Wing between courses—or even Wealth's Crossroads, though not to this degree or at this hour. Part of him wished he could have slipped into the lives of these Celestians, worried only about course projects due on Monday or where their friends were planning to meet tonight. Then he thought of the woman he'd loved more than anyone in his life, and the boy with his hair and eyes. His focus tripled, eyes scanning his surroundings. If he wanted to see them again—and soon—he needed to pass this test.

There wasn't a statue at the center of the plaza despite Thusia's persistence otherwise. This time, however, there also wasn't an empty square of cobbles. The crowd ebbed and flowed through the center. Quincy had told him the "civilians" who'd walked around the empty space had actually been members of the Celestian garrison—another thing Bryson hadn't known existed—who'd been instructed to act as if they were circumventing an object while blocking any passersby from stepping inside. Also, the maps given to Bryson had been a lie, at least in regards to that statue. They wanted him to think there was a statue, that way its absence sprung red flags in his mind. A brilliant ploy on their part, but they hadn't foreseen his lack of studying.

This time, he knew the layout of this plaza like Phesaw's campus. Garnetts—the luxury bar that didn't serve food—stood on the northern side, sandwiched between a premium inn and an abandoned, closed-down sweets shop with an owner who had likely bit off more than he could chew financially. Owning real estate in Founding Plaza was a mark of extreme wealth—or crippling debt. The successful establishments were staples of the plaza, while the failures went under within a year and replaced weeks later, making certain properties a revolving door of businesses. It was one of the most important details Bozani scouts like Aestys and Nora had to pay attention to, though Aestys purposefully avoided this place because of its lack of action with Gefal.

Bryson was thankful he had studied the plaza so intensely since his first test's failure, hoping they might bring him here again to redeem himself. Today, he was with two members of Squad One: the aforementioned Nora, scouting rival and good friend of Aestys, and Withornis Storm—also known as Thornstorm.

Withornis had led the first meeting between the five Pogu and Bryson. As the leader of Squad One, she held an air of superiority over her equals; although, according to the layout of the Bozani hierarchy stated by Empress Tonitrua, no Pogu ranked higher than the other.

She sported her signature outfit. Silver flowers dotted a maroon backdrop on today's kimono. She had many kimonos, but they always followed the color scheme of maroon and silver. Her waistband today was also maroon, tied at her back in a bow, its loops wide enough to look like wings. Her ivory quiver was long and slender across her back, carrying a bouquet of roses instead of arrows. The Intelamp hanging outside of Cluttered Shelves—a bookshop known for its quirk of holding more action figures, dolls, and memorabilia on its shelves than actual books—glowed against her bald scalp.

Nora walked with Bryson, holding pleasant conversation with him. He couldn't decide if he liked her or not. She was nicer and less eccentric than Aestys, but she could have been playing her role here: distract the test subject from his true goal. Besides, her green hair threw him off, reminding him of the Intel women. Most specifically, Shelly. Looking at her made him feel guilty, so he supposed he should have been appreciative of this, as it forced him to concentrate on the job.

"Aestys try jumping your bones yet?"

Bryson broke into a coughing fit, shock sending spit down the wrong pipe. Thornstorm turned from her pole position as they pressed through the crush, but said nothing, dark-chocolate eyes firm. He recovered and looked at her incredulously. "No."

"You're kind of her type, and she's terrible at impulse control." Nora's brows furrowed, mouth curving into a frown. "Figured that was a recipe for disaster. She would sleep with you and then toss you aside, effectively ruining any work relationship in the future. Honestly, I thought that was why you were assigned with Squad One tonight."

"I'm married."

"So you would sleep with her if you weren't?"

"No," he said. "I don't like her personality all that much."

"You don't like seeing a woman with a guy's sense of humor," she said.

"I ... That's not what I ..." he trailed off, tilting his head. Had she been correct? No, he liked Pilot Ophala, whose humor often ventured down more crass avenues—even if she was more subtle and clever with the delivery. He simply didn't like it in a partner. "I think of them as—"

"Did you know Aestys slept with eighty-two men in her mortal life?"

Bryson ran into the back of a civilian, who turned with an enraged glare before catching sight of his radiant wings and promptly stepping to the side. It had been Bryson's fault, but he was too shocked to offer the man his apologies.

"Seventy-one of them were married," said Nora, ticking off statistics as if they had no meaning. "Sixty happily so. Forty-two of them had children, a home, and career. And she enjoyed every bit of it. That sort of thing— luring men away from their happy lives—got her off. The more saintly the man, the harder she tried. Her favorite spots to hunt were schools, where fathers dropped off and picked up their children; parks, where fathers sat with their wives on benches or at picnics while they're children played; and event halls, where she looked to pluck a newlywed in efforts to destroy a marriage within days."

Bryson was disgusted. How was a person like that a Bozani? Quincy had told him not everyone up here was as holy as he wanted to believe, that even Magnifica—the woman who had deflected a meteorite in the First of Five—had pride and superiority complexes, but to lure that many men into infidelity? To purposefully seek it out? That destroyed lives. And to think Aestys was the one who'd been giving Magnifica heat about her pride. She made Magnifica look like a saint.

"Why are you telling me this?" he asked. "Aren't you her friend?"

"She likes to talk about the other Bozani behind their backs, so I figured she already had." She looked at him sidelong. "Has she not?"

"She has."

"Well, then she can handle the favor returned. And yes, she's my friend, but we're also rivals." She held up a finger. "Also, I wanted to warn you of her tactics. She can turn the most honest of men."

Bryson turned up his nose. He loved Shelly wholeheartedly. The crowd swallowed their silence, and he suddenly remembered why he was here, the significance of tonight. He was supposed to be looking out for any clues of a Gefal's presence; this was a test. He had zoned out for a few minutes, lulled by Nora's story. *Damnit.*

They walked through the plaza for a while, the crush not as lenient as it had been the night with Quincy and Aestys. Covering several paces took half a minute and a bruised shoulder. Thornstorm showed no patience, sometimes disappearing and sending Bryson into a panic.

The plaza went dark as every single Intelamp extinguished. Bryson froze, Celestians growing into frenzy around him. His wings were a luminescent white, but like anything made of Tahara, they didn't illuminate his surroundings. The only Tahara that proved otherwise was the substance spilling out of the Cavities above the Starlight. His first thought was that this was part of the test. *Awfully aggressive this time around.* He began formulating suspects in his mind, mentally perusing the abilities and notable crimes of every Gefal. Who was capable of extinguishing over a hundred Intelamps at once?

A hand grabbed his wrist, and Nora spoke into his ear to counter the dissonance around them. "Keep pace! The lights will come back on! Follow me. If you get lost, follow the flickering lights!"

This didn't feel like a test anymore. The Intelamps flickered back to life just as Nora had warned. The plaza was emptying quickly, Celestians fleeing into buildings or down branching roads. Darkness again, then back to light.

"Let's go!" Nora bellowed, running in the direction of Thornstorm.

Bryson hesitated, spotting bodies writhing in agony on the cobbles. People were in crippling pain.

Was this the test? It felt like a morbid joke. Flashbacks took shape in his vision.

The Generals' Battle. Fleeing spectators in the stands. Blades darting through the air. Bodies slung lifelessly over benches. The coliseum drenched in crimson at dusk as he scrambled to find Olivia.

The Phesaw invasion. A woman playing a frozen piano in the lobby of Lilac Suites. Olivia turning on him and the Jestivan to take her side. Students dying at the hands of Dev King Storshae and his soldiers. The revelation of his mother's identity and Olivia as his sister.

The Blizzard of Blood. War on the frozen Diamond Sea, armies clashing. People dying by the thousands. His hopelessness at the top of Kindoliya's wall. A demonic wyvern in the sky, raining death and suicide upon the weak souls below. Its red eyes turned toward Bryson, the dread within him. Stepping onto the ledge, preparing to end it all.

Toono's invasion of Dunami. King Vitio's fear. Bryson's own terror, knowing the proximity of life-threatening danger to Shelly and L.K. The clash of titans and shattering of the landscape. Revelations: a half-brother whose mother their father had also victimized. A suicidal sacrifice, the blood of a demon gushing from its neck onto Bryson's face.

Founding Plaza … He blinked. He was seeing the plaza again, the cacophony growing distant as the crowds retreated. Many of the writhing bodies were now limp … lifeless. This wasn't a damned test. Bryson had seen enough tragedy and destruction to know its raw, ugly authenticity when he saw it. His life as a Jestivan had been a montage of the evils this world had to offer, which was why he could never agree with a philosophy like Aestys's: *Evil doesn't exist.*

The Intelamps went off again, plunging the plaza into momentary darkness, stunning Bryson's vision. Then the lamps started flickering fast enough that it was a miracle some people didn't fall to seizures.

He bounded after Nora, who was sprinting toward an eastern road. He caught her in the blink of an eye, his speed percentage cranked just below his maximum. She looked at him, either impressed or surprised.

"Where's Thornstorm?" he asked.

She pointed up. A pair of wings, white and radiant, were stretched against the star-strewn night sky. Thornstorm glided effortlessly above the city of Celeste. She was already several blocks ahead of them, having put Bryson and Nora in the back of her mind.

Bryson clenched his jaw, either trying to will his Tahara out of his body or gain control of his Tahara wings. Neither worked, though he could feel it. Wrangling Tahara was a thousand times more difficult than his Intel Energy. They turned down two different streets, Intelamps continuing to flicker around them. "What's happening?" he finally asked.

"The Intelamps serve as the city's alarm system. Empress Tonitrua will manipulate them to communicate simple messages with any Bozani in the city. The code she gave in the plaza signaled something that hasn't happened in years." She paused, distress shadowing her face. "Wings of a Gefal. Not only is a Gefal in the city, but whoever it is isn't trying to hide their Mulawi wings."

"Isn't it only a few who can sprout wings?" he asked.

"And that's the scary part. If you've been studying like you said, you should know who that might mean."

He literally gulped as he ran, slowing his pace to not outrun Nora. He had no idea where they were going. Did the Dark Empire send a Versac—the equivalent of a Strasan?

"We're following the Empress's path right now," Nora explained. "The flickering lights ahead tell us which roads to follow and which to avoid."

He looked behind them and noticed the Intelamps stopped flickering as they passed. Clever system. But that wasn't all he noticed. In his early years as a Jestivan, he had trained his eyes to see minute details in the dark—a necessary skill when fighting a Passion Assassin like Himitsu, whose black flames seemingly vanished in the darkness. If it hadn't been for that, he wouldn't have caught the slight haze lingering above the rooftops in the direction from which they had just come. A massive shroud of blackness barely a shade darker than the starlit sky. If it hadn't been for the backdrop of the Starlight's Tahara-infused quartz, even *his* eyes might have missed it.

"Thornstorm can see everything from up there," Nora continued, oblivious to what was behind them. "She's headed directly for whichever area of the city is most brightly illuminated, for that would be the target of the suspect. The spot usually moves as the Gefal tries to avoid the Empress's spotlight."

"In the plaza," Bryson said, "did you not notice the peculiar response?"

"Celestians are also familiar with the Intelamp system," Nora said. "They know to run in the opposite direction of the flickering lights. Thus, they fled westward, deeper into the city and closer to the sentry districts, where it will be safe."

"People were hurt!" he screamed.

"Trampled. Not our problem."

The shortness angered him. How were people like Aestys and Nora Bozani? Noticing his anger, she said, "The Celestians have hospitals, garrison, and all of the public services a city needs. It's not the Bozani's job to heal every injury. We give them an alarm system, and that should suffice."

He looked back again, tuning her out. She may have missed it because of her instinctive nature to disregard the civilians, having seen frightened stampedes and the trampling injures that resulted from them, but he'd always been observant of the suffering of innocents. He had run past a handful of bodies on his way out of the plaza, none of which had any visible damage to their body. No blood, bruises, or twisted limbs ... not even a torn shirt. He saw two men convulsing and a woman simply lose her breath. He supposed someone could have blamed them as symptoms of shock, such as a heart attack, but he saw an entirely different scenario thanks to his studying—and the haze was affirmation.

He planted his foot, pivoted, and dashed the other way, back toward the plaza. He barely heard Nora's shriek of reprimand before he was already a mile away. Something along the lines of: "IDIOT!"

Why would the Gefal send an elite rank with exposed wings into the Light Empire, knowing their enemy could sense them? Catching whoever was responsible would have been too convenient. The person Thornstorm and Nora were chasing had to be a red herring. The real threat was in Founding Plaza, a notion the Bozani wouldn't have been able to believe because of the Gefal's trepidation when penetrating the inner districts of Celeste. Bryson, on the other hand, had only been in the Empire a couple months, so he ruled out nothing. He only hoped he wasn't wrong. While this wasn't the test, that only meant failing had more dire consequences than not seeing his wife and son.

As Bryson entered Founding Plaza, his sprint slowed to a jog and then a full stop. He stared at the expanse, eyes wide and heart falling to his feet. Bodies lay everywhere, the tangled mass thickening westward in the direction of the capital's heart, where Celestians thought they'd be safe.

The haze he had seen was now gone, but one figure stood at the center of the plaza—black hair stringy and unwashed, face reflecting the plaza's Intelamps with its oily sheen, and a grated mask of wood covering his mouth and nose. He slowly lowered to a crouch and, with a dangling arm, caressed the face of a young woman at his feet.

Bryson screamed, hoping a Bozani was around to hear him, and charged. There was a Fuhren in Founding Plaza—something that had never happened before according to Bryson's studies. He had known it when he'd seen the haze and linked it to the uninjured civilians squirming in pain on the cobbles.

Toxins. A man known as Plague.

Brenson Ulial, Fuhren of the Dark Empire's fourth unit.

47

The Tools of the Elite

Brenson looked up from the dead woman's body just as Bryson was within ten meters. A cloud of colorless smoke—a haze that camouflaged with its backdrop—blossomed from his grated mask, then jetted toward Bryson in billowing waves. Bryson planted his foot and ran to the side. The Fuhren turned his head and followed Bryson's circumvention, the poisonous haze sweeping behind.

Bryson was successful in avoiding corpses, but that didn't mean they didn't slow him. Each electric beam Bryson hurled was absorbed by one or both of Plague's wings, as he cocooned himself within. Bryson tried weaving an electrical storm from directly above, but Plague's wings then widened and morphed into a dome that protected him at all sides. Unfamiliar with the properties of Mulawi, Bryson couldn't penetrate the shadows. He felt his Intel Chains weakening the moment they contacted the shadows, then dispersing into nothing before reaching the other side.

A hole formed in the shadowy dome, from which shot a toxic cloud. Bryson ran again, this time losing balance as the left side of his right foot and its big toe landed on someone's ribs, the right side of his foot finding only air, causing his ankle to roll and leg to give way beneath him. Another corpse saved his head from smacking cobbles, face meeting crotch instead. He rolled off the body and clambered to his feet, but favored one side. Plague had used his wings as a defense mechanism. Could Bryson do that, too? Did Tahara and Mulawi possess similar traits?

He searched for Plague, but instead found a woman with skin like toffee and a heavy green coat adorned with golden tassels ... Sephrina Jordan, Pogu of Squad Four and the Second of Five. The Fuhren was nowhere to be seen and must have fled during Bryson's fall. Had Sephrina scared him away?

Sephrina walked toward him, but then ran as he collapsed. Lemon overpowered his sense of smell. Recalling his study material, he knew that scent as one of Plague's toxins, which were now attacking his body.

*　　　*　　　*

Rhyparia stepped out of the shadows of a shanty, her wings stretching to their full length as if welcoming free space. While she had gained some control over them, they were still mostly disobedient. It was a fight between her will and the Mulawi itself, as if it had a life of its own. That made sense, she supposed. It was a close link to the God, Mulawith. What was the will of a human to that of a deity?

Mendac exited the shadows to her left, his wings subtler in their motions. He had gained near mastery over them in only a couple of months, but he confessed to possessing an advantage of which he wouldn't disclose the specifics. Since seeing him in his cell across from hers, he had carried himself differently than her. He was a natural at the transition process, taking everything in stride. His wings seemed nothing more than another pair of arms. She wondered when he would learn to fly. His poise when confronted by Gefal spoke to his rigid self-confidence, even though they had yet to meet a Versac.

Tonight, however, their demeanors mirrored each other, invigorated by a sense of purpose. Training their bodies via simulations could only take them so far; they wanted the real thing, a way of knowing what they were really up against. This would improve their simulations, knowing what level they actually had to achieve.

Rhyparia wanted to meet a few of these Bozani. After reading the files of beings like Aestys, Magnifica, and Rhysel, the thrill of testing herself against vileness of their level was too enthralling. She was who she was. She had already wiped out a capital and hundreds of thousands with it; there was no turning back. She felt no remorse.

The outskirts of the Crust—which itself was the outskirts of Celeste—had no light aside from the stars and moon. Her eyes took a moment to readjust, a nuisance she wouldn't have to deal with much longer according to her superiors. As she established control of her Mulawi, seeing in the dark became easier. She'd originally seen it as an ability that would lend well to the Gefal at night, but then she'd learned the Bozani could also see in the darkness better than the average person.

The dirt road was silent, the windows of every shanty along its sides absent of light. Civilians were sleeping, preparing their bodies for the crack of dawn, when they'd wake for minimum-wage jobs. The Crust was poor, but it did have an infrastructure, avoiding the nature of the crime-ridden slums in Pasten, where they were poor *and* desperate.

Intelights sparked to life, illuminating the entire block, the shadowy recesses of potholes littering the street. They flickered over a dozen times, and Rhyparia, idiotically, stood still.

"Get out of the street," Mendac said.

She followed him into a barren side yard about ten paces wide between shanties. The Intelights continued flickering, but didn't reach this area, granting them a veil of shadows.

"So we know we're bait," he said, crouched against the side of a shanty, waving his hand to signal for her to follow suit. "We know the Bozani's common scouts are all Branian."

"Aestys, Kose, Boralis, Nora, Tricipidal, Dalonius, and …" Rhyparia blanked on the last name.

"Drog," he said.

"The Crust is commonly manned by Aestys and Nora," she added.

"Aestys is Passionian and the eccentric type; Nora, a Spiritian not fond of gimmicks—straightforward."

The two Dark Empire recruits spent the next minute overviewing their studies. They had come into this knowing exactly in which territory they'd wind up and with whom they'd have to contend. As bait, their task was to simply hold their own against whoever came to apprehend them. This meant they had reviewed Aestys and Nora's documents repeatedly over the past few days. This was their domain. The street's glow remained steadfast, the flickering coming to an end. Rhyparia didn't know what to make of it. The timing between the Intelights coming on and the arrival of the two Gefal recruits couldn't have been coincidence—it was past midnight—but they hadn't learned anything in their studies about Intelights in the city.

"An alarm?" Rhyparia asked.

"I think so."

She didn't like the Intelamps. They were brighter than normal—a translucent white that could be seen from leagues away. She wanted to inch down the side of the shanty and check both ends of the street, but thought she shouldn't risk it. They needed to last long enough for Plague to complete whatever his own mission was. "Let's move," she said, unease settling into the pit of her stomach—something she hadn't experienced in years.

Rhyparia sprinted through hard earth behind the homes. Mendac didn't argue and followed. The Crust was far enough out to yield space for pastures, but such a thing would require grass, which required rain. None of that existed out here. As they ran, the Intelamps illuminated parallel with their path ... tracking them. It didn't matter that they weren't in sight of the lamps, they still knew somehow.

"No one said anything about Intelamps with tracking abilities," she said. They had come to a stop in another gap between shanties, this only an arm's length wide. "They can probably see this from the Starlight."

Mendac peered that way. "Doubtful, but someone has taken notice. And I have a feeling Aestys and Nora aren't the only two we'll ..." he trailed off, gaze now resolute toward the sky.

A pair of ghostly white wings spread against the stars, a woman's figure suspended at the center. The wings flattened, and the woman dove directly for them.

Wings? How? They said nothing about someone capable of flying. Instinctively, Rhyparia grabbed at her hip only to find air. Damnit, Mialo! The Emperor still hadn't returned her ancient, which was part of the reason why she didn't possess her normal confidence. If she had her umbrella, she could contend with a winged individual—even a Bozani. Gravity conquered all.

"It's Withornis Storm," said Mendac, the woman now close enough to spot the roses extending above one shoulder, the smoothness of what could only be a bald head. She reached behind her back as she descended, grabbed the ivory quiver and held it under her arm, pinned against her ribs—a cannon, as the tales had called it. Her wings turned vertical, producing drag and bringing her to a stop, midair. The dozen roses were deceiving, hiding the real threat of hundreds of thorny rose stems.

She unloaded, expelling Spirit Energy into the ivory quiver, resulting in a volley of thorns. A voltaic sphere swallowed Rhyparia and Mendac, surrounding them in a dome of electricity that pulsed and crackled. Thorny stems hit the sphere and burned out before entering their safe area.

Rhyparia's eyes widened, hands limp at her sides. She hadn't felt this helpless since the Gravity Trials while at the whim of her mother's mercy. Without her ancient, what was she? If Mendac hadn't been here in this moment, that attack would have maimed her. She had speed to evade thanks to gravity training, but when staring down that many projectiles, she'd need the speed percentage of Bryson or Yama—which she didn't have.

The sphere dissipated, leaving Rhyparia with a permanent afterimage of blinding white. She blinked, but it did nothing to regain her vision. Mendac couldn't have warned her to close her eyes beforehand?

"We have to get out of here!" she screamed, sprinting behind the shanty to use it as a barrier. She felt along the wall to guide her path, eyes closed. She opened her eyes after fifteen seconds, but saw no Mendac. He wasn't at the side of the building. She looked up, mouth slightly open …

The man was airborne, black wings slapping downward as he ascended toward the Pogu.

*   *   *

Satisfaction blanketed Mendac as the eyebrows of Pogu Withornis Storm—also known as Thornstorm according to their material—furrowed, disbelief contorting her lips into a scowl. He had striven for godly levels of power in his life, searching for unorthodox methods of obtaining it through his intellectual prowess. At a young age, he had learned something about himself that set him apart from others, but kept it secret for most of his life until that final battle with Ataway ... and that one instance in Prayoga during his invasion of the Dev Kingdom. What he discovered about himself he then tried to recreate. For that, he thanked Kadlest and Apoleia.

The wings—a trait different from the aforementioned one—came late in life, months before Pogu Ataway Debonicus Kawi was sent to execute him. The shadows sprung from his back the moment he cut into Bryson's skin to begin tests. Strange timing, considering all the evil he had committed in his life. Even before Bryson, he had operated on a different son ... Toono.

Conviction replaced flabbergast on Thornstorm's face, her jaw stiffening and eyebrows crumpling deeper. She effortlessly undid her waistband with one hand and threw off her kimono, letting it fall victim to the night's calm breeze.

Mendac's hands and forearms cackled with electricity as he flew at her. He shot a voltaic beam from each hand. She didn't dodge, but slapped a luminescent wing in front of her as a shield, the electricity deflecting errantly into the sky.

Just like Debonicus.

His fight with Pogu Debonicus had started in his lab in Brilliance's sewers, but he had taken it outside after deciding he didn't like the idea of a fight with a Bozani in closed quarters. Once above ground, he had released his black wings and took to the sky, believing he'd catch Debonicus off guard. But the Pogu hadn't missed a beat, showing no signs of panic. Instead, he had sprout wings of his own—white and radiant.

The pair had fought throughout the streets of Brilliance in—what should have been—the dead hours of night. But when two powers on the level of Mendac and Ataway clash, the world is bound to wake. Even with Mendac's other unique trait catching Ataway off guard briefly, the fight hadn't lasted long because of his unfamiliarity with the specialties of the Pogu's wings. Ataway killed him within a minute, and ... that was it.

Mendac didn't know how the world responded after the fight, but the image of winged men must have alarmed every single person who had seen. He wondered how the world adapted, but during his short amount of time between his rebirth and abduction by the Gefal, he hadn't seen any evidence of anything being different.

Thornstorm's wing extended again to reveal her figure. The electric beams had done nothing to her person. Her eyes bulged as she widened them to their greatest extent, radiant halos of white light surging around her pupils and irises. They looked like two distant stars. A beam of light shot from both eyes. Mid charge, Mendac dipped beneath her, but a scorching heat ripped through one of his wings. He felt the hole, a massive blank spot in his sensory intake of the Mulawi that composed his wings. He quickly filled the hole, instinctively reforming the wing.

If he could only use his Mulawi to attack as an extra weapon added to his already-stacked arsenal. Honestly, if only he could use that other ability. Could he? Thornstorm might already know about it. He had used it twice, one of those times against Ataway, who would have likely informed the Bozani afterward.

A mighty gale swept him off his path, forcing him downward. He plummeted, his wings not strong enough to fight the blast of wind. He turned over, back toward the ground, gathering electricity in his hand and then releasing a barrage of lightning bolts that snapped the sky in two as if it were the ground.

The resulting flash of white was blinding, and he noticed Thornstorm evaded this attack rather than deflecting it with her wing. The hammering gale rescinded, but a bevy of roses shot toward him from another angle. He spotted it too late and could only fold his wing to protect himself, hoping it had the same effect as hers.

It didn't.

Dozens of razor thin cuts split open across his face, arms, and legs as roses passed through his wing as if it was air. They shredded his clothes and tore out chunks of his hair. He felt a few rip through the thinner areas of his body, such as his wrists and fingers. If it hadn't been for a desperate full-body carapace of electricity to disintegrate the thorns into ash just before hitting skin, they would have likely punctured vital organs.

The carapace disappeared, and he unfolded his wing to find Thornstorm eight paces away, plunging at him from above. She was moving too fast to react, and for a primal moment, he became enraged that this woman was besting him. He hadn't felt such disgust since the weeks following Thusia's death, when the idiot girl had died on his behalf.

A figure swept in front of him with black wings of its own. Thornstorm stopped immediately, wings catching air.

Poten Copor, Fuhren of the Gefal's third unit, hovered between the Pogu and Mendac. His massive robes were tied to his waist, knees, and ankles to hold the excess cloth, which billowed in the breeze. He was a big man, a being of muscle and nothing else. His back was turned to Mendac.

"Thornstorm," Poten said, voice deep.

"Poten." Her posture had relaxed, mirroring his. Neither seemed threatened by the other, which was either credit to their confidence or a product of knowing the fight ended here.

"We'll be going now," he said. He turned and grabbed Mendac by the wrist, dragging him down to the Crust.

Rhyparia waited between shanties, her eyes drawn to Mendac as the pair approached. She looked livid, but didn't say a word. They clustered in the shadows and disappeared from Celeste.

48

The Nature of Cynnish

The Unbreakable didn't mesh well with his neighbors. They saw him as a fraud—perhaps, even a predator who looked to take in young, hopeless children who could easily be taken advantage of. Those were the most insane Cynnish, their cynicism driving them to irrational conclusions, ignoring the man's wife and two sons or the manner in which he carried himself. They saw only what they wanted to see: the worst of things.

The age of three was an eventful year for Tashami Patter, for every nightmare was set during that time. It was the year when his father's hard work in bringing light to the souls of depressed children was coming to fruition and showing real results. But something about these scenes from Tashami's life felt ominous. They were leading to a turn in events. Spirits were too high; life was too smooth.

What goes up must come down.

Tashami's little feet pattered down the stairs to his father's foyer. The children were all sequestered in separate rooms around the house, committed to their studies. He could hear the turning of pages in books or the scratching of a quill across parchment, their sources coming from multiple directions and distances. Boiling water was poured into a pot in the kitchen a couple rooms away from the foyer, steam hissing as it rose into the air, his mother hard at work on another pasta dish.

Tashami, the one child still young enough to require only an hour of study time a day, wandered sheepishly, hoping his brother and friends were done soon. He looked up at the clock hanging high on the wall above the front door. He couldn't read time, but he knew when the small hand reached the three, it was time to play. That gave them until the small hand reached four, which would signal mother's dinner. That routine never changed.

Just as he was about to turn at the bottom of the steps and head for the kitchen, he paused, another sound barely audible among the rest. It was his father's voice, low and pleading, but muffled greatly by the house's walls. Another voice responded, this one more of a hiss, sharp enough to pierce the clatter of wooden dishes from the kitchen. It came from the direction of outside.

Tashami approached the front door and pressed a hand and ear against the wood, which did little to help. He looked back down the small hallway that ran below the second-floor overlook, through a dining room and breakfast nook before ending in the kitchen. His mom was currently out of sight, occupied with chopping vegetables on the counter. That *bang-bang-bang* noise only made hearing his father worse.

The demon in his stomach twisted it into knots, confronting him with that sensation of dread whenever he was about to do something naughty. It was a powerful demon, but Tashami was stronger.

He opened the door a crack and stuck out his tiny head, peering beyond the weed-tangled front yard. He scanned the dirt street and saw his father and their neighbor standing in the walkway leading to their neighbor's house. Their neighbor was a portly man, which was quite a sight to see in the Void. Most people of Cynnish descent—especially those who'd spent their entire life in the kingdom—were malnourished and sickly. Their hair had no color, their skin a ghostly white—if they had skin at all.

Only the Cynnish children still possessed some sort of vibrancy in their image.

Tashami could never understand why he, Joni, their father and mother looked so different than everyone else. The sight of his father and neighbor was like a newly painted canvas hung next to an ancient, cracked mosaic.

Porky—or that was what the orphans had begun calling the overweight man—hissed at his father, speaking in that language Tashami hated so much. He didn't understand the native tongue of the Void, and his father wouldn't teach it to him—not that he protested. When he heard the language, it did something to him, made the demon in his gut a little bit bigger. There was power to those words.

Makes me hate myself, the boy thought. He didn't like feeling empty.

His father waved a hand—not aggressively, but almost as a gesture. He spoke the same tongue as Porky, for most Cynnish didn't know Sphairian. The orphans only knew Sphairian because of his father's rigid language classes. If Tashami didn't know any better, he would have thought he came from a different land.

The exchange of words ended poorly, Porky waddling back toward his house after a sharp hiss, the sound trailing hauntingly through the atmosphere for several seconds. Father watched, face inscrutable. Porky's venom wouldn't dampen Father's spirit. Father tucked his hands in his pockets and looked toward his own house, spotting Tashami in the cracked door. A frown formed, and the shock and guilt of being discovered caused him to slam the door shut harder than he should have.

The sound was a loud snap through the house. Footsteps came from all directions. Doors opened upstairs as curious orphans looked out into the foyer from the overlook. Tashami remained still, back to the door and hands clasped behind his back as if that didn't look suspicious.

Mother stepped into view in the dining room in the back of the house, a cooking mitten on her hand and furrowed brows on her face. Anger overtook curiosity as she spotted her little boy, and he nearly wet himself. Her back straightened, stature stiffening as she removed the cooking mitten and tossed it onto the dining table. She pointed down at the floor in front of her, signaling a command for him to approach.

He did, hesitantly, reaching his mother with head bowed slightly, tears already mounting. Mother was full of passion; she loved deeply and made it apparent in her hugs and kisses. She took care of her children and made it apparent in her warm meals and clean clothes. Alas, those passions also brought forth uglier sides. She angered easily when crossed, making it apparent in her—

A scream sounded from upstairs, high-pitched and ear-ringing. A girl. Hurried footsteps drummed across the floorboards above as children rushed to the source. Tashami had winced at the sound, his mind having been prepared for the verbal assault from Mother. Instead, she ran past him, hiking up her dress and exposing flat shoes and the bottoms of her stockings.

He turned and followed. She reached the staircase in the foyer much faster. The front door burst open, Father disheveled as he wasted no time in racing up the stairs on his wife's heels while sparing Tashami no mind.

At the top of the stairs, Tashami found several children crowded around the doorway to the study. They split to make a path for his parents, his mother even placing a hand against Panelle's face to move him out of the way. Something bad was inside; Tashami knew it, but that didn't stop him from approaching. The other children who had been studying in the basement's rooms were just now arriving.

Much shorter than everyone else, he managed to maneuver through the throng until he was at the forefront, stricken with the sight of a ghastly mutilation. He wretched, and yellow sludge splattered against the floorboards. No three-year-old should have seen something like this.

Halice, at the age of eleven, had tried taking her own life. Her eyes were bloody sockets, one eyeball atop her study table, the other hanging from a string of sinew in her skull. A quill hung from the eyeball, punctured by its tip.

Coddling Halice's face against her chest, Mother screamed at Father to close the door, leaving the rest of the children outside alone, staring at each other in horror.

*　　　*　　　*

There were no games after that. Weeks passed, and all the work Father had put into helping the orphans combat their nature slowly regressed. No fault of Father. In fact, he hadn't been rattled, but how could one expect children to recover from such an image? Dinnertime was no longer a boisterous event at the long table, but hollow and filled with clattering tableware as Mother and Father offered conversation topics as bait. Hide-and-seek died. No one studied in sequester anymore, but in large groups spread out around the living room among a symphony of turning pages and scratching quills. Mother or Father always proctored, seated in the armchair.

Father had always carried out meetings with the children one on one. It was a tri-weekly affair for each child save Joni and Tashami, who Father claimed didn't need it. Tashami didn't know what the meetings were about since nobody shared information with him. Even Joni knew—an advantage of his age. Father shared more with him.

But since the day they found Halice's maimed face, those meetings doubled in length. And whereas before, the orphan would come out looking rejuvenated and happy, now they exited just as empty as they entered. Father didn't look the same anymore. That aged face of wisdom, the gentle smile that packed more spirit than any full-toothed grin, was losing life. Bags settled under the eyes, and his lips sat on a permanent downward tilt. It was like that day had hurt him more than any of the children.

Comparatively, Mother's lamentation—at least the visual aspects of it—lasted only a few days before returning to her normal self. She became the backbone of the foster home, keeping the children upright and motivated to the best of her ability. She cooked, cleaned, and even laughed a time or two, though Joni would look at her strangely each time she did. He noticed something different in it while Tashami heard only a laugh.

Her anger and discipline didn't dissipate, but neither did her compassion. When Tashami overheard Joni and Nina, the two eldest children, discuss Mother, Joni claimed the woman was overcompensating for Father's shortcomings in recovery. With Father out of commission in regards to being a presence around the house, Mother stepped up to fill his void. Her dedication to feigning normality in herself was to restore a sense of normality for the children. She would be the anchor to this home, grounding it during times of distress and hopelessness.

At three years old, Tashami couldn't comprehend the complexity of that thought process. But the sleeping him—at the age of twenty-two—interpreted the nightmare as such. Father was hurting because he felt he had failed the children. Because of that, the normally upbeat man was now downtrodden with remorse. The Unbreakable teetered on the verge of breaking, so Mother did everything she could to fix it.

Father took Tashami into his bedroom one afternoon at the heart of second-night. It was mostly dark. Three candles spread throughout the room cast flickering orange glows and long shadows in multiple directions. Father had Tashami sit on the bed, a rickety thing, but big enough to barely fit both parents. Father grabbed a bench that sat in front of a desk and mounted mirror, wooden jars of mother's face paints scattered before it, and placed it at the foot of the bed before taking a seat. He stared at Tashami for a protracted moment and then exhaled out of his nose, glancing down at the floorboards.

"We aren't Cynnish," he whispered. This was only for their ears, his whisper lower than normal.

"Yes we are," Tashami replied, ignoring the logical part of his mind that told him he'd been questioning the differences between him and the others for months now.

"We're called Spiritians," Father said.

"What's that?"

"People from the Spirit Kingdom. Every kingdom has an opposite; the Spirit and Cyn Kingdoms are that."

"Why are we here then?"

Father held his gaze, a twinkle illuminating his right eye despite not smiling. "No interruptions, Tashami. Let me say my piece. I didn't plan on telling you this until you were older, but given the circumstances and what you saw recently ... Well, plans change." He extended an arm and placed a mighty hand against Tashami's cheek, swiping a thumb beneath the boy's eye to catch a tear. Tashami didn't know why he was crying, which frustrated him.

"Learning you're different than those you'd likely call your brothers and sisters is heartbreaking," Father said, bringing clarity to the boy's emotions. He had a knack for that, as did Mother. "But know that differences don't make you any less the same." He paused, then chuckled, amused by the baffled expression on Tashami's face. "Joni loves ham, right?" he asked.

Tashami nodded.

"And you hate it."

"I like chicken." Tashami said it with resentment. Chicken was a rare meal. They were lucky to eat it once in a month's time. Something about chickens living in different kingdoms. "Do chickens live in the Spirit Kingdom?"

Father laughed, no longer worried about the secrecy of their conversation. Tashami hadn't heard him laugh in weeks. The man leaned back and slapped his knee, chest swelling and sinking in tune with the laughter. "I need to talk with you more!"

Tashami tilted his head, but smiled. He made Father happy again.

"Yes, yes," Father said, regaining his composure. "The Spirit Kingdom is one of them." He sighed, and lowered his voice again. The conversation came easier to him afterward. "Despite Joni's love of ham and your love of chicken, you're still brothers, right?"

"Yeah."

"And those differences make you all the more human, which make you all the more alike." Tashami didn't respond, so Father continued. "The difference between Spiritians like us and Cynnish like the other children here is that you begin life with a massive privilege because of your genetics …" He trailed off and narrowed his eyes, searching for something too small to see. "Because of traits only Spiritians are born with. Do you know what a soul is?"

Tashami shook his head.

"It's the life of your body." Father made a fist and flexed, tightening it. "The core of your body. The thing that shapes who you are, from the emotional to philosophical sides of things. It makes you resilient and …" he tapered off again, then rubbed his eyes with a slight groan. "This is why I waited until Joni was older. How do I say this without it sounding like a university class?"

"The life of your body, so what gives you reason to live," said Tashami. He didn't know what "resilient" or "philosophical" meant, but he understood the rest.

Father blinked, holding his son's gaze. "Wow. Yes. That's it! It drives you to keep living. All those reasons to live—the people you love, the goals you wish to achieve, the good for which you're destined—accumulate in your soul. For Spiritians, our souls naturally strengthen as we age because of our Spirit Energy, which is something that flows through our body. That's a lesson for a different day. Cynnish, however, they are the opposite. Their souls dissipate as they age."

Confusion twisted Tashami's features once again.

"It, uh … it degrades."

"Rot?"

"No, no," Father said, his voice getting lower while gaining an edge. "I don't like that word. Don't use it. Nothing about them rots. The Cynergy that flows through them *weakens* their soul."

"Oh …" Tashami became sad. That wasn't fair.

"This means they become empty eventually," said Father. "They slowly lose reasons to live, and their body drains their life force. It's why they look different than us, why someone like Nina has graying roots while only being thirteen. And it's why I came here a decade ago."

"From our real home?" Tashami asked.

"Our *first* home," corrected Father. "This is our second home, and just as real. I came here to inspire the children of the Void, most of whom are destined to become hollow shells that drift through the motions until death grants them turmoil. Cynnish never die peacefully. I wanted to make a change, become a positive influence." He held up a finger. "And keep in mind, none of this is their fault. They didn't choose to be born here. When you see a Cynnish adult who shows no kindness, know that they're a product of their genetics and environment. From birth, nature works against them. As they grow older, their environment doesn't help, for there is no one around who can show them otherwise."

"How do you do it?" Tashami asked. "With words? You make them happy by telling them stories?"

"Yes, I seem to do more talking than anything else, which can work in any other kingdom, where people seek out therapists. And it works a bit here, too. But with the Cynnish, the most effective methods are directly remedial ... or straight-to-the-point. I find the source—their soul—and inject it with life, little by little. My Spirit Energy can help others through special techniques. But I can't use it too much or too frequently, otherwise it'll have permanent effects on me that can't be fixed. Then what use would I be?"

A rare moment of silence passed, during which Tashami gave the revelations thought. Like most three-year-olds, he typically reacted without thought. Not here; not now. "But Halice still did what she did," the boy said softly. "No happy person would do that. You couldn't fix her. Are you broken, Father?"

The Unbreakable visibly quivered. His lip and eyebrow twitched, and he looked away from Tashami. If he wasn't broken before, he was surely about to shatter now. But he recomposed himself after a cathartic breath, refocusing on his son. "I am not perfect. I've healed so many souls in my past, which only happened because I had to heal the most broken soul of them all when I was a teenager ... my own. But the Cyn Kingdom presents different challenges. I've never battled Cynergy. Halice is the most difficult soul I've ever encountered. We were making progress, but then she regressed inexplicably. Cynergy is erratic and unpredictable. The Linsani don't help."

"Why do you try to fix everything?" Tashami asked. "That's not fair."

"Nothing's fair, Son. Look no further than the very existence of a kingdom such as this." He spread his arms to the sides. "I've never regretted the decision to come here. But you're right in some ways; I do need help. Your mother gets upset with me sometimes about it, but she sees the good we're doing here ... every time one of the kids cracks a smile.

Those games of hide-and-seek were her favorite moments. The exuberant laughter; the pitter-patter of cautious hiders as they moved through the house; the thuds when doors slammed shut on a seeker's face."

Tashami's eyebrows crumpled. "Mother hated that. She screamed at me twice the last game."

"She likes it," Father said with a wink. "Don't let her fool you. And just because she didn't play with all of you doesn't mean she didn't enjoy it just as much, listening and watching from the living room ... But nobody has played in a month. I wish you all would return to doing so. I can only do so much in my meetings. Your mother and I need help."

He paused with watery eyes, voice shaking.

"Tashami, can you and Joni help us?"

49

The High Warden

"Everyone has a specialty," said Arithmys, who was standing behind a seated Agnos, looking over his shoulder at what he was reading.

He had made it his mission to divulge nothing of his purpose here to her despite her being the forerunner of candidates to join him in the Warpfinate. He didn't know her that well, and he could only put so much weight into Evelyn's words of support. Also, there was a chance they couldn't get either of the Prim Diatia away from Ipsas. With that uncertainty, sharing secrets about Erafeen, the age before Known History and the title of the Thunder Queen's chronicle, seemed rambunctious. If he left here without the Prim Diatia, it was better they not know his purpose. Even if they were great people, that didn't mean information couldn't be tortured out of them by whatever kinds of evil led this school. Therefore, he read a book on the Primmish perspective on the nature of Goodness while Erafeen was stored in the desk's bottom drawer.

"Mine is mathematics," she said, leaning closer, her chest pressed against his shoulder. He shifted sideways and grimaced. "Or arithmetic, hence the name. I come from a town where your profession or skill is assigned to you the moment of birth. My parents took it a step further and decided to name me after my skill."

"What's two hundred and seventy-four times thirty-six?" asked Tashami, who sat on the floor against the bed, tossing a ball of socks in the air.

"Nine thousand eight hundred and sixty-four," she said after two seconds of mental computation.

Agnos turned and looked up at her, honestly impressed. He excelled at all subjects, far beyond ninety-nine percent of the population, but even he couldn't have figured that out without parchment and a quill.

"Is that right, Agnos?" Tashami asked.

Agnos grabbed a quill and some parchment, then did the math. He stared at the answer. "Yes."

"Maybe if you had asked me something more advanced, you could have stumped me," she said. "I can't do everything in my head. Anything involving advanced accounting, where I must balance revenues, expenses, and payrolls, requires tables and graphs. Then add financial forecasting, and that's a whole different beast … and a dangerous one if I get anything wrong. Companies rely on me."

"You're a professional?" Agnos asked, almost absentmindedly as he tried to imagine how she did the multiplication in her head.

"I'm a member of Ipsas's Accountant's Guild." She left the desk and leaned back against the wall, careful to avoid a hole that looked into the shadows between rooms. "I'm not the president or a director or anything, but I could be I think … Well, I don't know if I have the tools needed anymore." She paused, gaze falling to the floor, reflective. She then snapped out of it and looked up. "I am the accountant of a few businesses on campus, but none which are in direct competition with each other—a matter of business ethics."

"That's cool," Tashami said. "Phesaw doesn't have guilds or clubs."

Already familiar with Ipsas's guild system, Agnos glossed over that detail in favor of something else she'd said. "What tools?"

She smiled at him. "Nothing."

He cocked an eyebrow, but dropped the topic. She tilted her head and asked, "So what's your specialty? Like I said, everyone has one."

"Philosophy," he said, "with a focus on metaphysics. I've spent my life inquiring about the existence of human life and our world. How Kuki Sphaira came to be; the meaning of Earth's existence in our sky. A large part of what I do also pertains to the inductive reasoning of logical philosophy. I've been collecting data throughout my life that is leading me to a greater discovery."

"Ah," she said with little emotion. "The dry stuff. Don't get me wrong. As a Primmish, I appreciate that kind of intellectual path—it's probably the deepest, most convoluted scholarly route—but I could never fathom how anyone could find joy in it."

Tashami raised an invisible glass, as if to toast to that. "Here, here."

She smirked and mocked his gesture, then turned to Agnos again. "Classical idealism?"

He nodded. Religious and modern idealism had never been his belief, the former being illegal. "I want answers," he said. "The absolute truth and nothing else."

"The chance of you finding the truth about our world's origin is about zero percent," she said flatly.

"That would mean impossible, with which I disagree."

"Not impossible. I said 'about.'"

He shrugged. "Semantics."

Tashami groaned. "I hate this. It's like my brain's gone numb. Could you two be any more of a bore?"

"Ignore him," Agnos said, noting Arithmys's offended frown. "He's looking for a reaction. I think he got it from Himitsu."

"A friend?" she asked.

"Yeah." And that was all he said about that.

The three of them would go on to talk for another hour before Arithmys left, leaving Agnos and Tashami as a pair once again. They had spent weeks in this room, mostly without any other company. Evelyn had taken a room down the hall. In coming to Ipsas, he had expected an adventure, a mission. Years of being a Jestivan followed by years as a pirate had made him used to excitement. He thought he would have enjoyed the downtime, the opportunity to stand still. But he was growing antsy, and Tashami's presence was becoming more of a distraction from his reading then it ever had been since meeting the Spiritian.

He looked at Tashami, who glanced away, pretending he hadn't already been staring. Slowly, he looked back again, and their eyes connected. Agnos made a point to keep his eyes locked on Tashami's, to not let them drop lower. He didn't know why that was an urge in the first place. Then he returned to his reading, turning his back to Tashami. Heat flowered in his chest and face, and he could feel Tashami's eyes still bearing into him.

We're brothers, nothing else.

*   *   *

"All we want is Arithmys and Pistimi," said Evelyn, standing behind the chair in which she had been instructed to sit. She wasn't a student at Ipsas anymore, so she had no obligation to take orders from the High Warden. It was foolishly disobedient—perhaps, even childish—but there was history here, and she needed it known it was history for a reason.

High Warden Sylial sat across the desk in an opulent chair with burgundy cushions set into its back. Despite being seated, he barely had to look up at Evelyn, his height besting the two tallest Jestivan: Himitsu and Toshik. Surrounding him were trinkets that operated on Permanence Vessels infused with Dev Chains. A model of Kuki Sphaira rotated in a glass ball that sat atop a Permanence stand, a gem hovered in midair between two Permanence discs, and a small holographic display hovered to one side of his desk, its image projected from a large Permanence box set into the desk. In the display were the front doors to Ipsas's main building, granting an aerial view. Several guards stood outside the doors. It was a surveillance system that didn't require a person recording or broadcasting— the most recent technological marvel from the city of Prayoga.

The High Warden was a proud, disciplined man. He had the posture of a redwood even when seated, his face angled and jawline defined as if chiseled from the very same tree. His hands were folded in his lap, eyes slanted with fierceness only he could obtain. His long, black and silver hair must have seen a comb ten times a day to maintain its sleek straightness. The only marks against his aura of professionalism and high standards were the ripped sleeves of his robes. It was the one vice he granted himself, proud of the ropes of muscles that twisted along his arms, for most Devish didn't bother with physical training. He was that exception, and he'd laud it over them. To Sylial, the mind—something he possessed in great measure—could only do so much when faced with overpowering might.

One didn't find him telekinetically flinging daggers at enemies from the shadows. His battles were face to face, often littered with punches, kicks, elbows, and knees. His favorite method was grappling—a barbaric style of fighting that most modern day warriors believed belonged in back alleys or the first five centuries. Rolling around in the dirt was below skilled fighters. For Sylial, it was the only way to truly measure someone's strength in combat—and sometimes craftiness, for even a heavier opponent could lose to a smaller one if the gap wasn't too wide.

"Ipsas is down to three Diatia," Sylial said. His tone was deep and smooth, but short, cutting off syllables and words in a way that made his sentences sound like a series of drum strikes. "You suggest I make it one."

"Ronossius is a perfectly viable chore boy," she replied. "He listens to you without question, whereas Arithmys and Pistimi give you a hard time. If anything, I'm ridding you of two massive headaches."

"They are difficult, but pose no threat."

"Since when?"

"Since confiscating their ancients."

She paused but didn't betray her emotions. Confiscating an ancient wouldn't have been surprising if they had been the wieldable types, but both Arithmys and Pistimi had body augmentation types, which meant their ancients had been infused in their bodies.

"Yes," Sylial said, sensing concern in Evelyn's pause despite her blank expression. "It was not pleasant, but acts that are necessary for the well-being of this school are, often times, exactly that. And it takes someone like me who won't only talk about it, but be about it. If it is worth anything to you, know that Arithmys offered hers willingly. She was not hurt."

"And Pistimi?" she asked, afraid of the answer.

"He is unwell. I am sure you have noticed his absence since whenever you arrived on the campus proper. He has been out of commission, recovering from injuries sustained during the removal process of his ancient."

A flare erupted in Evelyn's chest, shooting up her neck and filling her head. Three weeks had passed since exiting the Infested Forest and infiltrating the main campus. Most of that time had been spent in the rundown dormitory buildings of Block Genevere—a five-hundred feet stretch of road that held abandoned buildings scorched by fires three hundred years ago. Students with little to no money lived there without plumbing or other modern day conveniences.

Evelyn hadn't seen Pistimi once during the past three weeks, but she had accounted that to her sequester in the dorms of Block Genevere. Only recently had she been able to walk freely through the campus after High Warden Sylial forced her hand. Either she came forward and presented herself and her reason for returning or he hunt her down, including the two companions with whom she'd arrived at the teleplatforms. She might have avoided punishment, but the same mercy wouldn't have been shown to Agnos and Tashami, who weren't just Light Realm foreigners, but Jestivan on top of that. They might have held their own against Sylial, likely even defeat him under the right circumstances, but not without repercussions. And there was more to this school than its High Warden.

She had questioned Arithmys about Pistimi's absence, but received only vague responses with intentions of circumvention. Arithmys didn't like discussing it, but claimed Pistimi was very busy with his first year of teaching the class: *A History of Failed Usurpers*. It was a believable story, considering the young man's knack for spreading knowledge to others— even those who didn't want it.

"You are angry," Sylial said, reaching for a glass of water and taking a long swig. He returned it to the desk and straightened once more. "Yet not at me ... Well, not mostly at me. Arithmys did not tell you, I assume."

Her silence was her answer.

"Shameful on her part," he said. "I expected a fight from her, not Pistimi. He is the coward—or so I had thought."

"Who did you threaten?" she asked, knowing Arithmys wouldn't have given in so easily had it only been her life or health on the line.

At this, the man's dark side materialized in the form of a smile. Warden Sylial came off as a good man to those too far removed to see him properly. He exuded honor, and that was true in most cases, but he also understood the political nature of possessing absolute authority. Might Commander Jewel was seen as the villain of the school because Sylial created that illusion. Students fell for his posturing, unaware of the fear—not respect—that subdued them. But his gentler methods of manipulation toward the student body and faculty didn't extend to those with whom he had direct dealings. With the Diatia and five wardens, they had to experience Sylial's more sinister puppetry.

"Drasys," he said.

Evelyn said nothing. Arithmys had forked over her ancient to protect her little brother, who was also an Ipsas student. As for Pistimi, he had only himself to value because he had nobody else. He was an only child, and his parents died shortly after his birth from a genetic disorder frequently seen in those whose ancestors belonged to the two towns that were massacred by Brenson Ulial centuries ago. Evelyn's swell of rage was now fully directed at Sylial.

"If you have their ancients," she said, "what do you need Arithmys and Pistimi for? Find another Primmish who can use them."

"You act like there is a pool of Primmish students from which to pick. There are fourteen total, none of whom have the weaving skill to operate either ancient. Besides, I want their minds. They are the two most intelligent students to grace Ipsas since Tazama Bandia. I cannot have a traitor bringing them to the Light Realm, where they will join the Jestivan and strengthen their ranks even further beyond the already-massive gap between us and them."

"Pathetic," spat Evelyn. "You're still griping about that? The Diatia failed, miserably. Largely thanks to your failed leadership. You do realize nobody cares about this school or the Diatia, right? The Jestivan have forgotten your existence, and consider that a blessing."

"Insults and threats serve no purpose other than to give me reason not to grant you permission to take the two Prim Diatia."

"You wouldn't free them anyways," she said. "So I'll do as I please. I'm not that little fifteen-year-old girl you recruited into the Diatia anymore. I can beat you."

Sylial crossed his arms and looked her up and down, though her bottom half was hidden behind the chair. "A moment to which I'm sure you look forward … in your dreams of delusion."

Evelyn didn't bite at the bait. She'd done enough of that already. Instead, she asked, "Are you going to let me see Pistimi?"

"He is not fit for company."

"Well then," she said, inhaling deeply and collecting herself to leave. "I trust that this meeting will keep you from hunting me or my companions down."

His jaw clenched at what he likely viewed the most damning insult of anything she had said up to this point. "I am a man of my word," he said, tone steady. "You may walk the campus as you see fit, but do so knowing you left bitter-friends-turned-enemies here when you abandoned the school. Nobody will face discipline if they choose to … accidentally attack you. As for your two friends, if they make the mistake of voluntarily revealing themselves, I will confront them personally. I promised you I would not seek them out. It's a different story if they put themselves in my sightline."

Evelyn nodded in understanding. She would deal with him properly in time, but there was someone else she needed to confront. Agnos had expressed concern with Tashami's mentality and actions recently, stating a steady growth in its severity since the night of their imprisonment at the teleplatforms. She wasn't blind, nor did she have to know Tashami for years to notice the unnatural downward trajectory of his spirit. Thus, she'd find Ronossius and have a little chat.

She turned to leave, weaving a thick carapace of ice along her back. With anyone else, this would have been a precautionary measure to shield herself from a blindside projectile attack. With High Warden Sylial, this was a taunt—another insult toward his character. He didn't believe in ranged attacks or blindside maneuvers. They were cowardly in combat, tactics reserved only for the political sphere. The fact that she armored her back implied she didn't trust him to stick to those beliefs. An attack on his honor—the greatest blow she could have dealt.

50

A Spy's Many Layers

With free exploration of the campus returned to her, Evelyn strode eastward through the Infested Forest. She reached the teleplatforms by evening, the light of second-day washing over the expanse of field between sea and forest. Alerted by guards who watched the path, Commander Jewel met with her before she had a chance of stepping more than a few dozen paces out of the forest. She was surprised to see him. Part of her assumed he might have fled after the fiasco of the night of her arrival, lacking confidence in himself to hold his tongue about his role in the ruse when confronted by Warden Sylial.

"Someone's either really bold or really stupid," he said, thinking he could simply stop in front of her to halt her progress.

She walked around him, sparing him a brief glance. "Definitely not stupid. Do I look like Bruut?"

He chuckled and turned, but didn't follow. "I miss that kid," he yelled after her.

"Where's Ronossius?" she asked, turning to face him while walking backward.

"In there." He tilted his head toward the inn.

She offered a whimsical salute and headed in that direction, leaving Jewel to bark orders at a nearby group of soldiers.

The inn's bar was as lavish as she remembered. Since it served as any visitor's first impression of Ipsas, the school had poured money into its upkeep, even blessing the innkeeper, who everyone knew as Neps, with a substantial salary for his skills. The High Wardens of the last four hundred years wanted students and guests to know what kind of wealth could be found here. What better way to do that than by starting people in a bar that functioned more like a lounge?

Instead of booths with wooden benches and small, circular tables with flimsy chairs, there were sofas and armchairs with fine burgundy cloth and gold string lining the seams; coffee tables and end tables of the deepest mahogany wood slicked with polish; and a lush brown carpet beneath it all. Oil lanterns stood atop some tables, basking everything in a warm glow. Wine glasses hung upside down from an extravagant wooden rack above the bar counter in the back of the room. Padded burgundy leather topped the bar stools. A hearth sat on both ends of the barroom, encircled by piles of plush pillows as large as Evelyn.

Evelyn missed this place. It had been an escape from school in the evenings, if one could ignore the presence of off-duty soldiers. The hearths were prime study areas for students, though nobody actually spent the night here. Lodging was reserved for visitors. Students could remain in the barroom through the night into morning, but only if they kept their voices down and didn't fall asleep. The risk of not making it back to the campus proper for classes the next morning fell squarely on the student's shoulders.

She gathered her breath as she spotted Ronossius accompanied by Josie, a soldier of the school and wife of Commander Jewel. She had stood guard of Evelyn, Agnos, and Tashami's cells and was responsible for bringing Ronossius to Tashami. If there was anyone worse than Jewel, it was her. Her complacency with the man's disgusting thirst for inflicting torture was shameful.

They didn't notice Evelyn until she reached their area, a gathering of four armchairs in a circle, a coffee table at the center. She stood between the two empty chairs and asked, "May I speak with Ronossius alone?"

Josie raised an eyebrow. As a Powish, she was tall and layered in ropes of muscle, all of which were on display in a sleeveless tunic—garb she couldn't get away with wearing had she been on duty. Her pairing with Ronossius—a spindly Cynnish man whose bone structure lent to shadowy recesses in his face and arms—was comical. She glanced at him before answering, because all of that muscle meant nothing when faced with matters of weaving and clout skill—two areas in which Diatia excelled.

Ronossius nodded, and Josie left without a word. Evelyn moved to take her seat, as it was the chair closest to him. There was something to prove with such a decision—a maneuver not lost on him.

"You have nothing to gain by that," he said, voice empty. "I don't emanate around you, so this isn't as brave as you think it is."

"Emanate" referred to the Cynnish weaving technique of creating a cloud of Cynergy around one's self, degrading the spirit and soul of whoever stepped inside of it. Most Cynnish could only create a bubble a couple feet wide, but someone with Ronossius's skill could encompass this entire building. And with Evelyn seated this close to him—the apex of the cloud—she'd receive the bulk of its power. He rarely emanated when in the vicinity of someone he respected, but she liked to remain close to show him she didn't care if he did or not.

"Did you emanate around my friend?"

"Of course this is what you come here for," he said, shaking his head in disappointment. "I am supposed to be your friend, not him."

"Come now. While you're more tolerable than Bruut, Gina, Halluci, or Groto, that doesn't make you a friend. We don't see eye to eye, and whatever that thing you did to Tashami only made my opinion of you worse."

"You don't have authority to comment on that," he said, drawing a genuine laugh out of her.

"And who are you to have authority on his punishment?" she asked. "You became a tool of Josie's anger. She sent you after Tashami because I goaded her into retaliation. Since when do you serve as an attack dog?"

He fell silent for a moment, eyes gazing into hers. "Call it what you will," he finally said. "But I know what I know, and you should shut your mouth on the topic." He sipped on a glass of clear liquor and returned it to the end table. "You're smart—smarter than I—but that doesn't mean your knowledge extends to the personal matters of others. You won't learn my life from a text book."

Her eyes narrowed, searching for the meaning in the cryptic words. What did Josie's petty anger and Tashami have to do with him, personally? Knowing he wouldn't elaborate on that, she returned to her original question: "What did you do to him?"

"Exactly what you thought."

"But he's still showing signs of melancholy, while emanation causes temporary symptoms. It's been weeks now."

"You're a Diatia, Evelyn. You know we don't follow ordinary laws of nature. We do things others can't. I heard you froze over an entire river ... and the Knowledge River at that. Isn't that one of the widest in the world? There are rumors of one of the Jestivan dropping a moon on Ulna Malen. Bryson LeAnce defeated the Rogue Demon—the very man who killed Chelekah."

They let that final name dangle between them as bait. Despite being one of the most damaged people she had ever met in her life, she had been drawn to Chelekah, viewing him as a project in need of fixing. He had also been a dear friend of Ronossius, the two Cyn Diatia having known each other since boyhood. During their short period as Diatia, the three of them had been an interesting trio.

"You think you knew Chelekah," Ronossius said. "And I'll admit you did to a certain extent. But I saw what came before his induction into the Diatia."

"I get it," she snapped, gaze flicking up to the ceiling in annoyance to avoid his face. "A childhood in the Void. Tragedy and suffering. But I came to you about Tashami, the man you hurt on behalf of Josie."

He shook his head and rose from the chair, movements sluggish but smooth like so many Cynnish. Grabbing his glass of liquor, he downed the rest and looked her dead in the eye, exposing his vacant soul and wrathful nature. "Emanation. That's what I did. It will wear off eventually. If you think it's something else, then ask him. The fact that you came to me tells me he's reluctant to share. Maybe you'll find your answer in his silence … or listen to the ramblings in his sleep."

He walked away and brought his glass to the bar.

"You're lying to me, Ronossius," she said, a little too desperately.

He said nothing and left the building.

*   *   *

Creep hacked at the front leg of a hanging pig carcass with a cleaver. He had no idea what he was doing; he was sure his technique was off. But people had to see him actually do some butchery once in their lives. Sunshine's Chopped Meat had ventured into regular territory, meaning he had repeat customers on a daily basis. Through small talk that led to full-blown conversations, he had learned of their home lives and families—even some vices of those with looser lips. On the flipside, they were beginning to question his role in the business. They had never seen him hack at meat—a flaw of the shop's layout. Anyone could look past the front desk and see into the ever-ice room in the back.

He was squelching those doubts today. York, whose father had been a butcher, had spent extra time with Creep overnight to show him the weak points of a pig carcass, the proper angles at which to hack, and when and where to use his other hand as an anchor point on the body. Creep wasn't perfect, and a trained eye would notice it, but he was good enough. York— the wily bastard that he was—had played down his butchery skills ever since opening the shop, knowing more savvy customers might notice the superiority of his technique when compared to the man who was supposed to be his master.

Creep looked toward the front of house, where a dozen customers crowded the small space. Five stood in line, one forced to stand outside, and the rest were seated on benches along the front wall. York wrote someone's order and then walked into the ever-ice room, pinning it to the bulletin board at the front. The bulletin board was around the corner and out of sight from the front room, so York took that opportunity to motion the proper hacking angle to Creep. The "master" butcher readjusted his stance as the "apprentice" returned to the front desk.

He heard a knock from the door in the side wall of the ever-ice room. It was one of two back doors, this one locked at all times. Creep's special clients used it, for it wasn't an easy door to find from the outside. The alley in which it sat wasn't accessible directly from the street. A person had to slip down a narrow alley two shops down, then traverse an even skinnier path that ran between the backs of two buildings on parallel streets. Anyone claustrophobic wouldn't make it more than a few paces through before the press of stone against their chest sent them shuffling back. If the person made it past that, then they'd find the alley where Creep's door waited.

He removed his butcher's gloves and threw them atop a bloody table, then opened the side door with Soraku's blade raised as a precaution. He really needed to install a peephole.

A woman with red hair stared at the blade, then blinked up at him. "Excuse me. Your mother ever tell you it's rude to point things in a woman's face?"

He lowered the blade, head cocking as he processed the implications of this woman showing up at his door for special clients. "Sally ...?"

She stepped past him and grabbed herself from a chill. She was wearing a striped green and yellow tunic and black trousers, the staff attire at the Electric Eel. It was half past three o'clock in the afternoon, which meant she was likely on her way to her bar soon—not without a pit stop here, apparently.

"Step inside my office," he said, opening the door and extending a hand. "No lady should stand naked in such conditions."

She swept into the room with a smile on her face. "*This* is naked?"

York had entered the ever-ice room to pin another slip of parchment to the bulletin board. He caught a glimpse of Sally just as she disappeared into Creep's office. He paused. Creep shrugged, then followed her.

"What a surprise," he said after closing the door and taking a seat at his desk.

"Is it though?"

"You've been hanging out in my bar for months now, eyes skittering every which way, but with a keen interest in the booths at the front." She had leaned back in her chair, a leg kicked over the other, hands folded atop her lap. *Getting comfortable.* "Don't get me wrong; you're good at what you do, but as a bar owner who makes a living behind the bar, I've picked up certain skills in observation. You see, in order to obtain substantial tips, I must decipher quirks in personalities and tendencies in actions or conversation—this way I know exactly how to pander to the customer I'm serving … make them feel like I care." She paused and twisted her lips. "Empathy and all that jazz. With some people, it's less of that and more direct truths, even if they're jaded or judgmental. People who frequent bars are the types who don't need sugar-coated air."

"And what did all your analytics say about me?" he asked.

"Easy-going. Too easy-going. A nonchalance that whispered 'I have no mundane, real-life problems, just a job to execute and objective to achieve.'" She paused, then asked, "Do you have bills, Sunshine?"

"How do you think I keep this place going?" he asked, speaking of the shop.

She nodded. "Family, taxes?"

"I'm a person just like you." Creep's expression remained indiscernible. He'd been backed into a corner by the last person he would have suspected, but he knew to remain in character. This bold play by Sally could have been a reach in hopes to land damning information. And considering her position as the bar owner of a hot spot for rebel congregation, he couldn't believe he hadn't thought of it before. This woman knew she harbored rebels. Was the Electric Eel a haven for them—one which she funded?

Creep, you idiot. Blinded by another mature, independent woman with an exotic hair color. Why did that have to be his thing? Better yet, why couldn't the bar owner have been an old man with a limp? That would have been more suspicious. Alas, it also implied he couldn't see women like Soraku, Rose, and Sally as power players above men. He frowned. He thought himself better than that.

"Awful lot of introspection going on in there," said Sally after waiting out the silence.

He had been the last one to say something, so the fact that she'd paused meant she'd done so on purpose. He grinned. *Oh, you are good … and probably dangerous.*

530

"Why do you think I'm here?" she asked.

"A visit? To do business with me? We both know your establishment has received a fair share of its revenue from me, so perhaps you're returning the favor." He paused. "After all, I do have bills to pay."

"Business of a different kind than mere commerce," she said. "What do you do with the bodies?"

"Usually chop them up and sell them to my paying customers."

She smiled. "I know you're being sardonic, but there are rumors that the butcher named Sunshine serves his prey to his customers."

He cocked an eyebrow. "We're talking pigs here, right?"

"Humans."

The word fell out of her mouth so bluntly, the impact might have left a dent in his floor. "Excuse me?" Something told him she knew what she was talking about. How else would she have known to use the side door? However, it was best not to assume these things. A common tactic to lure out intelligence was to feign knowledge with vague statements, hoping the mark would fill in the blanks with specifics. That's what this felt like.

"Colleagues of mine have done business with you," she said. "They pay a pretty coin, and you take out their trash, leaving no evidence behind. You've eliminated three enemies of the rebels already. Croinys, Dren, and Leland confirmed that the individuals they paid you to kill haven't been seen or heard from since. Where do the bodies go?"

She knew names, and he could see it in her face—the emergence of a glower—that she wasn't pretending to know about his operations. "They are disposed of," he said. "And, clearly, I'm not at liberty to discuss methods or locations."

Leaning forward, she slapped a slip of parchment on the desk. "Then I have a target of my own."

He stared at it from afar. "And you have payment?"

"Free drinks from now until the end of time."

"I'd take you up on that offer, if it could help me pay the bills."

Her lips quirked up into a wry smirk. "Touché."

He reached forward and snagged the slip. "So who's the pain in the ass this time? Another civilian vigilante who thinks he can topple the rebels and defend the crown?"

She laughed. "Oh, dear. Why would I target one of my own?"

"One of your own?" he asked incredulously. "You just named Croinys, Dren, and Leland as colleagues, all of whom are known rebels."

"Did I?" she said whimsically. "I see you're searching for clarity. York can provide that for you." She stood. "As far as payment, there is none. This is an assignment from your superior—which is me, mind you. Eliminate the person whose name is on that slip and you will be rewarded greatly in the Archaic Kingdom. Spy Pilot Ophala is willing to grant you anything within reasonable boundaries, Creep."

The last word—his real name—was a lead weight. As she reached for the door handle, she paused and turned. "Also, you're not the only one with this assignment. The person on that paper has a partner also in the city. The pair serves as the rebels' leaders. One mark has been given to you; the other to another assassin. So be on the lookout for a boy—sixteen, seventeen perhaps—with long red hair. You might cross paths. He is not an enemy." She left the room.

Creep visibly balked. What just happened? Had Ophala played him? How many layers were involved in this ruse? He unfolded the slip of parchment. He would speak with York at the soonest possible chance and receive answers. He didn't serve for ...

He blinked at the name: *Periphan LeAnce.*

*   *   *

"Help me understand," said Creep. He stood next to York, whose apron was bloodied from sawing at a cow's leg. Creep was supposed to be paying attention and mimicking the apprentice with the cow on his own table, but he couldn't focus on something that felt so trivial now.

It was just past midnight. The shop had closed for the day hours ago. Curtains were drawn shut over the expanse of windows at the front of the shop. Two Intelights, courtesy of York, cast the ever-ice room in a stark white glow.

"The Spy Pilot didn't trust you," York said. "Simple as that."

Creep placed gloved hands against the table and leaned forward, staring through the skinned cow. It made sense, but that didn't quell his frustration.

So the whole time he'd been working on this case—albeit, making progress while doing so—had been nothing more than a test. He was dumbfounded, but it was a clever tactic that proved Ophala covered all bases.

"You can't expect Pilot Ophala to implicitly trust you because you said you had ties with Praetor Poicus. Yes, it's a mammoth name with an even grander legacy, but what does it mean when Poicus isn't alive to provide confirmation?" He cut through the leg and held it aloft, inspecting it before slapping it down on a smaller table to his right. "You're a hybrid—and that's amazing. Nobody like that exists anymore, not officially. But you show up in the Intel Kingdom after not existing for decades, during which you apparently spent working for Primmish elites, and expect True Light leaders to not question your motives?"

"I was there under Mynute Senex's orders," Creep said.

"Another person who's not alive to confirm."

Creep began sawing at his cow's leg, using it as an avenue to redirect his frustration.

"Not only that," said York, "but Pilot Ophala spoke at length with the leaders of the operation to save the Powish slaves. They said you worked with Rhyparia NuForce, the Jestivan responsible for annihilating Ulna Malen and eradicating the entire Powish royal family. One man said you stoked her fire. That alone made Pilot Ophala want to move on from you immediately, lock you up and put you on trial, but there were enough conflicting opinions from SLO leaders to give her pause. She decided to give you a chance by placing you in this role."

York leaned back against his table, wiping his gloves on his apron. He stared at the opposite wall, not paying Creep's butchery any attention. "Sally and I were assigned to monitor your progress. I kept an eye on you here; she watched you at the Electric Eel. Her assignment was a little different than mine, however, for she'd been stationed at that bar long before we received roles. She's been hunting down rebels for a couple months longer and, in doing so, has infiltrated their ranks and acts as a double agent."

"And what if I had decided to scout a different bar over the past couple months?" Creep asked.

"Wouldn't have happened. Horos and I dropped hints that led you there."

"Horos?" said Creep.

"Yes. He's the Spy Pilot's husband and has been watching you during moments between here and the bar, when neither I nor Sally can focus on you." The shop fell silent, and a sigh escaped the apprentice—a title that no longer fit from Creep's perspective. He had been the rat in a larger experiment, York the scientist poking at him with a stick. "Listen. You still managed to help out a lot. Sally only discovered the identities of the leaders two days ago, which she says wouldn't have happened without your acting skills at the rally the other day when the poor kid was assassinated."

Creep dropped his tool, giving up on the task. He had wondered why he didn't receive a visit after that night. He thought someone from the rebels would have reached out to him after seeing his rage directed toward the crown. They had simply contacted Sally instead, having established a relationship with her and knowing she had developed a rapport with Creep at the bar. They must have asked for her opinion on him, and she, somehow, twisted all of that into a way of deepening her infiltration into the rebels' ranks.

He had a sudden nauseous sensation. "Was that entire rally planned?"

York closed his eyes. "No. Gore wasn't supposed to be assassinated. The rebels, unfortunately, suspected him a spy. And knowing they would dispose of him, they found a way to make it look like those who worked under the royals would have been responsible. Make him useful in some way."

"So is this real?" Creep asked, holding up the slip with his target's name. "The test is over?"

"Very real. Periphan LeAnce is one of many siblings who sit on the League of Weavineers' Board of Directors in Brilliance. She's been funding the rebels from the northern city for months now, but just recently has relocated to the capital with her brother, Commissioner Wendel, who we don't believe has any knowledge of the rebels or his sister's criminal funding."

"Anything I should know about her?"

"Not yet," York said. "Sally is collecting what information she can, while Horos is reporting directly to Princess Lilu, Spy Pilot Ophala, and other relevant powers. Princess Lilu is believed to have had dealings with the LeAnce family during her tenure in Brilliance."

Creep wanted to know who the other target that Sally had mentioned was, but knew he wouldn't be given the answer. Knowing both names was unnecessary, for he needed to focus on one target without distraction.

"Who is Horos targeting?"

"Minor rebel leaders," York said. "His face and identity are too well known, so he operates in secrecy and kills from the shadows. That sort of thing doesn't work with larger profile names like Periphan LeAnce, who are protected at all times, so we need assassins who can operate in the open and gain the trust of people close to the big wigs."

Creep picked up his saw and returned to carving the leg, and York took that as the hybrid's cue of understanding and acceptance. They worked for two more hours before retiring for the night. During his walk back to his apartment, Creep marveled at Pilot Ophala's methodical mind.

She was deserving of that position, certainly.

51

The Skylight's Gimmick

Strolls through the herbal gardens with Doctor Mengai had become more enjoyable over the weeks, as the elderly woman's sporadic questions on medicinal topics rescinded, noticing the progress in Kaylee's studies. The doctor was beginning to respect her pupil, finding satisfaction in Kaylee's astuteness.

Today, they focused on antidotes. Doctor Mengai did little speaking, allowing Kaylee to ramble on about each herb they passed, such as which part of the herb provided the required ingredient, what other ingredients it needed to be paired with, dosages, and which poisons they counteracted. This was information she had found only briefly touched on in texts back home, the subjects involving geographical locations and what the medicines treated. None, however, knew the technical aspects such as the technique of application or dosages. Mengai was a walking text book of everything Kaylee wanted to learn.

She had a specific question she wanted to ask during today's lesson, but had to wait for the proper moment to bring it up—a moment when the question would hold relevance and thus not seem random and desperate. Himitsu had no way of contacting his mother, which she understood must have been difficult. The two of them were close, and what kind of son wouldn't want to let their mother know he's okay? They hadn't prepared for the impossibility of no contact with birds.

When Kaylee reached a patch of herbs that grew like clovers from long, spiraling stems, she seized the opportunity. "False Clover. A spring herb that can only survive with plenty of rain. The stem vine on which it grows contains aux plasma within, which is a yellow paste that is most potent in the roots and most productive at countering poisons—when in antidote form—that attack a person's vocal chords. However, that antidote, Auxythm, also requires the barb of a songbird, preferably a swallow."

"And what's a fun fact about Auxythm?" Mengai asked. She liked to do that from time to time: add fun to their lessons. Kaylee hadn't been betting on her asking that question for this herb, but it was convenient, for it transitioned smoothly into her question.

"It costs a lot of money to make."

Mengai nodded. "Very good." She continued walking, but Kaylee remained by the False Clovers. Mengai turned.

"Why does it cost so much? Are the herbs that difficult to grow?" Kaylee asked, already knowing the true answer.

"Has nothing to do with the herbs, but the barbs," said Mengai. "How many birds have you seen since arriving to the Loess?"

"A few, but they were on the uppermost plateaus of the western wall, where the farmlands were."

"Exactly. None come near the buttes, for they have no reason to."

"You're telling me a bird has never seen the massive skylights in the buttes or tunnel openings in the cliffsides of the plateaus and decided to fly inside?"

"That is exactly what I'm telling you," she said. "Difficult to believe, but not when you know the secrets behind the skylights and tunnel openings."

Kaylee paused, looking for an avenue from which to attack her next question. Clearly, they were "secrets" for a reason, and she wasn't sure how willing Mengai was to share—or if she knew the specifics at all.

"My companion was taken to the Piety Mines recently," Kaylee said, "where he met a relative of yours ... goes by the name of Joselina."

Mengai didn't respond immediately, face pensive. "Is that who visited her?"

"You know?"

"Yes," Mengai said, looking off to the side. "It's one of the very few favors the Soteria family grants me: written communication with my relatives around the Piety Mines. But before I go any further, describe the visitor and explain the situation to me."

She was being careful—not sure she could trust Kaylee—so she wanted to hear Kaylee's story to make sure it lined up with what she knew.

"Young man with tan, almost caramel, skin," Kaylee said. "Black hair that falls to his shoulders. A scar on his face. He was physically assaulted by a Loess officer for, allegedly, stealing pious minerals from the smithy. Truth was that Joselina gave it to him as what we're believing was a test of loyalties. He took the beating without telling the truth, allowing the officers to believe he stole it. Joselina put her life on the line with the maneuver, which is proof to me of how desperate she is to escape her role in this place."

Mengai's face became grim, nodding to herself. "We all are."

"They have my companion under strict lockdown now. He can't leave our rooms. Kopios Soteria has lost trust, fearing him a victim of greed. I came here to learn from the best, not from prisoners. I don't like what's being forced of you. I want to help, but that's impossible if I can't contact a certain person that my companion knows very well."

Mengai's eyes drifted right and left. She turned and walked, and Kaylee followed. Mengai returned to lecturing about each herb they passed, but spewed facts Kaylee already knew. The doctor was feigning lessons, for their conversation had ventured into mutinous territory. Best not to be overheard by herbalists who traversed the gardens regularly.

They wound up in a medical supply chamber two floors above, Kaylee with an armful of herbs to make it look as if they would be bottling ingredients for several minutes. Mengai took her to the back of the chamber next to racks of jars of liquid. She began grabbing different containers.

"Every skylight and tunnel entrance, aside from the minor entrances on the upper plateaus, is rimmed with Permanence devices. You've seen the stairs that wind up the butte's interior walls, right?"

"Hard to miss," Kaylee said.

"They lead all the way to the skylight," Mengai replied. "They exist so an Archain by the name of Veil can reach the Permanence vessels up there. She wields an ancient that grants the ability to create illusions. Veil weaves Archaic Chains into the vessel, and it creates a permanent illusion of dirt to anyone who might see the skylight from above. In other words, while we see a skylight from within, a bird would see solid ground from outside. And the same is done at the mouths of tunnels that lead to the Loess's inlands. Veil has to replenish the Permanence vessels every week."

Kaylee dropped the last of her herbs into the liquid in a container. It was clever ... *too* clever. Why would Kopios Soteria feel the need to protect the butte's skylight from exterior sight? She could understand the mouths of tunnels in the sides of the precipices. Outsiders could stumble upon them; they were on level land. The buttes, however, stood taller than the Loess itself. Even from the Loess's elevated sides, a person couldn't see down into the skylight. They wouldn't know if there was a hole or land at the butte's top. That meant it wasn't being protected from people, but something that could fly over and see it from above ... birds.

She twisted on the container's lid, face hard with focus. Were the inlanders hiding from the birds? Did they know about an ancient that could allow someone to dip into a bird's memory and see what they saw ... like Spy Pilot Ophala?

She bit her lip, cursing her deductive reasoning skills. They made her jump to rash conclusions with no bearing, as she often thought further ahead than the common person. But there times when her intuition was correct. Now she was questioning why Pilot Ophala had sent her and Himitsu all the way out here in the midst of a danger such as Mendac LeAnce rising from his grave. Between what appeared to be the enslavement of the Accus family, Himitsu's strange side-missions he'd been getting into since arriving here, the Loess Lord's mistrust of Himitsu, and the lengths to which the lord went to mask the butte's skylights, she was beginning to sense a purpose here of which she had no part.

Her tutelage was staged—a false pretense to distract her from something else. She found herself unbothered by that. She'd play along. While it hurt to know Pilot Ophala didn't trust her fully, she respected that woman enough to trust her. Besides, she found herself pitying Mengai and Joselina Accus while despising Kopios Soteria.

"Thank you, Doctor Mengai," she whispered. "I must leave early today."

Mengai placed a hand on Kaylee's wrist. "Can the Accus family trust you?"

"Yes."

She left the supply chamber with a royal gate, knowing a greater purpose lay in this butte than her career goals. She would do what she could to help Himitsu; she was in love with him.

*   *   *

"I've come to request permission to visit one of the higher steppes," Kaylee said to Loess Lord Kopios as he nocked a bow in a courtyard repurposed as a shooting range.

An archer, good to know.

He took a moment to aim, tongue curled against his top lip in concentration. He released the string, and the arrow sailed fifteen feet to the right of his painted target, snapping against a stone pillar instead.

A terrible archer, better to know.

He lowered the bow and let his arm fall to his side, sighing as he stared at the two halves of shaft. "I'm afraid I'm not cut out for the marksman's life."

She shrugged, choosing to not push her question he'd glossed over. He would get to it; he was stalling as he processed the question, the intent of such a desire, and his answer depending on those first two factors. "You are a lord ... Milord," she said. "That's the life you belong to. There are others who will lay their life on the line on your behalf."

He extended the hand in which he held the bow, and an attendant stepped forward from his station behind the lord, taking the weapon from his grip. Kopios removed his gloves and handed those over, too. He had no quiver, for the attendant had already been carrying it for him, handing him an arrow whenever demanded.

"A correct assessment," he said, taking a glass of water from the attendant—the young man was quite skilled at his job as a pack mule. He turned toward her with a grin. "What does a newcomer want with the upper steppes?"

"A breath of fresh air," she said, causing him to glance upward and then around.

"I suppose you have a point there," he said.

"More importantly, a resemblance to home. I find the Loess extraordinary, but its marvel is waning day by day. I need to see real grass, a wooden home, farmlands, the sky unencumbered by rising cliffs … Heck, even an animal—domesticated, wild, or livestock." She frowned. "I haven't seen a single pup or kitten in this place."

He took a long swig of water, then sighed pleasantly. He twisted his lips and gave it some thought. "Horses," he said. "I can have you escorted to the stables."

She paused, forgetting she had seen horses in the Heresy Butte. In fact, she had ridden on one during her first journey here. *Stupid. Clumsy.*

"That doesn't cure my sky sickness," she said.

"When do you want to go?"

"The earlier, the better."

"And where is it you would want to be taken?"

"There was a very nice family we met when first arriving to the Loess," she said. "They fed and escorted us to the uppermost military caverns."

He groaned. "Oh, yes. Don't remind me. Did I ever apologize to you for making you suffer through living there for a week? The men and women up there are barely capable of fending off a swarm of gnats, forget potential military enemies."

"You didn't," she said, ignoring the insults. She wanted to point out that that was likely his own fault, for nobody up there was armed or trained properly. Their equipment was shoddy and old, their discipline nonexistent.

It was clear the Thousand-Layer Loess didn't provide proper funding to the sentries. Alas, she must hold her tongue in this instance.

He stared at her for some time before smiling. He never directed anger, frustration, or disgust toward her, like she had seen him do to so many others—including Himitsu. If anything, she sensed longing in those eyes … like he wanted something. A longing greed. He only treated her with the upmost kindness. At first, she had liked that about the man, but after weeks of learning more about this place, she didn't know how to take it. What was his motive?

"Well, my belated apologies," he said. "Anyway, you speak of a farm or forester family?"

"Farm."

"Name?"

"I didn't catch their last names, but the mother and father were Elana and Jacoby. They have three children, two girls and one boy."

He clapped his hands together. "The Libbins!" he exclaimed. "Their farm did wonders during their ten years. I was gutted when their service to the Loess ended. Their crops could feed two entire villages year after year. Miracles, some would call it. Did you know they won the Provider's Competition all ten years of their service?"

"What's that?"

"An annual competition where farm families try to yield the highest number of crops. Nobody beat them, ever. In fact, the record for continuous wins had been four years prior to that. Part of their reward when they broke that record in year five and when they won in year ten was a personal visit from me."

"So they know you," she said.

"That they do."

She fell silent, suddenly unsure of her decision to choose them. Receiving rewards and a visit from the Loess Lord was a big deal. And she hadn't missed Elana's reaction when she and Himitsu had mentioned the Archaic King during their visit. The woman's face had darkened. Did that mean the Libbins family was loyal to a fault? Would they watch Kaylee's every move while she was up there? Surely, she could transfer a slip of parchment to a bird without them knowing.

"Jacoby could have brought the two of you down here himself, and I would have listened," Kopios said. "That's how much I admire that man."

"He probably didn't want to travel that far," Kaylee said.

"True." He snapped his fingers and pointed at her. "Tell you what. You'll be escorted to the upper steppes by some of my best officers. Can't have you in danger."

She kept her mouth shut. She preferred not having anyone around her—especially not people who would report back to the Loess Lord. However, she knew that argument to be moot.

"While you're up there …" he paused, narrowing his eyes. "How long do you plan on being up there?"

"A day or two," she said, knowing anything lengthy could come across as suspicious. A couple days were plenty of time when involving the Pilot of Spies, but Kopios didn't need to know that. "I still want to return to my studies with Doctor Mengai, and considering the weeks-long journey between here and the upper steppes, that leaves only a couple days to relax."

"I admire that. You are …" he trailed off with a thoughtful gaze … "a magnificent young lady."

She cocked an eyebrow. Was he trying to court her? If it hadn't been for the disgust from their age gap—he was well into his forties—she would have been shocked by the analysis. After all, no one in Lost Wisdom paid her any mind because of her mismatching eyes.

Enough's enough, she thought. She wove out of her ancient eye to read his aura—a habit she'd been trying to kill lately. It was invasive and rude, so she thought doing it less often would make her a better person … with an added bonus of feeling less fatigued from not constantly weaving.

Light red, almost rose pink. Shades of maroon swirling within, and … tendrils of slate gray lining the perimeter with wisps of black that flared outward?

That … that wasn't what she expected. He wasn't lusting after her, but there was longing—a plutonic kind. But that was at his core and hidden beneath a shell of greed and resentment.

He cleared his throat, the significant pause after his unexpected compliment weighing on his conscious. "I'll make arrangements, and you'll leave tomorrow," he said. "If that's okay with you."

"Yes."

They said their goodbyes, and she watched as he turned and left the shooting range with his attendant in tow. His aura shifted as he walked away, the red innards rescinding as the gray and black shell crept inward from its extremities. So, the greed and resentment absorbs him when he's not looking in her eyes.

What were the actual depths of Himitsu and Ophala's lies?

52

His Return

One of the most outlandish thoughts Toshik frequently found himself contemplating was the lost possibility of a daughter. His relationship with Jilly had been more than spiritual and emotional; it had been physical, yet none of their nights of love had led to a pregnancy—not that either of them had desired it.

But now he wished it had happened.

If not for the likelihood that a daughter would have prevented Jilly from entering those mountains with him—eventually leading to her sacrificial death—it would have at least given him a conduit in which he could see Jilly again.

Illogical postulations. That was how desperate he had become, and he knew it. He was grasping at straws of hope, searching for a ray of light in the abyssal hole of his chest. Besides, it was selfish. He wished for a daughter only so he could see shades of Jilly in her, even if that meant the girl would grow up with a dead mother and a father who didn't love her for her? He'd grown up with a dead mother and a father who didn't love him at all, but at least his father hadn't feigned love by using him as a substitute for something or someone he truly loved.

For someone with a bottomless pit in his chest, Toshik lacked depth. He was bitter. Yama's death was the only endgame. He had separated himself from others in this hunt not because they were distractions, but because he couldn't continue to make them bear his burdens, which was exactly what the Jestivan would do. They were selfless, and when they saw one of their own hurting, they did, too.

But he needed help from someone. He had done all he could here at his family's estates, training for months in solitude, refining skills that Leon Suadade had taught him. What next, then? Most options were futile, incapable of measuring up to tutelage beneath a Bozani. He still didn't feel he had thanked Princess Shelly—or *Queen* Shelly now—for that. Adren King Supido and Director Buredo were both dead, and nobody else in the royal family was good enough. Master Ichi at the Adren Assistance Academy would want nothing to do with him.

That left one option: follow Simon's advice and take the long trek to Yinyon, a rural village not only on the edge of civilization, but the Edge, itself. The boy had promised he'd find what he was looking for there, and although Toshik couldn't fathom why Simon would know anything about Adrenians and swordsmanship, the fact remained that the very men who had taught Toshik to become a great swordsman—Debo and Suadade— were born in that village. Should that not be reason enough? He had already done enough of a disservice to himself as a young Jestivan by not taking Director Debo's advice more seriously. He wouldn't make that mistake again.

With newfound direction in his path to becoming a swordsman unmatched, he set his jaw, lungs finally succumbing to the lack of oxygen. Setting his feet in the muddy floor of the pond, he lifted his sword through the depth's pressure.

Then he swung straight downward, a roar of bubbles accompanied by tectonic shifts in the pond's depths. Water shifted right and left as the pond split into two tidal waves that crashed onto grassy banks at either side, giving him two seconds in which he could gather air again before the pond's water behind him crashed forward to fill the now-empty half of the pond.

Thrice more, he swung. Until the pond was empty.

He stood at the center of a muddy crater, clothes dripping wet. Tears of happiness and momentary satisfaction overcame him, only to become those of mourning once again.

*   *   *

"You didn't inherent your mother's genes."

The sentence hit Yama like a net of timber. It was one thing to be figuratively disowned by the words of her mother, but to then be disowned from her mother by nature itself seemed downright sadistic—as if gods were teasing her. She had Soraku's violet hair, sure, but what about the gifts that truly mattered?

Master Ichi's face was grim. She hadn't wanted to deliver that news just as much as Yama hadn't wanted to receive it, but the results of her weeks of exams had been telling. A child could have deciphered them. Yama's speed percentage was high—well within the territory of an assassin's—but she couldn't run on walls or air. Once an Adren Assassin entered the necessary speed percentile, he or she would be able to show signs of becoming airborne. It had less to do with weaving techniques and more to do with that trait that made an assassin's Adrenergy genetically different from a normal Adrenian. It was similar to how a Passion Assassin didn't have to weave in a specific way to create black flames; they just *did*, for their energy wasn't capable of producing anything else—reds, oranges, or yellows.

"Considering your misfortune," said Ichi.

"Deficiencies, you mean," Yama interrupted.

Ichi's gaze became fierce, pinched skin wrinkling between slanted eyebrows. "Stop the pity party." Yama's eyes widened. She hadn't heard that tone from the woman since the revelation of their blood relationship. "It ends today. Now that we have real answers about your genetics, we can begin training you properly. You don't need to run on air or walls to eliminate anyone. You could strike something airborne with a flick of your sword, the displaced air slicing through the atmosphere toward your target as a ranged attack. We focus on your agility. In all my years, I've never seen someone with a change-in-direction like you. The way you pivot, the twist in your hips. Don't even get me started on the acceleration and breakneck speed."

Yama looked down—a mistake.

"Look at me," Ichi snapped, eyebrows somehow angling deeper. The bear was showing hints of her lioness sister. "Enough of the auntie-niece act. Adrenians sit straight-backed. Adrenians hold their heads high no matter the circumstances. And most importantly, Adrenians look each other in the eye."

Yama lifted her head, which felt like dead weight on her neck. "I've never had family," she said. "But I heard from people who could have been my friends that family empathizes and supports."

"Has this not been support?" Ichi asked. "Have I not shown empathy? I gave you those, the latter of which I will now alleviate between us. Because you know what family also does? It motivates. It guides. It disciplines. And it knows damned well when a firmer hand is needed."

The woman was even cursing now; she had completely shed the bear image.

"I will get you where you need to be, but you must accept my guidance and drop the self-pity." She paused, lips pursed. "Do I make myself clear?"

And there was the commanding presence Yama needed, the Master Ichi she remembered as a child—albeit, much less animated. "Yes, Master."

*   *   *

Simon crouched atop one of few abandoned buildings surrounding Griza's plaza. It was the grayer hours of dusk, light from the sun's rays dying beyond the horizon. Intelamps illuminated the plaza in a steady white glow to help guide the construction crews as they wrapped up for the day. These newer Intelamps had become more commonplace over the past five years. Simon had originally hated their stark white light, the sterility of it reminding him of hospitals. But he found he enjoyed them as outdoor light sources rather than constrained within walls. Alas, their existence was threatened as Brilliance's provod store dwindled, forcing necessary powers to reanalyze its distribution. Intelights and Intelamps were frivolities, which meant the Intel Kingdom would see a return to candles and torches.

He had arrived to the kingdom a couple hours ago and decided to stop here before traveling to the palace and meeting Lady Lilu. He knew this was the place of the new Weavineering factory and the location of the first person killed by the rebellion's hands.

He marked a woman, blonde hair tied in a stiff bun, as a person of note. She was speaking with a man he believed to either be a head engineer or architect, judging by the massive canvas he held in front of them, arms spread wide to reach either end. Simon couldn't decipher its contents from this distance, nor did he care to move closer. He had no suspects at this point; he was entering this blindly. He wouldn't jump to conclusions, so he left the plaza, sprinting across roofs and skimming across air when gaps were too wide.

Eliminate the eastern gate, and the palace wouldn't have looked like it had experienced an invasion like half the city. Its structure was stable, walls unmarred, but take a closer look within and one would find its heart hadn't escaped unsullied.

A king's murder; a queen's suicide. Their daughter in a debilitating state of depression. Her husband abducted by divinities, leaving an infant without the care of his parents. The only person who kept it together on their behalf was Lilu, who needed help.

In came Simon.

After some asking around, the Adren Assassin found himself approaching a broad set of doors at the end of a corridor.

"Torchtop," said one of the dozen guards stationed around the doors.

Simon smiled and replied, "Brutes." A few of them chuckled. It was a running joke between the archery and melee divisions of the military. The men and women in the infantry were called brutes, while archers were known as ...

"Daisy!" shouted a guard at the end, chuckles strengthening into genuine laughter.

Because, clearly, archers were delicate and thus required positioning far away from an actual battle during war. It was all in good fun, so Simon grinned at the retort.

"High Princess Lilu told us to expect your arrival in the coming weeks," said Nonen, the man adorned with knots and patches along the chest of his uniform. He was the officer of this squad. "This is much earlier than that."

"There was no use in wasting time."

"You ride a comet here, Torchtop?"

Simon glanced at the guard by the name of Moon. "I jogged."

Three guards broke into laughter, one placing a hand on another's shoulder to hold himself up. He grinned, as if aware of the impossibility of his response. It was partly a lie, he supposed. He jogged only thirty percent of the way across the Adren Kingdom, walked fifty-five, and ran fifteen. He made sure to never sprint, however. Sprinting on long journeys could quickly kill an Adrenian … Not everyone was Ataway Debonicus Kawi.

"I'm guessing you're looking for the High Princess," said Nonen. "She's busy with some higher-ups at the moment."

"Who?"

"Wendel LeAnce, Lester Fray, Agatha Harling, and a couple representatives from Ipsa and Ferrous."

Simon cocked an eyebrow. Lester and Agatha were governors of Continon and Acu. When was the last time they had visited the capital for formal meetings? Surely, not in Simon's lifetime—not that sixteen years was much of a lifetime. Then again, when was the last time a LeAnce—outside of Mendac, who wasn't biologically a LeAnce—visited the capital? Had they ever?

If Lilu was meeting with leaders and representatives of the Intel Kingdom's major cities, that meant they were discussing logistical matters. Considering recent turmoil in Dunami with the invasion and Continon with the flooding, it was likely the logistical concerns of deploying supplies in aid and relocating tens of thousands of people—if not more.

The left door opened partly, and Lilu's head stuck out, her wavy green hair splashing down her back in a ponytail. She eyed the guards first, suspiciously, then found Simon, realization dawning on her face. "You know we can hear you buffoons through the door, right? This is important business, and you're interrupting it."

"Yes, Princess Lilu," said Nonen, snapping to attention, clearly embarrassed by his momentary slip in leadership. "It will be corrected, I assure—"

"How are we supposed to focus when the lot of you are clearly having way more fun?" she asked.

Nonen faltered, face twisting through five different expressions before settling on amusement. "Yes, Princess Lilu. The fun ends now."

She nodded. "Good." She looked at Simon. "I'll meet with you later. Your presence is a relief."

She slipped back inside, closing the door behind her. Nonen turned and adopted a more professional stance, his guards following suit. But the man grinned, proving that despite his promise to the princess, he would continue to have fun with his duties. "That woman is reminding me more and more of King Vitio every day," he said with the pride of a father.

Simon made sure to not let the smile slip from his face, lest they notice the impact the statement made on him. Shelly Intel, their rightful queen, was losing these men with each moment she spent secluded in her tower. Continue this, and she'd lose her kingdom, too.

She already was.

*   *   *

"I have a confession to make," Simon said, walking side by side with Lilu through the corridors of the palace's royal sector.

The royal sector had always been an empty area of the palace, where only a few of the most trusted stewards were granted access. They were the kind of servants whose family names had served the Intel family for generations. As king or queenship was passed down the bloodline, these servants passed down servitude. It was the highest of honors. Benedict Ronal, the head steward whom Queen Delilah had taken a liking to decades ago, was the lone exception to that rule.

"And what's that?" Lilu asked.

"I'm not Intelian," he said.

Pity darkened Lilu's heart as she regarded the boy. He was having an identity crisis. She had done this to him; this was her fault. "Look, Simon. I know how much I hurt you and pretty much everyone else when bringing the idea of socioenergenic classes to my father, but just because you're an Unable doesn't mean you're not Intelian. You don't need energy to claim a nationality. You're just as Intelian as Bryson, Shelly, or me."

"I appreciate that, but that's not what I mean. I know what I am, and that's not Intelian—nor an Unable." He sighed, as if what he was about to confess was the most difficult thing he'd ever do in his life. "Not only am I Adrenian, but I'm an Adren Assassin."

Lilu snapped her head around, eyes widening as she looked Simon up and down. He had grown taller than her, and in that height she saw his Adrenian roots. And she was just now noticing the scabbard at his hip. "A sky-skimmer?"

He snorted in laughter. "Of course you would know the old names."

She looked forward again, wrestling with the revelation in her mind. The only classes of assassins that were supposed to still exist were Dev, Passion, and a small number of Spirit. Adren Assassins were wiped out in Known History's earliest centuries according to text. When Pilot Ophala had sent a missive a couple weeks ago suggesting Simon as a capable assassin to eliminate rebel leaders, Lilu had assumed she had meant his skills in archery. His ability to strike a mark from a mile away—an achievement to which only Torchtop could lay claim—was ideal for assassinations. But a sky-skimmer? Had Ophala known about this?

"So you can kill from miles away, run on air and up walls, and wield a sword?"

"My Sky-Skimming is imperfect. I've only been training for a few years since I didn't figure out about my assassin blood until after experiencing wall-running with Debo over Generals' Battle weekend. Then I returned home with questions after he prompted me to. Apparently, he had known my secrets before I did."

Lilu suddenly thought of Bryson and laughed. Simon had envied the Jestivan and, most specifically, that idiot. The eleven-year-old boy had wanted to become Bryson, yet here he was, possibly excelling beyond that benchmark at the mere age of sixteen.

"Not the response I was expecting," Simon said. "Do you not believe me?"

"No, no," she breathed. "I believe you. My mind went elsewhere." She sighed. "Your secret is safe with me."

"It's not a secret anymore. While I won't be shouting our existence from the rooftops, I definitely won't be hiding it anymore. In fact, another one of my kind is in Dunami right now. She traveled with me, stating her presence is needed in case my 'big mouth', as she puts it, gets us in trouble."

"I get it," Lilu said as they proceeded up a staircase. "But it won't be necessary. I won't say anything because widespread knowledge of your existence wouldn't benefit the crown. It's better the rebels have no clue." She grimaced. "I know it sounds selfish, but can you wait to reveal your truths until after the rebels are handled?"

"Not selfish at all," he said. "I'm indebted to your family. Queen Shelly got me a position in the archery unit, which propelled me down a path of adventure and self-betterment."

Lilu paused as they reached a circular room, paintings of previous kings and queens circling its perimeter. "It's not good, Simon." She approached the center and said, "Stand next to me." She stepped on a switch in the floor, and the platform lurched upward. "Remember how my mother was after my father's death?"

"Yes," said Simon. "Distraught. Depressed."

The ceiling opened above them, revealing the stars beyond a ceiling of glass. They heard crying from somewhere above, which wasn't a surprise. "Shelly's worse than that," she whispered. "She is unmotivated to the point of immobility, miserable to the point of despondence. I don't think I've ever seen anything like it. And if my mother's condition was bad enough to lead to suicide, then I'm afraid what that means for my sister."

He didn't respond, and she took it as a sign of respect for her mourning. He couldn't put himself in her shoes—or so she assumed—and therefore didn't try providing empty hope. Simon was kind and hyper aware of emotional circumstances. That maturity mirrored Bryson's. Bryson may have been stupid in a scholarly sense and impulsive in regards to physical endangerment, but when someone was hurting, his companionship was medicine. He sensed pain in friends, and he'd risk it all for them.

As the platform connected with the floor of Shelly's glass room, the highest point in Dunami Palace, they found the source of the crying. The queen was curled atop the sofa, her head in a man's lap. A tear slipped from Lilu's eye as she absorbed the image of that man—that look of solemnity in his face, as if he'd just learned everything about what had happened since his abduction.

Bryson was back.

53

Passing of the Torch

An hour earlier ...

Bryson stood in the rotunda in which he had entered the Light Empire months ago. A chamber of white stone floors and walls, its ceiling a singular sheet of glass through which he couldn't see because of the rain from a passing storm hammering against it. At the center of the rotunda was a vast basin of radiant light. He stood at the edge, looking down into it.

"You've grown stronger since arriving here," said Naipa, the Strasan who had abducted him from his home and brought him here in the first place. Now she was accompanying him while he returned home for a visit. He was being granted sixteen hours, after which she would come to abduct him again. "So you should be able to traverse the gateway without dying."

"Should?" he asked, preferring more certainty.

"The odds are stacked highly in your favor," she said, as if that was reassurance.

He dipped a toe into the basin, then yanked his entire foot back. He felt a surge of heat, but that was commonplace here when passing through the quartz walls of the Starlight. His panic had come from the unknown, nothing else.

"Keep hesitating like that and the odds tip the other way," Naipa said flatly. "You must enter steadily. Walk in."

He inhaled, looked up, closed his eyes, and then exhaled. "Okay." He stepped into the basin, light rippling around his legs as he waded deeper. "Think of the location at which you want to arrive in the kingdoms," she said. "Think clearly, and you will find yourself there."

The radiance reached his chest, swarming the bulk of his body with heat. As it climbed his neck and touched his skin, Naipa said, "Sixteen hours. That's it. Then it's back here to meet with the Strasan and learn of your next objective."

Bryson's head slipped beneath the surface. Flame erupted within him, and he stepped into the glass room of Dunami Palace's tallest tower.

Shelly lay on a sofa, the only piece of furniture in the room. He had gotten lucky. He had chosen this spot for its seclusion, believing it'd be the safest place for him to appear out of light without the chance of bystanders seeing him. He didn't expect to find his wife here, but he appreciated it. His heart fluttered a sigh of relief at the sight of her very much alive, though he questioned the peculiarity of the situation into which he'd arrived.

He walked forward and placed a hand on Shelly's back. She was curled up, face and knees pressed against the back cushions. She stirred, then opened her eyes and turned.

She paused as her eyes skittered between his in efforts to process what she was seeing. Her eyebrows creased, then came a shove hard enough to make him stumble backward.

Rage ripped a scream from her throat as she got up and marched forward, shoving him again. Tears spilled down her cheeks, face twisted with disbelieving anger, as if his arrival displayed some sort of vile audacity.

He stumbled again, this time nearly falling onto his butt. She struck his right shoulder with a palm. "*YOU LEFT ME!*" Left shoulder. "*YOU ASS!*" Two palms to the chest, and this time he fell. She marched forward and stood above him, ire fading to sorrow. "YOU ABANDONED ME WHEN I NEEDED YOU MOST!"

He said nothing, looking up at her from a puddle of guilt. He had abandoned her. Logic said that wasn't true, that he'd had no choice, but his heart told him he should have fought harder. He should have found the basin of light the moment he had learned to navigate the Starlight and came straight here. Instead, he had waited for permission.

His ignorance didn't help. He didn't know what happened while he was away. That night Benedict had burst into the dining room the moment of his abduction, there had been distress on the steward's face. Shelly could have simply been attacking him over Vitio's death or something else that unfolded during his absence, but he didn't know what to say. Some stupid part of him had expected a desperate embrace and words of love upon his return—not this.

He rose to his feet and noticed a shadowy figure on the balcony surrounding the room. Someone was watching from outside. In his distraction, Shelly pounded a fist against his chest and screamed. He looked at her and caught the wrist of her other fist just before it landed. He pulled her in, wrapping his arms around her and squeezing her against him. She continued to struggle within his embrace, screams turning into sobs, rapid inhalation as she struggled to catch her breath in the fervor.

He pressed his lips into her hair even as she squirmed and bucked, her head ramming against and busting his lip. He closed his eyes, leaking tears of his own as the level of her pain dawned on him. He was partly responsible for this, unfulfilling in his duties as her husband. Eventually, the fight rescinded as she sobbed into his chest, body growing limp in his embrace. Her tears stained his tunic, and he fought to hold her up. She had exhausted herself.

He looked up and spotted the man on the balcony, who had now turned away from them and was leaning against the outer banister—a gesture of kindness to allot them privacy. He recognized that kinky hair and short, spindly stature … Frederick.

He helped guide Shelly back to the sofa. He sat at the end, and Shelly collapsed across its length with her head settling in his lap. He placed a hand in her hair and combed his fingers through it. It had lengthened beyond a pixie cut since he had last seen her, making it evident she hadn't been giving it any attention. Her skin was oily, reflective of the moonlight. She wasn't taking care of herself at all. He had seen despair like this before in his mother, but channeled into infuriation, revenge, and aggression. This was depression … desolation.

"You left me." The words tumbled over paralyzed lips, her eyes glued to his tunic.

He studied her as tears continued to fall. "And I will never forgive myself for it."

"You left me."

He closed his eyes, blinking tears onto her wet cheeks. "Is L.K. okay?" he asked.

"He's been away from me, so yes."

He didn't know what that was supposed to mean, so he panicked. "What … Is he safe?"

"Yes. Lilu is …" she trailed off, words difficult to come by … "She's been taking care of him, I think. She's doing everything."

He glanced toward Frederick on the balcony. Was he standing guard? "What happened, Love?"

The question ripped wails out of her, as her agony intensified once again. She burrowed her head in his lap, muffling her moans. It took twenty minutes for her to regain composure to speak, but once she did, the story took a fraction of that time.

"She killed herself." Heavy sob. "Mom. She just stepped out the window." Sharp breath. "In the nursery. In front of L.K." More sobs that turned into vicious coughs. "I sent for you. And you were gone." That was it, and now Bryson knew the reason for Benedict's tearful intrusion. It made sense considering the steward's relationship with the former queen.

The floor at the room's center opened. The mechanical sound of the platform in the chamber below clicked as it rose to fill the hole in the floor. Two heads appeared first, and they stared in the direction of the sofa. They were Lilu and Simon.

Bryson had no more tears left, but the evidence of prior tears streaked his cheeks. As of right now, he was solemn and needed more time to unwrap Shelly's words. He held a finger up to his lips to request their silence and pointed toward the balcony. They took the directions in stride, finding a door in the glass wall behind them that wouldn't involve passing the sofa. They met with Frederick outside, and Bryson's focus returned to his wife.

Shelly had always been a strong soul. Those less familiar with her would have called her callous; he knew it as toughness. She had lived nearly her entire life as a prisoner of royalty, locked away in this palace and barred from attempting anything deemed dangerous by her father. It was the life of any royal firstborn, but the misery of hers was embellished because of her little sister's privileges. The siblings of other royal firstborns lived a similar life of seclusion, but Lilu had been granted freedoms such as attending Phesaw as a normal student or living in Brilliance to become a weavineer. Lilu was off changing the world while Shelly felt like an outcast.

These facts led to insecurities in Shelly. She kept her hair cut short to differentiate herself from her younger sister. While developing a playful, instigative side to her personality from so much time spent with her father, she also became entitled and accustom to being served. Her opinions were loud and direct, for her power didn't extend much further than her voice. She didn't have a life like Lilu, who could make change with action because of her freedoms. Some would call her whims of flexing royal muscles by snapping fingers at the palace staff as overcompensation for her hopelessness, and that assessment would be correct.

However, that didn't mean the royal firstborn didn't love or empathize. No, if anything, nobody in the Intel family loved quite like Shelly. Lilu had an issue with overanalyzing. She found flaws in everyone and everything, searching for social injustices only to create social injustices of her own— the socioenergenic system, for example. Shelly simply loved, including those who served her. Alas, that empathy came with the downsides of passion. The loss of her father, mother, and husband shattered her tough exterior, and she had likely separated herself from L.K. fearing herself as some sort of disease that would rip the baby from this world, too.

After five years, Bryson knew this woman. He had fallen in love with her not just for her beauty, laughter, or the way her pixie cut swooped in layers from the part on the right side of her head to the left, but her insecurities and self-perceived flaws, too. The latter qualities humanized her—the lack of which had turned him away from Lilu now that he really thought about it. Lilu had always been enamored with perfection.

He brushed his fingers through her hair, then placed his hand against her cheek, feeling the heat of her skin through the wetness. Her sobs had reduced to sniffles, and he remained silent, knowing that was what she needed: silent comfort ... peace. When Debo died, Bryson had wanted quiet companionship. His carriage ride from Necrosis Valley to the Dev Kingdom's teleplatforms had been a lot of silence—the Jestivan too distraught to speak—but little comfort. When Jilly died, silence consumed Toshik, but again there was little comfort. Words could only do so much, and he hadn't possessed family or someone he loved to provide physical consolation.

"I love you, Shelly. More importantly, I admire your nakedness. You wear your emotions on your sleeves. Bottling them up is never healthy."

She removed her face from his lap, her left eye sliding to the corner to look up at him. "I've never felt this way about someone," she whispered.

He smiled softly. "Neither have I."

"Tell me you're back for good."

The smile faded. "I have sixteen hours."

Her gaze remained on him for a few seconds. "So, that means this time we can have closure."

"I don't like that word."

She hummed, then said, "Abeyance."

"Abeyance?"

"Suspension," she said. He thought he saw a quirk in her lips.

"Ah. Look at us, the two ironically dumb Intelians using big words." He looked up and spotted Lilu through the glass. "Why is Lilu never in the vicinity when we do or say something smart?"

"It's better this way," Shelly said. "She'll underestimate us, and when her and Frederick's future child is dumber than ours, we can laugh in her face."

He snorted, though he didn't know if it was from the possibility of Lilu producing a mentally inept offspring or her and Frederick conceiving a child in the first place.

"So," Shelly said, pushing herself out of his lap and rising to a seated position. She leaned her head against his shoulder. "Sixteen hours, which means no surprises?"

"No surprises."

She kissed his cheek, bubbling magma spilling from his head down his neck and through the rest of his body. Not even the quartz walls of the Starlight paralleled with the fiery sensation this woman brought him.

The pair sat in silence for at least half an hour until Lilu turned away from the balcony railing and noticed them sitting up and in good spirits. Bryson motioned her inside, and Frederick and Simon followed. Frederick volunteered to get L.K., so the boy could see his father and mother happy again. That left Bryson, Shelly, Lilu, and Simon in the sky tower.

"Catch me up to speed," Bryson said before Lilu could ask any questions about the Light Empire or her sister.

Lilu hesitated, eyes shifting toward her older sister, curious of her condition. She likely hadn't seen a functional Shelly in months. But when Lilu glanced back at Bryson, she saw the pleading look in his eyes. *Drop it for now.*

She sighed and proceeded to tell him everything about the efforts to discover the rebel group and infiltrate their ranks, from the important assassins and spies on the job to suspected enemies of high importance. She had to visibly bite back anger as she spoke of the person responsible for funding the rebel operations: Periphan LeAnce. Bryson understood what kind of betrayal that must have felt like, for Lilu had worked under that family for a few years now. He was pleased to discover that Wendel, apparently, was oblivious of her criminal activities. She didn't speak of the second important figurehead, but when she mentioned his or her existence, something akin to grief or pity flashed across her face.

"Okay, what do you need me to do?" Bryson asked.

Lilu's eyebrows skyrocketed. "Are you kidding me?"

"You're not doing anything," Shelly said.

"But I can fix this."

"I'm sure you can," Lilu replied, "but without any sort of finesse. You're an avalanche, and we need this handled covertly. We are plenty capable of executing a takedown. Look who we have on our side."

He looked at Simon, the boy who had idolized him as a child. He was standing at a forced distance from the trio, adopting the image of a personal guard as he observed from afar, knowing if he stood any closer, it'd feel like an intrusion upon familial matters. Though only sixteen, the boy was dangerous. Bryson waved him over. "Stop being an idiot. You're family."

His austere expression slipped to reveal that doughy-faced, wide-eyed boy of wonder. For a split second, Bryson felt he had traveled back in time to the morning before his induction into the Jestivan. Simon had been more ecstatic than anyone else.

As he approached and stood next to Lilu, Shelly squeezed Bryson's hand. "Besides, sixteen hours isn't long. Call me selfish, but I'd like to spend it with you." She paused and glanced down at their entwined hands. "I don't have to sleep alone tonight."

And that was that.

Frederick returned with L.K. and placed him directly into Bryson's arms. The infant, who was mid yawn during the exchange, paused at the sight of his father, mouth held open as he absorbed a god of his tiny world. He reached up with pudgy hands, grasping at air, and Bryson leaned over to kiss his forehead. Little fingers clasped onto hair and ears, and the father wept tears of relief.

*　　　*　　　*

The next morning, Simon sat on the floor outside of the war chamber after pulling an all-nighter. Sleep had been impossible. Seeing Bryson and Shelly together and happy—as happy as the two of them could be—had been medicine for the soul. The main part of his reasoning for returning here so quickly wasn't for this kingdom, but that family. He would die for them. He may not have been L.K.'s godfather—that honor belonged to Vistas—but he would be his guardian. Not only was he the son of two people who propelled Simon to fantastical aspirations, but he carried the name of two legends from his culture: Leon Kawi. There was legacy in that bundle of joy, and he would serve as its fortress.

"You're brooding intensely enough to set the palace asunder," said a voice to his right.

562

He looked up and found Lilu peeking through the open door of the war chamber. He hadn't even heard the door open. "You caught me."

"Not a look I'm used to from you."

He stood. "So, what can I do for the cause, Princess?"

"Stop calling me that, weirdo." She slipped back into the chamber. "Come in."

The war chamber was far humbler than its larger brother. For starters, a gigantic, wired three-dimension module of Kuki Sphaira didn't demand attention in the center of the room. A humble table stood at the center with a map of Dunami currently sprawled across it. A bald man with age spots and a scarred face stood next to it, draped in blood red robes and hemmed in black—a Passion Assassin. Simon had seen him around before, usually conversing with Spy Pilot Ophala when she had been here. His name slipped his mind, however.

"This is Fane," Lilu said. The Passionian nodded, and Simon returned the gesture. "Typically, he's in the field during covert operations such as the one presently happening, but considering circumstances in the palace, I needed him for other duties. He has, however, provided great counsel whenever I have to deal with new information that comes in from any active spies."

Simon approached the table and surveyed the map. Small copper figures—pyramids, cones, and cubes—were scattered across it, typically standing atop specific locations of the capital. He assumed each form signified different things.

"Most of this you don't have to worry about," Lilu said, taking her place next to Fane on the opposite side of the table from Simon. "It's the lone black piece that requires your attention."

Simon found it easily. Black and shaped like a heart, it stood out among the browns. Except it didn't sit on a specific location, but rested in the blank border outside the map's boundaries. He furrowed his brows.

"I'm sure you have questions," she said. "The truth is that we don't know where your target actually is. She remains hidden, but fuels the passion of the rebels as if she was their martyr."

"What's the silver bag of money?" Simon asked, eyes drawn to the only other piece that stood out from the rest.

"The rebels' financial backing. Without her, they don't have the means to launch an attack directly on the crown. But she's not your concern, for someone else is targeting her."

Simon noted the location of the silver piece: the heart of Griza's Plaza, exactly where the new Weavineering factory was being built. He had just been there hours ago. Had he seen the culprit?

"So the bag of money makes sense," he said before refocusing on the black heart. "And the heart makes sense, too, as it symbolizes the core ideologies of the rebels."

"Yes."

Fane cleared his throat and said, "The heart is far more dangerous than anyone else beyond enemy lines. I truly believe if the choice were to be made, the woman it represents would die a martyr. And I think it's a reckless decision to have her assigned to you as your mark."

"Watch it," said Lilu.

Simon raised an eyebrow. "Why?"

"Personal relationships should never interfere with this line of work," Fane stated coldly.

"Personal relationships?"

Lilu exhaled cathartically, gaze lingering on the black heart before returning to Simon. "Whistle."

Simon grasped the table's edge, head tilting, eyes widening. "Whistle?!" he hissed. The middle-aged archer had been his fletching master during his time in the Intelian archery ranks. Fellow archers would tell stories about her feats with a bow and arrow, how her arrows whistled at a pitch equivalent to a Linsani's scream when slicing through the sky. He had never seen her do it, but she had told him which supplies to gather to create the perfect bow-and-arrow combination and taught him the proper technique with which to shoot them. It was the inspiration behind the arrows in the quiver on his back—their spiraling feathers.

"Yes," Lilu said solemnly, "which is why I didn't want to give you this mark, but Pilot Ophala insisted during every meeting I've had with her. When I explained to her your prior relationship with the woman, that only strengthened her resolve. The Spy Pilot wants you to go after Whistle." As he remained quiet, she continued, "I know this a cruel twist of fate. If anyone's to blame, it's me. Whistle was cast out of the Intel Kingdom after discovering her lies about her energy during inspections to assign identification cards. Her not being Intelian shouldn't have mattered considering all she had done for this kingdom as if she belonged here."

Simon blanched. "As if?" he asked, disbelieving. "She *did* belong here."

"I know, and I can't change what happened. And now she's leading the rebels, viewing my plans to abolish the socioenergenic system and the identification cards that came with it as a slap in the face to those who have already suffered because of it—some in irreversible ways. There have been Unables who have died to entitled weavers—especially the wealthy—because they mistakenly infringed upon their properties." She paused, eyes growing wet. "I can't give those lives back. No amount of money that the Intel or LeAnce family has can repay such debts. And it's spiraling out of control now. Viewed as scum elitists who had taken advantage of their stationing in the socioenergenic classes, three aristocrats were murdered in the past week alone, all at the hands of rebels. And there is a common theme in all of this."

The war chamber fell silent. Fane was staring at the map, as if staring at the princess would shame her beyond the self-hate already suffocating her. Simon didn't care; he looked her in the eye. Was Lilu telling him to assassinate Whistle, the kind woman who had mentored him, the unfortunate woman who had done nothing wrong? No, that might have been what Lilu was thinking, but Pilot Ophala wasn't. He knew it. There was a reason why she had interfered and insisted his assignment to this mark. The wise Pilot sought out something different than violence, at least in this scenario.

"All of this blood is on my hands," Lilu said.

It wasn't completely true, but partly. She wasn't responsible for Flen's decision to flip sides and kill her father, leading to her mother's suicide. That had all been King Vitio and Mendac's faults from decades ago. But he didn't deny her claim, for she was responsible for the smaller issues within Dunami's populace that had been festering beneath the grander chaos.

"I don't know how you plan to stop this," he said. "But I'll do what needs to be done."

*   *   *

Bryson awoke the next morning with a stiff neck that wouldn't turn to the right, head twisted awkwardly against the arm of the sky tower's lone sofa as Shelly's body was tangled with his. He looked down at her and smiled, then cringed as another pain shot through his neck. The sun splashed over them, the Light Empire and its companion island hovering in the sky directly above.

He and Shelly left the tower an hour later. He walked the corridors of Dunami Palace while she resituated herself into a chamber closer to the palace's heart. She refused to take her parents' room, so a dozen servants were now moving their furniture and belongings again, as they had already moved into that room before his abduction. He didn't blame her. Sleeping in the quarters that had once belonged to your dead father was one thing, but *both* dead parents? Bryson hadn't returned to Debo's home in years, fearing that same discomfort.

Vistas waited at the door to the library with a tome held against his chest. Like Shelly and Lilu, the Dev servant wasn't the same as he had been before the Rogue Demon and SCAPD forces invaded the Intel Kingdom. Aside from the brief escape of Bryson and Shelly's wedding days, the man was distant … but not in a mistrustful way. This was the man who served as L.K.'s godfather, the man largely responsible for helping Delilah raise Lilu and Shelly. He had been to Vitio what Benedict had been to Delilah.

"There are no words to explain my happiness at the sight of your face again," said Vistas.

Bryson walked directly into a hug. Vistas let one arm wrap around the Jestivan, the other pinned between both of them with the tome. "Lilu told me how you've stepped up with L.K. during Shelly's ordeal and my absence. Thank you for everything."

"It is an honor."

In the library, they sat at a table in the study area. "I found it," Vistas said, sliding the tome across the table toward Bryson. "Not here—I searched high and low with no success—but I had one of the crown's acolytes search the Warpfinate at Phesaw. It took him a couple of days, but he returned with this."

Bryson read the title: *The Unforgettable*. It sounded similar to *The Unbreakable*, yet he had never heard of this story. Even Lilu and Agnos, whom he had asked for information on the woman this book was about, didn't know her. It was like she had been erased from the world. The title's irony wasn't lost on him. Beneath the main title was a subtitle: *The Tale of Naipa Levlin*.

Fearing the little time he had known he'd had left, he had asked Vistas about Naipa the night of their dinner and his subsequent abduction. The fact that she was the one who had abducted him had also been ironic. He had only wanted Vistas to find out about her in order to prepare for the Light Empire. Guilt swept over him. This felt invasive. None of the Bozani had answered his questions about the oblivious Strasan, claiming that it was not their place. And asking Naipa herself had felt abrasive. He sighed at the book. So, he would circumvent and discover her truths behind her back ... impertinent.

He looked back up at Vistas. "Two days, huh?"

"The Warpfinate is vast, as you know. Consider yourself lucky it was not two years."

Bryson lifted the book, his wrist giving way beneath the weight. Why did every legend require a thousand pages to hold it in words? "I don't want to take this to the Empire, and I only have seven hours until I leave again. I can't read all of this."

"I already read it," said Vistas. "I can summarize it for you. She was a great woman who was willing to sacrifice it all."

Bryson leaned back in the wooden chair, placing his hands behind his head. "I'm all ears."

54

The Unforgettable

When Naipa Levlin's mother, Slivial, came home from work, she did so with the aid of her secretary. The nine-year-old waited in the living room until her mother's arrival. She didn't charge the door when it opened, but waited hesitantly on the carpet, expensive dolls scattered around her. Slivial entered with her secretary—a man named Nonce—behind her. Her gaze roamed the entry foyer and attached rooms, eyebrows furrowing. "You don't have us barging into some stranger's home, correct?"

Nonce shook his head. "This is your home, Mrs. Levlin."

Her eyes paused on Naipa. She leaned close to Nonce and whispered, "Is that her?"

"Yes."

The whisper hadn't been that effective. Tears streamed down Naipa's cheeks after hearing the question. Today was a particularly bad day. Whenever her mother asked that question, it meant Nonce informed her before arriving home that she had a daughter. Slivial must have had a hellish day at the office, either treating an extremely damaged patient or simply a large number of average ones. The best days were displayed in her mother's knowing smile as she entered their home, ready to embrace her daughter, which were usually foretold by Nonce's absence. Today was not one of those days.

At the sight of Naipa's tears, Slivial rushed into the living room to comfort the girl. That only stung more because Naipa knew such empathy wasn't a result of their familial love—for the woman didn't know the girl as her daughter—but because Slivial was naturally a caring person. If she saw a beggar crying in the street, downtrodden and festering with disease, she would have considered it her duty to comfort them. This made Naipa as much a stranger as said hypothetical beggar—at least today.

Nonce sighed from the foyer. Of course, he had warned Slivial to not respond this way before arriving, that if she were to hug Naipa, it would only make the girl cry more. He knew this because he had seen it firsthand dozens of times before. Only twice had her mother listened.

Slivial backed away, sorrow shaping her eyes and lips. Naipa knew what she was thinking: *Apparently, I'm her mother, yet my presence doesn't make her happy. This can't be my daughter.* The girl sobbed harder. Why did her mother always forget? Why couldn't every day be like yesterday? She had come home early from work without Nonce's assistance and beamed at her daughter. She took Naipa to her favorite creamery, letting her taste-test every flavor even though she had done it countless times before and already knew what she preferred. It never made the clerk angry. He'd always grin at Mother and say, "Anything for the Selfless Sliv."

Selfless Sliv was the name that the people of Rim called Mother. Naipa never thought much of it or why they revered her so much, but she would come to know later in life, after her mother's suicide.

That tragedy occurred the very same night of Naipa's tears. When Mother backed away, noticing her presence only worsened the girl's mood, there was more hurt in her eyes than usual.

"I'll be spending the night here tonight," Nonce said. It wasn't unusual; he had slept over a handful of instances, but only when Mother had experienced a truly taxing day at work. Naipa didn't want to go through one of those nights tonight—a night where she couldn't fall asleep because she knew Mother and Nonce were in the same bed. He may have been Naipa's biological father, but she refused to recognize him as such. A real father wouldn't choose to spend the night only when Mother was at her worst.

"No!" Naipa screamed.

Mother's eyes widened, surprised by the outburst. She didn't understand the dynamics between her and Nonce—not today. He was only her secretary. He never bothered explaining the truth of their relationship to her. On the days she did remember, she knew the two of them were separated and to not bring him home to their daughter. Naipa's pain, which was rooted in her mother's forgetfulness, also came from having to see her father while knowing he wouldn't remain present for long.

"You know I must," Nonce said, still watching from the foyer. He didn't dare enter the living room because the reaction he'd draw out of Naipa would have made her present hysterics seem like a drizzle.

"*GO AWAY! I'll watch over her!*"

"You're just a child."

She pounded both fists into plush carpet. "I'm her daughter! I'm enough!"

Slivil's gaze softened. This was the first time Naipa had voiced her disdain of Nonce's offer to stay, the first sign of courage that she could reject him. Mother didn't need him.

"Perhaps, your offer is kind," said Slivil, "but crossing boundaries. I can understand why a girl would fear a strange man sleeping in such proximity."

Ponce's lip twitched. To have the ignorance of their relationship thrown in his face must have hurt. To be thought of as a strange man with possible ill intentions for their daughter broke him to the point of allowing his calm demeanor to slip—if only for a moment.

"I think it wise I remain," he said, pushing his luck. This was unexplored territory for them.

"I think it wise you leave," Mother said, an unfamiliar iciness coating her tone.

He lingered, glancing between wife and daughter. And then he left.

That night—despite thinking she could overcome it all—Naipa couldn't sleep in her mother's bed. The first ten minutes were spent as the little spoon to her mother's big spoon, but the embrace was rigid, her mother still uncertain about whom the girl was to her. Naipa broke free, got out of bed, and left the room, closing the door on her mother's apology. She acted as Mother's personal guard for the rest of the night and into morning, posted outside her door in a bundle of blankets.

Mother usually woke up at the crack of dawn. Her internal clock was wired that way, and Naipa couldn't help but find that crude of the universe. She was allowed memory of one thing, and that was time. In most instances her memory healed by morning, but this wouldn't be one of those instances. Based on the severity of her amnesia yesterday, it would take multiple days to recover.

Naipa became antsy when an hour passed after dawn. Not hearing any movement from within the room, she opened the door to wake Mother. During the walk toward the four-poster bed, Naipa saw massive stains of red across white sheets. Red liquid dripped from the ends of blankets that hung off the bed's side, soaking the carpet in … blood.

Naipa sprinted forward. She leapt onto the mattress and held her mother's face between two hands.

Nothing.

She collapsed atop her mother. Her right knee squished in the warm, dampened sheet. Slivil Levlin had sliced both wrists open, vertically. Resting in a limp hand was a metallic symbol that looked like crosshairs—a circle with four dashes in each side. The small tattoo of that same symbol, usually found on Mother's forehead, had disappeared, leaving clean skin in its wake.

*   *   *

In adulthood, Naipa became that hero her mother had been.

The crosshair-shaped pendant had been an ancient piece, and not just any ancient, but a relic. It was capable of powerful feats, and Naipa had taught herself how to use it properly to her father's chagrin. Losing Slivil under circumstances he felt were avoidable if he hadn't left her with Naipa that night was one thing, but to then watch his daughter follow the same path of mental suicide was asking too much. He had moved to a different town sometime during Naipa's seventeenth year.

She treated the same patients her mother had, but made sure to not make the same mistake of falling in love and bearing a child. She had experienced the life of a daughter forgotten by a mother, and she wouldn't place that burden on anyone else.

She accepted more patients than her mother ever did, forcing herself to a life of amnesia. Patients spilled their guts to her—their darkest secrets ranging from events of which they were victims to their shameful desires or evil acts. She helped them get through all of it. First, with typical therapy sessions. If conversation and time could heal their emotional and mental wounds, then why bother with the more drastic measures?

Alas, drastic measures are one's only option sometimes. If she determined a person was beyond saving, she could erase their memories—from the tiniest moment to complete obliteration. Her weaving skills determined just how finely she could narrow down the millions of compartments of one's memory. She wasn't on her mother's level, so oftentimes she erased more of a person's memory than she would have liked. The repercussions of such a technique were that her memories also vanished—and to a greater degree. This was why her mother forgot she had a daughter so often.

Naipa was forty-three years old when she died. Nobody in Rim would remember the events of that day. Some believed there were several earthquakes. Even fewer rumors spoke of an alien species of animals that came out of the Archaic Mountains. They walked on hind legs and could speak Sphairian, but they were also described as rabid and aggressive toward humans. The citizens of Rim slaughtered them before they ventured too deep into the city. At the demands of the mayor, Naipa obliterated the minds of over a thousand people that day.

In doing so, she obliterated her own existence.

55

The Haunted

Just because Olivia Still was in greater control of her emotions and better at shielding her heart and soul than even the most cynical war veterans, that didn't mean the Cyn Kingdom's atmosphere didn't puncture holes in her defenses. The feeling was foreign to her, as she had been the kind of person who didn't waver or doubt her convictions in the slightest for most of her life. But here, with the Linsani's screams in the distance, there was reason to doubt herself. The fact that she had already seen one of the wyverns in person during the Blizzard of Blood didn't make this any less mortifying. Vuilni shared those sentiments.

The two women theorized why that would be. Surely, when faced with a threat a second time—especially one which you had seen conquered before—confidence shouldn't be an issue. The unknowns were now known, giving you methods of defeating it again. However, Bryson had been the person to defeat Tongku Feilong, and only with the help of their mother and Thusia—meaning it had taken two royal firstborns and a

Branian. Olivia and Vuilni were just one royal firstborn and a woman. And now they were in the Linsani's kingdom where they thrived in the Cynnish atmosphere. Who was to say Tongku wasn't weakened during the Blizzard of Blood because of the foreign atmosphere? That was a scary thought, magnified tenfold as the Void continued to extinguish their hope and replace it with terrible emotions.

The western reaches of the Almawt Woods were a nightmare. Olivia thought they might be granted a reprieve after dealing with the Voidlands—they were the most discussed landmarks of terror save the Linsaniun Mounds—but it turned out the southern Voidlands were the tamest of the three because of their distance from the Mounds. Tame enough to make the Almawt Woods hellish in comparison.

They had yet to run into any of the Cynnish parasites, of which there were twenty-three species. The most notorious were the umbra fairies, but those were more common in the northwestern Voidlands. Call it a stroke of good fortune or mere coincidence, whatever it was they counted their lucky stars.

Most of their encounters were with decrepit animals that would have been dead in any other kingdom. Olivia could best describe them as walking corpses: a stag with pink muscles exposed through patchy skin; birds forced to walk the ground because of featherless wings; and a litter of leopard cubs squirming at the base of a tree, biting at each other with toothless mouths, not in playfulness but mindless aggression.

They were currently traveling during one of the Dark Realm's two nights. Best practice was to only travel when the sun was out, but they were desperate to escape the Almawt Woods. Having crossed Wraithful River earlier in the day, they knew they were halfway to Gangladesh, the closest city of note to the teleplatforms. Olivia couldn't fathom how difficult it had been for the Jestivan to reach Spachny all those years ago, which was farther away and involved crossing multiple rivers.

Olivia stopped walking and grabbed Vuilni's arm, raising a finger to closed lips. She felt something in their vicinity. The Void's atmospheric qualities were a double-edged sword. While their footsteps and whispers could be heard from miles away, so could someone else's. That meant the possibility of a threat was preluded by their sounds, granting ample amount of time for the two women to prepare. That made this presence unnerving. She knew someone or something was close, yet she hadn't heard anything until just now.

She scanned the scattered trees. The sparseness of the Almawt Wood was deceptive. While there were hundreds of trees within eyesight, the absence of foliage made sightlines stretch into forever. They were gray skeletons of dead bark, their canopies a lattice of interlocking claws.

Vuilni nudged Olivia's arm and pointed to her right. A humanistic figure was walking in their direction from a few hundred yards away. Despite its human build, it didn't possess any other human traits—no skin, muscle, or bone. It was gray and semitransparent, nearly camouflaged with the Almawt Woods' bleak atmosphere. Its walk was uneven, shoulders and head tipped slightly to the left, a limp from a foot that dragged through dead grass. Every few paces, it teetered sideways as if it was about to fall over, but then recovered with panicked steps. It caught a nearby tree and used that to prop itself up. Its motions were mostly silent despite their heaviness and clumsiness.

"You're seeing that, right?" Vuilni asked. "An apparition?"

Olivia closed her eyes and then reopened them. The thing was now a dozen paces closer. If they both could see it, it wasn't a hallucination. The Void truly was a mystery.

"Walk, quickly," Olivia said, possessing no interest in discovering what the specter wanted.

They walked briskly, checking behind them at regular intervals. Despite the specter's apparent lack of speed, it didn't lose ground. Every time she turned, it was trailing at the same distance.

"Try attacking it," Vuilni said. "I would, but my ability is all physical. You can hit it from a distance."

Olivia turned and shot a jet of water toward the specter. The water went right through its stomach as if nothing was there, disrupting the figure in a swirl of mist that reformed.

"Ghosts," Vuilni said in disbelief. "All those Void horror stories were supposed to be fake!"

"I think it's more complicated than that," Olivia replied. "They're people, but people who have decomposed differently than the typical corpses we've seen up to this point."

Vuilni looked back again, eyes widening. "*RUN!*"

The Powish woman wasted no time in sprinting ahead, kicking up divots in the dead grass. Olivia made the mistake of glancing back. The specter was running—or trying its best to while having one good foot. And still, its footsteps were only whispers. Then it did the unthinkable. It condensed itself from a human to a cluster of translucent mist that rushed toward her like a barreling cloud, kicking up withered leaves around it.

Olivia's legs moved before her brain registered a reaction, but that thing certainly moved at a speed that bested her own. While she had achieved high speed percentages because of the training in Rhyparia's gravity alterations, that didn't mean she was Bryson, Toshik, or Yama. Her build tended to put her at a disadvantage, as her extra bulk of muscles weighed her down. Her thighs were their own worst enemies, knocking against each other with every stride. They provided power, however, which meant each stride was a massive lunge. In her earlier years at Phesaw, several students made fun of her for her wonky running style, and Bryson usually silenced them on her behalf—not that she required his interference. She was perfectly okay ignoring them.

Vuilni continued to pull away, her calves swollen to twice their normal size while her thighs contained their normal bulk. It was a handy skill for the Powish. While specifying the enlargement of her muscles to the calves, she could still produce power in her lunges without the hindrance of her thighs.

Vuilni turned and noticed Olivia's distance behind her, but there was nothing she could do to help. Both women understood this. If she turned to help Olivia by carrying her—something a Powish could easily do—it would still slow her down to Olivia's current pace, if not worse. Thus, she would continue forward ... or she should have.

Vuilni ran back toward Olivia, footfalls obliterating fallen sticks on the ground. Concern of stealth had dissipated the moment they had seen the specter. They could have been heard from ten miles away by this point.

What is she doing?

Charging past Olivia, Vuilni roared as the muscles in her right arm expanded, starting from the right trapezius and rippling down the shoulder to the bicep and triceps, forearm, and fist. Flabbergasted, Olivia whirled. Vuilni was charging a cloud with a fist! Powish were foolishly confident in their strength, but there came a point when common sense had to take over. What wins in a collision between an unstoppable physical object and an unstoppable metaphysical force?

Olivia could leave it to chance and hope the answer was "neither." Maybe Vuilni's punch would pass through the specter without effect, and the specter wouldn't be able to affect Vuilni because it couldn't physically touch her. But that wasn't how Cynergy worked and Olivia knew this. Listening to her gut, she summoned *him*.

Shadows swirled up from the ground between the two forces. Vuilni stopped, but the cloud continued barreling forward. A decaying man then slipped off the cloak of shadows and caught the cloud with a single hand. The mist became human again, its neck crushed in Preloz Henye's grasp. It struggled; it writhed. It opened its mouth to scream, but released no sound.

Preloz turned his head toward Olivia, the specter still held aloft in his hand. Vuilni recoiled at the sight of his face, but said nothing. He looked angry—no surprise there. He knew where he was, and he likely knew why.

He turned toward the specter again, exposing the gory hole in the back of his head to Olivia and Vuilni, the latter of whom retreated to the former's side. Preloz whispered something in Cynnish to the specter, and it seemed to calm with each hiss, growing lax in his grip. He released its neck. It turned and silently walked the other way with a foot dragging behind.

The Bewahr watched it leave and waited for it to completely vanish in the distance. Once it did, he turned his head slightly to the left and right to inspect his surroundings. His shoulders rose as he inhaled deeply, then he exhaled and turned toward them.

"You don't know what you've gotten yourself into."

"What was that?" Olivia asked. Vuilni pulled her collar over her nose. She would have to talk to her about that later.

"A karzirp," Preloz said. "A weak one, thankfully." He glanced to the side. "I'm guessing we're in the Almawt Woods, but the deeper you go into this kingdom—specifically the closer you get to the Linsaniun Mounds—

the more dangerous those things become. They're creatures that were once humans, decayed past the point of a physical body, their souls bound to our realm by their Cynergy."

Olivia's hypothesis had been correct earlier.

"The weaker someone's Cynergy is," said Preloz, "the more difficult it is for them to die, for the Void's atmosphere overcomes their souls and traps them. The Linsani are largely responsible for this, which is why the closer to the mounds you get, the more frequent and dangerous karzirp become. They may have been weak and lacking in Cynergy in their human state, but when they've transitioned into a karzirp, they become deadly because of their enslavement by the power of the Void's atmosphere."

"This place sucks," Vuilni said, mouth muffled by her shirt.

Preloz regarded the woman, eyes gliding down her body. "Powish?"

"What gave it away?" she asked sarcastically.

His eyes drifted back up to hers. "Tell me. Is it worse to be a slave to nature or people?"

She blanched, collar slipping off her jaw and exposing pressed lips. "Who do you think you are?"

"I have that same question." He tilted his head. "Did you live in the capital?"

She didn't answer, gaze hardening.

"And what were you?" he asked.

"I was a slave," she muttered. "Once."

"You lived in Cascade's Closure." He didn't phrase it as a question. "You lived in the sewage of an entire population, under the whip of brutish officers who rode atop beasts."

"And what does that—"

"Because it's nothing like this," he said calmly, eyes glued to hers. "You're right. This place 'sucks,' as you so aptly put it. But, don't toss that accusation around so flippantly; it undermines the strength and tenacity of the people who live here, what they must endure. Because at least as a slave in Cascade's Closure you can choose something better, a salvation not found in the Void." He paused, his next words heavy and intentional. "You can kill yourself."

56

The Pilot's Command

Pilot Ophala stood in the bird tower of Phelos Palace. Mists furled around her, shrouding the ground hundreds of feet below and the city's buildings in the distance. The early morning air was humid and cool. She cupped a mug of hot tea with two hands in front of her face as she leaned against a pillar at the floor's edge. The tower was more silent than normal, the wintry conditions—which were a rarity in the Archaic Kingdom—driving most of the birds east to the Central Grasslands or into other kingdoms such as the Passion Kingdom, a daring flight that would cause the deaths of hundreds of birds.

The frigid temperatures didn't stop Ophala from her morning routine, however. She came to the tower every morning at dawn with hopes of receiving some kind of word from the Thousand-Layer Loess. Months had passed not only without seeing her son but without communication. As someone who could enter a bird's mind and see what they saw up to a week's time in the past, one would think she would have spotted them somewhere around the loess. But no, all she saw were farmlands and forests on the uppermost plateaus. The rest were vacant of civilization save for several tunnel entrances wherein sat meager stations for sentries. If President Mesitis Epidex, Skill Broker of the underground market, wasn't lying about the Loess housing a population that could rival the capital, with a leader, army, and equipment capable of marching westward, then where was all of it?

Was she missing things her younger self would have seen? Admittedly, she was spread too thin. On one front, her birds were searching for Mendac, Kadlest, Rhyparia, and Flen. Some were dedicated to tracking Yama, who was currently training in Katashi. She would have worried for the two young princes and the queen in the royal estates, but she didn't believe the former Jestivan a threat ever since splitting from Toono. Still, she would remain a person of interest to Ophala and a possible target. She had aided Toono and Ophala believed she had killed Adren Director Buredo. Plus, she and Toshik were headed for a collision course, the latter of whom Ophala had last witnessed training vigorously at his family's estates.

Another one of her flocks followed Rayne, Saikatto, Prakriti, and the dimiours as they traversed the Archaic Mountains and dealt with the Unboundants—a faction of dimiours that hadn't shared their forgiveness toward humans centuries ago and thus lived in the mountains, separated from Epinio. If the dimiours wanted to integrate with the humans of Archain society, they needed to first squash their issues with the Unboundants.

Matters directly beneath her nose required her attention, too. Archaic King Sigmund was finally gathering the confidence needed to lead a kingdom, but she had noticed a couple of his advisors leading him astray with selfish agendas. Not desiring a repeat performance of the Amendment Order's effects on the young man, she found herself attending meetings daily.

Perhaps, what she found taking up most of her time was the very thing she would soon let go of. The Intel Kingdom's issue with rebels was too difficult for her to focus on when this far from the epicenter. It wasn't her kingdom, and King Vitio had never been the most cooperative Royal Head.

Why was she fighting this hard on their behalf? She had already placed spies and assassins in positions. There were capable leaders above them. Targets had been established. What more could she do? She had the Loess to worry about. She had faith in her husband, who was one of the spies helping the Intel Kingdom. Princess Lilu could manage, and Queen Shelly had recently recovered from her emotional spiral.

A falcon startled Ophala, sweeping in from the mists and landing on the stone floor next to her. Icewing was one of the few falcons who thrived in cold weather. A slip of parchment was tied to her leg. Ophala fed her and untied the parchment, scanning its contents:

SPO,

The Power Kingdom is impenetrable from its Realm River. I can't put into words what it is that I'm seeing. Nobody in my crew believed the claims of a fallen moon, pegging a mission which involved the crossing of a whirlpool erroneous, but what you and Spirit Queen Apsa told us was true.

The moon has crushed, what appears to be, most of the northern half of the Power Kingdom. We can't even approach the gulf, for part of the moon sits in it, too. I can't see the top of it. Picture ten thousand mountains. We can't climb or circumvent it. And the Power Kingdom's teleplatforms must have been obliterated along with everything else. The Malanese Peaks are gone.

I'm afraid to say it seems access to the Power Kingdom is no longer possible. The Powish will have to fend for themselves … if any of them are alive. We must turn back and return to port … somewhere. But we'll be awaiting word.

Captain Yu

Ophala crumpled the letter and let her hand fall to her side. She raised her mug and took a sip, dreaming it was alcohol. *Time to brainstorm ways of infiltrating the Power Kingdom.* Without Ulna Malen and its infrastructure and economy, the Powish would enter a dark age as the kingdom's outer cities and towns became susceptible to anarchy. She would also have to get word to the Intel and LeAnce family, for they had interest in the provod mines of the Malanese Peaks. The technological boom that had sprouted from Permanence technology was about to take a mighty blow.

Another falcon entered the tower, landing next to Icewing. Ophala immediately recognized her as Skyrise. The poor thing was shaking, frazzled by the cold temperatures. Icewing tried playfully nipping at her companion, but Skyrise ignored her and stepped forward. She lifted a talon, revealing a note of her own.

Elation lifted Ophala's heart as she retrieved the small parchment. Skyrise had been in charge of finding Himitsu and Kaylee with clear instructions to not return without evidence of their sighting. The fact that she was here and had braved this cold could only have meant good news.

Pilot,

I don't know what you've tasked the idiot with, but I know this has been more than a friendly gesture to allow me to begin my career path.

And that's okay. I trust you. I don't need to know what's going on, but I have information for you.

The Loess Lord isn't a good man, and he hides the inlands of the Loess through crafty methods involving Permanence vessels. The dozens of buttes scattered throughout the Loess house the most important sectors of their civilization. The one you should focus on is the tallest one.

The tops of these buttes look to be covered with dirt, deceiving anyone or anything that might look at it from above ... birds, I'm guessing. Maybe they know about you and your skills. The truth, however, is that those surfaces are mere illusions created by an Archain who infuses the energy of her and her ancient into Permanence rims that border the butte's rim, masking what are actually massive skylights.

I don't know when, but you need to send the rats. The idiot and I need to get out of here and help the Accus family, but he's gotten himself into a situation he can't escape without the use of his abilities. As for me, the Loess Lord trusts me for some reason, which is why I've gotten into a position that allows me to send this.

On the back of this sheet is a terribly drawn sketch of the fortress in which Himitsu is being held, marking the general position of his room. He always told me your rats were capable of getting him out of a tough situation ... whatever that means. Something about the Rolling Oaks.

I trust you, Pilot

-Kay

Ophala flipped the parchment over. Kaylee wasn't lying about her artistic skills. Regardless, Ophala had been waiting for something like this, and while her son may have been struggling, there was a fix.

The rats.

She frowned at Skyrise. "I'm sorry, Sky."

The falcon bowed its head. Icewing lunged at her. The two raptors began brawling, darting toward the center of the tower in a mess of wings that scattered the smaller birds.

Ophala was confused by Kaylee's language in the missive. She had revealed a lot of information, which meant she wasn't afraid of it being intercepted. However, she had also refrained from using Himitsu's name, referring to him as "the idiot" instead.

She took a seat on the stone floor, unbothered by the mist-slicked stone that dampened her trousers, and leaned back against the pillar. She would send the rats, but not to help anyone escape. Himitsu still had an objective to complete over there ... a man to kill. There was no way around it. Ophala learned that lesson years ago, which led her to the assassination of Toth Brench. To banish evil, you take on bits of its form yourself.

"Pilot Ophala."

She turned and saw King Sigmund in a kingly fur coat at the top of the stairs, his ancient scarf wrapped around his neck. "Milord, you are just the man I wanted to see," she said.

His chest swelled and back straightened with a sudden surge of pride. It was rare when Ophala expressed needing him. "What is it?"

She looked out into the mists. "The Loess has been infiltrated. My son is in position to attack from behind enemy lines. Prepare the army. We need three divisions of fifty thousand men each."

He paused, then whispered, "It's time?"

She nodded. "We head east."

57

A String of Visions

Rhyparia spent three days in silence after returning from their infiltration of the Light Empire. She had gone as a pair with Mendac to the outskirts of the empire's capital, Celeste, where they were supposed to run into a low-level Bozani while Fuhren Brenson distracted any Pogu deeper in the capital's heart. Instead, a Pogu had flown out of its way to attack Mendac and Rhyparia. Had a Pogu also been sent after Brenson? That would have meant two Pogu had been deployed, which never happened according to her studies.

The anger consuming Rhyparia was palpable. The mission hadn't gone as planned, and part of her felt bamboozled. Her own incompetence hadn't been lost on her either. She had frozen out there. She, the woman responsible for dropping a moon, had been useless when faced with one person. Had the combination of her Archaic Energy and umbrella compensated for that much physical ineptitude? Without her ancient, she might as well have been a suckling babe.

Mendac had proven his worth, aggressively confronting the Pogu with brilliant use of his Intel Energy. And since when could he fly? She scowled at her own wings and flexed—the only movement she could manage.

"It takes time," Mendac had said upon their return to the Labyrinth. "I've had more time than you think to gain mastery over them."

The statement led Rhyparia back to questioning the peculiarity of Mendac's presence here. He had been locked up with her, and his first meeting with Dark Emperor Mialo had also been hers. When Yasmine walked through the wall of Rhyparia's cell that day, he reacted as if it was his first time seeing her. If that was the case, then didn't that mean he was just as new to this experience as Rhyparia? That didn't align with the timelines of their lives though. Mendac died sixteen years ago; it couldn't have taken that long for him to arrive here. She also would have questioned his presence here rather than the Light Empire because of his Intelian blood, but she herself had Archain blood, yet still managed a spot in the Dark Empire.

She looked up at the starry sky. She stood at the center of a courtyard in the Labyrinth's depths. She was getting used to the muted colors, which meant her eyes were adjusting. Soon she'd be able to see in the dark. That progress wasn't satisfying enough.

Her entire body tightened as she tried to manipulate the wings in her back, only to have them stiffen. She had no control over their directional movement, a frustrating reality for someone who had taught herself to manipulate Archaic Chains hundreds of miles away in order to flatten a tree of a distant forest or bring down the moon in the sky.

"Stop flexing your muscles." Mendac stepped out of the Labyrinth's wall, accompanied by that woman at his side. Her name was Kadlest. Ever since their mission in the Light Empire, she had been granted access into the Labyrinth as long as he was with her—a reward for his accomplishments during the mission. Rhyparia turned the other way, back toward them. She tried again and failed.

"You're too tight," he said. "You need to relax. When you weave with your ancient, you don't flex your muscles, right?"

"Of course not. The energy and muscular systems are separate."

"And that is why you use the elastic walls of your energy canals to propel your energy where it needs to go in order to exit your body, while simultaneously secreting more energy from your Morality Cavity in the right half of your brain to refill the canals. It's the firing off of neurons just like what happens when you flex a muscle, but it's directed elsewhere. You make a decision, which then sends signals to those areas of the body. With flexing a muscle or moving an arm, these are abilities you learn and master in your early childhood—in your infancy in the latter's case. They become instinctive, requiring no thought."

He rounded and stood in front of her, hands behind his back like a professor. "According to your backstory with your mother, even powering your Archaic Energy became instinctive early on. While most people don't learn how to ignite their energy until their preteen years, the feeling was forced onto you at the tender age of seven by your mother's will. She triggered those neurons to fire off and set your Archaic Energy into frenzy. Then when you tried doing it in the future under your own will, it was so instinctive that it activated without limiters, hence the instability and lack of power tempering. You needed to harness it, which Musku helped you do during those two decades of training.

"Alas, because you never actually learned to trigger your Archaic Energy on your own that first time in your early years, you never realized that your neurons are directed toward the left half of your brain when you make the decision to use your energy. It just happens, and you're okay with that. You know where to emit the energy from your body and how to weave it once it's outside among nature's currents. Now you must learn to use an energy for the first time again, and your mother's not around to force it out of you. This means you'll have to spark it yourself, which requires signals from neurons to be sent to the correct location of your body."

He paused, and Rhyparia waited for the rest of his explanation.

"Pay close attention," he said. His wings surged outward, like a raptor taking flight. "Focus on me, not the wings."

She looked him in the eyes and saw it immediately. Black haze leaked out of the pupils and into the irises, sometimes shifting as far out as the whites of the sclera. His wings slapped downward and lifted his feet off of the ground, but she continued studying his eyes, where the shadows shifted in patterns with the motions of his wings. He lowered himself to the ground and let his wings rescind into his back. The blackness in his eyes vanished.

"The secret is the Judgment Cavities in the eyes," he said. "That's where the majority of your mental flexing should be directed, at least the first several times until it becomes natural. Then you start worrying about the flexing of your energy canals. Relax your muscles though. They have nothing to do with it."

"Thank you," she whispered. "I know I'm unfair to you, but I'd be useless here without your guidance."

"You're not unfair. You're frustrated with being thrust into the unknown, which is a common response for any person. At least you're not scared, which is how most people would respond. Not everyone is like me. I embrace this sort of thing." He smiled and placed a hand on her shoulder as he walked past. "You'll figure it out, and we'll continue to dominate together."

She turned and watched him leave. Kadlest followed him, grabbing his hand as they passed through the wall. Had he come out here just to help her? Rhyparia was beginning to believe he was a good man, but misunderstood, thrust into unfavorable situations as a general that forced him to choose between lesser evils.

And seeing Kadlest's hand in his, she felt envious of that.

*   *   *

Mendac had fallen to his knees, vision flashing between the present and several unknowns. Confusion about his state of mind seeped into frustration. Kadlest crouched next to him with his hand in hers. To display this moment of weakness in front of her was shameful.

His eyes were fixed on the gray grass of a Labyrinth courtyard. The first two visions had been short and tame, but he knew more were coming, as they typically came in bursts of ten to twelve. He was living moments in time that didn't belong to him, but he had yet to discover the identities of the people whose perspectives he had been experiencing. The visions were too quick.

The grass disappeared. He was rushing down a long corridor with dozens of tall windows lining the left wall. A woman in a burgundy cloak ran ahead of him. She didn't seem to be running away from him, nor did he feel like he was chasing her. Either she was leading the way or he was struggling to keep pace. He tended to believe the latter, as he felt considerable bulk in his midsection. He glanced at the windows he ran past and could see he was a very heavy-set man, but couldn't decipher any finer details with the sunlight overpowering his reflection.

Their journey ended at an open door in the right wall. The woman who had been ahead of him didn't enter. She stepped to the side, and he rushed into the chamber beyond. The far end of the chamber was a prison cell occupied by an emaciated man. Mendac almost didn't recognize him because of his poor condition, but that was undoubtedly Archaic King Itta. Directly in front of the cell was a man in a burgundy cloak, like the woman he had been following through the corridor. He was twisted on the ground and bleeding. Mendac knew him, too. He was one of the prized Devish he had brought back to the Intel Kingdom, a truth extractor known as Marcus. Scattered throughout the rest of the chamber were the most important figures in the Light Realm: Intel King Vitio, Spirit Queen Apsa, and Adren King Supido.

Mendac gazed into gray grass once again, eyebrows furrowed. That was the first vision to offer him enough information to make an educated guess as to whose point-of-view he had experienced. Every Royal Head had been in that chamber save Passion King Damian. Mendac had been Damian. It explained his overweight build, as the mute king had always been an unhealthy man.

The scene brought to light many questions. Since his rebirth, Mendac hadn't questioned Kadlest about the nature of the kingdoms and their politics. He had planned to, but the abduction by the Dark Empire's Gefal had pushed such topics to the back of his mind. Seeing the Archaic King imprisoned and clearly tortured or neglected was jarring. And why had Marcus looked like that? What were the Royal Heads doing?

Questions vanished, as did the grass. He stood in a vast, empty atrium of eroded stone. The tops of walls crumbled away from ceilings, gaps allowing moonlight to streak through. Despite the structural damage, he saw no rubble on the ground. In fact, the atrium was clean and well decorated with portraits, furniture, and accent pieces. Distant screams pierced the atrium's walls from somewhere far away—likely, miles.

A perfect, gray cube stood in front of him. It was smooth and featureless, a paradoxical juxtaposition of architecture when placed in such a broken down chamber. He believed he was viewing the perspective of a child given how large a sofa looked across the room. The cube, however, was only slightly taller than him and a few feet wide. He couldn't think of any reason for its existence unless it was an abstract decorative piece. It might have helped if these visions allowed him access to the person's thoughts. He felt general sensations, like the anxious pit in this vessel's stomach, leading him to believe there was more to this cube than its aesthetic.

A rectangular section in the front of the cube opened, revealing a door that, previously, had blended in with the stone. It was a room—or a closet, considering its size. A woman stepped out. She had vibrant ivory hair and silver eyes. Gentle porcelain skin hugged every angle of her facial structure, not a wrinkle or blemish to be seen. She was nothing short of stunning, donning a silk dress of black that contoured her legs as she stepped out of the cube.

"Oh, sweet boy," she said, crouching low to meet the height of the vessel Mendac occupied. She spread her arms, and he entered her embrace after a moment's hesitation. He couldn't feel her, but he felt in the boy's soul that he was warm in her arms. She pulled her head away from his shoulder, looked into his eyes, and rustled his hair. "I'm all better now. That session should last me three days. And by that time, your father will be ready to pay for more."

The anxious pit returned. Mendac didn't know what she was talking about, but he knew this boy didn't like that cube or whatever it contained. The woman kissed his forehead, took his hand, and led him away from the cube.

Gray grass became Mendac's focus again. That vision had taken place in the Cyn Kingdom, a place he had mostly avoided during his first shot at life. He'd recognize those beastly screams anywhere, his time spent building the interrealm teleplatforms in the Void one of the worst experiences of his life. The Linsani could be heard for hundreds—if not thousands—of leagues. The only evidence that contradicted its location as the Void was the physical state of the woman who had exited the cube. Nobody looked that pristine in the Void, not even foreigners when exposed to its atmosphere for more than a day. The woman had been too perfect.

A series of four more visions occurred, each one lasting only a split second before transitioning to the next. They happened too quickly to leave a lasting impression. The last vision, however, stuck.

He swung through the trees of Phesaw Park, shrouded in the pink canopies of its cherry blossoms. The sensations of this vessel were jarringly different than the rest. Elation flooded his chest, a sense of spirit that made him feel as if he was flying. He couldn't hear himself, but he knew by the stress of his cheeks and jaw that he was laughing hysterically. He looked down and saw that he was barefoot, each toenail painted a different pastel: shamrock green, sky blue, rose pink, soft yellow, etcetera. The air resistance, caused by the speed at which he moved, tossed golden hair in his face. Something was tied around the front of his neck and hung loosely down his back. This vessel must have been a girl, and a very happy one.

He was in the grass again, Kadlest's hand now clammy in his. He ripped it away and looked up to the gray sky that hung above the Labyrinth. His gaze roved toward Kadlest, who recoiled from his fury. His question had bite. "*What is happening to me?*"

58

The Strasan

Naipa had been responsible for retrieving Bryson from his home again, proving the Light Empire didn't trust his willingness to cooperate despite his promises beforehand. He supposed he deserved that distrust given his prior track record. While he was relatively sure he would have returned to the Empire after his sixteen hours had ended, the difficulty of saying goodbye during that final hour had made him rethink that certainty.

During the walk back to Capsule Three, he waited patiently as Naipa tried deciphering their location without draining the walls of their ivory color. What should have been a thirty-minute journey ended up taking close to two hours, as someone who apparently loved pranking the forgetful Strasan had, once again, manipulated the signs she had posted around the many corridors. Bryson remained silent throughout their trek, admiring the woman each time she came to a stop and stroked her chin in thought. History called her the Unforgettable, and he agreed. It would be a sin to forget a human like this.

The entire world had.

He entered Capsule Three to find Thusia and Suadade arguing in the sitting area of the commons area. From what Bryson could tell since arriving here months ago, the two Branian—who were supposedly best friends—spent most of their days bickering with each other or looking for ways to pass the time. Aestys, meanwhile, stood guard throughout Celeste. That woman might have annoyed Bryson, but he respected the work she did. He didn't think any less of Thusia or Suadade, for both were active Branian and needed to remain in the Starlight to protect the firstborns to whom they were bonded in case of emergency.

Thusia turned upon his entry. He saw in her face that this argument was more than a mere squabble. She was flustered, face a bright pink. Suadade rose from the armchair in which Bryson had never seen anyone else sit. The Adrenian regarded him with an expressionless face—common among his type.

"What's going on?" Bryson asked, dropping his hoodie on the center table of the entrance area.

"Nothing," Thusia said.

He raised an eyebrow. If there was one quality for which most Spiritians weren't known, it was lying. Thusia was not an exception. He looked pointedly at Suadade, an Adrenian who would give it to him straight. "What's going on?"

Thusia flashed an irate glare at the swordsman, clenching her jaw as if to communicate, "Tread lightly."

When Bryson had first met Suadade and, shortly afterward, Thusia, the Adrenian had been known to keep the Empire's secrets while the Spiritian had a tendency of being loose-lipped. That had changed ever since their stint of imprisonment, and even a bit before that. What the higher Bozani had intended to be a method of striking fear in the two Branian actually became fuel to Suadade's fire. He was angry.

"Now that a few days have passed since the night everything happened, reports have finally begun trickling down to our ranks," Suadade said while Thusia stared at the ceiling in annoyance. "While your assessment of the situation that night had been correct, and you did well in turning around and finding Fuhren Brenson in Founding Plaza, he wasn't the only threat that night. The Intelamp distress signals that Pogu Thornstorm and Nora followed weren't false alarms, apparently. There were threats in the Crust, too."

"Did Aestys handle it?" Bryson asked.

"No, she was tied up with a different threat."

"How many were here?"

"Four total," said Suadade. "Brenson, with whom you dealt. Aestys fought with Fuhren Poten Copor, whom she managed to withstand for a few minutes before he broke away. She did well in avoiding a direct brawl with him, but did sustain critical injuries, which is why we haven't seen her since that night. The Strasan believe Poten was to serve as a distraction to Aestys while two others of their ranks roamed the Crust unchecked. Thornstorm eventually ran into those two, which were the two responsible for triggering the Intelamp signals because of their wings."

"They were diversions," Bryson said. "I already knew this."

"Which would be fine if it wasn't for the additional information we're now hearing about their identities."

"Were they Versac?"

Suadade's eyes widened. "Goodness, no. Thornstorm wouldn't be alive if that was the case. But they were capable of sprouting wings, and one could fly. And what makes it even scarier was that neither of them were traditional Gefal."

"What is that supposed to mean?" Bryson asked.

Thusia exhaled and plopped down on the arm of the sofa behind her. "This is your funeral, Leon. He meets with the Strasan tonight. You can't wait for them to tell him?"

"He needs to hear it from us."

"Spit it out," Bryson said, angst growing by the second.

"We don't know if they're new Gefal who took the place of old ones, but that would have implied a former Gefal died or retired, which isn't believable considering we're in the midst of war. Dark Emperor Mialo wouldn't risk sacrificing proven skill and experience in favor of unknown talents. This has led to the theory that the Dark Empire has acquired humans from the kingdoms who have tapped into Mulawi pre-death, adding to their normally-fixed number of twenty-four. That's similar to what the Light Empire has done by making you an additional piece to our forces."

"Maybe Empress Tonitrua already knew about this, and her sending for me was a response," Bryson said, surprising himself with his own intuition.

Suadade nodded. "Another theory, but that's not the most troublesome part of this news." He trailed off, eyes glued to Bryson's. "Thornstorm's descriptions of the two unknowns have also made their way down the ranks, and while one is a mystery still, for she apparently cowered in the shadows, the other is a big deal."

Bryson hung from a cliff for several seconds before sticking out his chin and shaking his head. "Who?"

"Oh, now you're having cold feet?" Thusia asked, a lazy expression directed at Suadade.

"Mendac," said Suadade.

Bryson's stomach froze, plunged, and shattered atop the floor. He blinked as the name rattled his brain. No longer did Thusia stare daggers at Suadade; she gazed pitifully at Bryson. Her face paled, then her expression darkened as she glanced down at the floor in thought. No matter how much both of them wanted nothing to do with the man named Mendac, they knew their realities. They both had ties with him. He had wronged her in his actions following her sacrificial death; he had wronged Bryson in the evils directly done to the boy and his mother.

"Mendac is fighting for the Dark Empire?" he asked, voice hollow.

"So it seems."

Bryson looked off to the side, sucking at the inside of his cheeks as he mulled over the implications. He had already known about Mendac's rebirth, but something about hearing how close he had been to the man that night sparked rage in him at the missed opportunity. Something icy ran through him—anger like cold steel. Thusia gripped herself, tugging her cardigan tighter around her shoulders, but he thought nothing of it.

He saw a silver lining. If Mendac was in the Dark Empire, that meant he wasn't hiding in the Intel Kingdom as a threat to any of his friends. He was serving as a soldier for a greater war, which made him Bryson's enemy. They had an opportunity to clash up here, away from anyone in the kingdoms.

"Would Mialo give Mendac the opportunity to visit the kingdoms like Empress Tonitrua just did for me?" he asked.

"We don't know," Suadade admitted. "But it would be difficult for him to access the Light Realm's kingdoms now that he has wings and his eyes are flooded with Mulawi. There's a reason why ranks above Branian or Bewahr don't enter the opposite realm's kingdoms. It's because they've reached a power level that would draw the attention of the Essences. They'd be risking their lives, so I don't think you should fear anything happening to your friends as long as they remain in one of the Light Kingdoms."

"The Essences?" Bryson asked.

"That I'll leave for the Strasan to explain," Suadade said. "I think your meeting today revolves around that very subject, and it has to do with the entity named Intelius that the Empress supposedly said you would have to slay during your first meeting with her. Beyond that, I am clueless, for it is far above my jurisdiction."

Thusia remained silent, either still jarred by the mentioning of Mendac or finding no reason to rebuke Suadade after he had revealed as much as he had.

"What's the news from the royal front?" Suadade asked, considering the previous topic over. "I sense less resistance from Shelly, though I haven't tried contacting her while you've been down there."

"I think you should visit her. She's ready."

Suadade nodded and vanished into light. Thusia locked eyes with Bryson, and they found solace within each other's gazes. They knew what needed to be done. Mendac needed to die by one of their hands. There was a cold resoluteness to that fact.

Thusia gripped herself harder and huffed. "Is it cold in here to you?"

*   *   *

Bryson was flying, but not by his own power.

Naipa held him against her chest like a rabbit dangling from the talons of an owl as they soared above Celeste. He was impressed by her strength, for she was considerably smaller than him. But considering her rank as a Strasan, he figured he shouldn't be all that surprised.

He looked down upon the city. The view was breathtaking. He had a sudden appreciation for Pilot Ophala's ability because there wasn't just awe that arose from this, but fear. Was this what it felt like when she entered the vision of one of her birds?

Part of him wilted at the sight of Founding Plaza, its vast emptiness a stunning contrast to the crowded streets branching off of it. Since the night of Brenson's attack, nobody had been allowed entry into the hub of commerce for Celeste University. The businesses there were shut down until the city's safety departments deemed it safe to return. Even then, Bryson wondered if the plaza would ever return to its previous vitality. Many students had died there, which could drive away anyone from wanting to visit.

Naipa was forced to fly around the castle that was the university itself. Other than the Starlight, it was the grandest building in Celeste. It was something straight out of ancient times, built of weathered stone and assembled as a scattered grouping of towers with geometrical forms and pointed roofs, similar to Phelos Palace. Students passed over bridges that connected towers while others walked in groups across the school grounds far below. Those who noticed Naipa pointed in her direction. How common was it for one of the winged Bozani to venture into the city, much less take flight above it?

They flew beyond Celeste, where the land became a grid of pastures and farms. Manmade structures dissipated in favor of nature. A carpet of green stretched below them, dotted by acacia trees with wide umbrella canopies and waterholes where animals Bryson had never seen before gathered at the edges. He became so enamored by creatures with necks taller than him and snake-like noses that extended from the fronts of their faces that he didn't realize they had begun their descent until Naipa was telling him to lower his feet and brace for a landing.

Thankfully, the landing was simple. The Strasan caught herself in the air just above the ground and lowered him gently. He almost collapsed atop legs like jelly, his heart pounding against his ribs. He wobbled and caught Naipa's sleeve. She looked at him and smirked.

"You did well. That's better than vomiting."

Unaware that he did in fact have that urge until she mentioned it, he gagged, bile creeping up the back of his tongue before he managed to choke it back down. She patted him on the back and laughed. "Let's go."

He followed her to the Empire's Edge. Like the kingdoms below, it was an island that floated in the sky. It was a wonder how when a person jumped, they fell downward, but these islands managed to remain in a fixed position in space. He supposed if he had paid any attention in science class at Phesaw, he would have known the explanation behind the wonder. Something about an array of magnetic fields.

A land bridge extended between the Empire's island and another smaller island a couple thousand paces in the distance. It was a narrow strip of grassy land that could perhaps hold four people shoulder to shoulder, with nothing but a meager rail along either side to prevent someone from toppling off the edge. Inspecting the island from this distance, Bryson couldn't recognize any landmarks or features of note. It looked flat for as far as the eye could see. There was a brightness to it that perplexed him.

"What's over there?" Bryson asked. "Besides my supposed target: the mysterious Intelius."

Naipa glanced at him sidelong as they both stood at the cusp of the land bridge. "I hope that light tone is due to discomfort and not a lack of seriousness."

He frowned, unsure of which one it was. "I guess a bit of both."

She stared at the distant island for a moment before turning back. Celeste was no longer visible, but the Starlight gleamed above the horizon. How far had they traveled? With Naipa's wings, it had felt like nothing.

A figure appeared in the sky, radiant wings growing larger as it neared. The person descended and landed a dozen meters away, wings rescinding into their back as they walked the rest of the way.

The woman had dark skin, hair coiled tightly in a thick braid that ran down the side of her head and spraying into loose kinks near the bottom. She wore elegant robes that rustled behind her, appearing to fall to about knee-level if undisturbed by wind. The robes were a sky blue, trimmed with silver along hems and dotted with diamonds that shined like stars at the collar. The light was unnatural, and Bryson realized they were bits of the

Starlight's quartz. He knew this woman without an introduction, for he had heard Aestys complain about her regularly. This was Magnifica Solaris, the woman summoned by Gatal Accus in the *First of Five*, responsible for saving the city of Balle from the doom of an incoming meteor.

Another person arrived—this time a man—but in such a manner that caused Bryson to jump. He seemed to have appeared out of nowhere. He was sunburned to the point of leather, wrinkles tight and pronounced around his mouth and across his forehead. His hair was short and rustled, graying at the roots. He had sideburns that stretched down to his jawline, fading into a five-o'clock shadow along his chin—a style which Bryson had never seen in the kingdoms. Beneath his robes, he wore an elastic skin-suit that molded perfectly with his chest and abdomen, highlighting features below his waistline more than Bryson would have liked. He was a physical specimen much like Debo, Director Buredo, and King Supido, but with a couple inches on each of them—and they were tall to begin with. The front of his robes came to a rest at his sides, tucked behind the hilt of a sword at each hip.

Bryson looked up at him after admiring his build, suddenly aware that he was a child despite being in his lower twenties. He didn't know this man, yet already wanted to stand by his side. He glanced at Magnifica … to think she might have been more powerful than the swordsman.

"Ah, we finally get to meet the brat," said Magnifica.

Bryson's eyes widened. He didn't become angry or embarrassed, but suddenly guilty about how he had treated Aestys's viewpoints on the Strasan. The Branian had been correct in her assessment. Magnifica was an elitist, and something about that squelched his fear.

"And I get to meet the pompous, prissy princess," he said, eyebrows falling flat to display an air of boredom. His mastery of facial expressions down to the minute details was credit to Lilu. He had always been defiant when it came to authority, but the royal Jestivan had strengthened that defiance with an arsenal of sass and wit—or what he thought was wit. He was quite dull when compared to even the average person.

Magnifica looked at Naipa, then said, "Children." Her tone teetered toward amused rather than reprimand. She refocused on Bryson, lip curling slightly downward in disgust, as if she'd had two lifetimes spent sneering to practice. This was a Bozani? This was the woman who saved the Archaic Kingdom? She had to be one of the eldest beings in the Empire.

"So, you're Magnifica Solaris. No need for an introduction," he said before acknowledging the taller man, as if shrugging off the woman's existence. She had pissed him off, and perhaps it looked like he was being petty, but it was more about a statement than anything else. He wouldn't let her treat him like a rat. "My name's Bryson Still. And you?"

The man grunted, resting a hand on each hilt at his waist. "Rhysel Kawi."

So much for Bryson's cool demeanor. He blinked, running the name through his mind twice more. "Are you related to Debo?"

"Debo?"

Ah, that's right. Nobody up here knew him as that. "Ataway … Debonicus."

"Yes. He was a very distant grandson."

Magnifica swept past the group and started down the bridge. Bryson paid her no mind, fixated on the Adrenian whom shared Debo's blood. "I've never heard of you."

"I'm sure they wiped my name from existence," Rhysel said. "Just like they tried my race."

"You're an Adren Assassin?"

"The very first."

Now Bryson understood how this man had seemingly teleported into existence just moments ago.

"Keep your pants on," Naipa said. "You look like a boy confronted by his first crush."

Bryson regained control of his facial muscles, realizing he had been sporting an open-mouthed grin.

Rhysel laughed heartily. "I admire you a great deal, too, young man," he said, causing Bryson to blush. "I've heard from a couple of the Pogu about your skills. Specifically, that speed percentage of yours, which is outrageous for someone who isn't Adrenian. And you must be something special for Ataway to have abandoned his friends here to take care of you."

Bryson's shoulders sunk at the word "abandoned," and Rhysel must have noticed. "A wound long since healed," he said. "We hold nothing against you." He paused, then asked, "You want to race me some time?"

"An Intelian versus the first Adren Assassin?" Bryson said. "That seems silly."

"I won't use my Adrenergy. What do you say?"

Bryson crossed his arms. "I'm definitely not doing that. If I race you, you use every advantage you have."

He lifted his chin and scratched at his five o'clock shadow, emitting a sound like a rake through dead leaves. "You asked for it." He grabbed Bryson's shoulder, turned him around, and guided him down the bridge. "I'll have arrangements made."

Naipa followed the two men. Magnifica led the group by fifty paces, robes billowing behind her. Bryson and Rhysel reminisced on Debo's life. While they had known the man at separate points of his life, it seemed he acted no differently. Rhysel asked about the current state of Adren Assassins, and Bryson wondered if Suadade hadn't given him any information. When he admitted to knowing only about his friend named Simon Skimentis, Rhysel barked out a single laugh and clapped his hands together.

"The Skimentis's are still at it!"

"Another old family?" Bryson asked.

"Yes, there are three family names that served as the foundation to future families. It started with me, a Kawi, but I had five children with my wife. She had been a normal Adrenian, for I was the only Adren Assassin in the world. I passed on the assassin trait to only three of my children, a son and two daughters. My son married and had children, carrying on the Kawi name. Each daughter married into a different family of non-assassins, adopting their last names and passing them onto their children. Those two families were known as Skimentis and Fuuna."

"Kawi, Skimentis, and Fuuna," Bryson repeated. "Like some sort of legendary trinity."

Rhysel smirked. "I do take great pride in my family and the lineage that resulted from it, even if I didn't get to live long enough to personally see the fruits of my labor ..." he trailed off, cocking his head curiously ... "I guess it was my wife's *labor*, literally."

They shared a laugh, and Naipa groaned. "Men are never as funny as they think."

Rhysel glanced back, offering the type of smile that enraptured someone with charm when gracing the face of a good man, but struck someone with repulsion when splitting the face of a bad man. He was the former; that was clear. It was reminiscent of Debo, which caused Bryson to practically melt beneath the man's gaze. There was no denying that the two men were blood.

Naipa pointedly looked away. "I'm not falling under your spell."

Rhysel slowed until he was at her side. Bryson turned, walking backward. The assassin's hands moved from his sword's hilts to the pockets of his bodysuit, which were just big enough to grant his fingers access. He towered over her, a two-foot difference between their statures. "My apologies, Naipa. You have my attention again."

She didn't respond, and Bryson raised his eyebrows at the interaction.

"She likes me, you see," said Rhysel. "And I like her."

Luckily, Bryson had superb balance. He almost fell over the side rail and land bridge as he tripped. The two Strasan didn't even feign a rescue attempt, either suspecting he could recover on his own or feeling he deserved his fate after such a reaction.

"I tolerate you," she said. "You're cruel."

Bryson studied the Adrenian, trying to find the cruelness of which she spoke. All he could see was an older, more weathered Debo. Then the name, Rhysel, sparked a memory from his first day in the Empire. During Naipa's struggle to guide Bryson through the Starlight to find Capsule Three, she cursed Rhysel under her breath for switching around the signs she had posted as directions for herself. Apparently, it hadn't been the first time. And now that Bryson knew Naipa's story—or the summarized version of it—cruel wasn't even close enough a modifier to describe the trickery. He was preying on her forgetfulness.

Bryson frowned. "Why do you mess with her directions?"

Naipa looked at Bryson, perhaps with a tinge of surprise. The accusative tone in the question was a sharp turn from the conversation's previous lightness. Rhysel's laughing face fell, hanging between hurt and understanding. He placed a hand on her shoulder and inhaled. "I don't do it often, but when I do, it's for good reason."

"Getting off on abusing her weaknesses?"

He pursed his lips. "Weakness? If anything, Naipa sees her ability as strength. She helps others find peace during dark times."

"At the sacrifice of her own peace."

Rhysel opened his mouth to respond, but Naipa lifted her arm and placed her hand on his, pressing it gently against her shoulder. "I appreciate your concern, Bryson," she said, "but I do what I do knowing full well the consequences. And I do have peace, for Rhysel gives me that. He doesn't change my directions to discombobulate me; he's actually giving me his own directions ... usually to him."

"Oh," Bryson said. He blinked, then narrowed his eyes as he chewed the inside of his cheek in uncomfortable thought. "OH!" He whirled and began walking forward again, whistling with hands behind his head. Rhysel's booming chuckle rocked the land for several seconds.

Bryson would have released a sigh of relief when they finally reached the other island thirty minutes later, but he was too enamored by the landscape sprawling before him. The ground was pure white—a prairie of quartz. It played tricks on his eyes, making him uncertain of how much land encompassed him.

Magnifica didn't break stride. More time passed in their journey, and Bryson's mind drifted. They started with positive images before giving way beneath the oppressive weight of darker ones: Mendac standing above Bryson, leering at him with a scalpel in a gloved hand; Mendac throwing his mother against the wall; Saikatto's half-burned face, courtesy of Mendac; Mendac rising from his casket, as organs, muscles, and flesh bubbled into existence, shadowy wings spreading from his back. Bryson stuffed his hands in his pockets and puffed out a breath. The man had only given him evil stories by which to remember him, and now he was back.

The sun began to set, and Bryson noticed a bluish light in the distance. He thought it a trick of the fading sun, but as they neared he found the source to be something on the island itself. Magnfica reached it first, coming to a stop and looking up at it. Bryson, Naipa, and Rhysel followed suit.

A massive crystalline structure rose like a stalagmite from a wide base until narrowing into jagged points at the top, edges cragged and layered. It was made out of the same white quartz, but more translucent. It was the source of the light, wherein neon blue sparks cackled and coursed throughout, illuminating a white core where the quartz was denser. Contained in that core was a darkened silhouette in the form of a human.

This wasn't a landform, but a prison.

Naipa caught Bryson's hand to keep him from walking closer, and despite that measure, he still had to squint to protect his eyes from the light. It didn't spread beyond the spire, operating like every instance of Tahara he'd seen before in his life—confined in a way that broke the rules of normal light.

"Intelius," Magnifica said, speaking for the first time since storming off across the land bridge earlier. "The most stubborn of the Essences."

Knowing Magnifica was considered a zealot, he listened closely. She would know more about lore like this than anyone else—what could only be mysticism to a mind as naïve as Bryson's, or any human for that matter.

"Before Empress Tonitrua's rebirth in the Empire, in her previous life—before Known History—she was known as the Thunder Queen, or the Originator who ruled the Light Knowledge Kingdom. There had been ten Originators, each possessing an Essence from which they harvested to monopolize the ability of magic. Queen Tonitrua harvested from Intelius, the elemental entity of electricity that could take on the shape of a human, in what is now known as Thunder Alley. This granted her the ability to wield electricity and lightning, while containing nature's magical source to that one location. It was a mutual relationship, granting Tonitrua absolute power and allowing Intelius a conscious life of freedom.

"Every kingdom housed a pair: Mialo and Devius, Stonebody and Powius, Galela and Spirish, Dimiourgos and Primitheo, and so on and so forth. When the era of Originators began to die, it started with Thunder Queen Tonitrua and Mind King Mialo. They were the first to *voluntarily* cease harvesting from their Essences. In doing so, Intelius and Devius exploded across the world as billions of invisible currents, a few of which were pieces of themselves. These were said to have been cataclysmic events that yielded natural disasters, but what also came of it were the first signs of weavists. Commoners began to wield electricity or psychic abilities depending on which kingdom they were in.

"The other seven Originators—Tonitrua originally believed it was all eight, but later learned Dimiourgos hadn't been present because of a feud with Stonebody—chased after Tonitrua and Mialo, deeming them traitors. The two of them couldn't fight back, for they had weakened and aged from not harvesting in years, but instead fled to an island at the center of the Sea of Light. They were caught and sunk, which was ultimately their deaths.

"The true tragedy here, however, lies in the fates of the Essences after essentially dying. While the Originators lost their power from harvesting the Essences, the Essences lost their freedom. Their metaphysical form was scattered throughout Kuki Sphaira's atmosphere while their physical form was locked away here. There are four other Quartz Spires similar to this one located on this island, each imprisoning one of the Light Realm's five Essences.

"While none were pleased with this fate, they accepted it. And their jobs were to serve as sensors to dark forces in the kingdoms they watched over. If anybody in the kingdoms used Mulawi—ranging from an attack to simply spreading their wings—the Quartz Spire of that kingdom would activate here, signaling danger's presence in a kingdom to Empress Tonitrua. The same system is in place in the Dark Empire, which is why truly elite Bozani or Gefal don't typically infiltrate the kingdoms of the opposite realm. They wouldn't be able to go unnoticed.

"Which brings us to this fool," Magnifica said, exasperation thick in her tone. "Intelius is the one Essence that has refused to resign himself to his parent's imprisonment."

"His parents?" asked Bryson.

"Tahar."

Ah, that was right. He had forgotten about that. The ten Essences were children of Tahar and Mulawith.

She saw the understanding on his face and continued. "He fights against his bonds even though it's impossible for him to break free. The sparks you see igniting within are his efforts to escape. It has been this way since I've been here, and apparently the same can be said for the Empress. Intelius is livid with her; he feels betrayed. He doesn't sleep, for he's not human. We don't even think he's actually a 'he.'"

Magnifica looked at Bryson, her expression severe. "His mulishness makes it so the Empress never knows what's truly happening in the Intel Kingdom. This is because his spire is always signaled by his electricity. It should be dull ninety-nine percent of the time, only activating when the royal firstborn is in danger by the presence of a Gefal of elite rank, like a Versac or one of the Fuhren capable of flight."

"Wait, wait, wait," Bryson said. He went silent, shaking his head as he studied the quartz spire. "You're telling me a Versac, someone of your skill level, could enter the Intel Kingdom right now without consequence because of this guy?"

"And thus you see the dilemma," she breathed. "The only sliver of hope is that Emperor Mialo isn't aware of Intelius's reluctance to cooperate with the Light Empire. Otherwise, he would have taken advantage of it by now and sent someone to kill the youngest Intel royal firstborn. That wouldn't tip the scales of imbalance to his side, but it would alleviate the pressure he's feeling. Instead of the Dark Empire having three Cavities to our five, it would be three to our four."

Bryson's expression was fierce. All of this implied L.K., the youngest Intelian royal firstborn, was a target. "Well, allow me ..." he said, stepping closer to the spire, finding the solution simple.

Naipa grabbed his wrist again, this time without gentleness. "If it was that simple, do you think he'd still be here?" she asked.

He looked back at her. "What do I need to do? It's imprisoned and unable to defend itself."

"Its prison is its defense," Magnifica said. "Tahara-infused quartz is special."

He figured that wasn't too surprising, seeing that it was the body of a god. "If times are so desperate and dangerous," he said, "then why don't one of you three go down to the Intel Kingdom to continuously watch over my son?"

"Because we can't last long down there," Naipa said. "It takes a lot of Tahara to keep the three of us alive, and there's not enough in the kingdoms. It's buried deeply in a boundless building. We need to be in immediate proximity to the Starlight or this island. I can last maybe ten minutes down there."

"Basically," said Rhysel, "we would have to descend to the kingdoms and hope that an enemy foolishly tries approaching the Intel firstborn during that ten-minute span, which is highly unlikely."

Bryson breathed deeply, irritated by these supposed laws. "So how does Tonitrua expect me to kill it?"

"We don't know," Magnifica admitted. "The Empress is keeping that silent. Our job here was to brief you on the issue at hand by giving you some background. This is simply a preliminary meeting."

Rolling his eyes, he said, "In other words, my fifth preliminary measure before getting to the point? I've been through a meeting with the Pogu, a nauseating amount of studying, a first exam that I failed, a second exam that became an actual disaster, and now a meeting with the three Strasan."

Magnifica turned on a dime, lifting her chin as she regarded him. "You're a child. You, a mortal still on his first life, were abducted from a land of mundanity and thrust into a land of, what your kind considers to be, gods."

"Which we're not," Rhysel said, putting in his two cents.

Magnifica waved at him, dismissing his interruption. "You thought such a transition would be easy? This is more than taking the training wheels off your tricycle."

Bryson hated this woman.

"Consider it a blessing the Empress is willing to go through this amount of effort to groom you." Wings spread from her back. "Because I consider it a waste of resources." Then she took to the sky.

He watched her disappear in the direction of the Starlight, the six Cavities of Tahar gleaming like stars in the distance.

"Her delivery is never ideal," Rhysel said, "but what she tries to convey is usually correct."

Bryson met the man's eyes, but without the ferocity he'd given Magnifica. He was being a child, and Debo would have likely supported the woman's scorn. He acknowledged the quartz spire once more, and then departed side by side with Rhysel and Naipa.

DAVID F. FARRIS

59

The Heart of the Rebels

Lilu had her sister back.

Intel Queen Shelly strode next to Lilu through Dunami Palace, her gate rejuvenated by Bryson's visit days prior. She didn't smile as much as she used to, but at least there was life to her aura. That smile would never become frequent again. They had lost both their mother and father; that would take years to heal.

The two sisters had spent most of their day in one long, informal meeting. It carried through breakfast, lunch, and mid-afternoon, transitioning between dining chambers, private corridors, Shelly's bedroom, and the war room. The day would end here in the palace's guest sector.

"I don't think you met him," Lilu said, "but Pilot Ophala met a man who had once worked beneath Grand Director Poicus and Archaic Director Senex when they were spies. He is a hybrid of spy and assassin. Goes by the name of Creep."

"Well, considering his profession, that's a promising name," Shelly said.

"He is strange. But yes, he's skilled at his profession according to Pilot Ophala. And he's apparently passed some tests she put him through to assure our confidence in his loyalties. In order to infiltrate the rebels, his role has been to establish himself a reputation as a hired assassin, which means he must appear to kill the people his clients pay him to. Obviously, he doesn't actually kill anyone." She stopped in front of a door guarded by two soldiers. Both men bowed and stepped to the side. Lilu withdrew a key from her pocket and unlocked the door. "This was my solution," she said, pushing open the door.

A room sat on the other side, lavish and comfortable like everything else in the palace. It was one of the building's interior chambers, so there were no windows, but plenty of Intelights to fill that role. Four men and a woman were stationed throughout the room: a couple at a chess board, a man reading a book off to the side, and two people seated at a desk that had been repurposed as a parlor bar, bottles of liquor crowded atop it.

They all turned, eyes widening at the sight of the sisters. They stood and bowed. There had been a time when Lilu thought she could rid people of that habit. She had tried in Brilliance to mostly no avail, and it seemed that trend would continue in the capital.

"These are Creep's marks, targeted by rebels for obstructing their cause. In other words, they're friendlies of the crown. In exchange for their acceptance of their sequestering here in the palace, we've provided them with fantastic living arrangements. They drink to their hearts' delight and livers' demise. They sleep when and for how long they want. They simply must wait here until the rebellion crisis is mostly under control. We've even accommodated their families if they have any that depend on them." The guests straightened out of their bows and stared at Shelly. "But," Lilu added, "there was one condition they asked of me. One that mattered more than any of these luxuries ... And now I can give them it."

"What's that?" Shelly asked.

"They've been dying to meet their queen."

*　　　*　　　*

"What's the meaning of this?" asked Periphan LeAnce, the woman who was funding the revolution that sought to eliminate the Intel family.

"Bad news with which needs to be dealt," Lilu said, seated in the guest quarters gifted to the two LeAnce siblings. She, Wendel, and Periphan sat in armchairs in their sitting chamber.

"Must be bad if you've delayed the tour," Wendel said.

A tour of the new Weavineering factory's first two floors was supposed to be held this evening. The event had been in the works for weeks in efforts to assure nobles that construction was going smoothly, which it had been. It was news that would have made everyone happy. Alas, information brought to her attention by Ophala about the Power Kingdom's abysmal condition had squelched any optimism.

It forced Lilu to make a last-minute decision to postpone the event, angering many of the project's financial backers. Their contributions were minor, however, so she felt comfortable dealing with the public relations backlash that might arise from it afterward. LeAnce, Intel, and Brench were the families accounting for the bulk of the investment.

"Spy Pilot Ophala has updated me on the Power Kingdom," she said. The siblings leaned forward, as their family's wealth and city's economy relied predominantly on the resource that came from that kingdom. "It's completely inaccessible."

"How?" Periphan asked.

"You know … a moon."

"That's a lie. City gossip to create legends of our time."

Lilu glanced at Wendel. He looked horrified. He didn't question her; he believed her. She wasn't sure how she had misjudged him so egregiously during her first couple of years with him. He had made a couple of remarks that didn't sit well with her, but they had risen from a source of ignorance that he had corrected since then. She felt even guiltier knowing he was clueless to his sister's criminal funding.

"It has been confirmed that the smaller of Kuki Sphaira's two moons— the one that's been missing from sky—is in the bay entrance to the Power Kingdom, likely crushing most of the land's northern half. That means their teleplatforms are gone. Also, the Malanese Peaks, the source of provod, are obliterated."

Each sentence was like a needle puncturing their soul, emptying them of morale until they were deflated bags of skin in their chairs.

"Good thing you've stockpiled tons of it in the Bastion," Lilu said.

Periphan's empty gaze, which had fallen to the coffee table, slowly readjusted to anger as she refocused on Lilu. "An emergency reserve for Brilliance itself."

"Seems a bit selfish considering Brilliance is a tiny fraction of this kingdom's population," Lilu retorted.

"Yet generates over half of its income, even more than your obliterated capital."

"Peri," said Wendel, the only sane one capable of understanding with whom they were speaking. "She is our princess."

"I don't care! Brilliance is the source of all the technology in their hospital and every other innovation across this kingdom and the realm. We generate revenue that could buy us a kingdom."

Her threat was awfully heavy-handed. She was comfortable in thinking that Lilu knew nothing about her support of the rebels. "No kingdom is capable of being bought," Lilu said calmly.

"Tell that to Toth Brench and the Archaic Kingdom."

"And where is Toth Brench now?" The question slipped out cold and frozen.

Periphan's lips pursed, but she didn't respond.

"Are those the footsteps you desire to follow?"

"It was simply a hypothetical to prove my point," Periphan said. "The LeAnce family powers this kingdom."

The two women eyed each other. Periphan was speaking like a woman bitter over the fact that she wasn't in power, as if she deserved it because of contributions she had made to society. They may have been grand, but who had given her the ability to be so ambitious and productive in the first place? Lilu could remind her of that. She turned to Wendel. "What Intelian resource sparked the trade deal with the Power Kingdom for their provod?" Lilu asked.

"Iron."

"Funny," she said, gaze sliding back to Periphan. "Who controls the iron ore in the Ferrous Mountains?" She didn't answer, so Lilu did. "The royals do. We control everything in this kingdom. This is a monarchy, Periphan; don't you dare forget it. My family runs this kingdom, not yours. We sparked that trade deal in which you received your precious provod. And without our iron, you get nothing." Lilu let her words hang in the air. Periphan's face became passive. She was changing her approaching, noticing her anger wasn't achieving anything. Time for Lilu to make the final blow: "If anything, that means the small town of Ferrous means more to Intelian society than Brilliance does."

Periphan blanched, and Lilu forced herself not express a satisfactory grin. Periphan looked at Wendel. "Are you not going to defend our family?"

"You kind of deserved that," he said, drawing wide eyes from his sister. "Not only does her point stand, but they have provided us with other support over the years, too … all while allowing us our freedom to experiment how we please. When was the last time King Vitio asked us for updates regarding our Permanence experimentation?"

Periphan laughed, but the amusement didn't show in her eyes. "Don't credit that man for his incompetency. It had nothing to do with kindness."

"I'm going to stop you there," said Lilu, leaning forward with elbows on pinched knees. "And I'll disregard the idiocy for a moment to steer this conversation back on track. What do you two think about postponing construction of the factory for a short period?"

Periphan's shoulders perked up at that, her body rising from its slouch. "Are we talking months?" Wendel asked. "Years?"

"A few weeks," Lilu said.

"I'd say indefinitely," Periphan said. "With the belief that it'd be a few years."

Lilu regarded the woman with feigned surprise. This was what Periphan wanted. While she might have expressed frustration at the beginning of their conversation about the cancelation of tonight's event, that had been an act. Periphan wanted the factory to fail, at least while under the royal family's jurisdiction. She'd wait out the rising rebels to initiate an attack on the crown before snaring the throne herself. Lilu admired the woman's gall. She wanted not only Brilliance, but the capital and its kingdom, too. This meeting had confirmed everything.

"I can't do that," Lilu said, fishing for more. "It would reflect poorly on me and my sister. How would the populace react if they learned the factory, one which many believe exists solely for the purposes of war and is heavily funded by the Light Realm's wealthiest families, was going to fail after only a few months' construction? We've finished—no, half-finished—only two floors. How will the rebels then feed off that failure? They'd ride the wave and turn hundreds more to their side, claiming the money invested in the factory would have been better directed toward rebuilding the foundation of eastern Dunami. And while we know that's already happening, they don't believe it."

"And whose fault is that?" Periphan asked. "We have our own city to take care of, and now that we know we won't be receiving provod ever again, our financial circumstances will change. We can't loan as much money here, knowing we won't have the sufficient funds to make up for the loss in Brilliance down the road." She shook her head and twisted her lips. "Honestly, it's not even the money. To maintain a Weavineering factory of the size you wish here in the capital, you'd need a large store of provod. Probably thirty percent of Brilliance's. You'll run us dry."

"I already told you that provod is as much ours as it is yours," said Lilu.

"You did," Wendel replied, his expression grave. "And as I expressed earlier, I agree with that. But I find myself understanding both perspectives here. You want to postpone the project, but you'll eventually want the provod, whether that's in three weeks or two months. I, however, cannot give that to you in good conscious."

Lilu's brow crumpled. "In good conscious? Is forsaking a portion of your stockpile to help the capital not an act done in good conscious?"

He tilted his head, honestly confused. "I can't direct money and provod into that factory knowing it holds no value in the long run. When the stockpile depletes, that factory becomes useless. Brilliance, which already has the infrastructure to handle provod and Permanence, and in doing so relies on it, would experience an economic crash from such an event. Meanwhile, Dunami can live on without such a factory because the capital's never powered itself solely through the successes of provod. As you've stated already, your money comes mostly from iron in the Ferrous

Mountains ... even the lumber of Lingen's Rainforest. Brilliance *only* has Permanence. That's what we trade with other kingdoms."

Lilu's heart sank as she recognized the logic of Wendel's argument. She had no counter. He was right, but he was also unknowingly aiding his sister's criminal activity with each sentence.

"So, in good conscious, why would I doom my city by depleting our gross domestic product?"

More silence, and it was Lilu's turn to feel the pressure. Periphan didn't smirk, but a hint of pride had restored her posture. She would twist this to fit her vision, steering the masses away from the crown. Lilu couldn't argue Wendel's point. She hadn't thought of it that way. She was basically asking to rob Brilliance of their one valuable commodity to take for her own, and she didn't even need it. They had other avenues to accumulate revenue.

"But," Wendel said, "I also, in good conscious, cannot withdraw the funds we had planned to contribute to this project. Dunami must return to its former glory for reasons you've already established. I think we can do that by rechanneling the money elsewhere. Let's forget about the factory and put everything into restoring the capital's physical infrastructure ..." He tapered off and frowned, then added, "No, not just restoration, but innovation. Look at this as our chance to make this city even better than what it was before."

Lilu felt herself trembling as he spoke, partly out of frustration that everything he suggested was exactly what she should have done in the first place and partly out of admiration for his selflessness.

Periphan leapt at the opportunity like a shark sensing blood in the water. "Build a hospital in the eastern half, that way if citizens wanted treatment from elite medical professionals, they don't have to travel across the capital. Rebuild homes that don't rely on outdated safety regulations. Lay new streets with tar unmarred by potholes."

"Brilliant," Wendel said, suddenly rejuvenated by a new direction, unable to recognize the suspect nature of Periphan's cooperation. Lilu saw right through the woman's scheme. She would spread this as the LeAnce family's idea, and Lilu supposed she wouldn't be wrong.

This was her fault. The Weavineering factory would become another failure just like the socioenergenic system. She was brilliant when it came to technological studies and innovations, but her knowledge didn't expand into politics, lacking the diplomacy at which someone like Agnos would have likely excelled. She was only twenty-three. How did she expect to outclass Periphan and Wendel, who were both well into their forties and possessed the experience to adapt to most circumstances.

"That's that," Periphan said. "Let's put one-hundred percent of our focus on the rest of the city. And Brilliance retains it provod. You don't need it; we do."

She was purposefully stating redundancies to rub salt into the wound. Lilu had come into this expecting to pull the strings of the conversation and manipulate the damned woman. Did she think she was Pilot Ophala? Why? Because she'd invented travolters? Those involved two completely different types of intelligence. She gazed into the empty hearth rather than Periphan's eyes. She was a coward incapable of facing her defeat.

Desperate, she thought of one more card to play. Ophala had slowly begun to withdraw her tactical support, so Lilu would try to spearhead this operation herself.

The populace hadn't seen its queen in months, a mighty blow to morale. It was time to put on a show.

*   *   *

There was an eyeball in his soup.

Creep looked from it to the man who sat in front of it with a spoon in hand. Luckily, the man was distracted by a servant who was tucking a napkin square into his collar. She then spread one across his lap while his eyes lingered on the collar of her shirt, which was loose and cut low, revealing more than she probably desired. Then again, when employed by a man like Gator, there was only room for his desires.

Creep waited for the other servant to approach him with his bowl. He crossed his fingers beneath the dinner table, then balled his fist and shook it triumphantly after seeing nothing human floating in his broth.

Gator lifted his butt from his chair and leaned over his bowl to get a better look at Creep's. He frowned. "Are we feeding our guest liquid?" he asked, voice nasally and high. He was skinny with a flabby neck and earlobes. His eyes sat behind half-moon spectacles. A string stretched between the two earpieces, looping behind his neck. He removed them and let them hang down his chest. "Get him some meat," he said, snapping a finger at the servant.

"No, thank you," Creep said, holding up a hand.

Gator cocked an eyebrow, then cracked a smirk and returned to his chair. "You'll kill the meat, but let it go to waste?"

Creep resisted a gag, not entirely sure he trusted the liquid anymore either. It was dark brown, but part of him wouldn't have put it past Gator to have mixed blood into it. He couldn't reject the food, however, as that would have been seen as rude, and his mission here was to win over Gator. He still found that unfair, seeing that this man was the superior to one of Creep's—or Sunshine's—biggest clients: Leland. Creep had now assassinated three enemies for that man ... or so he had made them believe.

"I don't knock you for your tastes," Creep said, "but I do not share them." He dipped his spoon in the broth and lifted it, then tipped its contents back into the bowl. He did that twice more before hearing a crunch and looking up to find a string of pink flesh hanging from the man's pinched lips, brown liquid dripping from its bottom end. After chewing, he slurped up the flesh like a noodle.

"But you have no problem serving the meat of your victims to the unknowing patrons in your butcher shop," Gator said. "That's cruel."

"A mere rumor. I take my actual career as a butcher just as seriously— if not more so—than my assassin responsibilities. I only serve beef, pork, chicken, and some of the gamier animals on occasion."

"Boo," Gator said. He looked into his soup and poked around before finding another string of meat. He twirled it, brought it to his mouth, and paused. "Legends aren't fun when they're demystified."

The conversation wasn't going anywhere, and Creep was growing tired. He was supposed to be establishing a productive relationship with Gator in order to climb the rebels' ladder of power and find a way to get close to Periphan. Sally had arranged this meeting, claiming Gator to be a higher-up in the rebel's hierarchy. Gator's real name was Benjamin Songbrook, a nobleman who had been born into wealth. Creep pretended to not know any of this. Like most of the rebels' figureheads, Gator was a noble upset by the rumored abolishment of the socioenergenic system that had been installed a couple of years ago, which had greatly benefitted the wealthy or Intelian weavers in society.

Creep stared into his soup and narrowed his eyes. Fine. He had a feeling he knew why this conversation wasn't going anywhere, so he did what his instincts told him to. He lifted the bowl and downed the soup. To his pleasure, there were no chunks, only broth. At least Gator had shown him that mercy. As he lowered the bowl and smacked his lips, however, the saltiness didn't bode well for his psyche. Broth was typically high in sodium, but so was blood, which only fueled that paranoid thought of his from earlier.

Gator grinned, dropping his spoon in his meatier soup and slapping his hands together with delight. "It took hours to drain the body properly!" he exclaimed. "I was afraid it would go to waste."

Creep bolted out of his chair just as fast as his ingested food rocketed back up his throat, into his mouth, and ... right onto the chest of a servant. It wasn't until he completely emptied himself when he realized she had been holding a trash bin for exactly this reason. They had been prepared for this, yet her response had been too slow.

"It's just blood," Gator said.

Creep heaved again, this time only managing spittle. He made it into the trash can this time. He placed a hand on the servant's shoulder as he bent over and breathed deeply. "I'm sorry," he whispered to her.

Gator's laugh was just as nasally as his speaking voice, and he snorted on four different occasions. The woman left with the trash bin in hand, her face showing clear signs of trauma. Another servant came over and assisted Creep, lifting his chin and standing him up straight. She wiped his lips and chin, then guided him back to his chair after verifying he hadn't soiled anything else.

He looked across the table at Gator, who was wiping a tear from his eye. Creep wasn't surprised. It was typically the leaders of these operations that were corrupt or in it for the wrong reasons, while the masses on the streets were the ones with legitimate gripes. Half of the city was annihilated, and they hadn't seen their queen in months. People like Gator were simply trying to benefit off of the public's rage. If the rebels ended up winning, the

Gators of the world would enter power, reestablish and strengthen policies such as the socioenergenic system, and then the masses would discover they only worsened their lives.

"Sally only has great things to say about you," Gator said, proving Creep's instincts correct. Now that he had drunk the soup, the noble didn't question the trust factor.

"I'd hope so. I've only been giving her about all of my life savings."

Gator shook his head disapprovingly. "Yes, Leland told me you frequent her bar quite often. You see, at least my cravings when it comes to taste, while peculiar, won't kill me. Your liver must be on its deathbed."

"I drink a lot of water."

"Fair enough. Anyway," he said, leaning back as a servant retrieved his empty bowl and utensils, replacing it with a slice of red velvet cake on a small plate, "before we get into the interesting stuff, I must ask to see your identification card as a sign of trust."

Did I not just drink your potentially poisoned bowl of blood soup? He stifled that thought and dug into his pocket, retrieving a thick card. He slapped it atop the table and slid it across. It came to a stop a couple of feet wide of Gator's plate. The man glanced at it, but stabbed at his cake slice first.

Creep didn't know what would happen next, but he was prepared for any possibility. His fingers were on the switch that would drop his blade into his hand. While it was hidden within his sleeve, its purpose wasn't concealment in this scenario. He had been checked thoroughly upon entry to the villa, but they allowed him access despite finding the weapon. Gator knew Creep was armed. He probably was, too. Creep's frantic eyes skittered across the room, pausing briefly on areas of interests: the pant legs, sleeves, and waistbands of the serving staff, as well as the longer hair of women. Searching for weaponry wouldn't matter if they were capable weavers, for that would make them weapons themselves.

Why had Sally put him in this scenario? Months ago, Lilu had given Creep a false identification card at the beginning of the mission just in case he needed to make use of it. He never did. Just two days ago, Sally gave him a new identification card upon also informing him of this meeting. The two cards were nearly identical save the information regarding Creep's ethnicity. The original fake had labeled him an Intelian, while the newest fake labeled him as his true ethnicity, Archain. She then warned him that Gator would ask to see it. This felt like a trap, and considering York's confessional about Spy Pilot Ophala not trusting Creep, that possibility wasn't unlikely.

After taking a bite of the cake and relishing in its delight, Gator equipped his half-moon spectacles, retrieved the card, and scanned over it. His eyes slowed and froze upon reaching a certain detail. He looked at Creep, then back to the card, jaw slowing as he chewed. He set down the fork and pushed his plate to the side, having only taken two bites out of the cake. He let the card slip from his fingers as he clasped his hands on the table. "I've suddenly lost my appetite."

"Join the club," Creep said, the saltiness evident on his tongue again. He gagged.

"You're Archain?"

"Is that a problem?" Sunshine had to ask that question, but Creep knew it was a problem—and a big one at that. The Mind War's significance may have yielded to recent events over the past few years, but the feelings of that fifteen-hundred-year cold war remained in the culture of both Intelian and Archain societies. Spy Pilot Ophala and Archaic King Sigmund may have been on allied terms with the Intel family, but the people still hated each other. And from what Creep had gathered since arriving here, the Spy Pilot hadn't been very fond of Intel King Vitio when he'd been alive.

"What does an Archain possibly have to gain from this?" Gator asked, speaking of the feud between Intelian rebels and Intelian royalty.

"I don't really identify myself as an Archain anymore … I haven't for decades."

Gator shook his head as he gazed back down at the card. "You don't belong in this business. I know your kingdom has suffered a lot over the past five or six years, from that lunatic Itta's betrayal at the Generals' Battle to the rise of foreign leaders over your people, so I'd understand your purpose here. You see this as an opportunity to dismantle the Intel Kingdom further than it already is. You believe we're responsible for the mess that was the Amendment Order and that businessman-turned-false-king. In reality, that was your own king's doing."

"I don't care about any—"

Gator cut him off with a cold retort. "You've been trying to infiltrate the rebels and act as a saboteur once engrained deeply enough, hoping to widen this kingdom's fracture into a fissure." The noble stood, face red. "Do you think an Intelian man like myself wouldn't see through your tricks?"

Creep remained seated, but didn't respond. Gator wasn't entirely off in his analysis. Creep was a spy trying to infiltrate the rebels, but not as an Archain with a motive to destroy Intelian society. Still, he was failing to find the doors of opportunity this should have opened according to Sally. This was an Intelian man blinded by his ignorance of the Archain peoples. He wanted to kill Creep.

As Gator continued his tirade, the door to the kitchens opened behind him. Creep saw the edges of a figure around the noble's scrawnier frame.

A whistle pierced the room. Gator's eyes widened, then dulled. He fell forward and hit the table with a *thunk*, an arrow lodged in the base of his skull and likely the medulla oblongata. The shaft was fletched with a spiraling golden feather.

Creep looked up at the woman in the doorway. She lowered her bow, marched forward, and casually shoved Gator's body off the table. She sat in the noble's chair and stood her bow against the table.

"Name's Whistle," she said. "Let's talk."

*   *   *

Creep had spent most of his life either in control or aware of situations in which he found himself. Even when he had left the Prim Kingdom to help Rhyparia's efforts in the Power Kingdom, he never felt shocked to the point of stupidity—except for the whole falling moon thing. But here, since arriving in the Light Realm and discovering just how stark the differences were between it and the orderly nature of the Prim Kingdom, he realized the depths of the water in which he now waded. This was chaos, and he was a fish at the mercy of circling sharks.

"Like most of my fellow rebels, Gator was a wealthy idiot pushing a selfish agenda," Whistle said, unfazed by the fresh corpse at her feet. "While we fight on the same side, we don't share the same vision or motive." She had pushed the chair back away from the table, giving her room to cross one leg over the other. She reached forward and grabbed Creep's identification card to inspect it herself. Then she held it up next to her head and acknowledged him again. "You're different than most of the rebel executives. You're like me."

Creep raised an eyebrow, genuinely confused by all of this. Sally should have prepared him better, a thought that made him nauseous. He was fumbling his way through these schemes blindfolded, prodded along by the sticks of greater spies at his back. He expected a bit of honesty would go a long way. "And why is that?" he asked.

"I was in the Intelian military," she said. "Its archery division."

"That doesn't sound like me. Laying my life on the line for the kingdom has never been my dream."

"It was mine, and I took the lives of a lot of the Intel Kingdom's enemies during my service. It was how I received the name Whistle ... the death that rained upon the field when my arrows screamed through the sky. That's not to boast, just a matter of fact. I normally wouldn't explain it to someone, but considering the name Sunshine, I figured you'd appreciate the story behind the moniker."

He did. Sunshine was a moniker, yes, but so was Creep. He had spent so much of his life with the name that he had nearly forgotten his birth name. "As a kid, I fancied butchering animals. Never hunting. That was my dad's work. But when he brought home a kill, he'd let me help skin, gut, clean, and cut the beast. My mom didn't like it. She'd rush me to the tub with three buckets of water already waiting for me. Scrub my skin raw for thirty minutes. When she was doing it, she'd always call me Sunshine, and I think it was her way of convincing herself that I wasn't going to envelope myself in darkness. You see, I wasn't like my dad. He hunted and butchered solely for the purpose of feeding the family. I did it for the adrenaline. Now I kill people if convinced."

She read his eyes throughout his story, but eventually nodded and studied his identification card again. She seemed content, and he was pleased with himself. That was the first time he had given his false backstory. Every good character had one, and those who wound up in Sushine's state had deeper ones.

"How did the socioenergenic system hurt you?" Whistle asked, dropping the card on the table.

"When I was in my twenties, I left the Archaic Kingdom to live here. I did it for financial reasons. The Intel Kingdom was considered the world power for centuries, and its economy reflected that. I found I could open a butcher's shop in the city of Acu and make good money, maybe start a family. I successfully accomplished all of that and established myself as a tradesman staple in one of the city's outer sectors."

Creep's face hardened in efforts to sell his anger. "Then word of the socioenergenic system reached Acu, and months later it was enforced." He paused, collecting himself. "I was exiled from the Intel Kingdom and forced to return to the Archaic Kingdom. My wife, who was Intelian, and kids, who were half-Intelian, were given the option to remain in Acu. She wanted to follow me, but I rejected such a ludicrous idea. We had a home in Acu, and I had enough coin saved up to allow them stability beneath that roof for a year or two. I also had an apprentice ready to step up and run the shop. He would provide for them. In the Archaic Kingdom, I had nothing and had to start over from scratch."

His gaze dropped to the table. Reflecting. Brooding. "Only recently did I return, a short while after the Rogue Demon's invasion of the capital. It was part of a program one of the royal sisters was installing to repair damage they had done to families with the socioenergenic system. York came to Dunami to help me start a new butcher's shop, using money he had earned in Acu. My family remains there, far away from this mess. Meanwhile, I've been working toward helping the rebels take down the powers that separated hundreds of families in a matter of a few years—including my own."

"I was banished from the military," Whistle said, gaze fierce.

Creep's eyebrows furrowed. "For what?"

"I guess the crown would say it's my fault, and partly so. I did lie about my ethnicity. I had entered the military as an Intelian, but an Unable. I served while living that lie, giving my all to this kingdom. When they began their investigations of the people who had direct dealings with the palace, which of course involved the entire military, they discovered I wasn't an Unable … or an Intelian for that matter. I'm a Passionian."

Creep remained silent, wise enough to know pointing out the obvious fault that fell on her shoulders for that lie. Sunshine had been a simple civilian. The military was a different beast, requiring a heightened sense of loyalty and trust. The crown must have felt she betrayed that trust. Sunshine also never lied about his ethnicity; she did. Still, he understood her bitterness. She had achieved a lot for the Intelian crown, to the point of achieving war hero status by the sounds of things. They couldn't have forgiven her?

"They didn't physically hurt me. There was no torture or imprisonment. Instead, they exiled me not only from the military, but the kingdom, too. That was torture in itself."

Creep became genuinely sorry for this woman. His gaze softened. "And your family?"

"No family—none of blood, at least. My family was my fellow archers." She paused and they stewed silently on that note. He felt a distant yet intense connection to this woman that stemmed from a version of himself that existed decades ago. Sunshine's story may have aligned with hers, but Creep's real story was eerily more similar. The legitimacy of that bond made everything about this resonate deeper.

When he had fled Yinyon and returned to Phelos, he avoided his superior, Praetor Poicus. He had gone to Mynute Senex in secret, circumventing Poicus in efforts to avoid discussion about his discoveries of Adren Assassins in Yinyon. Senex sent him on a mission to the Prim Kingdom, one with an indefinite timeframe, all to help Creep never have to answer to Poicus again. Essentially, he had been exiled to a secluded kingdom and ripped away from his peers ... just like Whistle had been taken from her comrades in arms.

"I've never hated a collection of people more than I do the Intel family, and specifically that girl Lilu," Whisper said coldly. She was opening up after seeing the emotion on his face, undoubtedly believing Sunshine's tragic tale of being separated from his family to be the root cause. It couldn't have been further from the truth. He could never fake this pain, however slight it might appear on his face. It wasn't even the banishment to the Prim Kingdom. No, he was thinking of Soraku, the woman he loved whom he had abandoned.

He thrummed his fingers atop the table. "What are we going to do about it?"

60

The Nature of Spirit

Joni and Nina were about to do a bad thing, and Tashami was going to tag along ... unbeknownst to them. He couldn't miss out on the adventure, but he would have to sneak out. Otherwise, the two eldest children would have locked him in the basement. A four-year-old had no business outside in the Void. Even they shouldn't have been doing this.

Father and Mother had had a lunch guest over the house earlier in the day. While they had kept their conversation to a whisper, it still traveled far enough for it to be overheard from the hallway outside, where Nina, Joni, and Tashami had been snooping.

When they had heard their guest complaining about a haunting in the town square, Joni and Nina exchanged wide-eyed stares and open-mouthed smiles, and Tashami knew the mischief already formulating in their heads. A child barely older than Tashami was bringing sicknesses to the townspeople. Disease was very common in Cynnish societies, but even this was irregular. The council was getting ready to vote on catching the child and condemning him to exile. Death was a rare punishment considering nobody knew how someone would react to it. Not everyone died—not even children. The next best option? Casting the suspect into the Voidlands to wander.

Now that first-night had arrived, Joni and Nina would use the midnight darkness to sneak out. All candles were extinguished and Father's snoring did well at smothering other sounds around the house. It was loud enough that it had become a topic of discussion throughout the neighborhood, for his snoring could be heard a couple houses down.

The doors and windows of the house were all bolted from the inside to keep antics like this from happening, but all of the orphans knew where the keys were. Only Joni, however, was brave enough to try to snag them from right under Father's nose, sneaking into their parents' room and expertly tiptoeing across floorboards, avoiding the many planks that screamed bloody murder and retrieving the keys from the second drawer of Father's nightstand. Even with the man's snoring, that took patience, litheness, and skill.

Tashami was proud of himself. He crept down into the kitchen just after Joni and Nina had climbed out of one of the smaller windows behind the counter, hiding behind walls until the older pair disappeared. He grabbed a stool, carried it over to the window, and then climbed it to get onto the counter. The great thing about the locks on the windows was that they only locked from the inside, so once Joni was outside, he couldn't lock it. He'd assume nobody was following him. After all, he and Nina hadn't discussed their plan to escape the house to anyone else. Knowing his brother's sense of adventure, he had simply assumed.

His bare feet crunched in cold, dead grass. He should have worn shoes, but if they were spotted missing from the line of shoes at the front door, it would have looked suspicious. He smiled, giddy at the promise of adventure. Thousands of stars dotted the blackened heavens. The air was still. He heard one of the neighbor's laugh from four houses down. He slapped a hand over his mouth to stifle a laugh of his own after noticing he could still hear Father's snoring.

He spotted two shadowy figures disappear between houses an entire street away. Assuming it was Joni and Nina, he bolted after them. He didn't know where the town square was, so he needed to keep pace with the two of them. He bolted after them, breathing deeper the more distance he put between himself and home. After only a few dozen paces, he had already traveled farther than he ever had in his life.

Despite penetrating deeper into the more densely populated areas of Spachny, he had never felt more secluded. This was unknown territory for him, and his brother was moving quickly. He was afraid he'd lose him. And those scary screams that were always constant in the kingdom's backdrop were even more unnerving now. He was sure they had intensified ever since leaving the house, growing stronger with each step he took. Panelle told him a story about those screams once. They gave him nightmares for a month straight. Something about dragon skeletons cloaked in shadows. The absurdity had been enough to make Tashami cry, and give Panelle a terse lecture from Mother.

Such beasts didn't actually exist of course. This kingdom was unforgiving and dark, but certainly not *that* outrageous.

Still, those screams made Tashami's spine crawl.

Buildings began to inch closer together, dead grass and dirt roads yielding to broken cobbles. Hiding became easier for Tashami, but tracking also became more difficult, as Joni and Nina dipped into numerous alleys and turned at frequent intersections. A few buildings were full of life despite the time of night. Windows were illuminated with golden light and chatter drifted into the streets. He felt less scared because of it … until a man drifted out of a side door in an alley without a shirt and his pants around his ankles, only to drop onto his knees and vomit across the cobbles. Tashami could have turned and ran the other way, but he had just seen Joni and Nina turn into the street on other side. He couldn't get lost here, so he ran forward and leapt over the filth, the man too busy looking at the ground to notice his surroundings.

No wonder Father tells me to never leave the house.

He turned down the street and ran. He had lost track of Joni and Nina. A metal sign post creaked on its hinges. The letters inscribed were Cynnish, so he couldn't read it, but he followed the arrow anyway, thinking the only landmark of note in Spachny would be its town square.

His strides shortened as he heard sobbing from somewhere nearby. He came to a stop and turned slowly, checking every angle, gaze drifting from rooftops to shadowed alleys to blackened windows. Where was it coming from? He thought it might have been Joni or Nina, but this wasn't their cries—not that he had ever heard Joni cry to know the sound of it. But it wasn't this, surely.

He didn't like it. The unnaturalness of it made him shiver. The sob was gentle, but hollow and vast and echoing off of a hundred points in the distance, drifting through despair in search of an anchor of which to grab hold. It drifted into the core of his body and twisted his guts. He grabbed his stomach. That was where Father had said his soul was. Something was disrupting its peace, infusing it with ice. The chill spread from his stomach down to his legs. From his chest into his arms.

His legs folded, knees smacking broken cobbles. Teetering toward the ground, he threw out his hands to catch himself before his upper torso hit next. He wanted to cry, but couldn't find the emotion from which to pull. The sensation was not human, but monstrous. Father would have known what to do, but he could no longer understand the concept of a dad.

Father? Who?

The sobs spilled into his ears and filled his head, finding that anchor it needed, infecting him with its misery as it now echoed against his skull.

He screamed. Fear enveloped him. His intestines slithered; his heart slowed. The tears came. The fight followed—not that he knew he was fighting, or how. He clawed at the cobbles, fingernails tearing free from cuticles, blood slicking the gray road with crimson.

His shrieks ripped through the atmosphere, eyes bulging as his hands moved to his head, fingers clawing at his scalp. Hair fell in ivory clumps as he pulled, trying to penetrate the flesh and bone that shielded the sobs haunting his mind. The noises that came from his mouth were now inhuman, matching the sensations dismantling his mind, body, and soul.

And then the distant sobs stopped, and his mind emptied. His screams, however, didn't. He continued pulling at hair and scratching at his scalp, unable to trust his senses. Someone grabbed his wrists and pulled them away from his head. The person's voice sounded like it came from a different room, muffled by walls until it sharpened and grew nearer. It was Nina. Thank goodness, it was Nina.

She pulled him into her lap and shushed him, kissing his forehead and holding his head with a delicate hand. He felt light-headed.

"Keep your eyes open, Tashami," she whispered, voice shaking. She was scared, too. He didn't know whether to find comfort or anguish in that. "You've lost a lot of blood. If you close your eyes, you might not open them again."

Tashami rocked in her embrace, the motion offering his mind a menial task to remain conscious. She nodded and looked up, tears staining her cheeks. Father had said she, like the other orphans, was born with a disadvantage because of their Cynnish genes. Their souls followed a natural downward trajectory toward nothingness. It was unfair, but combatable. This girl was crying for him. She could feel. She could love. She didn't look at Tashami the same way she looked at Joni—with loads of admiration that Father explained as adolescent love—but she looked at him like Mother did. She had a desire to protect him.

"This was stupid," Nina said, eyes drawn to someone else.

Tashami tilted his head and saw his older brother. Joni walked toward them, sorrow dulling his eyes. He squatted a short distance away from Tashami, inspecting the blood-slicked cobbles. His eyes found Tashami's hands, and he exhaled. "I should have known you'd follow," he said.

"Someone was crying," Tashami muttered. A crowd had gathered down the street, looking in their direction, but that didn't matter. "Are they okay?"

Joni narrowed his eyes, then looked at Nina, who scoffed. "He's definitely the Unbreakable's son," she said.

Joni flashed a smirk only for it to darken. "It was a boy. I believe the one Father's friend spoke of earlier today. He's not in good shape, but I took a page from Father's book and helped him … a temporary fix. We'll see what happens."

Nina looked toward the crowd in the distance. "None of them are going to help us. They'll just stand there and watch."

Joni followed her gaze and sighed. "Seems like it. Father was right about this place. I think we've grown so used to home, we forget it's not a representation of everything happening around it. It's a bubble."

"How can we forget?" she asked.

The question's implications brought silence to all three of them. She was talking about Halice, who hadn't been the same since the day she'd been discovered with her eyes hanging from her skull. She spent her days in Father's room mostly now, blind and also paralyzed—not because of physical inability, but spiritual. She couldn't will herself to move.

Nina patted Tashami's cheek gently. "Nuh-uh. Open those eyes, mister. Let's go." She stood and groaned, as if he was heavy enough to warrant that. She helped him onto Joni's back, who carried him all the way back home. During the walk, Nina asked, "How'd you do it?"

Joni shrugged. "The nature of Spirit, I guess."

61
Guest Speakers

Agnos had the fingers of one hand pressed against Tashami's pulse in his neck. His other hand was cupping his friend's cheek, sensing the temperature fluctuation in his skin. Tashami had been whimpering in his sleep, so Agnos had taken a seat on the edge of his bed to study his face. That was when he had noticed the empty chill.

Tashami's skin was cold, his pulse slowed to the point of concern. As of late, his slumber was frequently disturbed by nightmares that caused him to tremble, mumble, or lash out, but this was a first. This felt more like a chemical reaction. His body was becoming sick. Something inside him was now responding unfavorably.

Agnos was worried about his friend. The effects of whatever Ronossius did to Tashami should have worn off long ago. Many months had passed since then, and it only grew worse. Agnos counted the seconds between pulses.

Two and a half.

Three.

That's it. "Tashami," he said.

Nothing.

"Tashami." He gently smacked his cheek. "*Tashami.*"

Tashami's eyes opened, revealing unnaturally constricted pupils. They dilated a second later before landing on Agnos. "Joni," he mumbled.

Agnos cocked an eyebrow. "Joni?"

Tashami blinked, then groaned, bringing his hands to his temple and massaging his palms against it. "What?"

"What do you mean 'what'?" Agnos asked, incredulous. He pulled his hands away from Tashami's face, just now noticing how strange that must have looked.

"You've turned into my caretaker," Tashami muttered.

Heat flooded Agnos's neck and face. "Why did you say your brother's name?" He hadn't forgotten about their mission in the Void, when they had fled Tashami's childhood home while the ghosts of orphans hanged themselves from the overlook's banister. A ghost had been at the front door, neck sliced open with blood spilling over his hands. That ghost had been Joni.

"I don't know," Tashami said. "I could have dreamed about him."

"Could have?" Agnos found himself growing angry. He couldn't tell if Tashami was lying or not. It was possible he couldn't remember his dreams. People normally didn't, but dreams that caused night sweats, outbursts, and sleep-talking usually left lasting impressions.

"I'm sorry," Tashami said. "I don't know what's happening to me." He sat up, propping himself against the bed's headboard. "I think this imprisonment is getting to my head."

Agnos studied his friend's eyes, then was drawn by something in his peripherals. He glanced at Tashami's hair and spotted a gray strand among the ivory. He furrowed his brows and plucked it. Tashami winced. "What the …"

Agnos held it up between them. "You seem a little young for this."

"Premature grays. The worst."

"You're twenty-two. That's beyond premature."

"Don't age-shame me." He narrowed his eyes and puckered his lips, displeased with his phrasing. "Gray-shame? No, hair-shame."

Agnos ignored him and stared at the strand of gray. Was there a way to decipher if this was natural? His gut gave him the obvious answer, but part of him didn't want to seem desperate—and, in doing so, seem weak—in front of Tashami, who was rolling with the punches as if this was routine.

Agnos pinched and rolled the strand between his index finger and thumb, feeling for texture. He then broke it in half to test its tensility. Tashami watched dully until Agnos eventually brought it to his nose and sniffed. Tashami slapped Agnos's hand, losing the strand in the blankets. "Too far, weirdo."

Sticking out his tongue, Agnos returned to his desk to read more of the Thunder Queen's chronicle. This was his third time through, but he was focusing on entries that he had skimmed over in past readings—a good decision, considering the gems hidden in the filler. A lot of the chronicle was meaningless introspection about Tonitrua's relationship with Mialo. They had loved each other deeply, a plot point that had always steered Agnos away from fiction. The fact that this was non-fiction made it tolerable, he supposed.

Tashami had used the word imprisonment earlier, and it wasn't far from the truth. While they technically could leave this room whenever they so choose, the risks made it unwise. And even if they wanted to risk it, which Tashami had stated multiple times he was comfortable with, Evelyn had begged them not to. They were to count on her to fix this … whatever *this* was. This was her territory and therefore her battle. Agnos supposed he didn't need to be involved in the heroics of every mission. It was a nice change of pace. Tashami was a bit antsy.

"I hope Arithmys stops by to visit today," Agnos said.

"I'll kill myself."

Agnos whirled in his chair.

Tashami visibly recoiled. "Wow, you're really scared something's wrong with me. It was a joke."

"Not funny. Tactless, actually."

Tashami's head fell back against the headboard. "Sorry." His gaze grew distant, mind drifting elsewhere.

Agnos turned back to his book. He didn't trust Tashami at all.

*   *   *

Evelyn stood in Ipsas's main quad, an ovular field of grass dotted with a dozen trees, crisscrossed by four pathways that connected a track encircling the field's perimeter. A class was seated in a section of grass closest to the track, where students either on their break period or in physical education were walking or jogging past.

Professor Jahved, one of Evelyn's least favorite professors during her time studying at Ipsas, was lecturing the class, dressed in a comfortable tunic and pants. It was a breezy day, just warm enough to warrant short sleeves and open-toed sandals. The best part of taking a class outdoors—a luxury allotted to a teacher only once a month—was the casual dress code. They could shed themselves of oversized robes and collared button-ups that choked them.

Evelyn stood off to the side of the class alongside Ronossius. They were the cause of the lingering stares directed toward the class from the students on the track. Even those in the class itself would frequently glance over. She read those looks and found a mixture of reverence and disgust. A student would lean over and whisper to another, only to be called out by the professor and warned of greater consequences for repeated offenses. Knowing Jahved like she did, that would either mean writing essays if he was in a good mood or reliving their worst nightmares if he was in a bad mood. As a Devish, the man was a skilled manipulator of the subconscious. He specialized in memory diffusion, but the effects were temporary and didn't cause physical harm. He was downright miserable at anything else that didn't involve the subconscious.

"To complete our remaining ten minutes of class," Jahved said, "I've acquired two guest speakers who have quite a reputation on this campus. Their skills lend well to today's lecture, so they've offered to give demonstrations on the creative capabilities of weaving."

All heads turned toward Evelyn and Ronossius, no longer forced to feign focus on the professor. It was a class of ten and eleven-year-olds, meaning none of them had been in school when the Diatia was formed.

634

What they knew of the elite group of students was a product of word-of-mouth from the older students, most of whom also didn't know what they were talking about—a bunch of teenagers who wanted to make themselves seem cooler than they actually were by fabricating stories about their interactions with the Diatia. And if it wasn't from older students, it was the professors or wardens, both groups possessing biases that would reflect each Diatia in a different light. And who knew what kind of propaganda High Warden Sylial had been spewing since Evelyn's departure to join her queen's efforts?

"I think we'll begin with Evelyn Tesai," said Jahved, "who's known for both her brains and weaving." He waved her over. As she approached, he asked the class, "Who knows Evelyn's ethnicity? Don't raise your hand. Shout it out."

The response was a smattering of "Stillian."

"And her specialty?"

"Sculpting!"

Evelyn surveyed the group of forty students scattered across the grass as she walked in front of them. Their knowledge of her was actually flattering. Was this all from gossip around the campus or had the professors begun to include the Diatia in Ipsas's curriculum?

"Sculpting, yes!" Jahved exclaimed. He was always better with the younger classes, but as the classes became more advanced, he hardened his teaching style into something less desirable. "But there's something else!" He scanned the class eagerly. "What's the second part of her specialty?"

Evelyn came to a stop next to Jahved. Unlike the first two questions, this one didn't receive an onslaught of answers. Some students scrunched up their faces while others scratched their heads or discussed it with others, combining their brains to recollect information they felt they should have already known. A girl in the back raised her hand, hesitant to blurt out an answer now that it had been silent for so long.

"Yes, Yupi?"

"Animation?" It came out as more of a question, but Jahved's smile confirmed her answer.

"Correct!"

Evelyn eyed the girl named Yupi, who blushed and ducked. She sometimes forgot what she looked like to others. She wasn't a child, but an adult approaching her mid-twenties. Many of these children idolized the Diatia—not that that was a good thing. The Diatia were flawed beyond belief, including Evelyn.

Jahved turned to Evelyn and whispered, "Welcome back." They shook hands. He walked away and shouted to the students, "The floor—or grass—is hers!"

After a brief introduction, Evelyn asked, "How many Stillians do we have here today?" Five students raised their hands, a relatively small number for a class of forty. "How many of you have activated your clout already?"

Surprisingly, one person raised their hand. She hadn't expected any considering their ages. While exceptions existed, most people usually activated their clout at the cusp of their teenage years. Then, once activated, the rate at which someone advanced in their weaving abilities varied greatly. Evelyn had been a late bloomer herself, showing no signs of her ice abilities until she was fourteen while everyone else had been weaving for a year or two. Fortunately, once she did show that first glimpse of weaving, she excelled beyond the skills of her peers in a fraction of the time.

She smiled at the boy who had raised his hand. "Very impressive," she said, siphoning a proud grin out of him. He must have felt even more elated given his sex. In Stillian culture, girls were usually the first to activate their clout. She noted the resentment in the faces of the girls who had announced they were Stillian. "And what can you do with your ice abilities?" Evelyn asked.

The boy held up his hand, palm up. A pile of ice crystals formed, spilling over the edges of his palms and crashing into his lap. It was shoddy work, involving not an ounce of weaving technique. He was simply expelling Still Energy from his body using his clout, and given the sporadic nature of his release, the resulting ice came out fragmented and shapeless. But given his age, that was impressive.

"Thank you," Evelyn said, smiling at him. She surveyed the rest of the class. "Weaving techniques vary according to your energy, but one fact remains constant across them all. The greater control you have over your weaving, the greater the variety of tools you can use with your abilities. A common Devish can move medium-sized items at short distances without physically touching tem. A Devish with average weaving skills can fling smaller objects in straight lines over longer distances as projectile weapons. One with good weaving skills can fling multiple objects at once. The better they get at weaving, the more they can do: manipulate the projectile's trajectory mid-flight, move miniscule or massive objects, or even collapse a building.

"Those abilities, however, have more to do with the control of weaving rather than the creativity. Creativity involves learning how to deviate from normal patterns in your Energy-Current chains. Using different combinations of wavelengths, speeds, and EC strand ratios, a Devish can achieve more advanced abilities: recording, projection, memory transfer, subconscious manipulation, clairvoyance, hallucinogenics, etcetera."

"Teleportation?" a student asked.

Evelyn paused and laughed. "Sure, in astronomically rare circumstances. I believe a person capable of teleportation is one in a hundred million?" She looked at Jahved for verification, and he nodded. "Anyway, weaving Still Energy, as well as any other energy, involves those same kinds of layers."

"Then how do teleplatforms remain functioning for so long?" asked the same student who had inquired about teleportation. "Don't they have to be refilled with Dev Chains every so often? Or is there an everlasting supply?"

"That I don't know," she said. She looked at Jahved again, but he shook his head. The student's question had been a legitimate one, and she had to force her mind off the topic despite its intrigue. Teleplatforms were such a staple of everyday live that she'd never really questioned it, like how a city person turns the faucet to obtain running water without thinking about how plumbing and irrigation made that possible.

"A lot of Stillians can do this." She raised a hand and created an imperfect block of ice. It had hundreds of irregular edges and surfaces. "Many can do this." She raised her other hand and created a perfect cube of ice, its surfaces a smooth and reflective bluish-white. "Even fewer can do this." She tilted her head back, and a ball of ice sprouted from the tip of her nose. She balanced it there, standing as still as a statue in a display of balance and core strength. Laughter erupted from the children, followed by applause as she bucked her head, knocking the ball into the air and catching it with one hand. The boring lecture was now a circus, and she was the showman.

Tossing the ball back and forth between her hands, she said, "But that just has to do with directional manipulation of my Still Chains. What if I was to begin changing the density of the clusters I weave? What if I lessened the clout used to expel energy and slowed the thrust of the colliding Energy-Current chains? These are all creative techniques that will affect the nature of the ice produced." She tossed the ball into the air and caught it with one hand a couple times. "I'm going to throw this at that tree."

She tossed the ball, and it hit the trunk with a heavy thud. The ice didn't shatter, but just fell into the grass and rolled. She formed another ball in her hand. "Again," she said and repeated the motion. This time, the ball hit the trunk and splattered against the bark as wet frost. "If I were to have a snowball fight with the first ball, I'd hurt someone. But the second one would be perfect. Now ..." she trailed off and gave an evil smirk, forming another frozen sphere in her hand ... "this one wouldn't just hurt someone, but maim them."

Dozens of little eyes widened, and Jahved cocked an eyebrow. "Do I need to have a nurse at the ready?"

"No," she said. "But they should back up."

He hustled in front of the class, spread his arms and walked forward. The students scooted backward on their butts to create distance.

"Keep going. Keep going," said Evelyn, lost in the excitement of the class. Their whispers were now outbursts of giggles. "That's good." Jahved remained in front of the class, standing at the center as if he'd protect them from any accidents. Her weaving skills were too refined to make such a mistake.

She hurled the ice ball at the trunk. It hit the bark and exploded into thousands of tiny crystals in a hundred different directions—a supernova of ice. The crystals rushed outward in a billowing cloud of frost, swallowing the entire section of grass. It dispersed seconds later, leaving everyone covered in frost. Teeth chattered throughout the class. The Stillians were the only ones unbothered by the frost. Jahved didn't look amused, but he understood there was a point to this.

"You see," she said, sticking her hands in her pockets, skin dusted with frost. "That was a volatile projectile. The Still Chains that made up the shell of the sphere were solid and slow, while the cluster within was erratic and desperate to escape. I made them thin, which was what made the impact nothing more than a harmless explosion of dust. If I had woven those dynamic patterns inside with a lot more density, the explosion would have resulted in thousands of glass-like shards of ice. Some of you would have been covered with cuts; most would have died from puncture wounds. Blood everywhere."

Silence blanketed the field. Then she realized that the same way she forgot about her own age, she also forgot about theirs. She was so accustom to a life of the gore and death seen in battle, but these children weren't—nor should they ever be. She bit her lip and elected to change direction.

"Let's get back to the fun," she said. "I've shown you my creativity in sculpting and engineering, but Yupi also mentioned my specialty of animation." She lowered herself into a squat, knees bent and butt parallel to the ground. Her elbows were bent at her ribs, hands in fists. "This was a technique I used about a year ago while traveling the open seas." She didn't explain beyond that, figuring nobody in Ipsas wanted to hear about how she fought on behalf of True Light against Powish leviathans. "I bet I can grab one of you from here without moving my feet."

The first row of students sat a couple dozen paces away from her. Jahved had taken a seat in front of them, finding it necessary after her explosive showing with the ice ball. "Yeah right!" screamed one boy.

She looked at him, and he stuck out his tongue. She smiled and then punched. A pillar of ice shot from her fist. At the end was a clone of her own fist, but frozen and thirty times the size. The children scurried backward and formed an empty pocket in their ranks, screaming as the fist—bigger than all of them—shot toward the boy. The frozen hand opened, ice splitting as the fingers spread and joints extended. It then reached for the boy and clasped shut, but she missed him on purpose. She didn't want to kill him.

He screamed with real horror on his face. She let the frozen hand retract back into her arm. "I don't suggest gambling in your future," she said with a lazy stare.

Jahved stood and clapped his hands together. "Alright! I'd say that was an exhilarating demonstration!" The children who had been in the vicinity of the frozen hand were breathing heavily, no longer worried about their frost-dusted skin. Evelyn dusted off her hands, suddenly happy she went through with this.

Ronossius was next. He strolled to the front with his unnaturally slow lumber. Unlike Evelyn, who had required a show of skill beforehand, he received applause just for showing up. She supposed it was his one perk of remaining a lackey of the school. If he were to go anywhere else in this world, nobody would bat an eyelash at him.

Evelyn took a seat on a wooden bench and listened. Typically, Ronossius wasn't one for social interactions involving large groups—he had kept his social circle to a minimum of three people for most of the time she'd known him—so to see him on a stage like this was intriguing. She had never seen him speak publically in a formal setting, yet his reputation commanded the attention of every child. There were no smiles on their faces, only earnestness. A gravity had fallen on the class.

"Evelyn did a masterful job at demonstrating the creative process of weaving," he droned, body completely motionless. "But even someone of her caliber is limited because of her energy. Still Energy is considered a multifaceted energy, but not quite on the complexity level of Dev Energy or Cynergy."

Some of the students glanced at her, but she wasn't bothered by his comment. His point was valid and factual. And he hadn't presented it as an insult, for such a tactic would have been petty and beneath someone like him.

"I'm Cynnish," he said. "I can do something as straightforward as sucking the life from this grass ..." a circular patch of grass around his feet morphed from green to brown ... "to obliterating its will entirely ..." The brown grass now wilted, unable to keep itself standing. Gasps slipped out of the crowd.

"Someone like me could extend this death to great lengths around me without touching it, while most Cynnish must come in direct contact. Even then the effects are shallow at best. I can do more than rot nature; I can rot a person's mind, heart, and soul." His lecture was as lifeless as the grass on which he stood, eyes dull and tone monotonous. "I can empty your insides into a bottomless pit. I can then fill that pit with despair."

Evelyn turned up her nose. To think she had been concerned about her own demonstration. This was just morbid without any ardor to alleviate it. He was piling on the melancholy.

"I don't think I want to demonstrate any of that, though," he said. "As entertaining as a human subject can be, nature serves a more humane approach in front of the youth ..." His voice emptied as a squirrel passed between the students and him, oblivious to the trap into which it had just scurried. It paused and gnawed at an acorn, looking around without a care in the world. Evelyn groaned and sunk into the bench, noting Ronossius's sudden idea.

The squirrel noticed the dead grass sweeping toward it too late. It dropped the acorn and tried to run, but it collapsed as its legs became paralyzed first. Its fur wilted and shed in clumps, skin peeling back and exposing muscle, bone, and cartilage. Its agonizing squeals were drowned out by the screams of children, a seizure rapping its body as its torso began to rot.

Evelyn looked away. Ronossius was a sick man, and she didn't care if he had grown up in the Void. She knew it was likely her privilege that allowed her to disregard such an excuse, but she couldn't bring herself to empathize with the monster.

Whimpering slowly replaced the screaming. A couple children puked, which made her close her eyes and fight back the sensation herself. Slowly, she looked back at the area at the front of the gathering. A tiny skeleton remained in the grass, draped with tattered pieces of meat and flesh. Several children were being escorted away by teacher's assistants, heading across the quad in the direction of the medical building. Evelyn spotted the High

Warden standing in the distance, arms crossed and swords sheathed at his hips. How long had he been spectating? She turned back to the class.

"To those of you still seated here," Ronossius said, "especially those absent of tears and specifically those propped on their knees for a better look, congratulations ... you are strong and unflappable. I admire that. It's a trait many of my kind who live in Batilearsh have. Of course, even they can't completely resist the combined presences of the Linsani and the king.

"What you saw happen to that squirrel is only a minor fate when compared to what can happen to a person. You see, the soul of a human is infinitely times more complex than a mere rodent, which means they can be twisted in an infinite number of ways by several methods, not all of which require much effort on my part." His gaze drifted toward Evelyn, and she narrowed her eyes. "I have exercised these techniques quite recently, and they're irreversible."

She gripped her knee, enraged by his taunt. That wasn't a petty threat, but a very real implication—a confession. She wanted to retaliate, but what good would that do her? So she dug frozen nails into her knee. Frost crept from her scalp down her temple. Ice slithered outward from where she was seated across the bench. Ronossius noticed it and then acknowledged the students once more. "That's it for me, Professor."

Jahved hurried toward the front, circling the dead patches of grass on the balls of his feet. He placed a hand on Ronossius's shoulder and chuckled nervously. "Unfortunately, no time for a Q and A," he said. Some of the students groaned in disapproval, but most looked relieved. He turned and noticed the crowds spilling out of buildings and onto the quad's track and paths. "Seems we've ran well over our ten minutes, so class dismissed!"

The students scattered in every direction but the front, where Ronossius stood, avoiding both him and the dead rodent like the plague. Evelyn stood and watched Ronossius, who spoke briefly with Jahved before walking the other way, not sparing her another glance. She turned and found High Warden Sylial still standing in the distance.

He winked.

62

The Next Step

Himitsu didn't enjoy the life of resistance, but Kaylee had asked him to be patient while she worked to fix the mess in which found himself. It wasn't much of a mess in his eyes, seeing that breaking free of his guest quarters would have been simple. He doubted the Loess had anyone capable of stopping his efforts. They didn't know he was a Jestivan or Passion Assassin. If his skill wasn't enough—which he doubted—the element of surprise would compensate for that. His mom would have scolded him for being arrogant and delusional—two ingredients that had created a recipe of disaster for many assassins in their prime.

He remained docile for Kaylee, but he questioned her ability under these circumstances. She was intelligent, perceptive, and skilled with a knife, but she was also in the dark. She didn't know what she was fighting here, and he feared she'd discover the true nature of her relationship with Loess Lord Kopios without him around to steer her elsewhere. Kopios might grow tired of the game and reveal himself as her father forthright, especially now that Himitsu had proven himself untrustworthy—not that he personally cared much. The only people whose trust he desired were those suffering beneath the lord's rule.

The Soteria family wasn't a good one. They reminded him of Archaic King Itta and the stories he'd heard about the man's father, Dolomarpos. Considering this, it wasn't a surprise they had colluded with each other over decades. He wondered which side would have tried screwing over the other in the long run.

Himitsu hadn't practiced weaving in months, nervous that he'd be seen. Even when in one of his quarters' windowless interior chambers, he refused to risk it. While he was good at searching a room for peepholes and secret doors or compartments—a skill every child in a family of assassin learns at a young age—he didn't fully trust his eyes. He could have missed something. Then there was the matter of the scent of black flames. It may have been subtle, but a trained nose could still pick it up.

So he spent his days training with the sword, hearkening back to his lessons with Toshik, who had gifted his once-rival a pristine spunka blade. Himitsu didn't have that sword at the moment; his mom feared someone would recognize the insignia on the hilt, which wasn't wise to flaunt in an area that likely hated Toth Brench, the foreigner who ruled their kingdom for a year. He used a normal sword, switching between stances and katas, peeved by the clear downgrade in weight distribution. He couldn't swing it quite like Toshik's gift.

The door to the entry chamber opened, and Himitsu continued his motions without sparing a glance in that direction. He figured it was an officer or one of the many guards posted outside his quarters, barging in to either monitor him or remind him of their presence—as if they were any threat to him.

He froze in a front stance, front knee bent and back leg straight, his sword raised horizontally above his head as if to parry a downward strike from an opponent. His brows furrowed as he sniffed at the air. Roses? He shot upright and turned toward the arched entryway into the sitting chamber. Kaylee leaned against the wall, a flirtatious smile on her face. "I love it when you're all sweaty."

He lifted his collar and wiped at his face. "How long do you have today?"

"Originally? Thirty minutes. But I talked him into an hour."

He leaned over and gazed toward the bed chamber. "I don't know if that's enough time."

"Oh? I thought five minutes would suffice for you."

He frowned. "Cruel."

"Sit," she said, taking a seat herself. "We must remain focused anyway. An hour isn't much time to discuss this."

"Discuss what?" he asked, sitting on the carpet and leaning back against the coffee table.

She curled her finger toward herself, gesturing for him to get closer. He scooted torward the armchair until he was at her feet. He felt like a child in grade school, circling around the teacher as she read a picture book on her stool. Kaylee plopped a foot onto his thigh, waggling her eyebrows. He smirked and lifted the foot, pressing his thumbs into her arch. She moaned cathartically, toes wiggling with glee as she arched her neck, head tilting toward the ceiling.

"Okay," he said, "maybe five minutes was right."

She lowered her head and offered a wry smirk, but it vanished shortly after. "I don't know what your mother has you doing here," she said, "but I know it has nothing to do with my aspirations."

His thumbs slowed, and he stared at her for entirely too long. She narrowed her eyes and hummed in thought. "Are you ashamed?"

He looked down at her foot and said, "No." His tone betrayed the word.

"It's alright. I trust you and your mother." If her acknowledgment of a secret mission that involved manipulating her dreams was the knife to his stomach, then her faith in him despite the deception was the twisting of that knife. "I don't know the specifics, but I'd assume it's something dangerous and important."

He nodded, wondering just how much she knew. He couldn't look her in the eye, fearful of what that ancient eye of hers might see in his aura. She must have been using it now despite the promises made. She would have every right to.

As if she had read his mind, she said, "I trust you so much that even now I refuse to study your aura."

He looked up at her, slowly, like a child in a dark corridor turning to find out what had made the hair on the back of their neck stand tall. Her gaze was soft and understanding, loving and nurturing. She treated him better than he deserved. Unknowing to her, he had led her to her father with the mission of assassinating him. While he felt Lord Kopios deserved that fate after learning about the Soteria-Accus feud, how could he do that without letting Kaylee know the truth? Did his mom not trust her enough with that information? It seemed unfair, especially considering Kaylee's current display of loyalty. She was the man's daughter, and who was Himitsu to understand that bond?

"I can't remain locked up here for much longer," he said, admitting he had other plans to execute.

"And you won't," she said. The entire conversation was whispers barely audible enough to be heard by each other. "I contacted the appropriate person."

He lifted her foot higher and kissed her toes. She giggled and nearly kicked him in the lip. "Getting violent, are we?" he asked.

She shook her head, lips pursed and eyes asunder with delight. Then she bit her lip. He lunged forward, determined to stretch five minutes into fifty.

*   *   *

"Not only do I not think she's ready," said Benedict, "but I don't think the people are."

Lilu shrugged at the head steward's input, eyes fixed on a weavineering-powered serving platter. She was fidgeting with the gears connecting it to the vessel. Benedict stood behind her, browsing the shelves of trinkets and inventions derived from the magic of Permanence. Most of the items were useless, novelties with which she had been occupying her free time since returning to the capital—not that she had much free time. These were distractions more than anything else, something to keep her mind busy so she could avoid thoughts of her depressed sister and dead parents.

"It doesn't matter who's ready," she said. "Only what's needed, and the people need a morale boost."

Benedict sighed, feeling awfully relaxed in the vocalization of his dissatisfaction with her plans. She didn't like that. She wasn't her mother, and he needed to remember that. Besides, to think she'd actually plan something as dangerous as Shelly stepping into the public eye during a revolution without other schemes at play was preposterous.

Lilu knew what she was doing, or she hoped so. She didn't need Pilot Ophala's terse missives to remind her of her recent political gaffs. In efforts to correct such blunders, she had spent months backpedaling only to botch that, too. She'd never felt more incompetent in her life, and she was beginning to wonder if this was simply the universe reprimanding her for what it viewed as unforgivable sins in her policies.

People had suffered because of the socioenergenic system. Many died from abuse at the hands of those who felt themselves superior because of their socioenergenic status; others killed themselves after being ripped from their homes or ostracized by people who were once their peers.

She hadn't been aware of these statistics not only because of her status as a royal, but because of her residence in Brilliance. She had separated herself from the crown and those it should have been fighting to protect, yet thought it her prerogative to influence society by conjuring up discriminatory policies. And all for what? The protection of her family? How selfish could she have been?

She was now the corrupt royal she had always vowed to never become, but she wouldn't continue. Enough politics.

There was only one way to redeem herself.

*   *   *

Toshik stood at Yinyon's cusp, having just stepped out of the tall grass of the prairie that stretched between here and Spunka Forest. He surveyed it from a distance before advancing, eyes narrowed as he scanned the sparsely scattered homes, most of which had only one floor. A building at the front stood a couple stories high, possessing the architecture of a poorer inn. He also saw another building that had a third level somewhere at the center of the village.

His gaze landed on a hill that loomed over the pastures and farmlands, topped by two grand oaks. Headstones dotted the sides of the hill, growing sparser and more decorated the closer they came to the crest. He heard the moo of a cow, which made him sniff. The air was fragrant with grass and morning dew, but he caught hints of manure that only strengthened as he neared the livestock-infested village. He didn't care. Younger him might have, but younger him had also spent thirty minutes in the morning making sure the part in his hair was a straight line all the way to the back of his scalp.

The building that headed the village was in fact an inn that sat against a lonely dirt road. He entered the lobby—if it could even be called that, its smallness lending more to a cupboard. The front podium was unattended, and he couldn't hear a sound from anywhere in the inn. He stopped at the podium and looked down at a sheet of parchment. It was a sketch of a woman running, but the soles of her feet were pointed toward Toshik. Had the artist been sketching her upside down? Strange.

He sighed and began tapping his fingers atop the podium, trying to draw the attention of anyone in the staff. He looked around, spotting a humble barroom in the back. He leaned over the banister next to the podium and gazed up the narrow staircase. *This* was where Simon had sent him? He was beginning to—

He whirled, catching a young man by the neck and lifting him off his feet. Red hair dusted the man's scalp in a buzz cut. He pried at Toshik's fingers, trying to speak but only managing short breaths. Toshik loosened his grip.

"I'm Kolver, the innkeeper."

Toshik lowered him, but didn't let go of his neck. "What kind of farmland innkeeper can run like that?" Kolver hadn't been here a split second ago. He had sprinted here from a neighboring room, and Toshik only caught him because he saw the blur of color in his peripherals. A couple years ago, and he wouldn't have been able to track that speed and react in time.

"The son of a skilled Adrenian," said Kolver weakly.

Toshik relinquished his grip. The innkeeper hunched over with hands on his knees, coughing fitfully. He was lucky the impact from the combination of his speed and Toshik's hand didn't break his neck. "Why were you trying to sneak up on me?"

"A test."

Toshik sighed and shook his head. He didn't want to partake in games, so he decided to cut straight to the point. "A boy named Simon told me to come here."

"That boy is my little brother."

Toshik raised an eyebrow. Simon was Intelian. Why did he live here? Kolver just said he was the son of an Adrenian. Maybe their other parent was an Intelian, and Kolver got the Adrenian genes while Simon got the Intelian.

"He told us to be on the lookout for someone," Kolver said. "What's your name?"

"Toshik."

The innkeeper nodded and smiled, still releasing a strong cough here and there. He grimaced and popped his neck to the right and left.

"Sorry about that," Toshik said. "I've been on edge for a while now. Very reactionary."

"Understandable. Never know when Yama's going to strike, ay?"

Toshik lost his apologetic stance. How did Kolver know about that? Had Simon told him? Then he would have also informed him of the situation's serious nature. Bringing it up so casually seemed dumb on Kolver's part.

Kolver glanced down at Toshik's hand, which was grasping the hilt of his sheathed sword. He looked back up at Toshik and asked, "Want to meet the mayor?"

"Is he the person who will help me?"

"You have Simon's recommendation, so yes," said Kolver. "He's our dad."

*　　*　　*

Solace Skimentis was built like any other Adrenian. He was tall and imposing. Lean muscles squeezed tightly to his skeleton. His hair faded from gray to a light orange, and he wore spectacles. When Toshik shook his hand, the grip was firm but not strong enough to cripple the other. Solace smiled a lot, and not falsely. The man's eyes were friendly, embellished by abundant crow's feet. And he laughed just like Simon whenever the boy hung out with Bryson. And despite all of these qualities, Toshik vowed to never cross this man. The gentleness of his mannerisms and smoothness of his strides spoke of a person who was extremely confident in himself.

"Ahp-ahp-ahp," Solace said, waving his hand as Toshik tried to sit down. "Rumor is you want to make the most of your time."

Toshik hung in a strenuous position between standing and sitting, hands gripping the chair's arms as support. "That would be ideal."

"Then don't you dare sit down." Solace removed his spectacles and placed them on his desk. He turned and approached a door in the back of his office. He unlocked and opened it to reveal not a balcony, but open air. What a strange location for a door. "Come here, Toshik."

Toshik stood next to him in the doorway, gazing out at the back half of Yinyon. The land was mostly flat save the hill with the two oaks that dominated everything else. He thought he could see the Edge from here. Solace placed a hand on Toshik's shoulder and waved his other hand forward, presenting the sight. "You have four months to make it to the top of that hill."

"Is this a trick?" Toshik asked. He could run up that hill, and he saw nothing that would have impeded him.

"From here," Solace said. "With a single step-off, you must cover the gap between this door and that hill."

It wasn't a trick, and Toshik accepted its absurdity. This was what he needed.

63

The Price of Betrayal

Take Phesaw's slums and multiply its square footage by ten; that was Gangladesh: a vast town condensed into as little ground space as possible, two and three-story buildings clustered together so closely they might as well have been one.

Per Preloz's advice, they had arrived at the town while the sun was out. Gangladesh was dingy and poor, but the streets were as full of life as a civilization in the Cyn Kingdom could be. Citizens still walked with the Cynnish sluggishness and hunched postures, but they interacted with each other. Olivia witnessed two people laugh at one point, which had been enough to make Vuilni smile. She didn't care how unnatural the laugh sounded … it was still good to hear.

Reaching Gangladesh meant they were halfway to the Linsaniun Mounds. After weeks of travel in this atmosphere, they'd be fools to not take advantage of whatever little comfort the Void had to offer. Their bodies had weakened, hair graying at the roots. After waking with a foul case of halitosis, Vuilni searched Olivia's mouth and found the culprit near the back: a rotting molar.

They pulled it out that night after discussing the possible cons of an amateur handling it. Aggravating the wound and tearing more gum than necessary was the biggest concern, but they argued leaving it in would only lead to infection anyway. Olivia spent the following four days in agony, muffling her yells with her travel sack at night, which didn't achieve much in a place where whispers could carry over miles. Luckily, she only attracted undead animals that Vuilni could easily dispose. They hadn't encountered another karzirp.

They were met with their first major problem as far as cultural differences when speaking with a host at the front entrance of a tavern. The man didn't visibly express uncertainty when faced with two women whose condition was too clean and intact to have lived in the Void for long, but her dead eyes did linger between them for a moment. Before he spoke, Olivia cut him off by placing money on the counter.

Vuilni shrugged and winced to express her apology. The language barrier here was insurmountable, for Cynnish was a language that required a highly agile tongue. Better they eliminate the awkward circling of that barrier, for there was no getting around it.

The host eyed the change then used one hand to slide it into her other. One of his fingers was only bone. He picked through it, noting more valuable denominations with a nod and sliding them into a separate pile. While Olivia didn't understand languages outside of Sphairian, she did understand currency exchange rates. The five Light Realm kingdoms and the Power Kingdom used the same coin, but the other four Dark Realm kingdoms had their own. Seeing that her mother was Stillian, she had made it a point to teach Olivia about the differences in currencies. Thus, she eyed the host's piles curiously, looking for anything that seemed deceptive. If he assumed they were foreigners, he would likely assume they knew nothing about the true value of their coin.

After finishing his examination, the man pulled a calendar out from beneath the podium. He gestured toward the coin, then pointed to three days in succession. Olivia pointed to a fourth. His deal wasn't unfair, but it could have been better. He held her gaze, lifting his eyebrows as if to say, "So you're going to try me."

She pursed her lips and tilted her head. *I am.*

He shook his head and lowered the calendar. Scooping up the coin, he chuckled hoarsely. He returned it to the top of the podium and waved them away.

"What are you doing?" Vuilni asked, frustration straining her voice. It was rare she showed that, especially directed toward Olivia.

Her question and frustration was valid. Olivia may have known about foreign currency and economics, but that didn't make her a professional barterer. The host cocked an eyebrow as the two of them didn't move or grab their coin. He crossed his arms, tapping two fingers against a scrawny bicep.

Olivia smiled guiltily—she was getting so much better at that—and pushed the coin back toward him. She held up three fingers to symbolize three days, settling on his proposed price. He chuckled again, retrieving the calendar and now pointing at two days. Vuilni shoved the back of Olivia's shoulder. She turned and gave her friend an icy glare, but Vuilni didn't back down. *Be mad at me all you want; this is your fault,* her eyes said.

They spent the next hour scouring several blocks for another inn or tavern. They found many, but it turned out their first stop had been the most generous. Even the host's downgrade to two days for her amount of coin bested anything else. The two women returned to that same tavern with their tails tucked between their legs a couple of hours later.

Olivia plopped a bag of coin on the podium. The host didn't sport a triumphant grin or scornful scowl, but an unbothered look, as if this didn't surprise him in the slightest. He took the bag and rifled through its contents, this time taking more coin than he had the first. He marked three days on the calendar and guided them to their room on the third floor. He had even offered to carry some of their travel sacks, but both women clearly possessed stronger physiques than him and declined the offer with a gentle wave of their hand. Gratitude swept over his face at the rejection.

The room was small, possessing one twin-sized bed and a love seat with springs sticking out of its left cushion. If one of them wished to use it as a makeshift bed—and they looked to not have a choice—that errant piece of metal would require handling.

The sun had fallen behind Earth, marking the passing of noon and beginning of second-night. Vuilni took advantage of the darkness and resorted to a nap. Olivia lit a candle and sat idly on the loveseat, reflecting on the journey to this point and what was to come. She wanted to summon Preloz, but felt doing so would wake Vuilni, and she had already aggravated her friend enough today.

This mission was foolish, one in which the likelihood of death far exceeded any other. She could hear the scream of a Linsani through the cracked window—a taunt meant to remind her of that doom. Their cries had grown louder since departing Almawt Woods, and Olivia wondered what she could do if faced with one … or many. If Bryson could kill one, so could she … right? Her failure in the woods, however, when faced with that specter Preloz had called a karzirp wasn't a good sign. If her water couldn't hurt that weak creature, it'd do nothing against a Linsani.

She looked at Vuilni, who slept with her mouth ajar. Powish were a strange counter to Cynnish. Their abilities were purely physical, which did nothing against the metaphysical such as shadow and ghost. But when faced with physical beings such as a rotting corpse, Vuilni would obliterate them. Still, Olivia couldn't expect much from her against the Linsani. She'd have to rely on Preloz, who had sworn to fight by their side if it came to that.

She closed her eyes, picturing herself standing alongside Bryson, Lilu, Jilly, Toshik, Himitsu, Rhyparia, Yama, Agnos, and Tashami, before everything went to complete shit. Training in Phesaw Park, laughing in the Lilac Suites, or attending classes.

Then she slept and saw it in her dreams, waking hours later with tears in her eyes.

*   *   *

Evelyn stared at Tashami, taking advantage of the rare opportunity. Both he and Agnos were sleeping, and she had entered the room silently enough to not disturb them. She would have knocked first, but she was desperate to study Tashami in efforts to analyze what might be wrong with him.

The Spiritian was losing weight. His skin had paled everywhere except for the drooping black bags beneath his eyes. His breaths, even during sleep, seemed shallow and difficult to maintain. His lips were chapped to the point of splitting. His hair had faded from ivory to a dull gray, strands standing errantly as opposed to falling flat. She wanted to dump a bucket of water on him.

She stood from the stool on which she'd been sitting for an hour now, electing to observe from a closer perspective. She stood next to his bed and studied his entirety, most of which was hidden beneath blankets. The upward tilt of his head exposed a shadowy recess down the center of his neck, like what happened to the elderly, skin loose and aged. She had a suspicion of what was wrong with him, but she couldn't verify it with the layers of blankets. He had also begun wearing a tunic at all times—the most glaring red flag in her eyes.

She sighed and turned to acknowledge Agnos. The scholar was sleeping on his side, face turned toward Tashami so that he'd see him the moment he opened his eyes. She wished she had met these two at the beginning. She was certain their journey together had likely been one every playwright or director had tried to tell and capture since the beginning of theatre. That elusive blend of friendship, love, and ... she inhaled at the thought ... she would try to make sure tragedy didn't enter the picture.

While sailing the Sea of Light and getting to know Agnos, he had told her all about his adventures with Tashami: their mission in the Cyn Kingdom; the incredible voyages as members of Gray Whale's crew, from battling a storm for the ages and taking on an Adrenian fleet to siege the Brench Hilt; the assembling of their own crew; the unbelievable journey on the Mythmaker, diving into the sea and being swallowed by a supposed god. Just one of those adventures could have been an epic. She couldn't think of a word that suited their journey properly.

She blinked, then raised a finger to catch a falling tear. She had joined Agnos to learn about true camaraderie—something the Diatia had never acquired. He showed it to her in spades while on the Mythmaker, charging the leviathan that had climbed out of a whirlpool just to potentially save the

Whale Lord. Then she witnessed it again when she was blessed with the opportunity to hang out with the Jestivan in Dunami Palace after Toono's invasion. Whenever she didn't directly see them comforting or laughing at each other, she heard about the magic of their unity from the likes of Kaylee and Vuilni, who both had found themselves in Evelyn's shoes within the past few years.

She didn't want to watch a major part of that bond snap, yet it continued to unfold right in front of her.

"I love him, Evelyn."

Having zoned out, she looked at Agnos, who had opened his eyes and was now staring across the room at Tashami. He finally knew what everyone else already did, and it might have come too late.

She nodded, and said nothing.

*   *   *

This was the worst Tashami had felt since Ronossius's attack in his cell, but he had thought that yesterday and would definitely think it tomorrow. His spiritual disease wasn't healing, nor did he expect it to.

He was in the room alone, solitude granted to him after persuading the duo of Agnos and Arithmys to take their conversation about scholarly subjects elsewhere. He kind of enjoyed their enthusiasm, but he needed an excuse to shove them away. Seeing him as a less intelligent person, they understood and listened.

Standing in front of the mirror, he examined his face and hair. He had added one new wrinkle and a dozen new grays in the span of a day. These developments were already concerning to Agnos, and he didn't know the full truth.

Tashami sighed and lifted his shirt.

*   *   *

The door to High Warden Sylial's office blew open. Evelyn stormed in with one of the school's attendants rushing after her, shouting her apologies

656

at the warden. "She's unhinged, Warden Sylial," said the woman. "I tried telling her to—"

Evelyn slammed the door shut on the woman's face, and Sylial turned toward her. He stood to the side of his desk. He had been stacking parchment at the end of his desk. A student sat in the chair opposite of his. She turned with wide eyes, alarmed by the intrusion.

"I'm busy, Evelyn," he said.

She looked at the student again, this time with narrowed eyes. An older student, eighteen or nineteen perhaps, but still a baby in Evelyn's eyes. Pretty. Unlikely here for reprimand. The older students knew what the High Warden liked, and a few of the women were willing to entertain his vices for favor. Evelyn turned and opened the door, pointing to the hallway. "Get out."

Evelyn closed the door after her, and Sylial shook his head as he returned to his chair. "What do you want?"

She remained standing in front of the door, refusing to walk any closer. "You're going to fix my friend."

"Me?" he asked. "Shouldn't you be going to Ronossius?"

"I know you're involved."

"Of course, but that doesn't mean I can fix anything. Besides, I didn't get involved with that until after I figured out what Ronossius had done. I'm glad he did it though … gave me leverage."

She crossed her arms, expecting nothing less from the man who hated assassinations and cheap shots when it came to altercations of the body, but relished in the schemes of politics. His Devish intellect bested the muscles that twisted down his arms. "Spit it out," she said. "What are we bargaining here?"

"This isn't how matters of business are handled." He extended a hand toward the chair opposite him. "Take a seat."

She said nothing and didn't move. Maybe she would have sat had this actually been a "matter of business," as he had so elegantly phrased it. He was dealing in flesh here, which was more a matter of crime. And there were no rules in criminality, so she'd remain standing at a distance.

He breathed out a laugh and slapped a hand on his thigh. "Fine. I have something—or rather someone—you want." He paused, but she didn't reply. She knew he was talking about Pistimi, the second Prim Diatia who was locked away somewhere. "And you have someone I want."

"Who?"

"Your friend."

She balked. "For what? Do you even know which of the Jestivan they are?"

"Rasha provided descriptions, and I connected the dots. I'm the High Warden. You don't think I would keep tabs on every detail about the Jestivan? I'm guessing your two friends are Agnos and Tashami—a pair that's created quite a stir across the seas. Might be the most influential pair in the Jestivan despite individuals like Bryson and Lilu getting the spotlight, but that's life I suppose. They're Intelian, and Intelians have always received disproportionate amounts of glory."

"Get to the point," she said.

"I want Tashami."

"I still fail to see why. It's not like you'd turn him to your side."

He chuckled and shook his head. "No, that would be a fool's dream. You see … I want Tashami dead."

Her eyebrows furrowed. "That's not going to happen."

"That's fine. You won't get Pistimi. The beauty of business arrangements."

Evelyn stared at him, knowing she looked like an irate child. Going to this man had been a mistake. She needed to confront Ronossius a second time. He had threatened her indirectly during their guest lectures. She could make him fix Tashami—she was hoping he was fixable—and then she could worry about saving Pistimi another way. Coming to a decision, she turned to leave.

"At this point, death is a mercy to that boy."

Her hand froze on the handle, but she didn't turn to face him.

"I'm giving you an easy choice here, Evelyn. And know that his death must be by your hands. You will kill him, and I will watch."

She clenched her jaw, breaths quickening.

"You have some nerve. To return to this school after your egregious betrayals. Did you think I wouldn't serve you some form of punishment? You know while I might not be the man who holds the whip, I've always been the one who tells that man when to bring the whip crashing down. How to hold it. At what speed and angle. In this instance, you're both the person on her knees in the whip's path and the person holding the whip itself. A mental torture only worthy of scum like you. My only gripe is that Vuilni isn't with you.

"Bruut Schap died on Phesaw's campus while, somehow, all of the Jestivan lived. Vuilni then joined the Jestivan and abandoned us. Gina and Halluci died at the hands of a scheme developed by Pilot Ophala, the mother of a Jestivan. You abandoned us and joined a Jestivan. Then you had the damned nerve to come back here to take two more Diatia to join the Jestivan? That would leave me with one."

Her hand had fallen from the handle, eyes locked on it instead. She didn't bother pointing out the flaws in his logic, for there was no logic involved. Both Chelekah and Bruut had died at the hands of Toono, who the Jestivan fought against. Gina and Halluci had been in that position because of Dev Warden Gala's thirst to honor her king. He had twisted these circumstances to place the blame on the Jestivan, which were all the emotions and shattered pride of an arrogant man. He was bitter.

"Why do I need to kill him when it looks like he's destined for death already?" she asked, lips and tongue dry. "Whatever Ronossius did is already doing it."

"Ronossius isn't causing Tashami's degradation," Sylial said. "But he planted what's causing it." She closed her eyes, fears now confirmed. "And I think you know what that means, which is why I said this choice is an easy one. I couldn't have offered Pistimi on a more appetizing platter. If you don't do what needs to be done, that boy's *never* going to die. He'll spend an eternity in a state of suffering and wandering."

*   *   *

Tashami stood in front of the mirror and examined the hole in his chest, wherein nestled a graying heart behind exposed ribs. A black worm pulsed as it crept around it, feeding on whatever it was that sustained it. Spirit? Some believed the soul was located in the stomach while others believed it resided around the heart, but as a metaphysical organ.

He would have to kill himself soon, but there remained a thing he needed to do ... for Agnos and himself. If he waited too long, the umbra fairy would reach the stage in the process in which it killed his drive to do anything in life, including suicide. He also couldn't let Agnos find out about this.

Tashami was going to die, but not without a confession long overdue.

64

Masterpiece

"You're falling for her."

Mendac was seated on a bench in one of the Labyrinth's courtyards. He preferred the open air to the black tunnels. He may have created a secret laboratory in the sewers of Brilliance, but that didn't mean he had liked it down there. That had all been out of necessity.

He spiraled black shadows between his hands, extending his repertoire of skills into Mulawi weaving. He supposed he always had some control over the shadows, even before his death. It was the only reason why he had been able to take Ataway Kawi by surprise that night he had come to execute him.

"Did you not hear me?"

"I did," he said, leaning in to inspect the density of a shadowy tendril that twisted up his index finger. "It didn't warrant a response." He could hear the meltdown in Kadlest's mind at his lackadaisical disrespect. She hadn't changed after all of these years, and he cherished it. The way she contained all of her emotions, refusing to project them out of the fear of losing him. That was loyalty not even a dog could give.

"Because I'm right," she said.

The shadows vanished from his hands, and he turned toward her with a look of genuine disbelief. *That* was different. Had she really just persisted after he had made a statement that implied the topic was over? Where had she developed such gall in direction toward him? She recoiled at his sudden reaction, fearful he would hit her though he hadn't laid an abusive hand on her since rising from his casket.

His face softened. Her tongue might have become misguided, but at least her body still reacted instinctively. He had conditioned her well. He decided to take a different approach to this defiance of hers, knowing it stemmed from jealousy. It'll confuse her.

He grabbed her arm and pulled her closer to him. Her body tensed and remained that way even when he embraced her at his side. She thought she was being lulled into a trap. He didn't blame her. He had done something like this before, only to release a few surges of electricity into her at the most unexpected moment.

"Rhyparia intrigues me, but don't fret," he said. "I don't love her."

"You love things that intrigue you," she replied.

She had a point. He definitely didn't love Kadlest, nor did she intrigue him, but the child she could give him had. He hadn't loved that child though; he had loved the science behind it. "Let me rephrase," he said. "The person, Rhyparia, doesn't intrigue me. The science behind her does. What makes her power tick at such extraordinary levels? She removed the moon from the stars. Does that not intrigue you?"

"No, that's not the word I'd use." Her body was beginning to relax. "Petrify. That's better."

He smiled. "Science is the most beautiful thing in the world. Some people would say magic, but magic is merely untapped science. Everything has an explanation based in logic, and I've dedicated my life to bringing clarity to the unknown, as I, myself, am an enigma." He paused there, uncomfortable with his lecture's proximity to his own insecurities. "I search for nature's laws. I can find some in her."

Mendac wasn't lying, per se—at least not to Kadlest, more himself. He exhaled hard at that thought. Could he, perhaps, have been trying to downplay his fascination with Rhyparia? She was definitely a plaything, the ideal test subject. But there was something about her that genuinely attracted him, too. The fact that she didn't see him as a monster? He wasn't ashamed of his vileness, but there was comfort in interacting with someone who didn't see you as a threat. Kadlest had feared Mendac's strength and abandonment; Apoleia had feared Mendac's gender and motives. Rhyparia displayed respect.

These thoughts scared him. He hadn't truly felt for a woman since Thusia. When she died beneath the weight of that demon after saving his life, his heart died right along with her.

"Catharsis?" asked Kadlest, shifting her head against his shoulder to look at him. She was pointing out his forced exhale. "That's not like you."

He looked up at the Labyrinth's constant gray sky and scratched at the scruff on his chin. Kadlest was being awfully observant at the most inopportune times. He had told her he didn't have feelings for Rhyparia, but his reactions didn't correlate. He needed to shake this feeling … a distraction to remind himself of his purpose: dispose the world of the unknowns by finding all of its scientific answers.

He lowered his head and locked lips with Kadlest, a display of intimacy of which he typically steered clear. He had found himself in the Dark Empire, where there were countless unknowns to discover. Brooding on Rhyparia was not productive to that. Thus, as he kissed Kadlest with tongues entwined, he activated his clout and released a surge of electricity into her mouth and through her body.

She jittered, then convulsed. He grabbed the back of her head and kept their mouths locked, continuing to kiss her as he racked every single cell in her body with just enough volts to hurt her without killing her. She bit his tongue, and he bled. Not her fault. She was practically having a seizure.

He backed away from her and released his hold. He stood, and she slumped onto her side on the bench, jittering from aftershocks. Staring down at her, he frowned. He didn't really want her around anymore. Her presence had been beneficial while in the kingdoms, catching him up to speed after spending a decade and a half in a casket. He couldn't have foreseen being abducted by Gefal. Up here, she provided nothing of substance to him. He had decided that he didn't want to know the nature of how she and Toono resurrected him. He would wait until these visions of strangers' lives died out. They couldn't last forever.

He left the courtyard that day contemplating his next move with Kadlest. Well, he knew his next move. The question was when he would execute it. Maybe he could have Rhyparia kill her for him.

*   *   *

Rhyparia stood in the massive rotunda where she had first met Emperor Mialo, sable walls curving up to form a domed ceiling dotted with skylights, gray moonlight illuminating the chamber in a dozen streaks. Mialo's form was visible in a rectangular panel of wall that stood in the middle of the chamber, disconnected from every other surface except the floor. That wall seemed randomly placed, a sheet of black that glowed gold from a light somewhere behind it—a light that didn't stretch beyond the wall's edges. The only area of the wall that remained a glossy black was the shape of Mialo's body as it pushed through the onyx. She had yet to see the man's true self. Something told her if she were to walk behind the panel, she wouldn't find him. There was some kind of magic involving the Mulanyx.

Yasmine Cordelia and Poten Copor watched from the rotunda's entrance, while Rhyparia stood out in front. She was the subject here. This was her stage to show Mialo what she had accomplished in her several months training.

"Flex your wings," he said. Unlike their first meeting, he chose to speak the Sphairian tongue this time. His harsh accent and butchered syllables made it obvious he spoke it rarely.

Manipulating patterns of weaving, she was able to pull the ends of her wings inward.

"Extend them," he said. She did. "Flex again. This time harder."

Her wings pushed forward and curled in front of her, creating a barrier that protected her front side. As she remained in the shadowy shell, she heard whispering behind her. She looked back to find Mendac had entered the rotunda and was now watching her keenly while whispering with Poten. Mendac nodded at her as they made eye contact. She returned the gesture as one of gratitude. His advice about focusing on her eyes had been the turning point in her training. Without him, this would have taken much longer to happen.

"Rescind them."

Rhyparia followed the instruction and let her wings disappear into her back. She inhaled deeply, a feeling of relief settling within her. It wasn't until she first absorbed her wings when she realized why the Fuhren who had wings used them sparingly. She didn't know how to explain it exactly, but when they were out, she had an overwhelming sense of vertigo.

The ebony impression of a hand extended from the wall, a finger curling inward to request her approach. She walked closer, unafraid of what might happen, and stopped only when the hand opened with the palm out. Mialo's face protruded farther out, facial features becoming more pronounced in the onyx material. She could even see his eyes narrowing as he inspected her face closely. "Keep your eyes open for the next instructions. Do not blink," he said. "Release your wings."

The wings blasted from her back in a frigid rush, her eyes surging with the same coldness. That split-second sensation revealed Mialo's true form, his features adapting a more humanistic color and shape: eyes so dark a brown they were practically black, cream skin, black hair, and a beauty mark at the tail end of his left eyebrow. But that image was gone in a heartbeat, veiled once again by onyx carapace.

Mialo's face retracted back into the wall slightly, his inspection over as he waved her back to her original spot. "There are no such things as masterpieces," he said, "but you're as close as any god has gotten as far as creation."

She blushed ... She actually blushed.

"Given what I just saw in those eyes of yours," he said, "I shouldn't have to ask, but I'd be remiss if I didn't follow through with my own protocol here. Besides, I don't want to rob your spectators of the show."

She turned, no longer faced with just Yasmine, Poten, and Mendac. The remaining three Fuhren—Brenson included—stood waiting. And there were lights that glowed behind three separate sections of the wall, each exposing a person's silhouette in the Mulanyx. She didn't know for certain, but her gut told her they were the Versac, the highest rank of Gefal that wasn't Emperor Mialo himself. They were the elites meant to counter the Light Empire's Strasan.

She had spent these last several months noting this moment as a personal goal, but apparently it held much more weight. Her success could help sway the tides in the Dark Empire's favor. Fuhren Poten watched intently, engorged muscles twitching in anticipation. Fuhren Brenson smirked proudly, beady eyes glinting behind curtains of stringy black hair. He had been in charge of the squad that housed her and Mendac. Fuhren Yasmine watched with little emotion. If anything was discernible from her flat stare, it was either disappointment or fear.

Mendac smiled broadly, contorting the scar that ran from his scalp down his face—a sword wound from some mighty foe while in the kingdoms. There was no evil in that smile, only honest admiration.

Rhyparia faced Mialo again. Her wings of shadows slapped down to the floor, lifting her into the air. She climbed higher and higher, ascending within one of the cylinders of moonlight until reaching the hole in its roof. She hovered beneath it, all eyes trained on her from a hundred feet below.

Sinking the moon. Taking flight. There was nothing she couldn't do, and *she* had made it happen. Nobody forced her to do this. They weren't involuntary actions. She had control of her life, her body. And she would continue to prove to the world—her mother, the Amendment Order, even the Dark Emperor himself—that nobody but herself was responsible for her strength.

Something below her clattered, echoing throughout the vast rotunda and ripping her from her revels. She looked down and saw her pride and joy—the tool that made her dangerous.

A humble, tattered umbrella.

Now, she was a masterpiece.

65

Breaking the Ice

Creep stood in the Electric Eel's back of house. Based on the coal pit installed in the counter that looked like it hadn't been cleaned in years and a complete lack of coal storage in the drawers he had searched, this had once been a kitchen. There were copious amounts of counter space, too, and a walk-in ever-ice cupboard that held only a few bottles of colorful liqueurs. It was a waste of space. Either this building had once been a restaurant under previous ownership or Sally had abandoned that business model herself, electing to establish her handprint primarily in the bar industry.

It might have been a room now reserved solely for storage, but it was organized and clean—aside from the coal pit, which he figured there was no salvaging. Bored as he was forced to wait for Sally's arrival, he walked over to it and examined it more closely. He ran a finger along its surface. The grime was thick, but solid. It didn't flake or smudge. She had likely tried scrubbing this a hundred times, yet the only solution would have been to break the entire pit apart with a sledgehammer.

The door from the bar opened, and Sally walked in, wiping her forehead with a rag and tossing it in a bucket full of others in need of a wash. She acknowledged Creep with a cocked eyebrow. "Previous owners," she said. "An eyesore, really."

"Why not get rid of it? You can have it replaced." He crouched and looked beneath the pit, studying its base to see if it was hammered into the floor or the wall. He rocked his head side to side and gave it some thought, then he looked up at her with a smile. "It's a project I could handle."

"Are you offering to be my handyman?" she asked slyly. "Like some sort of midnight play?"

He laughed. Midnight plays didn't exist in the Prim Kingdom. He hadn't attended one since he was sixteen, when he and his friends snuck into a rather famous one involving the wheel of a lady's carriage falling off in the middle of the night. It turned out the coachman had conveniently forgotten his tools in the town they had last left, which was ten miles back. When he suggested they sleep in the carriage for the night together, the audience groaned, knowing what came next.

It turned out they didn't.

Long story short: the play ended abruptly in its second act when the woman stabbed the coachman in his neck. Gasps in the crowd quickly became screams as stagehands rushed the stage without costumes, trying to press their hands against the man's neck as blood stained the wooden floorboards. The actress was apprehended, which she accepted quietly and gracefully. She only asked that she watched as her co-star's body pumped out its remaining life. They let her, and she was released a week later after authorities discovered the actor's basement. Five stagehands had been found chained and naked, each with aspirations of becoming the actor's next co-star. She had killed the man not out of fear of losing her role and celebrity status, but out of rage for what he had done to them.

Creep had snuck in to learn more about adult relationships, hoping to pick up on a few moves of the more sensual nature. Instead, he left traumatized for the next three years, during which he avoided physical contact while keeping his eyes fixed on everything around him.

"When you go silent and glance every which way like that, it unnerves me a bit, Sunshine."

Creep refocused on Sally, who was looking at him with raised eyebrows. He closed his eyes and breathed a laugh through his nose. "Sorry."

"I don't want to replace it," she said. He paused, confused, but then remembered they had been talking about the coal pit. "It's special to me."

"I thought you said it belonged to the previous owners."

"My parents." Silence, but before he could reply, she added, "They're not dead."

He stood and returned his hands to his pockets. "Thank you."

"For what?"

"I was thanking the universe," he said. "Had they been dead, I wouldn't have known what to say, and then this would have been …"

"Awkward?" she asked.

He grinned, and she rolled her eyes. She walked to the back door and opened it, checking the alley to make sure nobody was outside. She then closed it and regarded him with a look of all business.

"I don't know what the princess is thinking," she said.

He grunted, unbelieving.

She raised an eyebrow. "Don't believe me?"

"You expect me to?"

She snorted. "No." She sighed. "But I've been kept in the dark for a lot more than you think. I have a suspicion that this spectacle isn't one of the Spy Pilot's schemes, however. The Intel ladies might be doing this behind her back, or simply without her consent. And if that's the case, I suspect the information wouldn't be distributed to the proper players, even if people like you and me should know about it. Intelians are too proud, and that extends into the royal family. They'll keep their plans to themselves and try to do it all by themselves."

"But, a public stage?" said Creep, shaking his head at the floor. "What kind of plan would involve such a stupid maneuver?"

Silence stretched for a couple of minutes as they mulled over their thoughts. Princess Lilu was organizing a speech for the queen that would involve her standing outside the western side of the palace, allowing anyone and everyone to attend and watch from the streets. He understood her concern about the lack of a presence from the kingdom's Royal Head over the past several months, but this was extreme. A better option would have been to broadcast the queen's speech across the city via Dev servants. Even if she didn't believe that would stop the uprisings, it would quell them at least ... surely, no?

"We've been working on relocating Whistle," said Sally, breaking the quiet. "It's impossible. The villa you met her in that night has been abandoned since then. She likely never stays in one place. Who knows if she's even in the capital at the moment?"

"She has to be."

Sally leaned back against the counter, looked up at the ceiling, and sighed. That was twice now. She was growing anxious. This news about the queen's speech had invigorated the rebels, according to her sources within their ranks. They would use that event as an opportunity to pounce, and who knew what that meant exactly.

But it had also given life to the populace who had yet to convert to the rebels' cause, because part of this speech was an awards ceremony. The crown planned on handing out prizes and medals to the most successful or notable men and women of each major field of business: butchers, smiths, chefs, librarians, doctors, farmers, weavineers, etcetera. The list went on for days. Most categories would be decided legitimately, but that of butchers would be rigged for Creep to win. That was what would put him in a position to take out his target.

"Damnit," Creep cursed. "All the body guards in the world wouldn't protect her from such a public forum."

"Agreed. I've heard amazing stories about the Jestivan, but none of them are here."

"Lilu," he said.

"That's right, but I don't know how I feel about the princess defending the queen. If they both die ..."

He narrowed his eyes. "The real question is where the hell Bryson is?"

"From my observations over the years, that boy's never been one to shy away from the spotlight. He always winds up in it somehow, whether it's placing himself there are tripping his way into it." Her eyebrows furrowed as she gave it some thought. "Matter of fact, maybe that's why the royal sisters are doing this. There has to be a reason why he's been absent from the public. He's going to strike back, if necessary … and unexpectedly. His absence has seemed to make the rebels forget about him. I'd imagine if he had been walking the streets these past several months, their confidence and progress wouldn't be the same."

"Shouldn't have come to this in the first place," Creep said. "He should have been out and about. There is no reason for him to barricade himself in that palace." He scratched at his beard. "Something's wrong in there. I don't know what, but I feel as if there is a development—or several—that have occurred over these months that only the royal family knows about."

"There's the threat of Mendac's return," she said. "Perhaps, they're fearful of his presence in the capital."

"What has Pilot Ophala had to say about that?"

"She doesn't know much, but she doesn't think he's here. There were many witnesses who said they saw someone flying away from the capital the day of Toono's attack. They didn't know what it was they were looking at of course, but the fact that it had black wings and seemed to be carrying someone else lets us know that it was Mendac and Kadlest."

Creep scoffed. "That Bryson kid—and granted, I barely know him—didn't seem like one to hide his face."

"I don't think he is, which is why I doubt my earlier explanation." She grumbled. "If only I could get in touch with the Pilot. All I know is that I need to be present during the speech, and you need to work on your butchery skills. All eyes will be on you after you accept that medal. Focus on your target. I've relayed information about Whistle to the necessary people. She is not your priority."

His lips thinned. He wasn't making progress on his mark. He had yet to find Periphan LeAnce, nor did he understand why this was his job. Periphan was the kind of woman who was always near important members of the crown. If she needed be dealt with, someone a lot closer to the crown could have done it … unless they wanted it not to look like they had any part. That made sense.

Creep was an unknown to the world after secluding himself to one kingdom—and the most secretive kingdom save the Cyn. Nobody knew about his recent ties with the royals. He was a creeping ghost.

*　　　*　　　*

It had been months since Bryson last stood atop one of the Starlight's six Energy Gates. Although he had dreamed about it on several occasions, the true breathtaking beauty of it could only be captured when actually looking down from the tower's edge. It was also terrifying, which explained his five-foot cushion between him and the edge.

He was on one knee, staring across the sky and admiring the Cavities of Tahar as they spilled liquid light into the structure's quartz. This was the body of a god, and the Tahara spilling from those spherical lights was its lifeblood. He looked down at the floor, the liquid light not splitting to avoid his body like it had during his first visit. Instead it crashed past him, colliding into his lower leg in a rush of heat. The light of his wings were fading downward as they stretched for the liquid. These were signs of progress. He had come a long way. Now he had not just electricity and speed, but light, too.

"You are everything I wanted my first attempt to be."

He turned, finding the impression of a woman's front side in the waterfall of Tahara that crashed down from the spherical light. She was a curvaceous woman—a shrewd way of describing someone, but it was all he could really grasp of her image. The impression didn't allow for more specific features to shine. He could tell she was tall. Roughly six feet?

He stood and turned toward her, tucking his hands into his pants pockets. "What does that mean?" he asked.

She stared at him in silence for a moment, then smiled—or so he thought. He had to read facial expressions by the shadows in the light. "I'll explain that in due time. For now, I want to focus on the half of you yet to be developed."

"Is electricity, speed, and light not enough?"

"It's a lot," she admitted, "but not your full potential. It's a shame that man didn't teach you his skills with the sword."

She was referring to Debo. "You want to teach me swordsmanship?"

"Oh, no. It's too late for that. You would learn nothing, and the people you would potentially fight against who use such a weapon would demolish you in seconds—if you were to try to use a sword, that is."

He actually agreed with her, which was why he'd never tried to pick up the weapon after Debo's death. He figured it was too late and he'd be doing his idol a disservice. He could see the man rolling in his grave at the thought of it.

"I'm talking about your Stillian genes," she said.

He paused at that, automatically thinking of his mother. He missed her. Looking down at the liquid light that rushed over his shoes, he said, "I don't think that extends into anything beyond my genes. I'm half Stillian, yes, but it only shows in certain traits."

"You've suffered from a chill throughout your life, have you not?"

He nodded. He had been told how that might link his abilities to the potential of ice, but had yet to see proof.

"That's not just genes. That is Still Energy."

"So I've been told."

"And you don't believe it?"

"Why should I?"

She tilted her head. "Because now it's coming from *my* mouth."

"But you're Intelian. What do you know about Stillians?"

A long pause, followed by a ridiculous laugh. "Oh, Ataway had his hands full with you." She laughed again until it waned to a chuckle. "I'm more than just an Intelian, Bryson. I've been alive for thousands of years. Do you not think I know things?"

"I'm sure you know more than me."

"According to Thusia, that's not much of an accomplishment."

He blushed, wounded but not surprised. "You speak with Thusia directly?" he asked, recalling one of the Pogu telling him about the exclusivity of meetings with the Empress. If Pogu couldn't get one-on-one time with her, then how could a Branian?

"I hear things from Naipa, Rhysel, and Magnifica, who hear things from the Pogu, who hear things from the Branian. Word always reaches me, which is how I've also learned about your relationship with your mother." His nostrils flared, but she continued going before he could retort. "It's not a lot, mind you, but I heard the two of you were distant. Then it became strained. Then you made peace."

He eyed her, hands lifting out of his pockets as he crossed his arms. "What does this matter?"

"Have you ever tried tapping into your Still Energy?"

He gave it some thought, but then admitted, "No." There were times he thought he might have, but in truth he had never dedicated one hundred percent of his focus on it. Ever since Director Jugtah had operated on him, he'd been scared to experiment with his body.

"Why?"

The question was valid, and he supposed he didn't have the answer. Yes, he feared it, but from where did that stem? "Never took it seriously," he said.

"Really?" she asked. "The idea of harnessing ice, the ability of your beloved mother, is not a serious matter to you?"

He shrugged.

She licked her lips—a strange motion in the liquid—to wet them, then asked, "Let me ask you this. Do you respect her?"

"Of course."

"How much?"

"Immensely." He looked down, gaze distant. That woman had endured so much, even before Mendac's arrival. Like most Stillian mothers, Still Queen Salia had not treated Apoleia well—a toxicity amplified exponentially given her position as a royal.

Tonitrua watched patiently, allowing him his introspection. She then said, "You know no matter how much you may resemble your father on the outside, that doesn't mean the reflection extends beyond that. You are kind."

He looked up at her, brows pinched. It had been a long time since someone brought up his resemblance to his father, and he didn't like it. "I don't even look like him!"

"You do. You know you do." Her voice was now soft and motherly, which only irritated him more. "Do you honestly think that hoodie you wear is for the cold? If so, then why do you never wear a shirt under it?"

"It's because I always hated the spotlight," he said, voice clipped. "The expectations I couldn't live up to. Social anxieties and all that nonsense."

"Partly," she said. "But I think you wanted to hide your face. When people looked at you, they saw your dad. You didn't like it. And that only worsened when you learned about what he did to your mom. What are you scared of most when your mom looks at you?"

Flabbergasted, he stared blankly, mouth agape. This was the direction she was taking? He exhaled and said, "Devish, Passionians, and Archains are the mentalists, therapists, and psychologists. Since when do Intelians pick brains like this?"

"As I said before, I'm not your typical Intelian. I come from a time long before the stigma of dividing social strengths between the kingdoms." She paused, then said, "Answer the question, Bryson."

"I'm scared she sees my dad." The sentence just fell out. He had lost any effort to either dismantle her recourse by misdirection or feign ignorance by stalling. His shoulders sunk and voice deflated. "And she does. She's told me."

"But she's learning to see past that, right?"

"So she says, but I don't know if I can ever believe it. I never could, myself. Then I saw the bastard rise from his casket and thought I was looking at a future me." He muttered the next words. "It was revolting."

"I know you see the issue here," she said. "Why you haven't been able to use your Still Energy?"

"Because I hate myself."

"Not quite. You don't hate yourself. You're married to the love of your life, a woman with whom you've had a son. But you are ashamed of yourself, and you think wielding ice would be spitting in the face of your mother. You don't think you, a young man who resembles the demon who hurt her, deserve to harness her power … as if you'd be tainting her culture, her spirit. Not just that, but I believe you don't want to wield ice and electricity simultaneously because then you'd be proving to your father that what he did to your mom resulted in a success, which would validate the measures he took."

Bryson's arms dropped to his sides, as this woman laid out every truth about his fears he hadn't realized himself. His ears grew hot as tears swelled in his eyes.

"I assure you that your mother knows you think these things," Tonitrua whispered. "As a mother, myself, I know that." He would have questioned the revelation about her motherhood if he hadn't been so focused on everything else she had just unpacked about him. "She's moved on."

"How do you know that?"

"I saw it," she said. "Or rather, someone I sent saw it and told me. Do you recall seeing Pogu Quincy at any point between his first arrival with Thusia and Suadade and the evening Naipa came to get you?"

"At my wedding reception." Quincy had been standing in the distance, watching from between two hedges.

"He was scouting you. The idiot thought it not important to tell me who you were marrying, but he did mention a moment you had with a woman at the piano. I knew that to be your mother because, well, I've had to deal with her and your dad in the past."

"When?"

"I'm the one who sent Ataway to execute Mendac, obviously."

The revelation shouldn't have been as mind-blowing as it was. He had so many questions to follow that up with, but she raised a hand, liquid trailing from her fingers.

"The only thing more dear to a Stillian woman's heart than their ice abilities is their art. It doesn't matter if it's dance, painting, or music, they hold that skill above all others. It's where they funnel their emotions after spending days in an apathetic state. And they hide this emotional discharge behind closed doors. What your mother did was a *big* deal. Not only did your mother play the piano in front of a crowd of a hundred people, but she did it with *you* by her side, playing in rhythm. She brought you into her most personal act. She shared that with you. It was more than a truce; it was a cry for love and bliss and … forgiveness. And I don't mean her forgiveness of you, but vice versa."

"I don't get it."

"When it came to her broken relationship with you, it wasn't your fault," Tonitrua said. "She was the one who did you wrong. That moment at the piano was the most sincere apology she could have made as a Stillian. And if she was willing to give you that, then she wouldn't care if you could use Still Energy."

Bryson sniffled and wiped at his nose. This woman was not the typical Intelian. She was the wisest person he'd ever met. Suddenly, the heat of Tahara rushing through his back and feet was accompanied by a familiar chill. He imagined his mother's hand on the back of his head, her frigid lips against his forehead, and he cried.

Tonitrua smiled. "How's that for breaking the ice?"

66

The Nature of Influence

Rain was rare in the Void. One would have a better chance spotting a Linsani over the horizon, for they sometimes did venture away from their homes in the Mounds. Today was a rainy day, and the orphans were gallivanting throughout the home's main floor. Panelle was the most hyper of them all, crawling beneath coffee and end tables and then hurdling over other furniture. Joni and Nina halfheartedly tried ending his tirade, but were more focused on each other as they conversed in the kitchen. She was attempting a recipe that Mother had taught her, offering to cook for and take care of the orphans for the day while the two foster parents relaxed upstairs.

Tashami was trying his best to pretend like everything was normal. He sat on the floor, shifting tiny soldier figurines across the coffee table in battle formations. Ropper sat across from him, occasionally ramming his cup through the toy ranks and knocking them over. He was only a year older than Tashami, making him the second youngest child in the house.

Tashami cringed as pain sliced through his scalp. Ropper looked up at Tashami's hair and frowned. "Want me to get Mr. Patter?"

Tashami shook his head. He had a hand pressed against the bandage circling his head. It would be months before his head recovered from the night he had followed Joni and Nina into the town. He had torn out enough hair to leave patches of bald spots. He had carved away enough skin to leave scar tissue. His fingernails were just now starting to grow back after disintegrating them across broken cobbles. While those would heal, his mind proved more difficult. He could still hear the wails of that boy.

"Lift your hand," Ropper said. Tashami did, and the boy propped himself onto his knees and leaned over the table to look. "It's not bleeding. Don't worry."

"Thanks," Tashami said, returning to his toy soldiers.

"You and Joni are so strong."

He looked up at Ropper, who was smiling with two missing front teeth. He didn't reject his compliment. To be grouped with his big brother meant the world to him, even if he had proven otherwise.

Ropper looked to the right, and his eyes widened. He pointed toward the kitchen, which was visible through a wide archway from the living room. Tashami glanced that way and dropped one of his soldiers. Nina was feeding Joni a ladle of broth, just like mom did for dad. A little bit dribbled over his bottom lip and down his chin. He backed away and tried catching it with his hand, but she closed the gap and kissed him on the lips.

Tashami and Ropper gasped. The kiss lasted no more than a second—a single peck—but for a couple of preteens, that was significant enough. While the kitchen might have been only one room away from the living room, Tashami felt worlds apart from his brother in that moment. Joni and the eldest orphan had forgotten there was a room full of children within eyesight. As they split apart, he blushed and looked toward the living room.

Tashami started to rise from the floor to confront his brother, but was interrupted by a bang and shattering glass. He looked toward the noise's source and found Panelle standing guiltily next to an end table, a glass mug in pieces at his feet.

"That was my dad's favorite mug, you squealers!" hissed Joni, who had run into the living room from the kitchen.

"Your dad may be the Unbreakable, but his mug isn't!" screamed Panelle, whose look of guilt had shifted to amusement. Giggles erupted, but then footsteps from the doorway caused them to stop.

"That was funny, Panelle," came a deep and gentle voice. The Unbreakable stood in the entrance to the living room. He walked over to the end table and studied the broken mug. His eyes drifted up to Panelle. "A fantastic joke."

Ropper leaned over the coffee table and whispered to Tashami, "What's a joke?"

"It's something that makes you laugh," the Unbreakable replied, turning to face the rest of the room. "A great tool to ignite your soul. Jokes make people feel better."

"Do people tell jokes in the Light Realm, Mr. Patter?" asked Unry, a brunette boy around the age of ten. He had been reading in the room's corner.

"All the time, but not all are so nice. Jokes that harm someone's feelings are bad."

A knock came from the front door. Tashami whirled. It was jarring, considering the aggression behind the knock and the way sound traveled in the Void. Nobody had expected company. Ever since his brush with death in the town, all of the orphans had been on strict lockdown. Even Mother and Father hadn't left the house.

"Guess what, children," said Father. "You get a new foster brother today."

Most cheered and rushed the foyer, but three remained in the living room, hesitant: Tashami, Joni, and Nina.

"Do you feel that?" Nina asked.

"Yeah," said Joni.

Tashami didn't respond, but the pit in his stomach agreed with both of them. While nowhere close to the severity, he had experienced this sensation that night in the town, listening to those inhuman wails. He gulped.

Joni took his arm and helped him to his feet, then hugged him against his side. Nina stood on Tashami's other side with a hand on his shoulder. They were protecting him. And just as their guts had told them, the boy who walked through the front door to a swarm of orphans was the same one Joni had described as the boy who had been haunting the town.

He had white hair like the Patter brothers, but his was thinning and brittle. His face was sunken in, eyes lifeless as they scanned the many orphans surrounding him. He was only a couple years older than Tashami—five or six, perhaps. The boy made eye contact with Tashami, Joni, and Nina. He looked sad, but nodded at them. Joni's embrace of Tashami tightened, as did Nina's hand on his shoulder. He stood between two pillars, both which he knew wouldn't break. Mother and Father might have been the gears of this orphanage that made sure it ticked, but Joni and Nina were the foundation.

Another boy entered the house, and Tashami could tell by the look on Father's face that he hadn't been expected a second guest. This boy's hair was stringy and black, but slate gray at the roots. He looked to be eight or nine when standing next to his companion. The pair wore the same dead expression.

Father eyed the second boy suspiciously as he closed the door behind them. He instructed the orphans to give them some space, and Mother appeared on the overlook. She paused and stared, then said, "I know he's Chelekah, but who is the other one?"

"What's your name, son?" asked Father.

"Ronossius. Chelekah's cousin."

Father looked up at his wife, her expression grave. She was communicating with him in a way only the two of them could understand—non-verbal communication only capable from a married couple of a dozen or more years. "Family!" Father bellowed, his voice likely traveling into the town. Mother didn't share his enthusiasm. Perhaps, she felt what Tashami did. They all must have. There was a shroud following these two.

"We're not here to separate families," Father said, looking down at the two boys. "We make families! You're both welcome here, if you so choose!"

And just like that, a crack formed in the Unbreakable.

*   *   *

681

Tashami stood in the study next to his big brother. Across from them stood Chelekah and Ronossius. Despite Father's successful strides to incorporate the two Cynnish boys into the orphanage—most of the children were beginning to like them—Joni couldn't accept them. And until he could, the cousins would never receive proper respect from their peers. None of the children fully committed to anything without Joni and Nina's approval. When Panelle was caught playing with Ronossius the other day, a disapproving glare from Joni had been enough to make sure that didn't happen again.

That brought the four boys to this study, where they committed to a standoff. Joni waited for one thing: an apology. Chelekah had been the boy haunting the town for months, leading to the unfortunate ends of several civilians. Tashami would have been added to that tally had it not been for Nina's and Joni's interference. Chelekah's wails had driven Tashami mad. Only now was he beginning to restore his spirit to its normal glow, thanks in large part to Father's daily spiritual therapy sessions.

"No know why we say sorry," said Ronossius.

Tashami never understood what either cousin was saying, for they had grown up only learning their native tongue, Cynnish. Their Sphairian was broken. Mother had only spent three weeks teaching them, building on the small words they had learned from a family they ran away from a year ago. Joni, however, could make sense of the broken Sphairian.

"Because it's the right thing to do," he said.

Ronossius glanced at Tashami, arms folded. "Chelekah no can stop his nature. He six. I try hard to stop him."

"Tashami just turned four," replied Joni, "yet he knows how to temper his spirit."

"Do he?" asked Ronossius. "Then why he was in town that night? Too ..." he trailed off, narrowing his eyes as he searched for the right word ... "eager."

Tashami frowned and looked up at his brother. Was that a word? Joni paid him no mind, instead countering. "He hasn't gotten anyone killed. Actually, his nature improves the people here."

Ronossius tilted his head. "You know wind from Spirit Energy can hurt my people?"

"Tashami can't make wind. I'm talking about his personality."

Suddenly, Chelekah stepped forward, separating from his older cousin to approach Tashami. He extended a hand. Tashami looked down at it, confused.

Ronossius snapped at Chelekah, but it was in Cynnish, so Tashami couldn't understand. He sounded angry. Tashami regarded his brother, who stared at the boy with furrowed brows. He then looked across the room at Ronossius. "Even your little cousin knows what he should do."

Ronossius scowled. He marched forward, and Tashami had to make a choice between fleeing or remaining stoic. It looked like the boy was charging forward in aggression. Ronossius reached for Chelekah's wrist to snatch it back, but not before Tashami grasped his hand. The two younger boys shook hands. Frozen halfway toward snatching his cousin's arm, Ronossius closed his eyes and exhaled.

"I sorry," whispered Chelekah, and Tashami could see the remorse vividly in his eyes. Chelekah reached up and brushed his fingers through Tashami's hair, stopping wherever bandages crossed. "I a bad person."

Tashami sucked back a load of snot, mucus building in his nose and eyes. He reached out and hugged the boy, smiling. "You're nowhere close to that. And if you don't believe it, we'll teach you. My daddy is the most spirited person in the world! He can't be broken, and he makes sure no one else can, too."

Ronossius had backed away, watching with that scornful gaze. Joni said, "I don't think Chelekah's the one who's truly suffering."

*   *   *

The coming weeks followed that same pattern: Chelekah meshing well with the orphans while Ronossius drifted further away. Chelekah partook in games of hide-and-seek, becoming best friends with Tashami and often times taking Nina's spot as his hiding partner. They were always caught first since they couldn't last longer than a few seconds without giggling, but neither of them cared. The enjoyment was all that mattered.

Despite Joni's original disdain toward Ronossius, he continued to try to mold his attitude into something better, but all of his efforts fell short. Ronossius had told several of the orphans to kill themselves. He began experimenting with powers of persuasion, manipulating the hearts of the more vulnerable Cynnish children to commit acts they normally wouldn't.

The breaking point came the night before Joni's birthday. Tashami couldn't sleep. He tossed and turned, which kept everyone else in the room awake. Nothing was worse than a squeaking bed in the Void, but who could blame him? He always got excited before a birthday. They were big celebrations in the orphanage. And any of the children who didn't know their birthdays got to choose a day at the beginning of every calendar year.

He rolled one way, drooling over the thought of a rare chicken dinner. He rolled the other way, smiling at the wall as he thought of Joni slamming a slice of cake in his face. He rolled again, this time facing the room and finding Nina in the darkness. She slept in his room as a protector. A couple days ago she tried sleeping in Joni's room, but she gave up after Tashami sobbed long enough.

Joni's birthday arrived, and everyone celebrated in the den. Mother played the flute while dancing around the floor, weaving between children and struggling to hit every note as she laughed at a few of the more awkward dancers. They had these celebrations in the den because the Cynnish weren't fond of music, and being below land helped stifle the musical notes from reaching other homes. Nina danced with Tashami, holding his hands and bending her knees to get closer to his shorter stature. He had stolen her from Joni twice already. Fighting for her attention during past birthdays was never this difficult. He was happy that Joni never resisted. He only watched the two of them dance from his spot against the wall with a smile on his face.

Father distributed plates of food to some of the orphans who sat at tables pushed against the opposite wall. He laughed immensely, chest heaving hard enough that Tashami would likely bounce if he sat on it. Father always treated birthdays like they were moments he'd never experience again. Tashami didn't know why. Everyone was so young; there were plenty of birthdays in their future.

Mother began playing one of her more upbeat melodies, so Tashami hopped with the beat like the rest of the younger children. Nina paused and watched, shaking her head but grinning. Whenever Mother wanted to exhaust the children for a while so she could take a break, she played this tune.

Tashami jumped and jumped and jumped, pounding his feet harder atop the cement floor. He looked down to make sure he didn't catch anyone's toes, arms above his head as they rose and fell with the beat. Nina joined, which encouraged other older kids to do the same. Soon, she and Joni were hopping around Tashami, and he became the center of a growing circle. They cheered him on and hopped in rhythm while he twisted his body randomly, forgetting there was a tune to which he should have kept in sync.

Mother circled the wall of orphans, watching her youngest son flail as she continued blowing into the flute. She smiled throughout, her feet coming to a stop as she reached Father, who placed an arm around her shoulder and kissed her forehead. They stood in front of the stairs that led up the side wall to the main floor above.

There wasn't much substance to the moment. It was purely fun. Silly. Euphoric. A rush of adrenaline that lifted Tashami to a high he had never experienced before. He felt unstoppable, his bliss unflappable.

Father placed a hand against his chest and bellowed laughs, his baritone a backdrop of drums to Mother's flute. Tashami wiggled his shoulders and made a funny face, showing some attitude he had seen from Nina when she danced. He lifted his legs and ran in place, thrusting his arms in front of him. Joni entered the middle of the circle and danced alongside him, leading him with more practiced moves. The children around them grew louder, singing the words to Mother's tune:

Let them free, let them free!
Climb a tree, scrape those knees!
Children run 'cus they're free!
Play with me, play with me!
Hide and seek, filled with glee!
Weeeeeeeeeee!

That last part was Tashami's favorite, and he loved when Joni danced to it because he would roll his entire body in sync with the last line's ebbing rhythm. Joni winked at his little brother as they spun around each other, but Tashami's eyes locked onto the staircase beyond, where Panelle stood with a giant cooking pot. Despite the pot's size and the boy's smaller stature, he shouldn't have been struggling as much as he was. He had to heave it over the staircase's banister, so something must have been in it. And was that steam?

Tashami paused, eyes widening as he noticed the spot in which Panelle stopped was directly above Mother and Father. Joni turned. Father looked up, but Mother continued playing the flute while the children danced. "*MOM!*" Joni screamed.

Panelle tipped the pot over. Father's reaction was too slow, only managing to thrust an arm over part of her body. Water crashed over her with a hiss, steam erupting from her body as a deathly shriek ripped itself from her throat. Father roared as a portion of the right half of his body was caught in the splash. Joni sprinted through the wall of frenzied children. He knelt next to Mother, who had fallen to the floor … still screaming. Her skin was bright red, blistering already. Wet clothes clung to her frame, hands pressed against her face. Joni grimaced as he knelt in the scalding water, but he grabbed Mother regardless.

Tashami's sprint was impeded by Nina, who stepped out of the circle to catch the boy. He fought against her, banging fists against her chest and trying to squirm free, but she clutched him tight. Then he burrowed his head in her chest, forearms pressed against his ears to block out Mother's agony.

Nina eventually let Tashami go, but he fell to his knees as the small ones were escorted up the stairs by the older orphans. He looked up at Panelle, who stood lifeless on the stairs. His eyes were dead. Face, blank. It was as if he wasn't there. He was normally so animated. This was the same child who had cracked a joke just a few weeks ago.

Another person walked down the stairs, against the flow of children who fled upward. He stood next to Panelle and placed a hand against his back. It was Ronossius, his expression just as dead as Panelle's. He looked down at Mother, Father, and Joni.

And then he spit on them.

67

Smallest of Worlds

Olivia felt as rested as she could in a place like the Void. After three days of little movement—aside from regular exercise to keep her body prepared for whatever might come—she moved with more gusto, the Cyn Kingdom's atmospheric drain mostly ineffective.

She and Vuilni were following a lead the innkeeper had given them. Vuilni had asked him about the Linsaniun Mounds without Olivia's knowledge. She didn't know how the exchange went down, but Vuilni said he was perplexed as to why they wanted to know. He was helpful, however, and pointed them in the direction of a guild that supposedly could help.

A building loomed at the end of the city street, its shadowed silhouette tilted just enough to make Olivia question her eyesight. Who built a crooked building? She stuck out her neck and blinked a couple times.

"I'm seeing it, too," Vuilni said. "It's as broken as the people here."

"How does that work?" Olivia asked.

"Well, I'm not an architect, but I'm sure while it's definitely not safe, it's *just* stable enough to not collapse. If it were any higher than a few stories, however ..."

"The innkeeper didn't tell you to look for something like that? Seems like an obvious tell."

"Come to think of it, he did tell me I'll only see it at a perfect angle." She narrowed her eyes. "But I thought he meant from a perfect perspective, like a sightline."

"Riddles," Olivia drawled.

They had been hearing laughter for several minutes now, and it was growing louder with each step they took. Well before reaching the front door, they realized it was coming from the crooked building. Its walls were made of rotting wood, raising the stakes of its gamble with fate. Planks were missing in some areas, revealing cloth beneath, which Olivia guessed was the guild's attempt to cover the holes. Vuilni trotted up the stoop and lightly tapped a knuckle against the door twice. That was a suitable knock in the Void. The laughter and buzz of conversation didn't stop, so she raised her hand to knock again, but then the door opened.

The liveliest man Olivia had seen since entering the Cyn Kingdom months ago stood on the other side, a gaping smile on his face as he turned back to yell at someone inside. "Hold on! Hold on! Don't tell it yet! I'll be right back!" His laughter evaporated, eyebrows crumpling, as he turned to the two women on his stoop for the first time. Vuilni stood directly in front of him while Olivia leaned against the banister at the bottom of the steps. "You're not from here," he said.

"That obvious?" Vuilni asked.

He looked her up and down, then transitioned to Olivia. "Cynnish don't develop muscle like that. It's impossible."

Olivia returned the favor, eyes roving down his torso. "Look who's talking," Vuilni said, noticing the same thing. This man had a spark to him, and some build. His eyes were a bright green and hair an almond brown. For once, Olivia felt she could have guessed someone's age. This man must have been in his lower thirties.

He looked down at himself, as if just now noticing he had a body. "Yes, well, we're different here."

"Then so are we," Vuilni said.

He paused, grinning. "You know what? I'll let that slide for now since I don't even know why you're here."

"Someone pointed us in your direction. Said that this place can help us get to the Linsaniun Mounds."

He chuckled and stepped to the side. "Come on in."

They strode in without hesitation. Upon entering a foyer, they turned and saw the man still staring at them either with a look of bemusement or admiration. He closed the door seconds later and shook his head. "That's a lot of confidence for foreigners."

Before Vuilni could retort, Olivia raised an arm in front of her. There was no use pretending. This man knew what they were, just like the innkeeper. While Olivia and Vuilni may have seen the effects of the Cyn Kingdom's atmosphere on their appearances—differences which seemed stark to their eyes—it was clear that others knew what to look for when addressing Cynnish genetics. Whatever it was, they didn't have it. "Can you help us?" Olivia asked.

He winked and walked past them, turning into a noisy room. "Why do you think I let you in?"

They followed him and found a living room filled with people. A few were huddled around a coffee table, seated in wooden chairs, backs bent as they hunched over a card game sprawled between them. Four people stood around a circular table, its height not accommodating to any form of chair—not even a bar stool. They drank out of martini glasses, elbows resting atop the table. Several others were scattered throughout the vast room, each group or pair holding conversations of varying volumes. Olivia's strides slowed as she entered, uncertain of what to make of the scene. This didn't belong in the Void. This exuberance. This camaraderie … This life.

Most didn't turn their way upon entry, and those who did only glanced before turning back to their conversation or game. The man who had greeted them at the door led them through the room, patting another man on the shoulder as he walked past. "I'll be right back, Killui."

Killui whirled, as if shocked. His expression brightened after noticing who had tapped his shoulder. "Hurry up, Lu. I've been eager to tell this story all day!"

Lu laughed and picked up his pace, forcing Olivia and Vuilni to lengthen their strides. He pushed open a door at the far end of the room, holding it open for the two women.

They entered a dining room, complete with a long table surrounded by more than a dozen chairs. Plates, silverware, crystal glasses, napkins, and unlit candles had been set up. The absence of food along with the clattering of kitchenware beyond a door on the opposite side of the room told them dinner was close to being served.

Two women mingled at the table's far end. They looked to be discussing the arrangement of food items and serving platters, pointing at empty spots down the middle of the table. Both acknowledged Lu's entrance, but only briefly before refocusing on their work. Maids or servants, perhaps?

Lu waited patiently, taking position in front of Olivia and Vuilni. No, if they were any sort of house workers, this man wouldn't have been giving them the respect of carrying on with their conversation. They would have stopped on his behalf, as his priorities outweighed any matters to which they attended … assuming Lu was anyone of note. He could have been a guest. But what kind of guest answered the door? This was clearly a dinner party. Only its host would welcome in strangers … or the host's staff. She addressed Lu's attire once more. A rather lackadaisical code for a servant's uniform.

One of the women vanished into the kitchen, and the other remained at the end of the table. She adjusted a napkin triangle, muttering something about its uneven edge, before finally looking up. "Lu, who are they?"

"Foreigners."

Her right eyebrow climbed three stories. "Foreigners … this deep?"

"Not deep enough, apparently," he said.

She crossed her arms, interest piqued. She looked between their two guests and asked, "The Mounds?"

"We were told this place can help us get there," Vuilni said.

"We can, but that doesn't mean we can help you survive when we do get there."

A pause, during which Olivia weighed the implications of her statement. She decided to bypass and deal with it later. She had Preloz to help if they needed it, and it was unlikely anyone here amounted to the talents of a Bewahr. Her first priority was convincing them to take her. Then she could worry about what would happen upon reaching the Mounds. She wasn't naïve enough to think their help when faced with Linsani wouldn't have been welcomed.

"You're lucky," the woman said. "Two convoys deploy in a matter of days. You can tag along, though any resources needed by the two of you during travel will have to be paid for."

"Money isn't an issue," said Olivia, who had a heavy coin pouch in her bags. The benefits of royalty.

"Very well." The woman looked back at the door to the kitchen, which had opened slightly to reveal a young man's face. She nodded to him, and he returned to the kitchen. "Dinner is ready, so I must give that my full attention. After the celebration feast, however, I want to talk to you both. We'll discuss more of who you are and your purposes with the Mounds. I don't bring just anyone along with me. You can wait in the front rooms while my family dines. I'll have someone bring out food to you." She smiled. "We can start with names, though."

"Olivia."

"Vuilni."

"No last names?" she asked. "I suppose that's only fair. I don't have one myself ... never did." The final words made her eyes glaze over, gaze distant. For a brief moment, she actually looked like a proper Cynnish, devoid of life. Then it was gone, replaced by vitality.

"I'm Nina."

*   *   *

"You know," said Vuilni, leaning back in the armchair after devouring a plate of grilled chicken and rice. Both were surprised when they saw the meal, for chicken was more than just a delicacy in the Void. "I don't know

692

whether to feel concerned or relieved about the level of spirit in this place. And the fact that I must question that in the first place is morbid. The Void sucks."

Olivia was kneeling on the floor, inspecting the playing cards scattered across the coffee table. It wasn't a card game she had ever seen, nor could she understand the Cynnish language on the cards. She appreciated the art style. One person's deck was full of black and gray cards that depicted ghastly creatures such as corpses, skeletons, and ghosts. Blue and white cards made up the other deck, complete with knights, fairies, and other spirits.

"You gonna eat your chicken?" Vuilni asked, eyeing Olivia's plate from a distance.

Olivia shook her head, running a finger along the surface of a card that sparkled. Its texture was rough, the card made of a special type of material. Vuilni leaned over and grabbed the plate. "Chicken. It must be a true celebration to demand such an expensive meat."

On cue, an explosion of laughter came from the dining room. Vuilni slowed her chewing and turned to look around the back of her armchair. "If this can exist here, it can exist everywhere," she said, facing forward again. "I wonder what they're doing right."

"How are we approaching this?" Olivia asked. She wanted to be prepared for their conversation with Nina.

"Tell her the truth?" said Vuilni. "Clearly, they know we're foreigners, and that guy wasn't even entertaining our attempted lies. If they're that good at reading people, maybe it's best we be genuine."

"I agree. Besides, the personalities around this place seem to be genuine themselves. When they laugh, it's lively. When they interact, it's engaging. When we pitch to Nina, we should seem earnest."

"Settles it," Vuilni said, taking her last bite of Olivia's chicken. "And if we tell her the truth, maybe she'll be willing to tell us the truth of what they do at those Mounds."

"Hunt something, obviously."

"Like Linsani?"

Olivia leaned back on two arms. "Highly doubtful. I've never heard of Linsani dying, except for the one Bryson killed at the Blizzard of Blood. There might be something else there that they find desirable."

The door to the dining room opened, and Lu, the man who had welcomed them earlier, stepped out. He walked past them and said, "Follow me. Nina's ready to see you."

*   *   *

They were brought to a conference room on the second floor. Nina took a seat at the head of the table. When Olivia and Vuilni tried sitting at the far end—the Cynnish typically enjoyed their space—she beckoned them forward with a smile and gentle wave to the chairs closest to her. Olivia had to keep telling herself that this building and the people contained within were anomalies in the Void.

"This meeting is simple," Nina said. "It's your chance to tell me where you came from. And I don't necessarily mean location, though that would help, but the nature of your upbringing. For me to allow you to join us, I must have a good read of your soul. We don't accept anyone with bad intentions."

Olivia felt Vuilni's eyes shift toward her, searching for any hint about how to approach this. She didn't know, honestly. Did she have more to gain or lose by revealing her royal status? These didn't seem like bad people. After settling on an approach, Olivia asked, "Can you tell us about yourself first?"

"Certainly. I was already going to. What kind of person asks for so much without proving their own trustworthiness first?"

"Most sane people," Vuilni said.

"True," Nina said, "but not here." She leaned back and crossed her arms, gaze drifting across the length of the table in thought. "I grew up in Spachny. When I was six, my parents took me to the market only to forget me there when they finished shopping. I remained in the spot where I lost them, hoping they'd return. They never did. I returned to our house several hours later. The door was locked. When I knocked, my father answered but didn't recognize me. He stared at me for a long moment before cursing at me and slamming the door in my face. Basically, he told me to go find my parents."

"Sounds like he just wanted nothing to do with you," Olivia said, earning a hard punch from Vuilni to her shoulder.

Nina smirked. "So you *are* foreigners."

"What makes you say that?" Olivia asked.

"A real Cynnish wouldn't have even questioned the possibility of someone forgetting a loved one. You see it as a couple of adults who pretended I wasn't their child for some kind of evil, selfish reason. The truth was that they had hit an age where their souls had degraded to the point of losing empathy toward others. That apathy affected their minds. They felt so little for me that they forgot why I mattered in the first place, which meant they forgot I was their daughter. I became nothing, just like the souls within them." She paused, waiting for something.

"Don't worry," Vuilni said. "No more interruptions. You got us."

"I wandered for two months after that, surviving on scraps of food from town. Most of it was scavenged, for nobody voluntarily gives away food in the Void. My journey was destined for one of two paths at that point: death or a very long life of teetering on the boundary between life and death. I would have welcomed the former, even at the age of six. I didn't want to become like so many of the Cynnish who spend their lives an animated corpse. Fortunately, I was given a third option when approached by a large man with gentle eyes. He had unnerved me at first. An aura radiated from him that felt like anti-Void. He didn't act like anyone I'd ever known. When he found me in that alley, malnourished and rancid, he scooped me up without a second thought.

"He took me to his home, where other children played and laughed without any signs of depravity. Turned out they were orphans just like me. He had an ability to restore our spirit, a pregnant wife who cooked and took care of us, and a child of his own around my age who led the children. It was one long dream that spanned across seven years, during which his wife birthed another son, orphans came and went, and I developed my first crush on the eldest son.

"It came to a tragic end when I was thirteen. The orphanage took in two boys who became the first children too broken to be fixed. Their haunted hearts and souls infected one of the more impressionable orphans to commit an atrocious act against the wife, leading to a shift in the house's atmosphere and morale of everyone in it, including its leader."

Nina's voice died on her lips as she stared blankly at the table, arms still crossed. The rest of her story came out in a raspy, weak voice. "It took one month for those two boys to dismantle everything. Some of the orphans were killed by their fellow foster siblings. Most committed suicide in order to avoid a soulless life. It remains the worst day of my life, making the abandonment of my parents a trivial, inconsequential matter in comparison. The man who rescued me that day in the alley—who led the orphanage and repaired the souls of so many Cynnish children—we called him the Unbreakable. It turned out such a concept's a myth."

"The Unbreakable?" Olivia repeated the name much louder than intended, and Nina must have read the recognition in both her face and tone.

"Yes. I'm guessing you've heard of him. I've learned he's rather famous in the Light Realm."

"That's Tashami's dad," Olivia muttered to herself.

Nina sat up, arms unfolding and resting atop the table. "You know Tashami?"

"He's a friend. A very good friend. We're both ..." Olivia paused, questioning the necessity of revealing such a piece of information about herself. She closed her eyes and shook her head. "We're both Jestivan."

Nina's eyes widened, somewhere between a scoff and laugh escaping her mouth. "He's one of them? That little pain in my ass?" She laughed harder, placing a hand over her face. "Every time I dream about him and his brother, I see them as kids. I can't even envision him as a man, much less a Jestivan." She sighed. "Good for him, and I'm happy to finally know my efforts to save him weren't in vain."

"You saved him?" Olivia asked.

Nina nodded. "Only four people survived that night of death: me, Tashami, Ronossius, and Chelekah. At the time I didn't know why, but Tashami wasn't affected to the same degree as everyone else by Ronossius and Chelekah—nor was I, mind you. I think older me realizes it has to do with our internal make-up. Something about us, whether that be the will, spirit, soul, or whatever you want to call it, is just stronger than most. We escaped just after Joni took his own life. He bled out next to me, and I rushed to find Tashami and get him out. What followed was a long journey to the teleplatforms accompanied by our neighbor. I took him to the Spirit Kingdom and traveled to the capital, where I found an old relative of the Unbreakable's. He had spoken of her to me once. Gave her credit for all that he had become. I figured it was Tashami's best bet at surviving."

"And then you ended up back here?" Olivia asked.

"I did. The Spirit Kingdom was a marvel, truth be told. I can't accurately describe what it's like for someone to experience wind for the first time in their life. That invisible pressure that blows past you, cooling your skin and sparking life, swaying the branches of green trees and tossing your hair to the side ... simply enthralling. It was frustrating trying to learn how to speak louder. The low volume of my voice, developed from a life of mumbles and whispers here, didn't translate well there. I also suffered from hearing damage that night everything went to crap at the foster home. But I learned a lot from my brief stint in the Spirit Kingdom, and I vowed to return to the Void to heal it. I don't want it to stay this way forever."

"Inspiring," Vuilni said. "To think you came from that and created this ..." she lifted and swirled a finger in the air, gesturing toward the building ... "it didn't break you."

"Oh, it tried. It still does from time to time. Particularly, tonight would have been a rough one if it wasn't for what you just revealed." She grinned, eyes wet with tears. "That cutie's still alive." She looked at Olivia, and then she laughed hysterically, tears falling down her cheeks. "What a small world."

Olivia tilted her head. She was still confused by one of Nina's earlier claims. She had said only four people survived that night, yet Agnos had told Olivia years ago that he had seen the Unbreakable during their mission in the Void. He didn't say much—whenever she asked about it, he had visibly squirmed—but he did say the man wasn't dead ... not fully, at least. She decided to not resurface that wound for Nina.

"I'm in the presence of Jestivan!" the woman exclaimed. She didn't seem to care that the rest of the building had likely heard her. "You'd be great help to our cause."

Vuilni cleared her throat, then said, "I'm not a Jest—"

"Oh, shut it," Olivia said. "Yes, you are."

Vuilni stared at her, but Olivia turned back to Nina. "What's this cause you're battling for?"

Nina tapped her finger on the table. "Nuh-uh. First, you'll tell me your stories. And I also want to know what you hope to find in the Mounds."

Olivia and Vuilni exchanged looks. Olivia nodded, giving her friend permission to tell her full truth. Vuilni began with her life as a slave in Stratum Zero of Ulna Malen, from a childhood of beatings and disease to her teenage years of transitioning into a prized weaver for the Power Queen. That led to her inception as a Diatia, her father's stint as a slave miner in the Malanese Peaks, and her eventual betrayal of the Diatia in favor of the Jestivan.

Nina's fascination was infectious. She remained quiet during the more somber beats, but asked a litany of questions during the light-hearted moments. She was anxious to hear more about Vuilni's life post transition from Diatia to Jestivan, but Vuilni reserved that part of the story for Olivia since their lives collided at that point.

Whatever engagement Nina had felt during Vuilni's story was amplified to a stage of silent awe during Olivia's turn. She didn't ask a single question, her facial expressions providing her communication for her. Olivia revealed mostly everything, from a childhood of seclusion with her mother in the Almawt Woods to the secrets she carried at Phesaw about the true identity of her mother and best friend, Bryson. She shared the moment those secrets came to light and the repercussions of choosing her brother over her mom. Nina actually gasped when Olivia said she was the Still Princess. During the telling of the Blizzard of Blood, Nina clearly bit her lip to hold back any comments. Olivia stopped after returning to the Intel Kingdom from her mission in the Prim Kingdom. She didn't bother giving the details of what she learned from Queen Inedibus, for it was irrelevant.

"Wow ..." breathed Nina, eyes wide. "So that's what happened to Tongku." She let out a long, low whistle. "That liar is in trouble."

"Who?" Vuilni asked.

"Leslie. She and her group came back from a hunt, claiming to have killed the Linsani of Fear, Tongku Feilong. Nobody believed her, obviously, but over the weeks not only could we not find Tongku when we visited the Mounds, but we noticed the absence of its screech from the atmosphere. When you live here your whole life, you develop an ear for their cries. I still didn't believe she killed a Linsani, but I thought it was clear she had at least done *something*. You two just proved that wrong. Bryson killed him."

Nina shook her head. "Anyway, not only are you friends with Tashami, but you're friends and family with a man whose inadvertently helped my cause here in the Void by eliminating one of the Linsani. Fate is on my side—a credit to the spirit instilled in me by the Unbreakable."

"I haven't told you what we hope to find in the Mounds yet," Olivia said.

Nina shrugged. "I don't see how it matters this point. I like both of you, but go ahead."

"As a royal firstborn, I have a Bewahr, and he's of particular importance to this kingdom's history. His name's Preloz Henye."

"Say no more," Nina said. "The captain of the Mound Guard who was found guilty for smuggling citizens out of the capital. His daughter, Pytatia, was fed a handful of umbra fairies and forced to wander the Linsaniun Mounds forever. He ingested a fairy himself in efforts to find her, but was slain by the king after he killed over a hundred soldiers, including the general." Her expression became stony. "Someone who goes to those lengths would never give up on their goal, which means you're trying to help him achieve it during his second life."

"Basically," said Olivia.

Nina inhaled deeply. "That works out. The Linsani we're closest to killing just so happens to be the one who's been giving us the most trouble for ten years now, ever since bonding with that girl."

"Bonding?" Vuilni repeated, an eyebrow cocked.

"Strange, right?" Nina said. "Nobody had ever heard of such a thing before. But yes, Pytatia has become a pair with the Linsani of Purgatory. Together, they rule over the Mounds."

68

The Secret to Slaying a Beast

"Before I explain to you our goals in the Mounds and how we achieve them, you must know more about the Linsani themselves," said Nina, who led Olivia and Vuilni up the stairs to the third floor. The stairwell was hidden behind a locked doorway to which only Nina had the keys. "Going into this uninformed will get all of us killed, no matter if you have a Bewahr by your side or not. It only takes one person to ruin everything."

The stairwell was windowless and dark. Nina had grabbed a candle from the entrance, using it as a waning source of orange light to lead them up a stretch of stairs that confounded Olivia. It continued in one direction, but she was sure they had crossed beyond the building's exterior walls of the lower floors. After giving it some thought, she recalled the structure's crooked state from the outside, the uppermost floor partly leaning over air.

Nina withdrew another set of keys from a separate pocket and then unlocked the door at the top of the steps. She had to use her shoulder to push it open, her face cringing in effort. That didn't make sense given the door was small and looked to be made of simple wood. Nina arched her back and exhaled after finding success, then stepped through. "Hurry," she said.

They followed, and she closed the door immediately. A paradox of sensations took over Olivia the moment she crossed the threshold: dread, angst, rage, hopelessness and, somehow, nothingness. The chamber beyond was almost as dark as the stairwell, the only difference lying in its walls, reflecting grayish-white in the candlelight. Olivia placed a hand against it and felt smooth stone. She narrowed her eyes as she processed it all. "This is Permanence."

"Familiar with it?" Nina asked. Vuilni drifted back against the wall where they had entered, any evidence of a door gone. Whoever had crafted his chamber had been highly accurate in its measurements. She couldn't even see slits where the door stopped and wall began.

"Somewhat," Olivia said. She had gotten to look at one of Lilu's travolters after the invasion of Dunami.

"I know I'm not the only one feeling that," Vuilni muttered.

Nina turned toward the Powish, face grave. "It's intense, isn't it?" She looked back into the chamber, which was swallowed by shadows. "If it becomes too much, let me know, and I will let you out." Olivia followed the woman as she proceeded deeper into the chamber. "Linsani lay eggs, not actively, but a long time ago. Each one has a nest of about five to seven. They don't hatch and are impossible to break, but they emit a potent amount of Cynergy from their shells. That's what you're feeling right now."

Olivia stopped next to Nina as she held the candle in front of them, illuminating a cluster of eggs the size of her head against the far wall. She counted five. She knelt and studied them closer. They were perfect spheres, slate gray in color. "Can I touch one?" she asked.

"If you're up for it."

Cynergy had never really concerned Olivia. The repression of her emotions throughout her life had created something close to immunity to its effects. During the Blizzard of Blood, she had continued fighting on the Diamond Sea while her enemies dropped dead, froze in fear, or turned their blades on themselves. When Vuilni, Toshik, and Bryson had discussed the effects of the Linsani's presence, Olivia couldn't relate. She had felt its presence—a bit of her soul hollowed out—but nothing close to the magnitude of what they described.

But Olivia was now a different person than that hardened Stillian years ago, having worked hard at freeing her emotional shackles. Happiness made her smile; anger made her scowl; anguish made her shed tears. Would that also shift how her body reacted to Cynergy? She didn't feel that way right now. Vuilni was still pressed against the wall, hidden in the shadows of the chamber's other end.

She reached out and touched one of the eggs. Her insides squirmed as she ran a finger down the egg. A chill coursed up the back of her neck. That chill reminded her of her mother, a woman ... Wait. Her mother? She had one of those? No, no she didn't. She didn't have parents, a family, or friends. She only had herself.

Someone slapped her hand away from the egg. "A second is long enough," said Nina. "Otherwise, you'll forget yourself."

Olivia looked at Nina with wide eyes, memories flooding back. She did have a mother—a mighty one who had overcome the most abhorrent evils life had to offer. Her violet hair, blue eyes, and pale skin came into focus in her mind. It took a lot to genuinely shock Olivia, and she found herself moving her lips with nothing to say, fumbling over words. Her reaction asked the question for her, though: *What just happened?*

"That was a power unique to the Linsani whose eggs you just touched," Nina said. "Each Linsani is distinguished by a certain characteristic. Bryson defeated Tongku Feilong, the Linsani of Fear, which forces people to relive their worst memories. These eggs belong to Lianyu Feilong, the Linsani of Purgatory."

Kuki Sphaira would never stop surprising Olivia. The surplus of wonders it contained defied logic. People had a habit of being lulled into a sense of comfort when they spent their lives in one corner of the world. The truth, however, was that most of them didn't know the nature of their own kingdom. How many Cynnish knew about these eggs?

"The Void's atmosphere is very much a life-sucking vacuum," Nina explained, "but it's intensified by the Linsani. When Bryson killed Tongku, the fear in the Void's atmosphere dissipated vastly. That was another reason why we believed Leslie's story about slaying it. Also, we had all five of

Tongku's eggs stored here. We had been working on collecting them before we'd eventually attack the Linsani itself. During Leslie's mission to the Mounds, one in which she was supposed to be scouting Tongku rather than attacking, one of Tongku's eggs hatched here.

"I had been keeping watch over them that day, which was fortunate. Seeing a Linsani egg hatch was startling, and my first thought was that our beliefs were wrong about how they hatched. Certainly, Leslie couldn't have killed Tongku—not while on a scouting mission with little support. This egg, which was millennia old, had to have been hatching on its own. When the baby wyvern emerged from the shadows that spilled out of the shell, I killed it. They're extremely weak at that stage. The next egg hatched, and I killed its baby before repeating the process with the final three eggs."

"Effectively killing Tongku for good?" Olivia asked, recalling Nina's earlier comments about a Linsani's reincarnation process.

"Yes," she replied. "Had we not had those eggs, Bryson's feats on the Diamond Sea, while still holding significance in the Still Kingdom, wouldn't have mattered here in the Void, for Tongku would have been reborn from one of its eggs in the Mounds."

"How can you be certain you had all of its eggs?" Olivia asked.

"Each Linsani keeps its eggs in a singular nest to which it usually remains in proximity. We emptied it, though it took fourteen years. And like I said before, Fear's screams are gone."

"And now you're working on raiding Purgatory's nest," Olivia said, connecting the dots as she studied the eggs in front of her.

"Correct. These are four of five. The next deployment comes in a few days, during which we'll try grabbing the fifth and final egg. We've failed our last ten attempts. Lianyu is a particularly difficult Linsani to deal with, given the fact that it's the one paired with Pytatia Henye."

Olivia turned and looked up at Nina.

Nina smirked. "Consider your timing lucky."

"So not only can you guys help us get to the Mounds," Olivia said, "but you will be targeting the nest of the Linsani who's partnered with the girl we're trying to find?"

"Not only that, but you can find comfort knowing the tenacity I possess when pursuing Lianyu's life. As the Linsani of Purgatory, it's the beast responsible for amplifying the Void's sense of emptiness. When Cynnish forget the people they love, like my parents forgetting their only daughter, it's because of Lianyu. It's responsible for the path I had to take in my life."

"I don't know if I can do this," Vuilni whispered. They turned, but couldn't find her in the shadows. "When that thing soared above us on the Diamond Sea, I gave up. I succumbed to images of my family being whipped by taskmasters, friends dying to diseases from a life of walking through sewage. Now, I'm in this room and can't even grasp onto my fears because I can't feel anything at all. Fears are fading with the memories, and I no longer have a reason to accomplish anything, much less pursue a Linsani to save some girl … a girl whose name and identity has left me."

Olivia and Nina looked at each other. The energy radiating from these eggs were affecting Vuilni more than them. Nina tipped her head toward the shadows, and Olivia took that as her cue to leave the room with her friend.

Nina turned back to the eggs and whispered, "Take the next few days to determine if she's ready for this. If she dies, I don't want you bearing any underserved guilt."

69

Preparations

The role of general was foreign to Ophala Vevlu, but the duties performed by one weren't. As the Spy Pilot, she had spearheaded missions in similar ways to a general, generating tactical maneuvers and overseeing the deployment of her inferiors, streamlining communication between assassins and spies while pivoting when necessary if plans went awry. She had advantages over an army general, however. Her surveillance of the many moving parts below her was clearer. Her magnificent ancient, Cheiraskinia, gave her unparalleled influence over a battlefield, as her birds gave her clear vantages of the ground from above while also acting as messengers to expedite the communication process.

Pilot Ophala sat in a carriage that rolled well behind an army of thirty thousand men and women. She was accompanied by four others, but they sat at the front of the wagon, giving her several feet of space. Their jobs were to await orders from Ophala, who would frequently give them information to relay to other officers scattered throughout the marching ranks.

The wagon was weeks old, built just prior to deployment from Phelos specifically for her strengths. There were more empty windows than walls, big enough for any kind of bird—including the massive wingspans of raptors—to fly through. The windows were built with doors that could slide shut in case of attack or rain, not that rain had forced Ophala to take such measures. She could handle getting wet. Three massive skylights ran along the wagon's roof. Wooden bars crossed the skylights, serving as perches for ravens and falcons, both of which disliked the wagon's confined space.

Ophala stood up, her staff protruding above the skylight. She closed her eyes as she occupied the mind and perspective of Slipswift, one of her top scouting ravens. Like most raptors, ravens were big birds, but they were perfect for long-distance scouting. The bigger the bird, the greater the distance at which Ophala could see directly from their eyes. She sacrificed control, but that didn't matter given the trust between her and Kuki Sphaira's winged wonders. She didn't need to manhandle them; they simply listened to her will.

With the sun having just set, it was prime hours for ravens, deep onyx plumage blending well with the night sky. Her falcons were resting on the dozens of carriages scattered around hers, awaiting their shifts the next morning. Those were special carriages, the hitched wagons windowless in order to contain hundreds of a certain species of winged animals that were the best friend of any assassin. Kaylee had requested them in her last message.

Ophala's eyes jarred open, exiting the perspective of Slipswift. "Wendy," she said, looking toward a middle-aged woman with dirty blonde hair. "Send word to Commander Lusian that the tunnels housing the Accus family and Piety Mines have been found. I need him to meet with me in one hour to discuss its exact location."

"Yes, Pilot."

Ophala carefully removed her staff from between rods in the skylight. She leaned it against a bench and took a seat. Commander Lusian was in charge of an elite stealth unit she had crafted for this mission. Constructing the unit had been difficult since all of her top spies and assassins had been executed during the brief reign of Toth Brench and Wert Lamay, a big reason why getting rid of them had involved such a convoluted strategy. Lusian's squad served a much different purpose than the rest of this army. They were to break apart from the main forces and approach the Thousand-Layer Loess from a separate position miles away. Then they were to find and infiltrate the inlands where the Piety Mines resided, establishing protection for the Accus family before the army invaded.

Like all matters of war, timing and communication were most essential. Even with the reported numbers advantage Ophala had over the Loess, victory wasn't guaranteed. The Loess was self-sufficient. Ophala could try a tactical siege by overtaking the farmlands of the western side's upper plateaus and using them as temporary bases while waiting out the inlands' gradual starvation, but the Loess had farmlands on the eastern side that would render such efforts useless. An army couldn't cross a loess of a thousand layers in any respectable amount of time or with any efficiency. And why would they want to? The eastern side of the Loess was a dead end, unless one counted the Edge as salvation. Also, if they were going to cross through the Loess, they might as well invade the inlands as they pass them by.

Thus, with a siege rendered ineffective, they'd have to rely on a direct assault. It would be difficult for the Loess to defend against an aggressive attack of this magnitude, especially when they had a mole in their midst. With the royal army descending through the layers of the Loess, the Soteria family would direct their army's attention to periphery defenses.

Little did they know, there was one man at the center of it all, with all the might of an army contained in the silent motions of a wraith.

*   *   *

Creep turned the key to lock the door to his butcher's shop. He had worked a late night, this front proving that no matter how much of a façade it was, that wouldn't stop the rise of actual business. He was generating substantial revenue here, none of which landed in Creep's pockets. Since this business was a direct creation of the crown in efforts to establish his life as a commoner, the money went back into the crown's hand. Setting up this ruse had cost money, time, and effort on the Intel family's part. They were lucky to be making all that money back and more—a credit to York's skills.

York had trained Creep well enough that he could now run the shop himself sometimes, hence him closing the shop without the young man's presence. He could send his apprentice home early, establishing a sense of normalcy to the infrastructure. Customers had been commenting on how frequently the master wasn't at the shop while the student worked like a dog.

His walk home was short; he lived two blocks over. Another major expense of the crown was housing its spies and assassins. Most lived in lower to lower-middle class apartments—butchers, barmaids, and trade apprentices don't tend to live in estates—but with the sheer number of people employed, the cost added up to the equivalent of several villas.

The lobby of his apartment building was lively despite the late hour, as tenants headed for the adjacent parlor, some in pairs or groups and others alone with aspirations of getting lucky. Friday evenings lent to flowing drinks and congregating patrons. Creep avoided it like the plague, receiving more than his fill of social interaction during his visits to The Electric Eel. He should have been there tonight, but didn't want a reason to see the authenticity of real people leading real lives. Even Sally and York, who were fellow spies on the same side as him, had found kindling between each other. Their relationship went beyond their roles as spies. The neighborhood truly believed they were a bar owner and butcher's apprentice destined for a life of love, happiness, and children. They wouldn't be wrong about that last part.

Creep entered his apartment and kicked the door shut with the back of his heel. He hung up his trench coat and placed his gloves into one of the pockets. He wrestled off his boots, gaze distant as he regarded the untreated hardwood floor. He then turned and fell back against the wall, closing his eyes with a long exhale. Using one hand to press a switch on his other wrist, a blade slipped down his forearm and into his grasp. He pressed his thumb and fingers against the hilt, absorbing every memory through its texture. He slid down the wall, stopping at a crouch and finally opening his eyes to inspect the blade. On the hilt, an "S" insignia with a spine of spikes ran along its two humps. The first letter of the name of the woman he'd abandoned out of love.

He thought he had effectively pushed her into his past over the years spent in Asalka. It wasn't until leaving the Prim Kingdom with Rhyparia when he felt hope resurface. With each step closer he got in his return to the Light Realm, his love for Soraku intensified. He had been attracted to women between then and now, but none were quite the same. With Rose and Sally, it was lust that didn't extend beyond the surface, their unique hair colors reminding him of Soraku's violet locks. With Rhyparia, it had been something deeper. Her determination and stern ferocity was a flame equally as hot as Soraku's. But what had been so alluring about Soraku didn't present itself the same way in Rhyparia, the flame becoming an inferno that destroyed hundreds of thousands of lives—something Soraku would have never let happen.

"Don't worry. They'll get theirs."

Creep shot to his feet, awareness finally spreading to his apartment proper. Curtains blocked the moonlight, but someone flipped a switch in the living room, illuminating the space with a weak Intelight. Seated in a rocking chair next to the switch was the heart of the rebels herself, Whistle.

He lowered his blade, eyes narrowing. Skipping the stupid questions of how she got in or what she was doing here, he asked, "Is it time?"

"For?"

"For me to get involved," he said. "I've been waiting."

She was scraping at an arrowhead with a knife, refining its point even though it seemed sharp enough to pierce steel. He didn't see a quiver or bow anywhere. Had she come here unarmed or did she plan to defend herself with a single arrow and her throwing arm?

"That blade," she said, steering the conversation her way. "What does it mean to you?"

The question was an attempt to learn more about his past. He had told her his story already—a story fabricated and refined through weeks of repetition in his head. He had never intended for this blade to a part of it, for nobody was supposed to have seen it. But not everything goes to plan. The mark of a great hybrid was his or her ability to improvise.

"I wasn't all that up front with you the first time we met," he said. Amateur liars would try to fit this unexpected circumstance neatly into their original story, but sometimes it was better to admit to innocent lies or incomplete truths. People had secrets, and when it came to strangers—as were Whistle and Creep that first meeting—they're going to be careful with what they say. If he tried to double down on his story being one hundred percent truth, Whistle would sniff out the deception, for blind honesty of that magnitude didn't exist. She'd strike down every inconsistency between the two versions of his story if he tried to conveniently place the role and purpose of the blade into the second telling. No, it was better he admitted to redacting elements of the original story. A revision.

"Nor was I," she said. "But there's still time for us to develop trust in each other."

He looked down at his blade and muttered, "When I returned here months ago, I killed three of the men who had taken me away from my family."

The silence that followed stretched uncomfortably long. Nina's eyes remained locked on him. Glass shattered somewhere outside in the street, followed by a fit of teenage giggles. The unmistakable voice of the apartment owner yelled in response.

"I can tell from here that it's spunka steel," Nina said. "How did a butcher end up with such an expensive weapon?"

"A gift from one of my favorite customers in Acu. She came by the shop five times a week to purchase meat for her family's dinners. I gave her discounted prices because of the frequency of her visits. One night, she was waiting for me when I closed. She came up to me in tears, offering me the blade and apologizing for betraying me, claiming she had been tricked. I tried getting answers in the moment, but she didn't possess the courage to give me any. Instead, I consoled her right there in the street, and the next morning I was being dragged away from my house by soldiers."

"She ratted you out," said Nina. "So it was common knowledge that you were Archain?"

"To family, friends, and the neighborhood, yes. I hadn't bothered hiding who I was because there had never been reason to. At that point, the socioenergenic system was in its infancy. We hadn't even heard of it, yet it was being implemented in the background. Her social circles were much higher than mine. She mingled with nobles and wealthy merchants, so I believe someone asked her a question as bait, and she unknowingly jumped into the trap by revealing information about certain people in the economic classes below her. I don't think I was the only person she had sent to their doom that day."

"What's her name?" Nina asked. "I have contacts in Acu who can take care of her."

Creep looked up from his blade and glared at her. "No. I don't hold any resentment for her. Quite the opposite. York told me my family has never been in a better financial state, and that is thanks to her. If anything, I pity her. She was a sheep among wolves. She had money and status, but didn't operate in the same predatory ways as her peers, and therefore was blinded to the traps set before her. That's why this blade is so significant. I'll be the ruthless one on her behalf, butchering the people who put us in this position in the first place."

Nina had dropped the arrow in her lap during the story and was now twiddling her thumbs, rocking gently in the chair. "How much blood are you willing to get on your hands?"

"My hands are already drenched," he said. "Might as well submerge my arms elbow deep."

She stood with a groan and wince, keeping one hand on the chair's arm as a brace. She was in her lower fifties, her body succumbing to age much earlier than most. He knew not to read too much into that. What made her dangerous weren't nimble feet or physical strikes. She was an archer, and a legendary one according to his superiors.

She paused at his side before stepping past him, placing a hand on his shoulder. "This spectacle the royal sisters are planning will be monumental in history. I don't plan to involve you with the rebels right now, for we met too recently; I can't trust you yet. But once that page is turned, I think you'd prove beneficial to us."

She left his apartment, and he thought of the Intel sisters. What were they thinking?

* * *

Lilu and Shelly stood at separate windows in a corridor on the twentieth floor of the palace. They stared out at the western grounds below and the city beyond, the coliseum which once held the Generals' Battle for the Intel Kingdom looming above everything else. An immense stage was being built by a team of carpenters and architects in the street just outside of the western gate. The section of road which usually served as an entrance to the palace grounds, lined by barracks instead of civilian structures, had been blocked off while construction was underway. But when the day of the ceremonies came, that road would be packed with spectators.

"You ever stop to think we Intelians need to stop making everything a spectacle?" Shelly asked.

Lilu placed her forehead against the glass, suddenly reminiscent of their father. He'd always wanted to put on a big show, not necessarily to flaunt the kingdom's wealth or power, but to breathe hope into his people. Spectacle was the Intelian version of spirit. The people here needed more than positive attitudes and inspirational words; they needed grand stages, lightning shows, and terrifying weapons. They were materialistic. She didn't find much fault in it, for that's the environment in which they grew up.

That made the ravaged eastern half of the capital an insult to their way of life, but not just because of its unsightliness. It was a constant reminder of this kingdom's recent habit of losing on a global scale. Sure, there were minor victories sprinkled between, but nobody could forget what the Dev Kingdom did during the Generals' Battle or the more recent invasion. They didn't care that Mendac committed greater atrocities first. That man had been dealt with a long time ago in their eyes.

"They need to see you, Shelly. We're not backing out now."

"You're gonna get us killed."

"If we continue cowering in this building, the public is going to believe we're scared of the rebels. And they already think we're weak after the invasion. They're losing hope in us. They think we're dragging this out as long as we can, hoping the rebels disappear on their own. Meanwhile, even the citizens who are steadfast in their belief in us began to doubt us. It's better we risk facing a few rebels now than a whole city later."

"What would dad think?"

Lilu recoiled from the glass and gaped at her sister. Shelly crossed her arms raised her eyebrows. "Really?" said Lilu, aghast. "What would dad think? Weren't you the one who despised how much he kept you locked up in here? Weren't you the one who claimed to envy my freedom?" She shook her head incredulously, waiting for some kind of answer. Shelly only shrugged. "This is your chance to be more than a glorified prisoner."

Shelly turned back to her window. "I used to think that way until I realized every time I left the palace, something bad happened. It was like my presence motivated the public to react ... and always negatively."

"What are you talking about?"

"When you, Bryson, and I went to Griza's Plaza to see the location of where the new Weavineering factory was going to be ... the decapitated corpse we found in the alleyway. You think that was placed there for fun? No, it was a statement. They knew I was going to be there, so they made sure I saw it. That young man died because the rebels needed a method of threatening me. That's it. That's all it took. If I hadn't gone out that day, he would have probably lived."

"You don't know that," Lilu said.

Shelly forced out a single laugh, though it lacked any genuineness. "You can try to speak that into existence all you want, I know the truth. Before Bryson went to Brilliance to get his powers back, he and I made a spectacle of shopping for his tuxedo—another brilliant idea of dad's, though admittedly I supported it at the time. We walked through the streets like civilians and entered a store. Doing so drew all kinds of attention. Crowds swarmed our guards, making us the eye of the storm. Politics were brought into play, and then dozens of people with different agendas and beliefs began to riot. A brawl broke out, resulting in the death of an innocent. Again, that would have been avoided had we simply had a tailor come to the palace." Shelly lowered her voice. "These are mistakes I don't want repeated."

"Look, there are people in place to help make sure nothing goes awry," Lilu replied. "While you've been ..." she trailed off, unsure of how to word her sister's seclusion in the tower ... "dealing with things, the world hasn't stopped moving, and that includes me. If you think we're on the defensive here, you'd be wrong. Our forces are making moves of their own." Shelly didn't respond, so Lilu asked, "Have you been practicing your speech?"

"It's not *my* speech if you wrote it."

"I could give you talking points if you prefer. Then you can form your own speech around it."

Shelly sighed. "No, I would only butcher it. I'm woman enough to swallow my pride and realize I've missed too much these past several months to be able to speak intelligently about matters of the rebels and the state of reformation programs in eastern Dunami." She paused, then added, "I just need to add a touch of myself to it by adding some words I more commonly use and removing the nerdy ones only you and your Brilliance friends think of."

Lilu smiled, her retort light and halfhearted. "We're not all nerds."

"Yes, you are. And I'm happy you found them," Shelly said. "It gave you Frederick."

*　　　*　　　*

Mendac circled Rhyparia, who stood at the center of the courtyard with her umbrella open and pointed at him. He was smiling from ear to ear and had been for several minutes. This was glorious. Did she know how much of a tease she was being, standing motionless and trying to bait him into an attack? And it wasn't a strategy stemming from trepidation, but confidence. She could very likely attack first and deal damage, but she wanted to react. She knew Mendac's speed and was going to test how quickly she could adjust.

He *loved* it.

He had never met a woman with this level of power.

Her eyes were focused, barely visible over the open umbrella's edge as they tracked him around the courtyard's perimeter. He had handled her easily in every battle before this, but now she had her ancient, presenting a new challenge and extra layer to her abilities. He was mentally ready to tighten his muscles and brace his joints in case she tried a surprise attack, knowing she didn't need to make body contact with him to inflict damage.

"This is tedious," she said.

714

He chuckled, walking past a bench occupied by Kadlest. Then he wiped a bead of sweat from his brow, and he noticed his leg muscles were tense. Lifting an arm to test a theory, he frowned with raised eyebrows, impressed. Rhyparia had already shifted the gravity, but just slight enough for his body to naturally react before his mind could process the increased weight. She was straining his muscles to gradually exert more energy, a maneuver meant for the long game as she tried to exhaust him.

Coming to a stop, he turned toward Rhyparia and stuck his hands in his pockets. "I don't think this is necessary. You're ready."

She didn't relax from her position. "Come on," she said. "I have a lot to repay you. You've been taking advantage of my handicaps during our sparring matches. You can't back down now that it's a fair fight. Take this loss."

His smile still had yet to fade. She was right. He'd probably lose if he went through with this, but only because he, too, was fighting handicapped. There was an entire realm of abilities he had yet to reveal to the world … Well, except Ataway Kawi, who had surprised him with that untimely visit. That had been a matter of life or death, however. He thought the Gefal might have figured out about that incident, but it seemed the Bozani had kept it secret. They might have tried erasing the events of that night completely, fearful of what an abomination like him could have inspired in others

A lightning bolt hammered the spot in which Rhyparia stood. Mendac squinted, the flash of white never growing less harsh no matter how many times he tried such a technique. His ears popped. Kadlest threw up her arms to protect her face and eyes. The voltaic stream lasted five seconds, its path twisting and splitting halfway up only to converge at the target on the ground.

After he rescinded the attack, Kadlest lowered her arms and bolted off the bench with a look of outrage. "That was overkill!"

He eyed her curiously, not expecting a response like that. He thought she would have been thrilled about the possibility of Rhyparia's obliteration—not that he believed such a simple attack would have any effect on someone like her. Sure enough, Rhyparia was crouched below her umbrella, unharmed and unfazed, eyes still focused on him. The umbrella stood on its own, the handle thrust into the sod as support, an electric current coursing down its rod and vanishing into the ground.

Kadlest balked, incapable of processing the scene before her. Mendac had seen his fair share of beasts—Ataway Kawi the worst of them all—but even he couldn't blame the woman for being floored by Rhyparia.

"Pesky thing about ancients," said Mendac. "Their indestructibility. Even then, that shouldn't matter when at the mercy of lightning, which strikes with speed that bests Adren Assassins."

Rhyparia stood, kicking her umbrella out of the ground and catching it with one hand. "Sure, if it's actual lightning created by natural reactions in the clouds. Your lightning is created from woven Intel chains that mix with chemicals in the clouds, which limits its potential. It strikes with quite a punch, but sacrifices the speed, allowing me time to react."

He burst into laughter, hands still tucked into his pockets. "While your explanation is correct, that doesn't mean someone should be able to defend against it. It's still a speed that shouldn't be traceable."

"My own speed helps," she said. "Nearly two decades of gravity training means I also have nearly two decades of speed and strength training under the pressures of exponentially greater gravitational forces. Also, you've never sparred with the people with whom I've sparred."

"Like whom?"

"Your son."

Mendac's smile vanished. Was she talking about Toono or Bryson? All of these months spent with her, yet he hadn't bothered discovering anything about her past aside from her training with Musku Rao. But she was much older than both of his sons, so what kind of relationship would she have had with them? Had she been a teacher? He looked to Kadlest for answers, who was supposed to have been filling him in on notes of interest. He turned back to Rhyparia. She had to be talking about Bryson. The world didn't know Toono was his son unless Kadlest had revealed that.

"You fought with Bryson?"

"Yes, and he was fast thanks to Debo."

"Debo?"

"The man who raised Bryson after you died. Became the Intel Director of Phesaw, but it turned out his identity had been a lie. He was actually a Gefal, once known in his first life as the Third of Five."

Mendac closed his eyes, face strained with concentration as he tried to process her words. "Ataway Kawi?" he mumbled to himself. "That Third of Five?"

"There wasn't another one," she replied.

He fell into the grass and laughed. After executing him, that ass added insult to injury by raising his son? He might as well have found Mendac's casket and spit on it. He let his hands fall into the grass. He stared up at the gray sky, a silver sun ducking behind the Labyrinth. If Ataway had taught Bryson everything he knew, then Mendac understood why sparring Bryson would yield such alarming results for Rhyparia. Mendac's fight with the Gefal had been a bitter dose of reality to swallow. Ataway had moved at speeds that defied Mendac's eyes, substituting his wings for his own two feet at times, sprinting along walls and through the air.

He heard the crunch of footsteps in the grass grow louder. Rhyparia stood above him, studying him impassively. "I lost contact with Bryson long ago, but if I know that idiot as well as I think I do, he's still influencing the world in a major way. Don't worry about your son. He's a great man, better than any of us."

Mendac forced out a breath through his nose. If only she knew just how much better. As far as goodness, he was sure the gap between him and his son was oceanic. But that wasn't what concerned him, for he didn't care if he was a bad man. It was their power. How large was that gap? He had forced himself on a princess in hopes to one day discover that mystery.

He would get his answer.

And Rhyparia, the fool that she was, proved she had no idea what was happening in Mendac's head. She squatted next to him and placed a hand on his chest. "I'm sorry," she said.

70

The Playground of Shadows

It was two days prior to the army's scheduled arrival to the Loess when Ophala's birds recognized movement by Loess soldiers. Enemy troops marched up the plateaus to the very top. They set up camps outside the Loess and were organizing their ranks. Tens of thousands of them sprawled across the grasslands, concentrating more densely at natural ramps that connected terraces, serving as the most convenient entry points into its depths. Precipices with sheer drop-offs saw the least protection, but just enough to handle anybody who might have had an ancient piece that could allow them passage past the cliffs.

She knew why they were doing this. Their army couldn't sit on the lower plateaus. It was a disadvantage nobody could overcome. Ophala's soldiers would have plowed through their ranks if they obtained high ground without resistance. The Loess army couldn't fight from a lower terrace without being fully exposed from above, arrows raining down on them like sharpened hail. The other option would have been to hide in the tunnels and caverns of their inlands, setting traps to stop the crown's soldiers from penetrating. But that was also a suicidal strategy, for they'd be trapping themselves underground. Even if they had emergency exits at other levels of the Loess, they'd either exit at a higher elevation where Ophala would have certainly held soldiers back or a lower elevation, doomed to repeat their previous mistake and delay the inevitable.

Cutting off the crown's advance before reaching the Loess was the best option, especially considering their numbers. The Loess's army was vast, possibly larger than her own. She wanted to believe her soldiers had an equipment advantage given their steel armor, but her birds—when successfully flying close to the ground—spotted about three dozen officers wearing armor she'd never seen in her life, an unknown that raised serious concern. She guessed it was the pious minerals of which Mesitis Epidex spoke, a stone so precious to King Dolomarpos that he'd been willing to merge his family with the Soteria's.

Ophala's intelligence of her enemy's forces had become less reliable. Her birds couldn't fly too low. Knowing to look for them, the Loess army had resorted to shooting them out of the sky. Either Loess Lord Kopios Soteria had pried intelligence out of Kaylee or his inferiors were intuitive enough to have recognized unnatural flight patterns of the birds over the course of a couple of weeks—something they would have been on high alert for if King Itta had ever warned them about Ophala's abilities.

Over the past twenty-four hours, the little information she had obtained was about the direction in which their enemies were moving. They were marching west in efforts to collide with Ophala's forces long before reaching the Loess. This was beneficial to the Loess in two ways: one, if they lost this battle, it'd give those back in the heart of the Loess time to react before the royal army covered the distance and reached them; and two, it created cushion between them and the Loess's edge, giving them a few miles of grasslands at their backs to use as wiggle room. Fighting with their backs to a cliff wasn't ideal.

Typically, an army suspended advancement before sunset. Not today. Not under the Spy Pilot. She committed to the most unorthodox, downright foolish battle tactic known to man. Under nothing but the light of the moon and stars, she pushed her soldiers forward. Not a single spot of their ranks was illuminated by torch or lantern. They walked in shadows *as* shadows, a roiling mass of black marching east across the grasslands. None of her commanders had questioned her when presented with the maneuver earlier in the morning. They believed in her, the legend of the Pilot of Spy and Sky. She didn't promise them a clean victory—in fact, she guaranteed a massive amount of death—but she did say this was the only way to win. And it was all for the dozen carriages at the army's rear. The battle between two armies in the pitch black would divert their enemy's attention from the true weapon stored within.

An hour later, the battle commenced in a chorus of screaming metal and roaring soldiers. Blood spilled as bodies fell, but in the backdrop rose a wall of black that drowned out the sky and drifted east. The sable cloud emitted a cacophony of shrieks, as the winged rats requested by Kaylee made their way for the Loess to aid Himitsu.

*   *   *

Himitsu sat on the sofa in his sitting chamber. Weeks spent in this luxurious prison were making him remember who he was. He loved and laughed, yes, but he was an assassin by blood. All that nonsense about settling down and starting a family was now nothing more than a pipe dream. As he spent his days contemplating the injustices committed by the Soteria family against the Accus's, his decision to kill Lord Kopios became easier. He didn't see him as Kaylee's father anymore. Besides, what did blood bonds really mean? He didn't care if Bryson was his friend. If he ever met Mendac, he'd kill him. What made this any different?

He sat on the middle cushion, arms spread atop the sofa's back, staring out of the double doors that led to a personal balcony on which he hadn't stepped foot since being sequestered here. Six guards stood on the balcony, three of whom faced the doors to watch him. The other three were positioned at the railing, facing the other way as if they had to worry about intruders.

His sword hung in one hand, its blade resting across the sofa's arm. He must have looked mad to the guards, but they didn't seem fearful. They met

720

his gaze with equal resentment. He respected that. Killing men who possessed conviction was a lot more satisfying than killing cowards.

These were thoughts that should have concerned him, but life as a Jestivan had numbed him to everything that accompanied killing. It was a necessary measure to save others. If he hesitated before burning one enemy, that enemy could find a way to make him regret it—a lesson learned from Mother. She had known Itta wasn't a good man, yet never acted on it. She allowed herself to be removed from the equation by taking a position in Rim to survey the Archaic Mountains.

During the Amendment Order's tenure, she never took care of Toth Brench and Wert Lamay when she had the chance. Those hesitations were the result of an ethical mind, leading to atrocities such as the Generals' Battle massacre and the uprising in Phelos. The next time she had a chance to make an influential decision, she seized the opportunity by assassinating Wert and Toth. She had done it on a grand stage in front of hundreds of civilians, including children.

Cold, but necessary.

One of the guards on the balcony pointed upward. Two others did the same, and the rest looked up. Himitsu tilted his head and leaned forward, dropping the point of his sword into plush carpet. One of them looked back through the doors at Himitsu with a mixture of confusion and rage. Himitsu narrowed his eyes, tilting his head further. Something was happening. Was tonight the night?

A guard left the balcony and entered the sitting chamber. As the door opened, Himitsu heard hundreds of high-pitched screeches echoing throughout the butte's interior. The noises were unmistakable. As the guard sprinted through the antechamber and burst through the suites' main doors, Himitsu stood and approached the balcony. Two other guards met him before he could reach the doors with swords drawn, but he disarmed them with his own before they could blink. They were slow. If they wanted to stop him, they'd need more numbers or better fighters. He slammed their heads together and continued walking over their fallen bodies.

The balcony air was humid and warm despite the late hour. After months deprived of nature's sounds, he welcomed the annoying noises of those damned saviors. He bent another guard backward over the railing, a single hand grasping his throat while pointing his sword at his partner who had tried attacking from the side. The tip was inches away from his neck. The man screamed as he looked up at Himitsu's face, his top half suspended over open air, legs kicking in search for solid ground.

"My advice is to run," whispered Himitsu. "And tell your friends, too. I have friends of my own who've just arrived." He looked up from the man's red face to the cluster of black wings streaming down from the butte's skylight. Six hundred, perhaps? His mother wasn't taking any chances. "This place will drown in shadows," he said.

He pulled the man back to his feet and tossed him toward the balcony doors. Both guards fled back inside, carving through the group of reinforcements that had just arrived. Himitsu heard the fleeing men shout warnings, but nobody listened. They stared at Himitsu with looks of resolve that would have made an Adrenian proud. No matter. He had seen those looks before, on the face of a friendly rival whose sword now occupied his grip.

Black fire sprouted from his hand and down the spunka steel of his blade, absorbing all light and washing the fortress in shadows. The bats found him and flew past, bursting through the balcony doors and spilling into the suites. Unable to see, guards screamed as they were pelted by the creatures of the night.

Himitsu ambled forward in search of one man.

*   *   *

Six guards fell to Himitsu's sword. They were hapless in the dark. Having trained his eyes in the darkness of his flames, his vision was better suited for this—even if only by a small margin. He saw shadows atop darker shadows. Several times he mistook a chair or desk that a guard had flipped for a person, hacking at fabric instead of skin. His enemies had realized that the more moving targets, the more difficult it was for him to distinguish between thing and person. Usually he would rely on sound—a glass vase shattering against the wall versus someone getting thrown against it—but the hundreds of squeaking bats and their flapping wings overpowered everything else.

He broke free of his suites and into the corridor outside, where more guards waited. He knew even without seeing them. Most of the bats flew right, but a couple dozen broke off to the left and swarmed around specific spots, a tactic that highlighted enemies in the shadows. Instead of charging that way and eliminating the unfortunate souls snared in the tangle of wings, Himitsu followed the main group of bats that were now following an empty path. This group would serve as his pilots through the castle, periodically diminishing as smaller groups broke off to target any enemies nearby. During missions in the pitch black, bats thrived as assassin partners. Their echolocation—rapid clicks at a frequency too high for the human ear to detect—mapped out their surroundings.

They reached a "T" in the path, where his corridor ended at the intersection of another. Bats swirled around the far wall to let him know of the dead end. Two other groups split to the left and right down the intersecting corridor, both of which separated further as they swarmed six or seven enemies on both sides. Himitsu turned down the corridor from which he just came, but he could still hear the wings of the bats that had stayed behind. He was boxed in.

He broke the Passion chains sustaining the black flame on his sword. The gray light of night washed over the corridors, and he took that second to visually absorb his surroundings. There were more enemies than groups of bats, so several people were left unmarked. They were staring at him while their peers screamed in the cluster of wings.

Himitsu charged left, but not before burning an imprint of each guard's location in his mind. The flame returned to his sword, which he held with two hands at his hip, sucking the little light from the corridors. An enemy's sword whooshed past his ear as he dodged, spotting the darkened outline at the last second. He then stepped to the right and swung upward, cutting through the chainmail with ease. The man gasped, but then he screamed as the flame from Himitsu's blade consumed him. Himitsu wove through their forces, serving the same fate to others. His fiery sword danced around his body as he followed the steps of katas taught to him by Toshik.

This was foolish and reckless, and his mother would have scorned him for making it a thousand times harder than it needed to be. He could have consumed multiple guards at once in flame, effectively wiping out an entire group in seconds. But he wanted to challenge himself. The last time he had effectively used this sword was during the uprising, which was years ago now.

He rammed his sword into the gut of the final woman on the corridor's left side, flame igniting around the wound and consuming the rest of her. As he pulled the blade out, bats rushed past him now that their path was empty again. Himitsu turned and sprung a wall of black fire between him and the rest of the guards who had been blocking the other end of the corridor.

He ran for a while without obstruction. He sprinted up a narrow staircase that spiraled between stone walls. Relinquishing the flame on his sword, he came to a stop and glanced out of a square window to find more bats outside. They flew around a different wing of the castle, slowly moving in one direction. They were probably responsible for tracking Himitsu's target, Loess Lord Kopios. He picked up his pace, choosing to extinguish his flames for an extended time. He didn't need them yet.

An atrium sat at the top of the stairs, vast and hollow, dotted with dozens of stone pillars throughout its left and right sides. They stretched from the floor to cathedral ceilings four stories high. Orange flame flickered on torches scattered across the pillars, providing plenty of light. And given the massive size of the atrium, the bats were no longer as threatening now that they were forced to disperse. Many of them hung from fixtures in the ceiling, scouting the space from above with ultrasonic clicks, while others darted between pillars.

Himitsu walked down the center of the atrium, visually raking his surroundings. Doors shut somewhere up ahead. He looked that way and found four enemies step from behind pillars into the wide center walkway. Each wore armor far superior to the metal chainmail of the guards he'd just finished fighting. They didn't have full body armor, but their most vital areas were protected. Sparkling pious minerals made up their chest plates and helms. That would make spunka steel ineffective, but their legs and arms were still exposed.

The bats sprung into motion again. They dove from their upside-down positions in the ceiling and converged at spots close to the outer walls, which were mostly obscured from his vantage point by the scattered columns. He looked away from the four officers at the front just in time to spot arrows spring from bows in the forest of pillars. He circled himself with a thick wall of black fire, incinerating the arrows before they could reach him.

He rescinded the ring of flame and replaced it with the special black fire he had learned from his father. Smothered by shadows, the torches became specks of orange light that didn't extend beyond the flames themselves. One enemy made the mistake of lifting a torch off its fixture and holding it aloft, proving not all officers were intelligent. Himitsu shot a billowing stream of flame that way. The torch dropped, and the woman screamed.

Arrows whizzed in every direction as archers shot blindly at the spot where they had last seen Himitsu. He was now wending between the pillars, cutting necks along the way as he followed the bats and sounds of snapping bow strings.

As he finished off the archers, bats swarmed a spot behind him. He whirled, extinguished his black fire, and threw up his sword, deflecting a spear thrust at his chest. His eyebrows furrowed in disbelief. A lucky guess and swing? Himitsu responded immediately by impaling him in the only spot left uncovered by the bats: the stomach. He pulled out his blade. The man dropped to his knees with his hands pressed against his bleeding gut.

Torch light returned. Archers lay in puddles of blood. How had they gotten in here unnoticed? The bats would have spotted them immediately had they been here upon his arrival. He spotted arched entryways in the side walls of the atrium. Of course there would be multiple points of entry into a space of this size.

Himitsu sprinted out of the pillars and back to the center. The four officers who had been standing at the front were now gone. He heard a series of thumps around him. All of his bats were now pinned to the floor by heavy, chain-linked nets. He looked up and realized the fixtures in the ceiling hadn't been for decorative or structural purposes, but navigational. They were sky bridges. An officer from before stood on one, palms facing down toward Himitsu. Chains snaked out from each of his fingers, bending and twisting like serpents in pursuit.

Himitsu ran, looking back to find the chains gaining on him. He tried wending between columns, but the chains followed him with ease, whipping against the columns and shattering stone. One snared his ankle. His face smacked the floor. Bells rung in his head as he dropped his sword. The chain tugged him back, but he caught the base of a column. He grunted as he used one arm to hug the stone, the other reaching for his sword's hilt. He could feel the chain trying to rip his ankle free from its socket. Himitsu snatched the hilt just as he lost grip of the column.

The chain dragged him across the floor. Each time he tried to gain control of his body to sit up and hack at the chain, he collided with stone as the chain backtracked through the maze of pillars through which it had pursued him. He tried weaving fire out of his ankle and across the metal to melt it, but found no success. This had clearly been the technique of an ancient-wielding Archain, so the chain wasn't normal metal. The reports hadn't lied about the skill of some of the Loess's weavers and their ancients.

With his awareness depleted with each impact, he hadn't been prepared for when his leg was tugged upward, the rest of his body peeling off the ground as he was lifted to the skywalks. He dangled for a moment, sword hanging in one hand below him. He used his core to curl upward and try severing the chain, but the officer yanked harder, forcing his body to straighten out again. He ran flames up the chain from his ankle in hopes to make his enemy release his hold.

It worked. The grip at his ankle slackened, and gravity took over again. His body rotated so that he faced upward, his back to the floor thirty feet below. The officer had already recovered, shooting chains out of other fingers and grasping Himitsu's neck. They coiled tight, restricting air to his lungs. He grasped at the chain with his free hand just in time to cushion the blow from the officer's sudden tug. It nearly broke his neck as he was lifted just above the skywalk. Two other officers who stood at the far ends of the skywalk, just outside of archways that led from outer corridors, threw spears his way.

He cloaked himself in a sphere of black flame that turned the spears into ash, but the chain remained around his neck. It held him in the air as if it was an arm, coiling tighter and tighter. His ray of hope was the part of the chain exiting the fiery sphere, its chain links glowing a bright red as they weakened in the heat.

His head was pounding as blood failed to climb past his neck. Incapable of gasping or screaming, he mouthed empty words. He lifted an arm and grasped the chain, emitting flame down its length toward his assailant outside of the ball of fire. Scared of bringing Himitsu too close, the officer was trying to wait him out by strangling him from a distance. The chain slackened as the fire reached his hand again.

The chain's grip released. Himitsu plunged. With focus returned to his weaving, he wove blacker flames and sucked the light from the atrium. Still, a chain snatched his wrist and pulled him up again. This time he let it pull him. His other hand held his sword, and now he was in a position to sever it. He coated his blade in fire, the combination of spunka steel and black flame severing the chain like butter.

He stopped weaving. Light returned to the atrium. He was close to the ceiling, the skyways now below him. All three officers looked around frantically, but looked up too late. The two at the ends of the skyway threw their only other spears, and the man in the middle thrust his hands upward, chains rattling out of his fingertips.

Himitsu spread his arms. Black flames spewed from each hand. He opened his mouth and breathed more flame directly below. Three shadowy infernos billowed in separate directions. The chain-wielding officer stared up at his doom with nowhere to run. The wave of fire swallowed him and spread across the skyway before cascading below into the atrium proper. The flanking officers turned to flee into the corridors, but were pursued, caught, and burned to skeletal husks.

Himitsu's arching flight took him just past the top of a column. He extended his sword and cut through a chunk of its stone to slow him down. His body rolled forward from the sudden shift in momentum, his head now pointed toward the skywalk. With no way of cushioning his fall, he cursed and tucked his shoulder.

His head didn't receive the brunt of the impact, but his shoulder blade hit hard. Air rushed out of his lungs. He rolled with the momentum and tumbled off the edge of the narrow bridge. He reached out his arms, letting go of his sword and slapping the top of the bridge with both hands. He hung off the side, legs dangling. His biceps strained as his arms tried holding him up. Below him, the bats beat their wings to fight the heavy chain net. Could he survive a fall from this height?

He tried looking down. Someone was on the main floor. He caught a glimpse of an officer approaching the trapped bats.

"They're not even birds," the woman said. "They're mammals with wings. Does that not disqualify them from that woman's powers?"

Himitsu panicked as the officer stepped out of view again. He couldn't see straight down. He grunted as he fought to pull himself back up. His head eclipsed the bridge, elbows bent as his hands sat firmly on stone. He looked down during the process and spotted the officer with a torch in each hand. "*NO!*" Himitsu yelled as he heaved himself onto the bridge.

The officer threw a torch onto each pile of struggling bats. Then, for good measure, she grabbed more from around the atrium and tossed them into the rising orange inferno. It was too late by the time Himitsu shot an attack of his own at the enemy; the bats were surely dead, and the officer avoided the black flame and sprinted from the atrium. Himitsu dashed across the skywalk in the direction the bats had been taking him before.

The skyway took him to less maintained, narrower corridors. They resembled attics, their ceilings not stone but wood. Gaps between planks provided slivers of light, but not enough to allow him comfort in his sprint—not without his bats. They were inside a butte, after all. The moonlight didn't always hit the castle. He'd be foolish to assume there weren't any guards or soldiers hiding up here. There were plenty of corners and intersecting halls from which to ambush.

The shadow of a person stepped into view thirty paces ahead. Himitsu skidded to a halt, vision blurring momentarily. He didn't know if it was a result of energy exhaustion or the pounding headache. He blinked a few times, and the shape refocused. It was the officer who had set his mother's bats ablaze. She had flanked Himitsu from beneath, knowing the castle much better than him.

She wore full armor of pious minerals, minus a helmet. She was a brunette, short hair pinched back in a tight bun. What drew Himitsu's attention, however, were her glasses. He couldn't see her eyes through the black lenses, which would have seemed impractical had he not been in the

Archaic Kingdom. If they were an ancient, that meant she was another officer with whom he must tread carefully.

"What do you want with our lord?" she asked.

"His life."

"Why?"

"He conspired with Kings Dolomarpos and Itta to build a force that could help them overpower the Intel Kingdom."

"The Soteria family isn't that petty," she said.

"The Mind War lasted fifteen hundred years," he replied. "A timespan too substantial to be considered petty by the kingdom that spent all of that time losing. Besides, King Itta pairing with Dev King Storshae and conducting a massacre at the Generals' Battle, which took place in the Intel Kingdom, verifies his motives."

"Even so, King Itta's dead now, so what threat do we serve?"

"I'm not going to assume you know more than you do," Himitsu replied. "So I'll let you know this: Loess Lord Kopios Soteria has turned his focus inward, at the capital of the Archaic Kingdom … the very crown which rules over him."

"Sounds like rubbish," she said.

"Sounds like denial," he countered. "But I'm not here to make you believe." He drew his sword and coated it in flame. Any semblance of light waned from the corridors, giving him only a slight advantage. With how narrow these halls were, he couldn't do much to pass her without notice. She could simply spread her arms to the side and feel him pass. He couldn't flee backward and try a different route because he knew that would be the wrong way. The only reason why this officer would have intercepted him was because he was on the correct path already. Kopios could have been directly beneath his feet for all he knew. He'd have to engage her up close. His energy was too depleted to attack her from a distance like he had in the atrium.

He charged through the pitch black, letting his sword lose its flame momentarily so he could see her. She wasn't there. His feet slowed, and he reignited the black flame. He focused his entire mental effort into his sense of hearing. Wood groaned above him. He skipped back, narrowly avoiding being pounced on.

He extinguished the flame and saw the woman lunging at him with a blade of her own. He swept his sword in front of him. A clang of metal, sparks flying in the night. She pushed, and he backed off in a flurry of parries and screaming metal. He was keeping pace, but couldn't find a gap in time or her defenses to counter. She was fast and skilled, and he was confused by her black lenses. He lit the flame on his sword to plunge them into darkness again, but she didn't relent. No matter which way he moved, she made precision strikes toward his neck, abdomen, and thighs. The suffocating shadows didn't slow or deter her.

Deflecting her blade to the left, he stepped right with an open hand and shot fire from his palm. Usually, a scream would tell him he had hit, but her silence accompanied by a swift counter of a fist to his stomach said otherwise. She wasn't just tracking his movements and locating his vitals in the dark, but reacting to his assassin's flames. Part of him felt like her technique was *improving* in the playground of shadows in which he was supposed to thrive.

Her armor was a nuisance. Pious minerals were weak against fire, supposedly, but it didn't melt quickly. She'd need to be swallowed in flame for more than a few seconds. Anything less would have minimal effects. He had been trying to conserve his energy. As handy as a Passion Assassin's ability was, its downside was its limited usage. He didn't have the same kind of stamina as Bryson or Rhyparia. His energy exhausted at an exponentially faster rate, which was part of the reason why assassins didn't seek out head-to-head combat. Passion Director Venustas used to scold him for his tendency of hiding in the shadows because of moments like this one. He had needed to work on his sparring in case he had no other choice. Toshik had taught him how to use a sword for this reason.

But this seemed like a lost cause. He'd been maintaining a reserve of his energy for when he found Kopios Soteria, believing he'd possess a guard or two far stronger than the rest with whom would needed to be dealt. It was unnerving to think there might be someone better than this woman. Even the man in the atrium who used chains had been a considerable threat. If he had been smarter, he could have bested Himitsu.

The officer continued to dodge everything. He decided to forget his fire and focus entirely on his swordsmanship. They had turned down a separate corridor. He saw that it ended in a dead end after hacking at her shoulder and missing. An idea came to him.

Finally on the offensive, he thrust his sword at her face. She tilted back while stepping back. He lunged, sticking his foot behind her heel. He redirected his sword downward to target her abdomen. She mistakenly blocked, forgetting her armor would have done that already, but he adjusted his attack by reversing the momentum of his strike into the butt of his sword, jabbing it into her face.

The back of her head hit the floor, black glasses thrown from her face by the precision strike. Blood poured out of her nose and the fresh gash across its bridge. Her eyes dazed from the sudden impact. Himitsu's sword erupted into flame as he took the opportunity to plunge them into shadows again. Then, with the pious armor giving him no other choice, he plunged his sword into her face.

She didn't roll or deflect, proving his theory correct. Those strange glasses had aided her in the darkness. Without them, she was just another soldier confronted by the superior skill of an assassin. His sword lost its flame, bringing an impaled skull into gray light. It had gone through her open mouth before getting lodged in the floor beneath. She gagged around the blade, eyes wide with horror. Her neck had been protected by armor. He had tried hitting the medulla oblongata, but that was difficult to do from the front.

She was suffering.

He grunted, pulling his sword out of bone and wood. Then he rolled her over and struck properly this time. The noises stopped, her body coming to a state of motionlessness, blood pooling across the floor.

He stood and stared at her for ten seconds. He would have stared longer if it hadn't been for the slapping of wings from somewhere in the maze of attic-like halls.

Around the corner just ahead, a group of bats appeared. Reinforcements. They didn't pause at the intersection, but continued through the corridor which Himitsu had occupied before turning down this dead end. He ran after them, careful to leap over the blood.

71

The Simple One

Kaylee was sure she was going to die, and it scared her.

Childhood at Lost Wisdom had been a paradox. As swollen as her mind had become with knowledge gained beneath the tutelage of Neeko Lefolli, her life had remained unfulfilling. She could have gone on that trip to Accus Canyon with the rest of the orphans and not cared about death. That wasn't what had scared her, for orphans typically didn't die during it.

Yesterday, she had been taken from her lessons with Doctor Mengai by about a dozen soldiers and then escorted back to the castle. They had thrown her into these luxurious suites filled with lavender and azure curtains, bedding, and other furniture. She had read about tales of princesses trapped in castles like this one, sheltered and caged by one of two types of men—an overly protective father or evil king—waiting for a hero to come save them. Their living arrangements were pristine on the surface, but nothing of substance lay beneath. They were her least favorite books whenever Neeko had instructed her to read his entire library, and now she found herself as that very woman. It was a cruel turn of events.

A knock came from the door in one of her other chambers. It sounded like the main antechamber, which meant a servant was likely waiting in the corridor outside. The timing made sense. They were bringing her food and drink at five-hour intervals. The portions were too large for someone of her size, which only confused her. She still had scrambled eggs and a slice of bacon on her nightstand leftover from breakfast, and half a salad from lunch on the other nightstand. Why had they abducted her from her studies only to treat her like this?

Loess Lord Kopios Soteria appeared in the entrance to her bed chamber. He looked to have seen better days. His mustache was uncombed. His hairline wasn't as immaculate without tidied bangs to mask its imperfections. Gray dusted his chin and jawline, which meant he had skipped shaving this morning. His beady eyes flashed exhaustion, and his crown sat at a slight angle.

"What's the meaning of this?" she asked.

"Trouble has come the Loess's way."

Hope filled her, but she remained stone-faced. Pilot Ophala must have received her missive. But what had she sent in response to warrant this look on a man with so much power? Kaylee would have worried that he knew about her involvement had he imprisoned instead of sequestered her. She asked, "And that's cause for me being locked up?"

"You must be protected," he said.

She raised an eyebrow, genuinely dumbfounded. "I would have thought you'd be threatened by me?"

He smiled. "You don't know the bigger picture here."

She had to stop herself from snarling at him. She didn't like being patronized. It was one thing to be left out of a scheme by someone she respected like Pilot Ophala and loved like Himitsu, but to have that ignorance rubbed in her face by a stranger whom she despised?

She started weaving, searching for tells in the colorful haze of his aura. She had to strangle another snarl at what she saw: admiration and love tainted by greed. Why were those emotions spilling from him when regarding her?

"That young man who brought you here isn't a good person, nor is he on your side," Kopios explained. "We believe he's an assassin of the crown who's looking to eliminate me and, by doing so, overthrowing the regime the Soteria family has created here."

"That's a bold lie," she exclaimed, brows furrowed to feign shock and disgust.

"Twenty years ago, I was at the apex of a relationship with an Accus." He paused, reading her expression. "That's exactly how my parents reacted when I finally told them. A Soteria and Accus in love? But, I was there son. They had been willing to forgive both of us as long as it ended immediately and was kept quiet. They never saw her … mostly because they didn't want to tarnish themselves by having to look at an Accus. Being treated by Doctor Mengai was shameful enough to them. As long as this woman remained in the inlands near the Piety Mines, they didn't fear word of our 'sins' spreading." He paused, then sighed. "That pride helped me hide my biggest fear from them."

Regret and shame began blossoming in his aura's center. Kaylee saw it in his gaze, too. He kept glancing away from her, unable to maintain eye contact for longer than a couple of seconds.

"She had been eight-months pregnant …" he said, voice steady. He looked at her for a long moment. "Pregnant with you."

A massive weight fell upon Kaylee. She wanted to call his bluff, but his aura didn't lie. The regret was overpowering, now accompanied by flares of rage. He studied her, trying to gauge her reaction. "You know this is truth," he said. "That eye of yours shows it."

"How do you know what this eye is?" she asked.

"I'm in charge of the Thousand-Layer Loess, an area of the upmost significance to the Archaic Kingdom. The Piety Mines hold the minerals that compose about half the world's ancients. The holy wood of the Prim Kingdom's capital, Asalka, make up the rest. The Accus family had connections to the primordial being that is believed to have crafted the Piety half. I've studied their ledgers thoroughly since I was a boy, so I know about most ancient pieces. Just by looking at that eye, I know what it is." He paused. "My aura must have been confusing since first meeting me.

What do you see in me when I look at you? Love, embarrassment, melancholy?"

Truth was that she had seen all of those things, but his guesses weren't that impressive given the sheer number of colors in his aura. It would have been more difficult for him to guess incorrectly. "Those, yes," she said weakly. "And admiration, regret, anger, pride ... and so much more." That last part came out with confusion rather than reverence.

"A complex array of feelings for a stranger to have when looking your way," he said knowingly.

He was right, of course. Whenever strangers met for the first time, their auras were either dichromatic or trichromatic, usually exhibited from snap judgments on physical appearance followed by the manner of conversation. Lust, disgust, or indifference from the way that person looked, then exasperation or appreciation from the way in which they communicated. A polychromatic aura—such as Kopios's when interacting with Kaylee— could have only been produced by years of knowing someone.

She tilted her head. He displayed brilliant intuition by detecting those clues. It showed understanding of a human's social nature, which raised the question of why he couldn't have fathomed Kaylee's involvement in Himitsu and Ophala's plans. *Probably because he believes you're his daughter, and family can blind even the most brilliant minds.* She had pegged this man as an imbecile weeks ago, a privileged child born into wealth and status. This conversation was a slap across her face.

"Let me explain to you some of those colors you're seeing," he said. "While I still have time." He looked toward the window, alarm bells ringing throughout the Heresy Butte. Guards began shouting. Seconds later, someone pounded on the door in the antechamber. He disregarded it all. "Even I know I can't withstand the royal army ... not yet. We weren't ready." He raised a hand, spotting her desire to race toward the window to see what was happening. "I'll make this quick."

She sat still.

"There was once excitement," he said. "Before reality hit. When I first found out she was pregnant, I dropped to my knees and pressed an ear against her stomach. It was too early and you were too small to make any noise, but I believed I heard something. In those first few months we kept it secret, we dreamed of an ideal world where my father had never allied with King Dolomarpos and enslaved her ancestors. Then came the regret as I made the decision without her consent to tell my parents, believing they'd practice ethical goodness in regards to what would have been their future granddaughter. They didn't. They threatened our relationship and her safety. Their first option was to kill both her and our unborn child. Eventually, finding that too evil even for them, they settled on sparing your mother's life but permanently separating her from you and me after birth. She'd carry you, go through labor, and then be forced to give you up and never see you again.

"And that's what happened. You were presented to the Heresy Butte as my firstborn, and your mother wasn't spoken of ever again. The community simply believed that I had impregnated a woman not worthy of our status … a noblewoman or even a servant, the latter of whom earned more respect from my parents than an Accus woman. I suffered through that existence for two years before caving in. I set up a line of communication between me and your mother, using one of my favorite officers as the middleman who'd exchange letters. She sent me poems to read to you, literature from ancient times. Nobody possesses as much knowledge about the pre-Known History timeline as their family."

Fists pounding on the door thundered through the suites, followed by distant, muffled shouts from officers in the corridor. He shook his head. "I said this would be quick. Alright then." He sighed. "My mother found out. You were three. My initial fear was that they'd kill your mother. But no, they managed to commit an act far worse. They took your eye and sent it to her, paired with a letter explaining why it was her fault."

The rage in Kopios's aura was palpable. A bloody red swallowed every other color. Kaylee wasn't capable of a response.

"I never heard from her again," he said. "I haven't visited the Accus inlands since then, ashamed to face her. I fear showing my face would only cause the wound to fester. The only information I've allowed myself to know over the years is the state of her life. She's very important to the treaty that my father and King Dolomarpos had created, and that was a big part of the reason why my father allowed her to live." He smiled. "That shouldn't make me happy, but it's my lone comfort. Selfish …"

"How have you made an enemy of the crown?" Kaylee asked. She didn't want to hear any more about this—even though part of her needed to.

They heard the sound of shattering wood as a door was kicked off its hinges. One of the honor guard appeared. "Lord Kopios, hundreds of bats have descended through the skylight, and that man we've been keeping an eye on has broken free of his chambers. He's a Passion Assassin!"

"Give me a moment," Kopios said, not turning to face his guard.

"We must get you to safety!"

"A moment!" the Loess Lord exclaimed.

Kaylee watched as the guard's face contorted between several contemplative expressions. He had received a direct order from his lord, but he also registered the severity of the threat to his life. Kopios's order contradicted the man's job. His jaw clenched, then he said, "Fine, Sir, but I'm placing some men on the balcony."

After four guards reached the balcony, shutting the glass doors behind them, Kopios said, "I suppose I should give you a deeper explanation. It started six decades ago, when my father partnered with King Dolomarpos to initiate a long-term plan to unite forces to one day invade the Intel Kingdom. Back then, the Accus family was just as powerful as mine, but they held an advantage because of their control over the Piety Mines and certain abilities unique to them. A special force of the crown arrived at the Loess, offering my father aide in putting the Accus family under heel. This was beneficial to both my family and the crown, seeing that both the Archaic and Accus families had a feud dating back to the beginning of Known History about their reluctance to stop practicing religion. Gatal Accus had been that straw that broke the camel's back in the first century.

"But to Dolomarpos, that was nothing more than a squabble when compared to the Mind War with the Intel Kingdom. By helping my dad conquer the Accus's, he demanded a share of the pious minerals mined from the Piety Mines be sent to the capital. My dad agreed, of course, but executed some underhanded maneuvers when it came to actually defeating his rivals. The royal soldiers who had helped with the task didn't know that there were only certain members of the Accus family who could turn pious minerals into useful objects such as armor or architectural pieces. When forces invaded Accus inlands, my father's soldiers targeted those specific individuals, leaving only one alive: a sixteen-year-old Joselina Accus, who still shapes pious minerals to this day, stationed right outside of the mines

"It was a slaughter. The Accus's surrendered within an hour. When the time came for my father to send his first shipment of minerals to the capital, he sent enough armor to equip only six men or women, once of which had very strange measurements requested by the king. It was apparently a valuable trade piece for a foreign kingdom—a transaction to be carried out by the Skill Broker. The rest of the shipment had been raw, unshaped mineral. My father explained to King Dolomarpos through missive that with only one Piety Smith, the exports would be slow. He promised he was working on breeding Accus men with Joselina to try to create offspring who adopted her unique gene. And he did. She bore two children at the ages of seventeen and eighteen, each with separate men. My father never ended up telling Dolomarpos. He got lucky, as the king died within those first two years following the treaty. Itta became king, and my dad thought we were in the clear.

"But King Itta was thirty-seven when he gained the throne, so he was no fledgling. It turned out Dolomarpos, who had been approaching his seventies and struggling with disease, taught Itta everything he needed to know well before his death. The new king sent messengers to us, requesting a fresh shipment of pious minerals and information on Joselina's progress in regards to her labor pursuits. This was when I had begun a secret relationship with her, trying to comfort her during a time when her family had either become graves or slaves. She had become a slave of sex with the purpose of churning out children. She was twenty; I was nineteen, which she probably saw as a breath of fresh air compared to the older men my father had been forcing upon her. Then came you, of course. You were her third child and my first.

"With tension rising between my father and King Itta, the latter feeling forgotten and disrespected by the terms of their treaty not being upheld, my dad decided to use toddler-you as leverage, knowing Itta had a son of his own who was only seven at the time. He presented you to royal messengers as not just a daughter of Joselina and therefore capable of her ability to manipulate pious minerals—an ability not guaranteed—but as the daughter of Kopios Soteria, future lord of the Thousand-Layer Loess. He suggested mixing royal blood of the Archaic family with the blood of Soteria and Accus, hypothetically creating future generations of the most powerful people to ever walk the Realms. In exchange, the Loess's exports of pious minerals would decrease sharply. Joselina was only one person. She couldn't meet the demands of both my father and the king. She would die if she continued at the rate she was going.

"My dad's biggest fear was that he had already taken one of your eyes, so he wasn't sure if Itta would accept you. When messengers of the crown came for an inspection, they made particular note of the wound. When they returned again months later with word from the king, it was with mixed news. They would take you, but not directly to the capital. Apparently, King Dolomarpos had informed Itta before his death about the late age of a Piety Smiths' first signs of their ability. They realized you wouldn't be of use to the crown until your mid-to-late teens, so they decided to take you to an orphanage ran by a man of whom I'm not very fond: Mesitis Epidex.

"When people speak of underground businesses and the black market, they think of terrible things … and it's justified. Believe me. Mesitis is the owner of that market, known by only a handful of the kingdom's most elite and corrupt leaders. Kings Dolomarpos and Itta along with my father were a few of those leaders. Lost Wisdom was one of Mesitis's experimental hubs, where he tested out new toys and brainwashed children at a young age. He had trade established with several kingdoms, even the Void, which didn't trade with anyone.

"My father agreed to send you there until King Itta deemed you ready to meet his son, Prince Sigmund. I figured that would probably be around the last half of your teenage years, when you would most likely be able to transmute pious minerals." Kopios finally paused. He asked, "You must be twenty, right?"

"Yes," she said, mouth dry from not speaking for so long.

He nodded. "Later than expected, but I figured plans had likely either gone awry or been forgotten completely with everything that happened following King Itta's rushed attempt to attack the Intel Kingdom by allying with the Devish and massacring innocents at the Generals' Battle. If he was going to do all of that, why did he even bother with the lengthier plans that involved the Loess? I guess King Storshae's proposal was just too good to pass up.

"Anyway, when Itta died, I didn't know what was to come of you. I sent scouts to Balle, but they never returned. I tried getting in touch with Mesitis, but he never responded. I believe he was responsible for the absence of my scouts since we never got along the way he and my father did.

"Yet you showed up here anyway … with a guard under orders from Archaic King Sigmund. I figured Itta had passed on intelligence to his son like Dolomarpos had done to him, and Sigmund was simply trying to reestablish a treaty with a rocky past. I should have guessed Pilot Ophala was involved, but information on her has never been reliable or certain. I had been warned about her by Itta, but there came a point when she was imprisoned, apparently, and destined for execution. I wrote her off. After his death, however, I lost all contact with the crown, and scouting the capital from this distance is impossible.

"I don't know what made her come this way with an army. King Sigmund may have told her everything Itta had told him. He might have decided to sever ties with my family. And he sent you along with that missive from the assassin as false pretense to lull me into a sense of security."

Kopios shook his head, shoulders slumping as he looked toward the balcony doors. The guards were staring intently at the butte's skylight. One was leaning over the railing to the side, as if trying to see something along the castle's wall. Kopios was acting awfully relaxed for someone with an army at his doorstep and an assassin in his home. He seemed resigned to his fate.

"King Sigmund didn't know about this," Kaylee said. "In fact, he knows very little of anything. He's not a brilliant king according to Pilot Ophala, but that doesn't make him a bad one … because at least he's not morally corrupt. She learned this from Mesitis, the Skill Broker himself. He was caught and imprisoned when Lost Wisdom was investigated in the past year."

"No wonder," he replied. "And I'm sure he's twisted truths to make me look like a greater evil than I am. He wasn't happy when I didn't respond to his first correspondence with me. He thought I'd continue dealings with him just like my dad. I suppose the Pilot's intuition was correct, though. This was the right move on her part. I did plan on marching west just like Gatal did in the first century, except with destruction and flame in place of faith and sermons." His face softened, his aura flooding blue. "I wanted my daughter back, and if I had to march all the way to Phelos, so be it. I would have taken the capital in the process."

Silence. Tears threatened to plunge from his eyes. She was seated in front of her father. There was no doubt in her mind. Reading his aura wasn't necessary. Her eyes scanned his face and hair. She saw the similarities now. Had Himitsu seen it when he met Joselina? Did he know she was her mother, or that Kopios was her dad? If he did, that meant he had planned on assassinating this man without telling her who he was. Her heart broke.

"I'm confused," she muttered. "Where are your parents?" She couldn't call them her grandparents. She didn't want to.

"Dead. Both came down with the common cold a couple years after giving you away without my consent. I told Doctor Mengai Accus about everything, from mine and Joselina's relationship to the deal that sent you to Lost Wisdom. During treatment of my parents, whom she had treated on several occasions over the years, she deliberately misdiagnosed them, prescribing them incorrect medicines and herbs. They experienced slow, agonizing deaths, and I visited them every day to watch. A couple nurses suspected Doctor Mengai of malpractice, but when they brought it to my attention, I did nothing about it. I'm the one who had set her down that path in the first place. It was revenge for both of us."

"And why is the Accus family still treated like dirt?" she asked.

"Because their inlands and the Piety Mines are too secluded from the Loess's main inlands. And the officers there would probably rebel if I began dishonoring my parents by unraveling their 'grand' accomplishments alongside Dolomarpos." He scoffed and glanced at the balcony again. "Who am I kidding? The soldiers here would rebel, too. I've done what I can, though, by easing their shift schedules in the mines. I suppose that's not enough. Part of me welcomes this invasion. The crown can fix this

741

place. But, before I let that happen, I must make sure you're safe. They clearly used you as bait."

"I'm bait, yes," she replied. "But willing bait. I've known Himitsu is an assassin, and he's Ophala's son." Kopios's eyes widened. "He rescued me from Lost Wisdom. She halted its operations. I'm in love with him. I didn't know he'd been given a mission here at first, but I figured it out over time. I also knew Ophala had imprisoned and tortured Mesitis, but didn't link him to this place until you mentioned him just now. I'm safe. That I assure you. It's you who's in danger."

Surprisingly, he smiled. "That's good." He sighed, slapped his hands against his knees, and stood.

"ASSASSIN!" someone exclaimed from the corridor, words clear without a door to muffle them. What followed were layers of roars, cries of pain, flapping wings, and screaming metal.

Unfazed, Kopios said, "Then that means I can face whatever's coming my way in peace. I deserve it for what I let happen to you and your mother."

The guards on the balcony rushed into the room in defense of their lord—not that Kaylee believed it would do them any good with who stood just around the corner. They disappeared into the front chambers where they were met by an enemy of shadows and darkness.

She raised a hand to her cheek. It came away wet. She was crying, staring at the back of her father as he stood in waiting. He turned his head, his smile stretching into his eyes. What had happened to that weak imbecile she had seen in the courtyard just a few weeks ago, missing archery targets as if he was blindfolded? He was simply a wonderful man who occupied a role of which he wanted no part.

A man who missed his daughter. A man fearful of his own father. A man robbed of the opportunity to prove he was nothing like him.

He faced forward just as Himitsu Vevlu stepped into view in the neighboring chamber, clothes painted in blood. His black hair was tied back, a few strands dangling in front of his caramel face. The assassin paused, looking over Kopios's shoulder toward Kaylee. His face, hardened from the task of taking multiple lives in one night, fell at the sight of them together. She saw his grip loosen around his sword. "You told her," he said.

"I had to."

"To save your life," Himitsu replied, venom in his tone. "You think I won't be able to kill you if she knows. That my conscious couldn't bear the weight … as if one more life taken matters to me."

Kaylee didn't plead for Kopios's life, but she wanted to. She remained silent and read Himitsu's aura instead, waiting for his decision. She would let him come to that on his own. Himitsu radiated anger, and she assumed it was directed at the Loess Lord. However, the wisps of silver were what caught her eye: genuine confusion, which in turn sprouted distress. He was disheveled, incapable of understanding a cluster of sensations. In a moment where she would have looked the victim from the eyes of a bystander, it seemed, from her perspective, that the struggle was concentrated on the young man who had just slain dozens of people. Was he not the one who made victims?

"Kaylee told me what you did for her," said Kopios. "I thank you so much for freeing her from the destiny her grandfather had given her. I thank you for bringing her here, no matter your reasoning. I needed to see my daughter again. And she deserves to see her mother."

Himitsu's gaze was locked on her in efforts to read her. How was he interpreting her tears? What war was being waged in his head right now? She wanted answers, but she needed to see what he'd do here … not that she knew what it would tell her.

Would he kill her father?

*　　*　　*

Himitsu had always envied his parents. He thought his father had the coolest job in the world, and his mother was the woman in charge of it all, seated on millions of winged thrones in the sky.

He had never thought of its toll.

He didn't know why it was dawning on him now. He'd killed before … a *lot*. But this felt different. When he'd been the first of the Jestivan to travel to the Dev Kingdom during their first year together, he had slain many guards at their teleplatforms. When Rhyparia escaped her execution, he eliminated those who gave chase. When the uprising in Phelos happened, he had drenched his hands in blood on his way through the palace. He had killed soldiers in Throno when staging a fight with Elyol Brekton. His body count was in the hundreds.

Each of those instances, however, had been responses to direct threats. King Storshae kidnapped Olivia; Rhyparia's life was at stake; Toth Brench and Wert Lamay attacked Phelos Palace to usurp the throne; and the battle in Throno was a key step to taking out King Toth. They were all enemies directly opposing his side—enemies with little moral regard.

The Thousand-Layer Loess, however, was completely out of the way of the crown's goals. His mom had sent him out here to assassinate someone because of the word of a man known as the Skill Broker of the Archaic Kingdom's black market, someone who likely possessed ulterior motives from pinning the crown and Loess against each other. He felt like the very people he had fought against in years past. How jarring must it have been for these guards and soldiers to watch their comrades be killed for no reason?

He stared Kopios down, uncertain of the validity of his mother's accusations of the Loess's desire to march west in conquest. The Loess had planned on uniting with King Itta to attack the Intel Kingdom. The only reason that fell through was because of Itta's botched alliance with the Dev Kingdom, which had stemmed from impatience.

He reminded himself of what he'd learned about Joselina and Mengai Accus. The legendary family had been treated poorly, enslaved by Kopios's father a few decades ago. He supposed their living conditions didn't compare to the horror stories he had heard from Vuilni about Stratum Zero, but that didn't make it any more just.

Most importantly, this man was Kaylee's father. And now that she knew, he couldn't will himself into action—certainly not in front of her. She was staring at him now, undoubtedly reading his aura. She had promised not to do that anymore, but he couldn't blame her. He had betrayed her trust. If his word wasn't sacred, why should hers be?

He was stunned into a standstill with a trail of corpses in his wake. If he didn't kill this man, then what had been the point of the lives taken to reach him? He had a job, and his mother was expecting him to complete it. He was livid at her for placing him in this position. She had become something rougher around the edges since her imprisonment after the freeing of Rhyparia from her execution, but even this felt too uncharacteristic … too dark and empty and cold. She was becoming everything she had worked to eradicate from this world, and she was dragging her son down with her.

The clattering of armor grew louder from a distant corridor as Loess reinforcements approached. The bats didn't move from their upside-down perches in the ceiling. They would wait until Himitsu sucked the torchlight from the chambers—something he no longer had any intention of doing.

Ten to twenty soldiers swarmed the antechamber and stepped over bodies as they ran directly for the assassin. Casually, he looked their way, sick to his stomach about what they were forcing him to do.

"*STOP!*" Kopios bellowed. They did reluctantly. "Do not touch him."

Himitsu faced the Loess Lord again. He had expected a fight, either with Kopios or some kind of premier officer. He was used to there being a climactic resolution, a formidable wall of resistance that pushed him to his limit. Were the four officers from earlier the Loess's greatest talent? They had to be, unless they had been stationed elsewhere. Why did Kopios not have an elite soldier with him?

The Loess Lord dropped to his knees, hands clasped behind his back and chin lifted to his expose his throat. A surrender.

The soldiers stirred, eyes finally flicking toward their ruler. Their demeanors shifted instantly, lungs deflating from expelled hope, bones wilting from weakening pride.

Kaylee and Himitsu looked at each other. He saw his wife. He saw a home. He saw children running circles around his legs. A life free of responsibilities to the world. A normal existence. The Sphairian dream. Not everything had to be on a global scale of grandeur. He had grown up as a secret, his parents constantly on missions abroad and without siblings. He was allowed to dream of a family and security.

Fulfillment from simplicity.

He dropped his sword and, with it, the world's burdens.

72

Shame's Deception

"Shame is fine if it's yours to own."

Leon Suadade was giving advice to Bryson as they watched Thusia and Aestys fight a squad of luzens in a training arena at the heart of the third sentry district. They sat in the bleachers, which were mostly empty save the luzens scattered throughout. Bryson had come to Suadade for his calm wisdom. He might not have been an Archain, but traditional Adrenians shared a similar mindset. Rarely did the Branian say anything stupid or without purpose.

"Everyone has something about themselves of which they're ashamed," the swordsman said, "but some unnecessarily burden themselves with the shame of others, focusing on it so much that they trick themselves into believing it's their own. For you, it became a subconscious state of being. It was always there, but only made evident recently with Empress Tonitrua's insight. In many cases, the victim blames themselves for what goes wrong, when it couldn't be any further from the truth. In others, the world views a person as a certain label based on preconceived notions with such intensity that that person then takes on that identity. That latter scenario didn't happen to you, which is credit to you."

"I could never become my father," said Bryson.

"Ataway made sure you didn't."

Thusia carried herself into the air on a gust of wind. She soared, laughing hysterically as she blasted craters into the quartz bodies of twelve-foot luzens in the back of the ranks.

Suadade snorted, pointing at the free spirit. "Not everyone can be like her. She fell in love with Mendac, going as far as sacrificing her life to save his. He would have died that day and never had the chance to commit the atrocities he did after that. There are a lot of people in Kuki Sphaira today, now that they know about the man's true actions, who blame her for unleashing his evils. And I don't just mean because she gave him a chance by saving his life. I mean they try to use her death as a scapegoat, as if he witnessing her death is a viable excuse to go burn villages, slaughter innocents, rape women, and carve open toddlers."

Bryson inhaled deeply, disgusted by the perspective. Talking to Suadade often offered a multitude of angles from which to inspect a problem, most of which were unpleasant as they highlighted the flawed organ that was the brain.

"Thusia has every reason to bury her happiness in a bottomless pit, believing her sacrifice wasn't just wasted, but taken advantage of and misused." The Spirit Branian plunged into the crowd of luzens and began blowing enemies away with mighty gales. "But she didn't. And she doesn't shoulder that burden because she knows it doesn't belong to her. It's Mendac's. And because she understands all of this, she isn't held back."

"That's freeing," Bryson replied.

"A trait I'm most jealous of in Spiritians," said Suadade. "They're potential is limitless because of how well they know themselves and how unrestrained they carry themselves. Vitality gushes from their souls."

They continued watching the fight in silence for a moment. A vendor—a normal Celestian woman with freckles and brown hair—brought them bison leg. As residents of the Starlight, they didn't have to pay, but that didn't stop Bryson from giving her a tip. The battle simulation picked up heat as a gate was opened on the western end. A vibrant ivory beast, constructed and armored with quartz, galloped out of the tunnel. Its four legs were as thick as tree trunks, but it had astonishing straight-line speed that made the crystalline horn protruding from its nose a terrifying weapon. Not all luzens took on a human's form. Thusia and Aestys were forced to turn their attention toward the newcomer.

"The reason why most people fall short of a goal is their mentality," Suadade said. "A Powish giant's body, in theory, might be capable of ripping a small home from its foundation, but good luck finding one who can actually maximize their potential and do it. They're held back by that voice in their head that's worried about a litany of consequences: tearing tendons or cartilage, losing respect from peers by failing, the safety of any people who might be inside, and so on.

"Or look at it this way," he said, searching for a better example. "What was your first time with Shelly like?"

Bryson choked on a chunk of bison meat, unwisely swallowing before chewing thoroughly. Suadade leaned away, an eyebrow raised as Bryson recovered. He straightened up with watering eyes, finally coming to grips with what the Branian had asked. "Are you serious?"

"An uncomfortable question, I know," Suadade said. "But the most relatable parallel to make for you."

Bryson stared at him, stupefied. He coughed twice more. Then he shook his head and said, "Not what I thought it'd be."

"And you thought it'd be the greatest experience of your life, sensationally speaking."

Nodding, Bryson reflected on that first time. He wanted to word it in a way that was the least awkward. Talking about this with the man who was Shelly's guardian? A man who Bryson had always seen as a much older brother to Shelly?

"Nothing worked properly," he muttered, clearly uncomfortable. "I didn't work properly, and the whole process of it was slowed by discontinuity. We weren't in sync, learning at different speeds. Even then, I was the biggest problem." Suadade smirked, and Bryson scowled. "There better have been a point to making me tell you that."

"Must have been frustrating," said Suadade. He wiped his mouth with a napkin. "You find Shelly attractive, right?"

"Downright beautiful."

"And it was a moment you had probably fantasized about countless times before."

"Yeah."

"Yet when the moment came, your body betrayed you."

"Is that normal?" Bryson asked.

Suadade narrowed his eyes. "Not completely. I think that in most cases a man responds exactly how you'd think a man would respond to physical intimacy ... especially their first time. But it happens more often than you'd believe—the dysfunction. Your anxiety was likely at an all-time high. You questioned your readiness and performance. That uncertainty and fear prevented your mind from focusing on the passion. It held you back." He gave Bryson a sideways glance. "But I assume once you conquered those insecurities, later attempts were much, much easier."

Bryson remembered that night when Shelly had visited his guest room in Dunami Palace. It was when he had been distressed and infuriated from King Vitio's refusal to allow him passage into the Archaic Mountains to pursue Olivia. She had come that day to comfort and distract him from his pain for a brief spell. It was one of the most memorable nights he'd ever had with her. The next morning he had woken to a forged note allowing him passage into the mountains.

"I'll take the silence as a yes," Suadade said, refocusing on Thusia and Aestys's training. "So it comes down to that first time. The Empress was telling you to conquer the negativity that holds you back from tapping into your Still Energy. You think using it will sully your mother and her Stillian culture, but she has already proven that she's healed from the past and wants to accept you fully." He paused, then whispered, "Make her proud."

73

The Ceremony

Creep stood at the third spot in a line behind a massive wooden wall. He wore his finest attire, composed of clothes he'd bought just days ago. He'd spent an egregious amount of money on the sturdy trench coat, its interior sewn with silk. It was the one article of clothing in his ensemble for which he wouldn't request reimbursement from the crown when all was said and done. His ancient piece was at the ready, gloves hanging loosely from coat pockets, boots looking suspiciously drab when compared to everything else. He had noticed a few pairs of eyes glance down at them during conversations throughout the day. Everyone else in line, most of whom possessed a respectable fortune, didn't have a single flaw in their outfits or makeup.

He was exhausted of this farce at which he'd been playing for months now. He was happy it ended today ... or soon, he hoped. They might ask him to continue the charade to maintain appearances. His disappearance immediately following the assassination would stir suspicion, and any of the more resilient rebels unperturbed by their loss might have looked specifically for him.

A shorter man stood on stage with a bullhorn to his mouth. Gishil was an iconic personality known mostly for his commentating during the annual Generals' Battles. The Archain's voice boomed across the crowd that stretched down the street for miles—a crowd unseen by Creep, whose view was obstructed by the massive wall erected next to the stage. In efforts to rile up the crowd to the crown's side, Gishil spouted propagandist nonsense, a necessary evil when confronted by the rising rebels. He was tearing down the rebels' platform with unfounded accusations. They may have committed a few terrible acts, but this was outlandish. The rebels weren't soulless—not to him, at least, which was the problem with being perceptive.

"Now, after a long hiatus due to an illness, I present to you your queen!"

The reaction was thunderous. Roars and applause thrummed through the air. He would have been elated by the response had he not been preoccupied with who was going to take the stage. The Intel sisters had been at odds about how this part of the ceremony would unfold. This moment would show him who yielded first.

He was baffled by the person who stepped up and onto the stage from the other side, previously hidden by the stage's elevation. It was a skinny, black-haired man with pale skin. His burgundy robes marked him as a Dev servant.

The cheering faded. He took position at the center of the stage and looked up, emitting a holographic display in the air above. The face of Intel Queen Shelly smiled down at her citizens, and Creep's tenseness melted away. It seemed Lilu hadn't gone through with her reckless idea.

The queen's speech wasn't anything like that of the commentator who introduced her. She was humbler and softer spoken. There were no sales pitches—just words of comfort and affirmation, like a mother coddling a son who had woken from a nightmare. The delicacy of her delivery was to counter the harsh realities that had blown through the city like a mighty gale. Between the Rogue Demon's invasion and the alarming rise of rebels, the citizens could do with a little subtlety … a gentler hand. All it would take was a poorly phrased sentence or a misused word or tone to send them over the edge. The rebels, who were undoubtedly mixed in the crowd, were waiting for a mishap of which to take advantage.

Shelly didn't mention the setbacks of the Weavineering factory they had been building in Griza's Plaza. She elected to vaguely touch on Dunami's eastern half, stating that progress was being made in its restoration faster now that they had shifted attention away from the factory. She conveniently forgot to mention the state of the Power Kingdom and the complete halt in the exports of provod, one of the most important economy-boosting materials for the kingdom. Lies of omission.

"Aside from the men and women who gave their lives when the Rogue Demon invaded," said Shelly, "there is no one more deserving of my gratitude than the working class. Despite losing family, friends, and a bit of pride in your kingdom, you all have continued to propel this economy by doing your job every day. That is why today isn't for me or the crown, but to celebrate you, the People. You are what holds us up. The crown is broken and hurting, and you are the crutch on which it leans."

There was nothing spectacular about her praise, no exclamation or raised fist, yet she siphoned the loudest reaction from a crowd Creep had ever heard in his life. The other honored guests in line with him stood taller, necks elongating and chins lifting. The woman in front of him—a renowned baker from a district Horos had overseen—even turned to smile at him and those behind him. Two or three brought their fingers to their lips, whistles piercing through the cheers. The man behind him slapped a hand atop his shoulder in congratulations.

The city was desperate.

They had spent centuries on top of the world. Over the last several months, they had experienced a plunge from that perch. They didn't like it. They weren't used to it. And it was the reason why the subtlety of Shelly's delivery wasn't only a defensive, cautionary maneuver in respect to the rebels, but an offensive one. Just as quickly and easily as the citizens would have pounced on any negative, they would in turn rise on the minutest positive.

Creep appreciated Shelly's genius here. The Intelian crown had enough sway, wealth, and external support to afford a couple of years with the workforce depleted by sixty to seventy percent, making her claim that the working class was the sole lifeline keeping them from economic disaster only partly true. But she had spun it as a complete truth, pandering to their Intelian pride by treating the blue collar workers as heroes. It was reassuring and invigorating.

"I wish I could personally attend the award's ceremony, but I will make sure I meet the representatives in private in the coming week. For now, to hand out the awards, I want to welcome the leader of Brilliance, Wendel LeAnce."

The man was welcomed warmly, for him and his sister, Periphan, had established a reputation among the people as a couple of the kingdom's greatest philanthropists. The entire LeAnce family was substantial financial backers to the restoration project of eastern Dunami.

Wendel, however, never walked onto the stage. A young woman with wavy green hair and a yellow sundress strolled to center stage in heels. The cheers grew louder at the sight of Princess Lilu Intel. Postures of those in line straightened even more, while Creep's guts twisted again. This was incredibly stupid.

A dozen glittering medallions hung from her left forearm as she waved toward the crowd with her other hand. She glanced at her esteemed guests and smiled. "She's stunning," said the man behind Creep. "Who would have thought? Me, a welder, meeting a royal!"

"A story to tell our family for decades!" said another man behind him.

That was promising, but Creep didn't take any of their words to heart. He was wary of these people. How many assassins had Whistle planted in this line of winners? Surely, Creep wasn't the only one. He had warned Sally of this possibility, who in turn passed the message onto her superiors. Alas, it seemed the princess had either ignored the message or not received it. His only solace was the intensity of the frisking he'd undertaken before entering the line. They had patted him down effectively and invasively, but that still didn't account for the very real likelihood that one of these people was formidable enough with Intel Energy to kill someone with electricity.

The line started moving forward as the honored citizens were called onto the stage by name, occupation, and district. A tanner, chef, innkeeper, a farmer from a rural town, an architect, Intelight specialist, a carpenter, dyer, and an apothecarist. A different section of the crowd roared louder than the rest with each award—likely the result of that district's homage. Creep's heart climbed into his throat each time one walked past Lilu, bowing in front of her as she placed the medallion around their neck.

After announcing the baker's name, Creep reached the line's helm. He could see the crowd now. Some spectators eyed him to see who was next, while most gazes trailed the woman across the stage. This was a grand moment for the populace: seeing their peers recognized by royalty. It breathed hope into their chests, instilling them with the belief that they were noticed and appreciated.

After donning the baker with her medallion, Lilu looked down at a leaf of parchment held in front of her by the Dev servant. She nodded and then announced the butcher known as Sunshine.

The walk across the stage was a little much. Stealth specialists tended to avoid spectacles. Their whole job was to be efficient and go unnoticed. But he played his part and waved at the crowd during his walk, using the moment to analyze every bit of the scene in only a few seconds. From this elevated position on the stage, he could finally appreciate the sheer number of people in attendance. It was madness, shoulders rammed against shoulders from one side of the street to the other. The sea of faces stretched for miles, possibly curling off at intersecting roads—certainly a safety and health hazard.

Holographic displays hovered above the crowd at various intervals, Dev servants projecting them from second and third floor windows of the barracks lining the streets. Soldiers stood in position on rooftops, keen eyes trained on the activity below. There were likely more in the buildings protecting the windows from archers. At least Princess Lilu wasn't completely mad. She had taken some precautions, but that didn't mean Creep could relax. He didn't know how skilled Whistle was as an archer.

He smiled at Lilu and bowed graciously. She masked any familiarity, presenting him with his medallion in the same manner as everyone else. He straightened, eyes drawn to her bangs where he was just now noticing the chrysanthemum. It was a brilliant ivory, hundreds of curved petals cradling each other as they fanned outward. He'd seen bouquets of the flower before, but only during funerals. They were called the flowers of death.

They made eye contact once more, and she saw what he noticed. She placed a hand against his back and nudged him toward the other end of the stage, playing it off as if he had forgotten what to do when faced with a royal lady. Some laughs came from the crowd, but they were swallowed by cheers as he walked off of the stage. He had to force himself to not look back.

*   *   *

Simon wasn't close to the ceremony, but he could hear the crowd from three blocks over. He had a sword sheathed at his hip and a bow and quiver slung over his back. The clunky gear hampered his movement, but not enough to rob him of his sky-skimming abilities. He just couldn't maintain speed on the walls or in the air for extended time, requiring him to be grounded more often than not.

He stood on the rooftop of Dunami's greatest smelting factory, twenty brick chimneys vomiting black plumes of smoke into the air. It was an ideal location for an assassin, especially an archer. The smaller chimneys, some of which stood at knee-height, served as smokescreens while the larger chimneys, many of which towered over a normal human, were excellent barricades. The only downside was the impossible task of simply breathing, forcing Simon to sport a mask that covered his nose and mouth.

He bounded between different elevations of the roof and wended between chimneys with grace. His familiarity with the toxic playground had come from training sessions with other archers up here in the past. After returning from his expedition to Lingen's Rainforest to learn to shoot from the trees and live off the land, he and his group, led by Whistle, had made this their new training ground. The chimneys served as trees. The uneven rooftop was akin to the forest floor. The added bonus was the age of the building, causing many of the chimneys' bricks to protrude irregularly while others crumbled.

There had been a running joke in Simon's squad of archers about the real reason for their leader's nickname, Whistle. She wheezed when she breathed, reaching a pitch almost too high for the human ear's registration. But Simon's squad knew her well, so it had only grown louder as they grew familiar with it. Her lungs and trachea weren't ideal. Already not athletic at a younger age, she had taken up archery as compensation. The decades she had spent training on this roof hadn't done her any favors. She was the perfect precautionary tale.

Simon pressed his back against the final chimney and rolled his neck. He had met several soldiers along the way. Now they lay unconscious, scattered throughout the maze of smokestacks across the roof. He wasn't shocked to find Intelian soldiers defending this woman. Whistle had been a respected leader in the military, earning the admiration of forces beyond archers, such as melee specialists and even a few weavers.

Intuition had brought Simon here. Queen Shelly had made the main street leading to the western gate the highest priority, stationing over a thousand soldiers in its surrounding buildings and on the roofs. It was smart to remove the easiest threat of a location from your enemies first. However, she didn't know the archery unit well enough to understand the level of skill possessed by Whistle. Simon had seen her in that rainforest. She wasn't just a good shot who could hit a target from a mile away without losing a bee-line trajectory; she was a fletcher and mathematician.

Simon had seen her mock-ups of archery technologies. She had hordes of books that covered hundreds of different kinds of feathers and wood that could be used in fletching. She knew which wood types lent to greater flexibility in the bow or a sturdier hold. Different arrows could travel different distances ... yet the bow string might have been the most important element.

She became truly dangerous when she setting up a difficult shot. She'd become a physicist with the complexity and number of calculations she'd scribble down before committing, taking into account not just the type of bow and arrow, but the wind, distance, gravity, projected trajectory, and too many other factors to name.

Simon glanced around the chimney and found her. Whistle was seated behind the small wall that ran along the roof's perimeter. The soles of her boots were pushed against the wall as she leaned back slightly, pulling back on the string of an invisible bow. The actual one was lying next to her. She was envisioning her shot through simulation.

He approached through the black smoke, pulling his mask higher up the bridge of his nose. This wasn't the approach of an assassin, but killing Whistle wasn't in his agenda. If anyone thought he was going to simply take the life of a woman who had made him the archer he was today, they were sorely mistaken. He empathized with her. He had been at work when the soldiers took her—men and women who had been her peers. He had watched from his stump in the backyard of her shop. He didn't fight for or run to her. He just sat, stunned.

She grabbed her bow and pulled an arrow from her quiver that leaned against the waist-high wall. The arrow wasn't equipped with her signature feather—the same one adorning Simon's arrows. He had learned the technique from her. His arrows screamed in flight in honor of her.

She didn't want her arrow to scream this time.

"Whistle," said Simon.

The woman didn't turn, instead nocking her arrow and taking aim at the sky. She had done her calculations. She knew the pull, angle, and trajectory needed since the crown had decided to broadcast the event on massive holographic displays, some of which hovered above the buildings. One was perfectly visible from this very roof, offering a live update of where Lilu stood on the stage.

"Simon," she said with the finality of a woman on the scaffolding. She knew it just as well as he did. This wasn't the act of a rebel leader, but of a desperate, vengeful victim. What she was trying to achieve wouldn't help the rebels; it'd probably hurt them.

It was utterly selfish.

"I'm giving you the chance to relinquish your bow," he said.

"That'd require relinquishing my animosity."

The black haze dissipated the closer he got to the end of the roof, the bulk of its chimneys now behind him. But it was still difficult to see clearly. The soldiers on top of barracks near the stage and palace gates wouldn't have been able to spot anyone in this toxic fog. And they probably didn't even bother looking this way considering the distance between here and there—not to mention the lack of a sightline because of the three rows of buildings that blocked it.

"I'd stop there, Simon," Whistle said. "You're not supposed to die in this."

She was waiting for the atmosphere to calm. A steady wind had been blowing northeast for several minutes now, but it would only take a brief recess for her to take advantage of it. If it weren't for that wind, she would have taken the shot a while ago.

He looked at her desperately, wanting to tell her this wasn't like her but knowing how much of a lie that was. She had killed before. She was no saint. He had watched her massacre a bandit tribe in the rainforest who had developed a reputation for stealing iron from ships on Knowledge River. Her mercy had extended only to the children younger than seventeen, claiming anyone older had likely participated in the banditry before. Those had been orders from Commander Magnolia, head of the entire Intelian archery division—orders likely passed down from Intel King Vitio himself. She had committed atrocities such as those on the crown's behalf only to then be betrayed by that very same crown.

The wind slowed, threatening to stop completely. Simon inhaled and gathered his courage. He heard the sound of bows being drawn. Several archers were barely visible in the smoke to his right and left, all arrows pointed at him. He saw a body on the ground between him and the archers to his right, an arrow impaled through its neck. Shock paralyzed him at the inopportune moment when wind settled to stillness, as nature relinquished Lilu's salvation.

*   *   *

Creep followed an escort behind another wall. They rounded a temporary fence and circled back behind the stage. People in different uniforms scampered across the backstage area as they made preparations for the litany of acts that would follow the ceremony. There were several stations scattered throughout the yard, some designed to serve a specific task for honored medallion winners: a fire for the chef and baker, a wheeled anvil for the blacksmith, and a table and pig carcass for Sunshine, the butcher. Not everyone had a station, for not every occupation could be put on display in these conditions.

He spotted his mark in the rear of the activities. Periphan LeAnce kept her distance from most people, watching as her brother, Wendel, conversed with people Creep didn't know. She was aloof to the ignorant eye, but suspicious to a trained one. Discomfort pulled her gaze toward every corner of the backstage area. Sweat trapped her bangs to the top of her forehead. She knew Whistle had something planned for today. Was she mentally preparing for the carnage that would follow?

He looked away. Staring at her would have been an immediate red flag if she caught him. He didn't need her making this more difficult. The royal sisters had already prepared the festivities in a way that would set up the kill, but the method was unorthodox for Creep. Poison wasn't his specialty.

The scent of soap told him his station had been sanitized beforehand. The table was glistening steel and heavy enough to require wheels. A pig cadaver rested on a vast board of pinewood, legs pointed toward him. He grabbed a cleaver from a variety of tools that hung from pegs at the table's side.

Sandwiched between the baker and blacksmith, he tried to rival their shows as spectators walked past and paused to watch. He skinned the pig with speed and finesse. He cleaved through bone with precision and power. He separated body parts in specific piles that would have made no sense to any eye but his own. A certain pile needed extra care.

With the pig's belly turned away from the onlookers, he reached inside and pretended to rummage through organs. No one saw the vial of powder in his hand. He didn't know what it was or did, but he knew it was fatal in some way. He could make no mistakes.

His goal was a particular strip of muscle that ran along the spine, which meant he had to gut the pig before he could reach it. He would have preferred operating from the back, but doing so would have made what he was doing more obvious. This way allowed the pig's hollowed body to act as a shell that covered his hands.

He found the tenderloin—the most expensive cut of meat on a pig and, therefore, worthy of only the most honored individuals—and slapped the powder onto the muscle with gloved hands. He couldn't help but think how impossible this task would have been had it not been for York's lessons. He didn't understand why he'd been the one tasked with this job. Sally had said something about Pilot Ophala's orchestration of this mission possibly being transferred to the Intelian crown. It made sense, considering the tumultuous, downhill trajectory this plan had found itself on. He couldn't fathom Ophala tasking him with poisoning someone. He had briefed her on his skills, and poison wasn't taking full advantage of them. His ancient piece lent better to stealth missions in the night: moving in silence and with a blade.

But who was he to gripe to Intelian royals? He supposed he could have fled and not gone through with this at all, but he had spent enough of his life in hiding. He couldn't live like that anymore.

After gutting the pig and retrieving the two sections of meat most important to his show, he grabbed a bucket of water, dipped his hands in, and lathered the meat in water. He started with a cut of pork belly, which apparently was Wendel's favorite part of the pig. He then worked the tenderloin, soaking the poison into the muscle and making sure not to rinse it too thoroughly. He washed his hands afterward, dipping his hand back into the bucket.

Periphan and Wendel LeAnce reached his station. Guards surrounded them while maintaining a generous berth to give them breathing room. Wendel watched with genuine interest, craning his neck to try to see past the pig. Periphan appeared apathetic—if not a bit annoyed—as she frequently glanced away. *Good.* That misguided awareness would get her killed.

Like the chef, Creep had a fire of his own at his station, but lacking the bells and whistles of kitchen utensils, pots, pans, and other items with names that escaped him. He had two pans, one for the pork belly and the other for the tenderloin. Each slapped its respective pan with a sizzle. Cooking was a skill he once had possessed long ago, but after decades of living in a kingdom where the consumption of meat was blasphemous, that skill had atrophied. He had learned, however, that his taste for meat never dwindled. Decades of eating plants had tricked him into thinking there wasn't anything better in the world.

"Would you mind adding pepper?" asked Wendel.

Creep held up a pepper shaker with a smirk. "I heard you were fond of a little kick, sir," he said, dousing the pork belly.

By the time he had finished cooking and plating the meat, the final award winners were arriving backstage. He handed the two plates to a pair of guards who broke away from the squad. They didn't trust him to approach either of the LeAnce siblings. He glanced at a small holographic display in the far corner of the backstage area. Lilu was still standing on stage, but the Archain commentator with the voice-amplifying ancient stood with her, shouting words of encouragement to the crowd. Her arm was empty of medallions; she had completed her show.

Wendel released a groan of satisfaction, beckoning Creep's eyes back toward him. The commissioner of Brilliance was halfway through a generous cut of his pork already, using the small wooden gate that separated the work stations from the public space as a table. Periphan approached her tenderloin more delicately, fork and knife working in unison to carve away small chunks. She held up a strip with her fork and eyed it.

Creep's stomach dropped. The visible differences between salt and hylile—the poison laced in her meat—should have been indistinguishable according to Sally, but now that Periphan was looking that closely, he couldn't help but doubt it. Also, hylile became tasteless when heated. The only tell came from its scent, which was earthy and nutty, but subtle enough to become lost in the meat's aroma.

Periphan held the meat aloft, extending it in Creep's direction. His head recoiled as he cocked an eyebrow at her. "What's wrong?"

"Does this look cooked properly to you?" she asked.

He eyed it. "Yes."

"It's raw."

He hesitated and glanced at Wendel, who appeared embarrassed. "Ma'am," said Creep, "if you're calling that raw, then you might as well slap my ass because I'm a newborn."

She balked, and Wendel choked out a laugh. Creep felt an immense sensation of satisfaction. She was halfway through calling the guards on the butcher before Wendel stopped the ordeal, grabbing the fork from his sister and taking a bite. He chewed and swallowed. "See, Phanny, it's magnificent. Give it a shot."

"Don't call me that around other people!" she hissed.

Creep stood, gob smacked. The mission had just backfired. His eyes raked the backstage crowd, as if he would find a friendly with magical instructions to undo what Wendel had just done. He found none. Sally and York weren't here, Lilu was still on stage, and Queen Shelly was somewhere in the palace.

"I still think it's a tad undercooked, but if you say so," said Periphan, drawing Creep's eyes back toward her. She took a bite.

"I'm grateful for this," Creep said. "Two people of your stature giving us the time of day."

"You're great at what you do," Wendel replied, offering a respectful nod. "Brilliance is taking notes. I plan on conducting an event like this up there."

Creep watched the LeAnce siblings proceed to the next station. He had done his job, but not without unintended consequences. In four to eight hours, Wendel LeAnce would die … and likely on a toilet.

Creep eyed the holographic display once more. He hoped Lilu had an antidote.

74

The Banshee's Cry

Whistle was seconds away from taking her shot. She wasn't going to relent, but Simon refused to kill her. He had to push the fresh corpse to his right into the back of his mind.

Himitsu's father was gone, and there was nothing he could do about it.

She drew back on the string. Steady. Careful. The muscles in her arm bulged, required for a longbow of such mass. She was taking her time because she believed she had enough of it, but these weren't ideal circumstances for her. She was in the vicinity of Simon—a young adult whom she believed was an Unable relegated to becoming an elite archer. In truth, he was one of the fastest people alive. And though he could stop an arrow even after she released her grip, he preferred to end this beforehand.

The archers surrounding him had other ideas.

Bowstrings snapped. A dozen arrows converged at an untraceable speed to the normal eye. He ducked at an untraceable speed to trained eyes. In his squat—arrows colliding above him—he drew and nocked his bow, then shot Whistle's arrow out of the sky. She had tried taking her shot just as her lackeys tried killing him.

She didn't hesitate. She loaded her bow again, and her lackeys joined suit.

Simon readied another counter, but a perfect shot knocked his bow from his hand. It skidded across the roof. He reached for it, but another arrow pierced and cut the string. Who the hell could shoot like that?

He looked back and saw a woman standing next to one of the larger chimneys. He wasn't sure because of the toxic haze, but her height and the size of that bow brought to light a friend of his. A long ponytail danced loosely in the breeze behind her. Tisa ... another one of Whistle's most skilled students. He had made a longbow for her just last year. She was a terrific assassin who would have just killed him had she been aiming for him. She clearly didn't want to kill her friend.

Whistle shot. Without his bow, Simon resorted to the next best solution. He accelerated. He ran off the edge of the roof and sprinted through the sky. He caught the arrow from behind, grabbing it by the feather before banking a turn in the air. He looked back at Whistle while letting his legs continue to churn away, becoming a blur beneath his torso. He had cleared a thousand feet of distance. The shock on her face lasted only briefly before she released more shots. She loaded and released in such rapid succession that he couldn't believe she was taking into account accuracy anymore. Did she even care about the stage at this point?

He was waiting for her to run out of arrows. Her shots became increasingly errant. She was trying to bait him into overextending out of her desired line of sight. He almost let the decoys fly past, but he couldn't help but think about the likelihood that one of them hit an innocent life. He wouldn't sacrifice a civilian just because he wanted to remain a shield for a royal. Sensing this, Whistle's shots became wilder. He bound through the sky, pivoting and pushing off in another direction to locate the next missile.

An Adren Assassin's energy wasn't meant to be used for extended periods. Either the muscles in his legs would rupture or his energy canals would run dry. He didn't know what would come first since he had never pushed himself this far. The thought of seizing up while hundreds of feet in the air and free-falling to the tar-paved roads below wasn't a good one.

He could see in the black smoke behind Whistle her subordinates readying their bows as if to shoot into the sky. They didn't worry him, however, as none of them had the strength, skill, or appropriate gear to shoot far enough to put anyone in danger.

Whistle rescinded her assault. Simon caught the edge of a neighboring building's roof. He had a hand grasped onto the ledge and the soles of his shoes pressed against the wall as he hung there, looking back at his former superior.

His roof was much lower than hers, directly in the factory's shadows. She stood and peered over the ledge with squinting eyes. The sun was at her back, partially masking her features in shadows of her own. His muscles began to lock from the sudden stop in movement, forcing him into action.

He pulled himself onto the roof. Then he used one of an Adrenian's greatest skills—their push-off, that initial step—to bound upward. It was as if he had teleported. When he reached eye-level with Whistle, their faces inches apart, she was still looking down. Her brain and eyes had not yet registered that he wasn't on the other roof anymore.

This could have been easier. He should have apprehended her the moment he had seen her lining up that first shot, but that would have involved a belief that he couldn't have changed her in that moment—something he never liked to imagine. He wanted everyone to be capable of change. He had spent his entire childhood known as not just an Unable, but a poor farm boy whose clothes were riddled with grime and holes. Most people didn't think he could become anything greater than that, questioning why he even bothered with a school such as Phesaw in the first place.

Bryson and Olivia never doubted him. When they became Jestivan, and their peers questioned Simon's "deal"—as they so eloquently put it—those two never wavered, defending the young farm boy with vigor until the rest of the Jestivan eventually saw him as a friend. It shouldn't have taken that much work, but it had. They had changed.

His faith in the ability to change nearly cost lives today. He had hesitated.

This time, he didn't.

He landed on the ledge and connected his foot with her face just as her eyes started to lift. She skidded backward at a speed that caused the smoke to billow outward, creating a clear line of sight in the path she had traveled. Tisa remained standing in the distance with her bow lowered, realizing she had no chance of subduing the Adren Assassin—a race these people thought long extinct.

Despite the unkindly nature of Whistle's intended actions, Simon felt for the woman. He hated that he had to crush her dreams of revenge with such ease. She had likely been planning this for months, rallying rebels who had experienced the same kind of discrimination from the crown as her. She had put in all of that work only to be defeated without much of a fight? He was the last person she would have expected to become her opponent, but that was the reality of life.

He strode toward her slow-moving body, smoke rushing in to fill the momentary space again. Not everything was climactic or epic. Not every conflict ended in a battle that toppled buildings and reformed the land. Not everyone was Bryson or Toono, sons of one of the most powerful—and evil—men to ever live. Most times it ended swiftly and messily.

He looked down at Whistle. She held her mouth and nose with both hands, blood seeping between fingers and tears slipping down the sides of her face. He had been in this same position not too long ago, standing above Illipsia as she grieved both the death and betrayal of Toono, racking her with conflicting emotions caused by a man she had grown to love— maybe as a father, maybe as a big brother. He didn't want to make a habit of this.

He had let Illipsia live even though she had helped Toono in his efforts, not because she had been his best friend for a year at Phesaw, but because he felt for her. She had put her youthful trust in someone who had taken care of her while giving her purpose, and that trust had been preyed upon. He couldn't blame or punish her for that. So much of what made Simon "Simon" was his understanding of human nature and the soul.

Now he saw Whistle in tears. He saw her grief. She had loved her role in the military. It gave her self-respect. She had been adored—no matter how rough she was around the edges. The crown showed her how little she meant by taking all of it away. He saw the hate in her eyes, and not just for this kingdom—for herself, underserving and false. She had lost her identity.

The crown had made her believe she wasn't worthy of respect or love because of her Passionian race.

They had made her an outsider. A dog grown old, brought away from its home and left in the alley of some faraway neighborhood.

Simon wouldn't kill her, but he had to apprehend her. Unlike Illipsia, Whistle wouldn't give up if he let her go. He regarded the other archers. "Get away from here. As far as the world knows, I never saw any of you."

They ran, and Whistle croaked out a sentence with knowing finality. "Despite the revenge, I don't feel any better."

He couldn't manage a response. *Revenge? On whom?*

A whistle screamed at a pitch that cut the sky in two. His head jerked upward, where he found Tisa perched atop a chimney. She stood tall in the billowing black smoke, lowering her bow after taking her shot into the distance.

He bolted upright and whirled. Even with his speed, he wouldn't catch that arrow. Tisa had called herself an archer assassin for a reason.

He tried anyway.

*   *   *

Fables spoke of banshees, screeches drowning the night in echoes to announce a looming death. They didn't exist, but even Lilu's rational mind questioned it for a moment as she heard the thing screaming its way through the sky. Turned out they weren't creatures … just a shaft of wood with a steelhead and feather.

Most heads in the crowd turned this way or that, searching for the pitch that overpowered their prior applause. Even the commentator gave up trying to use his ancient, realizing his amplified voice was drowned out. Some craned their necks to peer skyward. They had the right idea, though spotting the arrow would have been impossible.

The thoughts that rushed through Lilu's head were many. She stood in the correct spot, as planned, giving a potential archer a clear pathway to any of her vitals—a shot only possible by one or two people. Of course, she could move, for no archer could hit a moving target from that distance. A small step to the right or left and she was in the clear. But her feet remained planted, having given the commentator enough space to make sure he was out of danger.

Soldiers rushed the stage from the side, knowing what that sound meant. She hadn't briefed anybody about Whistle's involvement with the rebels, but anyone who had been part of the Intelian military for more than a couple of years knew that sound. When she discovered Whistle was the rebel leader, Lilu kept that information to herself aside from telling Simon, who she was hoping would hesitate if he did find her. The young man had a knack for seeing the best in people. While nobody confronted him about how Illipsia managed to escape the day of Toono's invasion, Lilu knew he let her go.

Most importantly, Lilu hadn't told Shelly about Whistle. If her older sister discovered a top-three archer in the Intelian military's history was among the rebels' ranks, she would have locked Lilu up in the bowels of the palace for the foreseeable future ... not that it would have worked.

She glanced to her sides. None of the rushing soldiers would reach her before the arrow, and none were skilled enough to zap it out of the sky. Was she being foolish? She hated herself for suggesting the socioenergenic system to her father years ago. At the time, it had seemed the correct move to protect this kingdom from the many outside threats. But, only recently had she realized that it was her desperate attempt to protect her family while living hundreds of leagues away in a fortified city. Fear—and mostly guilt from being so distant and safe relative to those here—had caused her to create a system of bigotry and violence. The system had spurred riots, the separation of families, and even deaths in some cases.

Bryson told her about the deaf girl who had attended the public viewing of his and Shelly's shopping adventures for a tuxedo. That girl's mother died in a brawl that resulted from an argument between people who belonged in different classes of the system. The fact that she was the one who created the system was ironic, considering how aggressively she fought back against the superiority complex of men that riddled Brilliance.

What she was doing on this stage was, by definition, sacrificial. She didn't want it seen that way. The last label she wanted was that of a martyr despite its purposeful end.

This was deserved.

This was karma.

This was due process.

Give those broken families and homes a victory. They mourn for a reason. They rebel for a reason.

She thought of her sister again. Shelly would be alone, down a mother, father, and sibling, all lost in the span of a year. But she would be without opposition, too. Periphan would no longer be in the picture, so her financial backing of the rebels would render their operations useless. And Whistle would have her revenge and either back down or be apprehended by Simon. The rebels would lose their financial and emotional pillars.

The banshee's screech gathered volume as it neared.

What hurt more than anything else was that she was forcing loved ones to witness this unprepared. Frederick, Shelly, and Benedict were watching through a broadcast in the palace. She never said goodbye to Bryson. The idiot's face was the last image in her mind just as the arrow …

… Someone threw themselves into her shoulder. She stumbled out of her spot by a few feet. She was confused. The soldiers couldn't have reached her that quickly, nor would they have moved her with such little force. That had been a weak shove.

She heard a cry of agony directly behind her where she had just been standing. A collective groan sounded from the crowd, followed by screams and chaos. The soldiers were on Lilu in an instant before she could turn to get a proper look. They swarmed her, rushing her off the stage while forming a tight wall around her. She looked back, fighting against the tangle of arms that tried restraining her.

It was only a glimpse, but she found the person responsible for the weak shove, dawning light on the goodness of that man. Home village torched. Childhood dreams stolen. Enslaved and beaten in the early years by a foreign kingdom. Two brothers gone—whether through death or abandonment—because of that same kingdom that had abducted them. That lanky, weak-bodied man who had helped raise the Intel sisters into the women they were was now knelt on the stage with a massive arrow impaled through the back of his shoulder.

Vistas looked not at his wound or the arrow, but at her. And he smiled. It appeared small and frail, but it carried more weight than the world could ever know.

Vistas had no family left from that village, but he made sure he wouldn't lose the family he had in this city.

As the Dev servant's eyes closed, he fell forward into the timely arms of a guard.

75

Cold, Steel, and Resolute

Disarray surrounded Creep. Citizens ran in different directions as they fought against each other to scramble toward their idea of safety. He felt like the anchor, motionless at the center of a spiraling vortex, cries of distress and commands of authority erupting from the masses but unable to penetrate the silent bubble of his own mind as he processed it all.

Soldiers had swarmed different areas of backstage. Many were apprehending the award winners at their stations, either viewing them as primary accomplices to what had just transpired on the stage or as people most worthy of being saved. He hoped for the latter, considering the former would have contradicted the preceding ceremonies.

Wendel and Periphan LeAnce were absorbed by the most guards. Their squad who had been escorting them between stations closed in on them with a practiced, disciplined efficiency. They, in turn, were swallowed by everything else, but Creep saw them disappear into the distance and between the western gates, which were closing quickly to protect palace grounds.

Only he knew the LeAnce siblings were no safer on the other side of that wall. Their demise was already within them, slowly degrading their stomachs. In a couple of hours, they'd feel the cramps, which weren't the worst of the poison's symptoms—nor were they fatal. It was the blood's absorption. He didn't know the science beyond that, but whatever chemical reactions followed caused a plunging body temperature and heart rate until it ultimately ceased function.

Wendel wasn't supposed to die today. It had been made clear to Creep that he was a good man here for the right reasons. And he had seen that in the commissioner during his brief glimpse. Often times that's all it took. Wendel was going to die, and Creep didn't know how to tell the right person to possibly reverse it.

Lilu was gone, taken by her own escort of soldiers through a side path that had probably been set up beforehand in case of emergency. The last he'd seen of her was on the broadcast from the perspective of the Dev servant who had charged and saved her. It was surreal to watch such an act of heroics from the first-person perspective. For most of the commoners in the crowd, that was the closest they'd ever get to feeling what it was like to save someone's life from immediate danger.

Creep managed to escape backstage without so much as a tug at his arm, but he had the foresight to collect the excess tenderloin Periphan hadn't finished, fearful of running the risk that another innocent bystander would eat the leftovers and consume the hylile laced within.

He slipped into the main crowd that blanketed the road, moving in the opposite direction of the palace just like everyone else. He needed to access a less secure neighborhood, where he could slip into an alleyway or building. Because of its proximity to the palace, security was too tight here and alleys didn't exist, forcing him into an impractical, roundabout approach. Any attempt at sneaking onto palace grounds amidst this chaos would have been foolhardy. Multiple soldiers would have not just stonewalled him, but caused him trouble.

The masses moved in deadly waves that pulsed down the street. Bodies were thrown against each other in bulk, weaker individuals thrown to the ground and trampled beneath hundreds of feet. A little boy screamed just ahead, lost in the madness and incapable of resisting the undertow. His drop wasn't smooth, but staggered and broken as his hands fumbled with someone's shirt. That person, who didn't much like the idea of being dragged down and slowed amidst the unrelenting stampede, absentmindedly reached his hand back and shoved the boy in his face. The boy let go, but found a grasp of a woman's handbag just as his knees struck tar. She dropped the accessory, valuing her life over her possessions and him. She didn't look back once, unaware of who she had just sentenced to death.

The boy was still fighting as Creep bore down on him from behind, the handbag now kicked across the street between a jungle of legs. The strap became tangled in someone's feet. One man down. Another. Another. Six more. A pile that pulsed, then ebbed, then flowed outward as the currents tried restoring themselves.

Someone's knee struck the boy in the back of the head. Nobody looked down. The woman right in front of Creep stepped into the small of the boy's back. He grabbed and shoved her to the side, meanwhile bracing himself against those who pushed at his own back. Shoulders jostled. Feet stepped on. Yet he had eyes for one hopeless boy as others drowned in the stampede around them, lungs filled not with water but ragged, desperate screams of misery.

He lifted the boy by his armpits, trying to drag him to his feet. The boy turned with wide, wet eyes—a frightened thing. His legs wouldn't work anymore. Fear had gotten hold of him. Creep would run for him.

Someone threw their weight into Creep's back, likely spurred by the momentum of several others behind them. The hybrid was thrown to the ground, the boy beneath him. Suddenly, both were victims.

But Creep did *not* break.

He was on hands and knees, back rigid as he stared down into the boy's eyes, which looked up at him in tearful wonder. Creep winced and cringed, but did not fold. More people fell around him. He heard a woman cry nearby, its pitch high enough to rival the assassin's arrow from earlier. That cry subsided, replaced by grunts that fell in line with each footfall atop of her, grunts that weakened until life was driven out of her. He wanted to cup his hands over the boy's ears—he didn't need to hear this; he shouldn't have to hear this—but those hands were what kept his balance.

He roared as someone had taken the effort to lift their knee high enough to step on his back, unable to go around him. Another foot crushed his calve, nearly shattering his shin bone. Someone did snap his ankle. Legs battered his ribs as people marched past, shoving him to and fro like a storm at sea.

The boy crumpled into a ball, making himself smaller beneath his human umbrella. He mistakenly let some of his hand fall outside of that protection. A heavy boot landed atop three fingers, triggering more tears and another wail.

Survival of the fittest.

It was surreal to witness the truly animalistic nature of humans when consequences were dire. Every man and woman for themselves, which proved to include the children at certain extremes. Had this boy's parents already fell victim to the chaos? Or had they been separated? If they were alive, Creep liked to think they were pushing through this chaos not for an exit, but in search of their son.

Bruised and battered, he grabbed the boy and rose from the ashes, shedding several people in the process. He held him tight and pushed onward, doing his best to avoid trampling others with his one good ankle.

He searched for an exit of his own.

*   *   *

Dunami Palace did have a throne room. It simply hadn't been used in centuries. Shelly broke the mold shared by countless royal predecessors. She occupied the grand chamber that rivaled the sheer square-footage of many manors. She didn't sit in the throne, but stood just behind it, hands resting atop its back while her fingers thrummed a rhythm of angst. It wasn't a gaudy or grand piece of furniture, its back short enough to be seen over.

Every piece of her wanted to move. She was horrified, saddened, and irate. Lilu had lied to her after promising she wouldn't have any public involvement in the festivities. Shelly had watched her walk out onto that stage with an arm draped in medallions. Then she was forced to watch her stand suspiciously still while the unmistakable scream of Whistle's arrow shredded the sky to the pieces, only for Vistas to move her and take the blow instead. The entire chain of events had been perplexing, solely because of Lilu.

The queen couldn't leave the palace at a time like this. Protocol was to contain her to one room, and preferably one with much fewer windows than this. That last precaution she had fought against. Now soldiers stood posted not only at the entryways to the throne room, but directly in front of the dozens of windows lining its length.

She wanted to rush down to the ceremony stage, where no amount of authority would rescind the anarchy that had swept over the crowds.

One arrow was all it had taken to create ... *that*.

Uliji stood several feet to the side of her, a notebook pinned against her chest with crossed arms. One of the crown's top advisors, she had explained why nobody should be surprised. She was also highly critical of Lilu's decision to walk onto that stage—maybe even more so than Shelly.

"Think of the state of morale in the populace similar to its economic one," the advisor had explained to an irate queen. "Financial advisors and accountants speak of an economic bubble. It definitely exists and is vital to be maintained. But there's also a social bubble, and with the rising tension—which I believe is nearing its peak—between the rebels and the crown, that bubble has swelled to an unsustainable size. It was only a matter of time before it popped.

"While Intelians have established themselves as an economic and military powerhouse throughout Known History, they've always been notoriously bad at matters of politics and ethics. Look no further than Mendac's invasion of the Dev Kingdom and what he did there ... or the meddling they attempted in the Prim Kingdom's affairs in the 500's, bitter that the Primmish guarded their culture with such perfection and believing Intelians had a right to all information. It's why you can't find anything constructed out of holy wood in the Light Realm. Our kingdom ruined that, severing any potential trade we could have had with the Primmish." She frowned. "Which goes to show we haven't always made the best business decisions either."

"How long are you going to crap on my ancestors for?" Shelly asked, already annoyed that she was trapped in the throne room.

"And then there was Lilu's socioenergenic system," said Uliji, "to which I was adamantly opposed."

"Now you're crapping on my living relatives."

"Yet you let me continue because you understand my point. Lilu stood on that stage and didn't move an inch ... even when she heard that whistle. She had planned on taking that arrow, believing that would, *somehow*, ease her faults and erase the conflict. And she did it all without telling any of us. She didn't even contemplate the effects that single arrow could have on a swollen social bubble. That arrow was just strong enough to burst it."

Uliji gestured toward a holographic display, depicting the perspective of a Dev servant on a barrack rooftop looking down at the stampede. "And now look. More conflict, fear, and death. She diverged from the path given to her by Pilot Ophala, much like King Vitio—may his soul rest in peace—had done multiple times beforehand. Why do we have this incessant problem with believing we can fix everything ourselves in this culture? We fault the Archains for their notoriously broken economy, but forget about their political and philosophical successes."

Shelly fell silent, then said, "I suppose the reigns of Kings Dolomarpos and Itta can make that seem like a distant memory."

"A valid excuse ... if we hadn't been suffering from this superiority complex for centuries before that."

Uliji had remained mostly silent after that, content with watching the events unfold on the display alongside her queen.

Shelly eventually separated herself from the throne room proper, demanding use of a windowless storage room in the back corner of the chamber for privacy. There was no way out aside from its entrance, so she met no resistance. Two soldiers stood guard outside the door, and she took a moment to let the tears fall once again. She had cried so much over the past year, and now she wept for what could have happened to her sister and what had happened to Vistas.

Then, she summoned her Branian.

* * *

Bryson was having his first experience of seeing Aestys and Nora—best friends and Branian from separate squads—conduct their jobs together. Separated, he didn't fancy their company much, but together they were comical and complementary. The same characteristics that annoyed him when spotlighted alone came together to create a harmonious symphony of laughter and fun. He supposed his one question was how they got anything done.

"What about him?" Nora asked, pointing at a trio of men who had just entered the hotel parlor.

Bryson studied each of them, looking for any distinguishable traits that would mark them as threats to the Light Empire. He saw no resemblances to any of the Gefal, so he then paid attention to their mannerisms and actions, searching for cues that would imply bad intentions. His studies had given him more confidence in these bi-nightly excursions into Celeste, spotting traps and threats planted by higher-ranking Bozani at a passing rate. His game was a little off tonight, however, as most of his attention was focused on his untapped Still Energy. He was busy trying to weave ice beneath the table.

"Double chin," Aestys said before taking a sip of her scotch.

"True," said Nora. "Odd."

Bryson turned back to the pair of women with a lazy stare. He plopped his head back in exhaustion. He thought they were pointing out a possible threat, not evaluating the male talent.

"If you're going to have a double chin," Aestys said, "then at least have some roundness in the body. His chins just slide onto a long neck. It doesn't mesh with the rest of him."

Nora snorted, then giggled. Bryson groaned at the ceiling.

"That's not how a man should groan," Aestys said. "Complete turn-off."

Bryson straightened his neck and fixed her a hard stare. He had never met anyone shallower in his life, and he hated that it was growing on him. Everyone had a quirk that defined them from the rest. Aestys was rude and direct, proving celestial beings were just as flawed as humans.

"That's not how a woman should act," Bryson said. "Complete turn-off."

Both women frowned at him, displaying disgust the likes of which he had never seen. "And how should a woman act?" asked Nora, her interest piqued.

He shrunk down in his chair. "Sorry."

"A bit out of character for you," Aestys said, looking back toward the parlor entrance. She was right, and he honestly hated himself for the comment. "What's he doing here?" she asked, already moving on.

A man of average height and red hair entered. A scimitar was sheathed diagonally across his back, and his eyes locked onto Bryson immediately. Given his status as an active Branian who needed to be available to his charge, Shelly, at all times, Suadade rarely left the Starlight. Seeing him all the way out here in one of Celeste's distant hotels was cause for alarm.

"Ladies," said Suadade, sparing Nora and Aestys a brief glance upon reaching their cluster of armchairs. His gaze became austere upon meeting Bryson. "We need to talk."

"We have him for the night," Aestys said. "Orders from Magnifica."

"And I have orders from the Empress."

Aestys didn't fire back at that. Nora asked, "The Empress gave you direct orders?"

"It doesn't matter how it transpired. I am to speak with Bryson." Suadade turned. "Let's go."

Bryson followed. He should have been thankful to escape what appeared to be a wasteful night, but what came next had him anything but thankful. The two men stood in an empty corridor that branched off to main-floor offices closed for the night. "There was an assassination attempt on Lilu," Suadade said flatly. "The arrow hit Vistas instead."

Malice solidified Bryson's blood to a standstill. It was rage like no other.

Something frigid. Something solid.

Cold steel locked everything in him.

76

He Will Lose No More

He would lose no more.

Debo. Jilly. Poicus. Senex. Vitio. Delilah. He couldn't have Vistas added. The list was long enough.

Bryson was in the circular chamber that held the Basin of Transference. He couldn't move between the Empire and kingdoms without it. Only an active Branian could because they were tethered to the mainland by their royal firstborn. Their one limitation was that they had to be somewhere in the Starlight when called upon by their charge, which was why they generally didn't stray away from the quartz structure.

The basin shimmered as he stepped into it. Heat crept up his calves and tickled his thighs before they were submerged themselves. The sensation rushed through the rest of him, concentrating in an inferno of wonder somewhere in his eyes. It gave him a split second of sight beyond reality, or what his mind thought to be reality … hurtling through blackness, white stripes blurring through his peripherals and lancing the edge of his vision.

His heart throttled upward, threatening to burst from his mouth as his body felt as if it would disintegrate against some inexplicable pressure targeting his chest. There was no comparison—not even when he cranked his speed percentage up to its highest point.

Then it was over, leaving him winded and gasping for air as his eyes brought a vast chamber into focus. He would never get used to it. He was happy it only ever lasted for a short second. The worst part was the fear, and not just his own from having to experience that unknown vision, but someone else's—a fear from a being so grand that it seemed it needed a different word to explain it, but one that didn't exist in any language Bryson knew.

He looked up into green eyes, above which the matching bangs of a pixie cut hung. His love for her would have been the first thought upon seeing that face, but malice had a steady, icy grip of his heart.

"Is L.K. okay?" he asked.

Shelly nodded, neither bothering with a proper greeting. He saw the anger in her, too—a change of pace from what she had suffered through following her mother's suicide.

"And Lilu?"

"On her way back here, unharmed. Vistas is being rushed to the palace infirmary, where emergency personnel and procedures have already been prepared and await his arrival."

"And the bitch who did it?"

Shelly gave pause, her icy stare finally yielding to a stubborn flame somewhere within. She gripped herself and shivered. "I don't know," she said, eyes searching his face.

He heard doors open far behind him. He turned and saw an adolescent boy who had found manhood far too soon entering the throne room. Freckles faded into fair skin. Red hair fell in a sloppy mess past his shoulders. A woman trailed him who Bryson recognized, but didn't know from where. She sported no signs of injury, but she walked with her head bowed in defeat.

As Simon approached, Bryson's eyes were drawn to the corridor beyond the open doors, where a body hung limp in the arms of a knelt man. That knelt man had the posture of someone who clearly grieved, though he didn't sound like he was crying. That knelt man was the Passion Assassin known as Fane. Bryson took a step forward, nearing the steps down to the main floor, trying to recognize whose body that was. Soldiers maintained their distance and exchanged whispers. A few covered their faces and shook their heads.

Even though it wouldn't have made sense considering the information Shelly had just given him, Bryson couldn't help but ask aloud, "Vistas?"

"Horos Vevlu," Simon said, still walking down the lengthy chamber.

Bryson emptied completely. The father of his best friend was gone, working to defend a kingdom that wasn't even his.

*   *   *

The tears silently gliding down Fane's cheeks were over his friend and colleague, Horos Vevlu, yes, but he wept on behalf of his superior more than himself. Spy Pilot Ophala had moved mountains to save her husband in the past. Horos had done the same for her. They were a matrimonial pair the likes of which seemed too good to be true, having gone through tragedies mostly unknown to the world, including their son. Fane knew about some of them: the slaughter of both of their parents that led them to their professions, two miscarriages, and the divorce that nearly followed. They had buried those catastrophes in the shadows much like their own careers.

Forty-six missions together. Fane and Horos had been an unstoppable duo in their primes.

Now there was only one.

*   *   *

"She did it."

The comment sounded distant and hollow, echoing in the greatest depths of Bryson's mind. A hand squeezed his bicep, but it released quickly. He looked to his side and saw Shelly. She stared at the part of his arm that she had just touched with concern in her eyes.

He looked to Simon, who repeated himself. "She did it." He pulled the woman forward.

Bryson glanced at Horos's corpse one last time before refocusing. "Where do I know her from?"

"You saw her when you visited the archery shop I worked at. In the backyard. Her name's Whistle. She was the owner."

A dozen questions rolled through Bryson's mind, but he couldn't manage to voice any of them. He stared at Whistle, recalling not the visit when he had seen her, but the second visit when he hadn't. Simon had told him she'd been removed from the military because of the socioenergenic system. They had discovered she was actually Passionian and not Intelian. Bryson knew nothing beyond that. He hadn't looked into it. It had either slipped behind other priorities or he had assumed her situation would be handled respectfully—as if having your career stripped from you weren't already disrespectful enough. Yet he found himself apathetic toward those struggles. He was focused on her responsibility in the assassination attempt.

"She's considered the rebels' heart. She's their leader, responsible for growing and organizing the group. She also orchestrated the attack on Princess Lilu's life today."

Bryson descended the steps of the dais and marched toward Whistle, grabbing her by the throat with one hand. She didn't fight or beg as her feet lifted from the ground. She looked down her nose at him, her chest heaving from constricted breaths. She was dying in his grasp, but those eyes remained rigid. He didn't relinquish his grip. Soldiers looked on with quiet, expressionless discipline. Shelly and Simon said nothing, nor did they attempt to move closer.

Tighter. Tighter.

Whistle's face was bright red, eyes livid. Bryson's face was calm, gaze resolute. It remained that way until the woman broke, mouthing soundless words, unable to gather air. Her chin lifted higher, legs writhing, toes reaching for a floor just out of reach.

The ice came next, creeping around the neck from Bryson's hands. It slithered down her nape and up the back of her skull. Crystals sprouted along the strands of her hair.

Bryson didn't yell or become animated. His jaw was locked, eyebrows now slanted atop fierce blue eyes. Anger shook him while a chill sent shivers through the rest of the people around him. This was the frozen ire of his mother and all of those Stillian women who came before him, their genetics finally wrangling and suppressing the Intelian in him.

Ice was terrifying because of its stored energy. It was bottled-up emotion that had accumulated until its bursting point. He had fought through the deaths of loved ones and revelations of an evil father, carrying those weights on his shoulders for too long. He had screamed out his pain and spilled tears.

This was something else entirely. *This* was a tipping point.

Vistas might have been the best man he'd ever met in his life. Lilu had been his first friend in the Jestivan, and his first crush. They had shared emotional trials and handled them poorly, as all humans do.

This woman had tried taking both of them from him—and most importantly, his wife. It would have shattered her, the love of his life. It would have shattered them. Their marriage. Their happiness.

Their son.

By the time those consequences stormed through him, each one locking the joints in his fingers tighter, Whistle's head was an imperfect shell of ice. It didn't mold with her features, but clumped atop them, making the front of her head indistinguishable as a face. He couldn't weave Still Energy like Intel Energy—in fact, he hadn't consciously woven at all. It had been a display of clout: slow-moving, steady, and coated with malice.

He dropped her, lifeless legs folding beneath the top-heavy, frozen skull. The ice shattered against marble, a blue face now exposed, lips and nostrils still.

The throne room looked upon the murderer, his blue eyes as frozen as the Diamond Sea.

77

The Insignia

Creep limped his way to his butcher shop. The front door was open to an empty street. The shop had remained open for the day despite the ceremonies miles away. The lobby was just as empty. Any potential customers were currently in the stampede that fled the stage's proximity. He stepped around the unmanned front desk and into the backroom, where York was busy tenderizing a chunk of meat. The apprentice stopped pounding at it and looked up at Creep. He dropped the meat mallet and wiped his hands with a rag that hung from his waist, eyes raking the damage to Creep's body before noticing the young boy behind him.

"I'm assuming you had plenty of first aid training at whichever stealth school you attended," Creep said, reaching back and guiding the boy forward. "Patch him up. I have to get back to the palace."

York nodded and waved the boy over. "Plan's gone awry?" he asked.

Creep turned and limped out. "To put it mildly."

*   *   *

Wendel LeAnce had a hand placed against his sister's cheek, feeling the warmth vanish. She rested on a twin-sized bed in a room meant for common guests, a far cry from the lavishness of their suites. It was closer to the main floor, however, which meant they hadn't needed to travel too far through the palace. Periphan had required immediate rest. Her legs had gone first, incapable of motion as they stiffened along the smaller joints, such as those in her toes and ankles. Soon, the knees would follow, as well as her hip flexor, shoulders, and elbows. Once it took over the spine, she was finished.

Wendel knew all about the effects of hylile, a poison gathered from the Passion Kingdom's Volcanic Quadrant. In his cozy position as Brilliance's leader and the commissioner of the League of Weavineers, society frequently viewed him as a figurehead rather than an intellectual savant, which he preferred, as it'd cause many to underestimate him. But everyone in his family was geniuses in their own right, their knowledge expanding beyond the realm of weavineering. Poisons were a particular topic of interest.

It had been six centuries since the last generation of LeAnce children were guilty of poisoning siblings. Since the title of commissioner was given to the family member who wouldn't bare children, only a few actually chased the position. Back then, instead of choosing based on merit out of those candidates, certain individuals would resort to more sinister methods. While there hadn't been a case of such evil since then, the LeAnce family continued to learn about poisons and train their tongues to detect certain tastes and textures. Wendel and his siblings hated those lessons as children, so of course they found ways to stop the taste tests in their teenage years. Now, his sister was dying because of it. A trained tongue would have recognized the hylile, no matter the subtlety of its taste.

He remembered how to treat it though, a gift of the LeAnce memory. He was waiting for several runners to return with his list of demands. If he could just concoct the antidote before the symptoms reached the final stage of spinal paralysis. He would need to administer it before he began showing symptoms himself. If his fingers and wrists locked up, he wouldn't be able to make the antidote. He assumed he had also ingested the poison—likely from one of the award winners at the ceremony, a planted rebel—but the effects took longer to initiate because of his body mass compared to Periphan's. He hoped one of his runners returned with the doctor he requested.

He felt his fingertips and toes losing heat just as the door burst open. A woman rushed in, pushing a wooden cart scattered with trinkets and ingredients. He rose from the side of the bed and met her halfway, stealing the cart and pulling it next to the bed. Going to work, he crushed herbs and measured liquids, fumbling every now and then with numb fingers. Only so often did he look beyond the graduated cylinders and flasks to check on his sister.

Her jaw was locking, and the pain was a strike of lightning through her eyes.

The spine was next.

*   *   *

Lilu's trek through the grand corridor that led to the throne room was one of nightmares. A stumble and pause to look down at Horos's corpse lying on the floor. Fane seated a few feet off to the side, emptily staring at his comrade. Nobody moved inward to gather the body or console Fane. They remained at a distance, but most eyes were drawn to the throne room.

The soldiers who had ushered her off stage after the assassination attempt now led her into the throne room. They remained at the open doorway, allowing her to finally break apart. She only managed a few steps before processing what she was looking at. Another corpse lay on the floor, this one topped with a misshapen sphere of ice. Bryson stood above it.

She shivered, and her gut told her he was responsible. He had found the gift—or curse—his father had stolen from his mother to give to him.

Bryson looked up at her, his wife just behind him, still marveling at the cadaver below. He stepped over the body and marched down the length of the chamber, his face plastered with conviction. It almost frightened Lilu—sparking images of that day she had seen Apoleia at the piano in the Lilac Suites lobby—but the rational part of her knew too well the bond they shared. He wouldn't hurt her. Still, she flinched as he neared. He arrested his approach upon seeing her reservations, allowing a moment to pass between them.

Then he pulled her tight and hugged her, the chill from which he had suffered throughout his life—now at an intensified stage—rescinding to a warmth somewhere deep inside. It was an embrace of friendship and family ... no matter how badly she wished it was more.

*   *   *

Toshik strolled down a dirt path somewhere deep in the maze of farmlands and pastures that was Yinyon. Kolver walked alongside him, finally deciding to give the grieving swordsman a proper tour. Toshik welcomed the distraction, desiring a break from Solace's speed training. Since Jilly's death, he thought it impossible to become so exhausted that he would mentally checkout, but apparently nothing he'd done with Suadade could have prepared him for the torture that was Solace's tutelage.

He eyed the hill where two mighty oaks loomed over the village and a couple of legend's gravestones. He was still nowhere close to reaching it from Solace's office, which was frustrating. He supposed the challenges didn't end because he could cut a lake in two.

"I don't recognize this area," Toshik said.

"All of this property belongs to one woman," Kolver said. "You haven't met her yet, but she's important to this village. Carries one of the oldest family names alongside mine."

"I guess that explains that." Toshik stared at a vast ranch house just ahead. They walked next to a beautifully constructed wooden fence that bordered the ranch's acres upon acres of land.

"And there she is," Kolver stated, pointing at a distant well. A tall woman with violet hair approached with a bucket. As she situated it in the contraption and began lowering it into the well, she peered up, either admiring the clear blue sky or having a moment of reflection. An orange cat with black stripes along its back hopped onto the well's rim, then up onto her shoulder, displaying a level of nimbleness Toshik had been working to obtain. The cat peered back at the two young men, its owner oblivious.

Toshik looked up above the woman in search of anything unordinary. Was she looking up at the floating islands?

"She's reminiscing," said Kolver. "You won't find anything up there."

Lowering his gaze, Toshik paused as they passed the main gate to her property. Carved in its center, where two diagonal planks of wood intersected, was an insignia he'd seen before. It had been burned into his memory ever since meeting that strange man in Dunami. The man had carried a small blade of spunka steel, flaunting the sharp edge and smooth spine of what could have only been an expert craftsman. But it hadn't been a Brench product. It had been marked with a foreign insignia instead: an 'S', its ends tipped to a fine point just like a sword. When he'd inquired about it, the man said little save a vague implication of some kind of sob story. Toshik studied the insignia on the gate, then looked back at the woman. She had turned and was now watching from several hundred feet away.

"What's her name?"

"Soraku," said Kolver.

He remained silent as Soraku returned her focus to the well, retrieving a now-full bucket. She walked in the opposite direction. The cat leapt into the grass. She was the woman responsible for the man in the trench coat's crippled heart.

78

The Duel

Rhyparia NuForce felt restored to her former glory. That power she had displayed in Ulna Malen coursed through her at an even greater rate now. Her stay in the Dark Empire had been maddening, comparing herself to beings that seemed to exist in a different stratosphere of talent than her. She couldn't best any of the Gefal or even Mendac, and to top it all off, she had lost control of her will, strings pulled and plucked by an emperor. But now those wings of black were fully hers. They were rescinded into her back. She felt none of that man's presence in her mind.

She had her ancient again. The umbrella's handle was sturdy in her grip, a familiar weight that she had missed like an amputated limb. It was bliss, and power, and dependence. She had never learned its name because the idea of naming an object was silly. It was a tool. And if it was anything close to alive, it was nothing more than an extension of her own existence.

She looked up from the umbrella in her hand, its point standing atop the Mulanyx floor. A man just less than six feet stood on the other side of the battle hall. He sported a buzz cut atop a cubical head, a jaw blunt enough to hammer a spear into stone. He had shaved his patchy beard today—perhaps out of respect for the upcoming event. But he wore the same convoluted tangle of oversized robes, blankets, and sheets, some which he wore as clothing and others tied around joints as if to keep the clothes from falling off of his frame. He was a big man with thick muscles that wrapped around his arms, legs, and core, but not big enough to warrant attire suited for Powish giants.

A crowd had gathered around the hall's perimeter. A large number congregated in groups against the walls, while a select few were nothing more than shadowy silhouettes against illuminated backlights in the walls, likely watching from a distant chamber in the Labyrinth through a means of Mulawi weaving she had yet to understand.

Despite the crowd, she was very much aware of one man's presence. Mendac LeAnce watched from a spot separated from their peers. He crouched low, elbows atop his knees, eyes drawn keenly on her. The scar from a sword wound in a past life sliced up his forehead and above his hairline. He had been training with Poten for several months now, while this was her first opportunity. Mendac had prepared her by revealing the Fuhren's strengths and habits, but he also admitted the Powish Gefal had likely held back many of his skills. Poten might show something new today.

Shadows coiled out of the floor between Poten and Rhyparia, rising to become a humanistic shape. "This will serve as a demonstration to why we recruited humans from the kingdoms," the figure said. It was a rare circumstance in which Emperor Mialo spoke in the Sphairian tongue. "The Labyrinth has lost two Cavities with the murders of the Prim and Power firstborns. It has weakened our empire, but Rhyparia and Mendac are here to supplement such losses. I think we all have witnessed enough of Mendac these past few months to know his role here. There have been questions about Rhyparia, however." The figure of shadows turned toward her. "To which she finally has answers."

The shadows collapsed into the floor as the emperor returned to the Mulanyx. It had been a short introduction with an abrupt ending—a way of Mialo telling her she would waste their time no more. Either she proved something right here and now, or … well, she didn't know the alternate outcome.

It didn't take an expert fighter to realize Poten's strengths between his build, ethnicity, and ranking. Just one of those three would have made him a man capable of splintering rock. Combine them and he could shatter boulders. Rhyparia had faced Powish opponents before, including two royal firstborns in Power Queen Gantski and her son. She had even fended off a Bewahr—a short, bony man who somehow packed more of a punch than any giant. That very man was in the hall right now, though she didn't know how he was watching with those damaged eyes. Still, none of them were Fuhren.

Without signal or instruction to do so, Poten charged, shaking the floor with each monstrous stride. Rhyparia could never create such disturbances with pure physicality. That was why she had her umbrella. She lifted the ancient and pointed it at the man, shooting a blast of clout from its tip. She didn't bother weaving at all, resulting in a lateral force that nearly lifted Poten off of his feet. He ceased his sprint and bent his knees, turning his head and lifting an arm.

Behind him, the wall of Mulanyx splintered from the gravitational force. Cracks webbed throughout the onyx, emitting a sound akin to a frozen lake cracking beneath someone's feet. The wall then caved inward suddenly, black rock raining down atop the floor. She relented, leaving a sizeable indent in the wall that yawned behind Poten. He turned, admiring her handiwork.

"Okay then," he said, chest heaving. "Clearly, I'd be an imbecile to not make adjustments now." He began to unwrap the excess cloth tied around his joints, watching her all the while. The rest of his clothes fell to the floor in a puddle of ivory.

She wove a force above him, funneling it downward to crush him. He hunkered down into a low squat, grunting with effort. The floor lowered as another pit yielded to the gravity, but he stood his ground.

Poten roared. His shoulders widened, chest swelled, and neck thickened. The growth extended down into his core and legs. His skin stretched to the point of bursting, veins bulging like the roots of a forest's undergrowth. He grew taller until he towered over her, forcing her to look up like a child faced with her father. He stopped just before his head reached the ceiling. His clothes were nearly a perfect fit now. They still hung loosely, leading her to believe this wasn't his limit.

Mendac hadn't warned her about this ability. She looked his way, and he smiled. It was nothing evil or ill-intentioned, but teasing and genuine. He had known about it; he simply hadn't wanted to tell her everything—another test of his.

Poten dropped a fist toward her. She leapt backward, weaving a force that increased her speed, carrying her in a beeline trajectory to the opposite wall. She landed on the wall feet first just as she heard the impact of fist with floor. She craned her neck and looked up—or her version of up, given her position standing on the wall in a lateral gravitational field. Poten had created his own crater next to her previous one.

She flew at him, once again darting through the air like a spear. He stood fully, presenting his entire bulk as if waiting for her to enter his embrace, which she had no intention of doing. She wasn't suicidal.

With his focus drawn to her, she altered the gravity around him, this time maneuvering Archaic Chains in intricate patterns to lighten it. His eyebrows furrowed, feeling the shift just as she was about to make impact. His feet lifted from the ground, and the point of her umbrella slammed into his abdomen. It didn't impale him, his Powish build too firm to break, but he was thrown backward without any anchor below.

Poten tumbled end over end back through the hall. His head smacked the roof. His arms slapped against the side walls and floor. Her wings extended from her back. She flew at him, a mere crow compared to his size. He came to a stop and reached for her with a mighty fist. She dodged with an agile shift to the left, turning her wings to bank a turn. He reached out with the other hand and she knocked it out of her way with another gravitational shift. She was flying at his face, wings of shadows slapping downward, converging with the floor and peeling away in stringy tendrils. He tried to rise, but she warped the gravity around his head, pinning it to the floor. He tried to say something but only managed a grunt, as his lips were locked closed in the overwhelming gravity. She pointed her umbrella at a spot his Powish attributes couldn't deflect. He writhed in efforts to lift his massive bulk, but what could a giant do against a woman who had overpowered the moon?

The umbrella impaled his right eye, and he finally managed a scream, the gravitational force lifted just as she had arrived. Her ancient was half a meter deep into his overgrown skull, and she stood with a foot planted on each shoulder. He pounded at the floor, looking to retaliate. She was saved—not that she needed it—by tangles of shadows rising from the floor and wrapping around his body. Dozens of them ensnared him until he couldn't move anymore. Rhyparia retrieved her ancient and hopped back to the floor.

She sauntered over to Mendac. Some faces around the room followed her, while others observed the struggling Fuhren in shock. It was silent save the swollen man's grunts. She took her place next to Mendac and leaned back against the wall, arms crossed. He eyed her and smiled. They were two elites of the kingdoms brought here to operate as a pair of empirical soldiers for which there was no rank. They were substitutes meant to fill the gaping holes of a god's two cavities, which would imply they were gods themselves. They were coming into themselves, growing as fighters while lessening as humans. The fall or rise of either empire would come down to only a few players.

Rhyparia NuForce and Mendac LeAnce were two of them, and Preloz Henye could see that.

79

The Linsaniun Mounds

The cacophony of screams and roars lanced Olivia's eardrums despite the plugs in her ears. They were made out of a dense foam material and apparently the most efficient earplugs one could find, but they did little to arrest the cries of the Linsani. Even so, that little bit was marginal enough to keep their ears from bleeding.

Having temporary access to one of the transit's carriages alone, she summoned her Bewahr. Vuilni rode in the neighboring carriage with most of the other travelers, and Nina rode a stallion at the front of the pack. She was that kind of person, a fearless leader willing to assume the roles from which others shied away. Her horse was a special beast for the Void, its skin and coat unmarred by the atmosphere's erosive affects. Perhaps, Nina's unrivaled sense of spirit kept the animal safe. Olivia had noticed a dip in the Void's melancholic aura ever since arriving at the hunter's nest. It made her question how differently this journey would have gone without Nina's presence—or maybe it was the collective, all of the Linsani hunters traveling together. They were a peculiar group.

Shadows spiraled up from the carriage's floorboards, then slipped away to reveal Olivia's Bewahr. Preloz Henye glanced at the curtained window with one good eye before greeting his charge. "You're close," he said.

"Hard to tell," Olivia replied. "I know they're getting louder, but their screams travel so unnaturally. Vuilni's finding out how much longer now."

"Fifteen to twenty-five miles out." He approached the window and peeled back a curtain, exposing the mutilation in the back of his skull to Olivia. Why did the hole always look recent? Blood caked the hair surrounding it, clumping strands together in red goop. "Ah, more like ten to fifteen."

"You remember it that well?" she asked.

"I guarded these Mounds for a long time." He turned away from the window and took a seat, old bones creaking somewhere in his legs. She wondered what they looked like, for she'd never seen him without long pants.

After a few minutes of listening to the beasts cry, she took the time to study Preloz's face. She was getting better at reading his expressions through the mangled skin and muscle, so she saw the anxiety. "I'm going to make sure we get her," she said.

He looked at her and smiled weakly. "Yes, because I will be there to help." He looked away. "But that's not what has me worried."

"What is it?"

"Business in the Empire."

She paused, sifting through her next possible responses. Anything related to the Empire was a delicate subject for the Bewahr. "Are you in danger?" she asked.

With a deafening finality, he replied, "We all are."

*   *   *

Olivia didn't know what she had expected of the Mounds, but it wasn't this. They were the opposite of the rolling grasslands she'd seen in textbooks, a blanket of vibrant green beneath a blue sky and drifting clouds of cotton. What stretched before her was a natural wasteland, marshes for as far as the eye could see. The grass was waist-high. Muddy water met her ankles, making her thankful to Nina for lending her sturdy leather boots.

What was most jarring was the color and light. Noon approached, so the sun was disappearing behind Earth to bring forth second-night. The light had yet to wane completely, but everything seemed to be blanketed in gray. The grass was the color of charcoal, the sky an icy blue that faded to steel. Tangled shrubbery peeked above the grass in the distance. A tree slouched here and there, charred skeletons against the smoky backdrop, branches wilting toward the ground as if their vine-draped canopies were too heavy for their trunks. The Mounds were gentle hills smothered by brutal soil.

Vuilni's shoulder touched Olivia's. She hadn't realized how close they were standing to each other. In the outer reaches of the Void, the stillness was evident. This place was unnerving, a silence that no longer existed between the Linsani's cries. A blanket of gloom that shrouded her soul. With the thinnest of air to siphon, breathing was difficult even while exerting no energy. She had to consciously focus on her breathing pattern … deeper inhales, longer exhales.

"Are you ready?" The question came from Lu, the almond-haired man who had greeted Olivia and Vuilni at the front door of the hunters' headquarters. His comrade and friend, Killui, stood at his side.

"Always," said Olivia, drawing a sideways glance from Vuilni. Like in the attic of the hunter's guild when faced with the Linsani eggs, the Powish was feeling the effects more than anyone else. The Void's atmosphere had done noticeable damage to her. Gray drenched her braids; wrinkles raced throughout her face.

"How do you guys usually kill it?" Vuilni asked.

Killui gave a lackadaisical shrug. "We don't know yet. Haven't killed one. Your pal took all the glory last time."

Vuilni sighed. "Great."

"But Nina has this old man who we think can get the job done."

That got Olivia to turn. "Old man?"

Lu gave Killui an exasperated stare, then regarded the two women. "Look, we've never killed one because we've never actually tried yet. Don't go into this thinking we've failed a hundred times."

Olivia thought she'd probably feel better if that was actually the case. At least then that meant they had failures from which to learn. She didn't voice her concerns, however, allowing Lu to continue.

"Every mission prior to this one has either been focused on scouting or egg retrieval, and we've been doing this for many years." He looked to the Mounds again, crossing his arms. "In fact, even today our main mission isn't to kill Lianyu. That's just something we'll do if the chance presents itself, given the weapons we have at our disposal at the moment ... Two Jestivan, the guild's best hunters, and I was told you have a trick up your sleeve." She didn't respond, knowing that trick to be Preloz. "But killing that thing doesn't have priority over our other objectives. We're here to steal its final egg, and you're here to rescue its rider."

"There's no rescuing that girl," Killui said, once again spouting off with a grating nonchalance. His hands were tucked into his pants pockets, posture slouched somewhat. His crossbow, unlike Killui's, wasn't strapped tightly to his back. It hung askew and loose. Olivia's lips remained pursed, choosing to not give the jokester the time of day. He reminded her of Toshik during the Jestivan's infancy. She *would* rescue Pytatia Henye. Then she could put her out of her immortal misery.

Two miles east, a wagon rode into the Mounds. It bounced on its wheels as the horses dragged it as if it wasn't there. Someone was standing in its coach, one hand grasping the guard rail in front, the other grasping a whip responsible for sending the horses into frenzy. Olivia knew that coachman to be Nina. Horses typically didn't need to be handled so aggressively, but when in the Mounds, animals tended to march by the beat of their own drums—drums driven by animalistic fear. Like a dog could detect a man's intent by simply looking at him, a horse could detect the atmospheric shifts created by the Linsani.

"She's mad," Vuilni said.

"The Void can make you that way," Lu replied. "But there are much worse things to become than mad."

They watched her race across two vast mounds, nearly being tossed from the coach once. The wagon looked like it had struck a root next to a skeletal tree.

"Not her fault," Lu said. "She can try to steer the best she can, but the horses won't always listen."

As it rolled down another mound, three of its wheels lifted from the ground, leading to a terrifying moment when the wagon rode only on its front-left wheel. Vuilni gasped. Olivia squinted as the wagon grew distant, the mounds becoming high enough to almost swallow it whole. She saw just the top half.

"Anytime now ..." Olivia said, growing impatient.

"Just calm down," Killui breathed. "Not until the signal is given."

"What are we waiting for?" Vuilni asked.

"What good is bait if it doesn't do its job?" he asked.

Vuilni balked. "Bait?"

"Nina's always the bait. She doesn't let anyone else do it."

A beast lifted into the sky. A scream shook the ground. It looked nearly identical to Tongku Feilong save its eyes, an abyssal black compared to Tongku's reds. Shadows engulfed its skeleton like wispy black flame, ivory bones cloaked within. Lianyu was smaller than Tongku, but faster. It took to the sky effortlessly, moving as graciously as parchment caught on wind. One of its black horns looked to have been snapped in half. At the apex of its ascent, it pulled back its wings and spread them wide, seeming to hang in the sky, a lethal tail of hundreds of bones whipping beneath it. Opening its mouth, it screamed for the entire world to hear before spotting the wagon manned by Nina below.

The Linsani dove.

The wagon jerked right, the horses increasing their pace. Nina was no longer visible with the distance now between them, but Olivia couldn't imagine the woman hanging on. Every hundred feet, the wagon bounced with a vicious tilt.

"Let's do this thing," Killui said, grabbing his crossbow from his back. Lu followed suit, though he lacked his friend's sinister smile. This was all business to him.

"And what are crossbows going to do to that monster?" Vuilni asked.

798

Killui scoffed, loading his weapon with a broad-headed bolt. Olivia had never seen an arrow or bolt that didn't have a sharp point. "You think there's only one type of monster in these Mounds? You know what the Cynnish call this place, right?"

Vuilni's look told him no.

"The Monster Mounds."

"Nobody calls it that," said Lu, having just finished loading his crossbow. Other groups of hunters were already charging the mounds from other entry points.

"I do," Killui replied, hurt.

"Yeah, and you should stop. It sounds absolutely ..."

Olivia didn't hear the rest, for she had already begun her sprint. The world darkened as she penetrated deeper, kicking through charcoal grass beneath a sky of gray ash, stars lain throughout like trodden gravel. Lianyu's screams were brutal and strained, but her own breathing smothered it. She could hear her pulse through her eardrums. She looked back and saw Vuilni running despite her apprehensions. Lu and Killui had taken a more careful approach, stepping through the grass like hunters trying to sneak up on an unsuspecting deer.

The ground around her shifted. Sod split apart and lifted as if something was being unearthed. She counted more than a dozen spots where the black grass didn't grow. Hands were the first things she saw break free of the crust. White bone lined with deteriorated muscle grabbed at unbroken parts of the land to pull themselves up and out of their graves, exposing skulls, some stripped free of skin and muscle, others still covered by stubborn bits and pieces. Unnatural didn't quite cover it. These were ungodly things.

Part of her was thankful for their lack of speed, granting her the opportunity to evade them easily. But they swarmed in large numbers, unearthing from hundreds of different spots both directly around her and in the distance. It was an army of the undead spoken about in campfire tales, which now proved to be more than mindless fiction. She caught a glimpse of Lu about a hundred paces to her right, wielding his crossbow in one hand and waving a stone bludgeon in the other. The bludgeon did little for him because of his lack of pure strength, but that crossbow was obliterating the undead. Now she understood why they were broad-headed: to shatter bone.

He looked her way and waved his bludgeon. She retrieved hers from her back. She had forgotten she was carrying it, deeming it pointless against a Linsani. Why hadn't anyone warned her of these obstacles? Why arm her with a weapon and tell her nothing else? It was a question for after all of this … if they managed to survive.

Olivia swung, and she proved just how dangerous a bludgeon could be when in the hands of someone with her strength. Lu's bolts ripped through individual bones, shattering joints and dismembering limbs, while Olivia's blows blasted skeletons into pieces. She was at the core of a storm of broken bones. She spun and swung with little grace, but enough force to compensate. The undead emanated nothingness. She could feel Pytatia's name trying to slip from her mind, her purpose here faced with a powerful vacuum.

Within moments, she had obliterated a few dozen of the enemy's ranks, a skeleton graveyard now scattered around her. Several more converged on her from more distant graves, stepping over their comrades—if they were even considered that. One skeleton still had a nearly entirely intact head. It was a woman, dull eyes draining gray liquid down her cheeks, hair white as bone. She appeared to be trying to mouth words, but all that escaped were moans. Both ears were gone, torn from the sides of her head. Olivia froze for that one moment, caught in that age-old debate of the Void: Was she alive or dead?

Olivia should put her out of her misery. But was she actually killing any of these things? And were they actually in misery to begin with?

A beastly screech. Distant shouts. She looked that way and saw a skeletal wyvern cloaked in shadow chasing down a rattling wagon. Her eyebrows furrowed. That monster was gigantic and unsightly … Wait, that monster was Lianyu. The Linsani of Purgatory had nearly dug its forgetful claws into Olivia's soul. And now she could see the girl on its back from this angle: Pytatia Henye.

Scared she would lose her purpose again, she stormed that way without sparing the final undead a second glance. They would continue to exist in this graveyard; she only hoped they didn't suffer.

Pytatia was mounted on Lianyu's long spine, cloaked in the wyvern's shadows. She was still the little girl from the story based on her size, but a reliable perspective was difficult to obtain when considering the distance and the sheer size of Lianyu in comparison.

Olivia adopted a new strategy. She put one hundred percent of her focus on Lianyu. Her theory was that it'd be more difficult for Lianyu to affect memories that held more of someone's attention. In doing so, however, she risked losing everyone else. She had lost awareness of where the hunters or Vuilni were located, but she found solace in the fact that she could remember they existed at all.

Someone yelled Olivia's name, then a blur of white passed in front of her. She planted a foot and stopped. Whatever had crossed her was now somewhere in the charcoal grass ten paces to the left. A woman approached from her right, breathing heavily. She held a foreign contraption that looked like a bulky crossbow, but with limbs and switches that implied it served a much different purpose. Her regular crossbow was strapped to her left hip. She had dirty blonde hair, freckles, and angular cheek bones. Olivia knew her as Leslie, the woman who had lied and claimed the glory of slaying Tongku.

"Pay attention!" she exclaimed, running past Olivia and then reaching down in the grass where that thing had landed. She dragged it back and then dropped it. It was some kind of four-legged animal, but skeletal. It was snared in a net. "Lions," Leslie said around a deep breath. "They prowl in the grass. This one just lunged at you."

Before Olivia could reply, Leslie hushed her and spun. She raised her contraption to chest level and held it just like a crossbow. A net shot from its mouth just as another undead animal leapt from the grass a few feet away. The net swallowed it, apparently traveling with enough force to carry the animal in the opposite direction of its initial momentum. A crash and thud as the beast fell through the black grass and hit land. It didn't make any sounds save the rattling of its bones as it struggled to free itself.

Leslie took a moment to reload her weapon with a thick ball of rope. She reset the limbs and approached the skeleton to make sure it was successfully detained. "Want to beat it?" she asked.

Olivia looked down at her bludgeon, then back to the squirming lion. The net had tangled itself around the skeleton, and there were metal weights all along the edges, complete with hooks that caught on bones.

"Either you smash it to pieces or it will slowly dismember itself. Brilliant design, really. As it presses on one part of the net too hard to free itself, it actually causes hooks elsewhere to pull and break bone." She raised an eyebrow and shrugged. "Personally, I like watching them kill themselves in the struggle … like a desperate rat on the verge of death. But most don't share my pleasures."

Olivia raised her bludgeon and slammed the skeleton. There was still meat hanging from its hind legs and neck. She pummeled it until it was indistinguishable from a pile of broken rock. If it hadn't been for Leslie, the first one would have tackled her. The last thing she wanted was to come in physical contact with any creature here. It was the whole point of the bludgeon; otherwise, she would have been using her fists and feet.

"Get going and pay attention," Leslie said. "The raiding squad is closing in on the nest for the final egg. You don't have much time left with our help if you want to get that girl."

Spotting Lianyu, the Linsani of Purgatory, Olivia's purpose returned to her. It had almost slipped away again.

She ran. The wyvern caught Nina's wagon and flew past, banking a sharp turn just ahead, displaying the agility that Tongku had lacked. As it turned, its tail came down and slapped land, breaking the strata in an explosion of dirt and mud. The power shook the Mounds; the sound ripped apart the sky and rattled the stars. The wagon flipped. Nina was nothing but a faint shadow tossed from the coach.

Lianyu's attack didn't stop there. It lifted its tail from the newly formed fissure and looked back, opening a mouth big enough to devour buildings and redwoods, its mandible a menacing collection of sharp angles and razor-like edges. A sphere of shadows as black as the ocean's greatest depths swelled in front of its mouth, absorbing the cloak that shrouded the rest of its body. As the sphere gained mass, the Linsani's mouth opened wider until bones along the sides of the skull cracked. It was *literally* breaking its jaw to hold the Cynergy in place, collecting potential energy. Its cloak of shadows thinned as it did so.

DAVID F. FARRIS

Olivia had run far enough to see Nina trying to flee, but she was hunched and limping, the toss from her wagon having done considerable damage. She was doing all of this in order to get that final egg ... in order to kill off Purgatory. Olivia could empathize with her. Nina had lost her mother and father because they had lost her, mentally and spiritually. They had forgotten her and casted her away as nothing more than a groveling urchin. Who knew how many other Cynnish had experienced that same kind of loss, and all because of this monster? Nina wanted to obliterate it, but she was now at its mercy.

The shadow ball was now thrice the size of Lianyu's skull. The Linsani had lifted its feet and back end, its belly —if it had a belly—facing the ground to make room for the attack's size. Knowing her abilities were useless when faced with a Linsani's Cynergy, Olivia summoned Preloz. She picked a location as close to Nina as possible without being far enough from herself that would make summoning him impossible. The Bewahr appeared from twisting black mist, causing a rare moment when the grass swayed with the resulting air current. Many blades snapped, proving the grass was just as lifeless as the monstrous corpses buried beneath.

Preloz stood in his natural habitat. He had been shaped by this very kingdom, these very mounds. He had patrolled them, and he sported the wounds and rot to prove it: holes, scars, mangled skin, exposed innards. The man stared at Olivia, then turned slowly to assess the situation.

"Help Nina!" she screamed, pointing in the fleeing woman's direction. He visually followed her finger, spotted her, then continued to turn toward the black ball. If he saw his daughter mounted on the beast, he didn't show it. He ran—a first from what Olivia had seen from him—in the direction of Nina. He was suspiciously fast—not anywhere near the speed of any of the Jestivan, but quick enough. This was the same man who had required a full five seconds to simply turn his head in every instance before?

Her focus became Pytatia again as she sprinted in the direction of the wyvern. An eerie silence had settled upon the land. Cries of the other Linsani carried from distant Mounds hundreds of miles away, but Lianyu remained mute as it compiled its energy. She didn't know what she expected from the energy orb, but she assumed there'd be some kind of sound, like the cackling of a Passionian's flames or the sizzling of an Intelian's electricity. This was nothingness.

A series of snaps overpowered all other sounds. It sounded like branches breaking beneath one's boots. She sought out the source while running and found tall, narrow shadows peeking above the crest of a southward mound. They were some kind of engineered contraptions of war. Her eyes were drawn upward as massive shadows flew past her. Seven boulders soared through the sky, each targeting the Linsani. So they were trebuchets, but from where? She didn't see any such armory when she left the city. Did they have another base elsewhere in the Void? How big were their operations?

Olivia picked up her pace. They were trying to hit the beast while it was stationary, or perhaps, more importantly, while its cloak of shadows waned in favor of the sphere. Did they not care that Pytatia was still mounted?

She increased the force in each stride, calves and thighs bulging to create more speed. Her feet sank in the muddy floor. The waist-high grass, brittle and black, broke as she crashed through it, carving a trail behind her. She caught the shadows of the boulders, her speed percentage now reaching a mark she had yet to achieve in her life. Bryson had taught her all about speed as children, lessons handed down from Debo. Rhyparia had aided speed training with heavier gravity—a large reason why many of the Jestivan were as fast as they were.

She didn't fully appreciate the size of the Linsani until she was nearly beneath it. Not only that, but it was higher in the air than she had thought. She was strong, capable of leaping great heights and bounding across vast gaps, but even this was out of her reach. She wasn't Powish. She looked back. While she had outrun the boulders, they were closing in fast. Lianyu's black orb looked ready to burst. Pytatia was still in danger, gray hair falling stiff around a little girl's body.

Olivia thrust her arms up toward the Linsani, palms open. A geyser of hot water burst from her hands, hitting the naked skeletal wyvern in its array of ribs, careful to avoid that girl ... that girl? Who was she again?

The impact did nothing. Lianyu was anchored into the sky like the moon. The logical part of her told her every attempt was hopeless, but she had watched Bryson take one of these monsters down. And if recent events were to account for anything, even the moon had proven it was impressionable. Someone had made it disappear.

"Olivia, run!"

The Jestivan rescinded her geyser, turned, and found Vuilni running toward her through the cleared path of grass, the ground quaking with each planted foot of the former Diatia's stride. Her thighs had ripped the seams of her trousers, bulging to an unnatural size, displaying the Powish abilities that had always made Olivia—a person who prided herself on her physical strength—a bit curious. Vuilni was conquering Purgatory's effects, the same effects that had almost crippled her while in the presence of only its eggs. The transformation was unreal and too convenient, and Olivia would have narrowed her eyes and gave the moment pause had it not been for the urgency of their situation. The boulders now soared above her again, bearing down on the Linsani.

Vuilni gestured with her hands, interlocking her fingers and throwing them upward. Olivia understood and turned back toward the beast, bolting forward in the same direction as Vuilni. They raced ahead of the boulders' shadows once again, and Olivia slowed to let her partner catch her.

"NOW!" Vuilni roared.

Olivia leapt. Vuilni came up behind her. Olivia's feet landed in Vuilni's cusped hands, fingers interlocked. Vuilni's clothing tore as every single muscle—arms, chest, core, and legs—flexed to heave Olivia upward. With the combined forward momentum of both women and the unfathomable strength of a Powish elite, Olivia was launched into the sky just ahead of the boulders.

Seeing the Linsani this closely and at a level angle was humbling. It had looked big from the ground, but its scale was something else entirely when right in front of her. Lianyu didn't notice Olivia or the boulders—its gaping jaw forcing its black eyes skyward—but Pytatia did. The girl was trying to get the beast's attention, shadows spilling from her wrists and hands around the wyvern's spine. She shook it, but such a small grip wouldn't affect the beast. The two of them locked eyes—if one could call them that in Pytatia's condition. Olivia would have shuddered had it not been for the blistering speed of her flight.

Pytatia Henye made her father seem beautiful. Her hair had mostly fallen out. Long, thin strands clung to a scalp covered in worms. Her left eyeball hung from pink string, socket gouged and mutilated. Her mouth looked frozen in a contorted oval shape, as if her body had settled into rigor mortis mid-scream, forcing her chin askew from the center of her face. The left cheek dangled from her jaw, a flap of muscle and skin that obscured half of her neck. The half Olivia could see was absent of flesh, exposing vocal chords, the esophagus, and countless other internal parts. She was naked, and everything below the neck was that of a corpse: skin a grayish-white, blemished with black spots that were peppered with holes of rot as maggots feasted on death.

Olivia was on her in an instant, the boulders looming behind. Pytatia screamed something ghoulish and shrill and unnatural, mouth unmoving. Olivia gagged just as she tackled the girl.

The scream did something to Olivia. Everything vanished save sight, starting with sound and air before moving onto more abstract concepts such as knowledge and emotions. Olivia's consciousness slipped away from her, but she remained coherent to the physical world around her. An overwhelming sense of apathy shed new light on her perception.

Grass. Hills. Sky. A person here or there far below.

All held no relevance, as did the fall she was currently experiencing. This could kill her, she thought … or it wasn't a thought, more a matter of fact. This *would* kill her. She would die, likely from a broken neck. That was that, and she could accept it.

Her impact with the girl—whose name and importance she no longer knew—had flipped her so that she faced back toward a hulking winged skeleton. A ray of black shadows shot from its mouth and pummeled the land. The shadows blasted outward, spreading thickly across charcoal grass for a mile before furling upward at the end of its reach. It was an attack too immense for any of those strangers below to avoid, yet she knew someone down there was doing what he could. Preloz Henye was one person outside of her own existence with whom she had familiarity, and he was fighting it.

She'd never felt the Bewahr's presence in her before, but right now she could. She knew that to be her genetic tie to the man. There was a piece of him inside of her, as all royal firstborns possessed the genetic trait that granted them a celestial guardian. No amount of Purgatory could break that bond from her, for its existence was too firmly rooted inside of her. It only took a moment like this—all other noise from her consciousness wiped clean—for her to become aware of that feeling. Decades of dirt and grime had been scrubbed away to reveal his power hidden beneath.

Olivia continued rotating in the air and crashed through the shadows feet first. Her body went cold. The girl she had been holding was now flailing out of her grasp. Olivia hit the ground with a crunch, brittle grass breaking beneath her weight, knees relaxed as she tried to absorb the impact as best she could. Even her strength couldn't stop her body from folding over. Her upper torso bent forward and then snapped back, the back of her head slapping rocks.

80

The Price of Purgatory

Preloz stood above his daughter, ashamed by his revulsion. The state of her face and body was ghastly. She lay with a broken neck—split at a full right angle—from her fall off of Lianyu's back, yet continued to wheeze oxygen into her lungs, her good eyeball locked onto her father—a stranger to her. The other eye hung from pinkish flesh down the side of her face. It was morbid ... this kingdom's existence was morbid.

Unlike Preloz, she had no hole in her chest that exposed a gray heart ribbed with black veins, just gray and black skin riddled with tiny holes and maggots. She was a twisted corpse, mouth frozen in a litany of the worst emotions she could no longer feel. The girl was trying to speak, but all that came out were haggard groans. He watched her vocal chords vibrate through a skinless neck.

He squatted next to her, elbows on his knees and an unreadable flatness to his lips. Logic told him she wasn't suffering, for the Linsani of Purgatory had emptied her vessel, but his heart screamed for him to end this. He was surprised to learn his initial reaction wasn't to try to find a way to save her. She was his daughter, and despite the mutilation and decomposition, he saw the truth beneath it all.

The problem with umbra fairies was their lack of weaknesses. They only had one: the wind of a Spiritian. They didn't die to electricity, fire, ice, or Cynergy. In fact, Cynergy only strengthened them. You could mutilate the host's body by dismembering him or her, but the heart would remain beating. And cutting the heart was impossible because the umbra fairy hardened it to a point beyond steel. Then there was the matter of the host's soul, which was an intangible organ—or at least that's what was believed. There was no cutting that in half.

In other words, the host would never truly die and move on until the umbra fairy was killed by Spirit Chains from an outside source. A Spiritian couldn't weave within their own body, so even they were doomed if they ingested one. There were plenty of horror stories about experiments in the earlier days when the creatures were first discovered, involving the research of methods to kill them. Many subjects—actual human beings and, mostly, the impoverished—became throwaways. They were dumped into pits behind Batilearsh. They became piles of humans who had been incinerated, drowned, dismembered, or decapitated—all of them still alive and suffering no matter the severity of their injuries. In the year 223 K.H., fearing overcrowding and disease, the pits were emptied and the bodies transferred to the Void's Edge.

Despite being Lianyu's partner for years, which had likely wiped Pytatia's memory and conscious clean, Preloz saw her despair now. The umbra fairy, whose effects had been overpowered by the Linsani, was already beginning to retake its hold of her in Purgatory's absence.

He had one option. The woman Olivia had told him to save from Lianyu's attack hadn't needed him. A man had already stepped in front of her and dispersed the shadows with a powerful gale from his hands, creating an empty corridor behind him in which she lay. Preloz didn't know how or why, but these people were staffed with a Spiritian. And now he needed that man.

Leaping to his feet, he spun to find anyone standing in the waist-high grass. He saw many, but most stood still, faces blank and eyes distant.

Those who walked did so without urgency or purpose, meandering through the grass and changing direction at random intervals. He didn't spot the woman, but he found the man who had saved her. He was easy to spot among the horde of mindless wanderers, for he was the lone being who seemed to possess awareness as he searched through the grass.

"Hey, hey! Over here!" Preloz shouted, startling the Spiritian. It had been a long time since he raised his voice.

The man hobbled over. He was in his sixties, mustache grown long and ivory. His matching hair was tied up in a bun barely the size of Preloz's knuckle. He wore a light blue tunic and gray trousers. "You know you don't have to shout here, right?" he asked, breathing heavily as he neared.

"I need your help." Preloz turned and gestured to an open patch of black sod in the grass where his daughter lay.

The old man's eyes widened, but he didn't shudder or cringe. "That is bleak." He paused and tilted his head. "Grave dweller?"

"Umbra host."

"Ah …" The old man's gaze became solemn. "Nasty little parasites."

"Can you kill it? She's my daugh—"

The man held up a hand, requesting silence. "You don't have to explain yourself, Mr. Henye." He stared at the Bewahr with eyes of silver grace. ""Not only would it be an honor, but it's my duty here." He lowered himself to his knees with Preloz's help, then bowed over Pytatia's body and cupped his hands over her bare chest. A blast of wind tore through skin, muscle, and bone, reaching the heart and ripping it to shreds along with the umbra fairy.

Preloz was knelt at his daughter's other side, eyes focused on hers. If only she could return that favor—a sense of comfort and closure of which he asked too much. Hosts tended to remain alive for quite some time after the expulsion of an umbra fairy, but thankfully Pytatia's physical state was bad enough for her to die instantly. Her one good eye fixed to the sky until the eyelids closed shut. A long overdue death buried her groans, steadying her vocal chords as she drifted into peace.

"Thank you," Preloz muttered. "Your name?"

The old nodded. "Reginald Patter."

*   *   *

Olivia's eyes opened to a sky of blue steel, the grays she remembered now gone. She supposed noticing that change was a good sign, considering how hard she had hit her head. A pounding pulsed from the back of her skull to her temple, racing around the sides like chariots. She squeezed her eyes shut and groaned, then tried to roll onto her side. She gagged, which brought her attention to something slimy on her chin. She had vomited earlier when Pytatia screamed.

Olivia's eyes shot open. She remembered the girl's name, and she remembered the fact that such a feat should surprise her.

She pushed her upper body off of the ground, then promptly turned her head and puked to the side, a sudden rush of vertigo laying its will upon her. She went to stand, but couldn't. She looked down at her legs. The left one was wrapped tightly in a makeshift splint, two curved planks of wood running down the length of the leg and tied together by thick brown string. Now made aware of the injury, her mind's focus on the pain of the thunderous headache redirected itself to that of the knee, which itself was wrapped in so many layers of bandage that it resembled a globe. It felt like shards of glass were stabbing through her joint.

She screamed. Hurried footsteps shattered charcoal grass. From her seated position low in the grass, she couldn't tell who the person was until they were right next to her.

Nina dropped to her knees and pressed Olivia back with a gentle palm to her chest. "Lay down. Your knee is shattered."

Olivia's scream of agony became an angry roar. It was shameful. Among the aftermath of the Linsani's chaos—filled with death and destruction—she prioritized the condition of her knee. But such an injury didn't heal, and she prided herself on her physical strength. She had been the strongest of the Jestivan—a hard body to accompany a hard heart.

Nina closed her eyes, waiting for Olivia's rage to succumb. Her hand remained pressed against Olivia's chest, whose eyes drained tears. She finished her fitful outburst with a fist into dirt. Then she wept softly, glazed eyes staring at the sky once more.

She needed to recognize the good that had resulted from this mission. She took Nina's presence and seemingly intact memory as confirmation. She had been the main target of Lianyu's attack. Preloz must have saved her. She didn't see Lianyu anywhere, though she could hear the screams of its siblings elsewhere across the Mounds.

"What's the verdict?" Olivia asked.

"Lianyu's dead," said Nina. "That attack was a double-edged sword. It was large in scope and catastrophic in power, but it required using all of the stored Cynergy cloaking its body, effectively eliminating its defenses against our trebuchets."

"How catastrophic?" Olivia's voice was weak and shaky, interrupted by a wince induced from her injuries.

"Nobody is dead."

Olivia regarded Nina. That was surprising … unbelievable even. There had been a lot of people in that mile radius of shadows, including Preloz, Nina, and … her heart dropped. "Vuilni! Is she okay?"

"Vuilni's condition is similar to the others," Nina said quietly. Her whisper dropped to something softer, the Void's atmosphere carrying the mutters with ease. "She's alive, but …"

"But what?"

Nina exhaled and glanced away.

"But what?!"

"Give me a minute. I need help to get you up." She got up and walked away despite Olivia's protests. Olivia grimaced and let out a muffled yell, bones splintering in her knee. She had questions, but only a vague answer addressing one of them.

Nina returned with Preloz moments later, and another man with whom she had no familiarity. The Bewahr carried a long white rod at his side, shaped imperfectly, one side curving out at the end. It looked like a bone, but was as tall as any man.

"How's Pytatia?" Olivia asked.

"You did well, Olivia," Preloz said. "She's at peace."

A small victory, but not enough to quell her worries. As Preloz and Nina helped her up, she asked, "What about Vuilni?"

She got to her feet. Preloz handed her the white rod and confirmed her suspicions. "A Linsani bone. Use it as a crutch until we can get you something more practical."

She placed the bone in her armpit. "Why is nobody answering …" The question died on her lips as she surveyed the Mounds. At first, she couldn't tell what was happening. Even when she began making sense of the situation, she didn't fully understand it. People were roaming aimlessly with dead expressions. She saw nobody mourning the deaths of comrades or celebrating the defeat of Lianyu. It might as well have been a field of nothing.

She found Vuilni standing next to a broken pile of boulders that loomed over her. She faced the wreckage, her back to Olivia, but those braids—gray from the effects of the Void—were telling enough. Her muscles had diminished back to their normal state.

Olivia attempted her best jog, but couldn't manage more than the pace of a brisk walk when obstructed by the crutches and splint. She suppressed a groan with every stride. "Vuilni," she said, not bothering to yell. Her voice would carry. "*Vuilni.*"

Her Powish friend finally turned. Everything about her seemed the same as it had before charging the Mounds, but there was something off about her expression. She was alive and had acknowledged her name, but didn't show recognition upon seeing Olivia. She didn't bother closing the gap. She stood still. A sense of unknowing clouded her face. Olivia saw the unsightly truth in Vuilni's eyes when she was only a few paces away. Vuilni wasn't dead, but those eyes were.

Olivia paused a few feet away from the young woman who had once been a member of an enemy group. She surveyed the former Diatia's gaze and tried refuting the evidence. She opened her mouth, then shut it. She did that probably four more times before she finally asked, "Do you know where you are?"

Vuilni said nothing, regarding her with vacant eyes. At the very least, she could have answered the question with a simple "no." Olivia fought the overwhelming urge to lunge at her. "Lianyu's dead, and Pytatia was saved," she said, attempting to spur her mind into gear with familiar names that might have been rooted deep in her subconscious. Vuilni remained speechless. Olivia planted her crutch farther ahead in the sod, closing the gap so they were a foot apart. "You know what that means, right?" She was pleading at this point. Eyes welling. Voice shaking. "We can go back home and see our families. You can see your mom, brother, and sister … your *dad*!" The last word was a strained shriek, foreign to her vocal chords.

Nothing moved Vuilni. Her eyes drifted past Olivia. Olivia turned to find three figures looming behind her: the old man, Nina, and Preloz. They watched patiently. Others stood or roamed in the distance behind them, as lifeless as Vuilni. She saw Lu and Killui standing only a few feet apart from each other, but looking in opposite directions and not interacting. They had been best friends, but now they were nothing more than statues.

She turned back to Vuilni and shook her. "Come on! Your family needs you back!" Vuilni simply tucked her chin and looked down at Olivia's hands, then back to her face. Olivia whirled. "How do we fix this?" she asked.

"You can't," said Nina. "She's gone."

"There's a fix for everything," Olivia retorted. Grief was overcoming her typically rational demeanor.

Nina looked at the old man next to her, who shook his head. She twisted her lips, eyes falling to her feet. The man said, "That attack was devastating enough to require Lianyu's complete use of its shadow armor. It covered well over a mile's radius. An attack like that was never meant to kill or physically harm. It focuses on the spirit, heart, and mind."

"She's not even talking," Olivia said.

"Because not only has she forgotten who anyone is, including family, she's forgotten words." He looked around Olivia to acknowledge Vuilni. "I'm surprised she can stand. There's no way to restore someone's soul. She's living in her own purgatory now."

Olivia turned back toward Vuilni with forlorn eyes, not scorned by the old man's bluntness, but appreciative. Vuilni had yet to move, but she did open her mouth. All that came out was a hoarse rasp, fumbling with her lips and tongue to form coherent words. This was the price paid for trying to achieve a goal that many might have argued as unnecessary, at least in respect to anyone outside of the Cyn Kingdom. She had one last desperate question. "Can she relearn?"

"Not from my experience," the man said softly.

"What do we do?"

Preloz came to her side and regarded the empty vessel of Vuilni. "It's your choice. This is rare. Lianyu's effects on Cynnish natives are usually concentrated to certain areas: the loss of a specific relationship, memory, or piece of information. They continue to live because there are still plenty of reasons for living. They don't lose everything." He paused. "She did. But that means she also lost the ability to feel, so her lack of purpose doesn't hurt her. She's not mad at it or suffering from depression."

"Quite a dilemma," stated the unnamed man.

"I don't think I can kill her," Olivia whispered. "There might be a fix." She heard the stranger sigh behind her, but he didn't rebuke. She was being stubborn, but who was he to truly know?

"He's right," Preloz said. "I learned a lot before becoming a member of the Mound Guard. We had to know the dangers. We learned extensively about each of the Linsani. When Lianyu attacks, whatever cognizance it steals from its target is gone forever."

Olivia inhaled deeply. Vuilni's dead eyes—dark brown circles pricked with constricted pupils—drifted between the four of them. She opened her mouth only to manage a wheeze.

"I'll take care of the others," said the old man, speaking to Nina. "I'll make it swift, even if they can't feel anything. I suppose that's for my own sake rather than theirs."

"I have to confirm the retrieval unit successfully grabbed the last egg and killed its hatchling," Nina said. "Whenever you're ready, Olivia, we'll be waiting at the rendezvous point."

The two of them left the Jestivan with her Bewahr. Vuilni watched them depart, then turned without sparing her friend a second glance. She roamed the perimeter of the boulders, Lianyu's skeleton crushed beneath and tangled between.

"I can leave you to deal with this on your own," Preloz offered.

"No." Olivia surprised herself with how fast she rejected the idea. She shook her head. "I don't want to be alone afterward."

Preloz nodded, then slipped a knife into her hand.

The decision had been made. Olivia pressed forward, limping on her bone crutch. She fought back the tears and locked her jaw, returning her expression to that brick wall she had worn throughout her childhood. But that didn't mean she wasn't hurting. This was raw pain that overpowered her headache or shattered knee. Her heart beat slowly as she worked to calm herself, reducing this to something methodical by reminding herself this was no longer Vuilni. These were the actions taken by a Stillian royal, a woman of conviction who knew when to prioritize rationality over emotion.

She reached Vuilni and grabbed a fistful of thick, rough braids. She pulled them up to reveal the back of her neck. She drove the knife through. Ice crept from Olivia's wrist, up her hand and fingers, and to the knife's hilt. Vuilni fell limp, dying instantly.

Olivia dropped to the ground, only allowing a grunt to slip between her lips as her injured knee protested the sudden movement. She caught her friend. A sheet of ice blasted out from Olivia's body, coating the black sod in a frozen blue. She held Vuilni against her, blood draining down her chest. Vuilni had been a Diatia; she died a Jestivan.

No longer able to hold them back, the tears crashed forth.

The ice around her melted to water.

81

The Nature of Wrath

Joni's birthday had only been a precursor to Ronossius's true horrors. His actions that night had been vile enough to warrant expulsion from the house—a measure Father had never taken before. Over the next few days, Mother tried fighting the infections that seeped into the wounds and blisters covering her body in bright red patches. Panelle, the one responsible for dumping the pot of boiling hot water over Mother's and Father's heads, wasn't kicked out, but he was quarantined in the parlor. Father frequently visited the room to help heal his spirit.

On the second day following the incident, Tashami asked Father why Ronossius was punished so harshly while Panelle received treatment. "It doesn't seem fair," Tashami said, seated on one side of his parents' bed where his mother slept.

"It wasn't Panelle who did that," Father said.

"But we all saw him."

Father exhaled, then twisted his lips in thought. "He was manipulated."

"Manipu-what?"

"Someone messed with his mind and made him feel like he had no other choice but to do it. And when it comes to someone as young as Panelle or you, that's easy to do. You're impressionable."

"And Ronossius did that?"

"Yes, Son."

"You couldn't fix him like everyone else?"

"First of all, 'fix' isn't the right word," said Father. He was applying an ointment to Mother's shoulders. "I help them. But yes, I couldn't find the success with him as I have with the other children. Ronossius is a special case, one which I had yet to confront until meeting him. I didn't even realize what I was dealing with until that night. If I had known, I wouldn't have let him enter our house with Chelekah. My overconfidence blinded me to my limitations—an issue for which my father used to drill me. 'Practice prudence,' he'd say. 'You're going to get yourself killed,' he'd say."

Tashami paused before replying. He'd never heard anyone mention his grandfather. "What's prudence?"

Father leaned in and narrowed his eyes at Mother's shoulder before dabbing a cotton swab to the skin. "Spiritians have a habit of believing too greatly, believing they can defy all odds. Prudence counters that. It's the ability to discipline yourself by using logic to determine your limits." He noticed Tashami's confused expression and added, "Not biting off more than you can chew. Otherwise, you'll choke."

That made a little more sense, so Tashami moved on to his next question. "What made Ronossius special?"

"You know those screams you hear all days and nights?" Father asked.

"The Linsani."

Father looked up with a serious gaze. "Joni has been sharing too much."

"He only told me what they're called. I swear."

Father's eyes remained still on Tashami for a moment. He returned to his caretaking and said, "Each one is assigned a feeling or state of being, and their screams or presence can affect a human. Usually, it takes a long time for someone to feel the effects—decades. For whatever reason, Ronossius is already showing symptoms of one despite not even being ten years old. He's been highly susceptible to Fennu Feilong, the Linsani of Wrath."

"Their screams can hurt us all the way out here?" Tashami asked, frowning.

"They can, which is why the Void is so dangerous. Ronossius's rage isn't human ... it's beastly, complementing the very monster from which it stems. And that anger he emits is explosive, causing those around him to fear it and, therefore, do anything to get away from it. I'd guess it's more commanding than manipulative. He's too far gone at this point. When a Linsani has its soulless claws in a person that deep, there is no cure or treatment. I had to send him away."

Someone sneezed from the doorway. They turned and saw Nina standing there. "How long have you been there?" Father asked.

She hesitated, then replied, "Not long. I wanted to see how she was doing."

"Not well, but she'll pull through," Father whispered, turning back to his work.

Tashami studied Nina. She didn't enter; she remained in the open doorway. She had been standing there for some time. That gaze was fierce.

*   *   *

Mother never did pull through. She died on the sixth day, and the man dubbed the Unbreakable finally broke.

The weeping was demoralizing, counterproductive to all of the good the man had done for the children. But how could anyone tell a person their suffering wasn't wanted? There was no gray area in matters of true love, not when the magnitude was as heavy-hitting as death. The neighbor—dubbed Porky by the children because of his size—visited a couple of times. He was concerned about the weeping that stretched along the length of road. That was when Tashami learned how good of a man their neighbor was. He vowed to never call him the nickname again. His name was traditional Cynnish and thus complicated to pronounce. Sizzloztick ... or that's what it had sounded like. He never tried pronouncing the name after learning it the first time.

First-night was the worst time of day for Tashami. He made it a point to fall asleep well before midnight and pray his dreams carried him until after six A.M. Those hours were the scariest. Noises carried farther than normal. He swore "things" watched him in his sleep, but as long as he kept his eyes closed, they'd remain banished to the corners of the room. This belief had led to dozens of bed-wettings since he was too scared to open his eyes, leave the room, and find the waste bucket. Only a couple of the children made fun of him for it, as most feared what Nina or Joni would do to anyone who bullied him.

This first-night, however, he couldn't sleep no matter how long he kept his eyes shut. His father was in the midst of one of his worst episodes, and the despair grated Tashami's soul. He refused to open his eyes, but wondered how many of the other children were experiencing the same unrest. Someone sniffled nearby. It sounded like Joni. The eldest Patter sibling had also struggled with their mother's death.

Tashami had to pee so badly that it hurt. He twisted his legs and rolled over onto his back, a position that always helped with relief. Tonight something was particularly wrong ... the air felt different, like it had thickened. One of the children coughed, and the sound didn't travel to his ears with the same ease. It sounded muffled. He didn't like it. It spawned fear within him. The density was heavy and suffocating.

BANG!

Tashami bolted upright, suddenly oblivious to his rule of not opening his eyes. The noise had driven every other child upward, startled out of their slumber. Everyone looked around, confused and afraid. Questions were asked, but they didn't travel. They had to speak at volumes well beyond a whisper to be heard through the strange atmosphere.

"It came from the foyer," Joni said. He was the only one moving, inching toward the door. It was open only a sliver.

"Don't go out there," said Roy, one of the older boys. "Wait for your dad."

Joni slipped out anyway, his courage and spirit always too grand to be contained in his own skin—the same problem their grandfather had apparently warned their father about. He was gone for a few seconds, and the children waited in silent anticipation.

A beastly, wretched roar erupted from outside, shaking the floor, beds, and walls. The reverberations reached Tashami's bones and jostled his organs, the violence of the sound striking the house like an earthquake. Glass shattered. Windows splintered and burst; portraits fell from their fixtures. A wardrobe rattled a few inches away from the wall then toppled over, flinging a heavy glass vase at Sienna's head with enough force to knock her out.

Children scrambled, the roar unrelenting, air growing thicker as it dragged. Joni never returned to the room. Nina found Tashami and escorted him to the window. She punched at cragged glass that clung to the bottom pane, cutting her fist in the process. She stuck her head out and looked down. She retreated and scanned the room. Children huddled in corners or in the closet, most electing to avoid walking out the door from where the sound emanated.

She ran to the toppled wardrobe and began gathering sheets that had spilled across the floor. Blood seeped from her ears and down her neck. Tashami's hands were clasped over his. He looked out the window and his stomach dropped, and the full bladder he'd been contesting finally won. Urine drained. His pants grew hot and wet, and he cried. The drop was too far; he couldn't do it.

The house was only two stories if looking at it from the front, but its backside revealed the half basement. That meant a three-story drop with no awnings below as relief.

"Someone help me tie these!" Nina had to scream at the top of her lungs to overpower the roar. Roy rushed over and lent a hand, starting his own end of the makeshift rope they were trying to make.

Tashami had never been so frightened in his life. He felt the wrath from whatever that thing was outside attempting to break him and this house. He stood with wet pants, looking for any alternative to climbing out that window. Besides, they were taking too long.

He ran to the door, believing he had a better chance next to Joni or finding his father. He was the Unbreakable, a man who wouldn't cave to anything. His mind conveniently ignored the fact that his dad had been weeping for a week straight.

"Tashami, *STOP!*"

Nina's cry was fruitless. The boy bolted onto the strip of walkway that overlooked the foyer. He ran for his father's room, but mistakenly glanced down through the banister's columns. He saw Joni's neck in Ronossius's grip, his feet dangling above the floor as he was held aloft. Blood ran like rivers down Ronossius's fingers and wrist, draining from Joni's throat beneath the hand. Joni was wide-eyed and smacking his lips, blood pouring from his mouth and down his chin ...Tashami watched his big brother die.

Ronossius's roar didn't relent. It morphed into a screech as his head turned to spot Tashami above. He released his grip, and Joni's lifeless body crashed in a heap atop the floor.

Tashami ran for his father's room, confused by the man's absence and traumatized by what he'd just witnessed. The scream proved worse than the roar. The children began spilling out of the room he'd just left, abandoning Nina's plan prematurely. Tashami rammed his shoulder into his father's door and twisted the handle, but it was locked. He slapped his palms against the wood, screaming at the top of his lungs to overpower Ronossius's screech.

"DADDY! DADDY! DADDY!"

He threw his shoulder into the door repeatedly, but it only rattled. His pounded against it with tiny fists, tears streaming down his cheeks as he wailed into the wood. The screech grew sharper and higher, and the cries of children joined the ruckus. He held onto the handle with both hands and pulled himself into the door with all of his might. Still no luck.

"Watch out!"

Tashami spun and saw Nina. She was in a ready stance several paces down the hall. He moved, and she charged. She yelled and hit the door with enough speed to knock it off its hinges, her momentum sending her into a tumble on the other side. Tashami sprinted into the room and froze only a few paces inside.

The Unbreakable occupied the rocking chair in the far corner. He looked nothing like Tashami's father. He was a shell of himself, muscles gone and skin loose. His hair was fully gray, eyes hollow. He hadn't looked like that just days ago. His gaze dragged toward the door, but he made no effort to move upon seeing Nina on the floor and his son in the doorway. Nobody else was in the room with them. Where was mother's body?

822

Nina pushed herself up and groaned. Tashami's mouth hung open, eyes wide and a nose that leaked mucus. The screech in the foyer had returned to its previous roar.

"Ronossius is back, Mr. Patter," Nina said, but it wasn't loud enough to be heard. "He killed Joni!" She leapt onto her feet and ran toward the Unbreakable. She grasped both of his shoulders and shook him. His right arm came loose from its socket. She screamed and recoiled, and he howled in anguish, looking down at his arm but doing nothing else. She stepped back, putting an extra foot of distance between the two of them with each second. His arm hung listlessly down the side of the rocking chair. She paused and then turned with instructions to leave the room. "Let's go, Tashami! He's no use!"

She grabbed his arm and pulled him back into the corridor. "*ROY, NO!*" she bellowed, stopping just outside of the Unbreakable's door.

Roy was placing nooses around the necks of several children, the other ends of the ropes tied securely to the banister of the overlook. He placed one around his own neck and climbed the banister. The rest followed his lead. Nina ran again, but with a limp from her destruction of the door. She almost reached them, but someone stepped onto the landing from the staircase to block her path.

Ronossius had gone silent for a brief moment, blood staining his hands, wrists, and forearms. His eyebrows crumpled at the center, eyes narrow with fury. Nina tried to attack, but he opened his mouth and roared. A blast blew both Nina and Tashami back into the Unbreakable's room. The roar died immediately, returning the house to silence. Tashami looked up, horrified. Roy and the other children stepped off the banister. He heard a series of snaps as the nooses caught their prey with broken necks.

Ronossius advanced, mouth twisting into an evil smirk. Rage fueled every inch of him, a product of Fennu's influence hundreds of leagues away. Tashami had been born and raised in the Void, so he'd grown accustom to the aura it carried. But even this was too far outside the norm. He had never been exposed to such depravity and wickedness, which said a lot considering what lurked in the Void.

The boy's mouth yawned at a contorted angle, wide enough to make Tashami question if he had a jaw. The screech came again, racing over tongue and teeth. Tashami clamped both hands over his ears and continued scooting backward across the floor. Nina grabbed and dragged him to the front window of the master bedroom, where the house was only two stories and an awning rested just below. Her feet crunched over fragmented glass, limping still. She cleared glass residue from the bottom of the window frame, then pulled Tashami by his collar and sat him in the window.

"Jump and land feet first!" Her instructions were barely heard over Ronossius. "It's going to hurt!"

Tashami turned back once more. Father stared out the other window, oblivious to what was occurring. A single finger tapped the arm of his rocking chair—the only sign of life in his body. Tashami's gaze shifted to Ronossius, who had quickened his pace. He turned back toward first-night, closed his eyes, and slipped out the window.

The awning came quicker than he'd predicted, the fear from the potential fall having tricked his eyes. His legs crumpled, and he rolled down the short slope before landing in a bush void of foliage. He fought his way out of the bush—every inch of his body poked and prodded by sticks—and planted his feet on solid ground. He spun and saw Nina leap from the window with more grace despite her injured leg. She hit the canopy in a squat, then sprung forward to avoid the bush and find land. She cursed upon impact, but didn't fall.

"Run!" she screamed.

Tashami couldn't run as fast as her, but she kept her pace even with his, grabbing him and helping him back to stable feet if he stumbled. He looked back one last time to see Ronossius in the window, watching them flee. His mouth had returned to a thin line, but a dull resentment now lay heavy in his eyes. Tashami could hear the dying gasps or cries of his friends, all of whom were still trapped inside.

But he couldn't hear Joni.

82

The Nature of Love

Tashami awoke from the worst nightmare of his life in tears. The memories of his early childhood in the Void had never been accessible to him, and he had despised that. Now he realized how blissful that ignorance had been. That night didn't deserve an encore, but the umbra fairy in his chest only cared about negativity. It was at its strongest, feasting on the parts of his soul that walled off his greatest spiritual detractors … horrors pushed back into the deepest, darkest prisons of his subconscious.

His hand moved to his chest, where tunic covered skin. The difference was slight, but his skin was weakening there. If he looked into a mirror, he'd see splotches of gray working to overtake the natural cream. His body was dying, a feat his mind had no chance of achieving. He would live forever in this state, and it would only worsen exponentially.

The night was young; the nightmare had visited early. The waning orange light of second-day's dusk split across the floor through the boarded window as midnight loomed. Agnos slept in the twin bed against the wall on the other side of the room. Tashami left his bed and did the inadvisable. He abandoned common sense by exiting the confines of their room. But, sometimes emotion trumps all, and one must listen to their heart before all else ... especially if there was barely anything left of that heart on which to cling.

He found the door to Evelyn's room and heard a discussion on the other side. He could tell it was her and Arithmys. He knocked in the pattern only the two women, Tashami, and Agnos knew. It changed on a weekly basis. Evelyn invited him in, and he entered.

Concern wrinkled the center of her brow, and Arithmys's eyes widened. "What happened?" Evelyn asked.

He had forgotten to wipe his face. He could only imagine what he looked like: hollow cheeks streaked with tears, eyelashes clinging to wrinkled skin, and a head of dead, gray hair. "Can I speak with Evelyn alone?"

Arithmys glanced at her friend, then back to him. She nodded and left swiftly, bowing her head in efforts to not let her eyes linger on him. The door closed behind him.

"What's going on?"

Tashami lifted his shirt, revealing a discolored splotch across his chest. It was his skin in the infancy stages of erosion. "Back in the cells at the teleplatforms, Ronossius didn't attack me with his Cynergy. He fed me a strange creature that I later learned to be an umbra fairy after the pericul attack."

She sat speechless for a moment, staring at his chest in subtle horror. He didn't have time to wait for her to process this. "You told me the warden wants you to kill me. I held back on telling you about my circumstance at first, but now, you have the excuse to do so."

"I already knew about the umbra fairy," she said, "yet I haven't been able to bring myself to use that as an excuse so far. So why would my mind change now? I *cannot* kill you, Tashami. I'm a woman of the ice, yes, but that doesn't mean I can abandon all emotion, especially not in regards to a man so dear to Agnos."

He paused. "Listen, he needs Pistimi. All he's ever talked about is finding the purpose of this world and whatever that blue planet is in the sky. It's a comet he's been chasing for well over a decade, an ever-elusive dream he's never been this close to catching."

"It's not *all* he ever talks about," she snapped, genuine anger tightening her features. "I think he talks about *you* more!"

The hair on the back of Tashami's neck stood tall, goose bumps along his arms rising in unison. Heat flooded his chest, rocketed up his throat, and nearly spurred forth more tears. He composed himself. He closed his eyes and exhaled softly. "I'm not spending an eternity with this thing in my chest. Give me a few hours, then you're going to do what I ask of you." He turned for the door.

She stopped him with a gentle voice. "We don't need Pistimi. Arithmys is plenty enough help for the Warpfinate."

He left the room without looking back.

*   *   *

Tashami leaned against the desk of his and Agnos's room for half an hour in the dark. First-night had descended, the campus outside at its quietest with early morning classes just six hours away. His eyes were glued to his friend, who was tangled in his covers in a rather comical way. Agnos snorted and twisted to his right. Tashami smiled.

He looked down at a book on the desk next to him. It was open to a page somewhere in the middle, a ribbon running the length of its centerfold. Agnos's relic glasses lay next to it, a stack of parchment with Sphairian translations beside those. He glanced at the first paragraph:

"I'd like to think Dimiourgos would have helped us had he still been alive during the other Originators' pursuit of me and Mialo, but I find it far more likely he would have rather not involved himself at all. The King of Ethos had never involved himself in matters extending beyond his own kingdom, especially if it involved any sort of violence. His nature as a philanthropist and pacifist were what led to his death in the first place. Stonebody crushed him ... several times. A shame an Originator known for gentleness was neighbors with a man dubbed the King of Brutes."

Tashami shook his head. He had never possessed the same thirst for historical knowledge as Agnos, so why would he have pursued that knowledge so aggressively these past several years? Because they were best friends?

He moved to his own bed and sat on the edge of the mattress, gazing at Agnos. A war raged inside him, a convoluted mess of emotions—a truth trying to lay waste to frauds and escape as the victor. Agnos's body mostly faced the wall next to his bed, but his face was turned toward Tashami, neck twisted, mouth partly open and eyes closed. His chest rose and fell beneath the covers, one arm crushed beneath his body and likely numb. Tashami wished he could achieve sleep anywhere close to that level of unconsciousness. But sleep for him was to exist in another life he had long abandoned and forgotten ... and he couldn't do it again ... never again. The last nightmare had been his breaking point.

The next time he slept, he would not wake.

Tashami approached his friend's bed and stood over him. He blinked out tears, and one hit Agnos's cheek. Agnos's eyes opened slowly, at first confused. Then, noticing the shadow that loomed above him, he recoiled against the wall and yelped. Tashami grinned.

Agnos looked up in search of a face. His shoulders relaxed upon recognition. "Why are you creeping over ..." His question died, eyes adjusting to the darkness and spotting the wetness of Tashami's eyes. "Another nightmare?" he asked. He scooted forward across the mattress, anger in his face. "Let's go. That's it. We're getting Evelyn and finding out what Ronossius did to you. And he's going to fix it. Come on, move."

Tashami did move, but forward and down, lowering himself and advancing on Agnos. The two men's lips locked. Agnos's head recoiled into his neck at first, but the initial shock and tension quickly melted away. He returned the kiss, and Tashami mounted the bed on hands and knees, climbing over him and pulling his mouth away only briefly to unbutton Agnos's shirt.

This was it. This was right. An indescribable, validating feeling of felicity. Tashami's heart didn't just race, but flew feathery light into his throat, spawning new life and vigor from a place the umbra fairy had yet to reach.

His hand moved down Agnos's chest as they kissed, the scholar's frame small enough for Tashami's palm to mold around his side, thumb pressed into the pectoral while fingers gripped part of his back. The absence of muscle and fat didn't detract from Tashami's perception of this man. This was beyond stereotypical conformations of beauty, an attraction too deep for any ocean to fathom; a rush that made comets stand still; and the love a high only the sky could envy.

Nothing could take this from them—not even death.

83

The Nature of Death

Tashami lingered in that doorway for what felt like an eternity, allowing his eyes to feast on Agnos one last time. Getting out of bed had proved a tricky ordeal, but luckily he'd been on the outside and not the side against the wall. He escaped Agnos's embrace with no more than a yawn as protest.

Tashami left the room, leaving his few belongings and a letter behind. He found Evelyn's room, and she reluctantly joined him in his late-night trek out of the abandoned dormitory and across the moonlit campus. Ipsas's grounds were completely vacated save a few patrolling guards, none of whom bothered stopping Evelyn and Tashami. They simply looked their way and continued their business. The High Warden must have forewarned them about this possibility.

Tashami rapped Sylial's office door with conviction. Evelyn lingered behind with uncharacteristic gloom. He was pleased that she was here, considering her disdain for this idea earlier in the night. But this wasn't the true test. That wouldn't come until she needed to act. He had faith in her. She was a Stillian woman after all.

"Could have picked a better time—"

"—to die?" he asked, finishing her sentence. "I'd say two A.M. is reasonable. Something poetic about the dead of night." He knocked again.

"Doing it away from Agnos isn't going to ease his pain."

"It'll ease mine."

She said nothing else, and he banged on the door. He heard a barrage of curses on the other side followed by heavy, purposeful footsteps. Warden Sylial was undoubtedly readying a verbal and possible physical assault on whoever had the nerve to disrupt his sleep.

There was a series of clicks as bolts were unlocked, followed by a strange sound Tashami didn't recognize. The door opened to reveal a haggard and tired Sylial. He looked nothing like Tashami remembered from the brief glimpse he had seen of the man in the forest months ago. His expression of rage took little time to soften upon recognizing his guests. He opened the door wider and stepped back, a toothy smile stretching his lips. He lifted a hand to rub the sleep out of his eyes as a chuckle rolled over his tongue. "Timing aside, this is too good to be true," he said. "Come in, come in."

Sylial closed a side door that led to a bed chamber before lowering himself into his office chair. Tashami and Evelyn elected to remain standing.

"Can we make this quick?" Tashami asked.

"Certainly. I'm sure you've been suffering long enough as it is. No need to drag it out any longer. Just give me a moment. My provisions weren't well prepared for a visit at this hour." He blinked, and both irises turned bright red and began recording. He spoke, but not to them—to whomever was on the receiving end of his telepathy elsewhere on the campus. "Look who I've got here." A pause. Then, a smile. "Yes, yes. One of the 'legends' themselves." Another pause. "More than ready. Listen, summon Ronossius to my office. He knows who to bring with him." His irises returned to their natural color, and he studied Tashami intensely.

"I'm not letting you do this until I see Pistimi is alive, well, and free of bonds," Tashami warned.

Sylial sucked in air through clenched teeth. "I can guarantee two of the three. While she's breathing, her condition isn't ideal." He waved the matter away with a flippant hand. "You can see for yourself when she gets here, and then you can reassess your commitment to this trade." His eyes met Evelyn's. "Awfully quiet there, Evelyn."

She said nothing, only stared at the desk.

"You've killed before," he said. "Just add this to the tally. Or think of it as you doing a friend a favor. It's not like he's destined for anything good considering his state."

Tashami gave her a sidelong glance. She was struggling with what came next. Killing soldiers on a battlefield wasn't the same concept as taking the life of a friend unprovoked. But he needed her to do this. And as much as Agnos would have denied it, he needed it, too.

Fifteen minutes passed before a knock came from the door. Sylial had been waiting patiently in his chair, slippers kicked up on the desk, while Tashami roamed the office to busy his mind, occasionally glancing at Evelyn to find her standing in the same spot and still staring at the desk. It was as if she wasn't present.

A woman entered first, tall and golden-haired. She was big, too, a tight-fitting uniform hugging considerable bulk. Was she a guard to make sure everything that followed went according to plan?

Ronossius entered next, accompanied by a young brunette woman. Her hair was cut boyishly short, displaying a round face and wide neck. The lack of emaciation ruled out starvation. Whatever she had endured while imprisoned didn't seem to be physical unless the evidence was hidden beneath her clothes. Knowing High Warden Sylial's Devish roots, however, meant the damage could have been deeper ... the mind.

Evelyn watched Pistimi pass. Sylial pressed a finger against the shackles bonding her wrists, and a series of locks unlatched, iron clattering to the hardwood. He did the same for those at her ankles. Ronossius took his post to the side of the room, watching from a distance. The muscular woman stood next to the desk.

Silence drowned the room. Sylial bathed in it, eyes drifting across the many faces with subtle delight. He had yet to bother lighting a candle, trusting the moon to cast a fitting luminescence for the mood. It was theatrical, and the perfect setting for a political man to posture.

"Are we all ready?" The phrasing of the question suggested it was meant for everyone in the room, but his eyes had fixed themselves on Evelyn. Tashami feared she might try something reckless. If she chose to attack rather than adhere to the transaction, she and Tashami would be faced with High Warden Sylial, Ronossius, and the mystery lady built like a brick house—a gamble not worth taking. She had spoken of Sylial's combat expertise on plenty of occasions. He was on par with Grand Director Poicus, but in his prime. That was something Tashami never wanted to witness, especially not in his weakened state. Poicus had been formidable enough in his nineties.

Evelyn said and did nothing. Something in her eyes must have suggested the answer to Sylial, for he instructed the blonde woman to approach Tashami.

"Elga here is Spiritian," Sylial said. He was still leaning back in his chair with his slippers kicked up on the desk. "She's lived in the Dark Realm for a couple decades now, seven of those years spent here as a healer to our Cynnish students. She will perform the banishment of the umbra fairy, after which Evelyn has approximately five minutes to plunge the blade in Tashami's throat before natural death occurs."

Tashami glanced at the ex-Diatia once more. Five minutes was too long. It gave her too much time to think and hesitate.

"If you fail to murder Tashami before the natural death," the High Warden continued, "then Pistimi returns to her imprisonment, and I will have the other Jestivan killed in front of you. Then, I'll feed you an umbra fairy and expel you to the Linsaniun Mounds where you can discover if that legend of Pytatia Henye is true."

A long pause followed. Evelyn's lips remained closed, eyes unmoving, body unflinching. Sylial nodded, and a resolute steadiness solidified his expression. "Proceed, Elga."

The fellow Spiritian stood in front of Tashami, a pitying curve to her brow line. Despite being strangers, she didn't want to do this, but it was her responsibility to see it through. He reassured her that. "I understand," he whispered. "This is what must be done lest I desire an eternity of rot, rage, and sorrow."

Her eyebrows and lips flattened, eyes expressing appreciation for his encouragement. She placed a hand against his chest. A cooling breeze broke through skin and swirled beyond his ribs. His heart—or something in its vicinity—fluttered. It became an enigmatic sensation of relief and agony, but while the relief was his own, the pain came from the parasitic fairy as it succumbed to the Spirit Chains. He could feel it crawling away from the heart. It burrowed through his pectoral muscle. He grunted and nearly doubled over, but Elga's hand grasped his shoulder and kept him upright, the other hand still firmly planted against his chest.

His skin bulged beneath his tunic, and the fairy broke free as skin and fabric tore. It fell and plopped onto the floor, where it then made a desperate attempt to crawl away. Elga's hands weakened, but she made an effort to guide him to the floor.

"Get away from him," Sylial said firmly.

She did so, leaving Tashami in fetal position, clutching at his bleeding chest. His groans were punctuated with violent roars that traveled beyond the office walls, black blood pooling beneath him like oil. Forehead pressed against the floorboards, he twisted his head and looked up at Evelyn, who watched with little to no emotion.

The room was cold. Her silvery-bluish hair sparkled with frost against the moonlight. Ivory clouds plumed in front of Tashami's mouth with each breath. It was then he realized she hadn't remained silent out of guilt, fear, sadness, or apprehension, but apathy. She had tapped into a Stillian woman's strongest trait in order to perform a monstrous task with the calmest, coldest of efficiencies, as if it was something menial.

Tashami found himself suddenly in fear. The calm into which he had slipped, stemming from a night of closure and thus acceptance, was now gone. There was something about seeing a Stillian woman at her emptiest that froze a person to the very core. Those were dead eyes, as barren and blue as the Diamond Sea. He couldn't blame her for making his final moments a terror. He had asked her—no, *forced* her into this position. Whatever she needed to do to ease the burden was understandable. If he searched for a silver lining, it was the numbing of the pain with the frigid temperatures.

"In the throat."

Sylial's reminder was casual, and ironically gentle. She would kill the Jestivan in the way he desired. This was a business transaction. At this point, she could do nothing to change the outcome. Tashami was minutes away from death. He felt his lungs struggling to retain oxygen.

Evelyn closed her eyes for a long five seconds, the only betrayal to her emotionless state. A sheet of ice spread around her feet, a testament to how hard she was trying to suppress the fury. Shivers overcame Tashami's groans, teeth rattling in his head. He looked away from her, eyes pointed to the floor next to his head, gaze distant to the memories he had shared with the boy he loved.

Evelyn lifted her foot. A stalactite of ice hung from the sole of her boot. He heard the words of his older brother, said after a mundane game of hide-and-seek in the orphanage, just before it plunged.

You were strong. You were brave.

Then, Tashami hurt no more.

84

The Nature of Humanity

Evelyn stared down at her boot, a neck crushed below it, sable blood trickling down pale skin to join the puddle beneath. She couldn't see Tashami's eyes; he had closed them right before the moment of impact. He had been frightened, and none of the images that she assumed raced through his mind in those final seconds had made it any easier.

The cold was bad enough to affect her, proving that Stillian genes had a limit. Her heart didn't beat, but tapped dully with several seconds passing between each one. Blood inched through her veins at a glacial pace. For Stillian women, these were the measures taken to commit atrocities like this one, and pulling herself out of this state all came down to this moment. If she didn't want to slip into the tundra from which there was no escape, she had to claw her way back to humanity right now.

She went to work.

She stared at the fresh corpse. No, it was more than that. She *studied* the *vessel* in which this man's soul had flourished for over two decades. She recalled the stories of this man. There were many nights spent in the captain's cabin of the Mythmaker as it sailed the Sea of Light, listening to Agnos's stories of his best friend. He had been in a somber place because of Tashami's absence on the voyage, so Evelyn's time and attention became his outlet.

This man—now robbed of life because of her action—had braved the Void as a child and again as a teenager. He had faced the mutilated and undead body of his father, then continued to function in life after the fact. He had defended Agnos in Sodai's Chasm, injuring the foolish pirate who tried mugging him. He was the sole reason why the infamous ship of Gray Whale, the Whale Lord, hadn't capsized in one of the wickedest storms it had ever faced. He had taken on an Adrenian fleet. He had saved Agnos from drowning in the Region of Raging Tides, making sure the scholar's mighty dream didn't die just moments after obtaining the chronicle. And he had done all of this while starving himself of what he really wanted. This had been a man deprived of love, and she wasn't sure why he'd denied himself it for so long.

She looked at his lips. They had closed around Agnos's tonight. Surely, they had. The possibility granted her some comfort. *Tell me your eyes closed with his taste on your lips, a hunger settled before death.*

To not consider all of this would be to spit on his grave. Envision him as the whole human he had been, encompassing spirit, heart, and mind. She wouldn't be overtaken by the ice. She wouldn't fall victim to the same disease of her mother, who had killed her father because he could no longer give her anymore children. Seed tainted, she had deemed him useless in his role as a husband. After that, she had slipped into the tundra, heart cold and desolate.

Evelyn wouldn't join her mother; she could prove it now. She removed her ice-spiked boot from Tashami's throat and knelt next to him, placing a hand against his cheek. She acknowledged what she had done. She absorbed his every detail, every story, and she stored them in a place where she would never forget. She'd bear their weight on her shoulders until the day she died.

White clouds dissipated more and more with each breath. The sheet of ice surrounding her retracted back to the center—her own body. The frozen numbness fled her skin as the temperature slowly restored itself to normal.

Somewhere in the background of her consciousness, Evelyn heard Elga inhale sharply. Then came her voice. "She did it."

"That's why she was made a Diatia," Sylial replied.

Words of admiration. They were impressed by what they saw, like it was nothing more than a show. That hurt Evelyn more than anything else prior.

The tears then came. Not for Tashami or Agnos, but herself.

The nature of humanity.

85

Lightning

Bryson carried himself with a new demeanor. With everything he had seen since becoming a Jestivan, his mindset had to change if he wanted to win. King Vitio and Queen Delilah were dead. Shelly had to be monitored to prevent attempted suicide. Lilu would have been assassinated had it not been for the selfless act of Vistas, who was currently straddling the fence between life and death in a Dunami Hospital emergency room.

Despite all logic, blame went to one man in Bryson's mind ... his father. Mendac had gone beyond exacting revenge when returning to the Dev Kingdom. He raped, pillaged, and burned. The atrocities he committed, which then extended into other Dark Realm kingdoms, spurred people like Storshae, Toono, and Apoleia into the directions they took. They followed a similar path of destruction to those around them in their search for vengeance or redemption, but they had been dealt with or confronted already.

Mendac was alive again, given an undeserved second chance at life. And now he was fighting on behalf of the Dark Empire? This was beyond personal vendettas, philosophical differences, or familial bonds. It was a matter of duty. Bryson had a responsibility to remove his father from this world, for the sake of the world. Shame, anger, and sorrow slipped away. He had severed his tie to his father's shadow after learning of his crimes. Murdering Whistle had awoken the part of him needed to involve himself in a war of this scale. Two empires were at odds. If he wanted to conquer enemies like these, a moral compass wasn't always the best navigator.

Most importantly, he needed to protect Shelly, Lilu, and L.K., which was why he found himself in front of the solidified stalactite wherein stood a captured Intelius—one of the five Essences of Tahar. This man—this *thing* was the last line of defense for a royal firstborn. Aside from a firstborn's own power and the assistance of a guardian in the form of a Branian, there was a third layer of safeguards unknown to anyone but the Empress. The Essences could detect the presence of an enemy Bewahr in the kingdom from which they originated. While they couldn't attack the threat—trapped in their solidified state—they could alert Empress Tonitrua through the quartz. She could then take the necessary steps to handle the problem.

Intelius had always been a thorn in her side. Ever since she became the first Originator of the Light Realm to stop harvesting her Essence, he became spiteful and bitter toward her. After bursting across Kuki Sphaira's atmosphere into currents, his physical self was imprisoned by Tahar—the mother of Essences who lived in the quartz—on this island. Since then, he refused to do his job, which meant Tonitrua was always in the dark when it came to the Intel Kingdom. She wouldn't know if Bewahr intruded, and the Intelian royals would be in danger. This final safeguard existed in case there was ever a royal firstborn who refused their Branian's help. Branian couldn't force themselves to be summoned if their charge wills them not to—even if their life is in danger.

This meant Bryson had a chance to become his family's divine protector. If he took Intelius's position, he'd gain the Essence's ability to detect the presence of any level of Gefal in the Intel Kingdom. And the perks didn't stop there according to Tonitrua. Unlike Intelius, Bryson wouldn't be trapped, which meant not only would he have the ability to roam the Empire freely, but he could travel instantaneously to any location in the Intel Kingdom. He could be at Shelly or L.K.'s side in less than a heartbeat.

For reasons unknown to Bryson, Intelius couldn't be killed by any of the Light Realm's energies: Intel, Spirit, Adren, Passion, or Archaic. It took an energy of the Dark Realm: Dev, Cyn, Still, Power, or Prim. This was why none of the Bozani could execute this task. It made Bryson the only suitable candidate.

Bryson stared at the spire of quartz towering above him, the vague outline of a human figure hidden deep within. The three Strasan— Magnifica Solaris, Rhysel Kawi, and Naipa Levlin—watched from a safe distance behind, nothing but a vast land of ivory stretching around them. His fingers were numb, temperature plunging and heart slowing, each inhale sharp and prickly down his trachea. The quartz beneath his feet responded strangely, splintering outward in an array of webs and climbing the base of the spire.

He appreciated this level of aplomb. He had a lot of respect for Stillian women if this was the emotional equilibrium they maintained throughout their lives. It cleared his mind of noise, granting him precious space only suitable for the necessities. He was thankful for how naturally this had come to him; it proved he was his mother's child. It had always lurked within him since birth. If his chills hadn't been a constant reminder, the vision following his surgery had been a cry for attention. It was a vision he had forgotten until murdering Whistle, when he climbed that snowy mountain and spoke with Stillinia from Thyella's perspective.

Tapping into that emotional equilibrium, he regarded the spire with a face that could make Olivia's brick wall crumble. He raised a palm. Ice shot from his hand and broke through the quartz prison with ease. A thunderous boom shook the ground. The frozen pillar extending from his palm impaled the Essence within and continued beyond the prison on the other side.

That was it. Nothing climactic. No life-or-death struggle. Not everything was.

The Essence flowed into him, and he *became* lightning.

86

Abandon the Path

The power jarred Bryson.

Whenever he used his Intel Energy in the past, it rushed through his body. His hairs would stand at end; his insides would prickle. This, however, was all-encompassing. His entire body—microscopic to macroscopic—felt like a constant buzz, similar to the sensation of numb, tingly lips after consuming just the right amount of alcohol. He moved his arm to check his skin, and that buzz deviated into a pulse with the motion. He blinked, believing what he had seen to be a trick of the light. Raising his other arm, he saw it again. His skin fuzzed around the edges, and electricity cackled around it.

He turned to the Strasan, each of whom watched with their own version of surprise. Naipa's head was tilted, arms crossed. Rhysel's brows were furrowed. Magnifica's eyes were wide, jaw set and lips thin. It spoke volumes to illicit such reactions out of beings of their caliber.

Pure power flowed through him. No, he *was* the power. He was Intelius.

*   *   *

Himitsu watched as Kopios Soteria, Lord of the Thousand-Layer Loess, was hauled away on an open wagon out of the Heresy Butte's entry tunnel. The man sat on the rear with both legs and arms bound to a bar, two guards seated on either side. He gazed back in the direction of his once-home, haunted eyes searching for either his fortress or daughter.

Kaylee wasn't here. She had made arrangements to acclimate the Accus family into the Loess society, using Doctor Mengai and the Piety Smith, Joselina, as the two other women to help spearhead the cause. As valiant of a cause that it was, Himitsu understood the real reasoning behind an important meeting being scheduled at this time. Kaylee couldn't watch her father leave so soon ... not like this. She had spent a lifetime without him; she could manage another.

Crowds converged behind Himitsu, clogging the street to watch their lord disappear through the tunnel. He didn't know what they were thinking, but the general silence hinted at sorrow. Kopios and his father had been great men to these people. They had contained the wealth to this small sector while the rest of the Loess died slow deaths. Most refused to wander into the inlands. If they left the Heresy Butte, it was to vacation at one of the few other sectors of wealth, like the hot spring resorts in the Steam Butte. The citizens here were surrounded by pious minerals, but ignorant of its origins. They weren't taught about the Piety Mines or the Accus family. That had been erased from their history over the decades.

Part of Himitsu felt badly for Kopios. He had grown up in this regime thinking it normal. He gained the position of its lord and simply continued the path his father had already been forging, manipulated and led astray by cruel minds such as Kings Dolomarpos and Itta. The positive influences in his life had been zero. He became a victim of his environment. But, despite all of this, Himitsu couldn't forgive a father abandoning his child. And that's what he had done to Kaylee.

Himitsu decided to walk alone back to the Soteria fortress. Archain soldiers, brought from the capital with his mother, walked a couple hundred feet ahead. They wouldn't grant him too much space, fearing an attack from civilians—an unnecessary precaution, as there was no one here who could hurt him. But they also felt they couldn't completely defy his order to leave him alone, given his status as the son of the Spy Pilot. He'd take what he could.

A rarity confronted him at the fortress's main gate: his mother, waiting patiently, unbothered by the horde of responsibilities she'd taken on since arriving to the Loess. Ophala Vevlu had quickly become the epicenter of all matters of political or economic importance. It was eerily similar to what she had done after assassinating Toth Brench, proving no matter how hard she physically tried avoiding the throne, she would always be there in spirit and mind. She wasn't a Royal Head, but most saw her as a queen.

Ophala dismissed the soldiers and waited for them to be out of earshot before taking her son in a different direction along fortress grounds. Here came a talk, and likely a heavy one at that. That was fine. Himitsu was ready. She needed to hear his truths, and he needed to vent.

"How long's it been since you've talked to Kaylee?" she asked, handing him a sweet she had been carrying in her robe pocket.

He took it and popped it in his mouth. "A few days," he said around the candy. "She hasn't exactly been around."

"You haven't exactly put in the effort."

He looked sideways at her, mulling over the accusation. He turned forward again as they strolled past stone monuments of ancient pieces that were taller than them. "I was just moments away from murdering her father. She saw me, covered in the blood of other people and prepared to hack down the man. And she knew I was going to do it without ever telling her the truth of who he was. So forgive me, Mother, if I don't feel like I'm ready to face her ... or, more important, I don't think she's ready to face me."

A starling flew in their direction, undoubtedly carrying more information from somewhere in the Loess that needed Ophala's attention. She wasn't carrying her ancient, Cheiraskinia, so she wouldn't have been able to access its mind. She dismissed the bird with a wave of the hand. It banked a turn immediately, darting toward a distant fortress wall to perch and wait.

"You know what," Himitsu said, cutting off his mother just as she opened her mouth to speak. "I think the better question is why are you so comfortable interacting with her? You don't find that concerning? You ordered a mission to have her father assassinated behind her back, using her own motivations to become an apothecary as false pretense to travel out here in the first place. You groomed and manipulated her, yet you can carry on afterward as if you hadn't. And you know you can get away with it because of the level of respect and admiration she has for you. Ever since she's met you, she's only wanted your validation and acknowledgement."

"I'm a spy, Son." The delivery was firm, absent of motherly tenderness. They rounded a corner of the fortress and found a stone garden, interestingly shaped rocks stacked in abstract formations. Vines, capable of growing with limited sunlight, wrapped around and between them. "Grooming?" she said. "Just one of the many tools of manipulation that I've learned over the decades doing this job. There are times when empathy must be cast aside. Unfortunately, there are no set rules for when those times are determined. It's purely subjective, but I like to think my perception is closer to the moral path than most."

Himitsu took a seat on a stone bench. Ophala remained standing, looking down at him with disapproval. "And I have all the proof to back that up," she continued. "That empathy has put people at risk. Look at my shortcomings. I couldn't see what King Itta was up to because I ignored my instincts in favor of believing he wasn't like his father. I accepted a position in Rim overseeing the Archaic Mountains when that had been nothing but a diversion. Then there were the Gravity Trials, where I was too empathetic and understanding of Rhyparia. I'm the person responsible for freeing her to commit some of the worst atrocities the world's ever seen."

Himitsu's brows furrowed. "What?"

"She dropped the moon on the Power Kingdom."

Ophala might as well have dropped the other moon on Himitsu's head. He was left speechless.

"The extreme measures I took that day to save her from the noose resulted in not only the deaths of several soldiers who had chased Senex down to recapture her, but of hundreds of thousands of people in Ulna Malen." She paused and gazed into the distance, her final sentence losing the firmness to dance along a nonexistent breeze. "All of that death to save one person."

Himitsu heard it. That was where his mother broke. If Rhyparia had done that—and he had no reason to doubt his mother's information—then he could understand why it would break her. He racked his memory of countless history lessons at Phesaw, unable to recall an event with such a massive scale of death. Rhyparia had wiped out a capital and much more beyond that. And then there were the floods wreaking havoc on port cities, damaging property and taking more lives.

"So forgive me, Son, if I found it fit to not repeat history. I spared Kaylee the details of the operation in fear that she would compromise everything by revealing confidential information to the enemy. Who am I to expect a girl to not explore the nature of a man who she knew to be her father? Knowing that would have only triggered her curiosities. And then to let her know we planned on killing him? Well, asinine, really.

"But what did it allow us to accomplish? I disregarded the feelings of one person, but we saved tens of thousands of lives here in the Loess from oppression. We freed the legendary Accus family from enslavement, and all it took was lying to one girl." Ophala shook her head. "And even then, she still had the intuition to figure out we were going to assassinate the man. And she helped us in his capture, even after discovering he was her father. Kaylee is a highly practical young woman, and I've seen that in spades over the past few days. I know I hurt her, but let me assure you I do not regret it."

Himitsu held his mother's gaze, then asked, "How did you torture him?"

Her lips thinned, and she saw her swallow through the motion of her throat. He was referring to Mesitis Epidex, the Skill Broker who had frequently served as the middleman between Archaic royalty and the Loess Lord. His mom had never told him how she acquired the information about Lost Wisdom's secret agenda from him, but Himitsu assumed a man like him would have had a very guarded tongue.

"Had you ever tortured someone before that?" he asked, realizing she refused to answer the first question.

She shook her head, and he got the response he wanted from her face. Humanity remained inside her. Even when torturing an evil man, there was no place for apathy or happiness—at least, not for a good person. The horror was evident in her eyes.

"I'm done, Mom. I can't be like you." He got up and hugged her. "Don't take that as an insult. Just not everyone's cut out to be ruthless. I thought I could when I killed those soldiers at the Dev Kingdom's telecluster my first year as a Jestivan, but it's wearing on me. This was a step too far." He let go and walked past. "Whether it's here or somewhere else, I'm finding a home, settling down, and removing myself from destruction."

87

The Cold Truth

Agnos woke alone and confused. He didn't feel the heat of Tashami's body against his back, so he rolled over to discover his friend's absence. He pushed himself up with his one arm and looked toward the other bed ... unoccupied. The room was also empty, morning light slashing through cracks in the wooden boards covering the window. Agnos's first cause for concern was the fact that neither of them ever left this room. The other was the state of Tashami's bed, blankets folded back hastily and pillows crumpled. That man *always* made his bed in the morning.

The worst came to Agnos's mind: abduction. Emotional fear squelched the logical improbability. He sprung from his bed and nearly regretted the swift movement. His muscles were sore in spots he didn't know could become sore. He fought through it and rushed the door.

He came to a screaming halt on the other side. Evelyn sat in the trashed hallway on the floor next to his door. Her elbows sat on bent knees, thighs pressed against her torso, forehead resting atop forearms. She looked up, exposing red-strained eyes. He couldn't tell if it was from sleep deprivation or tears ... or both.

"Where's Tashami? What's wrong?"

"He's dead."

"No he's not." His response came faster than his brain could process her implication. He paused, and swallowed, searching for something lighter in her expression. He saw only intensity. Warmth crept up his back and spread throughout his shoulders and neck. Tears flooded his vision, distorting Evelyn's face. She wouldn't lie about this, but he couldn't believe her. "He's not," he croaked.

"I wasn't given much of a choice," she said.

"What are you talking about?"

"I killed him."

Her tone was steel, and the chill became unnoticeable as he threw himself at her. He was acting without processing again. The impact knocked her over, but she didn't protect herself. He pinned his knee into her side and swung at her face, wailing all the while. His weak fist didn't give up, connecting with cheek, jaw, and eye. His body racked and convulsed as he wept, his lungs quickly losing oxygen from the physical and emotional strain.

He believed her. She was a Stillian woman. If anyone was capable of it, it was her. She had taken his friend ... his love.

And he was devastated.

Multiple hands grabbed and pulled him away from the icy witch. He howled at them, trying to break free as they dragged him backward. He had never experienced something like this—so raw and carnal.

He clenched his fist and just now realized it was broken and smattered with blood. He let his head roll back to meet the eyes of those holding him. They were two women: one familiar—Arithmys—and one not.

He didn't care. He wanted at Evelyn one more time.

*   *   *

Agnos was numb. He lay in bed with his gaze to the tattered ceiling, drywall peeling. Arithmys had pulled up a chair next to him and was tending to his hand. Evelyn lay in Tashami's bed while Pistimi applied ointments to her face. He had discovered who she was after Arithmys used her name in conversation. That meant both Prim Diatia were now here, which should have excited him. But he feared the price paid to achieve it. The timing of Tashami's death and Pistimi's appearance couldn't have been coincidental.

"Why'd you do it?" he asked, voice distant. "How'd it come to that?"

Evelyn gave him the story. She explained the ultimatum provided by High Warden Sylial and how she expressed her reluctance to Tashami, who didn't care to hear it. She acknowledged that she still had a choice. She ended up choosing to kill the Jestivan, tapping into the darkest, coldest dungeons of a Stillian heart to go through with it—a journey from which she was still recovering. That hollow look on her face was a sign.

Agnos remained silent after that, analyzing every detail. Tashami had been fed an umbra fairy. If he had continued living, it would have been in misery. It didn't matter if he had six months or six years left of healthy emotional and spiritual balance, eventually both would degrade. And the moment the umbra fairy had been expelled from his chest, he was set for death anyway. Evelyn simply shortened that span. Her hand was forced. Either his spirit and health died while hosting the parasite, he physically died following its expulsion, or she killed him and reaped some sort of exchange: Pistimi's release. All three options resulted in a form of death, and she had concluded that it best they got something in return. A highly logical conclusion.

Yet, bitterness lay dormant beneath Agnos's current numbness. He didn't hurt people, but he had just assaulted Evelyn. That aggression should have been directed toward Ronossius and Warden Sylial, the former having fed Tashami the umbra fairy while the latter extorted that act. Agnos was also confused. He was used to the Jestivan confronting immeasurable odds by force. When Olivia was taken, Bryson and company hunted her capturers down. When the Dev Assassins infiltrated Phesaw, the Jestivan entered the Rolling Oaks to find them. The Whale Lord clashed with an Adrenian naval fleet. The Mythmaker pursued leviathans down the Knowledge River. Anger rose within him again.

"There's always another way, Evelyn."

"No, there wasn't. If you're hinting at physicality, it wouldn't have worked. Not everything can be solved by violence. I am one person. You expect me to defeat both High Warden Sylial and Ronossius? Would you ask Tashami to defeat Grand Director Poicus and Toshik? The world doesn't work that way. A hundred grunts don't even equate to the skill of two such beings."

"You had help," said Agnos.

"Tashami wasn't at full strength because of the fairy, and Arithmys isn't a fighter—nor would I ever ask her to put herself in that moral dilemma." Both were valid points, but it was what went unsaid that sounded the most damning. She hadn't bothered mentioning Agnos, for he couldn't fight. He would struggle against one grunt, let alone a hundred of them—or even worse, Poicus and Toshik. His head rolled to the side as he studied Evelyn across the room's width. Her face was blocked by Pistimi, who was leaning over her head to dab at wounds.

Evelyn had gone silent on purpose. She didn't mention him to make a point, knowing it would have more impact. He knew what she was thinking: *I know you're mad at me, and you deserve to be. But don't pretend you are free of blame. If you were stronger, perhaps we could have saved him.*

She reached up a hand to touch Pistimi's forearm, then pushed her gently to the side, opening a sightline between the Archain and Stillian. She looked at Agnos, one eye buried by gauze, butterfly bandages strained by cuts in her cheeks. "I do appreciate who you are. I find solace in this world, knowing there are people out there who couldn't harm a fly. You know how many times I've expressed my upmost respect about that trait of yours. However, being that way means you also have to understand its weaknesses and the repercussions that can come from it. If you don't, then that respect is lost. Accept who you are." She paused and took a deep breath. "I'll shoulder my load of responsibility; you shoulder yours."

88

As Always

Yama was on one knee, a hand planted firmly in the grass in front of her, back bent as she heaved for oxygen. The only reason why she wasn't on all fours was because she refused to succumb to that point of exhaustion. She had always thought of Master Ichi's training when she was a child as extreme, but nothing came close to this. These were exercises reserved for no one but the master, herself. Not even her most elite students suffered through anything this rigorous. These were methods of Adren Assassins.

She rose to her feet, laboriously, ankles and thighs sporting weights meant for Powish giants to lift. She wore a jacket similar to chainmail, yet thicker and infinitely times heavier. It bore down into her shoulders, leaving permanent impressions in her skin.

The whip smacked home before she saw Ichi raise it. Yama leapt to the side just as the whip cracked the cobbles on which she had just been standing. Another lash, and she sidestepped again. She spent only a split second on each spot, forced to move if she wanted to spare her bare feet the pain of the whip. Her success or failure each day was determined by the number of lacerations across the top of her feet.

There were a lot.

Master Ichi may have missed the assassin gene that had gone to her sister, Soraku, but that didn't mean she lacked the speed. She was still a Fuuna. These weights granted Yama no favors in avoiding the woman's lightning-quick lashes. She was thankful for Rhyparia's gravitational speed training. It made these weights somewhat bearable.

Ichi paused and stared at her winded niece. It took all the energy Yama could manage to not collapse. Ichi smiled. "You are a marvel. That's it for today." She turned and walked away. "Can't wait for the storms."

Yama fell to her knees and looked at the sky. *Storms?*

*   *   *

The eyes on him were few, but Toshik still felt the pressure as he stood in the open doorway that led to nothing but open air. Solace Skimentis, Yinyon's mayor, watched from his office chair, leaning back with one leg kicked over the other, hands in his lap. Kolver Skimentis, innkeeper of the village's only inn, was a dot on top of the hill in the distance. He stood between the two oaks that protected the graves of Leon Suadade and Ataway Kawi. A goat stood next to him, but its focus was on chewing the rope that bound it to the tree.

Toshik spotted a few citizens tending to their farms and children playing in a pond. None looked this way, but he felt like the world was watching. That was the presence Solace had, and Toshik didn't want to fail in front of him after spending four months trying to achieve this. He thought of his own ponds back at his estates. The speed at which he ran on the pond floor near the end of his training had helped the transition into this task: clearing the gap between this office and that hill in a single bound. He readied himself, curling his toes over the floor's edge and bending the front knee.

"Don't forget your sword."

He turned to find Solace had already flung it at him. He caught it last second by the hilt, eyes narrowed.

"You have to be able to do it with a sword in your hand," the mayor said. "What if you need to cover that distance during a fight? Are you going to drop your sword before you take off or just gamble and assume you can move at the same speed with a sword as opposed to without?"

Toshik shook his head and turned back to the village. The first option was impractical—he wasn't dropping his weapon during a fight—and the second one was careless, for it didn't take into account the added drag of carrying a loose object. He would have to adjust his approach, but first he needed a new location for his scabbard. He had carried it as his side his entire life, but that would cause too much disruption.

He retrieved his scabbard from the armchair in the office's sitting area. Through some finagling, he managed to repurpose its straps for his back rather than his hip. He approached the doorway once more, toes curling over the edge, legs positioned for the perfect first—and only—step. He had hurt himself over a dozen times the past few months in his trial runs, none of which came close to this distance. Solace never let him practice using his doorway, so Toshik had resorted to the rooftops of the few families who would allow it.

He needed an extra push, something to will him into accomplishing this test. Then, he looked up and saw her, hanging from a lower branch of the oak to the right. Jilly swayed to and fro with a smile only she could manage, sunhat dangling down her back, a curtain of straight, golden hair splitting at her shoulders. She wore a pink sundress down to her knees, collar and hems bordered in ivory lace. Her shoes lay in the grass below her, for she only ever played barefoot. When Toshik used to give her foot massages at the end of the day, he could always tell just how great her day had been judging by the amount of dirt on the soles of her feet.

And just like that, the pressure alleviated, calmness swam through him. Adrenians prided themselves on their responsibilities and seeing them through. His was to avenge her.

He took that first step, and it was his only.

Kolver stood in front of him, grinning broadly. Two gravestones stood to either side, welcoming him to a culture long forgotten. A teasing breeze rustled the oak's branches, as if to tell him she was still in there somewhere ... as silly as always.

As Jilly as always.

89

A Gentle End

Creep spent his time in recovery limping his way around Dunami's many courtyards and hedge mazes with the help of a cane. Fresh air and seclusion was all he wanted. He was bruised and broken—an ankle wrapped firmly in a stiff cast—from the stampede, but he was happy to know the boy he had escorted out was in good health. He had saved one life at least.

He'd taken two others.

Wendel and Periphan LeAnce were dead. An antidote hadn't made it to Wendel in time. Creep had botched his assignment by killing an innocent, and a mistake of that magnitude was not forgiven. It didn't matter if poisons weren't his specialty. It didn't matter if Pilot Ophala abandoned advisement, allowing a clueless Intelian narcissist to take her spot. As the individual executing the objective, he should have taken all measures to complete it correctly. Accountability was an important virtue for Creep. Well, not all that important considering the state in which he had left Soraku decades ago.

He came to a stop next to a stone statue of a historical figure. He used it as a leaning post, looking down at the marble beneath his feet and reflecting on those mistakes. He never did reach his potential. Discovering what he did about Yinyon and the people who lived there halted his progress for several years. Even after that, he only managed small improvements while in the Prim Kingdom. He never became what he needed to be in order to take on a mission like this most recent one.

A spunka-crafted blade slipped down from his trench coat sleeve into his hand. He eyed the "S" insignia, longing for her presence. He was literally holding onto a dead dream. Decades of grief and shame had shaped him into what many would see as a sarcastic, callous man from an outside perspective. It was a paper-thin shell worn like stone.

A whisper touched his ear. Not that of words, but motion. A sound he knew only he could recognize, for it'd been lost to the grander world since its supposed eradication over a dozen centuries ago. He thought it a trick of the wind or his subconscious until he saw a shadow glide along the marble just ahead of his blade. His eyes widened. His body locked.

Only one person could move with silence that bested even his ancient.

His eyes roved up and met hers. Violet hair rooted in grays. The whisper that had shaped his regrets.

Soraku Fuuna was everything he remembered.

"You left me and Yama." Her voice was soft, but full of resentment.

He couldn't blame her. When he had deserted Soraku, she had been pregnant. They had never discussed baby names, but he knew in his heart of hearts …

Yama was his daughter.

*   *   *

Lilu and Shelly sat next to Vistas's infirmary bed. Professor Nyemas Jugtah was readying supplements with a pestle and mortar at a counter at the far end of the room, back turned to them. The two sisters held hands, arms dangling between chairs. Their gazes were fixed on the loyal Dev servant. His skin was paler than usual, but his eyes were open and trained on them. It was a weak stare, eyelids halfway closed. His raven hair fell in strings, cleansing and care neglected with movement barred.

He had been in their lives for nearly two decades, helping raise them when father was busy. The world saw them as two sisters, but Shelly and Lilu felt they also had an older brother—the kind who instilled wisdom and avoided enacting the proper discipline that they likely deserved on more than one occasion. The kind who put himself in front of danger to protect them, even if he had no business doing so.

Guilt racked Lilu. She had stood in that spot with the full intention of receiving the arrow. Not only had she realized how stupid of a decision that had been, but how selfish and reckless. How could she have not anticipated Vistas's heroism? *Because Flen would have never done the same.* She had allowed that man's actions against her kingdom to taint her perception of Vistas. And all because they were brothers? Had she forgotten Tristen so easily, the third brother of the Inson triplets who had gotten himself killed in order to reveal Olivia's location to her and Father?

"Do not fear my gaze, Princess," whispered Vistas. She looked up at him, and those gentle eyes of his managed to pierce her heart like a dagger. "Everything I do is in service of your father. I love his family. I swore to protect it to the best of my ability for as long as I breathe. Flen's betrayal, and my lack of wherewithal to foresee it, was a stain on my essence."

Lilu couldn't manage words. He was such a fool. He had always refused to acknowledge the Intel Kingdom's wrongs. Shelly seemed to think the same thing.

"It's time I ask the question," the queen said. "For as long as I can remember, you've seemed to disregard the fact that you shouldn't have any loyalties to us. I'm done blindly accepting that in order to make myself feel better. My father was the man who sent Mendac into your kingdom, who then ravaged the land and its people, including you and your brothers."

"King Vitio did not know what he was sending into my kingdom," Vistas explained. "The atrocities were not made apparent to him until well after the ordeal, and I am the one who witnessed the aftermath upon his discovery. The struggle that consumed him became crippling. He was best friends with a monster and had no way of addressing the problem. Mendac was an unmatched individual as far as combative skill and intelligence, after all."

"My dad seemed fine," said Shelly, who had been old enough to remember those years.

"Your dad put on a brave face around his two girls, the most precious gifts life had ever given him." Vistas closed his eyes and rattled out a laborious breath. He wasn't in good health. "I think the turning point for my brothers and I—or, at least, Tristen and I—was when we witnessed his greatest measure. I will never forget that night, and not only because of the impact it had on me. I committed a lot of my Dev Energy to storing that memory." His gaze flicked between both of them. "Would you like to see it? To better understand my perplexing loyalties."

Jugtah turned from his work. "I don't approve of this. Weaving isn't ideal in your condition. And Dev weaving that involves the manipulation of memories is highly volatile."

"I owe them this," Vistas said, his eyes not leaving the two royal women.

"I will intervene," Jugtah said.

"You may take your leave if you find it that troublesome."

Jugtah paused. He regarded Lilu and Shelly, waiting for either of them to take his side.

"You can wait to show us," Shelly said. "Or just tell us."

Lilu studied Vistas. His expression seemed peaceful.

"It will not kill me," Vistas whispered. "And I refuse to die before I show you your father's most vulnerable, yet *greatest*, moment. I refuse his legacy be that of a coward. Nyemas, please leave."

Jugtah hovered a moment longer before bringing the concoction he'd been working on to Vistas's bedside table. He then took his leave without even glancing back.

The Dev servant instructed the two women to face each other and touch temples. They did, and he extracted a wisp of silver from his head and touched it to the point of contact between them.

*　　*　　*

"I can't contain him! I can't stop him!" Rage and grief painted Intel King Vitio's face red. "Ever since his mission in the Prim Kingdom years ago, I've barely seen the man. Even when he's in the kingdom, he's in Brilliance, especially the past few years! Wendel won't tell me why Mendac feels the need to be there all the time!"

The king's rant had morphed into a tirade, sentences interrupted by mighty heaves to haul in oxygen. The outburst was occurring in an auxiliary atrium of the royal quarters of the palace, out in the open where anyone could see or hear. He didn't seem to notice or care that two Dev servants were hanging freshly-cleaned curtains along the room's many towering windows. Vistas and Tristen were the two servants, the former stealing a glance the king's way more often than not.

"Did you hear what he did in the Dev Kingdom?" Vitio asked, lowering his voice without losing its ferocity. "The unspeakable things!"

"I've heard the rumors," Delilah replied. "But they're only rumors, Love."

"Rumors my ass!" shouted Vitio. "Twenty-seven soldiers have taken their own life since returning from that mission. Seventy-one have disappeared! A couple thousand more are visiting Spirit Healers daily, most of whom are finding no luck because their depression has sunken to such an abyssal state. We have hundreds in the process of trying to relinquish their military status. They know what they did, and they can't live with it!"

A long pause followed, and instead of turning to regard the royals— Vistas had a sneaking suspicion their eyes might have finally fallen on him and his brother—he looked at them through the faint reflection in the window. The couple was still focused on each other. Vitio stood behind an armchair. Delilah sat patiently on a loveseat, studying her husband. "Can *you* live with it?" she finally asked.

Then, the king broke. He wept, back slumping and head bowed as he placed his hands on the back of the armchair. "I allowed that man around my family … my little girls." His words were nearly lost in the sobs. "Shelly's old enough to be impressionable. I've allowed a monster to play friendly with them, and as their father, that makes me a monster, myself."

A tinge of pity tickled Vistas, threatening the resentment he had harbored for the Intelian family and its kingdom over the past several months. This man hadn't known what he sent into Vistas's homeland. Mendac had been the true demon. He looked at his brother, and Tristen shook his head while continuing to hang his curtain—as if to say this didn't forgive anything. Flen would have agreed, even if he hadn't been banished to the stables and wasn't here to see it.

*   *   *

The royal quarters of Dunami Palace were already an empty place, but midnight was especially quiet. Vistas stood on the second floor of the royal's personal library, hidden behind bookcases as he perused the spines of books and tomes. It was a wasted space; he'd never seen anyone enter here to study or read. He expected more when considering the Intel Kingdom's reputation for high acumen. They had grown comfortable with their status as a world power for several centuries. They thrived off the past glories of its predecessors, and soon the remnants of wealth and power they had spawned would fade … as long as the royals continued down this track.

Vistas shouldn't have been here, but he knew how the malleability of the king's discipline. Vitio was a soft man. It was probably what had led the king to employing a man like Mendac. They were polar opposites as far as morals and attitude. Mendac could perform the deeds Vitio couldn't himself—a solid choice in theory. However, now that the Intel General was proving his capabilities, the king was learning he couldn't handle it.

Vistas heard the doors to the library open somewhere on the main floor below. He closed the book and returned it to its proper place on the shelf, then flipped the switch of his miniature Intelight. Of all the misfortune, of course someone would enter this abandoned place the exact moment he was here in the dead of night. What's worse was that it could only be someone of importance, for access to the royal quarters was reserved to a select handful of people.

He heard two whispered voices from below, but couldn't distinguish what was being said or by whom. After waiting to affirm they didn't seem to be moving away from the library's sitting area, Vistas crept toward the second floor's balcony that circled the main floor. There were no light sources save the dim night sky through the windows, so he was able to get close to the rails without being seen from below.

Intel King Vitio stood with a man Vistas had never seen before. This man was older, in his late seventies or early eighties. Despite his age and the cane which he carried at his side, he stood stoic and tall. He wore thin-framed, circular spectacles and a robe of sweeping black that blanketed everything from the neck down. He seemed the suspicious sort, but unthreatening. Vistas had caught them somewhere in the beginning of their conversation.

"I'm putting my faith in King Itta here," Vitio said.

The elderly man wasn't looking at the king, but instead focused on withdrawing a book from somewhere in his robes and placing it on one of the reading tables. He sorted through pages and said, "The Intelian king requesting a favor from the Archain ... desperation indeed."

Vitio leaned over the table and squinted at the sweeping pages of the book. "You can read whatever that is?"

The man looked up and grabbed the left side of his glasses as a gesture. "With these, yes." He then looked down to regard Vitio's tapping fingers. "Anxiety is up." He returned to flipping through pages. "Understandable."

"Because I'm playing with fire?"

"Try 'Gods,'" said the man. "Or the next closest thing, at least."

Vitio straightened at that, removing his hands from the tabletop and turning to face rows of bookcases. Vistas could tell the king was having second thoughts of committing to whatever this was. He was sure the unknown man was an Archain based on his statement about his glasses. They must have been an ancient piece capable of deciphering foreign languages to a relatable tongue.

"Ah," said the old man. "Got it." He straightened out of his bowed position over the book, then regarded Vitio, whose back was still turned to him. "A few preliminary topics before I attempt this." He waited, then said, "I'd like if I could see your eyes while I speak."

The king turned, if not with reluctance.

"What we're doing here is one hundred percent illegal, outlawed by every kingdom save the Prim since the first century. We don't know the repercussions that could follow, or if there are any at all. The last documented case of an attempt such as this was the First of Five." The elderly man glanced at the book before returning his gaze to Vitio. "You paid Archaic King Itta a substantial sum of money for my service here, but know that the individual behind the curtain who ties him and me together is infinitely times more dangerous … and that person is with whom this transaction is truly exchanged."

"I know of the Skill Broker, yes," Vitio said.

"You know 'of.' And consider yourself lucky that that's all. For the less fortunate, we know what happens when he or she is crossed. Take that from a man who's already tried." A long silence, tense and uncomfortable. He continued, "With that said, it's understood that my ability to weave and use this ancient effectively isn't guaranteed. This was an ancient only Gatal Accus proved he could handle, after all. If I fail, which is more than likely the case, there are no refunds. And if you try to take it out on me, know that I do have a means of escape." He grabbed the handle of his cane after the final threat, the action serving as punctuation. "And lastly, you will forget of this moment. You will mention it to no one. You spent money, but the act being done in return is insurmountable in importance and danger. My life is also on the line, for the weaving required places extreme pressure on my body. I will never be able to weave the same ever again. I'll simultaneously be using two ancients … my glasses and this book. Are we on the same page?"

"We are."

"Good." The old man placed a finger on the open page of the book. The king watched closely. Vistas was in awe, unable to get a grasp of what was happening. The Archain began reciting words from the book, tongue moving fluently with the foreign script. For someone who claimed to not know the language, he seemed to be a natural. Vistas wondered if those glasses extended its abilities into the ears and mouth, that way foreign languages could be deciphered not just by reading, but when spoken.

The book began to rattle. Pages tried slithering closed, but the Archain used his other hand to pin it down. The braced nature of his stance meant he was straining to fight it. The muscles in his arms—hidden beneath the flowing sleeves of his robes—were likely tense. He continued reading, though his words were even less distinguishable through the grunts of effort to fight the ancient. King Vitio had backed away several feet, face stunned between fear and shock. Vistas, on the other hand, had pressed his face against the banister's columns, wishing he was closer. He knew what was happening here. The *Of Five* series of fairy tales weren't well-known in the Dark Realm, but the *First of Five* was the exception. He knew what that book was, and thus knew what Vitio wanted out of this. Vistas was going to get his first—and probably only—glimpse of a celestial being that surpassed a Branian or Bewahr.

A brilliant white light shot out of the book, forcing Vitio and Vistas to look away. The light didn't fill the room or extend beyond its narrow beam, but it was still blinding. The light curved and hit the floor next to the table. Then it vanished, the book shut on its own, and a woman now stood in the room.

*   *   *

Vitas's body felt strange: the pit of his stomach warm, heart feathery light, and breaths slipping into his lungs with ease. The summoned woman had altered the atmosphere. He composed himself and studied her.

She was short with voluminous hair wider than her shoulders. Large eyes dominated a smaller face, and she wore brilliant golden robes. Vistas couldn't distinguish more beyond that, given the angle from which he watched.

"I don't know whether to be pissed or impressed," she said.

The old man had collapsed into a chair. He wheezed, eyes barely open. His energy likely neared depletion, making his earlier threat of using his cane as a weapon useless. He couldn't do much in that state, and the atmospheric effects of the woman weren't helping his cause. King Vitio simply watched, wide-eyed.

She looked between the two men before acknowledging the closed book. She picked it up and flipped through the pages. She stopped at a black one. "Good," she said. "So this is the first and only time this will happen to me." She flipped backward through the book and found another black page, then set it down. "Let's get this done with. What do you need from me?"

"It's that simple?" the king asked.

"I wouldn't say that. The immensely difficult part is finding someone who can both read the text in that ancient and weave Archaic Energy well enough to make it function. And you got that part done, so now comes the easy part." She looked at the old man and tilted her head. "Did you explain the prayer to him?" He shook his head, clearly lacking the energy to speak.

The woman sighed and turned to Vitio. "This man recited a prayer that calls upon one of the three Strasan. He chose my prayer, which means I'm here to erase a memory ... or several."

This gave Vitio pause. His eyebrows furrowed, mouth twisting into a snarl. Vistas's reaction was the same, though he didn't show it on his face. Had Vitio summoned a high-ranking Bozani to erase certain memories? That's it? He felt guilty about what he had sent Mendac out to do and now wanted to heal his conscious by erasing his faults? The Intel King had a cowardly reputation, but this was a low Vistas never could have imagined. And what would happen when the topic arose again in the future, when his wife or general confronted him about it? He wouldn't know what they were talking about ... Vistas's train of thought shifted at that ... He wouldn't understand why his palace was full of Dev servants. There had to be more to this.

After a stunned silence, the king looked at the old man and said, "*That's what you did?*" His face was red again—fury and frustration. "I needed someone strong. Someone who fights. I needed Magnifica!"

The woman summoned by Gatal Accus to redirect the meteor, Vistas thought.

"Magnifica cannot be summoned anymore. That ancient has rules," the Strasan said, speaking about the book. "When a Strasan is summoned, their pages in the book are burned black, their prayers no longer legible. The same can now be said for me, Naipa Levlin. After this, nobody can summon me ever again."

"So I've been given a Strasan who won't fight," Vitio said weakly. He lowered himself into a chair and buried his burly face into his hands.

"Correct. I don't do that—at least not in this situation."

"It was in the contract," the old man whispered, regaining consciousness. "I use the ancient to summon the celestial being who forgets."

"A conveniently vague title," said Vitio.

"That's how she's described in the text. It doesn't give a name."

Naipa's eyes narrowed. "How are you still breathing?"

The old man managed a smile that felt out of place to Vistas. "When you've explored the depths of the world's largest historical and intellectual vessel, you encounter much worse than this," he said. He turned to the king. "The prayer speaks of someone who can erase memories, so I was told to choose her. She's going to make sure you don't remember me or this transaction."

"This is no longer a transaction if she can't do what I need of her!"

"The Archaic Kingdom's side of this deal was to provide you with a powerful Bozani. Consider that done."

The Strasan observed the two men, displaying patience Vistas wouldn't have expected from someone of her station. Vitio's jaw flexed as he ground his teeth, nostrils flaring with each breath. There was history here. The Intel and Archaic Kingdoms clearly hated each other, yet Vitio had still gone to nefarious lengths such as this.

"I need someone killed," the king finally said, ripping his eyes away from the old man.

"I'm a Strasan, not an executioner," she said.

Vitio's fist hit the table. "He's destroying kingdoms and he won't stop! There's nobody alive who can defeat him!"

"The dramatics ..." she replied. "But I'm curious. What is this man's name?"

"Mendac LeAnce."

If the name rang any bells, she didn't show it. She either truly didn't recognize the name or was the greatest actor Vistas had ever seen—and he came from a town known for its theatre. "Give me a rundown of his atrocities," she said. "I'm curious."

Vitio didn't hesitate, going on a ten-minute spiel about the mission in the Dev Kingdom. He went on to explain that he didn't know the extent of Mendac's crimes. There could have been more that had gone unreported. The general had such a firm grip of his soldiers. Vitio assumed something went wrong in the Prim Kingdom because their trade negotiations with them—iron in exchange for holy wood—had fallen through, and Prim

Queen Inedibus never contacted the Intel Kingdom again after that mission.

Naipa bypassed all of that to instead ask, "Is he the one who killed Dev King Rehn?"

Vitio had left that part out, but he nodded. "Yes. He committed an Untenable."

"Well, that changes things," she said, which was news Vitio judging by the confusion on his face. "The problem with the Untenables is that there is no accountability. The Empires don't have an eye that sees everything in the kingdoms, so when an Untenable is committed, we can only know if a Branian or Bewahr is around to witness or hear about it. Unfortunately, the Dev King's son wasn't old enough to have awakened his Bewahr, and we've had the Dark Empire breathing down our neck in efforts to discover the person responsible. You may have just extended the years of peace between the Empires by a few more decades by telling me this."

She was rambling, and Vistas was surprised she was revealing this much. The Archain man echoed his sentiment. "Awfully loose lips," he said.

"Neither of you will remember any of what I just said," she said flippantly. "I like to speak aloud sometimes, so don't mind me." She frowned. "I can't go kill this man, but I will bring the information to the necessary person. It's out of my hands after that, but I suspect something will be done, considering the nature of the man's crime ... if we value the nature of peace between the empires, that is."

The space fell silent. King Vitio had resigned himself to staring down at the floor. The old man watched him curiously, no longer struggling to breathe. How had he recovered so quickly? Weaving two ancients—one of which was certainly a powerful relic capable of summoning deities—should have killed him or thrown him into a coma. He had already righted himself in his chair and was now holding his cane, as if to remind the king of his earlier threat. The Strasan also took notice and asked, "What is your name?"

He looked at her and then the king, considering the consequences of giving out such information. Then, perhaps remembering he had the ability to ask for memories to be erased, he gave it to her anyway. "Neeko LeFolli, but let's keep that between us."

"Good," she said. "I'll make a point of remembering that for when you're reborn."

"Reborn?" he said.

"There's no way Tahar would pass up a specimen like you."

"Tahar?"

That she didn't answer. She had mentioned rebirth as if it was a casual concept, stating Neeko would become a Bozani one day. One didn't just throw comments like that around ... not to humans. Who knew what kind of effects that could have on someone thereafter. Then again, Vistas supposed Neeko wouldn't remember any of this once Naipa left.

"So, what's the request?" she asked. "What memories need scrubbing?"

Neeko blinked, regaining his wits. "Erase King Vitio's knowledge of this transaction between him and the Archaic King. Erase his knowledge of my existence."

"Easy." She faced the Intel King and raised a hand to his temple. Vistas racked his brain in efforts to recall any historical information he may have had about a woman named Naipa Levlin sense, but had no success. Wiping someone's memory sounded like a Devish ability, but she was a Bozani, so she must have been from a Light Realm kingdom. Then that would make her an Archain with a memory-manipulating ancient, but he saw none on her.

"Wait," Neeko demanded. Her hand froze just inches away from Vitio's temple. Neeko regarded the king and pursed his lips. "Free him of his guilt. I see the suffering."

Vitio narrowed his eyes at Neeko with accusation. "And how would you know what I'm feeling?"

Neeko withdrew a balled fist from a pocket of his robes. He held it up and opened his hand, revealing a perfectly spherical eyeball. It had a glossy sheen like glass and didn't sport any pinkish flesh that should have trailed from its backside. "Your aura."

"How long have you been using that?" Vitio asked.

"Since I walked in here. Saw the fear radiate from you while I read the prayer. I don't blame you," he said, returning the eye to his pocket.

Vistas balked. *Three ancients, one of which was surely a relic?* And he was holding the cane like nothing was stopping him from using a fourth.

Naipa smirked and shook her head. "Give Gatal himself a run for his money. Wait until the old man hears about this."

"Erase his memory of Mendac's crimes in the Dev Kingdom," Neeko said.

Vitio's eyes widened. "No. That's the last thing I want. That comes with me to the grave."

Neeko looked dead at Naipa, whose gaze remained impassive. "I'm the one who said and wove the prayer. I want you to erase that memory."

She paused, then sighed. "This is the part of this arrangement I've despised since learning of this possibility when I became a Strasan." She faced Vitio. "I don't have a choice. If he wills it, then I must obey."

The king dropped to his knees so fast that Vistas's eyes lagged behind. He clasped his hands together and began pleading. It was the most shameful—yet, somehow, admirable—act Vistas could have ever imagined from a royal. A groveling king?

Naipa just as quickly snatched the man back up to his feet with a strength not seen in her tiny frame. "Don't do that," she spat. "What do I look like? I'm not the Empress or Tahar."

By this point, Vistas had crawled his way far enough around the circular overlook to have a clear shot of Naipa's face. His eyes were drawn to a tattoo on her forehead—a circle with four dashes intersecting each side.

"You have one more request," she said, not bothering to look Neeko's way.

"I want to forget everything I know about my involvement with the Skill Broker, which includes my knowledge of the true happenings in Lost Wisdom and how I pretend they don't happen. I'm a bystander and, in some ways, a benefactor ... the orphanage does pay my salary, after all. I tried to take a stance decades ago, but I lost my mother because of it. I could still lose more."

Vistas closed his eyes. And they called King Vitio a coward? Here the king was, meddling with underground bosses, playing with illegal ancients, and confronting deities all to dispose of one man. He also had the chance to forget everything, yet wanted to own his mistakes, going as far as begging for his memories to remain. Neeko was the coward here. Vistas didn't know his crimes, but they obviously existed. And when dealing with an individual with a title of Skill Broker, one couldn't even imagine what that must have entailed.

Showing a sign of pity, Naipa adopted a reassuring tone. "King Vitio, you can still work to regain a memory even after I take it. I'm not taking the memories of everyone else who knows the truth. It'll just take some strokes of chance and the connecting of dots on your part."

Vitio and Neeko approached Naipa, and she reached out to touch both temples with each hand. She closed her eyes, and the tattoo on her forehead began to glow, light streaming from her head to their foreheads, passing through her neck, shoulders, and arms. The process took no longer than five seconds. They collapsed afterward, and she stood there for a moment, looking down at them. "Great," she said to herself. "I hate dragging bodies."

But before she did that, she looked up and stared in Vistas's direction, though he was sure he was cloaked in shadows. Wings exploded from her back, radiant and massive. She flew up to the balcony and let her feet land next to him. He remained on the ground, gawking up at her.

"Awfully sneaky," she said.

He tried speaking, but his lips only trembled. Despite her smaller frame, those wings and his knowledge of who she was made her appear larger than life. She crouched, wings rescinding into her back, and placed a hand against his forehead. He quickly committed his focus on a weaving technique. She was going to make him forget, but perhaps he could remember if he stored the memory deep enough in his mind. He'd hide, bury, and lock it. That last bit was a risky technique that required elite weaving skills—something for which Flen was better known. But, he was still an Inson; he could manage.

Naipa's eyebrows furrowed as light streamed from her tattoo to his forehead. Then she frowned. With persistence, she found the memory and began to erase. Vistas grew tired, and he heard her voice as if it was muffled and distant: "So you're a Devish. This might not work."

*　　*　　*

Lilu opened her eyes from the memory, finding she was already crying. Shelly appeared sullen. They had spent their lives knowing the kingdom thought their father a cowardly king, but what they had just seen proved otherwise. Ataway Debonicus Kawi had been sent to execute Mendac LeAnce, but it would have never happened had it not been for Father. And who knows what kind of havoc that man could have created had he never been stopped.

Vistas smiled at the two royal sisters.

His eyes closed. His breathing stopped.

And he was gone.

90

The One

Bryson stood atop the Starlight's tallest gate, faced with Empress Tonitrua. She didn't possess the same awe-inspiring aura he remembered from her, which he suspected had to do with his recent transformation. He had a significant chunk of Tahara in him, which must have evened the scales. He had become the very thing that Empress Tonitrua once craved in her past life as an Originator. He knew this. He felt it, as if part of Intelius's consciousness had seeped into him. He also knew he had loved Tonitrua once ... until she neglected and betrayed him. There were many other feelings just out of Bryson's reach. He couldn't shake the sensation of his heart being lodged in his throat, cursing him with a nausea he feared he'd never lose. It was as if he was stuck in an infinite plunge, hurtling through time and space.

"To your generation—your timeline—we are gods," Tonitrua said, beginning the story for which she had summoned him to the Cavity of Judgment. "However, we are not, for gods are responsible for creation.

None of the Bozani or Gefal have created anything. My timeline had gods, but even they are only demigods. Gale Thrasher created the atmosphere. Land Molder created the crust. Tide Drifter created all bodies of water. But Tahar and Mulawith, the forgotten Gods, created the magic ... the Essences.

"Those two are unique, confounding entities. Both are conscious beings, but don't think of them as human in shape or mind. Their existence encompasses so much more than that. They think and feel, but they cannot reach out and touch the same way humans do ... not even the same way that Gale, Land, or Tide can. The most ancient tales I know of—ancient to my own time, mind you, which would make them primordial for you— speak of Tahar and Mulawith as lovers, once sharing a cluster of stars in a distant sky. They were at peace, in a state of pure bliss until something thrust them into a foreign sky with unknown stars.

"I gather hints of Tahar's consciousness from living in the Tahara that spills from these Cavities, but they come centuries between one another. I've come to believe Kuki Sphaira isn't in its proper home. We don't belong in this sky among these stars. The question is how did we end up here, neighboring the planet called Earth? And was Earth also thrown into a foreign sky like us or has this always been its home?"

She looked up. "That's not even the most unsettling part. The old wise tale about the man who could see far enough to spot other planets in the sky ... something tells me there might have been some truth to it."

"The Star Seer," Bryson said. It was a tale nearly as infamous as the Of Five series, but preposterous enough to warrant a poor reputation.

Tonitrua nodded. "There is so much more to this universe than Kuki Sphaira. That was what Mialo wanted to discover before we died. He thought he knew where to find the answers. I joined him on the mission. Then the other Originators caught wind of what we were doing and put a stop to it. Once he and I were reborn, that mission was lost. We couldn't access the Boundless Wonder. Since then, I think we've both been looking for the answers by searching Tahar's and Mulawith's souls, but as I said, it's been a slog. Centuries go by without finding anything, which has to do with the main chunk of their souls being stored in the depths of the Boundless Wonder."

"What's that?" Bryson asked.

"I believe your people call it the Warpfinate."

His nose curled up. "Ugh. I hate that place."

She paused, contemplating his remark. "To think you have it so easy. Anyone has access to it in your time, yet nobody has the wherewithal to take advantage of it. When I was alive, the disputes of who owned the island and the tumultuous waters of the Region of Raging Tides surrounding it made reaching it impossible."

"Agnos is the person you want," said Bryson. "He's been chasing that since I've met him. I'm more worried about Mendac and the Dark Empire's desire to crush the Light."

"That comes from desperation on Mialo's part. He's losing his subtlety though, as the Dark Realm loses royal firstborns and, thus, Cavities in the Labyrinth. It's forced his focus to shift from discovering the truth of our universe to simply sustaining his existence. But, I'm also guilty of this. Even before the Prim Prince was killed, I had already set into motion plans to topple the Dark. While he talked about it, I acted."

Bryson was tired of this. He already knew why he needed to win this war: because his father was on the other side of it. Not everybody's motives were heroic. He wasn't in this to save the world. That would have required him knowing the consequences of them losing in the first place. He was in this for himself, but more importantly, his mother. He loved that woman. Concern for Shelly, Lilu, and L.K. had softened since becoming the Intel Essence. He felt them in his being, and knowing he could sense a Gefal if one tried approaching them put him at ease.

"Twenty-one years ago," Tonitrua said, "I entrapped Mialo. We used to visit each other. Circumstances between the Empires weren't exactly peaceful, but they weren't volatile either. Our visits were frowned upon, but none of our subordinates would dare voice that." She released a long breath, then said, "Have a seat, Bryson."

He looked down at the liquid light that flowed across the floor toward its plunge over the roof's edge. "I'd rather stand."

"*Sit.*"

He did, the firmness of her tone reminding him of who she was. The liquid no longer split in front of him and converged behind him like it had when he first arrived in the Empire, but instead rushed through him, recharging him. Thankfully, it seemed he remained dry.

"Roughly fifty years ago, I relinquished a vow of celibacy."

"Thanks for telling me."

She smiled. "It's necessary pretext. You know, I loved Mialo." An inexplicable part of Bryson grew enraged at that, and he figured it was Intelius. "He loved me, yet we never made it a physical thing … mostly due to my uncertainties. It was unknown back then if Originators could reproduce—none had tried. I was scared to find out. There wasn't a lack of effort on his part. He tried—not to impregnate me, but to simply make love. I refused every time. Even after we died and were reborn, I stood by that decision."

"You went over 1,500 years without having sex?" Bryson asked, incredulous.

"We acted through verbal expression … and physical contact that didn't venture further than needed. But, as I said earlier, I abandoned my rule." She lowered herself to her knees, making herself nearly eye level with Bryson. "There is no such thing as a perfectly good person. Everyone has darkness in them. Some believe even the gods. I took advantage of Mialo's love for me by laying with him for a selfish motive. I loved him, yes, but I wanted something out of it … a child."

Bryson remained still, the story finally becoming interesting.

"Again," she said, "not even for the sake of having a child. I needed to create something that could defeat Intelius. The damned Essence has been a thorn in my side ever since my rebirth, refusing to cooperate. I never knew what was happening in the Light Knowledge Kingdom, the kingdom I had once ruled over, because he withheld information. At first, I thought there was no way to remedy the solution. He couldn't die naturally. I tried killing him with my own hands and the help of a Strasan, but that quartz prison was impenetrable.

"If I hadn't been scouring Tahar's consciousness for information about our world's origin, I wouldn't have found out about the Essences' weakness: they could die to an energy from the opposite realm. I thought it another dead end because the only beings strong enough to penetrate the defenses of Tahara-infused quartz was someone on a Gefal's level, and no

Gefal would ever help me with such a task—not that I would want them to anyway. That would require me revealing to them that one of our kingdoms was defenseless."

Bryson tilted his head, his brain functioning much better than normal. "So … you tried creating a baby of both realms, hoping it would have an energy of both realms. Like me." He said the last part weakly, unable to stomach the acts that had led to him.

"Yes," she said. "Not only that, but it would be the offspring of two Originators. Mialo and I are powers unparalleled by any human, Bozani, or Gefal, so what would our child become? I succeeded. Pregnancy followed, and I barred communication with Mialo from that point forward. None of the Strasan were allowed to visit me either. I spent a couple of years in solitude, throughout the nine months and even after labor.

"It didn't take long to realize the monstrosity I had created. Tahar wanted nothing to do with my son; it rejected his very being within the Starlight. It thought him an abomination. My hands were forced. I had him sent far away from the Empire, but I couldn't do it myself since I can't leave the Empires. I made it Naipa's mission to find him a home in the Intel Kingdom, and she did it without questioning anything—a perk of being the Empress."

"And you're telling me she kept her mouth shut?" Bryson asked.

"Afterward, I forced her to erase the memory. I also lost track of the child, and let fate do with him what it wished."

"That kid could have grown into something dangerous," Bryson hissed. It had been an irresponsible and reckless act by someone who should have been far above such nonsense.

"He did."

"Who?"

Her gaze cast downward, unable to look him in the eye. "Your father."

91

The Gap in Debo's Memory

One would think, given the amount of revelations unloaded on Bryson since becoming a Jestivan, he would have been used to it by now. Mendac being a war criminal and rapist. Olivia being his twin sister. Apoleia, his mother. Toono, his half-brother. Since discovering all of this, he supposed he should have questioned why everything in this world seemed to revolve around people who were his blood relatives. He figured it was because of his association with the Jestivan and Intel family. With such massive connections, he was bound to find himself in the midst of the storm. But *this*?

"That can't be right," he said. "That'd make me your grandson."

"Yes."

Bryson was suddenly thankful he was seated. His legs wanted to wobble.

"I believe you and the rest of the world knows Mendac was an orphan," she explained. "Naipa had brought him to the wealthiest family in

Brilliance. Also, how else could Mendac have become as strong as he did? Do you realize the fight he put up against Ataway when I sent the Pogu down to execute him? Ataway almost died that night. A human almost defeated a high-ranking Bozani. That's unheard of."

"Mendac doesn't have two energies," he said. "Someone would have known."

"He kept it secret, revealing it only when absolutely necessary. He used it when fighting Ataway."

Bryson furrowed his brows. "I watched that memory and never saw any evidence of that."

"Ah, yes," she said. "The memory Ataway had no business sharing with you. According to Thusia, he didn't share the entire thing, though. Was it not doctored?"

Bryson looked down, eyes widening. How had he forgotten? There had been a gap in the memory, right after Debo chased Mendac into the sewers. The vision had cut to black and then returned to Debo walking back from the fight. Vistas had said there was probably good reason for Debo redacting the fight when it transitioned outside the sewers.

"The fight took place in the streets of Brilliance," Tonitrua said. "I guess I should say *above* the streets. It was catastrophic. Mendac revealed two weapons from his arsenal he had kept from the rest of the world: a set of Tahara wings ... and Dev abilities. I had prepared Ataway for the possibility of him having Dev abilities, but not wings. I should have known, but, once again, Intelius's refusal to do his job made me unaware of any such events that took place in the Intel Kingdom. I also hadn't prepared Ataway for the extent of Mendac's mastery over his Dev Energy. He did things only a handful of Devish people across history have accomplished."

Bryson's mouth didn't move. Words failed him. Debo had omitted that part of the memory because he didn't know how the Empire would react to a human knowing that information. If the world knew humans could gain the wings of elite celestials or create children with multiple energies, who knew how far people would go to achieve those goals? Mendac had already proven the desperate lengths.

"Naturally, a fight of such magnitude woke nearly every person in the dead of night in that sector of the city. The aftermath did quite a number on Naipa, who had to erase the memories of thousands of people." Her voice grew solemn. "That woman still hasn't fully recovered. I've never seen her memory as shot as it is. Can't even find her way around the Starlight anymore."

"What kind of things did Mendac do in the fight?" Bryson asked.

"It was really only one thing. It takes something special to counter the speed of an Adren Assassin of Ataway's caliber, and Mendac had it."

*   *   *

Illipsia and Homina stood in front of the Confines of Consciousness, a massive building in the shape of a perfect cube and molded out of gray Permanence. It was windowless and smooth—surely, a true wonder for any architect. Illipsia had seen it many times during previous stays here in Cogdan Castle, but Toono had never given her answers when she asked about it. All she knew was that her mother had been held in this building, and she wanted to know why.

"Second thoughts?" Homina asked.

Illipsia shook her head. Her mother had been adamant about not letting her into the Confines of Consciousness ever since returning to Cogdan, but her resolve had been weakening over the months. She cracked a week ago, noticing her relationship with Illipsia was continuing to deteriorate. Today, she folded completely. She had led Illipsia to the Confines with hopes of healing their relationship. Illipsia knew this method of emotional manipulation wasn't kind, but she needed to know what kind of evils required fortification measures such as this ... and why her mother had been considered one of those evils. The guards stepped to the side, and the doors opened. They crossed through and were swallowed by blackness as the doors shut. Homina lit a torch and held it aloft.

Illipsia sensed madness the moment the sunlight of the outside world vanished. Millions of thoughts rushed through her head from outside her body, converging as white noise. Somewhere in the tangle were individual words, memories, and experiences, but picking through them was impossible. Ten seconds in and she already wanted out. Her mother had endured this for how many years?

Homina placed a hand on Illipsia's shoulder, and she didn't protest, which spoke volumes about her discomfort. They passed countless cages, but most were empty. The structure had no rooms or corridors; it was one giant cubical atrium divided by cages and metal bars.

"How many prisoners are in here?" Illipsia asked.

"A handful. The number could have changed since I was released, but there were seven at the time."

Illipsia looked up at her mom. To what class of villainy did she belong in order to end up here?

They traveled deep into the Confines until Homina stopped at a cell that almost looked like the rest. This one was pushed against a wall of the building. There were blemishes in the Permanence, as if someone had fought hard to get out.

"This was my prison," Homina said.

Illipsia's gaze shifted between dents and cracks in the wall. She knew the Permanence of the Confines was thick—several feet or so. To manage this level of destruction meant her mother had been both relentless and strong. "Energy blasts?"

"Yes," Homina replied.

Energy blasts were a technique involving the expulsion of Dev Energy from one's body, weaving it as an orb with Dev Currents. It was basically a concentrated ball of Dev Chains that acted as a blunt projectile, capable of knocking someone off their feet. In the case of Homina—evident by the damage to her cell—they could break bones.

Illipsia grimaced, a particularly violent thread of thoughts cutting through her mind from somewhere beyond. She shook her head and refocused. "What was it like?"

"When you crack an egg into a pan," Homina said, causing Illipsia to raise an eyebrow, "the yolk and egg white is released, but together they're a singular entity. If I were to add a second egg, however, the egg whites would combine. And that continues as more eggs are added. You have several yolks, but their egg white blend and encompass all of them. That's the experience of the Confines."

Illipsia turned to absorb the rest of the prison, but she saw mostly darkness. The prisoners were the yolks; the Confines were the egg whites. "Like many people sharing their memories and thoughts," she said.

"Somewhat," Homina replied. "I'd say more like many people trapped in the same mind—a singular collective of thoughts. Our minds are no longer contained to our skulls, but leak beyond until this building becomes a skull itself ... which is why we're only going to be in here a few minutes longer."

"Why did Dev King Rehn lock you away in here?"

They continued walking in silence as her mother either searched for the right answer or debated on giving it at all. "I don't fully remember," she said. "Like I said, this place scrambled me. I tend to believe it had something to do with a love triangle between me, him, and his wife, but sometimes I feel there is more to it."

"You were romantically involved with the king?"

"The queen."

Shocked, Illipsia had to will her legs to continue moving. That could have explained the king's decision to imprison her mother, but after mulling it over, it still felt extreme. "You're lying to me."

"I wouldn't."

Illipsia stopped and turned toward her mother. "Your voice is shaking. Your responses are hesitant. Among the voices in this place, I keep hearing yours. I believe you feel that, too, for you tremble each time it happens. What are you saying?"

"Illipsia," she whispered, "I don't like these thoughts. They were what ruined my life in the first place. And what you're hearing isn't *my* voice; it's the voice of my past self—a self I've worked hard at forgetting since Toono freed me."

Something clanged behind Illipsia. She whirled, backing up next to her mother. A man peered through the bars, hands clenched around the metal. He was old and dark-skinned. His forehead, eyes, and cheeks were folded in many wrinkles. "You know," he said, "this place has gone to shit since you've left."

Homina stepped forward, partially obscuring her daughter like a shield. "Draysil."

Illipsia knew that name. He had once been the president of the Consortium in Prayoga, the most accomplished research center in the Dev Kingdom, before relieving his position for unknown reasons just over a decade ago.

"When you were here," the old man said, "most of the thoughts swimming around this place were mindless babbling. Talk of Originators, Essences, Gods, and the balancing of it all. I could handle that. It was interesting enough to give me something on which to focus, but nonsensical enough to provide little to no substance of which my emotions could grab hold. Now those thoughts have nearly vanished, giving way to the horrors of the other prisoners in here." He shook his head violently. "And they're not good. Did you know a woman here had once been the mayor of some western village? She drowned the children of any family who couldn't pay their taxes."

"If anything," said Homina, "that should give us some comfort, knowing the Dev family felt it right to lock up such evil."

"True, true," Draysil replied. "But what did *we* do, Homina? I cheated on an ex-girlfriend when I was sixteen, but I can't think of much worse." He paused, looking concerned. "Oh, my daughter. I gave her little attention … no attention. My work took precedence, but I did that to maintain a lifestyle for our family."

"Tazama knows that, and she loves you."

The man's empty eyes refocused and then watered. "You've ran into Taz?"

Illipsia's brows furrowed as she regarded her mother once again. If Homina had known about Tazama's father being in this place, why had she never brought it up?

"Tazama is hurting," Homina said. "No different than this entire kingdom. She doesn't blame her pain on you. She blames it on Mendac."

The man's body crumpled atop his knees, and he slouched against the bars. He wept, a hand pressed against his tear-streaked face.

Homina approached and knelt next to him, only a few feet of distance between her and the bars. "Your thoughts always stood out to me. The two of us were wrongfully imprisoned here. I know the work you put in; I know the pride you had in your position. You did everything you could to protect those blueprints, so the secrets of the Teleplatforms wouldn't fall into the wrong hands. But you couldn't have foreseen that man's talents. He was a being that defied natural law. And in the end, you did do your job. He never obtained the blueprints. Alas, what you saw made you a threat to the Devish family ... just like I was a threat."

"You believe me?" he asked.

"How can I not believe your own thoughts? Unless you've been lying to yourself, and rather convincingly, all of these years. You became the fall guy. When Mendac began building teleplatforms abroad, King Rehn announced that it was because of the Consortium's failure to protect the blueprints, which put you—as its president—in the crosshairs. King Rehn couldn't have the world knowing the truth of what Mendac was."

"I couldn't believe my own eyes," Draysil said. "Right in front of me, the man ... he *teleported*."

Illipsia couldn't keep quiet any longer. "Who teleported?"

He looked up, as if just now noticing the girl. "Is that your daughter?"

Homina smiled. "Yes."

"What a beauty. She looks just like you."

Illipsia's face softened, as did her tone as she repeated the question. "Who teleported?"

"Mendac," he whispered.

"An eye trick," she retorted. "I know his son. He has a speed percentage too high for most people to track, so it looks like he's teleporting. He probably got it from Mendac."

"No. This man closed his eyes before vanishing and reappearing. People with high speed percentages don't have to close their eyes before sprinting to a different spot. But, as we know from the stories of the rare few who could teleport in this kingdom's history, they all closed their eyes before doing so—an action of clairvoyance. It was how they sensed the physical matter of the location to which they were going to teleport—a precaution necessary to avoid fazing into objects or arriving above empty space and thus falling to their death."

"Mendac is Intelian," Illipsia said.

"You're right. I saw him use electricity."

"So he can't teleport."

Homina turned to look at her daughter. "Illipsia, do you ever wonder why Mendac sought out the Still Princess?"

"No, not really."

"Bryson and Olivia aren't normal," Homina said. "You told me Bryson has a tendency to be cold, even during hotter months. He uses electricity, but his Stillian blood obviously affects him in ways we might not understand. As for Olivia, she's more than just an anomaly. Some would call her alien. I heard she displayed the ability of water when Toono and Storshae invaded Phesaw. You don't think that might have something to do with her genetics residing from separate realms?"

"You're saying Mendac hypothesized such results and did what he did to the Still Princess to prove them?"

"I'm saying it might have been more than a mere hypothesis. I think he believed he had proof, and *he* was that proof."

Illipsia stood with arms crossed, trying to sift through the white noise of millions of thoughts and make sense of what was being said directly in front of her. "Mendac didn't know his parents," she eventually said.

"He might have believed they were from separate realms, however," Homina replied. "And considering his ability of electricity and teleportation, it would make sense if one parent was Intelian and the other Devish."

Disgust filled Illipsia, and it pertained mostly to the fact that she hated the idea that a man as vile as Mendac could belong to her culture. It may have seemed hypocritical, given some of the atrocities committed by the likes of Dev King Storshae, but as much as she didn't share the same perspectives as him, at least she could understand the motivation behind them: the loss of his father and the destruction of his land carried out by an enemy. Mendac, on the other hand, possessed motivations that weren't human.

"I was nothing more than a servant to the royal family during those times," Homina said, "but I remember what it was like to be in the castle when news of Mendac's conquest across the kingdom leaked. The staff was terrified, and it showed. The soldiers tried to mask fear behind stoic faces and firm statures, but it was there. Queen Halys would leak me information sometimes at the end of the day, when King Rehn was away on a mission and we could have our alone time. She always spoke of the Intelian arrogance. They were a world power, after all. She said Mendac pretended he was fueled by revenge for the death of a girl he had once loved, but she believed he used that as an excuse to cover up more shallow truths. He wanted slaves and information. But maybe, he wanted something else."

"Like what?" Illipsia asked.

"Mendac was an intellectual prodigy," Draysil said. "Naturally, he believed his parents were geniuses themselves … geniuses that came from Kuki Sphaira's two most brilliant kingdoms. It's well documented that he had been abandoned in Brilliance, left on the doorstep of the LeAnce family. He grew up there and likely did everything he could to discover his ancestry. If he never found it, it's possible that when he first started showing signs of Devish abilities, he began contemplating the possibility of his parents living in this kingdom. And which city is this kingdom's intellectual equivalent to Brilliance?"

"Prayoga," Illipsia muttered.

Draysil nodded. "He might not have known it, and I could be wrong, but the death and destruction he wrought on his way through this kingdom could have been rooted in his desperation to find answers to not just the confusing nature of his multiple abilities, but to his ancestry."

Illipsia floated in those implications for several moments. Mendac had been trying to find his parents. When he couldn't find them, he looked to the future, which was creating children just like him.

92

Deeper

Preloz Henye couldn't squelch the images of Rhyparia and Mendac fighting. The two of them—mere humans—were defeating Fuhrens in sparring matches. Rhyparia had taken down Poten Copor, and Mendac had done the same to Brenson Ulial just recently. He hadn't thought much of the feud between the two Empires since his rebirth, but that was beginning to change. Olivia's efforts to rescue his daughter from the Linsaniun Mounds while risking her life made him feel like he owed her a great debt—especially since her friend had died as a result.

Olivia was the heir to the Still Kingdom's Frozen Throne, but she had greater ties to the Light Realm. She was half Intelian, she had spent most of her life in the Passion Kingdom or at Phesaw, and her friends fought on behalf of the Light Realm.

The Dark Empire had been in a weakened state because of its missing two Cavities, but the recruitment of Rhyparia and Mendac might have heavily swayed the tides in their favor. The two of them had potential to be on par with the three Versac—something they couldn't know for sure until they were tested against them.

Preloz wanted to help Olivia, but his position made that difficult. He could do nothing from within the Dark Empire. He didn't have the skill to best Rhyparia or Mendac, and the Cavities of Mulawith were protected at all times, not that he believed he had the ability to destroy them anyway—the Bewahr didn't know much about how the Cavities worked.

There were other methods of destroying a Cavity, however. It'd require a difficult conversation with Olivia, not only asking her to remain in the Void longer, but traveling deeper into it. She would have to forestall a return to the Still Kingdom indefinitely—perhaps, permanently. With were she'd be going, there'd be no guarantee of escaping alive, for Batilearsh was a harsh, decrepit city ... its leader was even worse.

The Cyn King didn't survive eight centuries without squashing a few enemies along the way.

*   *   *

Vuilni's corpse rotted in a makeshift grave some fifty miles southeast of the Linsaniun Mounds. Olivia couldn't leave it in the Mounds after seeing the corpses unearth themselves and attack her. She didn't want her to become one of those mindless monsters known as Grave Dwellers. The solace she received from relocating her friend's body, however, was minimal, as there was no predicting what would happen to Vuilni anywhere in this kingdom.

Olivia sat in a carriage with Nina and Reginald Patter, the man who she had learned was responsible for Nina's unscathed soul from the Linsani of Purgatory. She discovered he was Tashami's grandfather. A long time ago, Nina took Tashami away from the Cyn Kingdom in search of brighter pastures in the Spirit, so she followed the advice given to her by the Unbreakable long before his death. She had been told about relatives who still lived in the capital, Saido. It turned out they were the man's parents.

After hearing about what happened to his son and the foster home, Reginald decided to leave the Spirit Kingdom to help Nina achieve her goal of eliminating the Linsani. His wife stayed behind to act as a mother to

Tashami. Olivia found it all unnecessarily sacrificial … until she realized the nature of her own mission in coming here. She had abandoned her mother, aunt, and everyone she knew to come here. The one friend who had come with her was now dead.

Someone knocked on the carriage door while it was still moving. Nina stirred in her sleep, eyes eventually blinking open. Reginald glanced at the door, and Olivia decided to get up and open it. As the youngest, she thought it proper that she walk across the rattling carriage instead.

A young man named Erin was on the other side, jogging to keep up. He was one of the select few who had survived the hunt for the final Purgatory egg without losing his sanity. Most of the people who shared that fortunate outcome were part of the egg retrieval unit, as they had been separated from the main force that was focused on the Linsani itself.

Olivia extended a hand. He grabbed hold while leaping onto the bottom step. She returned to her seat, and Erin remained at the top of the steps with an announcement. "The final egg hatched, and it's been handled. Fennu is officially dead."

Nina, who had risen into a seated position, nodded. "That'll do. Thank you."

Erin left. There was no celebration. A second Linsani had been slain, leaving only five to haunt the Void, yet they could feel no elation or pride. There had been so much loss. It was difficult to see anything as a victory.

*   *   *

Olivia stood in a small wooded area—a rarity in the Voidlands. The transit back to Gangladesh had taken a reprieve, so she used the opportunity to summon Preloz away from everyone else. Her Bewahr had been persistent as of late. She could feel his presence in her mind, pushing for a way out.

"How are you feeling?" he asked.

"Hurt. Ashamed."

"What you did in those Mounds saved a lot of people from ever having to suffer from Purgatory's presence again. No longer will people forget those they love."

She didn't respond. She understood that already. It didn't make Vuilni's absence any less painful. "How are you?" she asked. "Everything okay up there?"

"No, it's not." He paused, then asked, "Do you know a woman named Rhyparia?"

The name ripped Olivia out of her gloom. "Yes."

"She and Mendac LeAnce are in the Dark Empire right now, being trained as soldiers."

"How? Rhyparia's Archain and Mendac's Intelian."

"I'm not sure, but they're there. I wouldn't lie to you."

She believed that. She stared at the dead grass in thought. Bryson was in the Light Empire, which meant Rhyparia and Mendac were now his opposition. Irritation surged through her at the thought of her being stuck down here. It was difficult to find solace in the fact that she had cleansed the Cyn Kingdom of one of its many curses while Bryson was fighting a much larger battle in the Empires. What he was doing likely affected the entire world. And now he was faced with their father. Olivia wanted that opportunity.

"What's Rhyparia like?" she asked.

"Terrifying. The two of them get along very well, which makes them even more formidable. I am confused, though. When I heard she was a Jestivan, I couldn't believe it. She looks much older than any of you … probably Mendac's age."

Olivia didn't respond. She had crossed paths with Rhyparia in Asalka, so she knew about the body transformation. What worried her was Rhyparia's state of mind. She wasn't the same timid girl she had been when first becoming a Jestivan, scared to use her ancient because of her lack of control. She was galvanized, possessing an edge that could cut steel. She had shot into womanhood in both body and mind. And when she had spoken about her mission to free the Powish slaves, her tone had hinted at subtext that meant a lot more than that.

Olivia closed her eyes, brows furrowing as she inhaled deeply. She must have done something cataclysmic to end up in the Dark Empire, similar to how Bryson's defeat of Toono spurred wings from his back. What did she do in the Prim Kingdom? How far into darkness had she fallen? And to think she was willingly fraternizing with Mendac … Olivia almost wretched, until she reminded herself that Rhyparia never learned about the man's truth. She had been undergoing the Gravity Trials and escaping an execution when Toono, Storshae, and Apoleia invaded Phesaw.

"There is a way to make your mark on the Empirical War without ever setting foot in the Empires," Preloz said, reading the flood of emotions washing over her. He looked down at her knee, which was locked in a splint. "But your condition would make the task difficult, and it would require you to remain in the Void for quite a while longer."

Her shoulders slumped. "I can't take this place anymore."

"It would aid your brother and the Light Empire. Without having died and been reborn or possessing wings, you cannot visit the Empires. That leaves this one option."

"What?"

"Head north. Cross the Linsaniun Mounds and kill the royal firstborn … the King of Rot and Cyn and Void."

93

Ten Creates One

The height was a welcome change for Mendac.

He stood atop the roof of the Labyrinth with three others. Rhyparia was in a fighting stance across from him, open umbrella in front of her as a shield, hair swaying slightly sideways in a gentle breeze. Poten Copor, Fuhren of the Gefal's third unit, sat cross-legged off to the side, hands folded in his lap as he spectated. He was in a moderately swollen state, his height pushing ten feet, biceps as round as watermelons.

The fourth presence was a newer one, a man who had become a regular to Rhyparia and Mendac's sparring sessions ever since their battles with the Fuhren. His name was Plash Slabos, a Bewahr of the Gefal's second unit, led by Yasmine Cordelia. He was elderly, short, and balding, a crescent moon of ivory hair wrapping around a wrinkled scalp. Mendac would have pegged him for a Devish or Primmish, considering his fragile build, but Rhyparia had warned him about the physical power the man possessed. She had fought him just before killing Prince Zorn and annihilating the Power

Kingdom. He had been the Power Prince's Bewahr. He was Powish, himself, and apparently capable of considerable damage.

When Mendac had expressed his curiosities about why Plash was suddenly keeping such a keen eye on Rhyparia, she seemed not to care. Not only did she doubt the Powish Bewahr would try to attack her unprovoked after Emperor Mialo had just raved about their value as soldiers to the Dark Empire, but she also doubted Plash wanted anything to do with her ever again. She had exhibited her dominance that night in Ulna Malen, besting two royal firstborns and a Gefal while dropping a moon. Attacking her after witnessing that would have been suicide.

Mendac smirked. Rhyparia cocked an eyebrow. "Find something funny?" she asked.

He shook his head and lowered himself into a ready stance, but the grin didn't fade. She really was special. If only she had the blood of the Dark Realm, she would have been the perfect mate had they met twenty years ago. He wouldn't have had to bother with Kadlest or Apoleia, both of whom had forced the ugliest sides out of him. Why couldn't they have made matters easier? Everything he did was for the sake of science and improving the future—an admirable purpose in a city like Brilliance, where he had grown up.

Rhyparia lunged at him with unnatural speed and movement, the toes off her shoes gliding across the rooftop from a lateral gravitational force. Mendac raised a hand, a voltaic orb already pulsing in his palm. He forced energy outward just as she was ten paces away and ...

... she was gone. The roof of the Labyrinth was gone. The monotonous gray of the atmosphere that overpowered the sun was now filled with the vibrant teals of painted drywall and shamrock greens of sheets, comforters, and curtains. He was in a lavish bedroom, and the perspective from which he looked was that of someone much shorter than him. The wardrobe to his right looked monstrous. It, too, was unnecessarily bright, painted a rose pink and embellished with silver floral patterns along the edges of its drawers.

The chamber was an example of a child's imagination left unchecked, a canvas of pastels that would make no sense to any adult mind. He felt plush beneath his feet, soft twisting around and tickling his toes. He looked down and saw that he stood on a thick carpet in the shape of a sunflower, the center a deep brown and the petals a bright yellow. White stars dotted sky blue toenails. He was a little girl, and this must have been her room.

But a man sat on the bed's edge, paying the girl no mind while staring emptily at a photo frame that he coveted in two hands. His expression was forlorn, eyes red from previous tears. Thick, golden hair stood atop his head at a couple of inches, stylized neatly and professionally with a sculpting product. His uniform was immediately recognizable to Mendac, given he had once been the general of the Intel army. Its sky blue color marked him as an officer of the Spirit Army, the number of silver knots ranking him at the position of major.

Mendac had known of this man—not because he was a man of any note, but because his position as the Intelian general forced him to familiarize himself with the officers of other kingdoms' armies. He had met him once upon a visit to the Spirit Kingdom, an introduction that had called for nothing more than a firm handshake. This man had never crossed Mendac's mind since then—his name even escaping him—so why was he seeing this right now? And why so vividly?

He approached the estranged Spirit Major. A tiny hand reached forward and placed itself gently on his knee, reminding Mendac that this was a young girl's perspective. The man looked away from the photo to the girl—to Mendac. He smiled sweetly and turned the photo her way.

It was a magnificent painting. The Spirit Major stood in a regal military uniform next to a beautiful woman in a pink dress, its skirt embroidered with butterfly wings of burgundy. It looked like a wedding portrait, but what kind of bride wore such a colorful dress? Mendac was beginning to think that this room didn't belong to the girl whose body he occupied, but to that grown woman. It would have explained the massive bed fit for two. Was this where a man of the Spirit Major's status slept? This cacophony of pastels and patterns?

"How can I not smile when I look at you?" the major asked, reaching down to lift the girl off her feet. He placed her on his lap, and she looked up at him. If only faintly, Mendac could sense spirit in this girl—entirely too much even for a child. "You are your mother's daughter." He held the portrait in front of them both, and she studied it. If she said anything,

Mendac didn't hear it or feel her mouth move. In fact, he felt nothing save that warm spirit.

The girl placed a hand against the image of her mother's face. Her pose was turned slightly so that she had one hand placed against the major's chest, her cheek resting against his upper arm. It revealed something rather large that hung down her back, and the girl's hand moved to touch it.

"It was her favorite," the major said. "The kind of keepsake that you typically take to the grave. She wasn't having that …" He trailed off, exhaling slowly through his nose. "In those final moments she held you in her arms just after giving birth, when she found out you were a girl, that we had created a daughter, she told me to pass it on one day. That had been a lofty request, for I could have never seen anyone wearing it besides her. But enough stalling."

He lifted the girl off his lap and placed her on the bed's edge, feet dangling well above the floor. He strode toward the wardrobe and opened its tall center doors, revealing not a curtain of clothes, but a single kimono that hung from a hook. Hanging with that kimono was a sunhat, wide enough to be comically large for any child's head.

It didn't matter. The major grabbed the hat, a string dangling beneath it, and stared down at it for several seconds. He held it with more reverence and love than he had the portrait that now occupied the girl's hands. He turned and approached her, then reached forward and placed the hat on her head. It fell over her eyes like a bucket, ending the vision in the muted brown of sunlight through straw and the booming laughter of a father who had lost his wife to give him a daughter.

*   *   *

When Mendac returned to his senses, smothered in the chalky gray atmosphere of the Labyrinth, the point of Rhyparia's umbrella was jabbed against his throat. She stared at him incredulously. How long had she been positioned like this? How long had he been frozen while experiencing a life event that didn't belong to him?

She said nothing, but Poten pushed himself off the ground and onto his feet. The giant crossed his arms. "You must fix whatever is happening in your mind," he said. "You freeze like that against a Bozani, and you're going to die."

Rhyparia withdrew the umbrella from Mendac's neck, but didn't step back. He was trying to examine himself with the same intensity of her eyes as they looked between his. These visions had started as miniscule curiosities, but they had grown into something larger and more perplexing—and most importantly, a distraction. He wasn't familiar with the tool that had brought him back to life. Kadlest had explained it to him as an ancient piece, called Dimiourgos, in the relic category, requiring ten powerful sacrifices to power the life of one that had vanished.

And judging by these visions, it seemed those ten lives were now inside of him.

94

The Sphere's Identity

Preloz Henye watched Mendac and Rhyparia with newfound interest. He stayed out of their way and didn't interact with them, but he always observed. A benefit of his reputation to mindlessly drift corridors was that nobody found it suspicious when he stared. They thought him insane.

Today, the rookie duo trained with Poten Copor. They were outside, allowing the Fuhren to make full use of his body-morphing ability. No longer was he handicapped by the constraints of the four walls and ceiling of the room in which he had sparred Rhyparia during her test. They quickly learned just how formidable the man really was, and Preloz sensed annoyance in Rhyparia's mannerisms. It had to sting knowing her victory had been a lie ... or at least in her eyes.

Poten currently towered at thirty feet, leaving the distinction between his shadows and that of the Labyrinth impossible. He stood taller than the building itself, body braced against Rhyparia's increased gravity. Something told Preloz she was holding back, scared of Mendac being caught in it, too.

Despite talking to Poten only a few times over the centuries, Preloz felt a bond with the Powish brute. Poten had been promoted from Bewahr to Fuhren only a decade ago. He'd be the only one to understand Preloz's situation, but it was difficult to trust him. Thus, he decided to remain quiet. He liked to think, however, that if Poten knew the truth about the man he was fighting right now—what that man had done to a certain princess years ago—he wouldn't handle him with so much care.

*   *   *

Apoleia entered the Icebound Confluence—the central corridor that connected the many sectors of Kindoliya Palace—from a second floor doorway. A breath escaped her as she admired the two new sculptures that stood in front of the Statue of Gefal—a physical representation of a new way of thinking for Stillian culture.

The Statue of Gefal depicted twenty-four women stationed around a tiered column: fifteen to the bottom step, five on the next, followed by three, and then one at the very top. The notion of an all-woman Empire had always been silly to Apoleia. It was a lie their culture had tried to perpetuate since the beginning of Known History, and most of the population believed it. The proof that said otherwise now stood in front of the twenty-four women.

Apoleia had refrained from visiting the Icebound Confluence for several weeks, wanting to wait to see the sculptures in their full glory. She was glad she did. One was a man whose skin rotted on one half of his face, jaw bone exposed. He donned a modest physique, a skinny frame with a hole in his chest. Her sculptor had done a marvelous job depicting the Bewahr, using only a description provided by her as reference. Preloz Henye was now immortalized in ice.

The sculpture next to Preloz held a dear place in Apoleia's heart. She had met him only once, the day she awakened him. She had been fifteen on that day, and despite knowing a male Bewahr meant doom for a Stillian woman, she had been excited to meet him. He was a big man, strong and sturdy. His bald scalp reflected the Kindoliya ice in mesmerizing patterns, and his clothes looked more like oversized bed sheets. Mother had shamed her for the gender of her Bewahr, as if she had any control over that. She had barred her from summoning him ever again, even if her life was in danger.

Apoleia stood in front of the sculpture, looking up at the man who had been so kind to her that first and only day they spoke. He had expressed his understanding of her kingdom's customs, but pleaded for her to call him if the situation was ever dire enough.

She never did, even when Mendac had been on top of her.

Poten Copor would have saved her.

*   *   *

Archaic King Sigmund huffed as he stared out a window of Phelos Palace. "I should know what I'm doing by this point."

A woman stood behind him, poised and patient. She carried a sword at each hip, hair of burned umber shaved close to the scalp. She was just north of six feet with an Adrenian's lean frame. "I think you've been serviceable," she said.

He scoffed. "Serviceable?"

"That's an improvement from what you once were."

He sighed. Elasia Lamont, Branian to King Sigmund, had always been blunt. She said what needed to be said, regardless of repercussions—not that there were any. He was a king, but she was a Bozani. If she wanted, she could deny his every request outside of saving his life. He was fortunate to have a Branian who didn't mind spending time with him away from the Empire.

Radon, one of Ophala's falcons, soared toward the palace. Sigmund opened the window, and the raptor came to a stop, perching itself on the windowsill. He untied the scroll from its leg and read through it, heart pounding as he did. He had been waiting too long for news from Spy Pilot Ophala. He never enjoyed her time away, no matter the importance of her reasoning for doing so. His smile widened as he sped through the sentences. When he reached the end, he whooped.

"Sounds like good news," Elasia said.

DAVID F. FARRIS

He turned and took a deep breath. "The Loess is under control. Kopios Soteria has been captured and is now being transported here." Radon flew away as Sigmund walked past his Branian toward the chamber door. Elasia followed him into the corridor. "And I've been given the go-ahead to execute Mesitis. One by one, we're eliminating every remnant of my father's and grandfather's reigns."

*   *   *

"Does this not seem asinine?" Elasia asked, long strides allowing her to walk more casually in comparison to Sigmund.

"His execution is long overdue," he replied. "He's not giving answers anyway. Pilot Ophala has tried every means of torture just short of killing him. The man doesn't budge."

"Are there not other means? An ancient that forces someone to reveal truths?"

"Ophala's never heard of such a thing. She dug through Neeko's extensive archives and also found nothing, and that was a man who knew a curiously vast amount about ancient pieces." Sigmund began trotting up a staircase, Elasia practically gliding up them two steps at a time. "There was a Dev servant of the Passion family named Marcus who could extract truths, but he was the only Devish who had that ability according to King Vitio. He died at the hands of Toono and Kadlest a few years back." He reached the top of the steps and turned right. "All options have been exhausted. And now I get to end the man who's hidden in the shadows of the underground for decades."

They were in one of the palace's tallest towers, where Archaic King Itta had been imprisoned leading up to his death. They passed the very cell in which Marcus's truth extraction occurred, leading to an ugly scene of blood and tears. A few empty cells down, they passed Elyol Brekton, son of former Archaic General, Inias Brekton, and the man who had headed the military efforts of Toth Brench and Wert Lamay during the uprising … the man who had been an older brother to him as a child. Both had been led astray by corrupt fathers. The only reason why he wasn't dead was because Sigmund couldn't work up the stomach to execute him. Elyol had, after all, seen the error of his ways and joined Pilot Ophala's efforts to retake the kingdom from Toth.

"Can you end it please?"

Sigmund paused, but didn't turn to look at the general's son who had mentored the king's son. If only he had gotten a little bit of Elyol's strength and tenacity. He had never been a fighter, yet Elyol never shamed him for it.

"Execute me."

Sigmund looked down, and Elasia observed quietly. They had made a point to not let the Branian be seen by anyone besides himself or Pilot Ophala, but the prisoners held here were exceptions. If anything, her presence was a mercy to them. A Bozani's natural effect on the atmosphere was to purify it. Maybe it alleviated some of Elyol's burdens—a solid thought in theory. Sigmund continued walking without acknowledging Elyol, verbally or visually.

Mesitis Epidex, Skill Broker of the Underground, occupied the tower's highest cell. Sigmund stood on a small landing at the top of the stairs, surveying Mesitis's scars and wounds. Pilot Ophala had obliterated everything about this man save his existence. From his body to his mind and soul, she had recruited the most dexterous surgeons to operate on his body and a somewhat skilled Dev servant to pick his brain. She'd even gone as far as placing him in the same room with the old woman who held the mysterious gray sphere, the treatment that had been given to children in Lost Wisdom. Nothing broke him. He had given information about the Thousand-Layer Loess and certain operations of the orphanage, but he wouldn't budge on revealing anything about that object the old Cynnish woman held.

The greatest scholars and scientists had gathered to study it, but none had answers. They had searched far and wide to find anyone who specialized in Cyn culture, but found no one. Acquiring a Cynnish was impossible, for none left the Void. They didn't travel abroad and surely didn't make permanent homes in foreign lands. The old woman herself was no help because she didn't talk; she hardly moved. She was a husk. Their final option was to destroy the sphere, and they tried every means possible, from brute strength to elemental attacks. It proved indestructible.

Mesitis didn't bother looking up, but he heard Sigmund's approaching footsteps. He grunted. "Where's your mommy?"

"She died a long time ago," Sigmund said.

"The bird lady."

"Gone. I'm calling the shots right now."

A deep, sickly laugh rolled up Mesitis's throat. "Such a strong king." He looked up, revealing empty sockets for eyes. Ophala had shown no mercy. "Your father would be so proud."

The retort died on Sigmund's lips. He shook his head, tossing excess length of scarf around his neck. He opened his mouth, and a snow storm escaped. Flurries spun throughout the cell, nearly blocking sight of the prisoner as a blizzard raged.

Mesitis didn't fight. He hung limply, wrists and ankles bound by chains that unnaturally stretched his limbs. Many of his joints were broken, his right knee the ugliest of them all. Snow carpeted the floor and climbed higher. It buried his legs and then his abdomen.

Just before it reached his face and suffocated him, the Skill Broker used his last remaining breath to bellow a warning:

"Death isn't always loss!"

*   *   *

There was a room. A vast room that stretched a mile each way. An empty room save the Cynnish woman, old and mute and dead in nearly every sense of the word. One item kept her alive. It sat in her lap—gray and solid like stone, but too spherical to be anything of the sort. She had held it for years, keeping her in a state of nothingness. To grasp the concept of memory would be like trying to move her foot. Not only did she not know how; she didn't know the option existed. Someone could have entered her field of view, and she wouldn't know to look their way. She existed only to weave, to amplify the object in her lap.

The room hadn't seen motion in weeks, though there was plenty of activity outside its walls. Soldiers stood guard, but mostly to keep anyone from entering. If only the Archaic Kingdom knew the monster it harbored.

The gray sphere cracked and splintered, and with it came the first sound to curse the room in weeks. A small chunk of gray fell away. Shadows spilled out of the hole. An ivory claw snatched at the shell and began tearing the rest away. A skeletal wing unfolded and extended, and the rest of the body tore itself loose from shadows. Another wing spread wide to the left, and the tiny creature flew upward, snapping a jaw around the woman's neck.

The sphere had been an egg, now hatched and splintered as it collected the blood of its first victim.

DAVID F. FARRIS

Sphaira Publishing and David F. Farris hopes you enjoyed the sixth book in the Erafeen series.

The series is not over. There is one book left.

GET MORE FROM THE ERAFEEN UNIVERSE

To remain updated on the author's work, receive discount offers, enter giveaways, and enjoy behind-the-scenes looks of the creative process, join his group of JestiFANs by going here:

Become a JestiFAN

www.erafeen.com
www.twitter.com/DavidFFarris
www.facebook.com/DavidFFarris

THE ERAFEEN SERIES:

THE JESTIVAN
THE UNTENABLE
THE UPRISING
THE CHRONICLE
THE SACRIFICE
THE EMPIRES

BOOK 7 – **THE FINAL BOOK** – RELEASES 2022